THE GREEN KNIGHT

THE
GREEN KNIGHT

IRIS MURDOCH

Chatto & Windus

LONDON

First published 1993

1 3 5 7 9 10 8 6 4 2

Copyright © 1993 Iris Murdoch

Iris Murdoch has asserted her right under the Copyright, Designs and Patents
Act, 1988 to be identified as the author of this work

First published in the United Kingdom in 1993 by
Chatto & Windus Ltd
Random House, 20 Vauxhall Bridge Road, London
SW1V 2SA

Random House Australia (Pty) Limited
20 Alfred Street, Milsons Point, Sydney,
New South Wales 2061, Australia

Random House New Zealand Limited
18 Poland Road, Glenfield
Auckland 10, New Zealand

Random House South Africa (Pty) Limited
P O Box 337, Bergvlei, South Africa

Random House UK Limited Reg. No. 954009

A CIP catalogue record for this book
is available from the British Library

ISBN 0 7011 6030 6

Phototypeset by Intype, London
Printed in Great Britain by
Mackays of Chatham

CONTENTS

ACKNOWLEDGEMENTS

The author and publisher would like to thank the following for permission to quote from copyright material:

For an excerpt from the *History of the Peloponnesian War* by Thucydides, vol. IV, translated by Charles Forster Smith: The Loeb Classical Library, and Harvard University Press, Cambridge, Mass., U.S.A., 1986; from *A History of Europe* by H.A.L. Fisher, first published 1936: Edward Arnold Publishers; from 'Happy Days and Lonely Nights', music by Fred Fisher and words by Billy Rose, © 1928 Fred Fisher Music Co. Inc./Advanced Music Corp., U.S.A., reproduced by permission of E.M.I. Music Publishing Ltd./Lawrence Wright Music Co. Ltd., London, WC2H 0EA.

For Ed Victor

I

IDEAL CHILDREN

'Once upon a time there were three little girls – '
'Oh look what he's doing now!'
'And their names were – '
'Come here, come *here*.'
'And they lived at the bottom of a well.'
The first speaker was Joan Blacket, the second was Louise Anderson, the one so urgently summoned was a dog, the little girls mentioned were Louise's children, the place was Kensington Gardens, the month was October.

The dog, whose name was Anax, a distinguished and unusual collie with blue eyes, and long silver-grey fur blotched with black and white, came bounding back to the two women. They were of youthful middle age and had been at boarding school together, though not for long since Joan (a bad girl) had been expelled two terms after Louise (a good girl) had arrived. However, that time had sufficed to establish a lifelong friendship. Joan's lawlessness had cheered the docile younger child, new to imprisonment, with visions of a larger freedom; while Louise, to Joan's disorder, had brought near a soothing possibility of order, at least of the permanence of affection. Neither, in later life, had profited much from the other's example. And now they were both widows with almost-grown-up children.

'This dog business will end in tears,' said Joan.

Louise, who also thought that it would end in tears, said, 'Oh no, he's quite settled down with us, he's forgotten his old master.'

'Dogs don't forget. He'll run away.'

The 'old master' referred to, Anax's former owner, whose name was Bellamy James, a friend of Louise's deceased husband, was by no means 'old', but had decided in the middle of life's journey to abandon the world and become some sort of religious person. This new existence, not yet fully entered upon, involved the surrender of temporal pleasures such as alcohol and dog-owning. So Bellamy had handed Anax over to the Anderson family.

'Besides,' said Joan, 'Bellamy is a fool.'

Louise who also, in her mild way, thought Bellamy a fool, said, which she also believed, 'He's a very kind generous man.'

'In a moment you're going to say he's a "good man"! He's had a messy life. I think he's become a bit batty, he has a death-wish. Is he really living in poverty in East London? Will he sell that seaside cottage you all go to, where the seals are?'

'Yes. The seals have gone.'

'Poisoned I suppose. That must be a blow to you and the girls.'

'I think I'll put Anax on the long lead, I usually do. Come, come, good dog. Sit. *Sit!*'

Anax sat while Louise clipped on the lead. He looked up at her with what his ex-master used to call his 'sly judgmental eyes'.

'And how is young Harlequin?' This was Joan's nickname for, not all that young though eternally youthful, Clement Graffe, also a friend of Louise's husband.

'He's all right, but he's terribly anxious about his brother.'

'That still goes on? No news of *him* I suppose.'

'No, none.'

'By the way, is Clement paying for this trip to Italy? I imagine Bellamy can't. He can give up the world but he won't miss a free jaunt! Where are they now, do you think?'

'Somewhere in the Apennines.'

'I wish I was. Paris has been so stuffy this summer. Now I come to London, and everybody's away.'

Joan, whose mother was half French, had lived now for some time in Paris. Her mother, whom she rarely saw, was living with a rich Frenchman in Antibes. Her father had died long ago in a railway accident. Her husband, who had left her after six years of marriage, had later gone to Canada and disappeared. Joan's life in Paris was mysterious to her London friends. She worked in a 'fashion house', but in what capacity was not clear. She complained of poverty while also implying that she was 'getting on perfectly well'. Louise, visiting her, was kept at a distance, not invited to her flat, meeting only in restaurants. Joan, once rated 'a beauty', was still, though a little haggard, very handsome and much stared at by men. She wore skilful aggressive make-up, dressed eccentrically but smartly, and liked to be taken, in some rather old-fashioned sense, as an actress. She was tall and had a long stride and fine legs. Her copiously flowing hair, dyed for many years, was a darkish 'Titian' red. Her pretty nose was faintly *retroussé*, and her blue eyes, outlined in black between heavy lashes, glittered and sparkled.

Harvey Blacket, aged eighteen and now in the Apennines, was Joan's son and only child. His father had defected when he was five, his birth having precipitated the disastrous marriage; and Harvey had lived since then in a tempestuous mutually possessive relationship with his mother. Money had come from somewhere. The father, while still in England, paid something, Joan worked as a secretary. She had, it was said, 'men friends', the cause, in due course, of quarrels with her son. When Harvey was fifteen Joan fled to Paris, leaving the boy, still at school, with a tiny one-room flat off North End Road, and a tiny allowance, under the wing of various self-appointed 'foster parents' of whom Louise was one and 'Harlequin' another. Harvey, evidently judged to be grown up, proved in fact quite able to look after himself, and at eighteen won a scholarship to study modern languages at University College, London. He had elected to spend a year off before taking up his place and had promptly acquired a bursary to spend four months studying in Italy. He had spoken French as a child with his mother and grandmother, and had learnt German and Italian at school. The Italian 'jaunt' was a preliminary treat before his settling down in Florence.

It was generally agreed that while Joan had led, and it was presumed still led, a rather rackety life, *une vie de bâton de chaise* as she herself expressed it, Louise by contrast led a life which, even after its great catastrophe, was quiet and calm, a sensible rational life, a decent satisfactory cheerful life, as presaged by her kindly gentle parents and her orderly high-minded school. The catastrophe was the sudden death by cancer, at a surprisingly early age, of her husband Edward Anderson. Out of a serene childhood Louise, after a year at a London college, had moved smoothly into that wonderful marriage. She had seemed to advance, as one guided, under a happy star. Edward, known as 'Teddy', Anderson, several years her senior, was an able and much respected accountant. Prudent insurance had left his family fairly well provided for. After the catastrophe sensible rational Louise struggled with a word processor and took a part-time job. Her orderly life continued. Her children were angels. Friends surrounded her: childhood friends such as Joan and Connie and

3

Cora, and also her husband's loyal friends from Cambridge days, Clement and Lucas Graffe, and Bellamy whom, even as students, they had called 'the chaplain'. Louise's calm bland broad face bore no wrinkles, no evidence of grief or mental strife such as marked, not unattractively, the more striking countenance of Joan Blacket. But Louise's heart had been broken and had not mended.

'Does it never stop raining in England?'

'It's not raining now.'

'Is there *nobody* in town?'

'Yes, a few millions.'

'Why do you always say what is obvious?'

'I say what is true.'

'Why can't you tell me something funny and stirring, such as whose marriage has broken up, who's in bed with whom, who's bankrupt or disgraced or dead?'

Louise smiled. They were walking over wet grass upon which a pert chill breeze was moving, like hands covering and uncovering in some swift mysterious game, the huge brown leaves of the plane trees heavy with rain. The Serpentine, in fugitive light, was grey and silver through the trees. The pinnacle of the Albert Memorial, which on a sunny day looked like Orvieto Cathedral (or so Joan said once), was streaked and formless like a melting icicle. The sky was black over central London but the rain had ceased for the moment. Joan, who had just put down her big umbrella, was wearing a smart green suit trimmed with narrow bands of grey fur, a black fedora, and high black boots. Louise, who quite liked a little rain on her hair, was wearing a voluminous shapeless black mackintosh with the hood trailing down her back. Her thick brown hair, straight and stiff like horsehair the girls said at school, swept back from her large brow and collected itself in an orderly way upon her neck. Her complexion was pale, freckled in summer, her attentive eyes a mild golden brown, the colour of plane tree leaves in autumn. Her expression was patient, calm, faintly quizzical, benign; someone said, always faintly smiling.

'Are you all right in Harvey's flat?'

'No. That folding bed is damp if you fold it up, and if you keep it unfolded all day there's no room to move. It's very uncomfortable anyway, and the place smells. But seriously, who is in town? I must be fed and looked after. We know who isn't in town, Harvey, Bellamy, Clement, Lucas. What about Tessa Millen?'

4

'I don't know. I suppose she's here.'

'Of course that girl is Adolf Hitler in knickers, but I like the type. Why don't you like her? You like almost everybody, why not her?'

Why not indeed? Joan liked Tessa, Louise did not. Sometimes she thought she knew why Joan liked Tessa, and she did not like that either.

'I'm afraid Connie is out of town too, the whole family is in America, Jeremy has a case there.' Constance Parfitt, later Constance Adwarden, who had also been at the famous high-minded school, had renewed acquaintance with Joan later in France in what they referred to as their 'unbridled youth'. Jeremy was a lawyer, Connie wrote children's stories.

'Pity, we need her boys. Don't we need her boys? Will they be back in time for the masked ball? Jeremy was always a bit sweet on you.'

'No masked ball, only a little party, the children are making masks. You'll stay?'

'I've no idea. I need to be amused. I suppose Clement and Bellamy will come back when they've deposited Harvey in Florence. Are Clive and Emil still together?'

'Yes – but they're in Germany at present.'

'AIDS frightens the young off sex these days, off all sex, such a pity, they don't have fun like I had at their age, they daren't try themselves out, they daren't experiment. We'll have a generation of monastics. That would suit Bellamy I imagine. You know, I think Harvey's still a virgin, I don't think he's had any sex life at all. Has he told you?'

'He tells me nothing,' said Louise. She was always careful what she said to Joan about Harvey. Louise had known Harvey, as her oldest friend's child, all his life. She had watched over him, she had kept her distance; perhaps she had become, out of loyalty to Joan, too distant. When Harvey's father vanished, Harvey needed a father. At first Teddy was this person. When Teddy died, Bellamy and Lucas and Clement became his fathers. When Joan went to Paris she sold her London flat, bought Harvey his tiny flatlet out of the proceeds, and also set up a bank account into which she paid a small sum, promising more sums, which did occasionally materialise. Lucas and Clement paid for Harvey to attend the austere boarding school which they themselves had attended, and quietly kept him in pocket money and in credit. It was impossible for Louise not, at that time, to make some signal to the boy. Louise, who had three daughters, had wanted a son. She loved Harvey. But she was not his mother. Perhaps she had been too scrupulous, she hoped the boy understood. Louise had often done for him what mothers do, mended his clothes, cooked for him, given him presents, given him advice. He was often in her house, her daughters were like sisters to him. For a time she had shopped for him and cleaned his flat, but silently judged this to be 'too much'. He could begin to think her intrusive. Of course it was not strictly that Harvey 'told her nothing'. At one time, just after his mother's departure, he had told her too much, for instance about the terrible unhappiness of his early childhood. Louise had not invited these confidences. Later, older, he said less. Louise did not know anything about Harvey's sex life, he had shown no inclination to tell her, and of course she had not approached the subject; although, more recently, it had been much in her mind.

'I wonder if he's talked to Harlequin,' said Joan, 'I must find out. So you don't know when Lucas is coming back?'

'No. We don't even know where he is.'

'He must have felt it awfully undignified to be in court, even though he was completely innocent. Did you go to see the show?'

'Go to the court? Of course not!'

'I'd have been dying of curiosity, I'd have wanted to know exactly what happened. I wish you'd told me sooner!'

'We kept well clear. Lucas would have hated us coming to watch like tourists!'

Earlier that year, now several months ago, Lucas Graffe, Clement's elder brother, had had a very unpleasant experience. Out walking at night he had resisted an attack by a mugger with such violence that his assailant had died from a blow on the head from Lucas's umbrella. There was some general indignation (for the incident was briefly in the press) when Lucas was taken to court accused, not actually of manslaughter, but of 'taking the law into his own hands' and 'using excessive violence'. For a few days Lucas was even something of a popular hero. The goodies who wanted to defend the poor mugger were routed when it emerged that he had been carrying an offensive weapon. Lucas, a quiet reclusive academic, a much respected historian, was of course extremely upset by having inadvertently killed a man, even though a bad man.

6

'He must have been very very distressed,' said Louise.

'He must have been upset by the publicity.'

'He must have been even more upset by killing a man.'

'Nonsense, Lucas is a hero. If more people hit back there'd be fewer muggers. Lucas deserves a medal. You would side with the rotten thief!'

'To end a man's life – he may have had a wife and children.'

'I know, we all treasure Lucas, but he *is* eccentric. It is just like him to startle us by doing something unexpected. He sits in his dark little house writing learned books, then he goes out and kills someone – that's instinctive courage, and instinctive authority.'

'It was a bit of a freak that the man died – Lucas wasn't trying to damage him, he was just fending him off.'

'I imagine Lucas was angry. It was hard luck on both of them. And now Lucas disappears for ages – '

'I can understand that, he wants to get over the shock, and he wants us to get over it too. He won't want to chat about it.'

'Oh, he won't discuss it with anybody, we won't be allowed to mention it, it will be made never to have happened. But where is he?'

'I expect he's working somewhere, he works all the time, he's in some university city, in some university library.'

'Yes – in Italy, Germany, America. Is he still teaching?'

'Yes, he's still teaching, but he's got some sabbatical leave from his college.'

'He's certainly not very sociable, he's led such a sheltered life, he's a quiet and reticent person, he can't have enjoyed having his name in the papers. You must all look after him when he returns. You take him too much for granted. He's lonely.'

'He likes it that way.'

'Clement must be worried stiff about him. You don't think he's committed suicide?'

'No, of course not!'

'I don't mean because of guilt, but because of loss of dignity, loss of face.'

'No! Lucas has plenty of ordinary sense!'

'Has he? Well – and how are the three little girls?'

Louise's children at nineteen, eighteen and fifteen, were not now so little.

'Aleph and Sefton have done their exams – now they are anxiously waiting for the results!'

7

'Surely *they* needn't be anxious!'

Teddy Anderson, having had a classical education, had given his daughters Greek names, Alethea, Sophia and Moira. The girls however, in quiet mutual communion, had decided not to be known by these names. Yet they did not entirely abandon the names either. When the youngest, so much desired by their parents to be a boy, turned out to be another girl, Teddy said 'It's fate!' and christened her Moira, which was easily and promptly shortened to 'Moy'. The other girls had more trouble finding their true names. Alethea, not tolerating 'Thea', decided at first for 'Alpha', but as this sounded presumptuous, opted finally for 'Aleph', the Hebrew name of the first letter of the alphabet, which retained the connection with the Ancient World, and a mysterious bond with her original name. Sophia, who abominated 'Sophie', worked even harder, but came up at last with 'Sefton'. How she discovered 'Sefton' she never explained. Aleph (nineteen) and Sefton (eighteen) were bookish, destined for the university. Moy, who was not academic 'but clever as a little mouse' in other ways, was preparing for art school. The girls worked hard, loved their mother, loved one another, were quiet and happy and lived at peace. Sometimes they seemed almost too contented with their lot. To look at, Sefton and Moy were not unattractive. But Aleph was voted to be very beautiful.

'Exams. How time flies! Cambridge, like Dad?'

'They hope for Oxford, but they have other choices.'

'It'll do them good to get away from home. They are altogether too sedate, there is an *atmosphere*. And still no television! You deserve to have poltergeists with three demure teenage girls about the place, they're just the kind to attract them. Those girls are like a drawn bow, they compose a field of force – that's Clement's imagery incidentally – it's time for violence, it's time for them to fly apart – '

'Clement said that?'

'Do they still sing, and cry?'

'Yes – '

'They are perfectly safe and lovingly looked after – now when I was their age – '

'You said you were having fun.'

'Well, yes and no, strictly speaking I was in hell. Perhaps I have always been there. One can have fun in hell. But why the tears, are they in love? Moy is, isn't she? She's in love with Clement, always has been!'

'She's also in love with the "Polish Rider".'

'Who's he?'

'A picture by Rembrandt.'

'Oh yes. I always found that picture a bit soppy. Isn't he supposed to be a woman? And anyway now they say it isn't by Rembrandt. But seriously, are they in love?'

'No. They've always had that gift of tears. They cry over books, not just novels, Sefton cries over history books, Moy cries over things – '

'I remember, like stones. She thinks things have rights. And she was always rescuing insects.'

'Insects of course, and they all cry over animals. But they laugh a lot too.'

'The all-singing all-laughing all-crying show. You call it a gift. I sometimes wish that I could cry more easily. Men don't cry. That's one of the many proofs of their superiority over us. It's all that caring. I suppose the girls are still vegetarians and saving whales and saving the planet and so on. Moy will die of her own sensibility, she identifies with everything. Save hedgehogs, save the black-footed ferret, abolish plastic bags. Of course Sefton is a swot, a brown-stocking. I see her as a sober bespectacled schoolteacher. Does Moy still eat that orange-flavoured milk chocolate? No wonder she's such a dear little roly-poly, she's the plump little woman who makes everything nice. I think she'll be a cook, or perhaps she'll live in the country and have a herb garden.'

Louise did not like these descriptions of her children. 'Moy draws very well, she will be an artist. Aleph will do English at the university, she wants to be a writer.'

'Oh, Aleph! With her beauty she can have anything, she can marry anybody. When you let her out she'll be *surrounded*. But she won't be in a hurry. That girl has her wits about her. She won't marry some penniless student. She'll choose a powerful older man who is rich and loves life, a top scientist, a top industrialist, a tycoon with a yacht and houses everywhere, and they'll have *real fun*. I just hope they invite us!'

Louise laughed. 'You used to say Aleph would have to pay for her beauty. I hope you're right about her wits and not being in a hurry.'

9

'So they still sing all those love songs, those sentimental thirties songs and Elizabethan ditties? Those are worthy of their tears. But I think I know – it's the calm before the storm – they are crying over the horrors to come, prophetically mourning their lost youth, mourning for their virginity, their goodness in which they heartily believe, their innocence, their purity so soon to be desecrated – and yes, I think they are innocent lambs, not like Harvey who has always had filth in his mind as boys do.'

'Yes, possibly,' said Louise vaguely. Joan liked to speculate amusingly about the girls, of whom she was fond, but whom now she hardly ever saw. Louise did not want to talk about such matters. The tears moved and distressed her, such strange tears as for some terrible frightful joy. 'Bellamy says they are wondering at the existence of the world.'

'Its misery, its cruelty?'

'No, just that it exists.'

'That doesn't make much sense. They've realised their whole lives are at stake. I heard them singing that song about every girl's a fool and every man's a liar. Well, perhaps they don't sing it so often now when they can see it's not a joke! Well may they weep over the wickedness of the men who will break their hearts! Have they taken to religion? Moy was confirmed, wasn't she?'

'She used to go to church sometimes.'

'She would, she thinks it's magic, she's a leprechaun, perhaps she'll be a witch when she's grown up and earn a fortune making love-potions.'

'She is a very remarkable girl,' said Louise, 'and she will be a very remarkable woman.' She was tired of hearing Moy belittled and laughed at.

'You mean she's fey, she has an aura, she imagines she communes with the paranormal, but that's all just a form of female adolescence, she'll pass through it into ordinariness, no love-potions, no broomsticks, she'll be arranging the flowers in the local church. I wish I still had some religion, even the beastly old Roman church which my beastly mother hangs onto, while she lives in sin. They say religion is a substitute for sex. You don't know what it is to want a man, any man. I wish I could discover some respectable male prostitutes, like civil servants or university dons who do it in their spare time for a bit of pocket money, there must be such people. Moy's still at school, isn't she? With the other two at home the female vibrations must be overwhelming.'

'They're mostly out all the time, they go to libraries, they go to lectures, they went to that cramming establishment.'

'Lucas used to coach Sefton, didn't he?'

'Yes, I think she found him a bit intimidating. But it was very kind of him.'

'You say he's kind, you say Bellamy's generous and you refuse to call him a fool, you think Harvey is a sweet good boy, you think Clement is a parfit gentle knight, you see Aleph as an angel who will never turn into a Valkyrie, I believe you don't even allow yourself to make moral judgments upon *me*! You smooth things over and say things you don't really mean. You inhibit your fears and hates, you are the most inhibited person I know.'

Louise murmured, 'Good old inhibitions.'

'You've led an easy life, other people have made the decisions. I have a perpetual frown imprinted on my brow. Your brow is unfurrowed. You have what Napoleon most desired in a woman, repose. My God, how much I haven't got it! Damn, it's beginning to rain.'

Joan put up her umbrella, Louise pulled her hood over her head. In an instant the grass became slippery and muddy. The wind blew the rain into their faces as they turned back.

'I'm so glad Harvey got that bursary thing to go to Florence,' said Louise. 'He must be so happy.'

'To get out of London and out of England, yes. But I wish he had a girl friend. Somehow or other it always turns out he's with men. He hangs around with Emil and Clive – what's the use of a pair of dedicated gays – now who's he with? Clement and Bellamy. All right, they're not gay, at least Clement isn't, but they're *men*. Men flirt with him, he's so pretty, they pet him, I've seen them, they pull his hair – remember how they all used to chuck him under the chin, I remember Teddy used to. You know, I think he's been retarded by your girls, they've inoculated him against women, against *sex*, they've played brother and sisters all their lives, he thinks all females are taboo, they're his sisters! Chastity is a potent magic, it casts a spell. Those girls are paralysed, they've become fairy-tale damsels, grail-bearers, sleeping princesses inside an enchanted castle. Harvey ought to be the prince who hacks his way through the forest, but he can't be, he's *in* the castle!'

'What nonsense!' murmured Louise under her dripping hood.

Anax was pulling her now, she could feel the collar tight against his throat.

'He's under the spell too. And all the time Eros is fluttering his wings above them all. How I wish he could descend like an eagle upon the whole scene and tear it to pieces! We need someone to come to break the enchantment, someone from *elsewhere*. I warn you, if Harvey turns out to be queer it won't be my fault, it'll be your fault!'

' "I feel your arms around me, your kisses linger yet, You taught me how to love you, now teach me to forget!" '

The singers were Aleph and Moy, Aleph seated at the piano, Moy standing behind her, leaning against her shoulder. The girls all played the piano, Aleph very well. Sefton, who when reading was deaf to sound, was sitting on the floor at the far end of the room, leaning back against the bookshelves which covered the wall. She read: 'The Anglo-Danish kingdom was personal to Canute. His sons were not of the calibre to sustain so difficult a structure. Our island, which had led Europe in culture in the eighth century, lost nothing of its native character under the brilliant Dane, reverted soon after his death to its ancient loyalties and recalled the son of Ethelred from his Norman exile.'

Anax was asleep in his basket, his long head concealed beneath his bushy tail. Aleph, the 'beauty', was pale in complexion, her skin (of course innocent of make-up) faintly glowing, her face from a large brow tapering into an oval form, her eyes, beneath long almost straight dark eyebrows, large and dark brown, thoughtful, expressive of sympathy, also of judgment, her hair, a dark shining chestnut colour, a lively complex of curls which framed her face and cascaded in orderly disorder to her long slim pale neck. Her nose was straight, descending in an almost unwavering line from her brow. Her mouth, with a full lower lip and a classically bowed upper lip, always seeming slightly moist, was sweetly pensive, faintly amused, 'clever, but loving and forgiving' as Clement once said. (Sefton found a resemblance to a girl in the Acropolis museum.) She was slim and tall, though not too tall, with long elegant legs, she was dignified, in company often withdrawn, seeming proud, as if superior, but among people she knew, lively and witty. She was indeed clever, esteemed by her school and by her more recent mentors. Her university entrance had been delayed by the bout of glandular fever which had penetrated the trio in the previous year. Perhaps being constantly told that she was beautiful had indeed made her a little haughty, or perhaps what was visible and sometimes unnerving was a kind of controlled absolutism, a capacity for passion and exigence which was usually well concealed beneath her gentle silences and sympathetic perceptive gaze.

Sefton was less tall than Aleph and less slim, her eyes were the greenish brown known as hazel, she had golden brown eyebrows and reddish brown straight hair rather jagged (she cut it herself) and square teeth which used to protrude until they were restrained by a golden band only lately discarded. Her complexion was pale, not with the glowing ivory pallor of Aleph's but like her mother's, readily freckled. Her mouth was firm, her lips pressed together, thoughtful, even said to be stern, her expression in repose somewhat austere, she wore glasses for reading and could stand on her head. She was said to be too bookish, obsessed with learning and passing exams, only interested in serious conversation. She had a clear lucid carrying voice and, like her sisters, sang well. She did not care for clothes but wore shabby, often second-hand, corduroy jackets and trousers, and cheap men's shirts. She was reticent, and by her family generally agreed to be the cat that walked by herself by her wild lone. Moy, who took after Teddy Anderson, had blue eyes, and golden hair which she wore in a long thick plait which was held together at the tail by a sturdy elastic band. She was shorter in stature than Sefton and secretly afraid that she had stopped growing. (When did one stop growing? She was afraid to ask.) She was rosy-cheeked and rather plump, not 'intellectual' like the other two, but 'awfully talented' in various 'artistic' ways still to be defined. She made and dyed her own clothes and wore shapeless shifts in various subtle colours, with wide sleeves. She drew well, and painted in the style of her art teacher, Miss Fitzherbert (for she was still at school), and more wildly in various other styles. She also made things, garments, jewellery, hats, masks, ritual objects. She hoped to go to an art school, but feared (again secretly) that she could do many things but not any

13

one thing properly. She could in fact cook well, but did not regard this as important.

The large room on the first floor, once the drawing-room, had become in time the girls' 'common room'. It was called (having been so named by Moy) 'The Aviary'. It occupied, together with a small landing and a very large cupboard, the full width of the house, the other rooms being, with the exception of the attic, rather small. The furniture, remnants which had come from the larger house in Hampstead which they had occupied while Teddy was alive, was handsome but had become shabby, as if it 'knew its place'. Even the piano, a good instrument, had a slightly battered look. It rarely occurred to the girls, or to Louise, to polish anything. There was no television set, the girls disapproved of television. The house was a four-storey terrace house in a modest street in Hammersmith, near Brook Green. A fanlight over the door (already present when Louise had bought the house) said 'Clifton'. The number in the road was ninety-seven, proclaimed by Moy to be a lucky number. However 'Clifton', though never used in the postal address (which would have been too pretentious for so unassuming a dwelling), was what the house was called among its friends.

It was evening. They had had supper which took place at eight, and on this occasion had consisted of (provided by Moy) tomato salad with mozzarella cheese and basil, lentil stew with curried cabbage, and apples (not Cox's Orange Pippins, which had not yet appeared in the shops). The family, in a spontaneous movement of spirit (or inspired by Moy, Moy said) had become vegetarians some years ago. The rain, which had started in the afternoon, had continued ever since, making a pleasant soft faintly hissing sound. The curtains were pulled, the gas fire was murmuring. Louise, who now did not enter the Aviary except by invitation, was reading in her small bedroom on the floor above, opposite to the bathroom and Aleph's even smaller bedroom. Louise's bedroom looked out onto the street, Aleph's onto the small garden and the backs of houses in the next street. The book which Louise was reading was *A Glastonbury Romance*. The large attic room on the top floor was occupied by Moy. Sefton had the room on the ground floor opposite the kitchen.

Aleph closed the piano. Sefton was now supine on the floor, looking up at the ceiling, her book open upon her stomach. She often lay thus upon the floor, thinking. Moy had gone to kneel

14

beside Anax. She watched him sleeping for a while, then wakened him.

'Don't disturb him,' said Aleph, too late.

Anax, removing his long nose from underneath his tail, licked Moy's face. She caressed him, running her finger lightly along the black line of his upper lip, then laid her head down upon his warm flank, gathering her long plait into the basket with him. Louise had of course, as Joan pointed out, been wrong to suggest that Anax had forgotten his master, Bellamy. (Nor did Louise in fact believe this.) However, Moy had certainly, in a short time, established a profound relationship with the dog. The children had been in mourning for their old cat, Tibellina, when Bellamy's surprising move had cut short their discussions about another pet.

Aleph looked down at Moy's long yellow plait lying upon the stiff light-grey fur. Then she went over to Sefton and kicked her gently. Sefton, without otherwise moving, took hold of Aleph's foot and pulled the shoe off. Aleph, relinquishing the shoe, moved to an armchair and sat down, opening Milton's *Poetical Works*. She read:

> Nay, lady, sit; if I but wave this wand,
> Your nerves are all chained up in alabaster,
> And you a statue, or as Daphne was
> Root-bound, that fled Apollo.

Sefton, abandoning Fisher's *History of Europe*, was now wondering: what would have happened if Harold had defeated the Normans? Or if Canute had lived longer? England would have become part of a Danish confederacy with its capital in Denmark. Europe would have been unified. Would that have been a good thing or a bad thing?

Louise, who was convinced that the girls never discussed sex, was in fact wrong. They did discuss it, but only in a certain style. Perhaps most of the things they did were in a certain style, tacitly agreed upon, since each cared what the other two thought and a standard had to be maintained. Now some time had passed in silence. They often stayed thus together in the evenings. Sefton was still lying motionless, Aleph was still reading Milton, Moy, the restless one, was sitting beside Anax's basket with her back against the wall, arranging beads upon the carpet to plan a necklace. Her hands smelt of basil. Anax, sitting up, watched her.

15

Aleph said, 'Has he been out in the garden?'

Moy, intent, said 'Yes.' Then she said, 'Oh how I wish we could get out of London. How I wish we could get to the sea.'

Aleph had put down her book and folded her arms across her breasts. 'I wish Bellamy wasn't selling his cottage.'

'Yes. I suppose there's no other way of getting to the sea.'

'Moy is a girl upon the land, but she is a silky in the sea.'

'I dreamt about seals the other night, such a strange dream. When are you going touring with Rosemary, not before my birthday?'

'No, no. I must be at your party!'

Moy's birthday was to make her sixteen. Rosemary was Rosemary Adwarden, daughter of Louise's friend Constance Adwarden. Rosemary was a year older than Aleph. Her younger brothers, Nick and Rufus, were the 'boys' whom Joan Blacket had deemed to be so necessary. The Adwardens, still away, lived in London, but also possessed a house in Yorkshire. Rosemary had a car. She and Aleph were to explore the 'North Country'.

'It'll be just a sort of family party this year,' said Moy. 'It's much nicer like that really. Clement and Bellamy will be back, and Emil and Clive, and Joan will be still here, and there's Tessa – I suppose – ' The girls shared Louise's irrational mistrust of Tessa Millen, but did not speak of it.

Aleph said, 'I think the Adwardens will be in Yorkshire, when they get back from America. A pity Harvey won't be with us.'

'Louie misses Harvey,' said Moy. 'She misses Bellamy too, since he can't come here because of Anax.' An unforeseen by-product of Bellamy's donation was that he could no longer visit Clifton in case the sight of him were to upset the dog. 'Louie' was Louise. Early on the three had decided against 'Mummy' and could not bring themselves to call their mother 'Louise'. They settled first upon 'Lewis', then upon 'Louie'.

'We all miss Bellamy.'

Moy said, 'This time next year you and Sefton won't be here either.'

The statement had a strange momentous ring. Aleph, her hands folded, did not reply at once. She said, 'Who knows? We may be at college in London.'

'No, no, you won't be. You'll be in Oxford. Everything will be different.'

'Well, and then you'll leave. You'll be a painter in Italy. You'll be married.'

'I shall never leave, I shall never marry. Oh Aleph, how I wish we could all stay like this forever, we've been so happy, why can't it go on and on!'

'Because it just can't,' said Aleph, anxious to change the subject. She called, 'Sef!'

Sefton did not reply.

Aleph said, 'She is thinking history, she is an ancient Egyptian, she is Julius Caesar, she is the Duke of Wellington, she is Disraeli – ' she called again, 'Sefton!'

Sefton in fact was being none of these persons. Abandoning the fortunes of Harold at the battle of Hastings, she had become Hannibal. If Hannibal had marched on Rome would he have taken it? There were arguments on both sides. And if he *had* taken it – ? Sefton loved Hannibal. For the last few minutes however she had been in a kind of trance which sometimes came to her when she lay on her back. It was as if she were being, as she lay, lifted off the ground, surrounded by a vibrating chord of atoms. This sensation was accompanied by a wonderful sense of total relaxation and of joy. She thought now, as with eyes closed she floated, oh how perfect this is, oh I am so happy! And yet, some other nearby thought-self was saying, how can I be happy now, when everything is going very soon to be dissolved into pieces and made as if it had never been.

Obeying Aleph's second peremptory call she sat up, feeling slightly giddy, raised her knees and put her arms around them, not looking at her sister.

Aleph said, 'I've been thinking of a question I want to ask you.'

'Yes?'

'Why did the Greeks never use rhymes?'

Sefton, already regarded as a polymath, had never reflected on this matter. However, she said promptly, 'Because they felt instinctively that rhymes were puerile and mechanical and inimical to the true nature of poetry.'

Aleph seemed content with this reply. She closed her Milton and let the book slide down her skirt onto the floor.

Moy returned to her subject. She said, addressing them both, '*You* will get married!'

'And so will you,' said Aleph. 'Throw me my shoe, Sef.' Sefton threw it.

'Never, never, never. I just can't imagine being married or – or sex – we're all right now, we haven't fallen into all those traps, I want to stay as I am now, not be in all that *mess*, you know what I mean.'

They knew. Aleph said, 'Innocence can't go on and on.'

'Yes it can, if you just *don't do things*.'

Sefton said, 'Being human, we are already sinners, we aren't innocent, no one is because of the Fall, because of Original Sin.'

'The Fall is ahead,' said Moy, 'and I am afraid of it. How can evil and badness begin in a life, how can it *happen*?'

'Sefton is right,' said Aleph. 'We are all sinners. Surely you yourself have occasionally done what you ought not to have done and left undone what you ought to have done?'

'Well, yes,' said Moy. The others laughed. Moy went on, 'But our lives are not in a muddle, we don't tell lies, we all love each other, we don't harm each other, we don't harm anyone.'

'We can't abstain from doing things!' said Sefton. 'Besides, how do we know whom we harm?'

'Don't you want to fall in love?' said Aleph.

'I don't want men and sex and all that roughness and disorder.'

'Life is roughness and disorder,' said Sefton.

'I can't see how anything can ever happen to us – I mean, I feel as if, if we leave this place, we shall crumble to pieces.'

'I sometimes feel that too,' said Aleph, 'but it's nonsense!'

Sefton said, 'You know, I can understand why people of our age commit suicide.'

'Sefton! Well, why?'

'Like what we've been saying, it's the future, it's so near and so secret and so different and so awful and so unavoidable and so *crammed*.'

'The calm before the storm,' said Aleph. 'It is true that there is a barrier between us and the world like a wall of rays.'

'You are romantic,' said Sefton. 'You like to think about what Moy's so afraid of.'

'No, I'm afraid of it too,' said Aleph. 'But perhaps I am romantic, I want romance!'

'Aleph, you are joking!' said Sefton.

'As for this stuff about being innocent and harmless and pure in heart, we are really just lucky and sheltered and naive. We are awfully nice to people, but we don't go out into the violence and the chaos and help people, like – '

'Like Tessa does!'

'Well, I wasn't thinking of her, she does of course. I wonder if it's harder to be good in this age?'

'I want us to stay together forever,' said Moy.

'As old maids?' said Aleph.

'Perhaps we could make our beastly husbands live near each other,' said Sefton.

'We won't have beastly husbands,' said Moy, 'anyway *I* won't. I'd rather become a nun.'

'Like Bellamy.'

'It's said unlucky love should last, when answered passions thin to air.'

'Who said that, Aleph?' said Sefton.

'A poet. I suppose there's a moral there. Shall we sing again? What about the "Silver Swan"?'

'I'm retiring,' said Sefton, jumping up. Aleph had gone to the window and was peering through the curtain. 'I think the rain has stopped. Oh – '

'What?'

'That man is there again.'

The other two joined her. A man was standing on the other side of the road under a tree.

'What's he doing?' said Moy. 'He seems to be looking at our house.'

'He may be waiting for somebody,' said Aleph. 'He's nothing to do with us.'

'Close the curtain!' said Moy. 'He'll see us!'

Sefton had already disappeared down the stairs and into her room.

In her bedroom above, Louise, moving the curtains to open the window slightly (for she liked fresh air at night) had also seen the man whom she had seen near the house twice before. She turned out the light, returned to the window and continued to watch him. He was a tall robust man wearing a trilby hat and a mackintosh, just folding up his green umbrella. He certainly did seem to be watching the house. She closed the curtains, turned on the lamp and prepared for bed. She put on her nightdress. Raising her arms to put on her nightdress gave her a strange feeling of being young again, a young girl, feeling a strange solitary thrill of vulnerability, going to bed and dreaming of marriage. Marriage, she thought. But I'm all confused. Marriage is in the past.

I *was* married. Besides, even when I was a young girl I didn't really think about *that*. It came suddenly out of the blue, suddenly like a storm wind. And now it's all over and I shall grow old.

Later, silence reigned in the house. The man was gone. Louise turned out the light. She dreamt that it was her wedding day and that she was dressed in black. She was in a room waiting for her bridegroom whom she had never seen. She kept saying aloud, 'How terrible! I'm late, I'm late.' The door opened slowly and a man in a black trilby hat and a black mackintosh stood outside. As he beckoned her to follow him, she felt a violent thrill like an electric shock. She thought, but this is *not my wedding day*, this is *that other* day. She ran sobbing in darkness, stumbling over black obstacles, the humped backs of animals; and she thought and *they are dead too*. Downstairs Sefton, not yet undressed, was thinking about Hannibal's tactics at the battle of Cannae, and pressing yellow gingko leaves between the pages of her Liddell and Scott. In the little room opposite Louise's room Aleph, in her long cotton nightdress, dark blue with little white flowers, was looking at herself in the mirror. She smiled faintly at herself, then by the tiniest movements of her face dissolved the smile into a pensive pout, then into an ugly demented gasp. Her teeth captured the fullness of her lower lip, her nose wrinkled, her eyes narrowed and filled with tears. She thought, it's a mask – and sometimes the mask is so heavy, and it is pulling me to the ground where I shall lie face downward. Perhaps this was a dream which I had and then forgot. Strange thoughts were in Aleph's head. She knelt down beside the bed, lifting the hem of her long nightdress and spreading it out around her. She knelt there for some time, open-eyed, breathing deeply. In the attic above, in *her* nightdress, dark red and voluminous, Moy was standing beside *her* bed. Over the bed hung the picture of her beloved, the Polish Rider. He was looking, with his authoritative pensive mouth and his calm wide-apart eyes, past Moy, over her left shoulder and away into some vast distance. He was a knight upon a quest. He was brave, innocent, chaste, good. But Moy was looking now, not at her hero, but at where her grotesque ugly flint stones were arranged upon a shelf. She was gazing at one stone in particular, golden brown, shapeless as crushed brown paper. She moved, reaching out her hand towards it. After a moment the stone shifted slightly, it rocked, then slid evenly forward off the shelf and through the air into her open hand. Moy knew about poltergeists and why, or at any rate when, they were present. She had said nothing to the others, but had, by investigative hinting, satisfied herself that she was the only one to whom the ambiguous gift had been given. She accepted it as a strange not unfriendly presence or form of being which joined her life with the life of things. Only sometimes, for it had various manifestations, it frightened her.

She put the stone, warmed and reassured by her hand, back on the shelf. She had, as usual, brought Anax's basket up from the Aviary, and put it in a corner where she could see it from her bed, and Anax was sitting in it, very erect, his tail neatly curled about his front paws, and he was gazing at her. She said to him, for he had watched the moving stone, 'Don't be afraid.' But his judgmental eyes said to her: 'Where is my lord, for you have taken him away and I know not where you have hidden him.'

'Well then, I dare you to walk across!'

In the bright morning light, somewhere in the Apennines, Bellamy James, Clement Graffe, and Harvey Blacket were standing on a bridge. On the previous evening, at the moment when Aleph and Sefton and Moy had been wondering where he was, Harvey had been taking part in the evening *passeggiata* in the square of the little town. The square, in warm waning light, was crammed with people walking, mostly young or youngish, mostly walking in a clockwise direction, though there were many older people too and many who chose to stumble into confrontations by walking anti-clockwise. In fact with so many people in the small square, it was impossible to avoid stumbling and confrontations. Harvey, who had experienced this phenomenon elsewhere in Italy, had never seen such a lively crush. It was like being inside a shoal of fishes who were confined by a net into a huge compact ball. His bare arms, since he had rolled up his shirt-sleeves, were being liberally caressed by the bare arms of passing girls. Faces, smiling faces, sad faces, young faces, ancient faces, grotesque faces, appeared close to his and vanished. People hastening diagonally through the throng thrust him gently or brusquely aside. Good temper reigned, even a luxurious sensual surrender to some benign herd instinct. Girls walked arm-in-arm, boys walked arm-in-arm, less often girls linked with boys, frequent married couples, including elderly ones, walked smiling, now at least in harmony with the swarming adolescents. Predatory solitaries pushed past, surveying the other sex, or their own, but well under the control of the general decorum. Eccentrics with unseeing eyes glided through, savouring amid so much society their own particular loneliness and private sins and sorrows. Clement and Bellamy, briefly amused by the show, had soon retired to sit in the big open-air café whence they viewed the intermittent appearances of Harvey, who with parted lips and shining eyes, in a trance of happiness, was blundering round and round the square.

'He's so happy,' said Bellamy.

'Yes,' said Clement.

They did not actually sigh, but the bleak tone of the statement and the laconic assent conveyed the fact that *they* were *not* happy. This was not the result of envy, they were both very fond of Harvey, they could have taken pleasure in his pleasure were it not that both were afflicted by grave and pressing uncertainties, even fears. Bellamy was feeling little less than horror at the prospect of the extreme self-denial to which he was now it seemed irrevocably pledged. While Clement was suffering a profound and secret anguish at the prolonged and mysterious absence of his brother, whom he knew to be quite capable of committing suicide.

The two men, friends since college days, brought together by their friendship with that enchanting sweet-natured *bon viveur* Teddy Anderson, could scarcely have been more unlike each other. Bellamy found simply *living* a task of amazing difficulty. It was as if ordinary human life were a mobile machine full of holes, crannies, spaces, apertures, fissures, cavities, lairs, into one of which Bellamy was required to (and indeed desired to) fit himself. The machine moved slowly, resembling a train, or sometimes a merry-go-round. But as soon as Bellamy got on (or got in), the machine would soon eject him, sending him spinning back to a *place* where he was once more forced to be a *spectator*. Perhaps, that was in some mysterious sense his place, his *destiny*. But Bellamy did not want to be a spectator, nor could he (having no money of his own) afford to be one. Moreover he had never really mastered the art, apparently so simple for others, of *passing the time*. His failure to find a *métier*, to find a task which was *his* task, caused him continuous anxiety, nor did it occur to him to emulate the majority of mankind who positively resign themselves, seeing no alternative, to alien and unsatisfying work. At one time he had suffered from depression, and was nearer to despair than his friends realised.

His parents were poor but not too poor, evangelical but not too evangelical, kind and well-intentioned like himself. He was an only child, he had a happy childhood. When Bellamy was over thirty his father (an electrician by trade) died in a freak accident and his mother decided to return to New Zealand, the land of her birth. Her death there was much later reported to him by a remote cousin. Bellamy was deeply grieved by these losses, but was able to deal with the pain in a fairly rational way. He often thought about his mother and wished that he had visited her in New Zealand as he had often intended to do. But *they*, perhaps (as he reflected later) because of the simple purity of their lives and the plain ordinary openness of their relations with him, did not enter into the torture chamber of his soul. About not having, in time, visited, even joined, his mother, he felt regret, but no anguish of remorse. In general, nobody *bothered* Bellamy. He worked hard at school and gained a scholarship to study history at Cambridge. Why after two years at that university, he left to study sociology in Birmingham, no one knew clearly. He suddenly, as he said, 'couldn't stand Cambridge'. He wanted to get closer to something – perhaps life. But life continued to reject him. Armed with his sociology degree, he went into local government, first as an administrator, then as a social worker. Later he taught sociology and religious studies at a sixth form college. Then he was unemployed, seeming unable to find *any* job. Then (to the horror of his mother – his father was by then dead) he became a Roman Catholic. One thread in his erratic life was (as he now felt he had discovered) that of a religious quest. He thought of becoming a priest, and even made some plans to enter a seminary. However, instead of doing so, he became a teacher at a comprehensive school teaching modern history. He soon lost this post through a complete inability to keep order. He then seemed to be intending to attempt a return to his earlier career as a social worker, and, in spite of the fact that his *curriculum vitae* was now patently so blurred, hopefully filled in some applications. Then *something*, which he felt was at last *that* for which he had been seeking, *overcame* him and he decided to 'give up the world' in the most extreme and complete manner possible by becoming a monk in an enclosed order. He made contact with a religious house, which he had now visited several times, and into which he hoped before long to be admitted as a novice. On this subject he was now in continual correspondence with one of the Fathers. How frightened and appalled he often felt at this prospect he kept concealed from his friends. He welcomed this fear into his soul as an intimation of something more irrevocable, the entry at last of Truth into his life. Much was made, perhaps too much, by those friends who saw in his plans only what Joan Blacket had called his 'death-wish', of Bellamy's homosexual tendencies. It was true that he did prefer his own sex, but seemed to find no difficulty in remaining chaste.

At Cambridge he had gained two good friends, Teddy and Clement, from whom he later acquired Lucas and Louise. Clement in fact had been the 'bonding agent'. Like Bellamy, Clement left Cambridge without a degree. He was, by temperament and in appearance, exotic. Bellamy was fairly tall, thick-set veering on stoutness, with a large face and a round head. He wore round glasses. He had light brown eyes, the colour of beech trees in spring one of the girls had said, and thick lips and untidy straw-coloured hair now hiding a bald spot. He smiled readily and had a mild and gentle expression. Clement was tall and slim, with copious dark almost black hair and very dark eyes and eyebrows and a long straight narrow Grecian nose, shapely red lips, and a fierce proud expression. His father was Italian-Swiss, his mother was English of a traditionally military family in Hampshire. His father, 'a financier', Clement was never quite sure what his father did, had worked partly in London, partly in Geneva, with residences in both cities. As longed-for children did not appear, the couple, then in England, had adopted a boy. This boy was Lucas. As sometimes happens in such cases, two years later the mother became pregnant and Clement was born in Geneva. At a later time, when Lucas and Clement were at an English boarding school, the tall good-looking father (whose striking appearance Clement had inherited) defected, departing for America with a mistress whom he subsequently married. The boys received affectionate, slightly apologetic, letters at intervals. Clement sometimes replied, but Lucas never forgave his father. The father paid for the boys' education, the mother in due course returned to Hampshire, Lucas took over the London house, the father disappeared, a letter which Clement sent to him when the mother died was returned 'unknown'. Over their mother, Lucas and Clement shed tears, but separately.

Life, which so much resented the advances of Bellamy, adored Clement. He swam through it swiftly, weightlessly, lively and slippery as a fish. He arrived in Cambridge stage-struck, after successes as an actor at his school, and immediately joined the Footlights. He enjoyed his academic studies too (he was reading English), loved literature, and mastered the latest fashionable critical theories. He published reviews in university periodicals. However, though tipped for a first or good second, he left Cambridge without a degree, lured to London by one of the talent-spotters who frequented Footlights' performances. Clement loved the theatre, he loved the buildings, the actors, the sonorous voices, the echo in the empty shell, the clothes, the smell, the perpetual glittering artificiality and transformation scenes. He was, in that great palace of true and false, versatile, some said too versatile. He was a good actor, a natural actor, born with it, grasping very early in life his talent to defend himself by mime. He was strong and agile and graceful, he could have been a ballet dancer, he worked briefly as an acrobat in a circus. Almost everything which could be done in theatre he did. He directed, he designed sets, he designed clothes. He was said to be lucky and to *bring* luck. Apt at everything, he settled down to nothing, but that, he said, suited him. He was good at what he chose to do, endlessly productive of fresh ideas. *Etonne-moi*, great figures in theatre land had used to say to him. He was known, but never quite famous. He worked in small theatres, less often in the West End. Older mentors were continually telling him to concentrate his talents, to stop playing the monkey, to stop imagining he was still twenty and in Cambridge. But this was just what Clement did imagine and joyed in imagining, finding little reason to doubt that the gods had given him the gift of eternal youth. There was no doubt in Clement's case that he loved the other sex; but here again he lacked concentration, he lacked constancy, and was even heard to preach that in *that* caravanserai it was better not to try to settle down. The theatre was essentially a scene of partings, a *métier* for free beings. Something like 'home life', in so far as it existed for him, was provided by his elder brother Lucas, by Teddy and Bellamy, then by Teddy and Louise, then by Louise and the children; the children being the girls and Harvey, for whom Clement had figured, if not

25

exactly as a father figure, certainly as the most delightful of uncles, and later more like a brother.

The human fish experience of the *passeggiata* was yesterday. Today they were at the bridge. They had intended to leave early by car, since they were a little behind with their timetable, but it was Harvey who had insisted that they must see the great fourteenth-century bridge, a little outside the town, famed for its grandeur, its great length and height, and for the large number of persons, including distinguished ones, who had chosen to commit suicide by leaping from it. They had had to leave the car at some distance from the bridge and proceed on foot, thereby losing more time, but when they arrived they agreed that it was worth it. The scene itself was grandiose, a deep valley, a chasm with a glimpse of the ruined Roman bridge and a scarcely discernible river, the valley floor and hillsides covered with a thick forest of mingled cypresses and umbrella pines, their dark and light greens creating in the brilliant sunshine a vibrant fuzz of undulating colour. Out of this vast surge the pale bridge rose on sturdy yet elegant piers, in the centre affording a drop of several hundred feet. The bridge carried only a long narrow footway, with a tall wall on one side and on the other a parapet about four feet high and four feet wide. The trio had crossed the bridge and were admiring the chasm from the other side. An argument had developed about what the great thing was now made of. Had it not, according to the waiter in the hotel, been damaged in 1944? Would they be able to drive along the valley so as to get a proper view, perhaps from the Roman bridge? How silly of them to have left the guidebook in the car. As they were about to walk back, the conversation had turned to suicide and how that would be facilitated by the comparatively low parapet. Then there was some discussion about the width of the parapet, Harvey arguing that it was really far wider than it seemed, and how it would be perfectly easy to walk along it. It was then that Bellamy had uttered his very ill-advised and ill-starred 'dare'. Even as he ceased speaking Clement had kicked him, called him a fool, and seized hold of Harvey's arm. Bellamy was explaining that of course he hadn't meant it, it was just a joke, an idiotic idea, not to be thought of – but it was too late. Twisting away from Clement's hold, Harvey ran on a few paces and vaulted up onto the parapet. He began to walk.

At the point at which Harvey had mounted, the tops of the pines and cypresses were only a few feet below him. As he walked now, steadily, not fast, aware of the ground falling away below, he fixed his eyes upon a mark at the far end of the bridge, a white post with a tree beside it. He thought, it's not far away, I must keep looking at it and simply walk *straight on*. However, a few steps later he found that he was losing the concept of 'straight on'. It was as if the space upon his right, where the chasm was opening, were turning itself at the level of his feet into a sort of floor, or sheet of faintly glittering water upon which some superior power was gently urging him to step. He took a quick glance downward and a shock passed diagonally through his body, and for a second his mouth opened and his arms rose. He stared instantly back toward the white post and the tree but could not find them. His eyesight seemed to have altered, refusing to deal with the distant manifold. Ahead now all was pale and swimming in sunlight. Yet his feet were finding their way, each foot replacing the other as if *they* were now in control. He was aware of his arms swinging and a continued impulse to raise them up to balance himself, or as if they were wings. With an effort he focused his eyes, gazing now upon the parapet itself some four yards in front of him. It seemed astonishingly narrow, and becoming narrower – could it actually *be* narrower? He tried to concentrate upon its texture which was roughish, as of tiny stones engulfed in concrete, what had seemed smooth was now becoming uneven so that even the little stones were casting shadows. The colour of the parapet which had seemed before, long ago, a light brown, now seemed a dazzling white, covered with little black shadows, like a tiny model, it weirdly occurred to Harvey, of a primitive village of little white houses in a bright southern sun. Then it seemed to him that the giant ponderous footsteps which had somehow taken him over were *crushing* the little houses. Amongst these thoughts he could hear behind him a whispered conversation going on between Clement and Bellamy. They were agreeing that they must not walk beside him, where they would distract him and disturb his balance, but keep close behind him. What use is that, thought Harvey, now irritably aware of them out of the corner of his eye, why are they there at all, when *this* is happening? Cautiously he drew his downward gaze, riveted to the parapet surface, closer to him. He was *keeping going*, but how? Must he not suddenly tire? He felt tired, his movements less steadily mechanical. The powerful spirit on his right was still subtly tempting him to move out onto that floor of void, to walk there, to *fly* there. He felt a pressure as of a strong wind. He wondered, *shall I look at my feet?* Surely he must not do that. He was suddenly aware of something approaching him, something dark just below him on his left, someone who was crossing the bridge, who would pass him, perhaps brush him, push him, *compel* him to *move aside*. The figure came nearer like an approaching wave, he could feel a force upon his breast. A voice said, '*Sei pazzo?*' That was over. Now he could feel, almost see, his moving feet, his dusty blue and white running shoes flashing to and fro, the white laces flapping. He thought, I did not check my shoes before starting. I shall trip over my laces. But there had been no 'before starting', just suddenly the thing itself. He resisted an impulse to bow his head, to let it descend onto his breast. He lifted his gaze, concentrating upon the lines, the receding straight converging lines, the limits of his ordeal. They now seemed, these lines, as if they had been very finely drawn in black ink, enclosing the terrible narrow, ever more narrow, path upon which and within which he must keep on walking. He thought, it's geometry, it's just geometry, it's like walking on a map. He did not dare now to seek for distant landmarks. But he allowed himself to think, is it halfway, surely it must be halfway – only I must not get tired, I must keep moving, above all I must not look *down there*. He was beginning to be conscious of his breathing. Suddenly the temptation overcame him and for a split second he glanced right and down. He saw no longer the appalling chasm but the roof of green colours still far off below him. He breathed again, he concentrated upon the lines, he thought it can't last forever. Then he tried again to find the white post and the tree – and suddenly they were there, in place, quite clear, nearer. He slightly slowed his pace. He became conscious again of the muted voices of Clement and Bellamy behind him. He began to have a collected feeling. The parapet seemed suddenly wider, no longer a punishment of inky lines. He was able to think, yes, it's an ordeal, it's something that *had* to be. Then he saw, in what seemed at last some quite ordinary sense of looking, a group of three girls standing beside the white post. He felt an impulse to smile and was aware of his mouth being open. He thought, I mustn't fall at *the*

28

last moment. The trees were close below him now, the end of the bridge, which he had not conceived of when he was looking at the white post, now clearly visible, and the brown stripe of the path behind it. Harvey now walked slowly. He was there, he had done it, he had *conquered*. He waved his arms. The girls were waving at him, he could hear their voices. The parapet ended, Clement and Bellamy were there saying things. Harvey turned and looked back at the way he had trod. He smiled at the girls. Then, with a yelp of triumph, springing high into the air, he leapt to the ground.

The ground was not exactly where he expected it to be. His eyes were dazzled as by a white flash. He hit the ground hard, his legs violently jarring his body, then slipping from under him, scraping a track in loose stones. He fell on his side, an outstretched arm jolted, his shoulder taking the impact. A surge of outraged annoyance bore him up, and in an instant he was on his feet, leaning against the wall and brushing earth and stones off his shirt. He felt a blush of shame and anger run up his neck and across his face. How could he have been, at the very last moment, such an *idiot!* He could hear the girls chattering in Italian.

Bellamy was saying, 'Are you all right? You haven't hurt yourself?'

Clement said, 'You bloody fool! I was going to shake you, only it seems you've shaken yourself! Now come on, get a move on, we're late, let's get away from this awful place!'

Harvey said, 'Yes, sorry.' He touched his cheek which had evidently also been grazed in the fall, and looked at the blood on his fingers. He had instinctively lifted one foot from the ground. When he put it down and placed weight upon it, trying to step forward, a sharp pain ran up his leg. He was conscious now of a continuous pain in his foot and ankle.

Clement repeated, 'Come on!'

Bellamy said, 'He's hurt.'

Harvey said, 'I'm all right.' He tried to walk, limped, then hopped as far as the white post and leaned against it. The girls, who had retired to a distance, were watching. 'Damn it, I'm sorry, I seem to have wrenched my ankle, I expect it'll be OK in a minute or two.'

'We haven't got a minute or two,' said Clement. 'All right, rest it – but then we must go.'

Bellamy said, 'Oh dear, I shouldn't have said it, it's all my fault!' They stood looking at him.

Harvey was panting. He felt breathless and suddenly helplessly weak. There was a raging furnace in his foot, which he was holding up clear of the ground. Rubbing his cheek with the back of his hand and trying to calm his face he put his foot down firmly and began to walk. The pain was great. But more than that, he realised he *ought not* to be walking. Whatever it was that had happened *didn't like it*, and was threatening that if *that* went on, it would get much worse. Harvey hopped forward, taking hold of the nearest support which was Bellamy's arm.

'It's not all that bad, is it?' said Clement.

'I'm sorry,' said Harvey, 'I'm *sorry*.'

'You'll just have to walk to the car, there's no other means of transport.'

'We could carry him,' said Bellamy.

'Don't be silly!'

A few yards further on along the path there was a seat. Hopping on one foot and leaning hard on Bellamy's arm Harvey got as far as the seat and sat down, burying his face in his hands. Kneeling before him Clement undid the laces of his shoe and with some difficulty eased the shoe off. The foot was dangling at an unusual angle. He gently rolled the sock off and revealed the swollen foot and ankle, crimson and blue, the distended skin burning hot to the touch. Opening his eyes Harvey looked at it. He groaned.

'Something must be broken,' said Bellamy, 'oh *dear*, oh *God*, it's *my fault*.'

'I can't walk,' said Harvey to Clement, 'I *can't*.'

Clement said, 'Don't worry. Just rest a little. I'm afraid we can't get the car any nearer, the way's blocked. Bellamy and I can hold onto you and you can hop.'

'We can still get to Ravenna in time – '

'We aren't going to Ravenna,' said Clement.

'Of course not,' said Bellamy, 'we must get a doctor in the town to look at your ankle.'

'If it could be just strapped up a bit,' Harvey was going on, 'it'll be better in a day or two.'

'We'll see,' said Clement, 'but if it's as bad as it looks I think we must head for the nearest airport and take you back to London.'

*

'Poor Harvey!'

Everyone was saying this.

The first news came to Louise, when Harvey telephoned her from the airport at Pisa, asking her to tell his mother. The news was that he had hurt his foot and was coming home, just briefly he said, to have it seen to. The gravity of the situation dawned upon his anxious friends, and indeed upon him, after his return. Harvey had first, after the mishap, visited the nearest *pronto soccorso* in the little town. The first-aid man had, after a glance, told them to go to the hospital. They decided to drive to Pisa to the hospital there, where they could also if necessary get a direct flight to London. At Pisa X-rays revealed a thoroughly smashed ankle. Harvey's foot and leg were immediately put into plaster for the journey home. At Heathrow he left the plane in a wheel-chair. At the Middlesex Hospital the plaster was removed, more X-rays were taken, and the grim diagnosis was confirmed, with hints of further complications. The leg went back into plaster, and Harvey was issued with crutches and *forbidden* to let his foot touch the ground. It was agreed at a conference consisting of Harvey, Joan, Clement, Bellamy and Louise, that it would be prudent, for the present, to keep Harvey in London near to the specialist who was dealing with his case. To the surprise of the others, Harvey had accepted this plan. He had, everyone said afterwards, more sense than they had realised! The walk over the bridge remained a secret however. Clement and Bellamy, present when Harvey telephoned his mother, noticed that he had simply told her that he had 'jumped off something'. This now appeared to be the story as generally reported, and Clement and Bellamy did nothing to disturb it. They were easily able to imagine that Harvey did not want, with this outcome, to talk about the exploit which had given him so brief a moment of triumph.

'You start, Moy, you're the artist,' said Aleph.

Laughing, sitting in the large armchair in the Aviary, Harvey rolled up his trouser leg and extended his heavy white plaster cast. Its weight, with every movement, still startled him. It was late evening, he and Clement had had supper with Louise and the girls.

The others stood watching while Moy, solemn, kneeling before him, armed with thick coloured crayons drew, round the top of the cast, a green wiggling design which turned out to be a caterpillar. Sefton, who was next, declined the privilege, declaring that the thing was already a work of art and should now be left alone. This was voted to be a negative spoilsport approach, the point being to cover the thing with random scribblings which would in the end, as Moy said, add up to a complex work of art. Aleph then quickly drew some sort of animal ('It's a dragon,' said Sefton) then criss-crossed it out. 'I can't draw!' 'Anyway, it's a something,' said Moy. Louise, saying she couldn't even manage a something, wrote in fine well-spaced capital letters – HARVEY GET WELL. Clement, sitting on the floor, drew a comical dog with a fancy hat and a sweeping line to make the dog say what Louise had written. Everyone laughed, Moy's caterpillar was voted best, and all agreed it was a good start. Harvey, laughing longest, thanked them all.

The atmosphere, thick with love and goodwill, was slightly forced. The company was still suffering from shock. Harvey's return had been so unexpected, after they had been resignedly bemoaning his absence and envying his luck. Of course his mishap was trivial, a ridiculous accidental fall, his recovery would be rapid, Rosemary Adwarden, when she had broken her leg skiing, had been quite mobile after a few weeks. It was just that it was surprising, even embarrassing, to find Harvey back so soon and suffering from *any* ailment, it seemed quite out of character! It was also surprising that he had not insisted on setting off at once for Florence.

Harvey was a tall slim youth with glossy blond slightly curling hair which at school he had worn ridiculously long; more lately he had trimmed it to fall flowing back to a length just above the shoulder, and had allowed himself the adornment of a sort of fringe which, though derided, was at once said to suit him, producing that 'raffish Renaissance look' which was his intention. He had a pretty nose, and a pouting mouth not too full-lipped, criticised as feminine, dubbed by its owner 'pensive', contributing to a certain forward pressing eagerness and air of lively curiosity. His eyes were brown and large, able (amicably) to blaze, and when narrowed and laughing, to glow. He was said, by Emil, to resemble the *kouros* in the Copenhagen museum. When Harvey managed to find a photo of this handsome and powerful youth he was suitably gratified. He played tennis and cricket and squash, ran faster than most people, and was a good wrestler, though not as good as Clement, and a good dancer, though again not as good as Clement. He had often wrestled with Clement and on some occasions danced with him too. He was sweet-tempered and popular, though in some quarters thought to be conceited, and by his schoolteachers lazy and facile, able to excel but unwilling to exert himself in pursuit of perfection. His air of cheerful self-satisfaction was reassuring to some, irritating to others. Those who knew him little could scarcely have guessed that he had had any troubles in his life.

The affecting little scene round Harvey was breaking up a bit. Sefton, leaning against the books, looking up something she had suddenly remembered to look up, was tapping her square teeth with her fountain pen. Moy, who had been dusting Harvey's cast with the fluffy end of her plait (known as 'Moy's magic whisk') had left the room followed by Anax. Aleph, sitting at Harvey's feet with her shoes off, was holding forth reassuringly about Rosemary's experiences. Clement and Louise were standing at the window looking out at the evening rain.

'So you arranged it all by telephone? That was clever of you.'

'Yes,' said Clement, 'they left their telephone number with me.'

'Everyone leaves their telephone number with you!'

'And they left the keys, so it was easy.'

'And they're staying on in Greece and going to buy a house on an island?'

'They' were Clive and Emil, the gay pair alluded to by Joan Blacket. Clement had 'cleverly' arranged for Harvey to move into their flat while Joan was to continue occupying Harvey's. This made sense as Emil's flat was reached by a lift, and Harvey's by several flights of stairs. Clive and Emil were a steady couple. Emil, the elder, was German but had lived a long time in London. He had been a picture dealer, and was said to be rich. He wrote books about art history which were published in Germany. Clive, Welsh, who said (presumably a joke) that Emil picked him up on a building site, had been a schoolteacher in Swansea.

'Yes,' said Clement, 'but they'll keep the London flat. I must say, I miss them, they are so entertaining and so sweet.'

'Didn't they make some advances to Harvey?'

'No! They just pull his hair!'

'You pull his hair too! Clement – any news of Lucas? Well, of course not, you would have told me.'

'No news.'

'My dear, I'm so sorry. I feel sure he's all right. He's such an eccentric creature. He'll turn up.'

'He'll turn up,' said Clement. 'I just so – very much wish that he would.'

'I know how close you are. I was thinking just the other day – remember that game you used to play with him in the basement when you were children. What was it called? It had some funny name.'

' "Dogs".'

'Yes, of course, "Dogs". Why did you call it that?'

'I forget.'

As Louise turned away from the window Clement, looking out into the dark rainy street, saw something odd. A stout man in a trilby hat was walking slowly down the other side of the street, now folding his umbrella. The rain must be abating. He looked familiar. Clement thought, haven't I seen that man before? He looks like that chap I saw a few days ago outside my place. He looked as if he were waiting for someone. He was about to say something about the man to Louise when something struck his foot. It was a red ball. As he stooped to pick it up a yellow ball followed, then a blue one, then more, reds, yellows, greens. Moy had fetched the ball box down from her room and was bowling them fast across the carpet, while with her other arm she restrained Anax. Swiftly Clement gathered the balls up, distributing them with magical ease about his person. Then moving into the middle of the room he began to juggle, with four balls, five balls, six balls, balls without number. The balls moved faster and faster, seeming to find their way, balanced upon air, making patterns which owed nothing to the juggler's swift hands. And to Clement itself it was as if the creatures themselves, innocent of gravity, were playing like birds a weightless game around his head. How do I do it, he thought, how is it done? I don't know what I'm doing. If I did know what I'm doing I would not be able to do it.

Louise, watching the spellbound children watching Clement, felt such a strange painful joy, tears came into her eyes.

A little later, Louise had descended to the kitchen where Sefton had already done the washing up. Moy, with Anax, had taken her beloved Clement up to her attic to show him a picture. Sefton

34

was lying flat on the floor in the Aviary and thinking. Harvey was sitting on Aleph's bed in her bedroom on the floor above. The room was small, accommodating a little desk, a chest of drawers, some shelves for books, a chair and a bed. Aleph's dresses hung with Sefton's in the large cupboard on the floor below. There was just enough space for Harvey's knees not to touch Aleph's as they sat facing each other.

'Does it hurt?'

'It itches.'

'Rosemary's itched too.'

'When are you going on tour with Rosemary?'

'November. She used to scratch inside it with a knitting needle.'

'Can you lend me one?'

'No one here knits. Perhaps I'll buy you one.'

Harvey had got through the evening creditably. He had eaten and drunk plenty at supper, he had praised the artistic efforts on his cast, he had listened patiently to the account of Rosemary's recovery, he had laughed at everyone's jokes, watched Clement juggling and said 'aaah!' at the right moment. But his heart was heavy and black and painful within him and he felt humiliated and defeated and miserable and afraid. He hated the hot heavy cast and was appalled when Moy suggested painting on it, he found the idea sickening. The cast he was now wearing was his third, the one put on after the first examination in England having been removed so that the damaged foot and ankle could be viewed by some grander specialist. This specialist had now gone on holiday and Harvey gained the impression that the present cast had been put on hurriedly just to keep his foot 'in a stable condition' until someone could decide what on earth to do with it. What he deduced from the murmurs and glances of the doctors was that he was 'an interesting case'. Broken bones were nothing. Trouble with tendons could go on forever. He had, moreover, gained the maddening information that if he had not walked on the damaged foot the situation would have been considerably better. He recalled how, out of sheer vanity and hurt pride, he had insisted on limping, instead of hopping, during the walk back to the car. The cast, even more uncomfortable than its predecessors, pinched his calf, there could be scarcely room for a knitting needle, his whole leg below the knee was burning hot, perhaps he was developing gangrene. His foot was persistently painful, he could not sleep, he felt exhausted and utterly alienated from himself.

35

And all the time he lived with the taunting mirage of what might have happened, what should have happened if only at one little absolutely accidental moment he had not been such a damn fool. A ghostly caravanserai of images accompanied him of the happy free life in Florence which he had so long cherished in his imagination. His first real freedom. And all this bitterness had to be kept absolutely secret and the strain of doing so added to his misery, to have *all that* and to laugh too and pretend that there were things, that there was *anything*, which he could now enjoy! He had to keep up the externals of his well-known merry confident triumphant self while really he was not that self any more, but something tattered. His early realisation that he was seriously damaged had made him decide to *give up* Florence at once and not prolong a hope which repeated disappointments must in the end extinguish. It was this, and not 'common sense' which had made him assent so surprisingly to the urgings of Clement and Louise, and of his mother who had promptly told him not for heaven's sake to go to Italy and run up endless medical bills when he could get better treatment for nothing in London. His upper lip trembled but there was no shoulder to lean on, no one could really understand how his life had changed and how he grieved over the wreckage of it which was so entirely his own fault. At his age, to be maimed, to be lame, never to play cricket and tennis again, never to dance again, with his perfect health some magical *authority* was gone forever. The two people who, in their imaginings, were nearest to him, Louise and Aleph, collaborated nobly with his miserable pride, stiffening him up, instead of, as he sometimes wished, encouraging him to break down! But of course they *saw*, and he resented this too, and felt ashamed before Aleph, unmanned, undone. Of course there were infinitely worse plights, he had good doctors and good friends, he might even get better, or if not, learn to 'live with his disability'. But something even more profound appalled him, his terrible devouring self-pity, his *fear*, and that he, Harvey Blacket, so successful, so loved, could have such a fear. No, no one must guess how craven he was, how unprepared to face this first challenge to his adult being. He had often imagined how well he would behave in the army, how brave and unselfish he would be in a shipwreck, how he would endure poverty, deprivation, solitude, without whimpering. It was as if *this* affliction had come at him unfairly, under his guard, unaccompanied by the contextual dignities of the situations in which he had imagined himself so strong. But of course what was so dreadful about this was that he had so wantonly brought it upon himself.

Aleph was sitting opposite to Harvey upon a pale blue upholstered chair with padded arms. Behind her, leaning against her little desk, were his crutches. She was wearing a long dark brown tweed skirt and a close-fitting light brown jersey with little brown beads around its high collar. During the knitting needle conversation she had folded her hands, placing them, nestling within each other, between her breasts in the attitude which so irritated Harvey's mother. She was staring at Harvey, her brow pitted, her dark eyes narrowed, with a look of calculating compassion. There was no doubt that she saw a great deal. But in the cramped vulnerability of the house, always it seemed full of people, there were few opportunities for long intimate conversations; and in any case she was still treating his wounded condition with a respectful caution.

'How's life at Emil's flat?'

'*Luxe, calme et volupté.*'

'You keep warm?'

'Oh *yes!* And what a kitchen! I think I'll give a party.'

'Are you all right? I know you're not all right, but are you all right?'

Harvey understood this shorthand. 'Yes. No, yes.'

'How's Joan.'

'Fed up, brimming with energy.'

'Does she mind staying on in your flat?'

'No, she loves being inconvenienced and persecuted. I'm going to see her tomorrow. And maybe I'll visit Tessa, see if she's all right.'

An uneasy sensation always prompted Harvey to tell 'the women' when he went to see Tessa Millen. Not that there was anything 'between them'. It was just that Louise and Aleph and Moy somehow 'disapproved' of Tessa. They had never 'seen the point' of her. Whereas Sefton liked her. Harvey was afraid of being detected making secret visits to Tessa which might be misconstrued. The result was these awkward declarations.

Aleph waved her hand, signifying absolution or perhaps indifference.

'You look tired, Aleph – are *you* all right?'

'Yes, no.'

'Been writing more poetry?'

'*Nyet.*'

'*Che cosa allora?*'

'*Non so.*'

'*Perchè?*'

'I am just waiting. Now you must go.'

Much of their converse lay in such laconic exchanges, signifying perhaps an *impasse* in which, most of the time, they found themselves amazingly comfortable, even the lack of privacy suited them somehow. 'It's like being always on the stage,' Aleph said once. But moments came when they had trampled the ground too much, nothing fresh was left, and they had to recover. They felt they knew each other too well. But also, and especially lately, they could announce that they had not yet discovered each other at all. 'Yes, we are players, actors,' Aleph said. Yet too they could agree that there was nothing in the world more natural than their mutual mode of speech. Now, it was as if her lassitude and his craven gloom came together, mingling like two opposing waves. A blue and green silk scarf was trailing over the back of Aleph's chair and touching her shoulder like an honour. She moved, drawing it across her breast. Harvey leaned forward and took her unresisting hand.

Sounds from above suggested that Moy's colloquy with Clement was over and they were now chatting on the landing.

Harvey and Aleph rose. Harvey reached out for his crutches. He said, 'She loves Clement.'

Aleph opened her bedroom door. 'Yes, she loves him. You know Moy will grow up to be an extraordinary woman.'

Clement, coming down the stairs to collect Harvey called out, 'Goodnight, Aleph.'

She called, 'Goodnight, magician.'

Behind Moy's closed door Anax could be heard barking. Harvey insisted on descending to the front door without help, keeping his wounded foot carefully off the ground.

My dear son,

Thank you for your long letter and please excuse this reply in haste. I hope that I have not misled you, and that we have not misled each other. 'A simple shelter, like a garden shed, unheated except for an oil stove in extreme weather, in the wooded part of the grounds', is not I am afraid to be envisaged. (Your reference to being perhaps 'immured' is I assume a metaphor.) I would advise you to reflect further before deciding that you really wish to come here on probation as a lay brother. You speak of a 'vocation', but there are many vocations in the world and opportunities to satisfy, at least to some extent, your expressed desire to 'do nothing but good'. You speak of 'preparing yourself', but the surrender of a few worldly pleasures conveys no picture of the austerity of the monastic life – and, moreover, the pride which you so evidently feel in these renunciations may tend to render them valueless. What is required of you is something more radical than, as it now seems to me, you have even attempted to imagine. You must realise that you are deeply stained by the world, the stain is taken deeply, deeply as the years go by. Your wish for a revelation or a 'great sign' should be put away, it is a mere stumbling-block. I am glad to hear that you are taking a more sober view of your 'visions'. As I have said to you before, religion is but too easily degraded into magic. The practice of 'visualising' is indeed not to be considered; I fear that you retain much of your early, and if I may say so half-baked, attachment to eastern cults! After your long and full confession I think you should abstain from brooding emotionally over early sins. An excessive cultivation of guilt may become a neurotic, even an erotic, indulgence. You should not imagine yourself to be in an 'interesting spiritual condition'! What is needed is a cool, even cold, truthfulness: I believe that you will understand me. I am afraid that I have no time to answer the list of theological questions which you append. Let me say again that you should reflect carefully and at length about your future plans. I am sorry that you have so hastily given up your employment – and your flat – and I advise you to *wait* before you (as you said you intend to) give up your dog! I fear you are in danger of being too romantic about the dedicated life – you say you desire its peace and its joys – but this peace is quite unlike

39

worldly peace, and its joys unlike worldly joys: such things are won only through deep pain in which there is no element of self-satisfaction. Please forgive this brief and I fear unpleasing letter! You know that I speak to you in love, and not in unkindness.

Yours humbly *in Christo*,
Fr Damien

P.S. About your friend who accidentally killed a man who was attacking him. As he acted in self-defence and without any violent intent I do not see that he need feel guilty. He should however, banishing any resentment and remembering that he too is a sinner, think with compassion about his assailant, perhaps finding out something about his history and circumstances – for instance, it might be suitable for him to assist the man's innocent wife and family. (You said little about the situation – these are but hasty reflections.)

My dear Father Damien,
Thank you very much indeed for your letter. Always your words lift up my heart. I particularly appreciate what you so wisely say about my friend who had the terrible misfortune to kill a man, what you say is so right, and that he might help the man's family – I shall tell my friend this when he returns to London, it could be a comfort to him, just something wise and good which he might do – not that he is guilty of anything of course, but I fear that he may be in a state of shock. I have taken what you say about my 'spiritual problems' very much to heart and am thinking soberly about my plans. I hope you will understand when I say that my uncertainty concerns means not ends. I am quite sure that I want to 'give up the world', but still unsure about how and where this can be done. (I have sent my poor dog away.) I think you know what my heart desires. I want to *surrender* at last to a yearning for holiness which has travelled with me all my life. I want to be, thereby, overcome and *destroyed*. I desire this *death*. You will understand me. As I at last grasp this need as a practical possibility and not a romantic dream I have had to think hard about certain matters, hence the list of theological questions which I sent you. (I hope you still have it, I kept no copy, and that you will find time to answer

some at least of my questions – if necessary I could try to indicate the most important ones.) I have no doubt that I am a Christian, but I have always left a certain area of my mind quite vacant as if I have already handed it over to God. I feel I can't be bothered, it doesn't matter – and, I hope, I feel it in a serious holy sort of way. I mean, of course I've read books, people, I mean scholars, say all sorts of things about Christ, that He was an exorcist, a magician, even a charlatan, that He was just one among other half crazy holy men, and the gospel writers just fudged them all together, that He never claimed to be God anyway, and of course there is no evidence for the Resurrection and the whole thing was really invented by St Paul – Paul who so clearly is an ordinary man – but *He – could* all that be true, could *He* be a sort of figment, He who spoke from the Mount? He who so clearly is *not* an ordinary man. So many things have been found out now, so many new ways of thinking. It is as if He is being *stripped*. Please don't misunderstand me, I mean I'm not naive, I know that faith in Christ need not be shaken by historical evidence, that the Resurrection is a spiritual mystery, and that what matters is the living Christ whose reality we *experience* (sorry, I know you don't like that word). These are just my jumbled thoughts, as you said you would accept them. But I do sometimes feel that, for me, there is this blank in the middle of it all. I want to be, here, in this, *in the truth*. But can I be if this last missing piece is *not clearly seen*? Putting it more bluntly, does 'evidence' matter? The Buddhists don't think so, they have a mystical Buddha – if we have a mystical Christ can that be the real Christ? Is a mystical Christ 'good enough'? Could there be Christ if *that* man never existed at all? It is almost as though He were telling us not to believe in Him! Is it necessary that I *clarify* all this before deciding to seek the monastic life? But – the fact is – I can't wait – I am already captured – I have opened the door and He has entered – I am in His hands. Sometimes I have felt that divine spirits surround me, as if angels. (What do you think about angels?) And I meant to say – all this about Christ, what about God? – Well, I think God can look after Himself. (What does that mean?) Forgive all this rant. I thought of tearing this letter up but won't. Sometimes I feel scarcely

41

sane. But when I write to you I feel you are already enlightening me! With love from your worthless pupil.

Bellamy James

P.S. Another thing. The creed says that after His death upon the cross Jesus descended into Hell and on the third day rose again. *What did He do in Hell*? Did He rescue the *good* people from the past who had lived before He came? Or *everybody* from the past since they hadn't known about Him, and might have led better lives if they had? Or did He go to see what really *bad* people were like and to sort of *experience* badness while He was still in human form? Of course I know this is a myth – though myth doesn't seem the right word. I can't help thinking what a bright light there must have been in Hell while He was there and how dark it must have been after He left.

Bellamy put down his pen and thrust away the blanket which he had drawn over his shoulders. He lived now in one room and it was small and cold. It was late at night. The light of the lamp illumined Bellamy's hand, and he thought, looking at it, how old my poor hand is becoming! He knew that his reply to Father Damien, swiftly written, was confused, even in places silly. But this impetuous outpouring was, he felt, the only *truthful* way in which he could write to the priest. Or was it, precisely, *not* truthful? Was not his letter 'picturesque', itself a case of 'romanticism' and 'neurotic erotic self-indulgence'? It showed no evidence of *hard thinking*. Should he not tear it up or rather use it as a text to be profitably *seen through*? He had not answered the questions, he had not replied to the charges. It was as if he immediately 'de-realised' the stern things which the priest had to say, softened and sugared and crumbled the grim language about being 'stained'. Yes, of course he was stained by the world, of course he knew that *that* existence would not be peace but the continuation of life under very unpleasant circumstances! In refusing to reflect on these things he was simply leaping over the difficulties. But was not this leap just what was now required of him? Was not this *faith*? Father Damien's letter, which he was now perusing again, expressed unease. The priest was troubled, startled, by the way in which Bellamy had rushed at the whole matter, and was retreating from the more come-hither position which he had occupied earlier. Bellamy had now known Father Damien for nearly two years, had visited him twice (Father Damien was 'enclosed') and written to him many times. Now Bellamy's letters were disturbing the holy man. But did not Bellamy intend to disturb, was there no end to Bellamy's duplicity? In his 'flirtation' with the doctrines of the East he had perhaps gone further than he had told his mentor. And there were the angels, the visions of which Father Damien thought so poorly and which had made Bellamy's doctor speak (though the idea was dropped later) of epilepsy. The visual experiences had now gone from him leaving only, and that was now less often, the strong sense of presences, inducing anguish, joy, tears. He thought, the images are withdrawing from me. That is as it should be. What is now is simpler, more humble, more absolute. Simple because it is just a matter of desire, of Love calling unto love. (Sex?)

Bellamy put his letter into an envelope, addressed it to the remote abbey where Father Damien was incarcerated, licked the envelope and stamped it. By this time his thoughts had wandered a little, returning to the image of Jesus, breathing His last upon the Cross, then hurrying away upon His mission to Hell. He now recalled that he had once seen (where?) a very moving picture of a scene (by whom – a disciple of Rembrandt?) entitled 'Christ in Limbo'. But surely Limbo was not Hell? Hell was where wicked people went, Limbo was where innocent unbaptised babies went. (He could not recall any babies in the picture.) And also presumably virtuous people who lived before the Incarnation. Perhaps Christ visited Limbo on some other occasion. What was He doing, anyway, in either place? What comfort could He bring, what good could He do? What greater torment than to see that light, and then to see it eternally withdrawn? This picture of the eternal withdrawal of light evoked another distant image: that of a slim fair-haired youth going away down a road, turning, looking, then going on, then vanishing. The figure was faded like an old photograph, just faintly tinted in colour, the pale blue of the boy's shirt, the pale blue of his eyes. The name of the boy was Magnus Blake, and he looked at Bellamy now, as he had sometimes looked in dreams, not accusingly, but with a mournful puzzlement. Bellamy had seen his tears but there were no tears now. It had all happened at Cambridge and it had all been so short and so simple. They had fallen in love. Magnus was two years younger. Shortly before this thunder-clap Bellamy had decided, after certain

43

messy and inconclusive experiences, that it was all right to love one's own sex, but in his case this must be done chastely. His brief glimpse of violent passion terrified him. He explained this to Magnus who thought Bellamy's ideas were mad. They argued fiercely. Bellamy, feeling himself on fire, not able to trust himself near the boy, broke off relations abruptly. It was the end of term. He left Cambridge and did not come back. He did not answer Magnus's letters. After he sent back a letter unopened the letters ceased. He killed within himself the voice which murmured 'it is not too late'. Several years later a Cambridge acquaintance, who did not know of Bellamy's relationship, mentioned Magnus, speaking of a 'broken love affair', but adding that Magnus had now 'found a lovely new partner' and emigrated to Canada. All Bellamy's anguish was renewed. A long time had passed and Magnus had probably had other 'broken affairs' since Bellamy had left him. Of course Bellamy *had* to leave him. But he did not have to do so in such a cruel way. He blamed himself for that sudden ruthlessness which he had felt then to be directed against himself only. Perhaps if he had been braver and better he might have talked it out drearily and made Magnus tire of him. But it was precisely this which he couldn't face. He had to be high-handed with himself, to wound himself and make sure it was his own blood upon his hands. It was *his* heart that must break, and his consolation would be to brood upon his own pain. He had told this story to the priest, Father Dave Foster, who had converted him to Catholicism, and later on to Father Damien. But somehow, when he told it, it changed, medicated in the telling and handed back to him as an instance of selfish irrational guilt and of youthful problems overcome long ago. The other person he told was Lucas Graffe; and to Lucas alone he told another of his secrets, that when he left Birmingham three years later he had suffered a severe depression, otherwise known as a nervous breakdown. The walking away down the road and the looking back had really happened. From the door of his lodgings he had seen Magnus walk away, look back and walk on. Bellamy closed the door. Magnus expected to see him again, he did not know that the argument was over forever. Bellamy left Cambridge the next morning.

Bellamy removed his black jacket and undid his white shirt. Since his 'decision' he had dressed always in black and white, a solemnity undermined by Clement who said he was just always

44

playing Hamlet. (A part to which Clement had so far aspired in vain.) Bellamy had given up his job at the further education college, and thereafter sold his large flat in Camden Town and moved into the one-room flatlet in Whitechapel. He had sold or given away almost all his belongings. He had given away his dog. These were steps upon the spiritual road of no return. Although Bellamy had had, in spite of his 'resolution', some strong 'temptations' after he left Cambridge, Magnus had had no successor. He was now thinking about Harvey, another blond boy with blue eyes. It occurred to him that now for the first time he was connecting Harvey with Magnus because of what had happened at the bridge, which had been so entirely Bellamy's fault. Supposing Harvey had fallen into the ravine. Oh if only Harvey could get absolutely better! For this he prayed silently in an old familiar childish mode of discourse which was one mode of his relation with God; there were perhaps for him more sophisticated modes but none more natural. Bellamy thought about Harvey, about his particular eager beauty and his affected raffishness of a quattrocento dandy and thought too of the crestfallen boy, so disappointed and so shocked, affecting courage and continually making jokes, whom he and Clement had shepherded back to England. And Clement too: everyone knew that Clement was upset by his brother's disappearance but only Bellamy knew *how* upset, how strangely, wildly upset Clement was. Bellamy understood. About Lucas's whereabouts Clement had said: I want to know and yet I don't want to know. Of course Clement was afraid: afraid that Lucas might have killed himself or else perhaps become insane, lost his memory and after an unsuccessful attempt on his own life be lying unidentified and raving in some mental home. It must be a terrible thing to have killed a man; and Lucas's reaction would have to be something extreme. The publicity, the ordeal in court when Lucas was accused of 'excessive violence' and virtually (as his defending lawyer indignantly said) of murder, would have shaken anyone. Lucas reticent, proud, dignified, secretive, eccentric, must have been overwhelmed.

Thinking of Clement, then of Lucas, then of Louise, Bellamy's thoughts returned homeward to Anax, pausing on the way to reflect that now, because of Anax, he could not go to Louise's house any more. He had not foreseen this separation when he decided to send the dog away; but of course it was implied, Anax must not now see him or hear of him ever again, he must learn

45

to forget him. Bellamy checked what might have been some awful grief. He missed the warm bundle upon his bed at night, tucked into the crook of his knees or lying stretched out long against his leg, silent and good, adjusting himself patiently to Bellamy's movements, aware of Bellamy's sleeping and his waking, knowing when it was morning time and Bellamy would take him in his arms and he would lick his master's face. Father Damien had said, do not send the dog away. That meant something. But the dog was gone. When Bellamy had spoken to Moy, who remembered everything, about Anax's judgmental eyes, he had not meant to indicate a censorious look. It was rather the look of perfect innocence, perfect love, which could not but be just. Bellamy thought, a dog is an image of God, better than us. He thought too of Louise and her children and of Harvey who also seemed to be her child, and how they and Clement had made up a family for him, provided him with a family life, something inherited from Teddy, a holy trust, a bond of duty, a place of absolute forgiveness and reconciliation. He loved them all, perhaps especially Moy with whom he had, since her earliest childhood, had some special intuitive understanding, so that they laughed at once, as at some private joke, when they met each other. The innocence of the children, the silent wisdom of the mother. Clement too upon whom that light fell – perhaps it was like a dream, something too perfect which was about to fall away into the distractions of the real world. Did it not depend upon the children who were so soon to lose that magic? Or do I imagine this, Bellamy thought, simply because *I* am losing it, and I want to believe that it will not survive me? He wrinkled up his face and put his hand before it as if to conceal it from some accusing stare, perhaps the just amorous gaze of Anax. He wondered, smoothing out his grieving mask, whether Anax was now sleeping on Moy's bed, or was he in his basket. That would of course be, not the basket of the defunct Tibellina, but his very own old basket, brought with him from Bellamy's flat on that terrible day of parting. Was he asleep, or perhaps awake and thinking of Bellamy, *could he forget him? But was not forgetfulness* the very goal, the thing itself, the blotting out of the world?

He got into bed and turned out the light. He lay for a while open-eyed, suspended, as if held in a dark void. As his eyes closed he saw himself walking in a strange twilight through endless huge empty halls, lofty halls with dim ornate roofs, empty yet full of being, the great unbounded spaces of his soul. Then, falling asleep, he began to remember how, at the Battersea Dog's Home, he had picked up Anax as a young dog, little more than a puppy, and how he had *chosen* him from the great yearning mob of other dogs, seeing his strange loving eyes and his brave intent face among the innumerable faces of poor doomed dogs, and carried him away in his arms. And he thought, it's like Christ in Hell. Why didn't He save them *all* and take them away with Him? Perhaps He *couldn't* – but why not? And as he fell into deeper sleep he thought, but *I* haven't even taken one away from death, I can't find Anax, I've lost him, *he's still there*, and he will be destroyed and his body will be burnt – and he began to run back, retracing his steps through the lofty empty halls which endlessly hopelessly continued to open one into the next.

'Now I see why you've been hiding it!'

'I haven't been hiding it!'

'Yes, you have, you're ashamed of it, you've been putting it under the bed.'

'Well, I've got to put it somewhere!'

The thing in question was Harvey's plaster cast. He was visiting his mother who was ensconced in his own tiny flat. Of course strictly speaking Joan should have been enjoying the grander scene *chez* Clive and Emil, but with Harvey crippled it was agreed that he must live in the large flat with the lift. Anyway, as Harvey pointed out, Clive and Emil were obliging *him*, not his mother.

Joan was lying back, supported by pillows, in Harvey's narrow bed which folded back into the cupboard when not in use. Harvey moved the cast, lifting its alien weight with his hands.

'Let me see. Who put all those scribbles on it?'

'Louise and the others.'

'Who did which?'

Harvey named the authors.

'How touchingly characteristic. Moy does a dear little creepy-crawly, Aleph does a dragon-cat, Louise does the obvious, Sefton can't think of anything, and Clement is a comic dog. It's all self-portraiture.'

'They've been so kind to me.'

'You are becoming as dull as Louise. Could you pour me some more champagne?'

It was the next morning about ten, and Harvey had found his mother in bed dressed in a white fluffy *négligé*, drinking and smoking.

He poured the champagne. 'No, I don't want any. Do you mind if I open the window?'

'I mind very much. It's raining outside.'

'The rain won't come in. This room is full of smoke. I can't breathe.'

'Of course you can breathe, why are you so *feeble* – why don't you go back to Italy, you aren't all that helpless, you can get about.'

'You said it would be too expensive, I'd have to pay doctors over there.'

'Did I? Well, you're getting better now. You're just doing this to punish yourself, since you made one mistake you want everything to collapse so you can call it fate.'

'Oh do shut up, *maman*!'

'Look, I want to write something on your cast. Why should I be left out?'

'Oh please not!'

'Give me a pen or something.'

Harvey produced a felt pen from his pocket and obediently propped his stone leg up on an adjacent chair.

'Here, hold my cigarette.'

Leaning over from the bed Joan wrote upon the cast the words which had been uttered by the man who passed him on the bridge and which Harvey had repeated to her.

He laughed, returning the cigarette and lifting down the heavy object, holding it carefully in his hands. He surveyed his mother. The white *négligé*, softness itself, seemed to be made of cotton wool, and some little white feathers had been sewn in around the neck where a pink nightdress discreetly peeped. Harvey did not want his mother to look too feminine. She had evidently powdered her nose, her pretty so faintly *retroussé* nose, making it look curiously pale, but had not yet donned the glowing mask of make-up which so magically composed her face. Her long slim hand emerged from the fleecy sleeve and adjusted her dark red locks which were snakily straying upon the pillow. Her eyelashes, not yet darkened, fluttered, her eyes, narrowed, sparkled. They gazed at each other.

'When I give them that stare, it hits them just like Bacardi!'

'I can do everything, but nothing with you.'

'That was a good song, I remember the girls used to sing it, there are no good songs now, nothing but repetitive shouting. How are the vestal virgins?'

'The same as ever. Beautiful and good.'

'All that will change in the twinkling of an eye. Aleph who folds her pretty wings like a dove will become a Valkyrie and marry a tycoon. Well, I suppose Sefton will tramp sturdily on until she's an old maid and head of some dreary college. But Moy – '

'Aleph said Moy will be an extraordinary woman.'

'Yes. Something amazing, perhaps awful. I never said this to Louise, I told *her* that Moy would be in church arranging the flowers. I see her as a witch – '

'*Chère maman, you* are the witch!'

'It's not just the sickening aroma of female adolescence, there's something mad there, it could become something horrid – '

'Never! She's so gentle, she loves little things – '

'All that will go too far. Heaven help her husband, she'll turn him into a mouse and keep him in a cage. I wonder if she thinks Clement will wait for her. He has the gift of eternal youth. He would make a good mouse. I gather she's in love with him already. Thank heavens you think *they* are all your sisters. Now *you* have got to marry a rich girl, listen Harvey, you've *got* to, you're so good-looking and it's time you started being serious. What about Rosemary Adwarden for instance – '

'Oh please don't *bother* me, please *leave me alone* – '

'You call that bothering? Wait till I commit suicide or go to Humphrey Hook!'

After some study Harvey had decided that this fictional individual signified drugs, or was another name for death. He did not take these threats seriously, but he hated to hear them.

'I wish you didn't go so often to that house. Actually those girls are zombies, they're all asleep. Louise has been asleep all her life. God, how the place reeks of females.'

'Louise is the widest-awake person I know, *she* isn't living in a dream world – '

'So you think I am? I know, of course Louise is your real mother – '

'*No* – '

'You always sided with your rotten father – '

'You mean at the age of six!'

'Yes, and then you poured it out to Louise – '

'Oh don't start up that old stuff, it's so *boring* – '

'My father gambled the money away, your father stole it, and now you – '

'Do you want me to give up the university and take a job as a clerk?'

'Yes.'

'Don't be silly, I get scholarships don't I, I'll earn more later on, I'll support you – '

'In my old age, which begins tomorrow. All right you don't want to think about money, you don't want a job, you imagine someone will always look after you – '

'Well, you earn some money somehow – '

'What do you mean "somehow", are you insinuating – ?'

'I think I'd better go away, I'm just annoying you.'

'So you find it *boring* when I try to help you! Go away then. I can always stay with my ma in Antibes.'

'You say you detest her.'

'Of course I do, but – '

'Mind your cigarette, it's boring a hole in the sheet.'

Such arguments occurred more frequently, now sometimes ending in his mother's tears, which he shuddered to see and blamed himself for occasioning. Her unhappiness had always caused him pain. But in the past he had felt, when they quarrelled, that somehow ultimately it was play-acting, and there was no background of a reality in which he was expected to play a heroic part. Now however, at this very moment of his being grown-up and *free*, he was being handed a terrible new burden of *responsibility*. He resented being made to think of himself as in some serious sense likely to *do wrong*. Of course he didn't want to think about money! He disliked the, also more frequent, references to his father. Harvey had, without any purposive intent, carried with him an evolving interpretation of his father. In this lively 'remembrance' his father, portrayed by Joan as a monster, appeared as reserved, laconic, silent, simply not framed by nature to control, or skirmish with, or be in bed with, an emotional passionate pugnacious woman. Joan had made scenes in order to stir him into some more positive relationship, to force him to respond, even to dominate. But this rough treatment, far from enlivening her husband, made him draw away, become even more laconic, until one day he vanished altogether. Harvey remembered that day. Some money, Harvey did not know or try to discover how much, did indeed vanish with him. About this truant father Harvey did not speak to anyone, not even to Louise. Sometimes he had dreamt of going to find him. But his love for his mother eternally forbade this move. Harvey adored his mother. She adored him.

Joan was staring at him. Her untended face looked damp and spongy, her cheeks were flushed, the grains of powder dabbed onto her nose were dry and visible. Aggressively she gulped down some champagne, spilling some on her nightdress, and put the glass down noisily on the side table. Adjusting her pillows she upset the overflowing ashtray onto the floor. Harvey picked it up, retrieving the cigarette ends and kicking the ash away under the bed.

'*Ma petite maman, ne t'en fais pas comme ça!*'

'*Tu es un moujik!*'

'Well, well! Have you heard any news of Lucas?'

'No, why should I? Why do you suddenly say that? Are you trying to change the subject?'

'I don't know what the subject is, I'm just making conversation.'

'Making conversation! My son comes here to *make conversation*! Why don't you go somewhere else and make something else. Have you, meaning you and Clement and Bellamy and Louise, had any news of him?'

'No. Clement is terribly worried.'

'Everyone goes round saying how worried everyone else is. I'm not worried. Damn Clement, I wish I could turn *him* into something.'

The doorbell on the flat buzzed from below. Harvey lifted the answer-phone. 'Hello.' He said to his mother, 'It's Tessa.'

'Good. Tell her to come up.'

'Tessa, come up. My ma's here.'

Harvey went out onto the landing. Tessa Millen came up the

flights of stairs fast, striding not running. She patted Harvey's cheek and sped into the flat. Harvey followed her in.

Tessa was, in the lives of what Joan called 'Louise's set', an anomaly, a misfit or enigma, liked by Harvey, Sefton, Clive, Emil, Bellamy, and Joan, a puzzle for Clement, treated with suspicion by Louise, Aleph and Moy, liked by the male Adwardens, disliked by the female Adwardens, loved by Cora Brock, and so on as the circle widened. She was said to be an odd bird, certainly a 'card'. She was not *comme il faut* and made some people uncomfortable. Others said there was nothing at all odd about Tessa, she was just a liberated woman, and if she seemed peculiar that just proved how few of them there were. She was handsome, had short-clipped blonde hair and narrow grey eyes, Bellamy said she looked 'angelic', and Emil said she had an 'archaic smile'. Said to be over thirty, she had a long obscure past. She kept her maiden name, but had been married to some (now vanished) foreigner, perhaps Swedish. She had been born somewhere in the north of England, had a degree from a northern university, had lived in Australia (perhaps with the Swede), was active in left wing politics, had worked in a publishing house, written a book, nearly died of cold in a 'protest camp', had affairs with persons of both sexes, and been a social worker but ceased to be one 'under a cloud'. She was said to have 'money of her own'. A photo, purloined by one of her 'patients', showed her on a horse. Bellamy, who had known her slightly in her social work persona, had introduced her to Louise and the others. Emil, it turned out, had already met her through Gay Rights. At present, having evidently re-established her relations with the social services, she ran a woman's 'refuge' and advice bureau. She had a clear cultivated voice retaining some northern vowels. She used to frighten Harvey, but he had got over that. He had, as he grandly put it, seen the point of Tessa.

'Hello, Teacher!' Thus Joan greeted her.

Joan had used the brief interim to effect some improvements to her face. She sat up, eager and alert, against her reorganised pillows, her thick dark red hair combed and patted.

Tessa handed over her wet mackintosh and dripping umbrella to Harvey who put them in the bathroom. She advanced on Joan and took away her champagne glass and stubbed out the cigarette which had been smoking in the ash tray. Then she opened the window letting in the hiss of rain and a waft of moist cool rainy air. Joan groaned. Tessa sat down on the chair Harvey had vacated, Harvey sat on the bed.

'This place is foul!'

'Sorry, Teacher!'

'Hello, Harvey, how's the leg?'

'Fine.'

'He lies,' said Joan. 'And how are you, saver of fallen women? Do save one for Harvey.'

'Someone said you were away,' said Harvey.

'I was in Amsterdam.'

'I think I know why.'

'I don't,' said Harvey.

'Don't hustle Harvey,' said Tessa, 'He's romantic.'

'I think *you* are romantic, Tessa, you don't want to explain the world, you want to change it.'

'She is the eternal student protester,' said Joan. 'Good luck to you, angel. Students will save us all.'

'Who told you I was away?' said Tessa.

'Sefton.'

'My ma sends her love,' said Joan. 'She was bowled over by you. You must come again.'

'So she is still with that old chap.'

'Of course. He is *beau comme Croesus* as someone said of – '

'You went to see my grandmother?'

This was unwelcome news to Harvey. He rarely visited Joan's mother, but he felt possessive about her. He felt possessive about his mother. He did not care for the bond between Joan and Tessa. He did not like to think they discussed him.

'Well, *you* won't go and see her!' said Joan. 'She has given up sending *you* her love!'

'I need love,' said Harvey. 'I hope she won't switch hers off. I'll send her a postcard.'

'Big deal!'

Since his accident the idea had occurred to Harvey that he might go to Antibes and be looked after by his grandmother and the 'old chap' who was *beau comme Croesus*. But the vision had faded. He lacked the will. Besides, Joan's mother was *difficile*.

'Let's send Harvey away,' said Joan, 'grown-up talk bores him.'

'All right,' said Harvey crossly. 'I just wanted to talk to Tessa.'

'Come and see me tonight at six,' said Tessa.

'Tessa loves to get her claws into a new patient, she thrives on

the anguish of others. Anyway I know you two have a secret
pact.'

'Don't be silly, *maman*!'

'Shall I help you down the stairs?'

'No!'

An hour later Clement arrived. Heavy rain was coming down,
straight, in long pellets, glinting. Joan was up, dressed in a dark-
blue and white kimono. Clement threw his wet overcoat into the
bathroom. He sat down on the tumbled bed. Joan, who had been
sitting by the window, drew her chair near to him.

'Hello, Harlequin. Your beautiful black hair is wet. You've just
missed Tessa.'

'Oh, too bad.'

'She frightens you. It's that ambiguous charm. Are you in love
with her?'

'Don't be daft.'

'Are you in love with me?'

'No.'

'Are you in love with – ?'

'Is there any champagne left in that bottle?'

'Can't you face me without a drink?'

'No.'

'Well, there isn't. Unless you'd like to open another bottle. Let's
open another bottle.'

'No, don't bother, *don't bother*!'

'Actually there's some whisky in that slit there, Harvey's so-
called kitchen. Get yourself a glass and put some in mine.'

Clement fetched a glass and the whisky bottle. He poured a
little into Joan's glass and into his own.

'Would you like a towel to dry your hair?'

'No.'

'Well, please yourself. Cheers, Harlequin. Why didn't you come
sooner?'

'I've been busy. Have you heard anything about Lucas?'

'No, I don't know anything about him, why ever should I, why
do you ask me?'

'I just ask everybody.'

'Harvey was here too, the poor little monster.'

'Yes, poor fellow.'

'You mustn't have guilt feelings about him.'

'I don't.'

'Well, perhaps you ought to. Never mind. He's smashed himself up accidentally on purpose. Tell me something. So it's still raining. We can agree on that.'

'I just hope Harvey isn't in for a depression.'

'If he is, Tessa will cure him.'

'Have you seen Tessa — yes, of course you just said she'd been here.'

'You aren't concentrating. Soon you'll be asking me if I've seen Joan lately. Aren't you glad to see me?'

'Yes. Yes.'

'Did you know that a man's sexuality ascends into the highest pinnacle of his spirit? That implies, no sexuality, no spirit.'

'I don't know what it implies or what it means.'

'Ah sex — a thunderstorm in the tropics when you are instantly soaked to the skin and in the lightning flash just for a second you see everything so bright and clear, including the tiger ready to spring!'

'Are you still in that flat in the rue Vercingetorix?'

'Yes, of course, why not?'

'You said you were going to move.'

'I can't afford to. All right, I don't want your money.'

'It's not on offer.'

'You can be nasty.'

'No, Joan, sorry, I'm not being nasty, I'm just so tired, and so terribly worried about Lucas.'

'So everyone tells me. But, damn it, he can look after himself. I know him, I know Lucas, he's a good deal better at self-preservation than *we* are. You make too much of it all. Could you fill up my glass, just *fill* it.'

'You drink too much. All right, all right.'

'*Ça revient au même de s'enivrer solitairement ou de conduire les peuples.* A great man said that.'

'Great men can be bloody stupid.'

'So can little men. So you haven't forgotten our tiny flat?'

'Not our flat, Joan, your flat.'

'Well, you know what I mean.'

'You mean too much. You annoy me.'

'Oh how young and fresh you look, no wonder you prefer the

55

younger generation! So, Aleph is up for grabs, and Rosemary, and – '

'Dear Joan, don't talk nonsense, *please*, I just want to be with you in peace.'

'Peace! When do I ever have peace? My life is scratched to bits.'

'For God's sake it was one night, and – '

'So you say. And you'll say we were both drunk.'

'Yes. It was only one – '

'How long is one? Sentimentally and in the soul it went on for ages, it still goes on, it goes on and on. I feel your arms around me, your kisses linger yet, You taught me how to love you, now teach me to forget! I'll get the girls to sing that song, and I'll cry, and so will you.'

'I won't cry.'

'And I won't forget. You lack loyalty, you lack generosity.'

'That's a serious charge, old friend.'

'So I'm old friend now, am I? You remember nothing.'

'There is virtually nothing to remember.'

' "Virtually" can cover a multitude of sins. Don't you remember *"si ça ne vous incommode pas je vais garder mes bas"*? The sexiest thing Sartre ever said. Don't worry, I won't talk. All the same – Vercingetorix. It suits me to have a secret, it gives me power over you.'

Harvey was sitting on Tessa's bed. Tessa was sitting beside him. Their sleeves touched. Harvey had stretched out his stone leg, not to exhibit its decorations, on which Tessa had already commented adversely, but in a vain search for a less painful position. Tessa had stretched out both legs, clad in sturdy shoes and high woollen socks pulled up over her trousers, making them look like knee-breeches. Her rather pale 'angelic' face, usually alert with attention and authority, often sardonic and amused, could become curiously blank, as if she were absent, her lips parted, her eyelids drooping. No doubt she was tired, resting, switching off her consciousness so as to regather strength. Harvey respected her withdrawal, he was proud that she could be thus withdrawn in his presence.

The rain had stopped. The thin house, in a battered terrace in

Kilburn, was, somehow always, rather cold and damp. This was Tessa's house, where she lived and slept and organised her 'social work'. The hostel for the unhappy women was several streets away. (It was rumoured that Tessa had, elsewhere in London, a luxury flat to which she secretly retired when it was all 'too much'.) The ground floor, which had been extended into the small untended garden, consisted of the office, a room for typing and interviews, and a very private primitive kitchen. The first floor was Tessa's bedroom and bathroom and a room containing clothes, books, and other items belonging to Tessa, and a few cardboard boxes full of give-away clothing. The top floor, now also colonised by Tessa, had housed a lodger, a Mr Baxter, who had made a tiny contribution toward the rent, but had disappeared suddenly, said to be in prison or perhaps dead. The house was cold, small electric fires, sparingly switched on, being the sole source of heat. Mr Baxter had had an electric fire on a meter, but that had vanished shortly prior to his own disappearance. Tessa had once explained to Harvey that the secret of keeping warm in winter was not to vary the temperature, to let the weather into the house and rely on warm clothing. She should know, having survived a cold winter in the protest camp, living in a makeshift tent which scarcely covered her body, and spending the day searching for firewood. (At least they lit fires there, thought Harvey.) It was like, she said, the rule well known to biologists that the way not to feel hungry was to refrain from eating. A little food brings on an urge for more. People who fast become used to it in a few days. By this method one could at least learn to do without breakfast and lunch. Harvey, who required food as pleasure and had not yet discovered it as a necessity, did not care for these lines of thought.

The doorbell rang downstairs. Tessa locked the door at six and could ruthlessly refuse to answer. She proclaimed that the evening was hers and that she was often out: perhaps, rumour had it, in chic clothes at grand houses. She moved a little away from him and they looked at each other. The bell rang again. Then silence. She murmured, 'If it was urgent they'd go on ringing. The telephone is switched off too.'

'It might be a friend.'

'No. Friends have codes.'

'Don't tease me. Everything wounds me now except perfect kindness.'

'I can't provide that at this time of day.'

'Sorry. I shouldn't have hinted that I wanted to see you. It's very kind of you to – '

'Yes, yes. Do you want to talk about your mother?'

'You make people talk about other people.'

'Only if they want to. What people say about other people says a lot about the people themselves.'

'I'm afraid she'll take to drugs, she talks about getting "hooked". She pretends to be desperate and suicidal. Or is it pretence?'

'Yes, it's pretence. Next question.'

'Please – '

'She has tremendous energy and a tremendous will to live. I don't think she is suicidal. Desperation is her mode of willing to live.'

'Oh well – you visited my grandmother.'

'Are you jealous?'

'Yes. That's another wound. Tessa, don't be cold and brisk with me. I don't want to talk about my mother, I want to talk about myself. I feel so depressed. I have to be merry and bright while I just want to cry.'

'Cry then, cry here, everyone else does.'

'You must be tired of weeping persons.'

'Do those girls still cry? You said they cried a lot.'

'Yes. Don't be nasty about them.'

'I'm not nasty, I'm just interested. I respect Sefton. But they are all sick with values, crammed with good behaviour. In a way I envy them. Perhaps they'll get away with it. Is the dog still there?'

'Now you're talking about the dog. Yes.'

'Bellamy ought not to have given the dog away. A dog is forever. The dog will run off and vanish. *Then* there'll be tears.'

'I'm afraid so.'

'Bellamy is totally mistaken about himself. He is a fool.'

'Perhaps a holy fool.'

'Ridiculous phrase. Holiness requires intellect. The Jesuits understand that.'

'Don't be cross with me.'

'Harvey, I'm not cross. I'm just very tired. I'm sorry I asked you to come, I have nothing for you.'

'Just being with you helps me, I feel you are in the truth.'

'Where do you pick up these bizarre phrases?'

'You regard my mother as a patient, as a case.'

'You like to see it that way. You want to feel that someone is looking after her. I love her, I calm her, she is so picturesque, she is a witch, a leprechaun, daft as a brush. What a tonic.'

'I have never understood why a brush is daft.'

'It is something to do with foxes.'

'Oh Tessa, I'm so miserable, I feel so unreal, so *sick*, as if my whole inside had been removed, I feel *vacant*, I'm a puppet, I feel I've *died*, I wish you'd take me on as a case.'

'It wouldn't do, dear child.'

'Why not? You can't imagine how unhappy I am.'

'I can. But your kind of unhappiness must cure itself. You have a healing substance in your own body and soul, it is called courage. Your mother has it too. Call upon it, let it flow. Besides you are young and have work and a place in life. Read, study, think.'

'I can't. I'm an orphan. I realise it for the first time. My mother is just like a child. I can't go near Louise, she's taboo, and anyway she doesn't want me – '

'Well, please don't elect me to be mother. Harvey, stop. Tell me something. Is there any news of Lucas?'

'Not that I know of.'

'You all need him.'

'Why do you say that?'

'He'll put you in order. He'll make you jump. He is the ring-master.'

'I didn't know you liked him.'

'I don't. But he's really real.'

'Let's go out and have a drink.'

'No, I've got to be somewhere else. With a beard St Joseph, without the Virgin Mary, as they say in Spain.'

Harvey had left the 'refuge' and was sitting on the sofa in the drawing-room in Emil's flat. The numerous lamps were softly shaded, the distant traffic hummed in the Brompton Road. Emil collected pictures. He possessed, for instance, a Bonnard and a Vuillard and a Max Ernst and a Caillebotte and a Nolde and a drawing by Picasso and an Otto Dix and some early Hockneys. In honour of such treasures Harvey faithfully remembered to turn the burglar alarm on and off and carry about him a jangling bunch of keys. The peach-pink walls were covered with pictures, not all of which Harvey, though often in the room, had asked Emil to identify. It was *very kind* of Emil to lend him his flat. He could intuit that Clive was less enthusiastic. In the afternoon he had tried to work. As he told everybody, there was plenty of work he could get on with, studying Dante for instance. But his 'study' seemed to consist of reading some of his favourite passages – and finding that their magic had faded. When he returned from Tessa he fried some eggs in Emil's dream kitchen, clearing up carefully afterwards. Louise had shopped for him, stocking the flat with goodies, but supplies were running out. Soon he would have to shop for himself: a first sign in a gradual process of being *forgotten*. Louise had said vaguely, 'Come over any time, come to supper'; but, and this was another sign, although he longed to see Louise, and to see Aleph, he increasingly lacked the will to go. He was afraid, he was ashamed, he was a cripple, he was *disabled*. He could not bear their all feeling sorry for him, their sympathy might reduce him to tears. The Harvey who had been once so handsome, so long-legged and athletic, *did not exist any more*. He couldn't even wash properly. He had lost, and lost forever, his youthful pride, his freedom, his nerve. All he could do now was attempt, but surely in vain, to conceal the extent of his loss. He watched television pictures of a war, of a football match, of worthy people in wheel-chairs. He thought about his father and wondered if his father ever thought about him. His leg was hurting alarmingly. They had spoken of taking the cast off again. What would they find underneath? Something decayed and rotting, suitable only for amputation.

' "And the many many times that I took her in my arms, just to save her from the foggy foggy dew!" '

'I like the descant,' said Clement to Louise. The girls were singing in the Aviary below.

'That's Aleph.'

'With that soprano she should have a singing teacher.'

'She had a piano teacher at school.'

Clement was about to protest against the weary irrelevant reply, why had *he* not, long ago, paid for Aleph's singing lessons? Everything in his life now seemed to signal: too late. The little flat in Fulham where he had lived for years remained provisional, a *pied à terre*. Of course he was often away, involved in some play in the provinces or else with theatre people he knew in Paris. He even thought at one time of moving to Paris. He did not exactly dislike his flat, but he lacked faith in it. He did not buy pretty things for it. He 'starved it', as Louise said. The only interesting object in it was an early picture by Moy of a girl among some flowers. Clement was still *waiting* for the storm wind or *tsunami* which would carry him to some much higher level.

He had made a habit (of course not unannounced) of, once or twice a week, walking over to see Louise in the evenings. He liked London walking. These evening meetings had become easier since Louise and the girls now took their meals at different times, Louise having 'high tea' about seven, and the girls having supper, cooked usually by Moy, sometimes by Sefton, at eight-thirty. Louise sometimes made special dishes for them which could be heated up. This arrangement, like many such customs in the house, had somehow come about automatically, as a confluence of desires or 'general will'. The girls, who had quietly 'acquired' the Aviary, had now taken over the kitchen. So Louise now retired earlier, disappearing to her bedroom before the girls, finishing their evening meal, returned to the Aviary. This regime made for her a slow elegiac ending to the day. She read, she sewed, she listened to music, she *thought*. She had never, in her married life, had so much regular solitude. Into this hall of meditation, however, as into a space prepared, Clement was now entering. Perhaps Louise, enjoying her new peace and quiet, was also aware of a new loneliness. Perhaps Clement sensed this, perhaps he was sorry for her. Their relations, though of such long and firm standing, were obscure, simple and limited, even awkward. Yet, with all this, they talked easily enough. Louise, who did not often 'go out' or 'dress up', wore usually in all seasons a uniform of cardigan, blouse and skirt. This evening she was wearing a richly nut-brown winter dress with a blue and green silk scarf. Clement thought, I gave her that scarf long ago. Then he thought, no, of course Teddy gave it to her. Her 'stiff' hair swept back off her pale unmarked brow, tidied in this way by nature. She avoided hairdressers, Aleph cut her hair. Her light-golden-brownish wide-apart eyes gazed benignly at her visitor, and her mouth pouted a little with friendly restful pleasure. She was sewing, mending the lining of an old corduroy jacket of Sefton's. He thought, how calm she is, I mean how calm she seems.

'So you won't come to the ballet? You ought to come out more.'

'Oh, I will, I will.'

'I can hear Anax walking about on the floor above, his claws are clicking on the boards.'

'Moy will fetch him down soon.'

'There's something organic about this house. Sefton cooking, Aleph playing the piano, you sewing, Anax walking, and Moy – well, being Moy, communing with a thing perhaps.'

'She thinks everything in the world is alive.'

'She gives it life.'

'Wouldn't you like something to eat?'

'No, I had some sandwiches when I left the theatre.'

'You're still working in that little place, someone was ill?'

'Yes. I don't like working on someone else's stuff, but it's urgent. I'll finish soon. Damn, I meant to ring Harvey, I missed him at – well – '

'Where?'

'Oh, at his flat. I thought he might be there, but he had just left, Joan seemed to be all right, Tessa was with her.'

'Oh. I've told Harvey he can come to lunch or supper here anytime but he doesn't come.'

'He thinks you're pitying him. It's not like it used to be. You must name a date.'

'He said he was working.'

'I bet he wasn't. I can't work properly. Oh God, I wish Lucas would turn up, I *can't stand this waiting. I begin to feel that I ought to go out and look* for him, I just want to do something, not just wait.'

'I know. But you've already used up every possible – '

'Yes, but I ought to *go* to all these places, I ought to go to America – or else – just set off into the blue, just *search* with – with faith – '

'Wandering penniless and at random?'

'How can I stay here and get on with normal comfortable life?'

'You want to suffer for him.'

'I feel he may be in some terrible state of mind. He was rather low even before that business.'

'You mean because he didn't get the Chair at Cambridge?'

'He's terribly sensitive and vulnerable.'

'He's lucky to have a brother who cares for him so much. Brothers don't always love each other. But you've always been close.'

'I feel I'm at the end of something – everything is going to be different – and terrible.'

'That doesn't sound like you, you ride every wave.'

'There is one that will drown me. You know, the theatre is a tragic place, full of endings and partings and heartbreak. You dedicate yourself passionately to something, to a project, to people, to a family, you think of nothing else for weeks and months, then suddenly it's over, it's perpetual destruction, per-petual divorce, perpetual adieu. It's like *éternel retour*, it's a koan. It's like falling in love and being smashed over and over again.'

'You do, then, fall in love.'

'Only with fictions, I love players, but actors are so ephemeral. And then there's waiting for the perfect part, and being offered it the day after you've committed yourself to something utterly rotten. The remorse, and the envy and the jealousy. An old actor told me if I wanted to stay in the trade I had better kill off envy and jealousy at the start. You know, sometimes, I feel I'd like to be back in the circus.'

'You said the life was hell.'

'I like circus people. They're quite unlike theatre people. They're crazy, they're gypsies, they don't make mean calculations. It's as if they expected death all the time, even if they weren't on the high wire.'

'But aren't such people under a terrible strain, without any privacy, and all that compulsory homeless travelling – ?

'And I could get out of London, London is terrible, full of dangers and punishments. Compulsory travelling, perhaps that's what I need, like being a prisoner and walking to Siberia. One would become depersonalised and ego-less. Sorry, I'm talking nonsense. I just feel I'm losing my nerve, I ought to be imprisoned. I've been on a high wire long enough.'

'You mean looked after. You feel Lucas's absence.'

'Oh damn it all. What are the girls singing now?'

' "Santa Lucia".'

'It sounds so sad.'

'I forgot to say, they want you to teach them "Porta Romana".'

'I'll teach them "Porta Romana". I'll teach them anything – how's Aleph, is she – '

'Is she what?'

'Oh happy, all right, upset about Harvey, anxious about her studies, going to stay with the Adwardens – '

'All that. You'll see her before you go, you'll see them all. Sefton will stand on her head in your honour.'

'And Moy – '

'I wanted to talk to you about Moy – '

'I don't lead her on!'

'I know, my dear – it's just that, as she's growing older, she simply mustn't settle down to imagining that she's in love with you! I don't want it to become a sort of problem, a situation. People could notice and make jokes – I think they do already.'

'Am I then to be distant, detached, unkind? I can't do it.'

'Not unkind – just rational.'

'Rational! Louise, you know I can't be rational! All right, all right, I'll try. I'll watch my step!'

'Won't you eat something? You starve yourself.'

'No, no, I must go. I've got to read a script. We'll just look in on the girls.'

'You go alone, they like that.'

The trouble with Clement was that he had been in love with Louise. He had fallen in love when he had first set eyes on her, when Teddy Anderson had introduced her as his *fiancée*. Clement's instant thought had been *it's too late*, oh *if only* I had met her first, before she met Teddy, it might have happened, it could have happened, she would have loved me, we are made for each other, and now she's *lost forever*! Had he succeeded in concealing his feelings? Had he *imagined* that he saw in her eyes some special understanding, some kinship? Of course he did not dare to think that she too had thought 'if only – ' What he saw might have been her pity for him, her sympathy. Or perhaps just her kindness, the way in which, ever after as he watched her, she instinctively made all things better, speaking no evil, disarming hostility, turning ill away, making peace: her gentleness, which made her seem, sometimes, to some people, weak, insipid, dull. 'She's not exactly a strong drink!' someone said. So secretly did she work in her courtesy.

They had met in an empty theatre. Clement had come early for a rehearsal and was standing contemplating the stage, observing what was wrong with the way it had been (not by him) arranged. He was expecting Teddy. Teddy arrived with a girl. Clement held her hand for a moment; knowing that after that moment the darkness would begin. Of course he had survived. He had loved the ladies of the theatre, and other ladies too, including more than one very much his senior. As for Louise, of course he never told his love, to her or to anyone. His evident merry life with various charmers discouraged any suspicion of a secret attachment. Louise was a jewel locked away; and after the first 'if only' period had passed and Clement had got used to 'Mrs Anderson', he felt that his love for her had not faded, but had suffered a sea change into something special and unique, causing a special and unique and much valued, pain. Later still he just settled down to thinking that, though he would always love her, he was not exactly in love any more. Then Teddy died. Teddy's unexpected death caused a great deal of grief and disarray in the small group which had in one way or other been his 'family'. He had also, it became evident, been a highly regarded friend of numerous colleagues and clients who thronged his funeral. Bellamy was deeply affected, so were Lucas and Clement. Clement mourned sincerely, but could not help having other thoughts as well. His instinct was to run straight to Louise and offer her every sort of help and support, in the course of which he would, in some natural manner, declare the love of which he now felt sure she must be well aware. The children loved him. He was a favourite visitor at the house. But somehow just this facility made him hesitate, as if his sudden presence or closeness might be unfair, unfair to *her* in her desperate and vulnerable state. He hesitated. Meanwhile Bellamy had moved in with spiritual, and Lucas with financial, first aid. Here was another 'if only' – if only he had acted quickly, spontaneously, throwing 'tact' and 'good form' to the winds. Just *then* she had needed him, and he had failed. This bitter reflection positively, for a time, hindered his strange friendship with Louise, he avoided her almost to the point of boorishness, almost deliberately seeming to have lost his interest and his affection. The pain of his 'might

65

have been' led him instinctively to devalue his loss, make it not a loss but something inconceivable and nil. This stage passed however, and he returned to her, was welcomed, as he really knew he would be, and found himself playing a role in her life which was somehow special, unlike that played by Bellamy, or by Jeremy Adwarden who was generally known to have an old *tendresse* for Louise. Yet, as more time passed, her kindly acceptance of him and the innocent harmless ease of their friendship began to sadden him. He was becoming used to 'things as they are' – was he still in love? Surely *this* wasn't being in love? He had occasional affairs with the 'charmers', now less often, recently not at all. He could not find anyone he wanted to marry. It seemed he simply did not want to marry. Gradually, Clement began to feel that his strange sadness with which he had lived so long was very faintly colouring his old friendship with Louise, as if there were now a tension between them, an awkwardness, a bond which vibrated with a significant melancholy. Clement connected this with the growing up of the girls, and of Harvey, whom Louise loved so much and regarded as her son. Of course Clement and Louise had, as the years went by, talked endlessly about the children. They still talked, but some topics were avoided. The problems were too evident, they sat together eyeing them in silence. The stage now belonged to the young people, there would be happenings. Yet nothing happened; and Clement felt as if a magic spell had paralysed them all – and in that paralysis he felt at times the realisation, between him and Louise, that really they were brother and sister.

Nothing happened; yet there were disturbing signs and portents. Some while ago Joan upset him with a joke about his being 'too young for Louise and too old for Aleph'. Clement had become aware that he found Aleph attractive. Well, everybody found Aleph attractive. Louise, later, had said, in random conversation with Clement, that she thought Aleph needed an older man, but, and, she was afraid of her marrying someone unsuitable. Reflecting on this afterwards the crazy idea occurred to Clement that Louise, who was always insisting how young Clement was, wanted him to marry Aleph! But this was totally insane, the notion made him sick and giddy! Then he found himself pondering upon Louise's question, which he had scarcely noticed at the time: 'You do, then, fall in love?' Was not that 'then' suggestive? But now he was dreaming, he was wildly imagining things. Nothing like *that* could be thought of seriously. Perhaps, in connection with him, nothing could be thought of seriously; he had played the ape and the jester too long, he was supposed and expected to play the fool, he was essentially a self-dramatising entertainer, who turns over twice in the air and fears that next time he will break his neck. He had spent too long up on the high wire. Now something else was increasingly troubling Clement: his relation with Joan. Of course, although he had sometimes flirted with her, he had *no* relation with Joan. The episode in the rue Vercingetorix was a matter of one drunken evening. But who would believe that if Joan asserted otherwise? He could not say that nothing had happened. A little shame-facedly he had asked Joan not to talk, and so far as he knew she had not talked. Hints that she might were uttered jokingly. Now, as he increasingly reflected, the note had become more sinister: she had a secret which gave her power over him. This surely was blackmail. Or was it just the same old nonsense, the nonsense within which he lived his clownish life? Anyway, did it really matter? Except that he would rather Louise didn't know. He had once overheard Joan, talking to Louise, mention him with a droll air of ownership. Clement dreaded the idea of having to deal with an inflated rumour. There was a potential mess, a blot upon the unblemished, almost holy, nature of his friendship with Louise. Of course it was, was it not, really something trivial, minor. Louise had surely never worried about Clement's affairs with the ladies of the theatre, people whom Louise did not know. Joan was too near home. Suppose Joan said he had proposed to her? In fact Clement had always been fond of Joan, he *got on* with Joan, when younger they had even had some vague feeling of being 'scallywags' together. He *must* now distance himself from her. There was such a sad meanness about it all. Anyway, as he was now reflecting, he had even darker troubles in his mind, problems quite unconnected with Joan and Louise, which would occupy him entirely as he walked home.

As he rose to go and held Louise's hand and gazed at her he felt for a moment his old love for her taking possession of his whole being. They looked at each other. I *feed* upon this looking, thought Clement, but does she? I don't know, and I cannot ask. I am terrified of saying something which would wound our whole precious relationship. We are well as we are. I love her, that's all, that is *my* drama.

As he released her hand and picked up his coat from the bed

there was a sudden loud noise from downstairs. Someone was banging upon the front door, hammering it violently with a fist or stick.

'My God, what is that?'

'Louise, you stay here, I'll go – '

'No – '

Clement began to run down the stairs. The noise continued. Doors flew open. Anax was barking in the room above. The light had been switched off on the stairs and Clement nearly fell. He passed Sefton and Aleph who had emerged from the Aviary and moved out onto the landing behind him, looking down into the hall. Someone turned on a light. Clement was conscious of Louise now touching his shoulder. Someone had bolted the door and he struggled with the bolts. Louise was saying, 'Wait, wait, put the door on the chain!' But Clement had already opened the door wide.

A figure with an umbrella was standing outside. It was Bellamy.

'You dolt, what do you mean by knocking like that!' He called to the girls above, 'It's Bellamy.'

'Sorry, I couldn't find the bell in the dark.'

'What on earth is the matter?'

'Lucas is back.'

Clement exclaimed.

Louise said, 'Oh Bellamy, do come in, come in out of the rain.'

Bellamy said, 'I can't really, I – ,' but stepped into the hall. Clement closed the door.

Louise said, 'Is he all right?'

'Yes, I think so, but – '

'He didn't tell me,' said Clement.

'Well, you see I got a letter, someone forwarded it, I just found it now, I've got a taxi, I thought – '

'Do take your coat off and come upstairs and tell us – '

'Louise, I can't, the taxi is waiting, I'm going to see him – '

'*Going to see him?*' said Clement.

'Yes, I was so staggered, I rang him up, I asked him if I could come and see him at once, he didn't seem to fancy it but then he said "All right, come, it may be a good idea." So I rang Clement's number, then I got the taxi, and then I thought maybe Clement was here, and I wanted to be the first to tell him, and anyway why shouldn't you come with me, Clement – Lucas must have been ringing you to say he's back – why not come along with me now, we'll both go, I feel a bit nervous – '

'But what did he *say*?' said Louise.

'Just that he was back, you know how he hates the telephone.'

'You go with him,' Louise said to Clement.

Clement said, 'No, he won't talk to two of us.'

Bellamy said, 'Shall I tell him – ?'

'Don't say anything, I'll communicate with him tomorrow.' Clement turned away as if to go back up the stairs.

Louise checked him, tugging at his jacket. 'Clement and I will wait here, you could telephone us when you leave Lucas, let us know how he is and what happened.'

'I must go home,' said Clement, 'I'm just going to fetch my coat.'

Bellamy called after him, 'I'd give you a lift home in my taxi, only I can't keep Lucas waiting – '

When Clement reached the landing Moy, who had darted up the stairs, gave him his coat.

Clement, coming down again, said, 'Thanks, I've got my car. Off you go.'

A strange terrible wailing sound came from above, a high-pitched howl, then another, then another.

Louise said, 'Oh heavens, it's Anax, he heard your voice.'

Bellamy disappeared, the taxi door slammed.

Clement occupied the open doorway, the taxi had gone, the howling continued.

'Clement dear, please stay, I'm so upset – '

'Sorry, I must go.'

'It's raining, is your car near?'

The sound above changed into desperate hysterical barking, combined with repeated thuds as the dog hurled himself against the door.

'Wait, take an umbrella – '

'No, I'm OK. Goodnight.'

Clement set off walking, then running. Louise watched him from the door until he turned the corner. As she went slowly up the stairs the dreadful noise diminished, then ceased. There was another softer rhythmical keening, the sound of Moy sobbing.

2

JUSTICE

Bellamy's hand had trembled as he paid the taxi driver, a lot of coins had fallen onto the floor of the taxi, others onto the wet pavement. Bellamy hurried to the door. He rang the bell.

Lucas's house in Notting Hill was the house which had belonged to his parents and in which he and Clement had grown up. It was a detached house with an iron railing in front and three steps up to the door. There was a pleasant garden at the back with a cast-iron staircase running up to the first floor and vistas of many trees in other gardens. There was a capacious cellar (where the game of 'Dogs' had been played) and a large drawing-room with doors opening to the garden.

Lucas opened the door cautiously, a slit only. When he saw Bellamy he opened it a little more and went back through the unlighted corridor to the drawing-room. Bellamy followed, closing the door behind him. The drawing-room was also unlighted. Lucas switched on a green-shaded lamp upon the large desk which stood at the far end of the long room. Heavy velvet curtains were drawn across the glass doors which led to the garden. The room was quiet, all the windows in the house were double-glazed, Lucas hated noise. There was a very faint scarcely audible sound of rain.

Lucas had seated himself on the desk, thrusting aside a pile of books. Bellamy closed the drawing-room door behind him and advanced halfway down the room. They looked at each other.

Once Bellamy was installed in Lucas's presence he felt calm, his heart beat less violently, he was able to feel a simple pleasure and relief at Lucas's return. Bellamy in fact knew Lucas a good deal better than he allowed 'the others' to realise. This secretiveness was instinctive, perhaps an insurance against the possibility, constantly envisaged, of Lucas suddenly 'taking against him'. He took off his mackintosh and dropped it with his umbrella behind him on the floor. As Lucas seemed intent on saying nothing he said, 'Lucas, are you all right?'

'Yes, of course.'

Lucas was dressed, over shirt and trousers, in a yellow silk dressing-gown. He had very dark narrow eyes, very dark straight hair framing his face, a narrow aquiline nose, a thin red-lipped mouth, and a smooth sallow complexion. He had dark thick eyebrows and long very white teeth. He was not hump-backed but often, because of his stooping attitudes, seemed to be. In fact he had grown slowly as a child and had a habit of crouching. He had small hands and feet. He was said by some to 'look Chinese'.

He spoke slowly in a precise authoritative voice which, to those unused to it, could sound affected. He wore narrow rimless spectacles for reading.

'But where have you been all this time?'

'Why do you ask me in that tone?'

'I'm sorry – it's just that we've all been so worried – '

'Why?'

'Well, in the circumstances, why not – we thought you might – we wondered whether – after all that – '

'I was in various places, in Italy, in America. I don't usually tell people where I go.'

'No, of course not. We were silly to worry! And you – now that you're back – well – I suppose it's business as usual!'

Lucas did not reply to this awkward jocularity.

'Clement has been terribly worried about you. He'll be glad to see you!'

'I find all this "worrying" rather impertinent.'

'Well, I'm sorry, we weren't to know. I saw Clement this evening, I mean I went to tell him you were back. I went there in the taxi, I mean to Louise's place, he was there, to tell him.'

'Oh.'

'He was very relieved.'

Lucas said nothing so Bellamy went on again. 'Have you heard about Harvey?'

'No.'

'He fell, in Italy, he was walking across a bridge, I mean up on the parapet, and he fell, not over the edge of course, but he jumped down and broke his ankle, so he can't go to Florence, you remember he was going to Florence.'

'No.'

'Nothing else has happened really, no births, deaths, or marriages. I told you I was going to retire from the world. That's still on. You remember that.'

'Do you still see archangels?'

'No – '

'Your friend Michael leaning on his sword and watching the damned falling into hell?'

'Not like that.'

'And how are the girls?'

'Delightful, innocent, happy. Well, except that we were worrying – '

'Apparently you all want to make a drama of my return. There is no drama. You ask if I am all right. I am all right. You can tell that to the others which will remove the necessity of their visiting me.'

'You wrote to me, but you didn't write to Clement.'

'That is true. You ask why. You are a harmless chatterbox who will rapidly inform all relevant persons.'

'Clement will want to visit you, he has been so upset – '

'Don't tell him to come.'

'But don't tell him not to come? Were you sitting in the dark?'

'Yes, I have been scalded and bleached, light hurts my eyes, in the dark they glow. In a century or two this planet will have been destroyed by external cosmic forces or by the senseless activity of the human race. Human life is a freak phenomenon, soon to be blotted out. That is a consoling thought. Meanwhile we are surrounded by strange invisible entities, possibly your angels.'

'I hope so.'

'Ah, you think they are good, they *cannot* be good, there is no good, the tendency to evil is overwhelming. One has only to think of the horrors of sex, its violence, its cruelty, its filthy vulgarity, its descent into bestial degradation. You had better go and dream in your monastery.'

'Would you come and visit me there?'

'Of course not. I do not visit. Only, unfortunately, am sometimes visited.'

'You don't want to discuss – you know – what happened? My priest said – '

'No.'

'I care about how you are, I love you.'

'You still fail to realise how this sort of talk sickens me. Now

72

please go. This will do for a welcome home scene. Tell them not to come. I desire to be left alone.'

'I must tell you this. My priest says that you should feel pity for, you know, that man, and think about giving some help to his innocent wife and family.'

'*What?*'

'All right, I had to say it. I'll tell the others. Goodnight.'

Lucas switched off the light. Bellamy picked up his mackintosh and umbrella and found his way out in the dark.

'It looked terrible when they took the cast off,' said Harvey to Bellamy, 'it didn't look like human flesh at all, it was all blue and spotty and rotten. I said "It's gangrene," and they said no, but I thought they didn't like the look of it either. I wanted, I so much wanted, it to be left alone now to breathe the air and the light, you know like a poor plant that has been in the dark. I wanted the sun to warm it, but they tied it up again immediately, not in the cast but these very tight elastic bandages, they're even tighter than the cast.'

It was the following morning. Harvey had arrived unannounced at Bellamy's flatlet, having taken a taxi direct from the hospital. Bellamy was touched and pleased that Harvey had come straight to him. He had already given the boy a suitably censored account of his visit to Lucas.

The rain had stopped, but London had a drenched drowned look, the pavements darkened with water, the gutters full of pools. Even the trees looked soaked and dejected. The low undulating clouds were a blackish grey. An east wind was blowing. Bellamy's one-room flat, now meagrely warmed by the tiny electric fire, was on the ground floor. The window looked out directly onto the street and the noises and presences of passers-by. There was a very small sick garden behind the house, scattered with dandelions which survived without actually growing. Bellamy's room contained a narrow bed, a chest of drawers, a table, a wash-basin and a gas ring. The lavatory was outside on the stairs. In a frenzy of excitement he had given almost everything away. He had

73

enjoyed this stripping with the joy which it is said sailors feel in hurling things into the sea. He congratulated himself on being able to hate his possessions. His flat was sold, his cottage was for sale. He had hoped to make some acquaintance with his new neighbours, first of course the people in the house, and be able to help them in some way. But except for an acquaintance with a shop lady he had had no success, and had not yet ventured to approach the local clergy. The first floor was occupied by a Pakistani family, a tall thin father, a beautiful mother with innumerable saris, and two boys of about six and eight, but except for smiles they were not very communicative. A silent shabby elderly man rarely visible was on the floor above. The third floor was an uninhabitable attic where rain poured in through the roof. Bellamy sometimes wondered, what's the matter with me, what do people take me for, what do I *look like*? Passing boys banged on the window. Harvey had just told him he looked weird. There was no mirror in the room, Bellamy shaved, now less regularly, by instinct. He thought, when I'm *in there* I'll give up shaving altogether and my face will *become invisible*.

Harvey was reclining on Bellamy's bed, propped up by pillows, with both legs stretched out on the counterpane. His crutches were propped up against the wash-basin. Bellamy contemplated his fine head of silky blond hair and his eager unmarked face.

'Does it hurt?'

'Of course it hurts, it keeps me awake at night, they give me sleeping-pills, but what do I want with sleeping-pills at my age? If only it were just the bone, it's the other things which are far worse, I'll probably be lame for life. Anyway, let's leave awful doomed me. How are you? You don't look up to much. Are you fasting?'

'Fasting? No.'

'Have you sold the cottage?'

'Not yet, I think somebody is going to make an offer.'

'What a shame about the cottage, our only outlet to the sea! I wish you weren't giving up the world, after all what else is there, all right I know you're a mystic. I can't really talk to anyone but you, well, that's not quite true. I wish Emil were here, I could talk to him. Oh dear, I suppose I'd better go and see Lucas now he's back. I've been thinking about him.'

'Why "suppose"? Why not just go and see him? You speak as if it were a duty.'

'I don't think he likes me.'

'Harvey, what nonsense, everyone likes you!'

'And I'm not altogether sure that I like him – well, I don't actually dislike him – I just feel he's – for me – sort of – impossible.'

'But you've known him all your life, he's like an uncle, a father almost!'

'*You're* like a father almost. Clement is more like my brother now. But I feel, in some crazy sort of way, that Lucas is my enemy.'

'This is absurd! Quite apart from anything else, why should he bother to be your enemy?'

'You're right. He doesn't *bother* about me at all!'

'Lucas is a difficult chap, he's very reserved and awkward and shy, he's anti-social, well, we're all used to that and you should be too. He's awfully rude to me sometimes, I don't mind, it's just his mode of communication! Look how close he and Clement are, and I've heard him being pretty rough with Clement too. He's rather nervy and touchy, that's all.'

'He was very rough with me once.'

'He told you off?'

'He hit me.'

'Really! What had you done?'

'I can't remember.' But of course Harvey could remember.

'How old were you?'

'Eleven.'

'Well, you should have forgiven him by now! But you'd like to make peace, formally, sort of?'

'Sort of, somehow. Perhaps it's vanity really. I can't bear to think that there's anyone in the world who doesn't love me.'

'Don't worry, you'll never be short of people who love you.'

'I think I'll have to give up sex, and I haven't even started.'

'Why ever?'

'I'm crippled.'

'Harvey, *I* shall hit you! You're not crippled, how can you be so spiritless and silly. Anyway Byron didn't give up sex.'

'Yes, my mother was on about Byron. But who wants to be like Byron? I despise him. O God, I don't think I can do it anyway,

I feel sort of paralysed about the whole business, I wish I was gay.'

Bellamy also wished that Harvey was gay, but had put away this wish together with many other worldly wishes. He replied cautiously. 'Harvey, be patient. It will all come to you, some god will explain it to you, it will all be clarified, it will all be *easy*.'

'I wish I was a lesbian.'

'Harvey! Really!' Bellamy could not conceive of what it could possibly be like to want to be a lesbian.

'Well, why not, I love girls like they do, and female arrangements are so much simpler. Not that I can quite imagine – '

Bellamy, who did not propose to think about female arrangements, hastily changed the subject. 'I hope you're able to work a bit, read a bit, at least it's comfortable and peaceful at Emil's place.'

'No I can't. I can't think of anything but Florence, my head was so full of Florence, it was bursting – and now it's empty.'

Bellamy sat silent, averting his gaze, speechless with remorse.

'Bellamy, don't, it wasn't your fault, I'd have done it anyway, I'm that sort of silly fool! Look, do you mind if I ring for a taxi?'

'I'm sorry, I haven't a telephone.'

'Oh damn, I'll have to walk.'

'No, you stay here. I'll go and find a taxi.'

Harvey had gone. Bellamy paid for his taxi. Bellamy felt sad. He had been surprised by what Harvey had said about Lucas. He hadn't *thought* enough about Harvey. Perhaps he hadn't *really* thought about anyone except himself. What would it be like when he was alone with God? Had he ever really been happy, like Clement was and Harvey used to be? Perhaps in his very early days as a social worker, perhaps for an hour with Magnus. Why had he given up his work? Because he had been disturbed by religion, by the Absolute, by the Hound of Heaven. Well, now, when he was about to give in, the question of happiness didn't really matter any more.

The boys were tapping on his window again, now banging the knocker on the door.

Clement had scarcely slept. When he did sleep he had a nightmare. He rose early and saw the soiled gloomy light reveal the wet street with its rows of sullen motorcars. At least it wasn't raining. He felt ill and couldn't eat. He kept looking at his watch. He dressed with care. *He must go and see Lucas*. Bellamy had telephoned late the previous night from a telephone box to say that Lucas was 'perfectly all right' and 'didn't want to see anyone'. Bellamy said, 'Of course he'll want to see *you*.' Clement was not so sure. But he *must go*. Not going, he would go mad.

Lucas was an early riser, usually starting work about six-thirty, his head clear, his concentration at its best. An early visit would be unwelcome. Perhaps ten or eleven? Or was Lucas at this very moment *waiting* for Clement to come? Had he perhaps telephoned Clement's number last night before he rang Bellamy? Of course Clement could telephone Lucas now, *now*. But that was unthinkable. Lucas hated the telephone, there could be some hideous misunderstanding or blunder. Lucas might simply say that he didn't want to see Clement. The essential visit might then be treated as a vile intrusion. He decided to wait a while, then to walk to Lucas's house arriving about ten. He set off at last, carrying a brown paper parcel under his arm.

He rang the bell. Silence. Nothing. He thought, he won't answer, he knows it's me. He pictured Lucas sitting hunched up, waiting for Clement to ring again, then for Clement to go away. Clement rang again. He was breathing deeply, audibly. He pictured Lucas lying dead. He thought, he's killed himself.

Lucas opened the door upon the chain. He peered at Clement. He unchained it and disappeared. Clement moved into the hall and closed the door after him. The drawing-room door was open. Clement went on into the drawing-room. Lucas was standing in an odd attitude beside one of the long brown velvet curtains, which perhaps he had just drawn back, revealing the garden where the trees still had wet golden leaves. Clement thought, he's hanged himself.

Lucas moved over to the large desk where the lighted lamp revealed the usual scene of open books, an open notebook, ink bottles, glass paper-weights. He sat down behind the desk facing Clement, he looked at Clement over his glasses, then took the glasses off and began to polish them.

77

Clement thought, I'm going to faint. He walked toward Lucas. He laid down the brown paper parcel on the desk. Then, as if propelled by a sudden force, he backed away to the end of the room and leaned against the bookshelves as if pinned there. Lucas watched him with curiosity. He did not look at the parcel. He said nothing.

Clement thought, he will remain silent. I shall talk, he will say nothing. Then I shall go away. After that I shall never see him again. And after that the world will end.

In Lucas's absence Clement had pictured this scene innumerable times. But in the pictures Lucas had spoken, Clement had responded. Now, Clement thought, I must talk and talk, and I must say just the right things. *But what are they?*

Clement said, 'Look, I know we can't discuss what happened – or how it will affect our future relations – but something must be said and really – I suppose – almost anything will do. I have had it all – that *enormity* – in my mind for so long now, and I've been alone with it. I want to tell you just – what I'm *not* thinking and feeling. I do not say or feel that this is or has to be the end, I mean *our* end. I mean, I don't want it to be. I've thought so much about this, about this *very moment*, and that's the only thing, I mean what I've just said is the only thing, which is at all *clear*. We have to say something, at least I have to say something – you may have the privilege of silence, I can't make you talk anyway, and I don't want – really I'm afraid of anything you might say. Whether this meeting, which had to take place, and this saying of mine turns out to be hail and farewell must depend on you. I don't want it to be like that – though equally I see how difficult – and what is now *possible* may depend on things which neither of us can control – or even at this stage imagine – sorry that's rather confused. I have no idea what you think and feel – and I had better not say anything more about what I – I believe I have said what is for me most essential. It occurs to me now that it might be best if I just went away and left you with – what I think about it – then you may feel later on – that we could talk more profitably – or you may prefer to leave it there, I mean not to talk about *that*, or not to talk any more at all – but I'd leave it to you to let me know – and I would come if you wanted to see me – now or later.'

Clement removed himself from the books. He realised that while he was speaking he had been tearing the spines of the books

78

with which his hands had been in contact. He did not look round. He stood still as if at attention. He would give Lucas perhaps a minute, perhaps two minutes, in which to speak, and then, for he did not now expect Lucas to speak, he would simply go quietly out of the door and out of the house. Indeed this might be best. He turned now and stood looking at the door, his hands, hanging, his head bent, his lips apart. He sighed deeply. His eyelids drooped. He felt very tired. He moved, as if falling, and took a pace towards the door.

Lucas said, in a calm slightly irritated voice, 'Pray do not go. I want, if you don't mind, to clarify one matter which, it seems, you assume to be already clear, but about which I would like to be certain. Please could you *sit down*.'

Clement took a chair and placed it against the bookshelves. He sat down facing his brother. He thought, this is like a court room – and *I'm in the dock*! That's absurd, it's *weird*, but – I'll think about it later – maybe there's sense in it – if there's sense anywhere in this business.

Lucas, after staring at Clement for some time, said, 'Are you sure that you thoroughly understood what happened, which of course includes what was meant to happen and might have happened?'

Clement was surprised by this question. He tried to speak, closed his eyes, then tried again saying softly, 'Yes. I thoroughly understood, it was after all absolutely evident, my memory is extremely clear.'

Lucas said, 'Good,' in a brisk tone, as if indicating: that is satisfactory. He placed his hands palms downward upon the desk; there was another silence during which Clement was able to *look*. Lucas was dressed in his usual shabby yet neat manner, with a dark blue corduroy jacket, a dark blue jersey, and an open-necked shirt appearing above it. As Clement watched him he took off his jacket and rolled up the sleeves of his jersey, the shirt sleeves showing beneath. He leaned forward slightly, peering at Clement, opening wider his slit eyes and narrowing, as it seemed, his narrow nose. His thin lips were indrawn. He waited.

Clement said in a forced cracked tone which he had intended to sound conversational, 'I believe you saw Bellamy.'

'I believe you know that I saw Bellamy.'

'Of course I haven't said – and well of course – '

Outside it was beginning to rain, a quiet sizzling blending with

79

the subdued sound of traffic. The sycamore tree in the garden bent under the rain, extending its heavy leaves. The rain hopped upon the paving stones outside the window where the creeping thyme showed black. The room was dark, darker, the only light illuminating Lucas's seated form.

Clement, feeling suffocated by stale dusty air, the smell of books, felt a desire to rush out into the garden. He could not *reach* Lucas, and this might be his only opportunity, before the whole matter was buried *forever*. He must not let the silence continue. He cleared his throat and said in his theatre voice. 'You spoke of what was meant to happen. Why was it meant to happen?'

It is necessary at this point to recount what actually occurred, as opposed to what was generally supposed to have occurred, on that terrible evening when Lucas killed a man. The story, so frequently run through, enacted, polished, probed and interrogated in Clement's mind, ran as follows. It was partly about glow-worms. It seemed to Clement afterwards that the history and happening of that evening depended on some memory, surfacing in Lucas's mind, a something which had been a bond between them when they were children: an interest in wild things, little wild things such as might live in city gardens, spiders, slugs, snails, insects. Glow-worms were a rarity, a treat. (Glow-worms are the larvae of a firefly which, lying on the earth, glow on summer nights with an eerie light.) Clement remembered how, when he was a child, he had been led by the hand by Lucas who had found a glow-worm, to see the creature (or creatures, indeed, there were several) one night under some bushes.

Perhaps it is better first to explain, or exhibit, since it is indeed difficult to explain, the relationship which existed between the brothers. Of course there was a built-in difficulty. Lucas, adopted, arrived first. Clement, the 'real child', arrived two years later. Lucas was acquired as a tiny baby. The parents, as is deemed wise, told him from earliest years that he was adopted. They did not tell him about his real parents and Lucas never asked. His strange eyes led some onlookers to think that he was a Down's Syndrome child. His complexion was yellowish, sometimes seeming positively dark. He had strange mannerisms, drooping his hands and descending his head into his shoulders. He grew slowly, and looked for a time like a dwarf. He had also as an adult, small hands and feet. His younger brother, who resembled the handsome father, grew fast and was soon taller. Lucas was a podgy child. Clement was slim, willowy, graceful, a beautiful child, a good-looking youth. Of course it was soon evident that Lucas was very clever; but Clement was clever too in his way, endowed with so many talents and so much charm. How could the parents, blessed now by what they had really wanted, their very own child, conceal their preference? The special care, the deliberate cherishing, which they had lavished upon Lucas when he was the only child, when they wanted, as adoptive parents must, to make certain that he knew he was loved, seemed later on, when the real son arrived, artificial, condescending, treats hastily given to one who has failed. After the defection of the father the situation was still worse since it was to Clement that the abandoned mother turned for consolation. There were, moreover, occasions when it was necessary to chide Lucas for being 'too rough' with his younger brother. Only once did Clement run to his mother to tell her that Lucas had hit him; he learned soon afterwards how counter-productive such informing was. He was afraid of Lucas, who unobtrusively bullied him. Yet, persistently, he also admired Lucas, even loved him; and in spite of everything the general idea that the brothers were 'close' and 'attached to each other' was by no means false. Lucas enjoyed his absolute power over his brother: absolute because he had soon taught Clement to accept in silence any degree of despotism. Yet he was also, in some way, grateful to Clement for his submission, and, in his sense of ownership, set himself up as the protector of the younger child. At school, no one dared to bully Clement for fear of Lucas's reprisals; and neither at school nor at home did anyone ever see Lucas bully his brother. The despotism remained a secret between the master and the slave. Something like this 'love-hate' relationship, so deeply established, continued in adult life. For instance, it was generally understood that no one was to criticise Clement in Lucas's presence; and Clement was never heard to speak of his brother except with esteem and affection.

As they moved apart into quite different spheres, Lucas into the academic world, Clement into the world of theatre, the strange secret bond remained. In fact to call it a love-hate relationship was not quite just; Clement, who had so certainly won the 'early childhood' game, however often his brother had beaten him at

'Dogs', was not really capable of hatred. He loved and feared his brother who, never attacking Clement in public, did not, in private, conceal his contempt for Clement's 'mediocre fiddling' in the world of entertainment. Clement was made to feel the inferiority of not being an intellectual. (Lucas had joined those who urged Clement not to quit Cambridge.) And behind the often spiteful continuation of the childhood warfare Clement could discern in his brother the old black bitterness and the terrible original never-healing wound. This dark thing Clement did not care to look upon. His natural cheerful and affectionate nature led him to believe, and there was some evidence of this too, that as the years went by the tension between them had become less of a damaging war and more like a strange ancestral game. The bond remained secret and mutually tacit; of course they would never have dreamt of discussing it. The 'outside world' continued to preserve the touching picture of brothers in amity.

Social relations between the two, which in other circumstances might have weakened, were sustained and stabilised by friends held in common, originally and especially Teddy Anderson and Bellamy, later Louise and Joan also, later still the four children. As already related, on Teddy's death both Lucas and Clement, though not formally 'guardians', became responsible, indeed in part financially responsible, for the children. Clement and Bellamy were loved by these children; their feelings about Lucas, though more mixed, were never questioned. He was a part of their family, an uncle, a pillar, a remarkable person. At an earlier period, both before and after Teddy's death, Lucas had been quite often on the scene. Later he withdrew and was said to be a recluse. He continued for a while to give Sefton history tutorials, but in time gave that up too.

On the summer evening in question Lucas had telephoned Clement about six o'clock and asked him, if he was free, to come over to supper. This had been, in the past, though lately rather discontinued, not unusual. Lucas, who disliked making arrangements beforehand, preferred, if any, *ad hoc* social encounters. On the telephone Lucas asked Clement not to mention this to anyone as he had refused two invitations and did not want to hurt feelings. He added that he would fetch Clement by car, soon, why not at once, since he had heard that Clement's car was 'laid up'. Clement, always pleased by any friendly signal from his brother, agreed. However, he said there was no need for Lucas to call for him, he would take a taxi. The afternoon had been hot and sunny, but as Clement prepared to set off a few drops of rain fell and he decided to bring his big umbrella – there might even be a thunderstorm. Supper with Lucas always consisted of pâté, cold tongue and salad, cheese and apples. Clement had brought an inexpensive bottle of Beaujolais just in case, as had been known to happen, Lucas had forgotten to buy wine; however on this occasion he had produced a rather fine claret. During the meal both bottles were drunk, mainly by Clement, whose glass was never empty. Clement had not eaten much during that day, which he had spent at an incompetent little theatre helping to arrange the hire of some furniture. (I'm a stage-manager, it seems, he thought, not a director!) He ate most of the tongue and almost all the cheese. Lucas, who was 'never hungry', behaved, as Clement recalled it later, in an unusually lively manner, smiling and looking about the sombre dining-room, his gaze lingering upon this picture and that vase, things which had been there unmoved since their mother died. It was as if he were listing those objects in his mind, since he was soon to go on a long journey and wished to fix them in his memory. Clement, when drunk in the presence of Lucas, usually felt anxiety, or in extreme cases shame. Now however, perhaps infected by his host's liveliness, he experienced a calm exaltation, a marked sense of *presence*, as if for both of them time had slowed down. This staying of time he connected somehow with childhood. The exaltation, which involved a form of slow-seeing, or entranced-staring, presence, consisted for Clement of two layers, one of good joy, wherein he was gladdened that Lucas had *survived*, that Lucas was a great man, and that after all Lucas loved his brother. The other layer, primal and less clearly discernible, was some awful strange old feeling, left lurking in his deep mind from long ago, of having *won*, having triumphed over Lucas, of being himself the loved, the cherished, the *real* child; whereas Lucas was a dummy, a garish puppet, a robot. Even, as Clement later recalled it, that supper table, the familiar objects, the silver-plated knives and forks, the four-footed silver salt-cellar with its blue glass interior (the little feet were lions' heads), the Wedgwood plates (as mother said, 'not to be used'), the Irish Waterford glasses ('for best'), enlarged and shining in Clement's slowed vision, seemed to come alive while standing *very still*, as 'witnesses'; the strange thought came to Clement as he reached out cautiously for his ever-full glass. He wondered, is time like this on *another planet?*

He had felt reluctant to go. When there was a silence in which he might courteously have expressed a wish to do so, Lucas always began speaking again. They had talked about childhood holidays, about schooldays, about Cambridge, about the dreadful state of education, about the girls (Aleph, Sefton and Moy), about New York, about the American election. At last, holding carefully onto the edge of the table, which had now become a vast dazzling landscape before him, Clement rose, said he must go, and walked with solemn dignity to the door. Lucas, following, said he would drive him home. At this point Lucas said that he 'wanted to show him something'. It was after midnight. The sky was overcast but no rain was falling. Clement went to sleep in the car. Lucas awakened him, repeating 'I want to show you something.' Clement's first thought was of the dream he had been having. He dreamt that Lucas was with him in a dark space, perhaps the drawing-room of Lucas's house. Clement thought in the dream, I have lived here all my life with Lucas, I have never really left this house. Why did I somehow forget this? Lucas was there too, they were standing facing each other in the darkness, and Lucas was smiling at him, a strange loving smile, a 'smile of power' was the awkward yet potent phrase which came into Clement's head. The drawing-room had become very large like a dark high-roofed hall. It's an old house thought Clement, a very big house, some-how I forgot about this room. The darkness is so strange – how do I know that it's a *room?* – It's all gauzy – that's a funny word – it's like dense gauze, like lots of knitted steel nets placed one above the other, only it's *floating* steel, it's so weightless and delicate. Only I mustn't keep looking up because Lucas is smiling at me – he's holding out something towards me, a sort of cup or *goblet* – that's another funny word – and it's a strange cup, so beautiful and tall, he wants me to drink out of it, perhaps it means peace at last – yes, I will drink, we will both drink, he is reaching it towards me, it is so beautiful, it is glowing, it is made of the purest silver, oh so pure, it is full of light – I think – oh I think it is *the Grail itself* – At that moment in the dream Clement fell down in a dead faint.

Hearing Lucas's words about 'show you something', he got out of the car. It was dark. He thought, he has driven me home. Perhaps he'll come in for a drink. I'll tell him that beautiful strange dream – then he thought, no, perhaps I won't. Then he realised that he was not at home. He held onto the car. Then felt Lucas taking hold of his arm and leading him under some trees into what seemed like a park or a garden, at one moment he saw a tall clipped yew, its blackness outlined against a slightly lighter sky, which was exhibiting a single bright star. He felt now, rather than saw, the presences of trees. Lucas was speaking to him now, 'Would you like to see some glow-worms?' Clement at once recalled what Lucas must be remembering, how on just such a summer evening, when they were children on holiday, Lucas had led him by the hand to show him a dell where a gathering of glow-worms made a positively brilliant light under some bushes. Clement even now fumbled for Lucas's hand in the dark. But Lucas, who had released his arm, moved ahead of him. Where were they? He stumbled on, then saw, a pile of bricks. Perhaps it was a building site, a 'development', where some big house had been demolished, and they were now in the huge wild abandoned garden. He shook off a snake-like bramble which had seized his ankle. Lucas had paused. Among some tall trees there was an arch of bushy leaves making a little dark cave. Lucas was pointing. Beside him now Clement leaned forward peering in under the leaves. What was to change many lives happened, and happened very fast in the next moments.

Clement (and how clearly and constantly he recalled and established this in his mind) became suddenly aware that Lucas was about to hit him. It seemed later like an intuition, something apprehended without sight or sound, then caught in the slightest swiftest sidelong glance, before even he could move: the arm, holding some weapon, uplifted against the faintly lighter sky. Clement recalled, as in slow motion, his realisation, his reaction, as his whole body was suddenly focused in an act of evasion. He transferred his weight from one foot to another, moved his head aside, began to straighten his spine, spread out both arms to balance and protect, poised his feet to run: but these movements, vulnerably placed as he was, were too slow. The blow fell – *but not on him*. Clement saw, as he half fell, half sprang away, the figure beside Lucas of *another man*, upon whom the savage force of the weapon now descended. The man fell, without any cry, with a heavy hideous sound into the bushes. Something fell onto the grass near Clement's feet. Lucas was kneeling down beside the fallen man. Clement, as he remembered, stood with his hands up to his face, holding his head as if it were likely to fall off, his mouth wide open, unable to utter any sound. Lucas rose and took hold of Clement's arm, pulling it down, and thrust something into his hand. 'Take this, put it under your coat, and go away, go home, *walk* home, go, remember, you were *never here*.' Lucas knelt again beside the fallen man. Clement turned back among the trees, hastening at random, moaning as he ran, losing what had seemed to be a path, and emerged at last onto a lighted road, quiet, empty, there was no one there. He ran, then walked, looking about him to find out where in London he was. At last there were familiar streets, no longer empty, through which he hurried, holding something under his coat, passing the late night people, men in evening-dress, girls laughing together, solitary sinister men with terrible secrets – of whom Clement now and forever after must be one. It started to rain, but he had left his umbrella somewhere. He dared not take a taxi. He reached his flat at last, stumbling up the stairs. He turned all the lights on, laid down what he had carried under his coat, looked at it, then took it to the kitchen and washed it. He had felt, throughout the walk, dreadfully clear-headed, no longer drunk. He thought that now he must sit up all night, with huge wide eyes and round open mouth, staring at the event. But he did not. He tore off his clothes, turned off the lights, plunged into his bed and pulled the bedclothes over his head and fell into a black pit of slumber.

When he woke next morning he rose as usual and pulled back his curtains. The sun was shining. The trees in nearby gardens were radiantly green and shapely, displaying their motionless leaves. He opened the window to a warm smell of roses. He thought suddenly: I had such a terrible nightmare. Then he thought: but it's true, it *all happened. What am I to do now*, what am I *ever* to do? He walked into the kitchen and looked at the thing which lay beside the sink. He thought, I must get rid of it somehow, I must take it somewhere. He wrapped it up in paper and put it away in a cupboard. He got dressed. He thought, Lucas will ring me. Then he thought, *no he won't*. But what has happened, what happened to that man, what did Lucas do after I left, is the man still lying there in the bushes – *ought I to go and look?* No, and in any case he had no idea, where, in what derelict park or garden, the terrible thing had occurred. It had occurred, it had *happened*, and could never in his life be unhappened, never removed, a huge deadly black scar lasting forever. But what has happened next, what *will* happen, to him, and to Lucas? In some dim light, perhaps the light of the glow-worms, he thought he had seen the man's face – but that was impossible – he had just gained an impression of him. What was he doing there so late at night in that dark place, by what accident was he, just then, just there? Who was he, had he been following Lucas, was he connected with Lucas? What did it all *mean*? Then Clement thought – of course – there were no glow-worms. And for a second he felt a strange terrible sharp pang, in thinking of the use to which that innocent memory had now been put. It was only in a secondary way, or at a deeper level, that Clement in his first state of shock, thought: Lucas intended to kill me. He made some tea. He sat beside the telephone. It was no use telephoning Lucas, who of course would not answer. In any case, Clement was *afraid*. Ought he to go over to Lucas's house? He was afraid to go. He tried to write a letter to Lucas. It was impossible. He rang the theatre, he rang his agent, cancelling appointments. An actress, an old friend, rang up asking advice. He gave it. Time passed. Clement made some more tea. His hand was trembling. He could not eat, he could not sit still, he walked up and down. His life, his whole being, had been suddenly destroyed. He had another thought: Lucas had gone home and committed suicide. Lucas had often talked of suicide, but Clement had not taken this seriously. But if Lucas thought of suicide was it not likely, in his character, to have the means? Clement then remembered his dream about the Grail – only it was not the Grail – it was the poisoned chalice, to be drunk first by Clement, then by Lucas. Clement began to groan and moan as he walked. Supposing Lucas had expected him to come, and then killed himself because he did not come. Clement rang Lucas's number and stood shuddering as he held the telephone. No answer. He also thought, if Lucas wanted to kill Clement and then himself he could have done it any time, anywhere, in his flat. Why that laborious stage set? Perhaps Lucas did intend suicide but simply did not want it to be connected with Clement. He continued to walk, now slowly now suddenly fast. He lay down on his bed, he lay there shuddering and trying to become unconscious. Time passed. He listened to himself muttering and wailing softly. He closed his eyes. The telephone rang. It was Louise. 'Oh Clement, have you heard what happened to poor

Lucas?' 'No, what?' 'He was mugged, someone tried to steal his wallet – he hit the wretched man and now he's in hospital, the man is, not Lucas. Wasn't he brave? He might have been murdered. It's all over the evening papers.' Clement thanked Louise for letting him know. He sat down. He resisted an urge to go out and buy an evening paper. He sat still and breathed deeply. Something awful had been even more degraded, it had been blackened. He couldn't *think* about it, it was unthinkable and inconceivable. He said aloud to himself, 'Lucas is mad.' Somebody had said that once. But he did not think, even now, especially not now, that Lucas was mad. He sat while tears came overflowing his eyes and running down his cheeks. Why was he crying? Was he not relieved that Lucas was apparently alive and evidently in charge of his wits? Did he want to think that Lucas had killed himself and was lying dead in his drawing-room, perhaps at his desk, while the summer evening darkened the room? He wondered again if he should go round and knock on the door; but he could not. He felt *too tired*. Later that evening Bellamy rang him. 'You know about Lucas.' 'Yes, of course.' 'Has he rung you to say he's going into hiding? I expect you were out.' 'I was out.' 'He says he's leaving his house and living somewhere else in London in order to avoid the press.' 'Thanks for telling me.' After that Clement had heard nothing more of his brother, except for what people told him they had read in the newspapers: at which Clement did not look.

There followed the court case, the charge of 'undue force', the 'unworthy suspicions', Lucas's brief fame for 'having a go' at an enemy of society, then the news that the 'assailant' had died without regaining consciousness, then silence. Lucas continued to be 'disappeared', thereby causing much anxiety to those well-wishers who regarded themselves as his 'family'.

'Why was it meant to happen?'

Lucas said coolly and without hesitation, 'You know perfectly well why. Why did Cain kill Abel? Why did Romulus kill Remus? I have always wanted to kill you, ever since the moment when I learnt of your existence. Do not let us waste time on *that*.'

'Yes, but wanting isn't doing – it's not my fault that I existed – I'm not your enemy, I've always done what you wanted, I mean I've always tried to please you – I like you, I love you, you're my brother.'

Lucas said, 'Of course you have an impulse to utter these empty words. Forces infinitely deeper and more ruthless and more real than your superficial blarney brought about that which was intended but did not happen. All right, it was necessary between us to mention it, now let us consign it to silence.'

'How can we, I must *understand*, all right, there are "forces" though I don't see why one should give way to them – but I don't understand the whole thing, I mean the thing as a *happening*, I don't know what *happened*, what did you do after I left, why did you *stay* there – I mean – '

'You are crude and naive. Can't you *think*? The man was alive. I was responsible. I had to see that he got prompt medical attention.'

'You could have just run out and told someone you'd found a man – '

'I tell you I was *responsible* – I *had to* look after him.'

'All right – but you didn't tell anyone, well, about me and – '

'Of course I didn't. Why should I? That was my affair. I did not propose to suffer a double penalty!'

'Double?'

'Yes, having failed to kill you, being accused of the murder of someone else.'

'You said you hit him with your umbrella – but you weren't carrying an umbrella.'

'No, but you were.'

'I thought I'd left it – oh heavens – so you faked it, you pretended – you told me to take the bat away – '

'I knocked the umbrella against a tree and stained it with blood. Remember, *you were not there.*'

'And – oh Luc, how awful – all right I understand – but what was he doing, why did you hit him?'

'He was a witness. He interfered with me at one of the most important moments of my life, perhaps *the* most important moment. I think I hit him out of sheer exasperation. Naturally I didn't mean to kill him, I just happened to have that thing in my hand. Thank you for bringing it back, by the way. Thank you for removing it, if it comes to that.'

Lucas was undoing the brown paper parcel which Clement had laid on his desk. Clement moved forward. What now lay revealed was a baseball bat: the very same bat which had played a major part in the game of 'Dogs', a considerably more ferocious game than was dreamt of by their mother, to whom Clement did not dare to show his bruises. Looking back, Clement saw the game as being, of course, simply an opportunity for Lucas to torture his younger brother. At the time however it had seemed like a game, and had at first the charms of secrecy. Lucas made the rules, under which he was officially batsman. On rare occasions when Clement held the bat a different set of rules prevailed. At one point Lucas decided to improve the bat by hollowing out a hole in the head and pouring in some molten lead, obtained by melting Clement's toy soldiers. Soon after this, as Clement was at last nerving himself to refuse to play, Lucas decided to put an end to 'Dogs', possibly because serious damage to his brother might endanger the myth of their mutual affection which Lucas had his own prudential reasons for preserving. In fact, as Clement later saw it, and as is the case in many human situations where such 'myths' play a part, that which was feigned could not have been successfully so if it had not contained some truth. Something mutual was involved. Clement persisted in admiring and indeed loving his remarkable brother, and Lucas, perhaps because this was so, moved, as it were, into the space which Clement thus made for him. He enjoyed (and not only in childhood) bullying Clement and seemed to appreciate the intelligent nature of Clement's response. So it seemed to Clement; who also told himself that their relationship was a mystery which he, at any rate, proposed to respect. Now, Clement and Lucas looked down in silence at the murder weapon. Then they looked at each other. Lucas sighed. Clement turned back toward the darker end of the room. He sat down on his chair against the books.

He said, 'Yes, but what was he *doing* – was he trying to assault you, to steal your wallet as they said in court – or what?'

'He was trying to prevent me from killing you. He succeeded.'

'Oh – my God – are you sure?'

'Yes. He rushed forward and tried to grasp my arm. I think he even said "No, no!" '

'So he wasn't a mugger or a thief, he was – But wasn't he said to be carrying an offensive weapon?'

'I think my defence lawyer invented that. All I said was that he seemed to be about to attack me. I said it was possible that he did not intend to do so. The press, the public, and my spotless reputation carried the whole thing along. I had no visible motive for killing him. The suggestion that I had used excessive force was soon disposed of. Some doctor suggested that I couldn't have caused so much damage with an umbrella but that was not taken up.'

'Did they ask you what you were doing in that odd place? Did you say you were looking for glow-worms?'

'I decided to leave glow-worms out of it. I said I was answering a call of nature.'

'Perhaps he was too, poor fellow – oh poor innocent fellow – and he didn't regain consciousness to tell his story – who was he anyway?'

'I don't know.'

'You mean you didn't want to know. We didn't either. We didn't follow the case – '

'I appreciate your delicacy. Yes. I didn't want to know, I was present as little as possible and I didn't read about it. I believe he was some sort of shopkeeper. I recall no mention of his family.'

'Yes. You blotted it all out. Don't you feel regret?'

'Don't talk foolishly. Of course I feel regret.'

'Well, where does all this leave us?'

'What do you mean?'

'Luc, something absolutely terrible has happened. You say you feel regret, I won't ask whether you feel remorse. I'm thinking now about how it all affects *us*, us two, what has happened and will happen to *us*.'

'Do you mean do I intend to try again? No. I think – this may sound odd – but one man can die for another – all that hatred had to go somewhere.'

'And it has gone? So he died for me?'

'Don't romanticise it.'

'And this means that you forgive me – '

'What horrible terminology. No I just mean I don't want to kill you. I did want to and I had to try – it was a burden I had long carried, like a duty – which I feel relieved of now.'

'I'm – I'm glad to hear it – but – '

'Do you want me to swear that I won't kill you?'

Clement hesitated. (What was the right answer?) 'Yes.'

'You disappoint me.'

'Oh.' (Wrong answer.)

'Never mind. I swear by my integrity as a historian that I will not kill you or again attempt to do so. Will that satisfy you?'

'Thanks. But I was wanting to say – to hope – that we can

now – without all that bitterness and horror and – be – well – friends – better friends – '

'What ideas you have! You mean reconciliation, mutual forgiveness, peace, a new understanding? No.'

'What then?'

'I don't know. What does it matter? I intend to go away soon to America and I shall probably stay there.'

'Lucas, don't be so cruel.'

'Really! I think I'm letting you off lightly.'

'*You* letting *me* off!'

'You wanted to "talk it over" and we've done so. I could simply have refused to see you. You wouldn't have liked that, would you?'

'Well, I don't like this either. I can't help feeling that you owe me something. I feel that we might at least try to salvage something out of this unspeakably awful business – I mean something like I said, we might become closer, like in bearing it together.'

'Some sort of mutual penitence perhaps.'

'I don't think I can bear it alone. I feel so terribly sorry for that man.'

'So we should meet at intervals to chat about it?'

'No, no – and of course I *can* bear it, I mean I won't ever speak of this to any other person ever in my life, you know that I shall keep my mouth shut – '

'You will be wise to do so.'

'But – oh let me speak *now* – I want us to be more connected – we have changed each other, I know I hurt you, I must have done, not just by existing but in other ways – I do so wish that out of this evil some good might come which we could make to come about together – this is what I meant that you owed me – '

'I owe you nothing. You're still alive. You asked me to swear not to kill you in the future and I have sworn. I hope you believe me.'

'Yes, yes. But you *would* have killed me.'

'*It didn't happen.* Who knows – I might have changed my mind. An angel might have stayed my hand. By the way, let me return this to you.'

Clement came forward. Lucas, still seated, handed him something across the desk.

'What – ? Why, it's my wallet! I lost it somewhere that night – '

'I removed it from your pocket in the car.'

'Why on earth – oh I see – to make it look like a theft – oh Luc – '

There was silence in the room. The rain, carried now by a gust of east wind, was tapping on the window. Clement put the wallet away. He felt his knees weaken as if he was about to kneel and then lie prostrate face downward. He was overcome by a sudden wave of intense misery, a blackness of soul.

'But that man died – I caused his death – I mean you caused his death – I feel we should do *something* – '

'What can we do? *Leave it alone*. Clement, please just go away now. I don't want to see you.'

'You mean you don't ever want to see me again?'

'Nothing so dramatic. Our paths have been diverging for some time. Now they will diverge more. We have had our talk and have nothing more to say to each other. *Go away*.'

Clement moved away from the desk. The rain was stopping. For one moment only a random shaft of sunlight fell upon the garden. Green leaves, washed with rain, glistened out there. The rain was lighter. He was appalled to find himself feeling so guilty, so touched by *evil*. He wanted from Lucas some reassurance, some liberation, some absolution. But what for? Of course for being so unkind to Lucas when they were little children. He must have been unkind. Of course he had been unkind for existing, for arriving, an outsider, an intruder, a spoiler, a wrecker, in that world of pure undivided love in which Lucas had first emerged in consciousness. *What had happened* had made him feel this wound. He must make sense of it *all*. He couldn't just drift away. Now everything had become tragically desperately important. Had he uttered the word 'evil'? He could not remember.

At that moment the front doorbell rang twice. There was something peremptory in the quickly repeated ring. Lucas scowled and uttered a sound of disgust. 'Who the hell's that? It's one of *them*. Tell whoever it is to go away.'

The bell rang again, this time a long ring.

Clement ran out of the room and along the dark corridor leading to the front door. He thought, yes it'll be one of the family, perhaps Louise. The idea was unpleasant. He opened the door.

A man, just folding his green umbrella, was standing on the doorstep. He was a tall man wearing a trilby hat. Clement recognised him. He was the man he had twice seen near his house, seemingly *waiting* for something.

The man, peering at Clement, said with a slight accent which Clement could not identify. 'Does Professor Graffe live here?'

'Yes – '

'I would like to see him.'

Clement said at once, 'I'm so sorry, he is busy and cannot see anyone.'

'I think he will see me. I shall certainly be glad to see him.'

Clement, feeling a strong distrust of the man, said, 'I'm very sorry, it is not convenient.' He began to close the door, but there was an impediment. The man had stepped forward and put his large booted foot in the doorway. He said, 'Excuse me, I must enter.'

Lucas's voice at the end of the corridor could be heard saying, 'Who is it?' Before Clement could stop him the man had pushed past and was hurrying toward the open door ahead. He entered the drawing-room where Lucas was still sitting in the light of the lamp. Lucas leaned forward peering into the obscurity at the far end of the room. 'Who – ?' Then he said to Clement, 'Put on the light, would you?'

Clement switched on the bright centre light. The man advanced to the centre of the room. He took off his hat.

At that moment Clement, still at the door, was staring at Lucas. An extraordinary expression had distorted his face. Lucas became not exactly pale, but yellower. His mouth opened, his lips drew back revealing his long teeth. After a moment he rose to his feet and said in a low but steady voice. 'So you are not dead, after all.'

The man, who had now folded up his umbrella and laid it together with his trilby hat upon a chair, came further forward, he said in an almost apologetic tone, 'Well, I *was* dead, you know, but they revived me.' He turned to Clement. He said, 'I think you were there too. Weren't you the third man?' He held out his hand. In a daze Clement nodded and moved forward. They shook hands.

*

My dear son,

Please excuse a brief reply to your long letter. You say your reading in critical historical books which are outside our faith gives you the impression that Christ is being 'stripped'. You should not be appalled by this image, but should rather embrace it. Christ is indeed 'stripped', stripped for the cross, and it is for us to follow Him into that ultimate place of our faith. The blank space you speak of *is* God, *is* Christ. This could be a theme for prayer and meditation. I think you would indeed be wise to clarify your ideas, and put your more ambitious plans, if I may put it so, *on ice*. You ask if the 'mystical Christ' is 'enough'. The mystical vision is the reward of a long ascetic pilgrimage and not to be compared with the emotional experiences to which you refer. The full reality of the acceptance of Christ is hard and plain, it is bread and water, the way is a way of brokenness. Your 'yearning for holiness' and 'giving up the world' are still, I fear, mere expressions of feeling, fancies which give you a 'thrill'. You think of the dedicated life as a form of death, but you will be alive and crying. The false god punishes, the true God slays. Sins must not be kept as stimulants, one must attempt to kill the evil in oneself, not simply punish and torment it. (I indicate a form of masochism to which many well-intentioned people are addicted!) You do not tell me whether you are attending Mass and availing yourself of the sacrament of confession. Your letters to me are not a substitute. It is not clear to me how you are spending your time. You should certainly find some *regular work* in the service of others; keeping in mind the possibility that this may, in the end, prove to be your whole true way of serving Christ. Do not sit all day reading Eckhart! Later you may meditate upon what he means when he says seek God only in your own soul. Please perceive the love which prompts all these, as they may seem discouraging, words! Sorry this in haste, yours in *Christo*,

Fr Damien

P.S. The 'descent into hell' signifies the universal nature of Christ's love and mercy.

My dear Father Damien,

Thank you for your enlightening and loving letter. I have

been to Mass and will go to confession. I recall your advice of some time ago that it is often better to find a confessor at random, than to ask for a recommendation or (worse still perhaps!) go to a friend. The priest speaks not as an individual but as the voice of God. (Sorry, this is not well put.) I also note what you say about Eckhart. You spoke earlier of my troubles with Our Lady, and how I shouldn't worry, and I don't. I know that innumerable sinners, unable (in the words of Claudel) to endure the stern gaze of God, run to fall at the feet of His Mother. (*Se blottir* was the French term, so expressive! Thank you for introducing me to Claudel.) I have no such instinctive wish. I certainly understand an unwillingness to face that stern gaze! But is it not enough to run to the incarnate Son? (I still cannot really understand the Trinity.) I keep using that word 'enough' as if I grudged the complete giving up of myself – well of course I do – but must hope, etc. May I in this context ask a question which I have hesitated to frame hitherto? What about angels? Does not the Orthodox Church represent the Trinity as three angels? Must that not have a deep meaning? If one is thinking of 'mediators' other than Christ (and Our Lady) may not these beings also be invoked to aid our stumbling steps? You spoke earlier of pure and holy things which are lights and guides. Are not angels everywhere in Holy Writ acting effectively as such guides and inspirations? I once had a remarkable dream in which an angel stood at the foot of my bed. I'm not saying that angels are to be worshipped, the Angel at the end of Revelations positively forbids St John to worship him, but can't they be thought of as it were as supportive elder brothers? (Does the Bible say somewhere that angels once consorted with the daughters of men? I hope *that* didn't happen!) Of course one cannot help being influenced by our great European painters: angels at the Annunciation, at the birth of Christ, at His death, at His resurrection, at the Last Judgment, *embracing* sinners in that heavenly picture of Botticelli. I myself feel an especial affinity with St Michael, blessed Michael Archangel. (Perhaps when I say angels I mean archangels?) I know that he can be rather ferocious, but are not his military characteristics meant for us as a spiritual lesson? I must admit I also love and venerate those old Byzantine images of the beardless Christ holding a sword and looking so wonderfully like a young soldier! Is not the soldier an icon of our human pilgrimage? Soldiers are rightly admired. 'Who would not sleep with the brave.' Excuse these spontaneous thoughts, of course I am not thinking of any form of idolatry. I understand what you say about regular work and am investigating this. By the way, is it true that Eckhart's excommunication was only revoked in 1980? I will, if I may, write to you again soon. I feel myself to be in the dark, yet moving, stumbling. I bow before you and send you my love, your infinitely grateful,

Bellamy

P.S. Is it true that Galatians 3.20 is the 'great text' mentioned in Robert Browning's poem? I can't see anything wrong with it.

Bellamy put down his pen. It was a dark morning. It was raining. He had pulled the curtains. He turned off the little lamp by which he had been writing. Through the space in the ragged curtains he could now see the rain coursing down the window-pane. It was clear and grey, seeming both still and in motion, accompanied by a soft humming sound caused no doubt by innumerable drops which were striking the pavement. Bellamy relaxed his hand and left it lying inert upon the page. He looked at it. He relaxed his lips and listened to his breath, he slowed his breath. When writing to Father Damien he always felt excited, he flushed, the words crowded onto the page faster than his thought, he had to prevent himself from abbreviating them into an illegible shorthand. He had been told not to write too often, he obeyed this command. Sometimes when he finished writing he felt a sick contingent sensation as if he had suddenly shrunk into something very small, a beetle, a piece of crumpled paper, a little dry lump of mud. He had once written to Father Damien about this state, calling it his dark night of the soul. Father Damien had replied that he could have no conception of that dark night, and should be humble enough to recognise ordinary boredom. At other times he could, as he released his pen, feel serenely tired and calm, sitting quiet for a while with his hands folded in a usual pose of meditation. Then there might come what he took to be the opposite sensation, the silent breeding of an enormous space, a chasm faintly lit, silently fermenting. In fact this experience now came to him quite often at times when he was sitting still. On more rare occasions he was gifted with tears. Time passed. He found himself thinking about how Father Damien had hinted, not for the first time, that Bellamy might in the end find his vocation in returning to social work. So what was going on *now* would seem like a holiday, perhaps later a dream. He thought I can't be content with that, I have come so far, I must have more, *more*. Surely I have felt it, I have seen it, it has *captured* me. Surely it is *true*. Before him he had sensed, and with his other eyes seen, the vast extension of his soul wherein God seethed and bubbled like a vast lightless underground spring. Now, as he moved uneasily, remembering the priest's 'discouraging words', something within him said, it's all imaginary, it isn't exactly false, it's just a sort of waking dream. Then he thought, that angel that stood at the bottom of my bed, he was a dream all right. But who was he and what did he say? Now the wind was driving the rain against the window. Something touched him, perhaps the delayed tears. He thought, Eckhart was deemed a heretic, he was lucky not to be burnt. He moved, turning, thrusting his chair away, attempting to stand up. As the hart panteth after the water brooks, so panteth my soul after thee, oh God. My soul thirsteth for God, for the living God. He took a step, then knelt upon the floor, then fell face down upon the dusty threadbare carpet.

'Perhaps he won't come back.'
'He'll come back.'
'He speaks so oddly, not like what one would expect. I think he just wanted to look at you.'
'He looked at you. You shook his hand.'
'Fancy his recognising me.'
'He didn't recognise you. You weren't there. If you had been you would have been called as a witness.'
'I – ? Oh yes. Indeed. Oh *dear* – but he knows – '
'God, have I got to *hammer* it into your head? We are not concerned with what he thinks he knows. We are simply concerned with what happened.'

'But he *saw* – '

'It was dark, he saw nothing, he has had a severe blow on the head and has lost his memory. I thought he was a thief, perhaps he wasn't. I shall be polite to him. He is certainly a damn nuisance and must be got rid of *at once*.'

'You must say you're glad he's alive, at any rate you must be pleased that you didn't kill him.'

'I am a fool to let you be here. The fact is, I don't fancy seeing him alone, and there's no one else I can ask – Oh *damn* – look, I require you to be *absolutely silent*. I shall do all the talking.'

'It's nearly time for him to come.'

It was the evening of the day of the unexpected stranger's visit. He had indeed stayed a short time. He had also, moving a little forward toward Lucas who remained seated, seen the baseball bat lying upon the desk. He stepped back and for an instant only exhibited the emotion which Clement had picturesquely described as turning pale. Apart from this instant he had maintained a tone of cool, almost considerate, politeness. He had announced that he would now have to go but would like to return at eight o'clock in the evening if that would suit Professor Graffe. Lucas had assented. Clement had silently shown him out. It was ten to eight.

Clement could not now conceal his agitation. 'Oh dear, what will happen? Shall we offer him a drink?'

'No.'

'I'd like a drink.'

'There is none in the house.'

'Oh, of course. I hope he won't stay long. I haven't had any lunch.'

'You may find yourself without an appetite for dinner also.'

'How terribly unfortunate about the bat.'

'Oh shut up. That didn't happen. Anyway it had no significance.'

Clement had left the house that morning very soon after the stranger's departure. Lucas, declining discussion, had told his brother to clear off. Clement went to the theatre where some sort of unruly committee meeting was in progress, stayed there a short time, went back to his flat, tried to eat something and failed, rang up Louise who chatted about Moy's birthday party. She also asked after Lucas. Then he lay down on the sofa, uncomfortably, so as not to fall asleep. Then he took a short walk in the rain, returned to change his wet clothes, then took a taxi to Lucas's house arriving at seven instead of, as Lucas had told him to, a quarter to eight.

The rain had stopped. The drawing-room, by contrast with the morning scene, was brightly lit. The room had scarcely altered since their father had furnished it, hastily but not cheaply, when he decided to make London his base of operations. The desk was handsome and huge, with an almost military look, its dark green leather glowing, its brass fitments gleaming. Lucas, who scarcely tolerated other people in the house, cleaned the place himself, hoovering the floors and dusting and polishing the furniture. Bookshelves covered the entire wall behind the desk, and also the opposite wall by the door. A large dark brown leather sofa, rarely sat upon, shiny as on the day of its purchase, stretched out beside the door to the garden, above it hung a watercolour of Lake Geneva showing the Château de Chillon. There were several powerful strong upright chairs with leather seats and ladder-backs. There was one soft low 'sewing chair' upholstered in golden brown velvet with an embroidered cushion on it which betokened the English mother. Her name was Barbara. There was a huge dark Persian carpet now pleasantly worn. Opposite the door to the garden a large Victorian marble fireplace surmounted a little crouching gas fire. The long mantelshelf was occupied by ornaments, again reminiscent of both English and Italian ancestors, china cats and dogs, lustre bowls, and hand-painted caskets of dimmed glass. Above the fireplace hung a portrait, by an obscure painter, of the Italian grandmother. In the picture she looked thin and startled, huge-eyed, one hand, curiously enlarged, clutching, above her silk *décolleté* dress, the end of a yellow amber necklace. Clement would have liked to have that painting, he would also have liked the sewing chair; but he had surrendered the house and all its contents to Lucas when his mother died. Or rather, he did not 'surrender' it, it simply never occurred to him to dispute the matter with Lucas. He wondered sometimes if Lucas and that frightened woman sometimes looked at each other in the dark evenings.

Tonight all the lights were on in the drawing-room, the big centre light with its bulbous *art deco* glass shade, and the four lamps, the green desk lamp, and the three powerful standard lamps. The thick brown velvet curtains, which reached to the floor, had been drawn against the twilight, now against the dark. The corridor, which led past a desolate book-filled front room to the front door, was also brilliantly lit by two high unshaded bulbs. Even the light outside the door, which Clement had not seen illuminated since his mother's death, was turned on. At eight o'clock precisely the doorbell rang. Clement, as instructed, ran to open the door. The stranger in the trilby hat stood outside, holding his umbrella now folded up into a neat packet. He smiled at Clement. Clement offered awkwardly to take his coat, but the man did not proffer it. Clement agitated and confused, forgetful of Lucas's prohibition, launched into conversation.

'I'm so glad to see you so well, you've made a marvellous recovery – '

The stranger, surveying Clement with a gentle yet quizzical look, said to him, 'I too must congratulate *you* on being still here.'

Clement said, 'Oh yes – but actually – '

After this ridiculous but important exchange, Clement turned and led the way into the drawing-room, and the visitor followed, retaining hat and coat and umbrella.

Lucas had turned the green-shaded lamp away from himself, but sat clearly revealed in the other lights with which the room was flooded. He sat quite still, upright, with his small hands evenly placed palms down upon the desk. He looked expressionlessly at the stranger with his slit eyes. The stranger, not taking his gaze from Lucas, now unhurriedly took off his coat and hat and handed them sideways, together with his umbrella, to Clement who, standing just behind him, hastened to put them, folding the coat carefully, upon one of the upright chairs. The stranger then walked down the room and stood before Lucas, a few feet from him. The sinister object was of course gone, but the stranger's gaze flickered for a moment to where it had been. Clement followed, standing again behind him like an attentive servant.

There was a brief pause, long enough for Clement to wonder wildly who would speak first and what on earth he would say. The scene seemed to him absolutely taut with terrible impossibility.

Lucas, moving his flattened hands slightly in relation to each other, spoke first.

'Good evening. I did not intend to kill you and I am glad to see you alive. I was unaware of your recovery.'

The stranger said in a low voice, 'Yes, I thought you might not know. My death was news, but not my resurrection.'

'Quite. Shortly afterwards I went abroad. It is kind of you to come and reassure me. It was an unpleasant encounter for both of us. I was under the impression that you intended to rob me, if I was wrong I am sorry. In any case nothing of that sort happened and we need not speak of it. You understandably wanted to see me, and now you have seen me, I have no ill feeling toward you, as I said I am glad to know that you are alive. It is extremely uncomfortable to believe that one has killed a man, however innocently. I think we may agree that this, though brief, has been a good meeting. Thank you for coming to relieve my mind. I hope you will now continue in good health. So – good evening to you, and goodbye.'

Lucas stood up.

The stranger who, as Clement observed him, had lifted his shoulders and closed his pendent hands while listening to the speech, now turned for a moment and darted a look at Clement. Then he returned to stare at Lucas. Clement had listened to Lucas's cold clear words with amazement – yet what had he expected? He felt ashamed and shocked, yet also in a way which was familiar to him, he admired his brother. However, when the stranger looked at him, Clement felt a shock, a flush, as if he had been scalded.

The stranger said to Lucas, 'Actually there is quite a lot more that I want to say. May I be quite clear? Did you really believe and do you still believe, that I am a thief?'

Lucas sat down and made a gesture, also familiar to Clement, which expressed the making of a concession tiresomely asked and grudgingly, yet generously, conceded. He said, 'I only speak of an impression, if you now wish to declare that you are not, then of course I am ready to believe you. All I mean is that this need not detain us any further.'

The stranger said, 'This impression was aired in court, where unfortunately I was not present, and I gather that you did not reject it.'

Lucas said in an irritable but matter-of-fact tone, 'I was not present either, except when I was ordered to speak. I know virtually nothing of what went on in court, I felt it did not concern me. If you can recall that unfortunate night, it was very dark. I am sorry that I struck you such a violent blow. Perhaps your memory of it all is less than clear. All I mean is that since we are now not in a law court we need not go over the details of an episode so extremely disagreeable to both of us.'

The stranger taking his time and speaking in a slow thoughtful voice said, 'I rather like details. Of course I was not attempting to rob you and I think you know that very well.' He turned suddenly to Clement and asked, 'How exactly are you two related? It is an unusual name.'

Clement, taken by surprise, said, 'We are brothers.' He flushed again.

The stranger murmured, 'Ah, I see.'

Lucas said sharply, 'May I ask you to go now? There is no point in our blundering over this confused and unpleasant matter which is now over and done with. I feel sure you do not feel disposed to chat about it. Please excuse my bluntness.'

The stranger, stepping back and speaking partly to Clement, said, 'Perhaps I may remind you of my name, which you will both of course have heard, but may prefer not to recall. It was I am afraid rather mangled by the press, misspelt and, I am told, mispronounced. My name is Mir, spelt M – I – R, and spoken as in 'mere', not 'mire', a word which in the Russian language means both 'world' and 'peace' – world peace, a felicitous combination you must agree. I expect you know Russian, Professor Graffe, I believe you are a very learned man, in fact I can see from here books in Russian upon the shelf behind you. When I recovered consciousness – '

Lucas came round the desk. Mir stepped back, so did Clement. Lucas said in a low voice, 'Please – go away!'

Mir was considerably taller than Lucas, he was broad-shouldered and solidly built, but with the look of a man who should have been more ample. Though his face retained a sort of plumpness, he had probably become thinner during his illness. His dark green tweed jacket, as Clement noticed, hung upon him a little loosely, and his big powerful hands, hanging at his sides during the conversation, were wrinkled and stained. His age how-ever might be guessed to be considerably less than fifty. His head was bulky and high-domed, his cheeks, with high cheek-bones, were plump, his nose, with wide nostrils, was short and broad and substantial, his mouth was thick-lipped but well-formed, his hair was chestnut brown and curly, his eyes, under copious eye-brows, were large, a dark and murky grey. He spoke with the odd accent which Clement had been unable to place until the man uttered his name. Clement had not hitherto known his name, had not read about him in the press, and did not want to know the name of the man who had died in his stead. He wanted this man to be no-man. Mir was still hard to place. He did not seem quite like an intellectual. He spoke slowly as if thinking slowly. He had a certain presence, a certain air of authority.

'All right,' said Mir, 'I'll go away. But I want to see you again soon.'

'I'm sorry,' said Lucas, 'that is not possible.'

'I think you can make it possible. May I be perfectly frank? I want something from you – and I propose to obtain it.'

'What?'

'Restitution.'

'What do you mean?'

'Sometimes called justice.'

Lucas was sitting on his desk. Mir had gone. Clement waited anxiously for Lucas, who had been walking up and down the room in silence after Mir's departure, to speak. Clement felt fear, breathing it in with the thick still air of the room, the smell of books, the presence of books. Lucas never opened windows. He felt also a curious shuddering thrill, somehow connected with Mir's resurrection.

Lucas, seeming suddenly to notice Clement who was standing by the fireplace, smiled. Clement was amazed. Lucas said, 'Well, what did you make of all that?'

'I don't know what to make of it,' said Clement. 'Do you think he's a bit mad? Poor fellow. It could be the result of the blow. Or could he be some sort of impostor? No, that's impossible. Anyway you recognised him.'

'Yes. That was the initial blunder. I should *not* have recognised him. He recognised you. Only that doesn't matter so much since you weren't there.'

'You mean – ? Oh yes – do you think he'll turn up tomorrow?' Mir had said departing that he proposed to return at six o'clock on the following evening and trusted it was convenient. Lucas had not replied.

'Oh he'll turn up all right. He's made a good start.'

'He wanted you to say you didn't think he was a thief. Perhaps that will do, I mean that may have been what he really came for?'

'That was just an introduction.'

'Lucas, I've just thought. He looks very like a man I've seen hanging around outside my place, and then outside Louise's house. I'm sure it was him. What on earth can that mean?'

'He knew our name. He must have been watching this house, he picked you up too, and you led him to Clifton.'

'He was waiting for you.'

'Yes! Did Louise notice him, did she say anything to you?'

'No. But I don't understand, when he came round, when he revived, why didn't he contact the police at once to tell them his story? Well, he may have been pretty confused to begin with – but he seems all right now. Why didn't he tell the police?'

'The fact that he apparently didn't is certainly interesting.'

'Perhaps he didn't feel certain and thought they wouldn't believe him.'

'He is either very stupid or very clever.'

'But anyway he can't prove anything, can he?'

'He may reckon that he can get something out of me, and if he fails he can always tell the police, and if he succeeds he can still tell the police.'

'Oh – Lucas – he'll blackmail you, he'll want money.'

'He was intelligent enough not to go public at once. His secret is worth more. Perhaps money – perhaps – other things.'

'But, Luc, if he did say what he thinks happened why should anyone believe him, they'd say he invented it, or dreamed it in his coma.'

'So he'd be discredited a second time, not only a thief, and not only not dead, the rotter, but a vindictive liar!'

'Well – anyway if he just thinks a bit he'll see you can't be blackmailed after all.'

'My dear boy, *you* are not thinking.'

'How do you mean?'

'You called him a "poor fellow".'

'Yes – so?'

'Would you stand by and let him be rejected and disgraced when he was telling the truth?'

Clement was silent. He fetched a chair and sat on it at some distance from Lucas. He said, 'Well, don't forget your promise.'

'You are priceless! I don't forget promises. The point is he could make a great deal of unpleasant trouble for me, and for you too. He might be believed anyway, without your testimony.'

'But I – '

'Don't say it. God what a mess. I want you out of it.'

'Thank you – but of course I'll come tomorrow and stand by – '

'No. I don't want him to see you again. But I must have someone here. It'll have to be Bellamy.'

'Surely you don't want him to know.'

'All right – hang it, you come. But I'd like you to see Bellamy, just say that the fellow is back, and not to tell anyone. Don't say you've seen the man. I may need Bellamy later.'

'You know – in all the conversations we've had we have not considered the possibility that I might – '

'As you said just now about him, who would believe you? For once you have said something quite amusing however. As you have not spoken hitherto I assume you had motives.'

'Yes, I had motives – but then I thought he was dead.'

'Well, review the situation now if you want to, only don't bother me. I doubt if you would be happy if you destroyed me. But you must decide. Be sure to come tomorrow. I don't want to be alone in the house with that man.'

'You are afraid of him.'

'Yes.'

In the evening of that same day Louise alone in her bedroom was restless. Nothing had happened during the day, she had done a lot of necessary shopping. Joan had telephoned her. The children had gone out. How did she know now where they went? The rain had stopped. There was a foggy darkness outside. She had had her early supper earlier than usual and retired as to bed. She had even put on her nightdress, lifting her arms as if in prayer or in the performance of a rite. She had brushed her stiff hair with a stiff brush. She was dressed to go to bed only it was ridiculously early to go to bed. She desired to be unconscious. She could not go on reading A Glastonbury Romance, she would not sleep, she could not sew. Upon a chair lay an old evening-dress which she had started to shorten so as to wear it on Moy's birthday. She paced up and down making little scarcely audible noises in her throat. At intervals she smoothed out her face with her hands and put on a smile and then let it vanish. Tonight, the presence of the girls tormented her, it made her itch and twitch as if she were covered with ants. Moy's noisy pounding as she ran upstairs, Sefton's firm martial tread, the cat-like footsteps of Aleph, their voices calling to one another like birds, the tinkle of the piano, the endless sentimental singing, the laughter: the silences, the whispers, the confederacy, not of course against her, but excluding her. Their budding womanhood, the milky smell of their innocence, their secret discovery of sex. She feared for them, she trembled for them, now sometimes she wept for them. Of course she loved them, of course they loved her. But love cannot always find out a way.

A lamp revealed her bed, neatly opened to receive her. She sat down upon the bed, upon the inviting sheet, folding her hands in a gesture not unlike Aleph's. She thought about Teddy and his *perfect command* of the world. The last days of Teddy's life had been terrible. She had lately read in a newspaper that scientists had now *proved* that there *could not be in the whole cosmos* any other beings in any sense like us. How could they prove such a thing? Not that Louise craved for aliens. It was just that the thought generated, out of her little local solitude, a vast cosmic solitude. The tiny solitary planet, the poor doomed little planet, for it too must die and its death will be terrible. To whom could she talk now? Clement came less often, and when he came she talked less. If she burst out, as she used to do, with any wild and impetuous speech, about the children for instance, she felt that she would embarrass him, even annoy him. She had asked him about Lucas and he had answered curtly. Louise wanted to talk to Lucas, she even felt she *ought* to go and see him, but she was afraid to. He was so difficult. Here a blunder, any blunder, might involve, for her, pain, regret, remorse.

Looking across the room she saw her pink and blue and white striped silk evening-dress, its high bodice lying on the floor, its sweeping skirt upon the chair. It could still fit her perfectly. It had been a bold moment when she had cut the skirt to make it shorter. Her needle and thread, at rest in the new tucked-up hem, were clearly visible in the light of the lamp. The thin needle was shining, glittering coldly like a diamond. Louise stared at it. It was so clean, so strong, so perfect, a needle at its work. But how little it was, in an instant it could be lost forever. So now all she could do was shorten her dress? She moved and the needle vanished. Among so many troubles she selected one: Bellamy's cottage used to solve all summer holiday problems. What would happen now?

Aleph had said that Harvey was coming to see her, Aleph, that evening. Louise had announced she was going to bed early. Not that Harvey was likely to want to see Louise. He often now came to the house without seeing her. Louise thought about the birthday party when everyone wore masks. Moy would be sixteen. She wished it was all over. She wished her visit to Lucas was all over and all right. She thought about Harvey whom she so much wanted to see and so much wished that he was really her own dearly beloved son.

Moy, upstairs in her room, had been thinking about the black-footed ferret. The black-footed ferret, an animal about whose preservation Moy had once been profoundly concerned, had become something of a family joke. Moy herself had become less ardent, having been unable to find out anything about the fate of the creature, or to discover anywhere a photograph of it. She was even at times ready to be persuaded that it did not actually exist, but had been, always and from the start, the invention of some jesting naturalist. Generally however she felt sure that it existed, or had existed being now extinct. What remained was its name, which had for her a certain magic, and a mental picture of it as somehow coming close, glad that she was thinking about it, reaching out its little black paws in gratitude. The lively presence of the ferret had perhaps been given substance by memories of a hamster, a real hamster called Colin, who had been Moy's pet when she was about seven. She had held Colin in her hands and let him move quietly from hand to hand, feeling his warm smooth belly and his little gripping feet, not, she felt sure, trying to escape, but communing with her in a friendly way. And when she held up the tame docile little beast before her face and looked at his gentle eyes she felt sure that he was happy with her and loved her. One terrible day however, when Moy was with Colin in the garden, letting him walk upon the grass, and was distracted from him for a moment, he vanished. Her mother and sisters assured her that Colin was perfectly well, probably now in some other garden, enjoying eating the plants and living free. They never told her that they had found his poor little body a day later, killed by a cat. Sefton and Aleph concealed their tears. Louise shed tears too, concealed from all.

Now she knelt down beside Anax, who was curled up in his basket, and began to stroke him. He looked at her with his strange light-blue eyes which could look so sad. She thought, will he never forget, never forgive? As if he knew her thought he thrust his long muzzle towards her, pressing it up gently against her hand as she drew her fingers back over his long sleek head into the dry bushy fur. His nose was moist, but his copious flag of a tail lay inert, not stirring for her comfort. She sighed and sat back on the floor, holding the side of the basket with one hand. What could she do? Every day she rescued the snail or slug or worm from the pavement where it might be stepped on, the spider from the bath where it was imprisoned, the tiniest almost invisible creatures who were in some wrong place where they might starve or be crushed. She was expert at catching them, coaxing them onto a leaf or into a vessel or into her hand. She was the one too who always found things which were lost in the house. But was this not something fruitless or even bad? How did she know what little living creatures, and even *things*, *wanted* her to do? The whole world was a jumble of mysterious destinies. Did the stones who were picked up by humans and taken into their houses *mind*, did they dislike being inside a house, dry, gathering dust, missing the open air, the rain, perhaps the company of other stones? Why should she think that they must feel privileged because she had, out of a myriad others, discovered them and picked them up? She felt this weird anxiety sometimes as she caressed a rounded sea-worn pebble or peered into the glittering interior of a flint.

Now she had taken Anax, of course not wantonly or wilfully, away from his beloved, and was keeping him prisoner. She was utterly responsible to him, suppose, because of her, he were run over? Or suppose he ran away and, trying to find Bellamy, got lost and was never seen again? Sitting beside him now, pressing her face against his side and hearing his fast heart beating, she murmured, 'I'm sorry.' She sat back, continuing to stroke him, feeling him trembling a little. Then she noticed that he was staring past her at something else. She turned in time to see something moving upon the shelf, a piece of grey speckled granite had shifted from its place. Moy was used to being called 'fey', not attaching much meaning to the word. Lately however she had developed a curious power, that of making small objects move simply by looking at them with a certain concentration. She had discovered this talent by accident, she even knew a scientific name for it, *telekinesis*. The fact that it had this impressive name might have served as a reassurance since it implied that other people had it too. However it frightened Moy and she kept it secret. What had just happened alarmed her even more. So now things could move on their own, perhaps whenever they wished? Or perhaps it was all due to her, her proximity, her *aura*? Did Anax know about it, did he fear it? He was gazing up and growling softly.

She went to the shelf and picked up the piece of granite and set it down again very firmly, saying 'There!' She said to Anax, 'Be quiet, don't fret.' She opened the window. Damp foggy air came in. She opened the door. She looked about her room which was strewn with cardboard, textiles, newspaper, ready to make the masks for the party. She heard, down below, Aleph talking to Harvey whom she had just let in from the street. She closed the door again. She thought, perhaps I am simply mad. It will grow worse. That will be my life. Anax was still growling softly.

Below in Aleph's room Harvey was sitting on the bed with his wounded leg extended. Aleph sat near upon the upright chair at her desk, her arms around his crutches.

'So, no cast. That must be good.'

'Not necessarily. They're experimenting. They've just tied it up very beastly tight. I think honestly they don't know what to do.'

'I bought you a knitting needle so you could scratch inside the cast.'

'How kind! Hang onto it. I may need it for some extreme act later on.'

'How does it feel?'

'It's burning, it's swelling. I may have to rush it to the hospital again tomorrow. It's like an evil alien thing which has been attached to my body. I can't attend to anything else. I've stopped reading, I've stopped thinking. *You* are working away I see! Everyone calls Sefton the swot, but you do it discreetly just as much. I even suspect you are cleverer than me.'

'Oh no! How can you say that!'

'You think you would stop caring for me if you believed it?'

Aleph laughed and clinked the crutches together. 'Well, one

must work, what else is there, what other meaning is there in life?'

'You've got that *ewige Wiederkehr* feeling again.'

'Nothing so interesting.'

'So you're not a romantic any more, youth at the prow and pleasure at the helm, not even the Magus Zoroaster?'

'Oh do not speak of him. So you contemplate an extreme act?'

'No, I wish I could. We have been so much loved, I can't give life any other meaning, am I supposed now to create new meanings?'

'We have been so much loved, yes. You agree that you have been too – '

'Aleph, don't separate me from the enchanted circle.'

'You know nothing about enchantment.'

'Don't talk death to me, sometimes you do. All right, my father and my mother both ran away. I was left abandoned in the forest. But I was found – '

'By Louie and Aleph and Sef and Moy. Well, that can't go on, the dream must end.'

'All right. And I know I shall never be happy as I once was. But there is a standard to be carried on, I meant a flag but in the other meaning too. Don't be a nihilist to me just when I need courage to go on.'

'You are thinking of your leg, but that will mend.'

'No, that's just a symbol, a reminder – I may or may not be lame forever – but it makes me see the rest – the horror – '

'We are pampered children,' said Aleph, 'we don't know *anything* about the horror. For us it's just an exciting bogy.'

'You are cut off from me today. It hurts.'

'Oh *silly* – it's just my old sick soul! Yet night approaches, better not to stay.'

'I feel so senseless and contingent and unmade.'

'That's simply the youth disease. Brace up, Harvey boy!'

'If only I had gone to Florence. Now I shall never go. I did it on purpose and I deserve it all. I love you, dear Aleph.'

'I love you.'

'Yes, but that's like ordinary responses in church. I love you but I don't deserve you, I can't really conceive of you, apprehend you, I have to go through some ordeal before I am worthy – '

'You have an ordeal, you have damaged your leg.'

'That's just a stupid accident.'

'You mean the gods didn't send it? Sefton says you are like Philoctetes.'

'What a perfectly beastly comparison! No, don't tease me. This contingent nonsense isn't the ordeal – '

'Whatever will count as one then?'

'I don't know, but I feel it's *there*, if only I were brave enough to reach it – '

'Perhaps it is I who am to have the ordeal.'

'Yes, like the girl chained to the rock.'

'No, *not* like the girl chained to the rock.'

'Sorry, you're the one on the horse with the sword – '

'You were always to be young Lochinvar.'

'Only he arrived in time – '

'Dear Harvey, perhaps we have to love each other, and to find each other run the risk of not finding each other!'

'You're not serious, you just make it all run away into the sand! Never mind, we'll try again another day! How's Clement, have you seen him since Lucas came back? I suppose he's seen Lucas.'

'I don't know, I suppose he has. He was here when Bellamy brought the news.'

'I know, Bellamy told me. Clement comes here a lot, doesn't he, so Bellamy thought he'd find him – '

'Unfortunately Anax heard Bellamy's voice and he started to howl terribly. Moy was very upset.'

'I'd have been upset too. I must go and see Lucas.'

'Oh – why?'

'I just have to, it's a compulsion.'

'Better be careful. What's the compulsion?'

'I just want to spend a friendly ten minutes with him so that I can dismiss him from my mind. Without that he haunts me.'

'He can haunt people.'

'He used to come to tea with you all. And he gave Sefton tutorials! I bet she was terrified.'

'It must have been a strain, but she says she learnt a lot.'

'Learning is her thing, she's *docile*, I wish I was. And you're really a scholar too though you put on that act.'

'What act?'

'Oh world-weariness, older than the rocks among which you sit, and so on. It comes of being so beautiful. *Tu ris de te voir.* I'm lucky to know you. You haven't started yet, and neither have I. Aleph, I'm a *fool*, forgive me!'

112

'My dear!' she reached out to take his hand. The crutches fell to the floor.

At that moment the sound of the piano came from the Aviary. 'That's Sefton.' They listened. 'Let's go down, Harvey, I want to sing.'

My dear son,

I write in haste to reply to important points and queries in your last letter. Let me repeat that the solitude which you seem to be imposing on yourself is not wise. Long periods of self-imposed solitude are only advisable in the context of some orderly spiritual discipline. Otherwise they may tend to degenerate into self-indulgent fantasy. I suggest once more that you go out and serve your neighbours. You have had experience of such service in the past and are now well placed to find out those in need. I would also advise you not to proceed with what appears to be your cult of archangels! The worship of angels is an idolatry against which we are cautioned. I connect this observation with your wish, expressed some time ago, for a revelation or sign. You must be humble enough to do without these luxuries. May I further urge you not to picture Our Lord as a soldier. This sort of 'dramatisation' of what is holy is, in your case, a form of egoism. See in Christ poverty, humility, service, love. Galatians 3.20, said by some to be what Browning had in mind, is of interest in relation to the doctrine of the Trinity, this could more profitably be discussed later on. Meister Eckhart was not excommunicated, nor was he, though inconclusively tried for heresy, ever declared to be a heretic during his lifetime. Certain of his writings were condemned as heretical in 1329 shortly after his death. These judgments were revoked in 1980. Please excuse a short letter. Work and pray, pray always, be earnest in your endeavours, consider seriously where your vocation lies. Yours humbly *in Christo*,

Damien

My dear Father Damien,

Thank you for your letter, you are very kind to answer my
letters so promptly. I take note of all your admonitions. I
have been to Mass and to confession and discovered a fine
young priest in this locality. I have also, rather less successfully, made some excursions in the service of others. As you
rightly say I have had plenty of experience – but organised
'social work' is unlike the solitary enterprises of the 'self-
employed'! (I remember we once discussed whether I would
not be happier as a Franciscan.) About angels and archangels,
of course I realise they are not to be worshipped like God
and Christ. I read in a book that physical pain can cure
mental pain, body silences mind and God can enter. I see
them as God's justice, purgatory, *cum vix iustus sit securus*,
I would like to feel I had a stern and austere guardian angel,
I desire to be struck down like St Paul. All this I connect with
my own notion of dark night against which I know you have
warned me. Please forgive these rambling thoughts which it
relieves me to pour out to you. By the way (I hope this is not
improper!) I went to a nearby Anglican Church which runs
a soup kitchen for poor vagrant people and attended a service
during which God was persistently referred to as 'She'. Is
it wrong to be horrified? After all, God is beyond human
distinctions of sex and changing the traditional He to She
raises a senseless problem, bringing God down to the level
of a human. You see what I mean. (I do not intend to connect
this with my earlier hesitations about the worship of Our
Lady.) As for women priests, that is quite another matter,
and I am well content to follow the teaching of the Church.
Please write to me again soon, your letters are as manna in
the desert. Yours ever in obedience, your loving son,

                                                    Bellamy

P.S. Is it possible that these are the last days of the world
and we are to look for an anti-Christ?

Bellamy usually enjoyed writing to Father Damien, letting his
doubts and exclamations flow free as to an old friend. He had
been rescued by that kind and worthy priest from a state of
depression which had been more alarming than usual. He had
been directed to Father Damien by a priest to whom he had at

last randomly confessed in a church in north London. Anax, who had sat patiently outside the confessional, had been made much of by the priest after Bellamy's gloomy recital was over, and it was after that they had sat down in the empty church and talked in a more personal manner. Bellamy had spoken wildly about death and leaving the world, and the priest had mentioned Father Damien. Since then Bellamy had developed his intense filial, almost childish, relationship with his secluded mentor, whom he had visited with trepidation at the lonely abbey in Northumberland. Bellamy immediately loved the place, its ancient grey walls conspicuous at the end of the valley, its solitude, its silence, its unworldly purity, its absolute and tranquil discipline, its evident benign existence as a prison. One thing disappointed him: he had expected to converse with his spiritual director dimly through the bars of a grille, but in the modern manner Father Damien had met him in a bright neat modern parlour with stiff shiny furniture and prints of local views upon the walls. The priest, not an old man, in his black and white robes, was pale, etiolated as if deprived of light, his faintly wrinkled face, and his long thin hands which lay stretched out motionless upon the table, were preternaturally clean. His straight dry hair was grey, his attentive clever eyes were light blue. He spoke quietly in a clear cultivated 'academic' voice, smiling at intervals a thin gentle smile, asking Bellamy a number of questions. His presence in the room was expressive of some infinitely great authority. Bellamy's voice trembled as he answered the questions. Beyond their conversation lay a vast silence, broken once by a bell. Bellamy, breathing in that silence and apprehending that authority, felt *I have come home*. He felt, here is purity and truth and love, and by those I desire to be *consumed*. The meeting lasted forty minutes, at the end of which Bellamy asked to be admitted to the order.

He was told to be patient, he was told to wait. Their correspondence began. After several months Father Damien saw him again, but without uttering encouragement, rather suggesting caution. Meanwhile Bellamy was busy dismantling his life. As time continued to go on Bellamy began to fear that his beloved mentor, after at first taking him seriously had on reflection become disappointed, had perhaps 'seen through' Bellamy, perceived him as a romancer, a chronic idolater, hopelessly given over to 'self-indulgent fantasy'. So, as such, he was being quietly given up. This doubt touched Bellamy at times with its cold finger hinting at a possible relapse into the old despair. Giving up his job and his flat, moving to the little room in Whitechapel, had for a time animated him, affording a seeming glimpse or vision of the contemplative life. But now more often the old stale hopeless weariness overcame him: the black sickness which *almost no one else*, certainly not his nearest dearest friends, could *understand at all*. The idea of giving up the world, which had given him for a time so much life-energy, appeared now as a sort of fake suicide, a ghastly play-image of his death. This fatal falseness-of-heart was what perhaps Father Damien, on further acquaintance, had now seen in him. The holy man now thought that *service* might be a cure, might at any rate arouse his penitent's interest in the suffering of others and lead him out into some real, more genuine, open field. But Bellamy's 'solitary enterprises' as he had described them, had been fruitless, it had been as if he were searching the neighbourhood for beggars and outcasts so as simply to sneer at them. Even the kind people at the Anglican soup kitchen did not want him. No one seemed to need him, everyone, like Father Damien, saw through him. Bellamy had been here before. Sitting now stiff with loneliness and fear in his cold little room he found himself tapping on the table. He thought, I am turning toward evil. This tapping is to summon it. I am crammed with darkness. Thrusting his letter aside he stared at the rain streaming down the window. He thought, tears, if I could only have the sweet warm gift of tears! But I am cold and hard as a stone. Oh if only I could have a visitation, an angel, a star, a lightning flash, a *sign*.

He became aware that a man was standing outside and tapping on the window, interrupting the straight courses of the running rain. He stared. It was Clement. He ran to open the door.

'You were just sitting there like a statue, I couldn't attract your attention. Your bell doesn't work, you know. Are you all right?'

'Yes, yes, I was meditating. Why, you're soaked.'

'Of course I'm soaked, I came out without an umbrella. I've left my car on a building lot, I hope it won't be attacked, everything around here seems to be being knocked down. Do you mind if I put my coat here and let it drip? This place smells, is the sink blocked? It's hellish cold in here, no wonder you're wearing two jerseys.'

'It's so kind of you to come and see me, I'm so glad you've come! What time is it?'

'It's three o'clock, in the afternoon in case you aren't sure. Bellamy, *sit down* – '

'I'll put something in the meter and turn on the fire – '

'No, no, I'm only staying for a moment, *listen*. Lucas asked me to tell you, it's in the strictest confidence.'

'What, what – ?'

'That chap that Lucas killed, you know – '

'Of course I know!'

'Well, he's not dead. The doctors evidently thought he was dead and the press said he was dead, and Lucas thought he was dead, but he recovered and he turned up at Lucas's place – '

'What, and Lucas didn't know – ?'

'No, it was a complete surprise.'

'But, Clement, how marvellous, how *wonderful*, Lucas must be so glad, so *relieved*, he didn't kill a man after all, it's like a *miracle* – '

'Oh yes, it's great – '

'It's like Lazarus, how *splendid*, raised from the dead, and he *liberates* Lucas, doesn't he, takes away that black cloud, when I saw Lucas he was so – I'd love to meet him, have you seen him, what's he like?'

'I haven't seen him and I don't know what he's like.'

'How kind of Lucas to send you to tell me – '

'Well, don't tell the others please.'

'I won't tell anyone, but – '

'Why do you live in this awful dump, what do you do all day? Can't you either get yourself into that bloody monastery or else live an ordinary useful rational life? Or do you want to be a freak living in a wood and picking up sticks like Tessa Millen? You're such a hopeless muddler, always arranging to make yourself fail and be miserable – all right, I know, I know, I'm sorry – '

'Clement, do stay here, don't go, let's spend the rest of the day together, we can walk though the City and look at the churches – '

'In this rain? Anyway I can't, I must rescue my car, anyway I've got to go to the theatre, I've got to rescue someone's botched design, and arrange a bloody poetry reading, oh never mind – I'll come another time, to see you I mean, if you haven't been removed – '

'By men in white coats?'

'No, fool, by your priest, or by God or – oh *hell* – '

'What's the matter?'

'Nothing. It's just the rain. Look, your window leaks, it's coming in, it's not just my mackintosh. Goodbye.'

'You lost us some cards, I did too. I was taken by surprise.'

'You mean we should just have denied it all or pretended not to understand?'

'It's still not too late to try, his memory may be hazy. Damn it, I haven't *time* for this wretched business – he may be a fool after all, a weak man putting on an act, the thing is to settle him quickly, confuse him and send him packing. He must be sent away mystified.'

'Suppose he wants to take you to court.'

'Us, Clement, us. I don't think it will come to that. I'm afraid he wants money. We must treat him like a poor confused creature who had a blow on the head. Perhaps that's what he really is. Still, I can't make him out, there's something wrong. He seems intelligent and cultivated, yet he's some sort of outsider, intruder –'

'He's an immigrant, or his father was.'

'It's more than that, I don't like him, he's a cursed nuisance, I don't care for ghosts, why couldn't he die decently.'

'Perhaps he just wants you to say you're sorry.'

'What for? *Think*, my dear, *think*.'

'All right, all right. But he did want to make you say you didn't believe he was a thief.'

'Yes, but that's a trifle. Well, we shall see what is to come. It is nearly six o'clock. I don't want you in the room. He may turn out simply to be mad, that might be best provided he isn't violent. Stay in the front room, but keep the doors open. There's the bell. Let him in.'

Clement had let him in, smiling and saying nothing. The visitor smiled too and said nothing. He followed Clement to the drawing-room. Lucas, standing behind his big desk, bowed his head slightly and pointed to a chair placed facing the desk about ten feet from it. The visitor returned the bow. He pulled the chair forward and stood beside it, looking back at Clement who was still at the door. Clement raised a hand, then slid out through the door leaving it ajar. The visitor turned to Lucas. Lucas sat down and immediately began to talk.

'Please sit down, Mr Mir, I expect you must be feeling a bit weak, after all I imagine you are still convalescent. If you remember you kindly told us your name. I must congratulate you on your recovery and I am glad to see you so alive and well. It is kind of you to visit me again. I am sorry that I cannot give you much time and we must have a brief, though I am sure pleasant, chat. What a blessing the rain has stopped. When did you leave the hospital, on what date?'

Mir had sat down and placed his umbrella and his trilby hat upon the floor. He was wearing a long black mackintosh of which he now undid the buttons. He replied, 'I can't remember exactly.'

'I quite understand. A certain confusion must be part of such a condition, areas of the memory are lost. I hope you have good doctors. I expect they are still keeping an eye on you. Do you see them regularly?'

'I have stopped seeing them.'

'Surely that is not wise? I imagined you would still be having helpful therapy? Who was the specialist in charge of your case? I'm afraid I can't remember what hospital you were in.'

Mir did not reply to this question, he simply shook his head slowly.

'Well, all that is your affair. I am glad to see you again and to express my sympathy. I would like to be able to help you, but I am afraid I cannot see any way in which I could. This brief quiet talk is certainly in order, and may be, in its way, a relief to both of us. Let us be gracious to each other and be content with just this meeting, for which I can well understand your desire. There is little to say. Perhaps we have already said it. I say sincerely that I wish you well.'

Mir, who had been looking at Lucas with a slight frown, said, 'Where's the other chap, I mean your brother?'

'The other chap is working in the front room, he assists me sometimes.'

'I thought he was an actor.'

'He sometimes acts. This does not make him an actor. I am sure your family must be very happy with your recovery. I expect you are staying with them.'

'I have no family.'

'Well, that too may be a blessing.'

'You evidently thought so. Why did you want to kill him?'

'I am afraid you are confused. I never wanted to kill anybody. I am very sorry for the damage and disturbance to your mind which I sincerely hope is temporary. As you know, I was under the impression that you were attacking me. I am very willing to admit that I may well have been wrong.'

'I saw you trying to kill that man. You were holding a club. I think I saw it lying on your desk when I first visited you.'

'You are talking wildly. Indeed you are *dreaming*. I fear our conversation is getting nowhere. Look, let us be reasonable, I do not want to waste your time any more than my own. I have agreed to see you again, I have spoken to you with sympathy. Your conjectures and your, perhaps unintentionally, portentous tone, are not assisting our discussion. Come, that won't do! I am sure that you do not want, after your unpleasant experience, to land yourself in further fruitless complications which would only damage yourself and not me. Truly, I do not want to cause you any more harm. You spoke of restitution, but I think that is better forgotten. Perhaps you are short of money? It occurs to me that this may be what you want. But of course – '

'You are offering me money? I can assure you that I am not after money. I have plenty of money.'

'That is just as well, as I have not. That being so, Mr Mir, I cannot see how I can assist you, and as I said I do not want to take up more of your time.'

'Oh I have plenty of time, indeed I have nothing but time, since thanks to you I am now unemployed. What is your brother's first name by the way?'

'His name is Clement – '

'A good name. Would you mind if he were to join us? I imagine he is listening at the door in any case.' Without waiting for Lucas's gesture Mir rose and strode to the half-open door. Clement, standing outside, almost fell into the room. 'Please come in, Clement, if I may call you so.'

'Mr Mir is about to go', said Lucas. 'You sit *there*.' He pointed to a chair near the door against the bookshelves. 'By the way', he said to Mir who was returning to his seat, 'how did you know he was an actor?'

'Well, I have, as I think I said, had plenty of time on my hands while I was waiting for you to reappear, some of that time I have employed studying your family and your friends, to whose houses after all, you might have returned.'

'You mean – detective work.'

'No, just watching and enquiring in a friendly manner and coming to certain conclusions which you might be interested to hear – '

'No doubt as a result of your disability, you are beginning to ramble. May I suggest again that a gift of money may be in order? Within my means of course, or a gift or indemnification of some sort, *something* positively good, may I put it so, to compensate you, even symbolically, for the distress I have accidentally caused you? Please *think* about what I am saying. By thus accepting something from me you would bring relief to both of us. I realise that your mind is not entirely clear – '

'I am not interested in symbolic compensation. It is true that I have to some extent lost my power to concentrate, and with it my ability to *work*, that is to do the difficult and valuable work to which I was dedicated, and thus, to put it briefly, my life has been ruined.'

'I am very sorry, but I have neither the time nor the talent to act as your therapist. For that you must go elsewhere.'

'I am really following our conversation very carefully and do not, contrary to your belief, think that it is getting nowhere. You have, perhaps inadvertently, given me quite a lot of valuable information. You keep expressing a wish to get rid of me and have twice offered me money. I have told you that I do not want money and have explained that I have lost forever a job which I prized – '

Clement, from the back of the room, said, 'What was your job?'

Mir paused. Then said, 'I am, or rather I was, a psychoanalyst. I hesitated to tell you, since not everyone likes psychoanalysts. And I do not want to be told, physician heal thyself. Of course neither of you would suggest anything so silly. Anyway, leaving this aside, let me continue with my explanation. You recall that when you asked me at the end of our last encounter what I wanted, I said "restitution", and when you queried this I said "justice". Well, since you seem to be giving consideration to what I want, let me repeat that what I want is justice.'

Mir had turned his chair somewhat sideways so as to include Clement in his observations, and every now and then turned

121

towards him. Clement, leaning forward, his elbows on his knees, was listening intently to the conversation which was becoming more and more baffling. Lucas was leaning back impassively, speaking softly and clearly. His yellowish thin-eyed thin-lipped face expressed a weary, sometimes faintly amused, obduracy, as of someone, capable of ruthlessness, temperately addressing a tiresome child. At that moment, as if taking advantage of a momentary silence, a gust of wind shook the garden doors, hurling pellets of rain, perhaps even little hail stones, against the glass. Mir frowned, looking at the well-drawn velvet curtains which were shuddering slightly. Lucas moved the lamp upon the desk so as to cast more light upon Mir, less upon himself. Mir was fumbling with his mackintosh, thrusting it off onto the floor. Clement took note of his expensive well-cut suit, the now visible waistcoat and chic green tie.

Lucas continued, maintaining the same tone, 'I am sorry that you have these persistent gaps in your memory. We agreed that there is nothing to be gained by involving lawyers and law courts. That would not *in any way* benefit you. Particularly after your recent admissions concerning the state of your wits. You must dismiss any such idea.'

Mir, smiling now and leaning forward and gesturing with both hands, replied, 'Oh, but I have no intention of that sort, not at present anyway. I agree that it would involve, as you put it, more tiresome unpleasantnesses! Justice does not dwell only in courts of law. Please let us talk for a moment or two about justice, a respectable and ancient concept, expressed in my book, if I may put it so, as an eye for an eye and a tooth for a tooth.'

Lucas, who had been concentrating upon his visitor, observing his facial expressions and bodily movements, said 'Are you Jewish?'

'Yes. Are you?'

Lucas, after a moment's pause, said, 'I don't know.'

'What does that mean.'

'I was an adopted child. I do not know, or wish to know, who my parents were.'

'I see – and he – ' Mir turned for a moment toward Clement, 'yes, indeed. I am sorry. But really, you know, I feel sure you are Jewish, yes, I'm sure you are, I can see – '

Lucas, who had frowned for a moment, interrupted, resuming his cool silky tone, 'You have spoken of restitution, you do not want money, I do not know what you want, I dare say you do not know what you want, what am I to offer – ?'

'I will tell you – *exactly appropriate payment.*'

'Come, come. I hit you impulsively because you startled me. I called for assistance, I saw that you were looked after, this promptness saved your life, I could have simply gone away and left you, then none of these problems would have arisen at all! I admitted my responsibility, I confessed before the law of the land that I had damaged you, and I was acquitted. That was justice. I have offered you money out of pure *ex gratia* kindness, sympathy, regret, if you like, for the unintentional result of my impetuous reaction. May I suggest that you drop this melodramatic demand for "payment". I owe you nothing.'

Mir did not reply at once and seemed for a moment to be bewildered. He turned his head toward Clement, then said in a low apologetic tone, 'Would you mind moving the lamp a little?'

Lucas moved the lamp, then pointedly looked at his watch, then at the papers on his desk.

Mir went on, 'I stopped you from committing a crime – and your graceless response was therefore a crime.'

Lucas was ready for this. 'No crime and no therefore. My dear sir, let us deal with what *actually happened*, and not with your conjectures and fantasies.'

'Let us deal with what I saw, and what your brother has confirmed.'

'He has confirmed nothing, and as it happens is not my brother, though it pleases him to use that cosy terminology. You have been very ill, I think you are suffering from loss of memory, I cannot understand you, I have nothing to give you and I cannot help you, I am sorry.'

Mir turned again and looked at Clement. Clement, prepared for this appeal, was looking at the carpet. Mir went on, 'I saved you from the sin of Cain – and in return you have ruined my life. Well, let us say that, for the present, you have one view of the matter and I have another. And let us return to my crude irrational conception of tit for tat. You thought I was dead, perhaps I was dead, perhaps I am dead. But this *desire for equity* has lifted me up and will not let me rest. I have sought for you as for my salvation. I have pursued you because I need you. We are eternally connected.'

As Mir uttered the final words of this speech he rose to his feet.

He stood, swaying slightly, then murmured in a low intense voice. 'You have wickedly wronged me, and you know it. I desire your punishment.'

Looking back upon the weird conversation, Clement saw this as a turning point. The speeding sky was dark outside, the room was dark, the rain now, no longer bothered by the wind, was falling with a steady faint sizzling hiss. The lamp illumed only the surface of the desk and one of Lucas's hands. The figure of Mir, suddenly rising up in the gloom, broad-shouldered, rectangular, seemed uncanny, unnaturally tall. Clement too, as if compelled by a kind of respect, or alarm, rose to his feet. Mir turned to him for a moment and Clement gained an impression of his head, suddenly like the head of a large animal, a boar perhaps, or even a buffalo. Then Mir, noticing Clement also risen, smiled, his glinting teeth appearing as out of dark fur. Then he sat down again, and Clement, discreetly moving his chair forward and a little to the side, sat down too.

Lucas waited as if expecting Mir to say something, then said, not in his previous cold sarcastic tone, but as if more thoughtfully, 'Surely in your book it says that vengeance belongs to God.'

Mir replied at once, as if saying something obvious, 'I am His instrument.'

Lucas then said, as if puzzled, 'But what *do* you want? Do you want us to fight?'

'I had great physical strength once, but now alas – well, a duel – no – I would prefer something rather more – refined – '

'I do not understand you. Why can you not take the path of reason, indeed of *virtue*, overcome your obsession and let us part company at peace with each other? Perhaps *that* would be sufficiently refined?'

'Peace? Are you begging me to forgive you, give you absolution, kneeling at my feet perhaps?'

'You jest. I am not concerned with the sickening concept of forgiveness nor with the pleasures of masochism. I do not want you to forgive me and I imagine you would not be satisfied by my grovelling. Perhaps I should say the path of reason, let us leave virtue out. Just let us not waste time – '

'Dear sir, as I said before, thanks to your assault I have all the time in the world!'

'What *can* you want me to do? Punishment, mentioned just now, is usually analysed in terms of deterrence, rehabilitation, and retribution. You can now have no need to deter me from assaulting you a second time, nor do I imagine you are interested in reforming my character. I certainly do not propose to suffer at your hands, but I do not believe that you intend to murder me. So let us say, instead of retribution, reparation. This leaves me with nothing to offer you except money, which you have refused. You say you sought me, and I can understand that you might have had a craving to see me. Now you have seen me, we have talked, even conversationally sparred a little. Can you not count that as an achievement which will satisfy whatever obsessional urge you may have had? After all, such irrational states of mind are your field not mine. You seem to be in good health and still endowed with a lively intelligence. Why waste your life and poison your mind with fantasies of revenge? Why wantonly pursue a course which is *bound* to lead to misery, disaster, and remorse? You have money – why not spend it on the higher pleasures – the enjoyment of art, the cultivation of friendship, generosity, charity? Indeed at this very moment you are in a position to use your power for better, or for worse. Please *think* about what I have been saying.'

Clement had quietly moved his chair a little farther forward again. From here he could see more of Mir's face, the short broad nose, the big shapely curling mouth, the high cheek-bones, the smooth protruding cheeks, the curly brown hair, showing no sign of grey, which ran down in thick dense growth onto the back of his neck. Why does he look so like an animal? Clement thought, he smiles like a dog. He has proud nervy nostrils like a horse, and his hair is like a close pelt, and he has big prominent dark eyes. He is horrible, yet he is pathetic too. But what is he doing *here*, what a nightmare it is, oh God if only he could *go away* and be just a dream. What was Lucas saying, is he serious or is he just joking? Is he *appealing* to the man? If only it could be *all* just a dream. And he thought, but this man saved my life. And he saw before him as in a cloud the darkness of that scene and the slow motion of what occurred. He began to feel sick and faint.

The visitor too had sensed, was perhaps conscious of having induced, a change of atmosphere. He sat back in his chair, staring at Lucas and allowing the silence to continue. Then he said in a soft confidential tone, 'There is one thing.'

'Yes?'

'When I last visited you I saw something, a sort of club, lying in front of you on your desk.'

Lucas threw back his head, frowning, and almost closing his eyes. He said after an instant, 'Yes.'

'I would like to see it.'

Lucas pushed his chair back and opened a drawer. He placed the object upon the desk. Mir rose and advanced. Clement rose too. Mir lifted the object up and weighed it in his hand. Clement stepped quickly forward. Lucas, seated, with an almost dreamy look upon his face, watched. Mir said, 'What is it?'

Lucas said, 'A baseball bat.'

Mir gave a long sigh and put it down. He said, 'Thank you.'

Lucas put the object away. He said to Mir in a gentle voice. 'I hope you listened carefully to what I said. I have come a long way to meet you. Can we *now* part in peace?'

Mir sat down again. Clement also retreated and sat down. Mir said, 'I am afraid not. I must tell you what is in my mind. You said earlier that you could not be my therapist. But you *can* be and you must be, you and you only, I require it of you. Please do not interrupt me. I do not see that you have "come a long way", you have not moved from your first position, you have not *understood*, you are just using fine words in order to mystify me, you think I am a fool. You indulged just now in a somewhat pedantic analysis of the concept of punishment – when you reached the third term, retribution, you quickly translated this grim idea into that of reparation. In fact the idea of retribution is everywhere fundamental to justice, where it has mitigated punishment just as often as it has amplified it. Recall that men were once hanged for stealing sheep. An eye for an eye and a tooth for a tooth serves as an image for both restitution and revenge. The punishment must fit the crime, being neither more severe, nor less. In some countries, as you know, some crimes, stealing for instance, are punished by the severance of a hand. So in this case, your just punishment would seem to be the reception of a blow upon the head delivered with equal force.'

There was a moment's silence. Clement, suddenly short of breath, put his hand to his throat. Lucas, who had been listening intently, now said, 'May I ask if you have been entertaining fantasies of this kind all the time you were waiting for me to return?'

Mir replied, 'Yes. These thoughts have raised me from the

dead.' After another silence he continued, 'I was training to be a surgeon before I turned to the science of the soul. It is very easy to cut off a hand or a foot, it is like slicing cheese.'

'But do you also admit,' Lucas promptly continued, 'that these were merely fantasies, *evil* fantasies, which you have no intention of enacting?'

'Not at all. I have been doomed to live with, and feed upon, these pictures. They are with me at this moment. You, sir, must be well acquainted with the relation between evil fantasies and evil acts. I am quite capable of enacting any one of them, and I may say there are many more, more foully ingenious and extreme, than the ones I have just mentioned. However, if I desire to ruin your life as you have ruined mine, I have also a choice of less crude methods.'

'Such as?'

'I have only to write a letter to a newspaper telling the truth about what happened on that terrible evening, including your vile intent to kill your brother.'

Clement cried out, 'But he did *not* kill me, how can we tell whether he intended to or not? A mere intention is nothing. No, he would never have killed me, I am sure!'

'Charming!' said Mir. 'An interesting testimony, which may sound touching in the witness box, but will carry little weight. Anyway let us leave aside these unfulfilled conditionals. I would maintain that you had that intent. The whole amusing story would be back in the papers, your brother appearing as a fascinating extra. The whole history of your relationship would be scrutinised and publicised and invented. You would then have to accept these accusations with their consequence, or sue me for libel. I would drag you back to the law court. How long would this poor fellow here, easily confused and not used to lying, last out? His recent outburst is an instance of the damage he could unintentionally do to your case. I said I did not need money, let me now vulgarly say that I am extremely rich. I would employ the best and cleverest lawyers to prove you a liar. And do not think that you could escape me by leaving the country, going into hiding in America for instance. My well-paid agents would find you. Your peaceful days as a secluded scholar would be over, your precious books, your silent libraries, all gone. I could *haunt* you to the end of the world, I could *very easily* make your entire life a misery and drive you to suicide.'

Mir had been speaking in a calm slow matter-of-fact voice. Lucas, again waiting with close attention for the speech to finish, said, 'If you are offering me a choice, it is certainly an unappetising one. Are we to bargain about it, am I to beg you to accept a severed hand? At the very least the speech you have just made seems intended to make me fret myself to death, expecting the catastrophic exposure or the lurking assassin. So, you are a terrorist. I do not care for blackmail. My answer is that I defy you. I felt some sympathy for you, and I have enjoyed your rhetoric, but now that you have revealed how extremely nasty you really are, I have finished with you.'

Lucas stood up abruptly and switched off his lamp. He said, in a voice now trembling with rage, 'Clement, see this gentleman out.'

Clement rushed forward to Mir who was still seated, and seized hold of his sleeve. 'Don't go please, and please say you don't mean any of this, you were just trying to frighten him, please say you won't do anything to him – '

Mir, gently shaking off Clement's hand, said to Lucas, 'You have an eloquent and potent defender, I hope you feel how little you deserve his loyalty. Now you sit down, my child, bring your chair nearer, and you too please, Professor, sit down and check your anger, I have more to say.'

Clement brought his chair forward again, placing it close to Mir. Lucas pushed his chair back against his books and sat down. For a moment only he covered his face with one hand.

'I should have explained, Professor and Clement, that I have also something else in view. I said earlier that, in the course of my long vigil, I had come to certain conclusions which you might be interested to hear. It was *necessary*, and you, sir, will surely understand this, to rehearse aloud, to spill out if you like, the truly terrible thoughts and images which have been tormenting me during this interval. I have not mentioned the physical pain which I endured and must continue to endure, we need not speak of that. I wish you to know what you have done. I have also wished, another natural reaction, to display to you the power I have to punish you for it. Let this be put away in parenthesis. Now please listen while I trouble you with some brief autobiography. I have been a successful man, but a lonely man, not really a happy man. My work filled my life, its success was my satisfaction. I have not hitherto sought for happiness, assuming it was not my destiny. Now I cannot work. You spoke reasonably enough just now when you advised me to cultivate the higher pleasures. Why should I not intelligently seek for happiness? If I were to revenge myself upon you, as I could certainly and easily do, that would be an act of despair, and incidentally an evil act, in which I too might perish, a form of suicide – and such a desperate idea has indeed travelled with me. But I have also thought, why should I not use my power to coerce, or let us say persuade, you into making me happier.'

During this speech Lucas had turned his chair a little, facing toward the curtained windows. Not looking at Mir he spoke now wearily, even sadly. 'What you say is interesting. Do not ruin the effect by being pathetic. In any case you know you are invulnerable – what is in parenthesis is easy of access, and your "despair" at the "evil act" is only a possibility. You must also envisage, as equally likely, the pleasures of a just revenge. I too have had nothing to do with happiness, and I certainly cannot create it for another. Indeed, in our situation, the concept is odd and out of place. And you have rightly implied, the only pleasure I could afford you would be that of being your victim.'

Mir replied. 'I am sorry, what I still have to say will seem strange to you and will embarrass me. I wish I could say it more carefully and at length, but I fear you might not listen, so I shall be brief. I was an only child, early an orphan, I have never married. I have never, to use a crude phrase, had much success with women. I have no close friends, that is, no friends. Now in the long time during which I was waiting for you I have had the opportunity to study your family and your friends, I have watched them, I have speculated about them. Studying them has indeed been a crucial occupation whereby I kept my sanity and my reason during that long agonising vigil. You,' he said to Clement, 'I discovered in the telephone book, and you led me to others, to the man with the grey collie dog, to the young man who now has a limp, to the fashionable lady, French perhaps, and to other persons, including the four ladies, a mother and three daughters, who – '

At this point Clement cried out, 'For heaven's sake tell us what you want!'

'All right, I will state it simply, I have come to like these people, they interest me very much, I want you to introduce me to them,

I want to get to know you all, I want to become part of your family.'

Clement, utterly astonished, instinctively horrified, said 'Oh!' He looked at Lucas. Lucas said, 'Well – ', then began to laugh quietly. 'Well, Mr Mir, you really do turn out to be a comedian after all! So this favour is to be a substitute for severed hands!'

'Yes, and an intelligent and humane one I think. Of course I do not know how far I, just as my person, might be welcome. You yourself have opened a way for me when you spoke of friendship, generosity, charity. What am I to do with my money? I could leave it to an institution. But why should I not also play the part of a rich uncle? I am not suggesting that I bribe my way in! What I want, if I may be blunt, is *love* – at least loving kindness, friendship, the chance visibly to *benefit* people, to assist in the children's education for instance. I have not been able to achieve such things, which I have often longed for, alone – if you will help me I may now achieve them, as it were, ready-made. Do you understand me?'

After saying all this, addressed to Lucas, Mir turned to Clement. Mir's large eyes, seen at close quarters, were very dark, nearly black. Clement was about to say 'Yes' when Lucas spoke.

'Thank you for telling us about your life, we have listened with interest to your various reflections. Now please at last it is time for you to go.'

'You haven't answered him!' said Clement. 'He has asked you to do something.'

Mir intervened, 'Of course I could simply go and introduce myself, but it would be so much better – '

Lucas said, 'Who and what are you anyway? What are your motives? No, I am afraid I do not understand you.'

'It would be so much better if you would introduce me.'

'I am very tired of this conversation which has gone on far too long.'

Lucas rose abruptly. He marched to the door and opened it. Clement picked up Mir's trilby hat and his umbrella and proffered them to him. Mir took them with a smile and a little bow. He said to Clement, 'Don't worry, there is no hurry.' Pausing half way to the door he said to Lucas, 'So, will you work with me, or against me?'

Clement expected Lucas to explode in exasperation, but he did not. He said, holding the drawing-room door wide, 'I'll think about it.'

'I have intended,' Mir went on, 'to require you to confess to these people.'

'Humiliate myself? Bow to the ground? I am not a Russian Jew.'

'How do you know you are not? But there, I will think about that too. I am tired also. I will come back on Monday at this time. Be here please. Till then, farewell. By the way, my first name is Peter.'

Peter Mir had departed, Lucas was sitting on his desk. He was again laughing. Clement watched him with anxiety and amazement.

'It's too funny for words! He wants to be adopted into our family, he wants security, affection, shelter, love. It's too touching. Who knows, he may decide to buy one of the girls!'

'You shouldn't have let him see the bat.'

'Perhaps not. I felt I owed it to him!'

'You must get rid of it, you must destroy it, it must never have existed – like me. But, Luc, what are we to do? You said you'd think – '

'Oh let him have what he wants! Why shouldn't he meet all those charming people? I think it's a wonderful idea!'

'But we don't know him – and he made such terrible threats – you called him a terrorist, he may be dangerous, he may be raving mad.'

'Oh, he's dangerous all right, he's very dangerous. I'm just relieved that at last he wants something that I can give him. You said you'd seen him hanging about, pressing his nose against the window-pane, poor fellow! I'll brush him off on the family, what a priceless solution!'

'But he said he wanted you to confess to them all – '

'Confess what, dear boy?'

'All right, but he might talk – isn't he bound to talk?'

'Let him talk, they won't believe him, they'll be mystified, they won't understand, you must see to that.'

'*Me*?'

'Yes. I'll tell you what to do.'

*

Harvey was sitting on Tessa Millen's bed, Tessa was sitting opposite to him on a chair. They had been talking for some time. 'It's like philosophy!' Harvey had exclaimed at one point. It was evening, it was dark, a little squat lamp, a bulbous blue bowl and a yellow shade, was alight on the bedside table. A gentle wind was blowing, pensively rattling the ill-fitting windows. Harvey's crutches were leaning against the wall. The damaged limb, its discoloured flesh damp and softened was, where visible, the consistency of lard. His ankle and half of his foot were bound in thick bandages. The remainder of his foot protruded pathetically, plump and red. Harvey had rolled up his trouser and removed the big unseemly slipper which was supposed never to touch the ground. Tessa had promptly lifted the wounded leg, laying it across her knees, placing her cool hand upon the hot unhappy toes.

Tessa now released his toes and laid his foot gently upon the ground. 'And cheat the poor girls?'

'Don't make jokes. Anyway I've changed my mind.'

'So be it, my child.'

'I can't fall in love, I just can't, I can't even imagine it.'

'Well don't complain. It leads to dangerous and distressing things like sex and marriage. The end of freedom, the end of romance. Don't be in a hurry. Go on having romantic friendships.'

'Like with you? Do you think I'm gay?'

'No, you've just had too much cold milk.' (This referred to 'the girls'.) 'You don't realise you're in clover. Relax. Work, think, learn languages, read books, read poetry, write poetry, attract people, make lots of eternal friendships, parade your beauty. Youth is a great green field. Romp in it.'

'Surely romping means sex.'

'No, that is the mistake all you young people make. You don't colonise all the potential joys of being young. Later you'll look back and wonder why you made so little use of your freedom. Sex means anxiety, fear, servitude, and being *forced* to be unkind. Watch and wait.'

'I feel everything's too late already. It isn't just the leg — that's a sort of symptom, or a label, or an emblem. What's wrong is in my soul. I'm *maimed* and that shows what I'm *like*. And I'm putting on weight. I need help.'

'Do some good. Go and see your mother. *She* needs help.'

'All right, all right! Have you seen Lucas?'

'That creature? No. Why do you suddenly bring him in?'

'You know he's back?'

'Of course. You don't imagine *he* could help you?'

'I sort of want to see him. I think I'd feel better if I'd – just – seen him.'

'Like touching a big black stone. He'd make you cry.'

'You said he was real.'

'That's what real does. Just ask your mother about him.'

'Why? What does she know?'

'Oh, well, just what everyone knows.'

'I feel unreal.'

'That feeling is self-pity.'

'Perhaps I need the tears which reality would make me shed. *You* are real. Tessa – could you just – do it for me?'

'Do you mean now? Do you mean what you said before?'

What Harvey had said before was that he wanted Tessa to initiate him into the mysteries of sex.

'Now I've said it again, I suppose I do mean what I said before.'

'Make up your mind.'

'I do mean it.'

They sat looking at each other. Evidently it had now begun to rain, Harvey could hear the mild rain which now enclosed the little room on all sides, tenderly holding it in space, a continuous sibilant presence. He saw, with the huge rounded eyes of a dragon-fly, the global room, the meagre chairs, the battered chest of drawers, the crumpled flimsy curtains shuddering in the continuous draught from the faintly rattling windows, the fat little blue bowl and dusty parchment lamp-shade, the double divan bed, jammed up against the wall, upon which he was sitting and at whose faded Welsh quilt he had been unconsciously picking, his hands, he discovered, holding little balls of dusty textile which he now surreptitiously released onto the floor. He saw Tessa, leaning forward, her long hands on her knees, her old worn tweed jacket, her brown shirt open at the neck, her thick trousers tucked into her boots. Her pale straight yellow hair, as pale as primroses, cut neatly short, gave her a tranquil authoritative air, calm with the gentle serenity of some sibyl who through millennia has observed the foolish helpless grief of mortal men. Her lips reflectively parted, her grey eyes narrowed, expressed as she perused him the gentle whimsical pity of a superior being. Harvey, motionless, felt the impulse to kneel at her feet and kiss her long hands. He wanted to groan and weep. He wondered, is this *it* after all?

He said, 'Yes, yes. But forgive me.'

'Don't be silly. Get up. One has to undress, you know. What about your leg? Is it hurting now?'

'No. You don't mind?'

'No, you fool!'

'Suppose someone comes.'

'No one will come.'

They moved, avoiding each other in the little room. Harvey thought, it's like *chess*. Tessa pulled back the quilt and blankets, and sat on the bed to take off her boots. Harvey, standing, watched her. He took off his jacket. He stepped back and felt a pain in his leg. He had forgotten his leg. He sat on one of the thin rickety chairs and took the shoe and sock off his good leg. By this time Tessa had removed her boots, socks, jacket and trousers. Harvey began to ease off his trousers. He thought, now she will take off her knickers. In his brother and sister upbringing with the girls, when they went on holidays to the sea together, he had often seen them undressing, even undressed. He had often watched them, before the time of the taboo, dropping their skirts in circles round their feet, and then hauling off their knickers. This had interested him only in retrospect. Much later, remembering those times, he had noticed how just that action, that movement, had something so thrilling about it, so crucial, so holy. Even the word 'knickers' had for him a kind of charisma, like a religious charm or mantra. As carefully and deftly, keeping his bad leg outstretched, he was removing his under-pants with his trousers, he became aware that Tessa had performed the action in question and was looking at him with nothing on except her rather large and long shirt which he now saw to be not just brown but khaki, and evidently bought at some army-surplus shop. A *soldier's* shirt. Harvey had pulled his own shirt and vest down as far as he could. The room was cold. Now Tessa had unbuttoned her shirt but not removed it. She was not wearing a vest. Looking back at her Harvey wondered whether now they would burst out laughing. Perhaps it would all end in crazy helpless laughter. Sex was funny, it was *ridiculous*, how had he got himself into this absurd situation! For a moment indeed they might have laughed, but by a silent compact they did not, but smiled at each other, gentle smiles, as Harvey recalled it, full of deep and complicated sadness. Harvey felt the presence of those tears.

She moved across the bed, sitting up and clasping her knees.

'Tessa do you mind if I keep my shirt on, just for now – '

'I don't mind! Harvey, whatever happens *don't worry*. Come here.'

He knelt on the bed, then lay down awkwardly as she stretched out beside him, lying on her back, the khaki shirt unbuttoned but still on. The shirt, that was something holy too, as if she were robed for a ceremony, as if it were all happening inside some great serene temple. He saw close to him her breasts, rising up suddenly out of the landscape, miraculous, pale and luminous in the faint light. His good leg pressed against her, felt the hem of her shirt as he began to turn, cautiously lifting his bad leg. A flash of pain shot up his thigh. He paused. Then, with a further determined movement of his adjacent hand, burrowed in under her waist which arched to his pressure, and laid his heavy head down into the hot softness of her bosom, while his other hand, tugging the khaki shirt back, gently explored the extension of her body. They lay quietly thus, breathing deeply. Then she moved slightly, dislodging his head, tilting onto her side, so that, with lips apart, they breathed each other's breath. Harvey thought, as he withdrew his hand from beneath her, damn, it's too late now to take off my shirt and vest. He moved his other hand vainly trying to haul the recalcitrant garments up a little. Someone's heart was beating violently. Her questing hand fleetingly touched his genitals and he glimpsed her closed eyes as their lips met. He found himself shuddering. He suddenly thought, how clumsy, how awkward, how *absurd* these fumblings are, we might as well be two machines trying to mate. He resisted an urge to thrust her away. Aware of this incipient movement Tessa withdrew a little. Their lips parted, their eyes opened, their hands stopped exploring. Harvey thought, it's not passion it's fear, it's miserable *timidity*, I'm cold, I'm no good, nothing is happening, I might as well be castrated. He turned on his back. He said, 'Sorry, my leg is hurting.' Tessa murmured, 'Just lie quiet for a while.' Supine they lay side by side. They both sighed, deeply. Then Harvey thought, is she laughing? No, she's smiling, I know she's smiling. She's a goddess, I can't serve her, I can't even *touch* her properly. What a perfectly awful business it all is, any other creatures can do it better. He moved again and his heavy leg fell over the edge of the bed, jerking him up with a gasp of pain. He sat up on the bed with both his feet on the floor, leaning forward and holding his head in his hands.

He felt Tessa slipping past him. She stood buttoning up her brown shirt, then drawing on a black and white kimono and tying its belt. Now he saw her smile.

'Sorry, Tessa, it's my bloody leg. No, it's bloody me, like I said before, I'm under a curse. I'm terribly sorry. I couldn't – there was nothing – '

'You think that was nothing!'

'I've just proved I'm no good.'

'Try to understand that you have learnt something. It's not just a matter of male and female mechanics or male and female roles! Love and trust and gentleness between two humans is very rare. Love is rare and expression of love is rare. I am grateful to you.'

Harvey had seized his trousers and was hastily dragging them on, manoeuvring his bandaged foot through the slit which had been made in the trouser leg. He thought, *what's* this, she's *grateful*, it's about *love*? How does *love* come in? What was I after anyway? Oh *God*!

He said awkwardly, staring at Tessa's pale bare feet, 'I'm grateful to *you*. I know it's of value, I mean it's been *useful*, I mean I'm very glad I've had the feeling – you were very generous – I suppose, I expect, that it will make things easier later on, I don't just mean between us but – I'm sure I've learnt something – I'm sorry, I'm talking nonsense – but I'm sure you'll understand. Oh hell, I'm sorry, it's all my fault!'

'There is no fault. You have taken an important step. We were closer, we are friends, friends help each other, friends trust each other, friends love each other. We won't forget this being together.'

Harvey had put on his trousers and his jacket and his socks and was frantically donning his shoe and his slipper. He moaned with exasperation. 'But I *failed* – !'

'Oh shut up, Harvey. Nothing has damaged you. You are young, your life is a great big place. If you need me I'm here, that's all. Now clear off.'

Tessa was sitting on one of the chairs, her long hands upon her knees. He said, 'You are an angel.' He put a hand to the floor and fell awkwardly onto one knee. Smelling the fresh clean innocent smell of the kimono, he touched her hands, he kissed her feet.

Harvey summoned the richly appointed well-lighted lift. He pressed Emil's various keys into their various keyholes and entered Emil's beautiful flat. He turned all the lights on. He sat down heavily upon one of Emil's Chippendale chairs and looked at the Bohemian glass and the silver goblets and the alabaster Buddha and the eighteenth-century snuff-boxes and the Persian rugs and the Caillebotte and the Nolde and the Bonnard. He recalled the previous occasion when he had sat beside Tessa on her bed and their sleeves had touched and they had sat as silent as two statues. Had it started then? But what was *it*? Was it his idea or hers? And that sad remote angelic smile – was that *because* they were not in love? What on earth had she expected? Oh God, what a sickening mess he had made of it all! He got up and fetched Emil's malt whisky from its cupboard and poured it into one of Emil's Waterford glasses. He felt better. He decided to go to bed. He undressed and got into bed and switched off the light. At once a heavy dreamy peace descended on him. He lay on his back, floating, breathing deeply. He thought, I have slept with an angel, and it was nothing but good.

'I have something to tell you – and something to ask you.'

Clement was with Louise. It was the next day, the day after Peter Mir's last 'manifestation', as Lucas called it. Clement had telephoned Louise in the morning and had asked if he could come round before lunch. He could not help sounding, as he heard himself speaking, rather pompous and mysterious. Now facing her, he felt even more so.

It was Saturday and the house was full of the girls. He could hear Moy above moving rhythmically to and fro. (He wondered, is she *dancing*?) Downstairs in the kitchen Sefton was clattering the plates. Aleph was singing softly in the Aviary, occasionally touching the piano, producing a little note like that of a bird. He could not make out the song.

Louise was looking smart and neat, her face, not always so tended, discreetly powdered. Clement was aware of the faint smell of the powder as they stood close to each other by her bedroom window. She was wearing a straight brown tweed skirt and a close-fitting light woollen brown jerkin, with a white blouse showing at the neck. She kept touching the collar of the blouse, now smoothing it down, now pulling it up. As she listened to Clement's solemn statement it seemed to him that she blushed a little and her eyes widened. Was she expecting something from him, something perhaps very different from what he was going to say? As this suddenly occurred to him he felt himself blushing and staring. Then he thought, maybe she thinks it's *about Aleph*! At that moment the words of Aleph's song became clear: 'When maiden loves she sits and sighs, she wanders to and fro.' He thought, confused, but it is Moy who is wandering to and fro. And now I shall upset Louise and alienate her and it's all *crazy* anyway – Luc is *crazy*, that terrible dead man is *crazy*!

He settled his tie. He too had dressed up. He said, 'Listen, Louise, this is something strange and odd, and you may not like it.'

'Oh?'

'It concerns Lucas.'

Louise's hand stayed at her collar, touching her throat, pressing it, then unconsciously undoing the top button of her blouse. She frowned and took a step back.

Clement, aware that he was somehow blundering, went hastily on, assuming a chattering tone which he knew to be entirely unsuitable. 'Well, there has been a surprise, you know that chap Lucas accidentally killed, well of course you know, well it turns out that he isn't dead after all, he's come back, he's perfectly recovered and he came to see Lucas, isn't that extraordinary?'

'He's not dead? Why did they say he was dead and cause all that trouble?'

'He was very ill and – you know the way people seem to die – their heart stops and so on – honestly I haven't got the details – he was just thought to be dead, or what they call clinically dead, and then somehow recovered.'

'But when did this happen, why didn't they tell Lucas, why

didn't the doctors tell him – poor thing, all that time thinking he had killed a man when he hadn't – '

'I don't know when it happened, but anyway Lucas went away at once, he vanished, you remember – I expect they tried to tell him but he wasn't there – the first Lucas knew was the man turning up.'

'Thank God!' said Louise. She recovered her hand from her throat and made a gesture as of relief and thanksgiving. She pulled the window curtain across a little and sat down in a chair. She neatly adjusted her tweed skirt. She said, 'Clement dear, thank you for telling me, I shall tell the others. How intensely relieved Lucas must be – and all of us – it's wonderful! And the poor man, he's recovered, how splendid! Thank you for coming – did Lucas ask you to come?'

'Yes, but – '

'I will write him a letter. I'll go to see him – in a little while – what a wonderful ending to this terrible time.'

'Yes, isn't it, but – '

'Of course the man wasn't a mugger, was he, or a thief, or anything – ?'

'No, of course not – he was perfectly innocent, all that was settled in court, the whole thing was a mistake.'

'Why did you think I wouldn't like what you had to tell me?'

'I don't know why I said that, I was stupid to say it – it's nothing awful – it's just that – well, he wants to meet you and the girls.'

'Who, dear?'

'The man, the chap Lucas hit.'

'Why on earth should he want to meet us, how does he know we exist?'

'It sounds silly, but when he came to look for Lucas, to reassure him, and Lucas wasn't there, he went around to look at people he thought knew him, as he thought Lucas might be staying with – '

'But how did he know?'

'He looked me up in the telephone book and then I suppose he followed me – '

'But didn't he *tell* you?'

'No, perhaps he was too shy, he wanted to wait for Lucas to come back.'

'Of course, to give Lucas that lovely great surprise – I can understand that.'

'Yes, yes, that was it – '

'So you mean he watched us – how odd – I think I saw him – a man in a trilby hat and a green umbrella – '

'That's him.'

'I was a bit frightened. So it was that man! How extraordinary! Yes, I can understand he was waiting for Lucas – it's a bit weird all the same – and now he wants to meet us – but *why*?'

'Oh, I think it's a sort of a whim, he just got interested in you, he thinks you all look so nice, and so ordinary – '

'*Ordinary?*'

'I mean, it's home life, he sees you as home life, he has no family, he's lonely, he just wants to say hello to you, it's just to oblige him, I thought you wouldn't mind seeing him, I know you'd be kind to him, he's rather shy, a little awkward and slow – '

'Slow? You mean he's a bit *damaged*? Was he mentally damaged by – ?'

'No, no, he's perfectly OK, he's just sort of diffident.'

'If it means simply saying hello just once – is it me or the girls too?'

'Actually he wants to see everyone, all the people he was studying, getting interested in, while he was waiting for Lucas, he wants Harvey and Bellamy too, it's like a sort of little celebration.'

'You mean a party, all together, here? That's a bit much – '

'Well, if you don't object.'

'I'm not sure whether I object or not. He sounds rather eccentric, I hope he *isn't* dotty – oh, all right, whenever you like, only let us know. There's the bell, I'm expecting Harvey, he rang up and we've invited him to lunch. By the way, when are you taking the girls to the *Magic Flute*?'

The kitchen was a large room, almost as large as the Aviary, benefiting from an extension made when the family first arrived in the house. It was also as a result of Sefton's meticulous orderliness, probably the tidiest. Louise had been gradually, to use Sefton's phrase, 'phased out' (in the kindest way of course) of kitchen operations. She was permitted to cook, or more usually put together from pre-cooked items, her high tea or early supper.

Major cooking was done by Sefton and Moy. Breakfast, not cooked, was an unorganised scuffle. Lunch was a serious meal only at weekends. Tea, if it occurred, consisted of tea and available biscuits. Dinner was always (for the girls only) a serious meal. Louise occasionally, now more rarely, joined them, on invitation or by her own request. On weekdays Moy had lunch at school, Sefton and Aleph if out took sandwiches, if at home ate bread and cheese and apples. A long scrubbed table occupied the centre of the room and a long tall dresser with open shelves covered one wall. A table-cloth appeared only for guests. The enormous fridge had been painted blue and green by Moy. There was a washing machine and (in spite of stiff resistance by Moy) a washing-up machine. Moy (Art) maintained a certain feud with Sefton (Order) since Moy had favourites among the plates and cups and mugs which had always to be washed by hand. Knives and forks and spoons were also individuals. As a result (in spite of Art and Order) of persistent breakages, there were no complete sets of anything. Moy preferred this state of affairs, as favouring individualism, and held strong views about the stations, upon the open shelves of the dresser, of particular plates and bowls, and the order, upon their hooks, of the cups and mugs. These patterns, which inevitably varied, had to be learnt by heart by Sefton, who was severely chided if she got it wrong. Moy and Aleph had a habit of buying, if *very* cheap, pretty china at junk shops. These additions caused, sometimes, contentious alterations in the order of battle, occasioning the dismissal of one-time favourites into invisibility. Washing up or consignment to the machine occurred after every meal however scanty, everything, including the spotlessly clean saucepans, was put away onto shelves or into cupboards or into the capacious larder, and the emptied table was brushed and scrubbed. In these daily and hourly operations Aleph played a fleeting though reasonably regular role, appearing at intervals and inquiring, 'Can I do anything?'

On this day, warned of visitors, Sefton had put on the best table-cloth (a king-size sheet from Liberty's sale), and placed a white cyclamen from the Aviary upon the dresser. She had brought in an extra chair from the hall and one from her bedroom. Clement and Harvey had the sturdiest and most comfortable chairs. Louise sat at one end of the table with Clement on her right and Harvey on her left. Aleph sat next to Clement and Moy next to Harvey, Sefton sat at the other end of the table, nearest to the stove. The main dish (Moy's creation) was mozzarella and spinach pie with salad. Some cold tongue and salami had been hastily brought in for the carnivores. Then there was to be a treacle pudding and ice-cream (which was supposed to be for dinner.) Then Wensleydale cheese and (on sale at last) Cox's Orange Pippins. There was no alcohol. Aleph suggested running out to buy some but nothing came of that. Louise kept some sherry for visitors, but confused and bothered by her two self-invited guests, she found no occasion to offer any. Clement's news had been so extremely odd, she did not know what to think of it, and Harvey had arrived before she had been able to put together any further questions. She was upset by Clement and annoyed at the hasty way he had announced it all, assuming that Louise would agree to meet the mysterious survivor. Of course she felt curiosity, but she also felt anxiety and irritation. What was this gathering or encounter to be like, who would be there, would they want to eat and drink? Would Lucas and his 'victim' make speeches? If Bellamy came then Moy and Anax must be absent, unless they could leave Anax with the Adwardens' housekeeper, and would Moy agree to that? She did not like the idea of this homeless stranger, she had enough troubles without *him*, he might want consolation, he might want money, he might *hang around*. Meanwhile, she was aware of Harvey being cross that Clement was present, he had evidently expected a private chat with Louise, and having forgotten it was Saturday was startled to find the girls at home and planning to entertain him. Clement was also on edge, not pleased to see Harvey, and in no mood for a jolly lunch party. The girls had already intuited some sort of chill, and it was already clear from certain arcane signals passing between Sefton and Moy that there would not be enough to go round. The kitchen looked out onto the small garden with its two trees, a birch tree and a cherry tree. Rain drops on the remaining leaves of the birch gleamed blue and orange in the cool clear light of the faintly veiled sun. Moy, who always opened windows, had opened a window. There was a soft noise of traffic and intermittent chirpings and fragments of song from the birds in the garden and in the many other tree-filled gardens. Heavy with rain-water, dark creepers hung upon the brick walls.

When they had assembled Louise had felt a nervous hasty urge to forestall Clement by telling the news. She did not want Clement to be portentous and make a drama of it, she wanted to calm herself by letting it out quietly, as if she could then see how little it mattered. 'You know, Clement has just been telling me that that man Lucas was supposed to have killed didn't die after all, he got better, he's been to visit Lucas, he's being very nice about it, he even wants to visit us.'

'Why us?' said Sefton.

'He recovered!' said Aleph. 'Lucas must be relieved.'

'Did he really seem to be dead,' said Moy, who was very carefully cutting the pie, 'or was he really all right all along and they made a mistake?'

'I don't know,' said Louise.

'When Lucas was away he came round to look at my place,' said Clement, 'and he came round here once or twice and waited about in case Lucas was with you, of course he didn't want to say anything until Lucas turned up, he's very shy and modest, he's really awfully nice.'

'Why, I suppose he was that man we saw,' said Sefton, 'do you remember, Aleph?'

'Yes,' said Aleph, 'how odd!'

'What's his name?' said Moy.

'Peter Mir,' said Clement.

'How do you spell "Mir"?' said Sefton.

'M – I – R.'

'That means 'world' in Russian,' said Sefton, 'it also means peace.'

'World peace,' said Louise, then thought, that's a silly thing to say!

Moy shifted some of the tongue onto a plate and handed it to Clement. 'Have some salad. There's basil in the salad.'

Clement said, 'Oh good, so that's the lovely smell.' He was dying for a drink. There was silence as everyone looked at the various foods. It was evident that the news of 'the man' was not proving so sensational after all.

Harvey felt surprise, but instantly returned to his own troubles, the burden of his leg, and now the terrible thing which had happened yesterday with Tessa, and which he himself had wantonly brought about. How had he been so crazy, so stupid, so *depraved*? And how could he last night have felt so peaceful and so calm and so good? That must have been the whisky. *Now*, when it was too late, he realised how valuable, how *precious*, his innocence, his naivety, his blessed lack of 'experience', had been

– and *what* it had been: freedom! Now, he was suddenly the slave of another person. Of course *that* would never happen again, he would never see Tessa again. But Tessa had stolen a part of his being, or rather he had forced her to purloin it! She said there was now a bond between them – but a bond was the very last thing he wanted. How could she keep her mouth shut? It was not just disgrace, *his* disgrace, but ridicule, something which would occasion laughter and be passed around as a joke, told to anyone, *told to his mother*. And even if Tessa were silent – and how could she be – he himself would have to tell, was bound to, was compelled, fated to tell, perhaps with terrible consequences. He had become a deceiver, a liar, and would inevitably blurt out some garbled version of the truth to Aleph, to Louise, to Emil, to Bellamy, to Nicky Adwarden, and finally and catastrophically lose his dignity, and lose his *honour*. Tessa had made a little speech about love and friendship, and even he, last night, had dreamt about some higher chaster purer love. But what he had done was to destroy forever whatever bond of friendship he had had with that strange girl, and replace it by embarrassment, contempt, disgust, horror, lies, fear. And now as he looked around the table at all these amicable innocents he realised how much he had now become an *outsider*.

Louise was saying to Clement, 'Will Lucas come to introduce him? How are we to do it? It really is a lot to ask!'

'Oh Lucas will come!' said Clement confidently, though he had in fact no idea what Lucas was going to do.

The girls, talking to one another, were now piling their plates high with salad.

Harvey said to Sefton, 'Would you like some of my salami?'

'No, thanks.'

'Oh, of course you – I just haven't any appetite today.'

'Anax would like some of the tongue. He doesn't like salami.'

There was a pause in the conversation. The silence was broken by Moy who said to Sefton, 'Did you know that sharks have to keep moving or else they drown?'

'Can fish drown?' said Louise.

'Sharks are not fish,' said Moy, 'they're more like mammals.'

'Why do they have to keep moving?' said Sefton.

'They have no swim-bladder. Fishes have a membrane which retains oxygen and gives them buoyancy. The shark has to get oxygen by continuous motion.'

'How interesting,' said Sefton, 'in what respect do they resemble mammals?'

'No wonder they are so bad-tempered,' said Louise.

'Moy will be a biologist,' said Clement.

Harvey rose abruptly and said, 'I'm sorry, I must be getting along – ' He had just thought, perhaps she does this all the time with young boys!

'Won't you stay for the pudding?' said Louise.

'No thanks.' Harvey looked at Aleph.

Aleph rose. 'I'll ring for a taxi for Harvey.'

'Have you got enough money?' said Louise.

'Yes, thanks. Emil sent me some taxi money.'

'How kind of *Emil*.'

Out in the hall, the door closed and the taxi summoned, Harvey sat down on a chair. A livelier chatter was to be heard in the kitchen.

'What's the matter, boy.'

'Nobody noticed I had a stick today, not the crutches.'

'I noticed.'

'You said nothing.'

'You are better?'

'No.'

'That ordeal you were looking for, have you had it? You look rather distraught.'

'Nothing has happened, nothing.'

'Well, we can't talk now. What is this thing of Lucas's?'

'I don't know. It sounds gruesome.'

'Have you seen your mother lately?'

'No.'

'You ought to see her.'

'Everyone says that.'

'Tessa keeps an eye on her.'

'Oh – !'

'Poor Moy, she wanted to sit next to Clement.'

'He ignored her.'

'He ignored us all. He is in a dream, he is overcome by some spell or potion.'

'You perhaps.'

'I don't think so. Cheer up. Here is your taxi.'

*

Aleph was in the Aviary, but silent now. Sefton and Moy had cleared the kitchen scene as usual 'by magic'. Sefton had folded up the table-cloth, after shaking the crumbs out of the garden door, and returned to Thucydides. Moy had run up the stairs to her room, her heavy steps followed by the click of Anax's claws upon the upper uncarpeted flight. Clement had hoped now for a continuation of his talk with Louise, but it was not to be. They had mounted to her bedroom but only, he realised, in order to pick up his overcoat which he had left there. Louise led the way down again and they stood in the small hall where the space was taken up by the chair lately on duty in the kitchen and a much carved dark oak hall stand with a lion's face in the centre, two mirrors, and a great many knobs. Clement absently stroked the lion's nose, then gripped one of the knobs. To detain Louise who was reaching out towards the front door, he said, 'How's Moy getting on?'

'All right.'

'I hope she's getting over you-know-what.'

'If you mean her crush on you, no.'

'Oh dear. Perhaps I shouldn't have stayed to lunch. Of course it would be Saturday. Do you think I should have some sort of explanation with her, I remember you said something about cooling it? Not that there's anything to cool as far as I'm concerned!'

'No, leave it. She's a strange girl. She's full of supernatural fears. It will pass.'

'Of course Sefton is no trouble, she just strides straight on regardless of other persons.'

'Yes, she'll be a powerful headmistress, as Joan exclaimed to me the other day.'

Clement did not like hearing about conversations between Louise and Joan. Wanting to go on, he was about to say 'that leaves Aleph,' but checked himself in time.

In the moment's pause Louise opened the door and said, 'I don't feel at all happy with the idea of that man coming here to meet us, could you ask Lucas to explain it to me? I imagine there's no hurry.'

Back in her bedroom Louise took off her brown tweed skirt and her light woollen jerkin and her white blouse whose collar had for some time been distinctly turned up. She put on an old warm dress which had many times narrowly escaped being given away to a charity shop. She sat down on her bed. She thought, I will *not* let that man enter this house. Lucas and Clement are *mad*. And I will *not* allow any more parties after this one. I *hate* masks, I *hate* dressing up, this whole house is vibrating like a taut string. It was all Teddy's idea, he loved parties and noise and masks and fancy dress and new people. Well – it was all right then, in the big house, in the old days, when Teddy was alive –

Upstairs in her room, Moy was sitting on the floor watching Anax drinking milk. She had only lately discovered that he liked milk. She liked to watch him drinking it. But was it good for him? He lifted his long grey muzzle and looked at her. He looked sad. When she came back to him after school he wagged his tail and put his paws up. But she never saw in him the wild overflowing ecstasy of his reunions with Bellamy. She reached out her hand and he came to her with milk upon his furry mouth. She lightly brushed it away with the end of her thick plait. She stroked him. They were both of them poor fugitives. Moy had been making the masks for her birthday party. She made them out of various materials, *papier mâché*, cardboard, stiff furnishing fabrics, pliant tin, she fixed them together with glue, string, plasticine, sellotape, bent paper-clips. Guests who were invited to the party made, bought, or hired their own masks, but the family wore Moy's masks which were of course secretly handed round before the event. This year, partly because of the absence of Clive and Emil and the Adwardens, and also necessarily of Bellamy, partly for other more mysterious reasons, the party was to be for family only. Moy put the masks completed so far in a cupboard. She had put them on an open shelf but did not like to see Anax looking at them. She rose and opened the cupboard door for a moment. The masks were evil. She closed the door. Why were they evil, because deception is evil? Even the happy masks were bad. She thought I won't make them any more. She picked up one of her ugly flint stones and gazed through a tiny fissure into its glittering interior, she watched a fly alight upon her hand, probe her skin with its tongue, then wash its paws and draw them down over its bowed head. She laid down the stone, the fly flew away.

Anax now slept upon her bed at night, not in his basket. She was glad of this, but uneasy too. There was so much mysterious alien *life* in the room, so many radiant centres of being. Was Anax

afraid of the stones as he had been afraid of the masks? At one
moment she had thought he might attack the masks. Were the
stones *hostile* too? She had picked them up, so many, in so many
places. Any stone she touched she had to keep. The garden was
full of stones. She had felt they must be glad, out of such an
infinite number, to be chosen. But perhaps she was wrong? Now
she touched cautiously a large conical stone covered with golden
lichen runes which she had found near a big grey rock in the
hills near Bellamy's cottage. Later, remembering, Moy had been
overcome by the notion that the rock and the stone, who had
stood there alone together on the grassy hillside, for centuries, for
millennia, were now pining for each other. Perhaps she ought to
take the stone back? But she could not recall exactly where she
had found it, and anyway Bellamy was selling his cottage and she
would never go there again. Stones walked sometimes. Perhaps
this poor stone would set off one day through the streets of
London seeking its lost friend who was now forsaken. Once,
coming back to her room, she had found the stone upon the floor.

Turning away from the afflicted stone she was aware of the
calm infinitely sad gaze of the Polish Rider, travelling in the golden
light of the dawn, thinking of his mission, perhaps of his home
which he may never see again, emerging out of darkness into
light, and looking far away at the still dark shapes of mountains
invisible before, courageous, gentle, truthful, wise, alone.

As she moved away now towards the door she nursed the pain
that was with her always. Destiny, solitude, grief, the sea. I am a
girl upon the land, I am a silky in the sea. And she thought about
Colin and the black-footed ferret. She thought about the pool of
tears.

Sefton, lying on the floor in her little bedroom, was reading
Thucydides' *History of the Peloponnesian War*. She lay flat on
her front, propped up by her elbows, her bare feet, protruding
from her corduroy trousers, crossed. Of course she had read this
work many times before, but there were certain parts to which
she passionately returned: so cool, so elegant, so beautiful, so
terrible. As she read tears began to stream down her face.

'When the day came Nicias led his army forward, but the
Syracusans and their allies kept attacking in the same fashion,
hurling missiles and striking them down with javelins on all

sides. The Athenians pushed on to the river Assinarus, partly because they thought, hard pressed as they were on all sides by the attack of numerous horsemen and of the miscellaneous troops, that they would be somewhat better off if they crossed the river, and partly by reason of their weariness and desire for water. And when they crossed it they rushed in, no longer preserving order, but everyone eager to be himself the first to cross, and at the same time the pressure of the enemy now made the crossing difficult. For since they were obliged to move in a dense mass they fell upon and trod one another down, and some perished at once, run through by their own spears, while others became entangled in their trappings and were carried away by the current. The Syracusans stood along the other bank of the river, which was steep, and hurled missiles down upon the Athenians, most of whom were drinking greedily and were all huddled in confusion in the hollow bed of the river. Moreover, the Peloponnesians went down to the water's edge and butchered them, especially those in the river. The water at once became foul, but was drunk all the same although muddy and dyed with blood, and indeed was fought for by most of them. At length when the dead now lay in heaps one upon the other in the river and the army had perished utterly, part in the river and part – if any got safely across – at the hands of the cavalry, Nicias surrendered himself to Gylippus.'

Clement was pacing about in his sitting-room in his little shabby flat in Fulham. Why didn't he move into a larger place, not like Emil's of course, but a bit larger, with higher ceilings and views of trees where he would hang up pictures and put vases on mantel-pieces and have room for his books? Many of his books were piled in corners and those on the shelves were disorderly, unclassified, unsorted, unarranged. He did not *deserve* to have books. The books seemed to reject him, gathered sulking into their own concerns like a disaffected tribe. He did not *read* enough. He used to be always reading. Now he watched television. He was demoralised. He ought to *think*, he ought to *decide* what he was doing with his life. So, at this age he was still 'going to be something'. How much longer could he continue to be young? And when was he going to take the girls to the *Magic Flute*? He went out onto the little dark landing and looked at himself in a mirror. Even with the light on, a fuzzy darkness surrounded him as he peered at his sharp face and his dark surging hair and his fine eyes. He turned back into the room where everything was a little dusty, a little elderly, a little dark red. He touched his breast, spreading out his hand to contain the rending movement of some dark awful kind of grief.

What continually amazed him was the way in which he had 'taken', and now continued to 'take', the recent doings of his brother. The word 'brother' had for Clement something sacred about it. Perhaps this was because his parents had dinned into his earliest consciousness the fact that Lucas, who was in a way not his brother, *was* his brother. Even without this disturbing reiteration, Clement knew he would always have felt brotherhood with Lucas, as if it were somehow to be his duty to *look after* Lucas. This idea seemed absurd, given Lucas's evident intellectual and physical domination over the new arrival, and the latter's docile acceptance of his brother's exercise of power. It may be that Lucas had from the start intuited Clement's timid sympathy, his desire to cherish Lucas, to serve him, to 'make things up' to him; and Clement sometimes believed that Lucas was actually grateful for these silent attentions, although they seemed more often to incite him to greater acts of despotism. And now, had recent events profoundly altered their relations? Incredibly it seemed not. During the period of Lucas's disappearance Clement's anxiety had largely taken the form of fear for, not of, his brother. Clement had been blessed by a gift of self-satisfaction. He had liked himself, he had loved himself, on the whole he had approved of himself. This was fundamental, and his many doubts and fears had floated above this felicitous foundation. He became aware at an early age that not everyone resembled him in that respect. Lucas hated other people, and also hated himself, and during his absence after the 'event' Clement had felt it possible that his brother might be moved to suicide. When Lucas returned this speculation seemed absurd. There was Lucas again, assertive, contemptuous, full of power, innocent of remorse, *in charge* as he had always been. It was after this robust reappearance that Clement, relieved of his first preoccupation, began to think more deeply about what had happened. He had yearned for Lucas's return but had also dreaded it. What he had feared, as he later realised, was that Lucas might return, changed, *broken.* He was not afraid that his brother, having failed once to kill him, might try again. Somehow that seemed impossible, and Clement had not required Lucas's declaration. It was not simply that he forgave Lucas, in fact the idea of forgiveness seemed, as between them, an absurdity. He had not expected 'what had happened', but given the event with its curious outcome he knew that some bitter stoical pride on the part of Lucas would preclude any replay. Clement did not want to brood upon the 'attempt upon his life', after all it had not succeeded, as far as he was concerned nothing had happened, and nothing might have happened. But what about the victim, the man who had taken his place? Of course Clement did not believe that he had been a thief. The man had seen what looked like a murder, and in attempting to prevent it had been murdered himself. He had saved Clement's life at the expense of his own. During Lucas's absence Clement had kept this terrible picture, and the *problems* which it posed for him, Clement, at a distance. When Lucas returned the accusing image returned with him; the appearance of Peter Mir followed mercifully. But what relationship was now implied, or imposed, between Clement and Mir? What had really happened? Would Lucas have killed him, did he really intend to, would he have succeeded? That both Clement and Mir were still alive were important *facts*. Clement had, obeying his brother's bidding, *run away*; he had also carried away the weapon – and he had *brought it back*. Why on earth had he done that? Why, when one has been unjustly beaten, should one bring back the rod? Was this too something to do with childhood, was it because of something owed, since Clement had, by existing, ruined Lucas's life? And now there was another ruined life in play, and another question about justice.

Of course Clement was glad, very glad, that the man was alive, and that he was able now to see his saviour and to express his gratitude. But what next? Mir had uttered terrible threats, he had spoken of an eye for an eye, and a blow delivered with equal force. He had recalled the fantasies of revenge which had raised him from the dead. Was he capable of enacting the direst of these

– and would it not also be characteristic of Lucas to *let him do so*? Clement knew, Clement had seen, how Lucas had been *saved* by his education, by the Greeks, by the Stoics, by his success as a scholar, as a historian, by the adulation of his students, by all the mysterious substances he had imbibed from his mastery of the past. His chosen mentors in that land had taught him pride, contempt for the weak, and also a cold dignified resignation to destiny. Fate was justice, justice was fate. As for the 'something else' which Mir had said he had 'in view' which was to 'make him happier', could that make any sense at all? Had Lucas been serious when he spoke of 'brushing him off on the family'? What could such a weird ridiculous introduction scene be like? What would Lucas say, what should I say? Would we be required to *tell the truth*? No, that is *impossible*.

Bellamy was reading a letter, it was from Clement. It had been dropped in through the door. Bellamy had been there at the time and had heard it arrive. He went to the door but whoever had delivered it had already vanished. If it was Clement, why had he not knocked? Bellamy thought, he is beginning to avoid me, my presence embarrasses him, my problems irritate him. I am becoming an unperson. He opened the letter.

Listen, could you come over to Clifton tomorrow evening about six? There's to be some sort of gathering, Lucas is to bring the chap, you know like I told you, the one who didn't really die. He wanted him to meet the family and that includes you. *Please come* – I shall need support!

C.

P.S. Anax won't be there, he's spending the evening with Mrs Drake, the Adwardens' housekeeper, I think you met her.

Bellamy was pleased to receive the invitation. Of course he would go, he even felt a beneficent twinge of curiosity about the man who didn't really die. But the matter-of-fact P.S. about Anax pained his heart. Anax, who had once been so close, closest, was utterly banished, never to be in his vicinity, exiled – or rather it was he, Bellamy, who was exiled – had exiled himself from warmth, friendship, love, and all the ease and comfort of the affections. He missed Anax terribly and had to console himself by thinking that after all Anax was only a dog, an ephemeral short-lived creature, from whom death would have parted him soon enough if they had stayed together. So this was his consolation! Only the pain now was different, less innocent, less pure, carrying with it the poisonous taint of regret, remorse, self-deception, treachery. He had received a letter from Tessa which said, 'Dear Bell, so you are trying holy poverty, why not come and help me, I need all the spare help that's around, we aren't enemies, are we?' He had not replied. Of course he would, he supposed, somehow, reply. Only the idea of all those battered moaning women filled him with aversion. Yet how could he feel this about these poor people who so much needed help? Had he not been searching for people to help?

He had dreamt last night that he had entered a dark hallway, not unlike the dark hall of Lucas's house only much larger, and had become aware that at the far end a man was standing holding an axe. The man was resting the axe with its head upon the floor and his hand lightly holding the end of the long handle. Bellamy felt a thrill of terror which was like a sexual thrill. The man's face was dark, as if veiled in thick darkness, but Bellamy seemed to perceive him as beautiful, he thought, he *must* be beautiful. Awkwardly shuffling he began to move towards the man, then he fell on his knees. Then he awoke. His first thought was, how heavy that axe must have been, and how lightly he held it, just touching the top of the handle with the fingers of one hand. Now remembering the dream and holding Clement's letter in his hand he thought of Lucas. So the victim had risen wonderfully from the dead like Lazarus. Bellamy found himself feeling jealous of the risen man who was now Lucas's friend. Lucas had been a person of authority in Bellamy's life. Now, because Bellamy's Commander was Someone quite other, his relationship with Lucas must belong to the past. But *all* this, all this shift and change, thought Bellamy, is part of the *vast lie* which surrounds me and wherein I move from one fantasy to another. I wanted to escape to solitude and darkness in a holy place, but the dark is just the old dark of meaninglessness and falsehood, which separates me from my friends and from the real world where people love and help each other, I even reject those who could help me to help others. (Bellamy had decided not to renew his acquaintance with the young Catholic priest.) In this blackness every way leads to evil. Of course, the man with the axe is the Archangel Michael leaning on his sword, he whom I revere most next to the soldier Christ (in Bellamy's vision of him dressed in khaki) – only this Angel is also the one who strikes down those who are to go to Hell. At this point Bellamy suddenly remembered another dream which at the time had made him smile. He dreamt he was a little tiny frightened animal called 'Spingle-spangle'. Later he did not smile. The little doomed creature was an image of what he most feared, insanity. He set aside Clement's note and read again the letter which he had just received from Father Damien.

My dear son,
Please excuse a brief letter in reply to yours. I understand your feelings concerning reference to God as 'she', but, as you yourself say, these are superficial human matters, irrelevant to the Mystery of the Divine. About the ordination of women, you know the view of our Church, which rests upon both theology and history. As for 'God's punishment' and wanting to be hurled to the ground like St Paul, these are but worldly obsessions in disguise. You are in danger of exalting a senti-mental Christ. You are secretly attached to magic, which is the enemy of religion. Often we enliven our sins by 'punish-ing' them. When you think of Purgatory as a consolation you are seeing beyond it yourself purified! God's justice is outside our understanding and concerns Him alone. The 'darkness' you referred to earlier is, I fear, but the obscurity of the restless self. I begin to think that perhaps the way of abne-gation is not your way after all. You are depending too much upon me. It may even be that you will 'better your condition' by seeking some form of secular, even medical, advice. Reflect upon this. It is of course a matter to be considered at some length. I am sorry not to be able to write more, I shall shortly be in retreat.

Yours lovingly *in Christo*,
Fr Damien

P.S. Pray always. God purifies the desire that seeks Him.

Bellamy was deeply disturbed by this letter. He began at once to write his reply.

Dear Father Damien,
Thank you for your letter. I do not think that I require medical attention! We have spoken earlier of 'depression', which may be what is in your mind, but this isn't it. I earnestly hope that you will realise how much I need you, it is no accident that I encountered you, you are my lifeline. I am not thinking of suicide. I just know that I need a purification by suffering, a sort of way of brokenness, a way of *truth*, which is what I have been seeking in my desire to enter, on whatever terms, the cloister. Yes, I have wanted a sign and I still feel I may get one. But I do crave for suffering, perhaps physical suffering, something so extreme that my false fantasising mind may be shattered, and into that great dark void God may enter. I wish I could be in Hell and see Christ and see Him *pass me by*. I thirst, I thirst like Our Lord upon the cross, like the hart thirsts for the water brook and the soul for God. Only I want not consolation but to be destroyed. Please excuse this outpouring which perhaps makes no sense but is the utter darkness of my spirit pouring from me like black blood. Please do not tell me these are empty exaltations. Please write to me, please let me come and see you. The mouse which ate the sacred wafer of the Host was damned. I am that mouse. Please do not think me ridiculous. Forgive me.

Yours most affectionately,
Bellamy

'Well, he's late too!' said Louise to Clement.

'No, he isn't, he's sitting in The Raven.' (The Raven was a nearby pub.)

'Oh. Why?'

'He's shy. He doesn't want to face you all until Lucas is here to introduce him.'

'I don't understand,' said Sefton, 'is it quite clear that he did not attack Lucas?'

'Yes,' said Clement.

'But Lucas said he did.'

'Lucas's lawyer said so, not Lucas.'

'But Lucas wasn't sure?' said Sefton. 'If he thought he didn't he should have told the lawyer to shut up.'

'No one was to blame, it was all a mistake.'

'I still don't see why Lucas wants us to meet him,' said Louise. 'Perhaps it's natural, like a way of saying sorry.'

'Giving the man a treat,' suggested Sefton.

'Still, it's very rum. Isn't it rum? And fancy him sitting in the pub! It's awfully foggy outside. How will he know when to come?'

'I'll fetch him!' said Clement.

'Suppose he really did attack Lucas, supposing he's dangerous?'

'Lucas is satisfied he didn't, and isn't!' said Clement exasperated. It was a quarter past six and there was no sign of his brother.

The gathering in the Aviary consisted of Clement, Louise, Harvey, Bellamy, and the girls. Anax had been banished to the Adwardens' house to be looked after by Mrs Drake who loved dogs, the Adwardens being still absent. There had been some discussion at Clifton beforehand concerning what sort of event the 'event' was to be: was it a sort of public explanation, or vindication, or even confession, offered to the family? Who would speak, who would explain? Or should it be thought of as a celebration, and if so, what of? The fact that Lucas had not killed a man, or that the man had recovered? Should light refreshments be served, or drinks, or would such entertainment be out of place? As a precaution Moy and Sefton had set out plates of biscuits and two thermoses of coffee and two bottles of white wine and a tray of cups and glasses in the kitchen, ready to be brought forward should the atmosphere prove congenial. The audience were disposed as follows: Harvey seating himself between Aleph and Moy on the sofa, Sefton on the floor leaning against the bookshelves, Bellamy on an upright chair by the window, with another chair beside him for Clement, Louise on the piano stool, Clement now standing at the open door. The sofa and chairs thus occupied (including one for Clement) had been placed in a semi-circle facing the piano, while beside the piano and facing the audience were two empty 'grand' chairs intended for Lucas and his – how to put it – *protégé*, erstwhile victim, new-found friend.

'Be nice to him,' said Clement looking at his watch again, 'he's a very decent chap really, he won't stay long.'

'Of course we'll be nice to him! I haven't put the centre light on, I hope that's all right. Do you think we should ring Lucas, can he have forgotten?'

'I've tried, he hardly ever answers the phone.'

The attentive audience listened respectfully to these exchanges. There was a tension, even a nervous excitement, but no glances were exchanged. Bellamy, sitting on the edge of his chair, leaning forward, his lips apart, had taken off his glasses and was fiddling with them. Without moving his large head he kept glancing round the room, as if checking on some place he had once known. He thought he could smell Anax. He was cheered by the presence of Clement and the expectation of Lucas, and the bright warm touch of curiosity which he felt about 'the man'. He was, for the rest, overcome by shyness and unable to speak to the young people. I *am* becoming cut off, he thought, that's as it should be. Everyone greeted him with exceptional cordiality, and he bowed silently in return. Harvey was, so far as he could manage it, motionless, his good leg bent, his bad leg stretched out. He had arrived by taxi and mounted the stairs with the help of his stick, and been congratulated on having relinquished his crutches. In fact the doctor who had sanctioned the stick had done so with dubiety and spoken of a possible operation. Harvey told everyone he was getting steadily better. As he stared down, keeping his eyes fixed on Louise's feet (she had small pretty feet and a large supply of smart old-fashioned shoes) he felt on one side of him the sturdy warmth of Moy's plump body, which she kept modestly but vainly trying to edge away, and on the other side the silky slithery presence of Aleph's thigh and of her blouse as it touched the sleeve of his jacket. He felt, in the tense atmosphere of the room, a special sense of unity with Aleph, of their understanding each other perfectly. At the same time he felt an excited fear at the thought of seeing Lucas.

The doorbell rang, everyone jumped, shifted, Clement ran down the stairs, Louise went onto the landing. There was a sound of voices below. Louise called to Clement, 'Is it Lucas?'

'No.'

Clement returned, followed by Joan and Tessa. There was a faint murmur of surprise, even disapproval, at the arrival of uninvited outsiders. How did they know? Harvey, receiving a telephone call from his mother, had mentioned the gathering as a reason why he could not see her. In fact, Peter Mir had actually mentioned Joan, 'The fashionable lady, French perhaps', as one of those whom he wished to meet, but Clement had not passed that invitation on.

Bellamy rose and, proffering his chair, sat down on the floor. Moy, getting up hastily, also sat on the floor, beside Sefton. Louise ran to fetch a chair from Aleph's room. The newcomers stood in silence, not sure whether proceedings had started. Tessa, smiling at him, sat on Bellamy's chair, with Clement's chair empty beside her, Joan sat on the new chair beside the sofa. She was wearing a black velvet coat and skirt and a pale-blue silk blouse, its collar lifted up under her chin by a large intricate golden brooch. Without turning her head she reached along behind the sofa, pinching Harvey's ear and unwinding one of Aleph's curls. Harvey, gritting his teeth, emitted a hissing sound. Determined not to look at Tessa, he looked at Tessa, who smiled and waved. He did not like seeing Tessa and his mother together. Tessa was wearing a smart corduroy jacket and trousers and a tie.

Louise said, 'I'm afraid Lucas hasn't come yet.'

'We didn't come to see *him*,' said Joan. 'We know all about *him*, we want to see – you know – *the person*.'

'He's in The Raven,' said Sefton.

'What?'

The telephone extension in the Aviary rang, Louise seized it. 'Oh Lucas, we're waiting – But Clement said – Oh dear, what a pity – Yes, I quite understand – Please don't worry – Goodbye then.'

She turned to Clement. 'He's very sorry he can't come, he has to see someone, it's urgent, about something in America. He says you can manage much better without him.'

'What a shame!' said Tessa. 'We all love a glimpse of Lucas, it's a religious experience.'

'Hadn't you better fetch him from The Raven?' said Louise.

Clement said Oh *hell*, oh *damn*, to himself, and ran away down the stairs. He had considered the possibility of Lucas's defection, but had made no emergency plan, and had no idea what he was to say or do. Lucas had uttered various suggestions, and prohibitions, but Clement had paid little attention, sure that in the end Lucas would be there to do the talking. He felt very frightened. The distance to the pub was not great, but as he emerged from the house he was startled to see the tall burly figure of Mir standing on the far side of the road. It had started very slightly to rain and Mir was putting up his umbrella. Closing it he crossed the road.

'Oh Clement, hello, I've been waiting for Lucas, but I expect he came earlier.'

'He can't come,' said Clement, 'I'm in charge. Come on, you'll get wet.'

'Oh, I'm very sorry to hear this. The Raven was rather nice but I got impatient. I hope you will forgive me?'

As this sounded like a question, Clement said, 'Yes, yes, of course – '

'But I hope – *they* are here?'

'Yes, they are here.' Checking Mir on the doorstep and putting his hand on his expensive overcoat, Clement said, 'Look, since Lucas isn't here I suggest we make this business pretty short, yes? I'll just introduce you to the company, and they can say how pleased they are that you – that you're still there and – and so on – and then suppose you and I go and have a quiet drink at the pub – I'd like that, I'd like to – to ask you about your life, I'd like to know about your life – '

Clement, who had closed the door when he came out, was about to ring the bell when Mir said, 'Wait a minute. Why do you want to know about my life?'

'Sorry, I didn't mean anything intrusive. I just – well, you're interesting, and I – I sort of like you, well, not sort of, I just like you.'

'You have reason to. I am *extremely sorry* that your brother is not to be here.'

'I'd rather we got this whole business over. Or do you want to postpone it?'

'Certainly not, I want to see these ladies now. But I shall want to see them again in the presence of your brother.'

Over my dead body! thought Clement. He rang the bell.

Louise opened the door. Clement entered quickly, Mir rather more slowly mounting the two steps which led up to the door.

'This is Mr Mir.'

'Peter Mir,' said Mir, bowing slightly.

'Peter Mir.'

'How do you do, Mr Mir?' said Louise. 'May I take your coat and your umbrella? We are so glad to see you.'

Mir surrendered his coat and umbrella murmuring, 'Thank you, how kind of you to – ' He took a comb out of his pocket and quickly combed down his curly hair.

Louise said, 'Clement has not introduced me. I am Mrs Anderson. Will you come up? Will you – would you like some coffee?'

'Please come up,' said Clement, taking hold of Mir's arm and guiding him to the staircase. 'Never mind about the coffee, Louise, for heaven's sake, Mr Mir won't be staying long.'

Mir allowed himself to be guided by Clement, who opened the door of the Aviary and pulled Mir into the room after him, Louise following.

The audience, who had been silent since the bell rang, at once rose to their feet. Clement, thinking about this weird episode later, was struck by the instinctive way in which they all so promptly greeted Mir's arrival.

Mir in fact, as Clement was able to notice in what followed, was an impressive sight. His broad-shouldered erect figure paused, towered in the doorway. Clement thought, he is over six feet, he seems to have grown since I last saw him! Mir frowned, pouted, narrowed his prominent dark grey eyes, and surveyed the room, turning his head with slow deliberation. His silky curly brown hair shone in the lamplight. Clement, again taking Mir's arm, as if he were an invalid, pointed, then guided him to one of the grand chairs. He sat down. The audience sat down. Clement quickly picked up the other chair and moved it to the side, leaving Mir alone in the centre. Still standing he spoke, addressing his remarks toward Louise.

'Well, my friends, this is Mr Peter Mir, who is as you see alive and well, much to the relief of Lucas, and of all of us I feel sure, and he has kindly expressed the wish to come here, and Louise has kindly invited us all, to say a friendly hello and make acquaintance, and we, do we not, welcome him and are happy to celebrate with him his wonderful return to health.' Clement, usually a fluent speaker in any situation, could hear his voice assuming a pompous and affected tone, not unlike that which many actors use (wrongly in Clement's view) when playing Polonius.

There was a pause; then someone, Clement was not sure at the time (in fact it was Tessa), out of nervousness and to end the silence or else (Clement later supposed) in mockery of his speech, began to clap. Everyone clapped. Mir bowed his head slightly, still frowning.

Louise hastily, so as to avoid another silence, said, 'I think we might have some coffee, perhaps one of the girls – '

Mir, raising his hand, said, 'Not yet, if you don't mind.' This remark had a chilling effect.

Clement said to Mir, 'Perhaps we should let you know who we are – I suggest each one of us introduces himself, or herself. Is that a good idea? Suppose we start on the left on the floor. Suppose you start, Bellamy.'

Bellamy, surprisingly, said nothing. He just shook his head. Clement said quickly, 'Tessa?'

Tessa, fingering her tie and using her slow deep voice, said, 'My name is Tessa Millen. I am unmarried, I am a social worker and a feminist. Let me say how interested I am to meet Mr Mir, and I congratulate him on being alive.'

'I'm sure we all do that,' said Clement.

'I should add,' Tessa continued, 'that I am not a member of the family. Neither is this gentleman at my feet who refuses to speak.'

'Joan?' said Clement.

'What family are we talking about?' said Joan. 'I'm not a member of the family either, though my son Harvey over there thinks *he* is. I am no one in particular, just Harvey's mother.'

Sefton proceeded to say that she was a Miss Anderson and a student of history. Moy had some difficulty in describing herself beyond saying that she was a Miss Moira Anderson and a – well, sort of a – painter. Harvey said he was the aforementioned Harvey and a student of modern languages. Aleph, who was the first person to smile at Mir, said she was the eldest Miss Anderson and a student of English literature. Louise, also smiling, then felt bound to say that she was, as he knew, Mrs Anderson, she was the mother of the three girls, and her first name was Louise.

Clement said in a hearty voice, 'Well done!'

After another, briefer, silence, Joan said, 'Is this supposed to be a party? No one has told me, no one tells me anything, least of all Harvey. I suggest that rather than sitting mum like a prayer meeting we should all get up and mingle, and what about drinks? I agree with Mr Mir in not requiring coffee. Louise, can't you rouse out some sherry or something?'

This speech seemed to amuse Mir, who smiled. The children giggled. Louise said, a little sternly, 'Later, Joan, later, we can have coffee and drinks, but we are doing all the talking, and I'm sure Mr Mir hasn't come here just to listen to our little speeches.

Perhaps he would like to talk to us, to tell us something of his – his work, his ideas – '

'What job do you do?' said Tessa.

Mir, after a deep breath, turning his big solemn face towards her, said, 'I am, I was, a psychoanalyst. As I explained to Professor Graffe and his brother, I am no longer able to continue this work owing to a lack of concentration, the result of Professor Graffe's blow.'

Louise said in a surprised tone, 'Oh, a psychoanalyst?' She added hurriedly in a sympathetic tone, 'Of course you have been through a terrible time and suffered a terrible – you must have had – we sympathise very much – '

'What was it like being dead?' said Joan. 'Were you really dead? Well, you can't have been because here you are!'

'I don't suppose Mr Mir remembers much,' said Louise, 'perhaps he doesn't want to talk about it.'

'I can't remember it,' said Mir. 'I can't remember – many important things.'

'Of course such experiences affect the memory,' said Louise.

She said to Clement, 'Do you want to ask Mr Mir any questions, or tell us something about him? It must be quite an ordeal for him to confront us like this! We must not keep him with us too long or tire him out! Now, if he would like a little coffee, or if he prefers tea – '

'I agree that we should not prolong this gathering,' said Clement, rising to his feet. 'I'm sure we have all been very glad to see Mr Mir, who has had this miraculous recovery. He so kindly wished to show himself to us and to meet us all, and now we have had our little conversation – '

During these sympathetic exchanges Mir's frown, as he looked from one speaker to another, deepened, and his thick lips pouted with annoyance and distress. He looked, as Louise saw it and said later, as if he were thoroughly confused and upset and would soon have to be led quietly away.

Interrupting Clement's bland mollification, Tessa said, addressing Mir, 'Did you try to steal money from Professor Graffe, or is that not true?'

Clement began, 'Of course he didn't and now I think we had better – '

Mir said, his frown clearing and his mouth relaxing, 'No I certainly did not try to steal anything from the Professor. I am not a thief or a violent person. In fact what I did do on that occasion was to save Clement's life, as I trust that he will now, in front of you all, confirm – '

Clement felt himself flushing violently, the heat running fiercely to his cheeks. He put his hand to his head, clutching his dark hair. The audience, silently embarrassed by Tessa's intervention, now shifted, looking anxiously at one another, then at Clement. Clement heard Louise murmur, 'Poor fellow!' and then aloud, 'Your memory of that terrible evening is naturally a bit confused. It is your own life which has been saved, not Clement's, after all he wasn't there!'

Mir, now patently clear-headed and master of the situation, said to Clement, 'Were you there?'

Clement sat down. He looked intently at the questioner and made a supplicating gesture. He said softly, '*Please*, you are dreaming.'

Mir said, 'These people are your friends. You need not fear them. What are you afraid of?' His tone seemed now slightly mocking.

'Well, were you there?' said Tessa. 'That's news to us!'

There was a moment's silence. Clement, blushing and sustaining Mir's gaze, said, 'Of course not!'

There was a perceptible rustling in the room as everyone changed position, sat up, leaned forward, drew breath.

Louise said, 'I think poor Mr Mir is having a fantasy, perhaps he thought he saw another man, he must be tired and ready to go home. Clement, perhaps you could drive him – or has he got his own car?'

'I have my own car,' said Mir. Then to Clement, 'Come, come. I think you should tell these good people the whole story. This is what I wanted, on this interesting occasion, in this so deeply concerned gathering, to hear Professor Graffe doing. However, since he has elected to be away, it may be better for you to do it. You are a truthful person, tell them the truth, the whole truth, now is the time.'

Clement was aware of having now reached the exact point at which, in his last conversation with Lucas, he had realised that he ought to *think* about what was going to happen at this scene, but had been *unable* to think and had *preferred* not to. He had imagined Lucas as, *somehow*, handling and conducting the whole horrible business. Now he saw himself as trapped, he had been

163

trapped by Lucas, and was now trapped by Mir. He found himself thinking: what does Lucas want me to do? One thing, a terrible thing, seemed clear. He must *not admit* that he had been there. Mir's appeal to truth was in his ears. But, Clement thought, if I tell it *here*, later on *they* will get it all out of me. By 'they' Clement meant, not his family, but the authorities, the lawyers, the police. He thought, all I can do is *appeal* to Mir, make him see the impossibility of my answering his question.

He said, 'Mr Mir is a kind and honourable man, *not* a thief, or an aggressor. He is absolutely blameless. He has behaved bravely and nobly and virtuously throughout. Now I suggest that we close down this conversation, which he must have found extremely tiring – we thank him very much for coming to see us this evening.' There was a faint murmur of assent, then silence. Clement, who had risen, sat down again. Breathing deeply, he put his hand to his throat and looked at Louise's feet and her shoes.

Mir, who had been leaning forward, now leaned back. Gazing at Clement he searched slowly for a handkerchief, drew out a large one and unfolded it. He put the handkerchief to his mouth, pulled at his tie and undid a button on his waistcoat. He said to Clement, 'You are a liar.'

The audience moved. Louise said, 'No! Really – '

Clement said, 'Look – '

Louise went on, speaking fast, to Mir, 'You mustn't say such things. You are mistaken. He has said that you are blameless. What more do you want, what is he supposed to be lying about? This is ridiculous!'

Mir said to Clement, 'You have the impertinence to speak of my honour, you graciously declare me blameless, as if *I* were the criminal who is now to be forgiven!'

Clement said, 'No, for God's sake try to *understand* me!'

'You mean "spare me" – why should I – I despise what you want me to "understand". I am asking you now to tell these people what happened! If you won't, I will.'

Clement tugged violently at his hair, dragging it down and scratching his neck with his fingernails. He held his hands out toward Mir. 'I did what you wanted, I assembled them here. As for what happened, how can we know? Let us *leave it alone*. You *can't remember* – '

Mir uttered a loud violent hissing sound.

Tessa said, 'It may indeed be possible that Mr Mir now admits he can't remember things and may be making mistakes. But I think we may reasonably ask him to say what he *thinks* happened.'

'Oh shut up, Tessa,' said Joan, 'who elected you to be the *juge d'instruction*? The poor man is having a fantasy, I can't see why he has to torment Clement about it. Let's not get cross with each other, let's leave it at that, as Clement suggested, and for heaven's sake, Louise, let someone bring us something to drink.'

No one moved.

Mir said, looking at Tessa, 'The lady who is a feminist and a social worker and whose name I have forgotten, has asked the appropriate question. I will tell you.'

Clement said loudly, 'No, no – it's all a *dream*.'

'I will tell you what I saw, and what he, here, knows to be true. I saw two men under the trees, this man and Professor Graffe. I saw Professor Graffe raise a weapon, a sort of club, with the evident intention of killing his brother. After all, brothers do kill each other, it is a well-known phenomenon. I moved forward to intercept the blow. Graffe then deliberately changed the direction of the blow and hit me instead. I knew nothing more until, a considerable time later, I regained consciousness in hospital, and heard an account of how a man had mistaken me for a thief and struck me with his umbrella. No mention was made of the other man or of the club which I had so clearly seen. I assume that the Professor gave the weapon to his brother and told him to run.'

After a moment everyone began shifting and looking about. Joan said, 'Oh what nonsense!' Louise said, 'He must have imagined it all. It's a fantasy, perhaps a dream he had when he was unconscious.' Moy whispered to Sefton, 'Oh do let's stop this, it's all *wrong* somehow.'

Tessa said, 'Why didn't you say all this at once to the police?'

Mir hesitated. 'I wanted to find my murderer myself.'

'What were you doing underneath the trees?'

'I just like walking about in the evening.' He added, 'It was a summer evening.'

After this there was a short silence. Tessa said, 'Won't Clement – ?' Clement, who was sitting with his hands over his face, said nothing. Then she said, 'I'm sorry, I know I'm an intruder – but when someone is called a liar shouldn't *something* be said?' She kicked Bellamy. 'Why don't *you* say something, what do *you* think?' Bellamy was silent. He carefully moved a little farther away.

Clement stood up, turning to Mir who was sitting with his hands in his pockets and his long legs outstretched. For a moment Clement, his face contorted and blazing, was hardly able to utter. Then he spoke, choking, sounding almost tearful, 'Please go away. You have upset these people by talking like this. You don't understand. We wish you very well. Now just go *please*.'

Mir rose. 'All right, I'm going. I didn't realise this was to be a charade arranged by you and your brother. I shall certainly not talk to *you* again. I shall talk to other people, I shall take other steps. I'm sorry I have upset these ladies – I thought perhaps – but I was wrong. I'm sorry.' He bowed to Louise, then marched out of the door. After a moment Louise followed him down the stairs, but he had already taken his coat and umbrella, and the front door had banged after him.

Everyone had now risen and was 'mingling' in the fashion prescribed by Joan, who had now taken it upon herself, with a perfunctory 'Louise, you don't mind, do you', to instruct Sefton and Moy to bring up some refreshments. Coffee appeared (no tea) and white wine and sherry and various biscuits, so that it did become a party after all, and 'Did we need it!' as Joan said to Tessa later.

'How outrageous, about Lucas trying to kill Clement, the man is crazy, it's just a mad dream, like Louise said.'

'He may be covering up something else. Perhaps he's an impostor, not that man at all, but a blackmailer, someone who simply wants money.'

'You mean a crook, who read about the case in the paper – after all, Lucas hardly saw the man.'

'What did he mean about "talking to other people" – does that mean the press?'

'Or the police. If this goes on we may have to sue him.'

'Lucas is one of us, we must close ranks.'

'Where's Clement?'

'He's washing his face in the bathroom.'

'No, he's down in the kitchen helping the girls.'

'What do you think, Tessa, you were the one who made it all spill out?'

'I don't know what to think – there's something bogus about him.'

'Yes, he *admitted* he was confused and can't remember, he even forgot your name – '

'Oh anyone might! No, it's – '

'He's ill,' said Louise, 'poor thing, they must have let him out of hospital too early, he needs looking after.'

'But fancy inventing all that stuff about Lucas, it's *libellous*! I think he's really a mugger and he's putting all this out to defend himself.'

'I think Joan is too suspicious,' said Tessa, 'actually there is something naive about him – '

'Yes,' said Louise, 'something childish – '

'It's certainly odd – and *very* interesting.'

'Interesting!' cried Joan. 'When he dares to attack Lucas *and* Clement in that rotten way! Louise thinks he's ill. What does Clement think? Is he ill or wicked?'

Harvey and Aleph had been listening to this conversation. Clement had just returned from the kitchen with Sefton and Moy.

Clement said, 'He's certainly not wicked – '

'What do you young people think, what does my son think, that profound student of human nature?'

'I don't know,' said Harvey, 'I believe there's something more behind it all, something *quite strange*. Of course he may be mad, but – '

'Mad, yes, what Louise calls ill. That's why Clement kept trying to stop him talking, he didn't want the mad stuff to come out – there's something *awful* about him.'

Harvey, who was also standing, leaning on his stick and holding a glass of sherry, had been observing Aleph. He could see that she was excited, her eyes were bright, her lips parted in a strange dazed smile. Now she kept looking at Clement.

'And what does Sefton think?' cried Joan. 'Speak up, Sefton, you sober sibyl!'

Sefton said, 'The main thing he said was that Lucas wanted to murder Clement, and that just can't be true.'

'Of course it can't be true, that goes without saying, but is it mad, or vindictive – *why* did he say those weird things?'

'Sefton is right,' said Tessa, 'it's *that*, the impossibility, that suggests it's all an elaborate lie to conceal the fact that he really is a thief and a mugger, didn't the police talk about an offensive weapon – but I don't see – '

'Yes, that's what's important,' said Joan, 'that he's a thief, he was after Lucas's wallet, no wonder Lucas fought back, he *would*! What do you think, Moy, you funny little oracle?'

'Well – ' said Moy slowly, 'I don't know – he seems to me to be – dead.'

Joan and Tessa laughed. The others looked worried.

'Really!' said Joan. 'And what about Alethea, goddess of truth and beauty?'

'Oh – ' said Aleph, 'I think he's *an absolute pet*.' There was now some, rather uneasy, laughter.

'And Bellamy? Where's Bellamy?' But Bellamy had gone.

'I must be off', said Clement. 'Louise, *thanks*, it was jolly kind of you to – I'm very sorry it all turned out so – '

'Clement, darling, don't grieve – let the others go, stay here with me – '

But Clement was anxious to go, and ran away quickly down the stairs.

Moy had gone up to her room, Sefton was already downstairs finishing the washing up. Tessa had telephoned for a taxi for herself and Joan, and had offered to take Harvey too.

On the landing, in the doorway of Aleph's room, Aleph said to Harvey, 'Go with them, dear Harvey.'

Harvey said, 'There's something I want to tell you – '

'Not now. Whatever it is, don't worry. *Whatever* it is – oh Harvey, how *strange* that was – '

'Yes, wasn't it. Aleph, I love you.'

'I love you too. There's the taxi. Goodbye.'

'Wait, please! Please let me talk to you!'

Bellamy had sat for a moment, stunned by Mir's sudden exit. Then, as everyone, recovering from their surprise, had jumped up and began talking, he had pushed his way past and out of the door, colliding apologetically with Louise upon the stairs. He was delayed at the front door because, although he had so often passed through it, he had never discovered, or could not remember, how it opened. He opened it at last, nearly forgetting his overcoat, pausing to seize it, and rushed out, stumbling down the two steps outside. Inhaling the keen cold, he looked wildly, desperately up and down the road. The pavements were glinting with speckles of frost. The fuzzy foggy night air had assembled the lamplight into thick localised yellow globes. He glimpsed a tall figure disappearing into a remoter dark. Slipping, nearly falling, upon the frosty surface he ran. Reaching out his hand he pawed, trying to seize hold of a sleeve.

Mir stepped back quickly, gripping his umbrella, startled, even alarmed, peering closely at Bellamy. Then he walked on with Bellamy hurrying beside him. After a short silence he said, 'Now you are the one who said nothing.'

'Yes, I'm sorry, I'm Bellamy James – '

'You're the man with the dog.'

'No, not now, I've given the dog away. He now lives with *them*.'

'Why? I liked the look of that dog. What was his name?'

'Anax. I have to live alone – I'll explain – I'll explain *everything* – I do so much want to talk to you, to ask you – '

'What do you want to ask? Would you mind walking a little faster?'

'Yes, yes, I want to, oh so many things – is there somewhere where we can talk?'

'Let us walk on please.'

'How did you know I had a dog?'

'I observed you, as a friend of Professor Graffe, when I was waiting for him. I thought he might visit you. Never mind, those days are over. What do you want?'

'You said such extraordinary things. Surely you must be mistaken, I mean it can't possibly be – all the others thought – '

'Never mind what they thought, what did you think?'

'I don't know. I think it is impossible, what you said. But somehow I believed, I had to, I believed in *you*. So you must be mistaken. I think I see how it is, how it must be, how it happened – look, here's The Raven, can't we go in, it seems to be quiet – '

'I think not. It's too near to – let us walk on, if you don't mind going some distance. I like London walking. There's a pub called The Castle. So you doubt the truth of what I said?'

'Well, no, I mean I don't think you – '

'Never mind, we can talk later. Let us walk now in silence. Hmm, a little mild rain. I'm sorry I cannot accommodate you under my umbrella, perhaps you should put on your overcoat.'

The Castle turned out to be a very quiet almost invisible little pub in a cul-de-sac. Mir seemed to know the host. Bellamy obedi-

ently sat in a corner letting Mir buy the drinks. With some difficulty he pulled off his damp overcoat. The well-lighted little bar
was indeed quiet and almost empty. The transactions (he suddenly
thought of them as transactions) taking place at the bar were
conducted in murmurs. He thought, it's all so bright and clean
and empty, it's like science fiction, it's like in a spaceship, loss of
gravity, all movements slow, like swimming. He felt the dampness
of the rain which had fallen on him before he put on his coat and
the aching of his body within his damp clothes. He was *so tired*.
He could not remember when he had last eaten anything. He had
spent the day sitting on his bed waiting for the time to go to *see
the show*. What had he seen? Something terrible – a *conjuring
trick*. He felt his eyes closing. He thought, it's a dream, it's a
dream place, like the dream Louise said *he* had when he was
unconscious. Mir arrived with the drinks. Bellamy had asked for
a lager, only when it appeared he remembered that he had given
up alcohol. He seized it and drank some. It tasted wonderful. Mir
was drinking what looked like lemonade.

Mir began the conversation. 'What do you do?'

'Well, I used to do various things, I was a social worker, a civil
servant, now I do nothing.'

'I congratulate you.'

'I'm waiting to go into a religious order.'

'I congratulate you even more.'

'Only I don't know whether they'll accept me. I want to be a
hermit, I want to wall myself up. But of course I'm not worthy.
I just can't live an ordinary life, I can't *pass the time*. I can't
organise myself, I don't have ordinary *motives* any more. I can't
even manage my body, when I go to bed I don't know where to
put my arms.'

'That can be a problem.'

'Don't laugh at me.'

'I'm not laughing.'

'You see, I'm not mad, I suffer from depression. It's not like
ordinary misery. It's like dying of boredom. It's *black*. But you
must know all about this being an analyst. Really – it just occurs
to me – I think that you could help me –'

'I have given up my work, as I said, I can't do it any more. I
just live from day to day, I value every day that I see the light of
the sun.'

'But you *could* help me, if you just talk to me. I sometimes see a priest, a monk, I write letters to him, but it's not the same. I have a feeling about you.'

'But you have friends – '

'Yes, but they can't help me, they can't *understand*, they haven't got what you have.'

'This is most gratifying, Mr James. I wonder if you would like something to eat, a sandwich for instance?'

'No, no. I'm so glad just to be with you, it's like being with a king. With you I can always tell the truth, I will *have* to tell it. Please do something for me, I want to bare my breast to God and let Him smite me, please enter my life, you can, like a great beating of wings, like an angel – oh send me a sign, send me a significant dream – let me be with you – I need help – '

'I am very touched, I am sorry, perhaps once I could do such things, perform such miracles, but now I cannot do them any more. Perhaps rather there is something that you can do for me. Tell me, how well do you know Lucas Graffe, let us call him the Professor.'

'I know him well, indeed very well.'

'And do you believe he is capable of intending to murder his brother?'

Bellamy swallowed some more lager. He said after a pause. 'Actually I think he is capable of anything.'

'So if he is capable of anything he is capable of that.'

Many things which Bellamy had seen and heard over many years seemed now to be rushing together. He said carefully, 'No, *that's* impossible – I mean – Lucas, the Professor if you like, is a very strange man. He is the *bravest* person I know – '

'You like him.'

'I admire him. I love him. He lives absolutely outside ordinary conventions.'

'Including ordinary morality.'

'He is very truthful – '

'But prepared to deceive.'

'I mean he's *honest*, he *sees* the terrible things, he doesn't try to cover them up or imagine them away – the evil of the world, the senselessness of it all, the rottenness of us ordinary people, our fantasy life, our selfishness – '

'You seem to want to see him as a saint.'

'In a way I do – I mean a sort of counter-saint – I mean he's above, beyond – '

'Beyond good and evil.'

'You are a psychoanalyst, you must have met – '

'You know the circumstances of his childhood?'

'Being adopted and – yes, of course.'

'Do you not think it *possible* that such circumstances might lead a man to build up a murderous hatred for his brother?'

'He loves his brother! Of course it is conceivable – '

'That he also hates him.'

'*No*, I *meant* in the case of some *other* person this might be conceivable, but not in *this* case! He is a very unusual man.'

'I think you believe what you said was impossible.'

'Look,' said Bellamy, who was beginning to feel a little estranged from himself by the lager, 'it's not *like* that! You are bringing in this *dream* of yours that Lucas tried to murder Clement! All this psychological stuff is simply *irrelevant* – he happens to love Clement but even if he hated him it would be *irrelevant* – Clement *wasn't there!*'

'Clement was there. Clement lied.'

Bellamy was trying unsuccessfully to think clearly. Another glass of lager had appeared as if by magic. 'How could he – he just wanted to stop you from telling us your dream! Anyway, what are *you* up to, why did you fix up that business this evening?'

'I wanted to make the acquaintance of those ladies, whom I have observed from afar and for whom I feel esteem. I also wanted to persuade your very unusual friend Lucas to exhibit some of the truthfulness with which you credit him. I thought it possible that it was the sort of thing he might suddenly do. He may be an evil man and a murderer, but there might have been a streak of nobility, I thought he would not be willing to lie. However, he chose to leave the lying to his brother. I am disappointed in him. I am disappointed in the brother too, but that doesn't matter, he is a silly weak man. The Professor may be, as you said, brave. We shall see.'

'I don't understand – '

'I was giving him a challenge, more precisely a chance. He refused it. His refusal leaves me with no alternative, it precipitates another less amusing phase of our relationship.'

'What do you mean, what do you want?'

'If I may emulate the ruthless frankness of the Professor, I want his death.'

*

The Saturday after Peter Mir's appearance before the esteemed ladies Moy had agreed to visit an art school to talk to a teacher there, a Miss Fox, who was a friend of Moy's art teacher at school, Miss Fitzherbert. Miss Fitzherbert had fixed this visit for Moy, saying of course it was not an interview, just a matter of learning a few facts and picking up a few tips. Moy did not inform her sisters and her mother, but slipped quietly away. (This was a usual procedure.) She did not bring Anax with her, as the journey would involve a long bus ride, and she did not like to take him too far afield for fear of being somehow separated from him. She was constantly haunted by fears of losing him; and also worried that he did not get enough exercise. She was carrying with her a big portfolio containing paintings and drawings.

Sefton and her mother, especially Sefton, were constantly impressing upon Moy that, whether or not she were going to be a great artist, she must acquire some sort of academic status, pass some serious exam or exams, before leaving school, as such titles might always come in useful later. They had exhorted her to work hard, it need only be for a short time after all, at 'dull school subjects', such as English, French, History and Maths. Moy, who hated these with the possible exception of English, had decided some time ago that she would *not* work at these horrid subjects, would *not* take any of the beastly exams, and would leave school as soon as possible. She occasionally tried to communicate this decision to her family, but they simply refused to listen. Now she was beginning to be more fully aware of the *gamble* she was making with her life. Suppose she never got into art school, suppose she was not a painter after all? Suppose the talents which others had persuaded her she possessed were to abandon her overnight, or turn out to have been unreal all the time? Suppose she had to take a typing course or live with a word processor? I would die, she thought, I would kill myself or *make* myself die of grief. Already there was one great deep grief in her life.

The meeting with Miss Fox was not a success. Miss Fox was clearly very busy and had obviously only agreed to see Moy to please her friend or acquaintance Miss Fitzherbert. Their conversation took place in a mean little room, an *office*, into which other people constantly intruded. Miss Fox glanced perfunctorily at Moy's offerings, made no comment on them, but said if Moy wanted to go to art school she should show up with something really *original*, something *striking* and *strange*, not just tame

173

copies from nature. A lot of girls, Miss Fox told her, thought they were artists because they could do a watercolour of a daffodil, and regarded art as a pleasant occupation to dabble with while waiting to get married. Such people had better not apply, Miss Fox said, the study and practice of art was difficult and arduous, and required absolute dedication, as well as of course considerable talent, which very few people possessed. She added that anyway it was extremely difficult to get into art schools as hundreds of applicants were chasing very few places. Moy, who felt the tears rising in her eyes, thanked Miss Fox and left hurriedly.

She realised that she had been very stupid, she had deliberately chosen her more 'accomplished' and 'traditional' paintings to show to Miss Fox, figurative paintings of (yes) flowers and trees, the pagoda in Kew Gardens, Anax asleep. She ought instead to have brought her wilder more outrageous work, crazy unfinished sketches, dotty fetishes, one of the masks, even one of her stones! Well, there was one art school where she would *not* be admitted, Miss Fox would damn her from the start. Clutching her paintings, which kept sliding away from under her arm, she walked at random, unwilling to go straight home, and after a while found herself beside the river. There was a fuzzy grey mist over the Thames, the tide was out, the narrowed stream looked dull and sluggish, like thick grey oil oozing along. Moy came to some steps, then saw, looking down, that there were some stones upon the muddy beach at the foot of the steps. She went down, stepping carefully upon the wet surfaces. She propped up her handbag and her portfolio against the stone wall of the embankment, and began to examine the stones. They were disappointing, shapeless and mud-coloured. As Moy felt a personal obligation to any stone which she picked up, or even noticed, after guiltily discarding some with a murmur of apology, she felt obliged to pocket some of the senseless stones. She walked down over the sticky mud to the water's edge and saluted the river by dipping her hand into it. Here the sound of traffic had become a woodland murmur, remote from the calm pace of the eternal Thames. Moy still felt tearful and tried to calm herself by standing very still and gazing at the fuzzy mist which was motionlessly pendent above the water.

Then she became aware of a disturbance, the sound a little distance away of violent splashing. She moved, trying to see through the mist. Some horrid *fight* seemed to be going on in the water. Moy hated to see animals fighting each other, she rushed at feuding birds to stop them, and shouted at aggressive dogs and cats, once trying to separate two snarling dogs she was bitten by both. Something very improper now seemed to be taking place in the water involving a swan, and something else, some creature whom the swan was attacking, a dark squirming thing, perhaps a large rat, perhaps a little dog. He's trying to *drown* it, Moy thought with horror. The little dark thing kept coming to the surface, to be violently thrust under again by the swan. The bird was leaning forward, its long neck doubled, its wings spread and beating, using its great distended breast as a weapon, battering down the little black creature, pressing it under water and frustrating its repeated attempts to rise. Meanwhile the swan was uttering a terrible fierce loud hissing noise.

'Stop that!' cried Moy. 'Stop it at once! Leave him alone! Stop, you *wicked* bird!' She took one of the senseless stones from her pocket and threw it toward the swan. It missed the bird, and Moy did not dare to throw another for fear of hitting the poor victim. She cried out again, 'Oh stop, *please* stop!' The swan continued to clap its wings, which made a loud cracking sound as they struck the water. It continued to hiss and to press its great white breast down upon the black struggling thing.

Moy stepped into the water, waving her arms and shouting. She stumbled, trying to lift her feet from the mud, and blundered forward. The water splashed about her, its shocking coldness clasped her. She saw now, in a sudden glimpse of the scene, that the creature which the swan was trying to drown was not a dog, but a small black duck. In that instant the duck became free, it leapt away, spread its wings, and rose from the water uttering a strange cry of terror, and flew away into the mist. Then as Moy steadied herself, the swan was upon her, she saw the great wings, unfolded and in the surface water the big black webbed feet trailing like claws, as the swan fell upon her, pressing her down with its descending weight, as it had pressed down the little struggling duck. Moy lost her balance and slipped backward seeing the heavy curving breast above her, the snake-neck like a rope of greying fur and for an instant, as if in a dream, eyes glaring in a mad face. As she felt the terrible weight upon her she tried to free a hand from the rising water to hold it away, trying to move her clogged feet and attempting to scream. The next moment it was over, the swan passed from her, beating the water violently with a loud sound with its wings, rushing away over the surface of the river, then rising into the silence of the gathering mist.

Moy made her way slowly back to the shore, her shoes full of mud, lifting her feet with difficulty. It had all happened in a minute, perhaps two minutes. No one had heard, no one had seen. She slipped on sudden stones, crawled out of the water on hands and knees, and stood shuddering, uttering little moans. Her coat was heavy with mud and water and she managed, fighting with it, to pull it off and shake it. Dropping the coat, she stood there helplessly, weakly, trying to wring the water out of her skirt. She found herself crying and knew that she was crying because the tears were warm upon her cheeks. Trembling with cold she gathered her wet hair and thrust it in a tangled jumble down the back of her dress. She was thinking, as the tears flowed, I do hope I didn't hurt the swan. She picked up her coat, realised she must wear it, and managed to haul it on again. Hanging her head she made her way to the steps and began slowly to climb them. When she neared the top she remembered her portfolio and her handbag which she had left propped up against the wall, and went down again. Her chilled muddied hands dropped water in upon the pictures. She climbed up again and began to walk along the embankment. People passed her, staring at her and looking back after her. Moy thought, I can't go on the bus like this, but it's too far to walk, what am I to do, oh what am I to do! She went on crying, her wet coat heavy upon her.

'Why Moy, whatever has happened to you?'

'Darling, what's happened? You're so late, we couldn't think where you were!'

'Oh *dear*, are you all right?'

'I'm all right,' said Moy, tottering in through the door at Clifton and sitting down at the bottom of the stairs.

'Why, you're soaking wet, and muddy, oh poor thing, and –'

'So sorry,' said Moy. 'I had a fight with a swan.'

She had at last nerved herself to get on a bus, where her plight occasioned various comments, some sympathetic, some hostile.

Of course she did not venture to sit down, but stood as near as possible to the exit, drooping her head and hunching her shoulders. She felt like a mad person.

'Quick, run a hot bath,' said Louise to Sefton, 'Now come upstairs, you must get those clothes off, no, better take them off here – '

'I'm so sorry, I'm making such a mess everywhere – '

'Shut the front door, Aleph, don't let the cold in. Why on earth were you fighting with a swan, I thought you liked swans.'

'It was – it was – trying to – to kill a little thing – ' said Moy, as Louise now hurried her up the stairs, and she began to cry again.

Moy had put on a special dress to visit Miss Fox, who already seemed to belong to the remote past. Now emerged from the bath, dressed in warm trousers and a woollen sweater, she was sitting in the Aviary telling the others the story of her adventure.

'And then what happened?'

'Then it turned upon me, it sort of *sat* upon me – by the way,' said Moy, interrupting her narrative, 'where's Anax, I want him to hear it too!'

'He's probably up in your room,' said Sefton, 'I'll get him.' She came down a moment later, 'No, he isn't there, he must be in the kitchen or the garden.'

'He was in the kitchen,' said Aleph, 'Sef was just making his breakfast. Sorry we forgot it earlier!'

Moy leapt up and ran out onto the landing calling, 'Anax, Anax!' then hurried downstairs with the others.

'He's not in the kitchen, he must be in the garden. Of course, because he would have run to Moy immediately when she came in – ' They ran out calling. But there was no sign of Anax.

'Perhaps he's asleep on someone's bed.' They hunted through the house looking into every room and every corner. They stood at last and stared at each other appalled. Anax was gone.

'He must have run out just when Moy arrived,' said Aleph. 'Remember we left the door open.'

'He'll try to find his way to Bellamy's old flat,' said Sefton.

'No, no, he'll just be hanging about quite near,' said Louise.

They went out into the road, and into the nearby roads, and called and called – then returned miserably to the house. 'At any rate,' said Louise, 'he's got his collar on.'

Sefton uttered a cry of woe. 'I took his collar off! He'd got it all dirty digging in the garden. I was going to wash it. Oh *God*!'

'Oh, if only – '

As they went on bemoaning the situation and wondering what to do next, Louise suddenly said, 'Where's Moy?'

'She's gone upstairs, she's probably having a good cry.'

They hurried up and down and called her name. They even ran out again into the road. But Moy was nowhere to be found. She too had vanished.

On the previous evening when Louise had come down the stairs with Clement they had exchanged few words at the door. Both were horrified and appalled, they could not face each other. Louise said again, sounding almost in tears, 'Don't be distressed, I can't bear it.' Clement replied, 'It's all my fault. Oh Christ, I'm so very sorry. Goodnight.'

He awoke the next morning to an instant consciousness of disaster. As he got up slowly and dressed clumsily he wondered in amazement how he had managed to be so cool about it all *before*. Why had he not realised what a terrible thing he had done, what a terrible situation he had put himself into, when he obeyed Lucas and ran away carrying that awful weapon with him concealed under his coat? Yet what else could he have done? At the time, it now occurred to him, he had run off simply because Lucas had told him to; and, when he reflected later, his thoughts were mainly of how Lucas had protected him, sparing him, as had happened sometimes in childhood when Lucas took the consequences of some blameworthy event. That he had placed himself in a position of falsehood, made himself into a liar, into something like an 'accessory after the crime', had not occurred to him at all. He had simply thought, well, what else could I do? It was better to keep out and let Lucas handle it all, as indeed he did! I would just have made every sort of blunder, and made things worse. Like I did when Peter Mir first appeared! Now I've messed things up completely, perhaps *fatally*. I've utterly discredited myself with *them*, I've virtually admitted to being some sort of liar, and I've lied again, and it will be proved against me. They will despise me, it's the end! *He* said he would now talk to 'others' – that means the police, the press. I would be put in prison. And Lucas – The whole case would be reopened. But how did it all happen? Why didn't Lucas come? He trusted *me* to carry it off! He was crazy. He might have known I'd break down. My whole life is ruined. What shall I do? I must do something. I can't just sit here, until they come for me. Oh I've behaved so stupidly, so rottenly, so badly!

He rang Lucas's number but there was no answer. He rang at intervals, still no answer. He sat gnawing his fingers. About ten o'clock he could bear it no longer and ran out and drove to Lucas's house, which had once been his house too, and rang the bell. No one. He introduced himself into the paved space behind the railings and peered into the front windows. One was curtained, the other showed the empty derelict dining-room now never used. He tapped on the windows and called out. He went to the side of the house where a passage with a gate led to the back garden. The gate was locked. He returned to the front and crossed the road and waited a while, watching the house. Then he drove back to his flat. As he had to do something or go mad he started to write a letter to Lucas.

Why didn't you come yesterday? I ruined everything, you might have known I would, Mir wiped the floor with me, he was just determined to tell his own story, someone, that is Tessa, asked if he had tried to steal your wallet, and he said no, what he had done was save my life! And Tessa asked me if I'd been there and I said no of course not, it was all a dream – he admitted earlier he could not remember some things, and the others picked that up, of course it was a fantasy he had in hospital and so on, but then he called me a liar and that really upset them, and I was all pathetic and trying to persuade him to *understand* and to *go*, and then he just told them the *whole thing*, that you had intended etc., and he said you had sent me away to get rid of the weapon, and all I could do then was repeat it was all imaginary, and he must be tired and please go away, and of course the women said the same, and at last he went away in a rage and said 'Now I shall talk to other people and take other steps'. And God knows what *they* thought or what *he'll*

do! For heaven's sake see me soon, I'll keep on calling and
ringing.

C.

When he had finished this missive Clement put it in an envelope
and was about to take it round to Lucas's house. However, he
was filled with sudden misgivings. Suppose it were to fall into
someone else's hands? Suppose Mir were to get hold of it somehow? There couldn't be a more incriminating document. After
some reflection he tore it up and threw the fragments into the
wastepaper basket. After more reflection he carefully picked up
all the fragments and burnt them in the kitchen sink. After that
he rang Lucas's number and then drove round to his house again.
No good. He thought of going to see Bellamy but decided against
it. He drove back to Lucas's house and shouted and waited, but
now senselessly and without hope. This waiting reminded him of
his long agonised waiting when Luc had disappeared and when
he had wondered every day whether his brother had committed
suicide. He imagined it now, as he became so sure that Lucas was
inside the house. Perhaps he was indeed inside, lying dead, on the
carpet in the drawing-room beside the gun (had Lucas once said
that he had a gun?) or upon his bed beside the bottle of sleeping-
pills. Realising the game was up he had taken his life. This idea,
increasing in strength, was beginning to make him feel faint. He
was also, by other faculties, being reminded that he had eaten
nothing all day. Suddenly he decided (which he had considered
earlier and rejected) to go to Clifton. He had thought it impossible
to face Louise. Now he realised that he must go there, he must
see her, he must.

He parked his car and rang the bell. The door flew open. Sefton.
He heard her call out in a tone of evident disappointment, 'Oh –
it's Clement.'

Louise ran down the stairs. 'Clement, come in, come in. Such
awful things. Anax has run away, and Moy has run away after
him.'

Standing in the hall Clement gathered something of the situation
from Louise and the girls who were all talking at once and interrupting each other. Of course they had searched the neighbourhood, of course they had telephoned Mrs Drake and all sorts of
people all over the place, and yes, of course they had considered
that Moy would assume that Anax was walking back to Bellamy's
flat in Camden Town, and yes, they were at this very moment,

see there's the map laid out on the kitchen table, trying to decide which were the best routes to follow, and the girls were going out on their bicycles and Louise was going to stay at home in case, and please would Clement help.

Of course Clement would help. It was decided that it would at this stage be a waste of time to try to fetch Bellamy who might not be there, but that the mobile three should set off at once along the most obvious routes between Hammersmith and Camden Town. Clement was able to remind them that Bellamy, who loved walking, had used to walk with Anax from his flat to Clifton, crossing Regent's Park and Hyde Park and Kensington Gardens. But how did he get from Regent's Park to Hyde Park, and then from Kensington Gardens to Brook Green? There was no one obvious way, given that Bellamy, as they all now between them recalled, had liked to make various detours and visits on the way, to the canal at Little Venice, to the Victoria and Albert Museum, and there were more recent visits, while Anax was still with him, to Brompton Oratory, and so on, in fact there were hundreds of possible ways and they must decide something at once. What would Moy be likely to think that Anax would be likely to do? It was hurriedly agreed that Clement by car should take the route via Kensington High Street, over the Serpentine, Bayswater Road, Marble Arch, Baker Street, and the Albany Street side of Regent's Park. Aleph on bicycle, should go via the Cromwell Road, walk her bike across Hyde Park, then via Gloucester Place and Marylebone Road and through the middle of Regent's Park. While Sefton, on bicycle, was to go by Hammersmith Road, Kensington Church Street, Pembridge Villas, Westbourne Grove, Bishop's Bridge Road, across the canal, Blomfield Road, St John's Wood Road and so to Prince Albert Road and Regent's Park, converging with Aleph.

While the girls were checking their tyres and lamps in the garden shed, Clement and Louise were left alone for a moment. Clement, who had for that brief time forgotten his terrible troubles, wanted to say something quickly, something which, in an instant, would be the uttermost confession which would evoke the most absolute pardon; and as he thought that that was what he wanted he also thought what a coward he was, what a liar he was, how irrevocably rotten it all was. He was also feeling terribly hungry and wanting to ask Louise to give him something to eat. He said, 'Forgive me for being a liar and a fool and an utterly worthless man.' Louise replied, 'I love you.' He took her in his arms for a moment and they held each other with closed eyes.

Anax had, since the terrible moment when he realised that Bellamy was not coming back to Clifton to fetch him home, been obsessed by one great thought, that of escape. He did not whine or claw at doors or do anything foolish which would reveal his intent. He was quiet and exceedingly watchful. He was fond of Moy, he understood her, but could not help sometimes looking at her reproachfully, knowing that she understood him. More remotely he liked Louise, still more remotely Sefton and Aleph. But these people were *aliens*; and the smell of the cat Tibellina still hung about the house, perceived by him alone. He grieved and waited, aware that his kind captors were careful not to let him stray. Sometimes he pretended to be happy, sometimes, quite accidentally, he was happy because for an instant he forgot, and then remembering was a greater grief. He did not reflect upon any reason why he had been deprived of the one he loved and to whom he had given his life. He knew simply that there was no other. He did not believe that his master rejected him or found him unworthy, indeed he could not imagine this. Nor did he imagine that his master might be dead, since Anax could not conceive of death. He felt only the painful unnatural severance from the loved one and the utterly poisoned wrongness of the world while the severance lasted. Of course he had expected, then later hoped for, then trusted in, his master's return. Only lately had he realised that there would be no return and that it was for him, Anax, to seek his Lord, who might be somewhere in need, perhaps captive too, waiting, deprived and unconsoled. Nor did Anax doubt the authentic authority of the magnetism which would, when the time came, draw him back to his master. Surely the moment of liberation must come, a moment conceived of by Anax as one of almost instant reunion. If he could only *run* towards the beloved he would be with him, nothing more was needed than that flinging of himself into the great void of that dreadful absence. Only very vaguely did he think of what would happen, what he would do. He did not picture any plan, but simply knew that as soon as he was free he would be guided.

When the instant of liberation came it came as a surprise, like a lightning flash, a sudden rending of the whole so sadly familiar scene. His collar had been taken off, his breakfast was late but it was being prepared, he was sitting quietly in the kitchen, his paws stretched out, his head upon his paws. Then all at once there was a lot of noise, Moy was standing there dripping and crying, and the others were shouting. Anax was distressed and wanted to bark. But then he saw, as they all crowded up the stairs, the front door standing wide open. Just for a second he hesitated, some craven atom in his being held him back. Then he bounded out, sprang down the steps, turned to the right, and ran away through the maze of little streets.

He ran so fast that people turned and stared after him, turning again to see what dreadful pursuer had inspired such speed. Once he had started Anax found that he knew his way perfectly well, he was *guided*. He was sure that when the moment came to use the knowledge he would possess it. Following a way which he must have traversed some time, but certainly not many times, he passed through the little streets, behind Olympia and down to Hammersmith Road, where it joined Kensington High Street, which was familiar territory. Here he had to stop running, partly because he was tired, and because of the dense moving forest of people's legs. Cannily he turned away into a quiet road which was parallel to the High Street and loped along it. He crossed Kensington Church Street, waiting for the lights to change.

By this time Clement Graffe, in a very distressed state of mind, had set out in his car on what he deemed to be a hopeless quest. He drove down Hammersmith Road in an easterly direction toward the parks. The women had so burdened him with their fears and their imaginings, he was unable to gain any satisfaction from his attempt to be useful. The misty haze was thicker, cars were turning their lights on. He pictured Anax run over, Moy raped. He drove slowly along, examining the people and the dogs on the left-hand pavement. At first he drove very slowly and attracted the attention of a suspicious policeman, after that he increased his pace a little. Sometimes one trouble can drive out another, but this miserable catastrophe seemed simply to intensify his confused grief about Lucas and his fear of what Peter Mir might now decide to do. His intense piercing desire to find Lucas and confess to him now merged with old old feelings which he had had about his brother, feelings of terror, feelings of love, feelings of – not exactly hate – it was somehow clear to him that he could never hate Lucas – perhaps because of – some deep eternal guilt, the guilt of having been his mother's favourite, the guilt of having been born at all. And now he was wasting his time looking stupidly for a girl and a dog, when he should have been waiting at Lucas's door, and even now the two miscreants might have reappeared at Clifton, while he was methodically performing a pointless task well in tune with the grinding hell he had made for himself lately. Why had he wantonly made himself so unhappy? It had all started with Harvey's idiotic fall. He could have stopped Harvey, why didn't he stop him, he seemed to *want* things to go wrong. Louise had embraced him because she was sorry for him, she was sorry because he had pathetically exposed himself as an incompetent prevaricating bungler. She had made some cheese sandwiches for him and he had eaten one and in his haste left the others behind. He said to himself, they won't really *think* about it, what Mir said, they'll just regard it all as some sort of bizarre mystery. That was the best he could hope for. Would Aleph think about it? She too would be sorry for him. His attention was failing, his stare, directed at the moving people, was glazed over. He could see nothing except Aleph's bright eyes, sparkling with delighted interest, and the way she had looked when she said of Peter Mir, 'He's an *absolute pet!*'

Anax, following without hesitation his computer guide, had reached his first main objective, Kensington Gardens, and was now beside the Round Pond, where he stopped to drink the muddy water, chilling his throat and his paws. He (too) had had no breakfast and was feeling hungry. He was also uneasily aware that he was not wearing his collar, and that troubled him. He felt undressed, unsafe. A mob of water-birds, ducks, swans, Canada geese, even a moorhen, were gathered jostling and fighting in the shallow water for pieces of bread which some children were throwing. Pigeons and sparrows were waiting hopefully upon the path for crumbs. A crust carelessly thrown fell near Anax and he snapped it up, just forestalling a pigeon. When he tried to seize another piece of bread he was threatened by a goose advancing from the water and he retreated. The children laughed at him. He looked at them with his baleful blue eyes and they stopped laughing. One of them shouted at him. He turned and ran away with a purposive air. A little way away some dogs were playing and he paused with them for a moment and pretended to play too, but his heart was not in it, and anyway they were rather rough. Anax did not really like other dogs, and regarded them one and all as an inferior species. A little further on some boys were playing football with a big black labrador who had learnt to dribble the ball with his nose. People passing by were laughing. Anax scorned the animal's undignified behaviour. Nearby some gardeners were burning a pile of dead leaves, and the fierce burning smell mingled with the chill fog smell. Anax sneezed. He paused in the longer grass and stood quite still. Suddenly the spirit that directed him had seemed to fail. A woman came up to him and spoke kindly to him and stroked him, and he wagged his tail absently. He walked on, moving his long grey muzzle slowly to and fro.

Clement had by this time left the High Street by the road which led to the Serpentine bridge. Pulling himself together and trying to imagine what Moy would be likely to do, he decided that if she had come to the Gardens, she would stay there, at least for some time, conjecturing that if Anax got that far he too would stay, and converse with other dogs. (Neither Clement nor Moy reckoned with Anax's contempt for these animals.) He parked his car near the bridge and set off on foot along the edge of the Long Water, calling out occasionally, 'Moy!', 'Anax!' When he neared the Fountains he gave up these cries which sounded so bizarre and unnatural, and turned back, making a detour across the grass. In doing this he passed in fact quite close to Anax who, the magnetic ray having resumed its force, was now running diagonally in the direction of the Marlborough Gate. As they passed Speke's Obelisk, Anax on the west and Clement on the east, they were scarcely more than two hundred yards apart. If at that moment Clement had caught sight of the dog and had managed to capture him, the fates of a number of people in this story would have been entirely different. Such is the vast play of chance in human lives. However, this did not happen and as Anax disappeared in the direction of the Gate, Clement had decided to return to his car. He sat quietly in the car for a few minutes, suddenly entertaining a vivid mental picture of Aleph long-legged upon her bicycle, and for a few seconds it was as if it were Aleph whom he was so anxiously seeking and running to earth. Perhaps they would meet at Marble Arch. In fact at that moment Aleph, following Clement's intuition that girl and dog might both be somewhere in the park, had left her bicycle, carefully though perilously chained up at Speaker's Corner, and was exhibiting her long legs by hurrying in the direction of the Reservoir. At that moment also Sefton, having mistakenly turned left at the Blomfield Road bridge, was lost, quite unable to find her way back to the canal. As Clement set off again, driving slowly in the direction of the Victoria Gate, Anax was already running up Sussex Gardens.

When Anax reached Marylebone Road he crossed it confidently at the traffic lights at Lisson Grove. He did not (another fateful decision) go up Lisson Grove, but set off 'across country' passing Marylebone Station and Dorset Square and entering into a complex of small streets. The conception of Regent's Park may even have been by now present to his courageous mind. But here, where he might almost have thought himself on home territory, his daemon really began to fail. Perhaps his loss of certainty was simply due to exhaustion, he had travelled a long long way alone, his paws were hurting, his high heart was daunted. Several times now he hesitated at corners, even retraced his steps. He was going on, farther and farther – but perhaps in the wrong direction. He kept pausing and looking about him. When he raised his leg at a sack of rubbish he was confronted by a mouse. The mouse seemed fearless. It regarded Anax. Anax felt pity for the mouse, or something more like affinity, respect. He did not wantonly kill other creatures as cats do, and some dogs are taught to do. He felt such a strange feeling, as if he had lost his identity and become part of some immense world being. He ran on quickly, then walked, hoping still to regain the magnetic message, along a road which prompted no recognition, where railings enclosed the front gardens of big houses. As he passed one of these gardens Anax received an unmistakable communication, the smell of food. The iron gate was open. He entered. He traced the smell to its source. Near to a side door of the house there had lately been laid (for it was still warm) a bowl containing a mixture of meat fragments and biscuit. The meat was *good*. Anax set about the bowl, pushing it along with his nose. After a mouthful or two of the excellent food he was interrupted by a sharp exclamation and a smell which he disliked extremely. He lifted and saw, two yards away from him, a large black and white cat, clearly the legitimate owner of the bowl and its contents. Anax's attitude to cats was conventional. His master had taught him not to chase them. (Whereas squirrels could be chased but of course not caught.) But the instinct of enmity, the dislike, the contempt, also the fear, remained. The cat was an alien, a foe, unlucky, dangerous. The sound it had just uttered was neither a hiss nor a mew, but a loud violent utterance which might have belonged to a large bird, a hoarse piercing squawking cry of hate. Anax, facing the cat, retreated, he growled but softly, not a ferocious threat, more like a firm admonition. The cat followed. Its large luminous green eyes horribly slit with black stared hypnotically at Anax and its large white paws moved majestically as with evident intent it advanced. Anax felt that if he turned tail the cat would spring upon him, he pictured it landing upon his back. He continued to retreat, growling, and watching the luminous eyes. Then suddenly the cat leapt towards him. Anax saw the animal rise, all four paws leaving the ground, and seeming to hover, arrested for a moment in his attention, as he stared at the open mouth of his enemy, its white teeth, its red tongue, its open throat, and breathed in the vile effluvium of its breath. At the next moment Anax had leapt too, twisting sideways in the air and streaking for the open gate. The cat's claws touched the thick fur of his tail. Then he was running as fast as he could along the pavement. There was no pursuit, only a distant trilling bird-cry of mockery.

Meanwhile Clement had passed Marble Arch, been delayed by a traffic jam in Oxford Street, and turned up Gloucester Place. He was so tired and fed up that at moments he forgot what he was supposed to be doing, though he continued to look about him and to follow the 'trail'. He kept on going over and over his new awful situation, the mistakes he had made and the sins he had committed. When Lucas had handed him the weapon and told him to go away and keep his mouth shut, Clement had simply *obeyed* his elder brother. Nor did it occur to him during the trial that he, Clement, was potentially a very valuable witness, or that his silence might do damage to an innocent person. When the victim 'died' Clement felt some vague pity and a considerable relief. They had all kept away from Lucas's ordeal, they did not want to embarrass him by being inquisitive spectators, they had preferred not to reflect about it, only hoping for it to be over and Lucas, of course, cleared of any shadow of wrong-doing. During the period of Lucas's disappearance Clement had as if *forgotten* the dreadful happening. He was taking refuge in this respect with 'the others', more occupied with worrying about Lucas's whereabouts, his welfare, even the possibility that he had killed himself. He had missed Lucas, he had *wanted* Lucas, as a younger brother might want an older brother who had always been kind to him, a protector, like a father. Am I mad, Clement wondered, am I not aware that he intended to kill me? I have busied my mind with wrapping up that fact, de-realising it, making it not to be. Anyway, he didn't kill me, and he might not have done, even if I hadn't been rescued by poor Peter Mir. Very likely he wouldn't have done it, he would have found it impossible. Now it's all got mixed up, Mir has an extra motive for hating Lucas, for not forgiving him, Lucas not only damaged Mir, destroying his life as he says, he was also engaged at the time in an attempted murder and so is revealed as an evil man, who cannot get away with it by talking about accidents. The picture of Lucas is darkened, it's lurid, it's bloodstained, he is presented as a villain. Well, he is a villain, perhaps he ought to be punished! But what, in all this, am I to do, what will happen now, if Mir tells the police and the press and they start to interrogate *me*? I'll figure as an accomplice in my own murder! Or else – in *Lucas's* murder. If Mir exposes Lucas I shall be blamed too, I shall have to give evidence, Lucas will be put in prison, and perhaps I shall as well. If Mir decides to go it alone and employs someone to do the job, if Lucas is found dead and I have been silent, never revealed to anyone that Lucas might be in danger, then I shall be guilty of Lucas's death.

These thoughts, like sharp roving pains, occupied the deeper parts of Clement's mind as he drove slowly in the evening traffic along Gloucester Place. Trying to concentrate upon the task which Louise had put upon him, to find Moy and Anax, he told himself that probably by now they were both safely back at home. He said to himself, 'I'll find a telephone box, I'll ring Clifton and – ' He suddenly jammed on the brakes and swung the car aside out of the traffic, mounting two wheels onto the pavement. He had seen Moy. Or was it an apparition, a *thought* of Moy? He jumped out of the car and ran back, then forward, bumping into people. Had he really seen her, little Moy, walking slowly along, dressed in trousers and a jersey? Yes, it was Moy, she had seen him, she had run to him and he was leaning down to embrace her, putting his arms round her as she leant against him.

'Oh Moy, *thank God!*'

'Have you found Anax?'

'No, but Sefton and Aleph are out looking for him. What a miracle that I saw you, I'm so glad, I was looking for you, I'll take you home, we've been so terribly worried. Anax has probably gone back to your house by now, he wouldn't have gone far away. Come now, why you haven't got a coat, we'll go back home.'

'No, no, I must go on, I'll walk on, you go on by car, he must have gone back to Bellamy's house, where Bellamy used to live – you go on, *please*, in the car.'

'I'm not going to leave you, now that I've miraculously found you! Do as I tell you, come. All right, if you like we'll drive on as far as Bellamy's place. Heavens how cold it is and you haven't any coat!'

With murmurs of protest Moy climbed into the car and Clement drove on in the slow procession of evening cars. Moy beside him was shuddering. He reached out his warm hand and touched, then held, her hand. It was icy cold. 'You're frozen! I'll turn up the heating, you'll soon be warm in here. Poor little Moy, fighting with a swan, they told me, and now this!'

'It's all my fault, I should have closed the door, we'll never find Anax, he'll be run over, he may be dead by now, oh why didn't I – '

'Don't worry, he's all right, we'll find him, he'll come back – '

Moy was holding tightly onto his hand and had lifted it and was pressing it against her cold cheek. Now it seemed she was kissing it. She moaned and said, 'Oh Clement – '

He withdrew his hand, giving her a brisk pat on the shoulder. 'There, there, Moy. Don't expect too much of me. You know I'm very fond of you. But you're so young and I'm getting on in years! Don't waste your love on me. It's not real love, you know, it's just a childish fancy! You'll find love later on, when you've grown up, I'm sure you'll find lots of young men – ' As soon as he had uttered this absurd tactless speech Clement regretted it bitterly. Why on earth had Louise told him to trouble the child with such a lecture, her simple hero-worship did no harm! He heard Moy draw in her breath and felt her move away, gathering herself against the door of the car. For a second he pictured her opening the door and jumping out. He tried to think of something emollient to say. Louise had asked him to try to cool this childish passion and now he had blundered and caused pain, what did it matter anyway if she imagined herself in love with him, he ought to be grateful! He heard a slight sound and realised she was crying.

Anax was now completely lost. He had hurried on, then wandered randomly on, trying to recognise some landmark or be guided in some direction, but now he had given up hope, he had lost all sense of orientation. The magnetic beam was quenched, the purposeful certainty, the energy, which had made him able to run so far and so fast, had vanished from him. He felt tired, hungry, and now frightened. Darkness was falling, the street lights were on. He could not conceive of retracing his steps, he did not know where he had come from, he felt no motive to go on, yet was unable and unwilling to stop. When he stood uncertainly at corners people stared at him. He had to pretend he was going somewhere. He felt shame and misery at the idea of being seen to be a *lost dog*. A little rain was falling. The night would come, the night when he had used to settle to sleep in safety – but *this* night would find him still walking, still wandering, homeless. What could he do, walk till he dropped? He feared everything, everyone, every human was now his enemy. Even the thought of his master, the great certainty which had illumined his life and made his joy, was confused, made senseless, covered in darkness, as if it had never been. He had no identity, no being. A horror had seized him like a black dream, a memory of a time before time, before his master had come to him.

Anax began to run. He was now once again a dog without a master, a dog without a name. So *they* would find him and take him back to that terrible place, among those poor degraded dogs, who smelt of sickness and doom. Desperately he ran through streets of bright shops, stared at, knocking against legs, uttering a little whining sound. He ran on into darker emptier streets where there were big houses and many trees. He felt his heart breaking. He stopped at last, breathless and panting, breathing in the thick foggy air. His coat was wet with the little mild rain. The pavement was wet and cold. He walked on slowly, his head down, his bushy tail drooping to the ground.

A man, holding an umbrella above his head, was coming towards him. Anax lifted his head and lifted his muzzle. He breathed. Something very strange was happening. The man passed close to him. Anax sniffed at his trousers. The man stopped. There was a faint gentle reassuring smell, a smell almost it might seem of Anax himself. He raised his head further and looked up at the man above him. The man leaned down and stroked him. Anax began to wag his tail.

The man said, to himself, 'Wait a minute.' Then he said to Anax, 'Haven't I seen you before? I saw you outside their house with your master. I think you're Anax – yes, you know your name, don't you – ? But whatever are you doing here all by yourself? *Are* you by yourself? I think you are, you must be lost – there, there, poor fellow, I'll look after you – in fact I'll take you back to the house where the ladies live – you won't run away, will you, you'll come with me, my car is just here.'

Anax, trembling with relief, walked beside him, breathing in the magical reviving smell. When they reached the black Rolls he leapt in through the door which Peter Mir opened and settled himself in the passenger seat. As the car set off Peter continued to talk to him. 'Anax, I'm ready to bet they are worrying about you down there. You know, you're miles away from home. Whatever were you up to, to come here? Perhaps you were running away to where you used to live. Yes, that must be it. Anyway, *they'll* tell me – if they let me in. Well, they'll be so pleased to see *you* – Perhaps some god sent you to me, little one.' Mir's deep liquid voice with its strange caressing accent murmured on. As they moved slowly through the evening traffic of central London, Anax fell asleep.

Meanwhile Clement and Moy had arrived back at Clifton. They had driven on to where Bellamy used to live, rung the bell of the flat getting no answer, looked about outside, and left messages with sympathetic neighbours. Moy wanted to stay, standing at the door all night, but Clement of course insisted on taking her home. There were cries of joy for Moy's return, and then various attempts to invent how it would somehow 'be all right' about Anax, how he would come back and scratch at the door any moment, how he was so clever and would find some warm place to spend the night, how no harm could possibly come to him and so on. While Clement and the girls were away Louise had telephoned the police (why didn't they think of that before?) and given them Anax's description, and the police were so understanding and sympathetic, and now policemen all over London would be looking out for Anax, and as he was such an unusual and beautiful dog they would be sure to find him. Clement reflected less optimistically that Anax's unusual beauty was more likely to lead to his being kidnapped, only he did not say this. He was deeply disturbed by his conversation with Moy, why had Louise suggested such a thing, and why on earth had he felt that it was his duty to utter those stupid wounding words, Moy would never forgive, certainly never forget, he had made a deep wound in his relationship, which had been so perfect, with these girls. Would Moy tell the others of his boorish conduct? He thought not. He thought, she'll brood upon it silently. We shall never be friends again. Oh God!

They were all standing in the kitchen with the door open and the front door ajar. The cold foggy air was blowing in. The rain had stopped. Louise had feebly suggested something to eat, something to drink, but no one had the heart for any refreshment. Clement felt hungry, but also that food would make him sick. Louise looked very tired and could not banish a look of intense grief which invaded her would-be calm face at intervals. Clement could not make out whether or not she wanted him to go. Aleph and Sefton, still in their cycling gear, looked dejected, half-heartedly joining in the chorus of false hopes. Sefton had managed to fall off her bike beside the canal and her trousers were muddy. Clement kept composing speeches of farewell which could get him out of the house without embarrassment. At the same time he wanted somehow to communicate with Moy, to catch her eye, to find something affectionate and apologetic to say, but she refused to look at him. She was wearing a big woollen cardigan belonging to Louise. Her long hair, its bright colour dimmed, hung about her in long damp strings, her lips moved, trembling or uttering silent words as, gazing down, she kept rapping her knuckles upon the table against which she was leaning.

A silence had fallen and Clement was trying to find a form of words to break it, when suddenly, swiftly, silently Anax was among them. He darted in through the open front door and into the kitchen. Amid the joyful tumult he perfunctorily greeted Moy, then hurried to his bowl, in which the meal that Sefton had made for him so long ago was still waiting. Tears of relief were in Louise's eyes, Moy was kneeling on the floor beside Anax. Clement went to the front door to close it.

A tall figure was standing on the doorstep. 'May I come in too?' said Peter Mir.

'So you all play the piano?'

'Oh yes, but Aleph is best – this is Aleph, these two are Sefton and Moy.'

'I know which is which, I've learnt quickly. What do you do, Moy, besides piano playing?'

'She collects stones!' said Aleph, 'and paints pictures!'

'We all sing,' said Sefton.

'Oh good, I sing too!'

'Those funny names,' said Louise, 'are of course not their real names.'

'What are their real names?'

'Alethea, and Sophia and Moira, but they decided to be called Aleph and Sefton and Moy!'

'Aleph – that's Hebrew, it's the letter A.'

'I know,' said Aleph. She blushed.

'Didn't you want to be Alethea? It means truth, well of course you know that. It's such a lovely name.'

'I just – '

'May I call you Alethea? I think I will!'

'Oh – of course – '

'The Princess Alethea. And will you please call me "Peter".'

'Fancy your just finding him like that,' said Louise, 'it's like a miracle!'

'He came to me, he recognised me.'

'But he's never seen you, and you've never seen him!'

'I encountered him outside this house in the days when I – I hope Clement told you – '

'Of course, when you used to wait about outside, we all know that,' said Louise.

'I hope you forgive me.'

'We forgive you everything!' cried Sefton. 'But my theory is that some of Anax's hairs got onto your coat when you were sitting in *that chair* – '

There was much exclaiming over the miracle and its explanation. They were all now in the Aviary drinking wine and talking away with such extraordinary happiness and freedom as if they had known Peter (as he insisted on being called) all their lives.

('Like an uncle,' as Sefton later said to Aleph.) They had run over and over all the events of the day, Moy's dramatic encounter with the swan, how Anax ran off, how they all searched the roads, how they decided Anax must be going to Bellamy's old flat, how Clement appeared, how they studied the routes, how Aleph and Sefton set off on their bikes, how Sefton fell off her bike, how Clement set off in his car, and how he so wonderfully found Moy, and how Peter so wonderfully found Anax, it was a day of miracles, well, a day of terrible things and then wonderful things! They were standing up in a circle, too excited to sit down. The only calm being present was Anax who was curled up on the sofa. For a while he watched them with his sly blue eyes and responded with a faintly quivering tail to Moy's caresses, then he fell into a deep sleep.

'Wouldn't you like something to eat?' said Louise. 'I'm afraid we are all vegetarians here, well Clement isn't are you, Clement?'

'I am a vegetarian myself,' said Peter, 'I am very much for ecology. I am a member of the Green Party.'

'That's why you dress in green,' said Aleph, 'you've got a green tie and a green umbrella, and your suit is a sort of green too.'

'Yes. I care very much about animals.'

'Anax must have known that instinctively.'

'But wouldn't you like a sandwich, a vegetarian one?'

'No, no thank you, I must be getting away now, my car is parked on a double yellow line! I'm just so very glad about what has happened this evening, it's so perfect, like a gift from the gods – I must not outstay my welcome. But I do hope I may see you all again?'

'Oh – indeed – '

'Well, let us say *au revoir* then, *au revoir* Moy, I wish I'd seen you struggling with that swan. Of course you know the story of Zeus and Leda.'

'But Moy fought him off!' said Sefton.

'So it seems, but who knows what will happen later on! Of course, I'm jesting, don't mind me!'

'Please come to Moy's birthday party!' said Aleph. 'That's all right, isn't it, can't he come?'

'Yes, do!' said Sefton. 'It's Tuesday next week!'

Peter looked at Louise. 'Of course,' she said, 'do come if you'd like to. It starts at seven but – come any time – it's quite informal – just family really – '

'So, I trust I can count as family! It is evening-dress?'

'No, it's fancy dress!' cried Sefton. 'Everyone has to wear a mask!'

'Oh, don't worry about that,' said Louise, 'not everyone wears a mask or fancy dress, it's just the children!'

'But you can if you like,' said Aleph.

'I'll see you down,' said Louise.

Beside the front door they paused, 'Please, I don't know your first name.'

'Louise.'

'I like that name. May I call you Louise?'

'Of course. But listen – '

'Yes, yes. You have things to say to me.'

'Yes, but I can't say them. You know what I want to say – '

'Of course, you were distressed by that scene.'

'I don't know what's true, but – can't it all be explained – can't it all end peacefully?'

'Peace. Women always want peace. I thank you from my heart. I shall think of you and of those lovely girls, and perhaps – well I shall see you at the party. Goodnight.'

When Louise returned to the Aviary the others were playing the game of what character in fiction Peter Mir reminded them of.

'I think he's Mr Pickwick,' said Louise.

'Oh no! Never!' said Sefton. 'I think he's more like Prospero.'

'I think he's the Green Knight,' said Aleph. 'Come on, Moy, what do you think?'

'I think he's the Minotaur.'

'The Minotaur isn't a literary character, he's a mythical character,' Sefton objected.

'Oh really – !'

'What does Clement think?' said Aleph.

'I think he's Mephistopheles.' said Clement.

'Surely not, he's so nice!' said Louise. 'Do you think we should tell Bellamy about Anax?'

'No, not now, later maybe. Better not tell him at all. He's got enough troubles.'

'Anyway, all's well.'

'Oh I forgot, I must ring the police and Mrs Drake.'

They all went downstairs together declaring how hungry they were. Clement was invited to supper but declined. He had hoped to have a private audience with Louise. She had granted one to Peter Mir. But she waved him off without a *tête-à-tête*. Clement let himself out of the front door. The fog had lifted, but the air was very cold and an east wind was blowing. His car was already coated with frost. He got in and lowered his head onto the steering wheel.

'How interesting about the dog.'

'Oh bother the dog!'

'The dog has done what we have failed to do.'

'Introduce him to the family! Yes!'

'The man has uncanny properties.'

'He has spent some time being dead.'

'Why didn't he stay dead!'

'Perhaps he did. Moy said he seemed like a dead person. But that was before – '

'Indeed, before – What a mess you've made.'

'Why didn't you turn up? He suddenly asked me whether I'd been there on that night. I couldn't say yes, it would have been the end, I couldn't pledge them all to secrecy, besides – '

'But that was after he'd said that he'd saved your life.'

'Yes, yes, and *that* was after Tessa Millen had asked him whether he'd tried to steal your wallet. Oh God, who will keep Tessa's mouth shut!'

'Come, come, you admitted nothing. Still I ought to have briefed you. I thought if I said I wasn't coming you'd call it off. I relied upon your wit and your common sense. You should not have given him that opening, you should never have let the situation arise. You should have arranged it all with Louise beforehand.'

'But we were waiting for you!'

'Yes, but when you decided I wasn't coming– '

'You mean tell her – ?'

'No, you fool – you should have said what a poor old fellow he was, likely to be confused and upset, how he wouldn't stay long and they mustn't expect him to say much – making a party of it, that was another mistake. After all, he gave them a lead by saying that he was unable to remember important things. They would have lapped it all up.'

'They did lap it up, but – '

'All that was required was a few introductions and some general talk. You should have just kept on saying that he must meet the ladies who had so kindly invited him, and that would be that. Why were you all sitting down? That made it look like a law court at the start. He should have been hustled straight into a crowd, he should have been chatting with the girls, after all that's what he came for! Instead you sat there mum and let him take the stage.'

'Oh all right, all *right*!'

'I'm afraid we were in too much of a hurry. If only the dog had happened sooner.'

'But why didn't you come?'

'I didn't want to see him,' said Lucas, 'I abominate him, the very thought of him makes me feel sick.'

'You are afraid of him.'

'I thought my presence might enrage him. I thought it was better to let you muddle through. Oh what a shambles – you don't know how much I loathe this scene, this vulgarity, this kitsch, these lies, these people. It interferes so with my work – '

'But my dear Luc, if you had killed me, would not that have interfered with your work?'

It was the next day. Clement outside Lucas's door in the morning, had been let in. He had already told his story, indeed both his stories, about Peter's 'introduction' which had turned out so unfortunately, and the episode of the lost dog, with its miraculous ending, resulting in Peter's establishment in the bosom of the family, even in his invitation to the birthday party.

Lucas was sitting at his big desk, tilting his chair, leaning back, his hands behind his head, Clement at the side, was leaning forward, clutching the edge of the desk and scratching the old green ink-stained leather with his fingernail.

There was a low grey sky outside. A quiet dull rain was falling, tossed gently by the feckless wind against the glass doors, sounding like waves of the sea. The long heavy brown velvet curtains were quivering slightly. The room was chilly, all the lamps were on, above the lamps a darkness hung like a baldaquin. Clement felt cold, he had run out bareheaded to the car, his hair was wet. Lucas was wearing an expensive brightly patterned high-necked

jersey which Clement had given him many years ago. The jersey
gave Lucas a more youthful, rather weird look, as if he were an
actor whose natural appearance had been skilfully altered.

Lucas looked at his brother and smiled faintly. 'My dear Clement, we do not know what would have happened, who can say
what I intended? I find it difficult to picture at all clearly the state
of mind I was in at that time. But the general condition goes back
very far. I have always wanted to kill you, all my life led to that
blow. Jealousy and hatred compose my earliest memories. I have
killed you every day in my thoughts. Please don't scratch the
desk.'

'I'm awfully sorry,' said Clement, 'but it wasn't my fault.'

'It was your fault. Not just because you were preferred. But
because you were cruel.'

'Luc, don't torment me with this, I was a child.'

'You were a cruel child. There are things which are never
forgotten or forgiven.'

'I'm surprised you didn't kill me earlier, or *then*! But now you
say you don't know what you intended.'

'Perhaps all I mean is that I find that I don't want to now.
Something has gone out of me.'

'It went out when you struck him, so he has really given his
life for me.'

'Don't be sentimental. It's more that I can't be bothered. What
did I intend? You might have stayed in the picture. It might just
have been a joke, play-acting, trying to frighten you – or part of
a childhood game or – ha ha – a sado-masochistic love scene!
Perhaps we should have played it that way from the start!'

'For the police – ?'

'You in the witness-box saying it was all part of a family game!'

'Yes. Behind it all we have seen an intent to kill, but there is
no reason why anyone else should see it.'

'We were not ingenious enough, we didn't think quickly
enough, we lacked imagination. Never mind. And now he wants
to punish me not only for killing him, but for killing you!'

'But you haven't killed either of us!'

'He says I have ruined his life. I may yet ruin yours.'

'Luc, I have thought of that too.'

Lucas had taken off his narrow rimless glasses. He looked at
Clement with his dark slits of eyes, pulling his thin lips into his

mouth and combing back his black oily hair with his pale elegant little hand.

He went on, 'You are wasting my time. You came here to ask me something. What is it? Perhaps you could be brief.'

'I came to tell you what had happened and to ask you what we are to do about it!'

'I don't know. Why should we do anything? Let him make the moves.'

'But Luc, don't you see, he said he'd *talk* now, that he'd talk to *other people* – of course that was before he was received into the bosom of the family. But do you really think this might distract him, flatter him, so that he'd give up – ?'

'It remains to be seen. It will be interesting to see. And now could you kindly clear off.'

'Do you think for *their* sake now he'll just forgive you – ?'

'You will use this disgusting terminology. No, I don't. The mutual attachment may well be short-lived anyway. I took him for a kind of buffoon. Now I see he is a devil.'

'So he'll go to the newspapers, to the police – ?'

'You know,' said Lucas, 'I don't think he will. I see him as something of an artist – and a gentleman. He will feel that this is now strictly between him and me. He'll want to deal with it man-to-man – like a duel – or rather, he'll want to torture me personally. The police would just spoil the fun.'

'Tessa asked why he hadn't told it all to the police. He said he wanted to find his murderer himself.'

'A good exchange. He is a witty fellow.'

'But, Luc, you'll be in terrible danger – hadn't you better move, go away, go to America – ?'

'And hide somewhere, waiting every night for his hired assassin? No, he went into all that, remember. He's in earnest. I shall stay here and wait for him.'

'Suppose it's blackmail?'

'He doesn't want my money, he wants my head.'

'You should be protected, we must make plans, we must take it in turns, there are problems which – '

'Problems have solutions. Extreme problems have extreme solutions. Don't worry, I don't value my life all that much one way or the other. Now, I have already told you to go.'

Lucas had risen and Clement reluctantly rose too. He wanted to prolong the conversation. 'You need a bodyguard – '

'This is not your scene, dear Clement. Get back to your theatre world. Has anybody asked you to play Hamlet yet?'

'No. Luc, please, I want to be with you in this – '

The front doorbell rang.

Clement said at once, 'It's him. Keep quiet. We won't answer.'

The bell rang again.

Lucas said, 'Go to the door. If it's him, let him in.'

'But – '

'Do as I say, Clement.'

Clement left the room. He hesitated at the front door – he opened it as the bell rang again. It was Bellamy.

Passing Clement, Bellamy strode on into the drawing-room, putting down a suitcase which he was carrying on the floor. Lucas, now sitting, closed a drawer of his desk. Clement followed Bellamy.

Bellamy began speaking at once in a loud voice. 'Lucas, I must tell you, I've been talking to Peter, I kept ringing you all yesterday and – '

'Please sit down, Bellamy, is it still raining outside? You can take your coat off. Now who have you been talking to? And please don't shout.'

'I've been talking to Peter, Peter Mir – '

'Has he sent you as some sort of emissary?'

'No, no. I believe he wants to kill you.'

'All right, but what do *you* want? Do be brief.'

'I want you to make peace with him.'

'Well, I would like him to make peace with me – '

'Communicate, do something, make a connection, have a conference, don't just wait, make a move, tell him you're sorry – '

'What for?'

'For what happened – '

'Well, who knows what happened. For heaven's sake don't be so portentous.'

Clement, standing by the door, said, 'I'm going.'

'What is that suitcase doing, Bellamy?'

'I want to stay here and protect you. Can I, please, *please* – ?'

Clement repeated, 'I'm going, I'm *going*! Oh *God*!' As he ran from the room he could hear Lucas talking quietly to Bellamy.

*

Moy was sitting on the floor in her bedroom watching a fly which was walking upon the back of her hand. She watched and felt its little tongue as it sipped nourishment from her pores. Then it began briskly to clean its wings with its back legs, then to wash its face with its front legs. As she moved slightly it flew away and walked high upon the window pane. Moy kept the window closed so that the fly should not go out into the cold. It was morning. Anax was out in the garden. She had had to persuade him to sleep in his basket at night, and not come onto her bed as his restlessness woke her up and his paws tangled with her hair. He seemed to understand this banishment, as Moy talked to him continually, but he sometimes uttered little whining sounds when it was still dark. Perhaps he was dreaming. Moy thought it must be like God hearing the endless wail of suffering humanity and realising He can't do anything about it. It seemed to her terrible that she had so much power over Anax, but was unable to console him.

It was her birthday. She thought, I am always unhappy on this day. She was sixteen. She could scarcely believe it, or perhaps it was simply that she realised that other people could scarcely believe that little Moy could move out of childhood. The exams which she was supposed to stumble through were near. She would do badly, dismally, and disappoint the others, even shock them, especially Sefton and Aleph for whom working hard and getting top marks in exams was an ordinary way of life. Well, Moy worked hard too in her own way. Only lately she had felt, coming like cold gusts of wind, new sensations, demoralisation, doubt. Her visit to Miss Fox had been the very first time that she had entered an art school. Of course she could have walked into one anywhere, any time, but she had refrained. She had postponed the experience as if it were something holy, preserving it as a long-awaited admission to a sacred place. She had, in some similar spirit, awaited her confirmation; but this magic had faded and she no longer crept out to church early on Sunday mornings. She had her own dark celebrations, her heart had beaten even faster when she entered the art school. But after Miss Fox everything was different, and it now occurred to Moy that she had been living for years upon a kind of happy confidence which had no foundation except her own childish energy and the loving praises of her mother and sisters. *She* felt she was an artist, *they* said so; and Miss Fitzherbert said so, but perhaps Miss Fitzherbert had been simply rewarding a pupil who so evidently enjoyed her classes. And as to her family, Moy now felt they had been, of course, it was clear now, simply encouraging, indeed tending, a funny eccentric dotty little child.

And after Miss Fox there had been the swan, and that too was a portent. She had told *them* about that, but they had not really taken it in, they had not understood, they exclaimed, they laughed, but the next day they scarcely mentioned it, they were distracted by other things. More terribly perhaps they simply did not believe the story as Moy had told it, thought she exaggerated, invented a little, after all she was a very odd little girl. About the swan, Moy was suffering from shock. She had woken at night breathless, suffocated by some great round thing bearing down upon her, she had sat up and turned on her torch and seen Anax's eyes glowing in the dark, and heard him utter a little humming sound as if he *knew*. There were scratches upon her arms which she had not shown to anyone. She had washed the grey muddy stones which she had brought home, the dull dirty Thames stones. Only one of them had any distinction, having a strange hole in it which the mud had concealed. This one was special, but she felt she must keep them all together, and she put them at the bottom of a drawer with other stones since there was no room upon the shelves.

The thought of her birthday party gave her no joy. In the past this party had been quite a large affair, but now, owing to some impalpable social attrition, it had become almost family only, including as such Bellamy, Harvey and Joan, also the Adwardens who on this occasion were still away, and Clive and Emil who were away too. Moy had used to make masks for her party, for the family and for privileged others, to match particular costumes or to please her own imagination. They had called her 'the Wardrobe Mistress'. Moy regarded these creations as ephemeral and would have destroyed them, only Sefton, with the instincts of a historian, stored many of them away, bringing out a few every year. In the past Moy had used *papier mâché*, only it made such a mess in the kitchen and once blocked up the bath. Later she made do with plasticine, cardboard, stiff textiles, cloth stretched on wire, any odd flexible materials. By now the old customs were lapsing, there was minimal secrecy, guests might wear old masks or worse still buy their masks in shops. Moy thought, I shall make no more masks, something is over forever. Anyway, she thought, this time next year I shall probably be dead. When Moy was unhappy a particular memory image always came back to her. She had visited Venice only once, four years ago, when Emil had persuaded Louise to let him take the girls to Italy for a few days. The marvel of it all had ceased for Moy (luckily upon the last day of her stay) when she had seen, stared at, and finally understood a pair of pictures by Carpaccio, representing the exploits of Saint George. In the first picture a captive princess was being defended by the soldierly saint against a handsome long-tailed winged dragon. The girls had an old joke about how Aleph was to be a sacrificial princess menaced by some monster and rescued by some gallant hero, as it might be Perseus, in this case Saint George. In the first picture the dragon, with wings spread and tail whirling, is leaping up, lifting his front paws, while the very long lance of the saint has passed into the dragon's mouth and out apparently through the back of its head or perhaps its cheek. Moy shuddered at this picture. Then she looked at the second picture. Here the saint with drawn sword raised, standing before an admiring crowd, has beside him a small animal on a lead, as if it were his pet. It took Moy some time to realise that this miserable diminished creature was the dragon, still alive, its wings clipped and folded, and the end of the lance still embedded in its bleeding mouth. Its shrunken body, awkwardly crouching, and its grievous face expressed its agony as the triumphant saint raised his sword to despatch it. This picture filled Moy with horror and distress and tears came into her eyes. Oh poor dragon! So was she on the side of dragons and indifferent to the fate of princesses? Well, couldn't he have killed the dragon quickly and mercifully, and not exhibit its misery and its pain? Anyway, why kill it at all? Didn't Saint Francis make a pact with the Wolf of Gubbio? The dragon was innocent, all beasts are innocent, and princesses should be careful and not make themselves attractive to monsters. Also, by some twist of thought which made it worse still, Moy found herself connecting the poor diminished wounded 'pet' dragon with her little hamster Colin, who had run off one day and been killed by a cat. (For Moy knew Colin had been killed, though she pretended to believe the comforting lies the others told her.) She could still feel the touch of Colin's little claws upon the palm of her hand.

As tears again came into her eyes she saw, gazing down at the carpet, a very small black thing moving. She knelt down and inspected it. It was so tiny that she could not discern what it was, whether a spider or a beetle or some almost microscopic creature whose name she had never heard. She thought, I must put it somewhere else or I may step on it, or Anax may find it, but it's so small, I might hurt it unless I pick it up very carefully, I'll get it to walk onto a piece of paper. As she rose, stepping carefully away to find some paper, there was the familiar rattle of Anax, let in by Sefton, rushing up the stairs, and thrusting the door open with his strong muzzle. He ran to her, scuffling and lifting up his paws. When Moy looked again she could not find the tiny black thing. She sat on the bed with Anax beside her, combing out her hair and using its long strands to dry her tears.

'Whatever possessed you to invite him?' said Clement to Louise.

'Aleph invited him actually.'

'Oh did she! You should have shut her up.'

'It all happened so quickly, I thought it was all right. We did intend it to be just family. He'll think we're very – well rather naive and childish – not grand and – '

'Louise, what *nonsense* you talk! You think he's grand and he thinks we are too?'

'I think he's – '

'What?'

'He *is* rather grand, there's something great and powerful about him, he has authority. I suppose someone in his job *would* be like that.'

'Oh hell – you think he's wonderful because he found Anax and now he's charmed you all, you're eating out of his hand.'

'By the way, Bellamy rang up yesterday morning and said he isn't coming, because of Anax I suppose.'

'I wish you'd told me you asked Mir.'

'I'm sorry, I thought it wouldn't matter.'

'Oh, really – you are a goose!'

'All right, all right, I should have thought, after that scene, I should have rung you – '

'What do you think of him anyway, after that scene?'

'I feel very sorry for him. I feel he's some sort of great person who has been damaged. It must be terrible not to be able to think clearly any more or remember important things. I see now perhaps I shouldn't have asked him – but he was so nice to us after he brought Anax, and so quiet and sane, and Aleph said – '

'Oh damn Aleph, she's a mischief-maker.'

'I can understand that you may feel embarrassed – '

'*Embarrassed*! Oh Louise – ! Anyway I certainly can't stay now, I'm off. It's getting awfully foggy out there, I'd better go home.'

'You mean you aren't staying for the party?'

'I mean that! Here's my mask, you can give it to him.'

'Clement, please, please stay – perhaps he won't come.'

'Well, maybe he'll have thought it over and realised I'll be there. All the same – '

'I felt so sorry for him, it's terrible to see somebody so confused and suddenly inventing things. His head was perfectly clear when he was with us and – '

'So you don't think he was really a thief and invented it all to protect himself?'

'Certainly not. I think he's innocent. Don't you?'

'Yes.'

'Then why do you want to avoid him? You must make allowances! Oh don't go away, you've upset me.'

'What's all that row?'

'It's Harvey and Aleph. Harvey has arrived early too.'

Clement and Louise were in the Aviary. Roars of laughter came from Aleph's bedroom. Clement closed the door noisily.

Sefton had let Clement in and he had run up the stairs to find Louise rolling back the carpet in the Aviary. She had already put on her mask. For her mother, Moy always made a special mild gentle mask, not like the grotesque inventions which she often imposed upon the others. When Clement came in the face he saw raised by the kneeling woman was a pale yellow, faintly speckled like the moon, and almost round with jaggedly cut-out eyes, and a green mouth drooping very slightly, expressing a sort of amused clownish sadness. Louise removed the mask at once.

According to recent custom the 'grown ups' did not feel bound to dress up much for the party, apart from perhaps having a mask, whereas the 'children' (and this used to include the young Adwardens) wore full fancy dress. Louise was touched to see that Clement had made a little effort, wearing a silvery satin-tinsel jacket and trousers, doubtless discarded from some theatrical wardrobe, and a long tassellated white silk scarf, such as used to be an essential part of male evening-dress. As Louise watched him he unbuttoned the jacket, removed the black evening tie and stuffed it into his pocket, then brusquely ruffled up his sleek black crest of hair and nervously scratched his dark eyebrows. His face looked to her thinner, almost gaunt, his unusually red lips pouting and vivid. Louise was wearing a long pure white evening-dress which had belonged to her mother. She put the mask down on the piano. Her arms hung down heavily at her sides, something about her own attitude and the white dress made her feel helpless, like a sacrificial victim. She quite often felt like this. As she continued to stare silently at Clement he took off the white silk scarf and put it gently about her neck. A purple light flashed in the tassels of the scarf as they swung.

'It's lovely!' said Louise, stroking the scarf, then beginning to take it off.

'Keep it. It's yours.'

'Oh but – '

'It belonged to my father.'

'The dress belonged to my mother.'

'So there we are. And there's to be dancing.'

'A bit. As we always do. *Please* don't go, dear, dear Clement, I want you to stay here and look after me, you will stay, won't you?'

'Louise, just don't be *silly*.'

Louise thought, yes I am silly, I am a goose, and now I'm going to cry. This evening is going to be a disaster.

The bell rang, Clement opened the door, voices were heard below.

Louise said, 'It's Joan.'

'Oh God. Who's with her?'

'Tessa.'

'I thought she'd given us up.' Tessa went through phases of hostility where Clifton was concerned.

'Joan's brought her. I think she finds us more amusing after recent events.'

Still talking Joan entered the room. Her face was white, with scarlet cheeks and lips, and gold dust widely encircling her sparkling eyes, a wreath of golden leaves crowned her flowing dark red hair. She wore a heavy purple robe with a golden girdle. 'My dear, you don't mind my bringing my bodyguard?'

Tessa had simply dressed up in her smart riding gear, complete with hat and whip.

'Isn't she perfectly brutal? Just look at her boots. Of course I am the Delphic priestess. Hello, Louise darling, when is drinks time? Hello, Clement, kiss me please.'

Tessa in fact looked much as usual, dressed in an only slightly accentuated version of her usual clothes. Clement gazed at the tight handsome material of the breeches. Tessa, after clicking her heels, and bowing to Louise, had put her whip upon the piano and walked to the far end of the room to look at the books and at a few masks put on display there by Sefton. Louise had gone downstairs to fetch drinks. Clement and Joan stood together.

'Hello, Harlequin.'

'Hello, Circe. Sorry, you're the Delphic priestess this evening.'

'And you are her master. Clement, let's *come out*, shall we? Come to Paris with me.'

'As we aren't *in* we can't come *out*. Goodbye, I'm just going.'

'Why are you going, I'll go with you, don't go, what are your motives? Is it because that madman is coming?'

'How did you know he was?'

'Aleph told Harvey who told me. Let's stay and see him. He's rather fun actually, he's like a big circus animal. Darling, please stay with me.'

'All right, for a little while. What's that stuff on your face?'

'Flour. Would you like to lick it?'

Sefton came in carrying a tray with glasses, which she put down on the piano next to Tessa's whip. Sefton, who never took much trouble on these occasions, was wearing black trousers with long black socks over them up to the knee, a black jacket and a black shirt with a purple scarf at the neck. Joan suggested that she was a Nazi, but she claimed to be a bishop, indicating a pendent cross, the property of Moy. ('What's the difference!' said Joan.) Moy had also made her a mitre, which unfortunately 'wouldn't stay on'. The drink, invented by the girls, was imaginative. It consisted of chilled white port, white vermouth, ginger beer, a discreet amount of vodka, and a good deal of apple juice. It was at least guaranteed to taste nice.

'Where's Moy?'

'Upstairs finishing her mask.'

'Or rescuing a spider or communing with a flint.'

'Tessa should have a mask.'

'She says she'll use her face.'

'She could have one of those.'

'This drink is stronger than it seems.'

'It's meant to be.'

'Where's my crippled son, by the way?'

'He's with Aleph.'

'Won't this party *go*?'

'It's only starting, give it a chance.'

'Let's have jollity, Louise will play the piano.'

'Yes, yes, coming, coming!'

At that moment the door was thrown open and a tall military figure entered in a blue uniform with a blue helmet with a blue plume, and a blue beard and a ferocious blue face with bulging cheeks, and leaning upon his arm a dark-haired woman in a long black gown wearing a mantilla and a black veil. There was laughter and clapping. Harvey hastily took off his veil and his mantilla, suddenly irritable and shy, as one who has made himself ridiculous to amuse the children. He was about to remove the wig of long curly black hair, when Louise, coming to kiss him, begged him not to. He limped to the piano and leaned against it. Aleph however stood still, stiff and tall in her uniform, staring out through the sinister blue face of her mask, her arms and gloved hands pointing downward to her jackboots. Sefton cried, 'Oh Aleph, *don't*!' Joan said, 'Really, it's too much.' Someone said, 'Aleph is born to command!' Then everyone started talking at once. Clement, going to Aleph who was still standing as if paralysed stiffly at attention, gently lifted the helmet off her head, releasing a tumble of dark curly hair. Aleph, taking hold of her blue beard, pulled the mask down, letting it hang about her neck. Then taking the helmet from Clement she smilingly donned it again. Meanwhile Sefton was drawing attention to her little exhibit of former masks on one of the shelves from which the books had been removed, and inviting the guests to try them on. Joan put on a Greek mask which was voted terrifying, and Tessa admired, but would not touch, a genuine Japanese, made in Japan, a mask which Joan had donated, gift she said of a rich friend. Sefton then persuaded Tessa to put on the stripy Cheshire Cat mask, 'So that she could be a real puss-in-boots.' Tessa wore this politely for a short while, then put it carefully back on the shelf. She then showed Sefton the proper way to put her mitre on, it was quite easy really. By now Clement had put on his own black elegant, bought in Venice, Venetian mask, which had a long thin tailpiece sweeping down his back, 'Somehow like a gondola,' Joan said. Harvey was sitting beside the piano which Louise, having laid aside her moon mask, was preparing to play. He was fiddling clumsily with the high neck of his black dress (an evening-dress of Aleph's) and pulling at it. A button flew off. Hitching up his skirt, he found it and put it on the piano beside Tessa's whip. Louise began to play.

'Oh good – !'

'What's the music?'

'It's a song – '

'I know, it's that fourth of July thing.'

'Is it the *fourth* of July?'

'It's wonderful to dance to.'

'You can do anything to this tune.'

'Where's Moy?'

'She'll be down in a moment.'

Tessa was dancing with Sefton, Aleph was dancing with Joan. Clement stood behind Louise and put his hands on her shoulders.

The sound of dancing was loud enough to drown the sound of the doorbell which Moy up above heard and ran down to open the door. The fog had thickened and cold air together with a speckled sheet of brown fog atoms flowed quickly into the hall. Outside, motionless, was a tall being. For a moment Moy thought, 'It's a frog footman.' Then she saw that it was not a frog. It was a bull: a big savage bull with great curling horns and huge wild dark eyes fixed upon her. Moy stepped back. Peter Mir stepped in, closing the door behind him. Moy uttered a little cry, a sort of mingled cry of dark fear and strange awful pity. Her guest was already attempting to remove the evidently heavy superstructure which encased his head and shoulders. Moy thought, he'll suffocate, he'll die, fall and die, here in front of me, he'll *die*! Standing on the bottom stair she reached out her hands, helplessly pawing, towards the hard cold muzzle of the beast. The great head rose at last, carrying with it the black velvet drapery which had covered the shoulders. Peter Mir laid it down on the floor, where it stood upright, glaring.

'I hope I didn't frighten you.'

'No, yes – '

'I'm not too late? Or am I too early?'

'No, no, just right. But how do you breathe inside that?'

'Oh quite easily, through the eyes and the mouth – you see it rests on my shoulders and there's lots of space inside.'

'You didn't have a coat.'

'No, my car is nearby, illegally parked as usual. What a merry sound is coming from upstairs, they are dancing and singing too.'

'Yes. Well, do come up.'

'Do you know, I feel shy!'

'Oh don't, I'll go with you. Shall I announce you?'

'No, please not. Tell me, would you mind? I'd like just to talk to you for a little while, just you, in your room. Can we get there without their knowing?'

'Yes – '

'You don't mind?'

'No, no – '

Moy started up the stairs, Peter following carefully carrying the heavy bull's head. The door of the Aviary was slightly ajar. Moy gently pulled it, closing it a little more as she passed. They reached the top landing.

'Anax is in here, we mustn't let him out, we'll slip in quietly.'

They slipped in and closed the door. Peter put the bull's head down in a corner. Anax who had been sitting in his basket, gave a little bark and ran to Peter wagging his tail and beaming. Peter sat down heavily in Moy's little armchair, receiving Anax's paws upon his knees, as the dog licked his face and hands. Moy sat and watched. Peter, speaking to Anax in a soft murmurous tone, perhaps in another language, calmed the dog down, and when Anax was sitting quietly at his feet, transferred his attention to Moy, who was sitting on the bed. 'That must have been a terrible experience with the swan.'

'Yes.'

'But wonderful too in a way?'

'Yes – '

'Would you describe it to me?'

Moy described it. Peter asked questions. 'Did you hesitate before you rushed in? Were you afraid? Did you fall over in the water? Was it as high as your waist? Did the swan fly up and come down on you? Was it on top of you? Did you touch its wings? Did the duck escape? Did you think you'd drown? Did you get all muddy? Did anybody try to help you? How long did it take you to decide to go by bus? How long was it before you got on the bus?'

Moy thought, that's more than *they* ever wanted to know! Then she thought, of course, in his profession, he's used to asking people how they felt!

Moy and Peter looked at each other. Moy, busy earlier preparing the Aviary and making last-minute adjustments to masks, was still in her working clothes, a long straight shift of thick white cotton over black trousers. She had bundled her long pale yellow hair up into a big hasty bun. She was barefoot. She stared at Peter with her wide-apart royal-blue eyes, the eyes of Teddy Anderson. Peter, beneath his disguise, was found to be wearing a very dark green suit of light fine material, with a white shirt and a black bow tie. He seemed to her neater, more somehow 'in order', than when she had last seen him. His closely shaven face was smooth, his plump cheeks rosy, his hair, above his slightly lined brow, abundant and curly, a glowing brown, his eyes, she could see now, a very dark grey, or grey-brown, like a deep pool.

'Did you buy that thing?'

'No, I hired it.'

'What's it made of?'

'Some sort of plastic. So you collect stones. I knew that anyway.'

'How did you know?'

'Aleph told me. Many happy returns of your birthday. How old are you now?'

'Sixteen.'

'Ah – it is a lovely age. I wish you, with all my heart, a happy fate. I have brought you a birthday present, I wanted to give it to you by yourself, not with the others, here it is.' Leaning forward he put a package wrapped in fancy paper into Moy's hands. It was heavy. Moy, surprised, held it in her lap, then put it on the bed, looking at him speechless.'

'Open it, open it, I want to see you open it.'

Moy tore off the wrapping, opened the cardboard container within, and pulled aside a lot of tissue paper. Out of this nest she lifted a little blue box with golden trimmings. Moy saw at once that the box was made of lapis lazuli and that the trimmings were real gold. She had seen something like it in the British Museum. 'It's Russian.'

'Yes. How did you know? Well, I'm Russian myself. Do you like it?'

'I like it *very* much, I *love* it – but it's so – grand – and – '

'It belonged to my family, the family motto is inscribed inside the lid in Latin, *virtuti paret robur*'.

Moy opened the box.

'Dear me, it's empty,' said Peter. 'How silly of me, I ought to have put something inside it, I'll send you something to put inside it.'

Moy reached up to the shelf by her bed and picked up a round pure white pebble and put it inside the box. 'Oh I love it so – it's – But it's too much – I mean – '

'Well, I certainly won't take it away again! Perhaps I shall send presents – to all of you – but this is specially for you. Now shall we go downstairs?'

'I must change – '

'Oh yes, and put on your mask, I think I can see it there? I'll wait outside.' He jumped up and went out onto the landing closing the door.

Moy sat holding the precious box. Her heart was beating hard. She thought, it's too much. Do I have to go this way into the enchanter's palace? But of course, it isn't *me* that he – She hugged the box, then put it away carefully in a drawer and covered it over with clothes.

She pulled off her cotton shift and quickly donned a white blouse and over it a golden brown velvet jerkin, with trousers to match, then brown socks and sandals. Then she donned her mask which was, as always, much less elaborate than those of the others, but (as she was always told) more simply beautiful and impressive. It consisted of a three-sided cardboard box, making a hat, and over her face, held simply by elastic bands and paper clips, a piece of thick white paper, with two egg-shaped eye-holes, upon which Moy had drawn, simply, with a few lines, the face of an owl: the outline of his face, his pricked-up ears, his fierce commanding eyebrows, his long pointed gracefully curving beak, his thin mouth and the two dots of his nostrils. The eye-holes were disposed so as to show only a little of the outside corners of Moy's eyes, as if the eyes were tiny. The effect was disturbing. She emerged, talking to Anax and closing the door upon him.

'Oh you are so delightful – so full of power, you have your *wise* look – what a fine pair we are – but look – I want you to lead me down – ' Peter had donned his huge bull head, his voice echoing inside the structure.

'How – ?'

'I am your pet, tell them I am your pet, the owl shall lead the bull, beauty and the beast, quick, have you got a piece of rope or – '

Moy opened the door again and pulled a long green girdle out of her smart dressing-gown, which she had inherited from Aleph, and handed one end of it to Peter, who knotted it round his bull neck. They moved cautiously down the stairs, hesitating at the now closed door of the Aviary, beyond which the sound of the piano, the dancing, the intermittent singing, was now deafening. Moy threw open the door and stepped in leading Peter behind her. The noise died down, then ceased. Moy announced in her high nervous voice. 'Look, I have brought my pet with me!' There was another instant's silence, then laughter, clapping, voices. Then Peter, who had been solemnly nodding, was seen to be again in trouble with his head-dress. 'Help him!' cried Moy, tearing off her mask. Clement ran forward and pulled the heavy simulacrum off, depositing it upon the floor. Those who were still masked took off their masks respectfully.

'Everything deep loves a mask? Who said that?'

'I've no idea,' said Harvey testily.

'Never mind. What were you talking about so earnestly with Tessa?'

The party was over. Peter and Tessa and Joan had departed. Peter left early, saying that he had better go, since at midnight he would turn into a bull. It was now after midnight. Moy had gone to bed. Louise had retired. Clement had left. Sefton, now, without her mitre and her cross and her purple scarf, all in black, was moving about soft-footed, tidying things up, as usual, although everyone had said, as usual, that it should all be left until tomorrow. She could be heard carefully, quietly, placing glasses on trays and padding up and down the stairs. Harvey and Aleph were in Aleph's room, Harvey sitting on the chair by the dressing-table, Aleph, her feet tucked under her, upon the bed. Harvey was dressed in shirt and trousers which he had discreetly resumed before the end of the proceedings. Aleph who had soon discarded her savage blue mask, still wore her, as they called it, 'dictator's' uniform, now rather unbuttoned, and had just replaced the plumed helmet upon her curling dark hair. Harvey, who had drunk steadily throughout the evening, was flushed and had tormented his straight blond hair into a positive tangle. He had looked forward to the evening with horror, wanted to refuse to come, but knew he had to come: not to come would have been impolite, cowardly, an admission of defeat, a gesture of despair. In fact, though awful, it was not quite as awful as he expected partly, he realised, because no one paid any attention to him! Apart from a very few perfunctory 'sympathetic' commonplaces, his presence as a spectator was taken for granted: much as if, as he had said later to Aleph, he had been born crippled! Every day he wondered whether his wounded foot had become a little better. Sometimes he thought it had, more often he thought it had not. He had, for the time being, abandoned doctors, and consorted now only with a physiotherapist, who seemed to be accepting him as a chronic case and speaking of alleviation not of cure. His experience at the party of being somehow patently classified as a cripple had been very distressing, yet he also grimly accepted the distress as a kind of refuge, a cover. How had he endured without crying out aloud the sight of Aleph dancing with Clement, dancing with Peter Mir? He so longed to dance himself, his foot, his poor foot, yearned to dance. Yet he stayed quietly in his refuge, only Sefton and Tessa had sat down beside him.

'With Tessa?' he said. 'Nothing much, I forget. Actually we were talking about Lucas.'

'What about Lucas?'

'Oh, about the Mir business, why Lucas seems to hate everybody, then about Lucas's sex life, we agreed he obviously hadn't any – Mir is another matter. He's not married, is he?'

'He doesn't seem to be.'

'I must say he dances well. What was that number you all danced to at the start and kept on coming back to it?'

'I forget. "*Numeros memini si verba tenerem.*" '

'Oh stow it. Did you talk to him? Is he sane? I heard you saying just now that he was something out of *Beowulf*.'

'I didn't talk to him. He has come out of the darkness. I think he is sane.'

'But sinister? That bull's head was going too far.'

'He doesn't yet know our simple ways.'

'You mean he proposes to stay around?'

'Don't you think we owe him something?'

'No. You women are so naive. Oh Aleph if you only knew how grievous all is within.'

'Your wound will heal.'

'I have been struck down before my life begins. I have already died in the war.'

'Youth at the prow, and pleasure at the helm?'

'Ah, we were young *then* – '

'Shall I call you a taxi? Have you got enough money?'

'Emil sent me a cheque to pay for taxis. Why won't you come and see me at my grand flat? Come tonight. Oh never mind. A fine romance with no kisses.'

'Harvey, I have given you many many kisses, you have forgotten them.'

'In your dreams – or in mine. Children's kisses. Goodnight, dear sister. Kiss me now. Oh Aleph – '

'I know – I know – '

'It's still terribly foggy.'

'And he called her "Princess Alethea".'

'He said, "I feel you are my family". He says he's going to buy a flat near here.'

'How sickening.'

'I thought it was rather touching.'

'It was impertinent, even sinister.'

'Well, he's probably joking a bit.'

'We don't even know where he lives.'

Clement had not left after all. He was in Louise's bedroom. They were standing beside the window, where Louise had drawn back the curtain to study the fog. Clement had thrown his overcoat onto the bed. He had given his Venetian mask to Moy, and

215

now regretted it. She had said she would keep it for him till next year. Next year! he thought. God knows where we shall all be next year! Louise was wearing her long white dress, with Clement's silk scarf clutched closely round her neck with one hand, while with her other hand she was nervously disordering her stiff brown hair. She let go of the scarf, letting it hang, and pulled the curtain back into place. The gesture reminded her of her first glimpse of Peter Mir when she had seen him down below, standing in the street and seeming to watch the house. She had been about to undress when Clement had knocked on her door. She had felt very tired and had looked forward to reading a little more of *A Glastonbury Romance* and then going to sleep. She had felt relief at the evening being over without any catastrophes. And now Clement had arrived, determined to tell her awful things which she did not want to hear.

'I think he means it.'

'Who? Oh, Peter – '

'So he's Peter now!'

'He kept insisting on it. Why are you so against him?'

'Oh I'm not *against* him!' said Clement turning impatiently away. He sat down heavily on the neat bed. 'Except that – I've *got* to be – !'

Louise sat down at her dressing-table, now laying the long silk scarf across her knee. The smell of her cosmetics seemed suffocating, disagreeable, as if they were all *old*. Lately Louise had decided to give up wearing make-up altogether, but had not yet acted upon the decision.

As Clement did not elucidate this saying, Louise said, 'He was kind to Moy, he – '

'Yes, what was that charade, I was meaning to ask you?'

'She let him in and he went up to her room and they had a long talk and he asked her about the swan – '

'He had no right to go up to her room! He pushes his way into this house and marches up to the girls' rooms!'

'I'm sorry, Clement, I asked a silly question just now. About that other time – and what happened – surely it was clear that he was simply mistaken, he was having delusions, he admitted he was all confused – he must have recognised this by now, he *must* have done, or he wouldn't have come here and been so nice to us all.'

Clement gave a long sigh and looked at his watch. 'I'm afraid *you* are mistaken. What he wants is something in return.'

'In return?'

'In return for his life, for the ruin of his life. He wants revenge. He may seek it even here. He is a dangerous animal, he is ruthless.'

Louise listened. She felt very tired, she felt confused, she found that she *could not remember* exactly what had been said by Clement and by Peter in that confrontation. 'But he was perfectly nice to you at the party.'

'No. He evaded me, he ignored me, we avoided each other, it was easy, it was like a dance, like a terrible dance. Louise, I must go home. I've talked too much.'

'I don't understand, is Peter angry because Lucas said he was a thief – he's not a thief is he – surely you can't believe *that*!'

'Oh Louise, do leave it alone, you will never understand, at least I hope you will never understand! Leave it alone. Only – please – don't let that man into our lives.'

'I can't leave it alone. What does Lucas think?'

'I don't know, to hell with what Lucas thinks. I've drunk too much. I must go home now.' He rose and began to pull on his coat.

'Clement, I can't believe it's as awful as you say.'

'No, no, it isn't, I'm exaggerating.'

Louise rose and went to the door, putting her back to it. 'But, Clement, there must be some solution, some *clarification*, I can't bear it – '

'You don't want to lose your picture of Peter Mir as a sort of teddy bear.' He came and stood before her and said softly, *'Just don't meddle.'*

They stared at each other. For a second Clement closed his eyes and his face was contorted with pain. Louise held her hands together as if each hand were capturing the other. She stepped aside. The long white scarf which had been upon her knee had fallen to the ground. Automatically she picked it up and folded it and held it out to him.

'Louise, I gave it to you!'

'Oh yes, of course, I'm so sorry! Well – goodnight – drive carefully.'

They stood still for another moment not moving, then he slipped quickly out of the door, quietly closing it behind him.

Louise stood quite still for a time, until well after the sound of his footsteps had died away. Then, moving slowly, she turned to the bed and drew back the wrinkled coverlet. Then she sat down on the bed and buried her face in the scarf.

Later, when she had at last undressed and gone to bed and turned out the lights, she lay on her back open-eyed. I run, I run, I am gathered to your heart. But no, she thought, it's not like that. I am alone. I cannot *reach* anybody.

Clement, realising he was indeed rather drunk, carefully held onto the banister as he descended the stairs. The lower flight of stairs was dark, the hallway was dark, the house was silent. He fumbled for some time at the door, dreading to discover that it was locked in some special way and he would have to crawl back up the stairs to Louise. At last the door, with a little noise, opened itself, and he paused in the doorway, letting in the cold muzzy air and the cold darkness outside where the street lamps could not penetrate. Then he heard in the silence a little sound, someone, breathing, softly, regularly, deeply – it was Sefton, fast asleep, within a few feet of where he stood. He edged out carefully, closed the door, unable now to prevent its sharp locking sound. He stumbled down the two steps to the pavement and stood there, fumbling for his car keys and trying to remember where he had left the car. His bare head felt very cold. He began to walk along the darkened empty street.

Oh God, what an absolute bloody fool I am, Clement said to himself. Why did I stay and talk to Louise? Now I've upset her and I've set her off *wanting to know*. *God*, I don't want her probing into this. Suppose she goes to Lucas? But no – she wouldn't dare to. All the women are frightened of him. But oh – what a dismal wretched part I am playing now. Surely I could have *got out* of it all – yet how? I am condemned to lead an utterly false life – now and – how can it end? It can't end. I've got to go on and on living with lies and mystifications. How on earth have I got into this trap? I see now, *now*, how I am condemned to be cut off from all the people who were so near and dear to me, who esteemed and loved me – I've got to be a liar forever – and somehow – oh I don't deserve it, it wasn't my fault!

Clement, walking a little erratically and now murmuring his thoughts aloud, was suddenly, horribly, aware of another person, a huge form looming up beside him and bumping violently against him. A lightning flash of terror pierced him. He thought, it's the end, now I shall be robbed and killed. He tried to cry out but could produce only a little high sound and flutter his helpless hands in pathetic supplication as his assailant, gripping his shoulders with terrible force, drove him back against a wall. Then as the force became an agonisingly painful pressure there was a kind of silence as he helplessly ceased to struggle, became aware of what had so abominably happened to him, and gasped out, 'Don't hurt me.'

Peter Mir, slightly loosening his hold, continued to pin him against the wall. Clement could feel his scalp being scraped against the bricks. He tried feebly to remove the hand, the huge giant hand, which spanned his throat. He could feel the bones of his throat giving way. 'Why did you lie? You didn't tell the truth. Why did you lie to them?' The pressure was released and Clement slipped down, almost falling to the ground. Mir now gripped him brutally by the shoulder, pulling him up and peering closely into his face. When Clement tried to turn his head away, Mir gripped his chin with his other hand. 'Why? Why?' Mir let go his hold, still leaning his heavy body against Clement. Then he moved suddenly gripping Clement by the arm and hustling him, dangling and dragging, across the frosty pavement. Clement lost his footing and stumbled against the long wet slippery surface of a large car. Mir, opening the car door with one hand, propelled him violently into the dark interior, then plunged in himself, roughly jostling Clement, who felt a sharp pain in his ankle.

For a moment they sat together in the back of the car, both gasping, Mir uttering an audible 'Pah! Pah!' and pressing up against Clement. Clement, trying to find his voice, was interrupted by Mir.

'But *why?*'

'Why what?'

'Why did you lie to them?'

'What did you expect me to do? Why should *they* be upset and made miserable? They at least are out of it. There's no need to involve me – not just because I don't want to be involved, but it would *do no good*. Why confuse and upset all those innocent people? Consider *them*. What was I supposed to tell them? After all what do *we* know – we don't *know* – '

'What do you mean, what don't we know?'

'What would have happened if you had not intervened.'

'It is obvious what would have happened.'

'It would not be obvious in a court of law. And it is not obvious to me. I am sure Lucas didn't want to kill me, he couldn't have done, it was a charade, he just wanted to frighten me! You don't know him, I know him! I told *them* you were innocent and they believed me. There is no point in stirring it all up. Why should we burden them with all this horror? Please now leave them alone. *Please*. Enough has been said.'

'Enough has been said! That is your solution, is it, that solves everything? What I desire and what I deserve is justice, and I shall have it. You admitted to me that you knew – '

'When did I admit anything?'

'When you thanked me for saving your life.'

'I was simply recognising you! Can't you take in that it is *not possible* to prove that Lucas intended to kill me? He sent me away simply to protect me – I swear that he did not – '

'Now you have changed your tone, and what you say betrays you. You shall be exposed as a liar. Justice and truth will destroy you both. *They already know – '*

'*Please* do not see them, leave them alone, leave the girls alone – '

'And you have mean despicable motives. I shall talk to them in my own fashion, they must know the whole truth.'

'Don't threaten us like this. I shall tell them you are dangerous, I shall tell them you are mad.'

'Dangerous, yes. With the innocent I shall be innocent, and with the devilish, a devil. As for you, I shall see that you are punished. Now *keep out of my way*.'

Mir leaning across Clement opened the door of the car and pushed him violently. As Clement was stumbling out he was pushed again, then punched in the back. Wailing, he began to run away at random.

My dear son,
Thank you for your letter and please excuse a delayed reply, I have been in retreat. Our communication with others can

have no value unless it is truthful. We must be, for each other, in the truth. Your recent letters are becoming, it seems to me, increasingly more expressive of Byronic romanticism than of the spiritual ecstasy which I believe you imagine yourself to be experiencing. The fault is partly mine for having encouraged a correspondence which I now think to be at the moment not helpful, but a positive obstacle. I beg you to reflect humbly upon your situation, making a serious endeavour to distance yourself from the self-gratification which you mistake for adoration of God. The greedy cunning self has many ways of deceiving; as I know well in my own imperfect struggles! He said, 'I am the way, the truth and the life'. We are all of us far distant from that way, that truth and that life. Always tell yourself that the truth lies beyond, and ponder this quietly and darkly. A true ecstasy is the reward of very few. A positive desire to suffer, to be, as you put it, in hell and spurned by Christ, a desire to be destroyed: these are familiar daydreams, fictions contrived by the evil one who dwells at home in the soul of man. I begin to feel that our correspondence may be engendering in you simply illusions, and that anything I say to you becomes in you illusion. This is of course my fault. One of the greatest temptations is the self-consoling wish to be the saviour of another's soul. There is only one Saviour. Think about your happiness, and how you can be happy in helping others. You need society and ordinary friendships. I begin to think that you ought not to live alone. Your 'depression', if I may continue to use the word in a general sense, may be partly caused by a lack of regular employment. Do not spend your time 'waiting for the call' or imagining that you will shortly be entering a religious house. I suggest that you do not write to me now for a considerable time. I think an interval may refresh us both! (Regard it, if you like, as a penance!) I will write to you later on. Do not answer this letter. You are in my loving thoughts and my prayers.

Yours in Christo,
Fr Damien

P.S. As for the famous mouse who ate the Holy Sacrament, I have been told on good authority that he has become a favoured pet of Our Lady!

My dear Father,
Please forgive this instant reply to your last letter. Yes, yes,
I understand about what you are telling me about being in
the truth and how far away from it I am. But I must see you.
I feel it is a time of crisis in my life. In fact I have found
another person, I mean a *spiritual* person, one whom I *revere*,
who is quite literally struggling with the devil. Only I can
help him. But you must help *me*. I would like very much to
bring him to you, though I fear he might not agree to come.
Please say that I may come to see you in the near future, with
or without my noble but unhappy friend. I am so sorry to
write like this, disobeying your request, but the matter is
urgent. *I am very sorry.* Penitentially and with love,

Yours,
Bellamy

My dear son,
Please *do not come* here. I shall be *absolutely unable* to see
you. As for your spiritual friend, I think you should proceed
with caution. This is not a moment for you to form strong
emotional attachments, such attempted 'rescues' often drag
down both the 'saver' and the 'saved'. This can be the region
of the demonic. I hope you will understand me, though I
write without knowledge of the case. As I said, *do not write*.
I will communicate with you at a suitable time. *Pray* – pray
every moment. I pray for you. Pray for me.

in Christo,
Fr Damien

'So he wouldn't see you? And you even suggested bringing me!'
    'Yes. I still hope to bring you to him.'
    'You forget that I am Jewish.'
    'Peter, what on earth does that matter! All salvation is in some
way the same.'
    'I think you mean that all religions are in some way the same,
which is far from being the case.'

'All right, never mind. I just thought you, we, might be helped by a man who has lived for so many years alone with God.'

Bellamy and Peter were once again sitting in The Castle. Bellamy was once again drinking lager. It was the morning after the party. On the previous day, after Lucas had laughingly refused to let Bellamy be his bodyguard, and had sent him away, Bellamy had sat in his room wondering if after all he *would* go to the party, even though it would upset Anax, and even though he didn't like that party with its noise and merriment and masks and dancing (Bellamy couldn't dance) and screams of laughter and the youthful gaiety of children. He had not enjoyed it last year. Of course he did not go, he sat thinking miserably about things which Peter had said. Something must be done. He did not even know where Peter lived, no one seemed to know where he lived. He was not in the telephone book. He ate no lunch but went out in the afternoon and bought some sandwiches. He went round to the house where the young Catholic priest lived but he was not there. When he returned to his room he discovered Father Damien's latest letter. He stood reading it, then stood thinking about it, looking at the dirty window pane and the half-closed curtains. Then he sat on his bed and ate two sandwiches. Then he read it again, together with two previous letters. As it had become dark he pulled the curtains. Roars of laughter came from the Pakistani family in the flat upstairs. The taciturn elderly man on the second floor had moved out. Bellamy felt guilty for not having made serious attempts to befriend him. Where was he now? He ate another sandwich, but it was already stale. A sense of futility and nullity came quietly to him like a mist. He boiled some water and filled his hot-water bottle. He had intended to give up sleeping-pills, but took two pills and went to bed. When he woke in daylight his watch had stopped. He noticed that since he had gone to bed in his clothes he did not have to dress. He fed the electric fire and made some toast but there was no butter. He read the terrible letters again. He decided to go out to get some food and ring up Clement. But instead he sat hunched up on his bed. He found himself saying aloud 'Spingle-spangle'. Then he decided to go to The Castle just in case.

By daylight, there was even a little mild sunlight, The Castle looked less stark and metallic, less positively weightless and spherical, less like a spaceship. It was certainly small, but Bellamy now noticed, which he had not noticed on the first occasion, that there were little shallow alcoves, saucer-like depressions, in one of which he and Peter were sitting, set in a neat semi-circle. Perhaps it was like a little theatre, or a tiny chapel, where the bar took the place of the stage, or the chancel, and the landlord (for he clearly was the landlord) that of the actor or the priest, as he stood there with his arms stretched out and his large hands gripping the counter, gazing with benign inquisitive satisfaction upon his clientele (or spectators or sinners). There were a few small tables in the central space, but those were empty. The alcoves were different colours, the one occupied (as on the previous occasion) by Peter and Bellamy was green. A few customers were occupying the other alcoves and talking in low tones, thus adding to the ecclesiastical atmosphere. Bellamy and Peter also spoke quietly. Bellamy wondered what time it was.

'What time is it? How wonderful that you arrived just after I came!'

'Nearly twelve. No, no. Ascetics are not saints, they are just as likely to be madmen seeking for magic power or miserable remorseful wretches with a spite against the world. It is more likely that *you* could help *him*. That is what he wants to conceal! Why don't you stop playing at destitution?'

'Please – '

'I am sorry. You have intruded upon my troubles and must take the consequences. You know that I have lost something. There is something, perhaps the most important thing of all, which I have forgotten.'

'Is it a good thing or a bad thing?'

'I don't know! If I knew – anyway it has got to be finished.'

'You mean about Lucas?'

'And then there are the women.'

'Is what you have forgotten something about a woman?'

'I tell you, I don't know! I mean there are *those* women.'

'Yes, and surely for their sakes – '

'You know nothing about hatred. There is an old maxim, let your enemy think he can escape, cornered he will fight to the death, fleeing he may be cut down – let him think he has an alternative to death.'

'These are evil thoughts. Can you not kill these thoughts?'

'They say a murderer returns to the place of his crime.'

'There was no murder.'

'And where a murder has been committed – something remains.'

'You mean something evil?'

'I feel if I returned to the place where I lost my memory I might regain it.'

'Well, I would go with you.'

'Let it all happen again.'

'Perhaps as a sort of rite of purification, like a sort of redemption – perhaps something like this cured some of your patients?'

'We could re-enact the scene!'

'You mean by doing it again, miming it, to disperse, to melt away all your anger and your hate? Surely you mean it like that? Oh please let it be like that! Peter, can't you just *forgive* him. *Forgive* him and then everything will be well. And *then* you will find out – '

'For me, nothing can ever be well again. If he were kneeling in front of me, I'd kick his eyes out.'

'But it wasn't his fault, it was a mistake, it was an *accident.*'

'There was no accident. That man was about to kill his brother. He killed me instead. I have given my life for that brother. Justice must be done.'

'But no one else was there! You had a dream and you wanted to tell it.'

'Go to your friend the younger brother, go and ask him, ask him to tell you the truth. There must be a final solution. I must damage him as he has damaged me. I want to maim and cripple him as he has maimed and crippled me. All the evil of that blow has entered into me. Now he must pay. I invoke blind justice with her sword and scales. It has got to be finished even if it comes to pistol shots. Wickedness must be punished. Nothing will bring me peace except revenge.'

'Peter, please be quiet and don't talk in this mad awful way. You are trapped by hideous thoughts and dreams, if you could only put them away and show forgiveness and mercy, you could heal yourself, you could set yourself free, you could set us all free. Perhaps that *could* happen if we returned to that place. *Think* about it. You have this great power. You could enact a miracle.'

'So you still imagine I am an angel?'

'I am certain of it. You are a good angel. This is what you *have* to be. And something in your soul knows it.'

'By the way, did they tell you about Anax?'

'No, what?'

'He got lost and I found him. I happened to meet him.'

'*That's* a miracle. I knew you could do them! You sent out a signal and he came to you! He perceived your goodness! There you are! You must believe in your good powers!'

'I charm only the innocent. That's not much good.'

'Peter, I'm sorry, but I am terribly hungry.'

'Well, let us eat. And, if we can, talk about other things. I went to that party.'

'To the birthday party? So they invited you – that's wonderful!'

'Yes, after I found the dog they had to!'

'And did you talk to Clement?'

'Yes.'

'I'm so glad!'

Breakfast at Clifton was no formal feast, no sitting down together with a blessing implied or otherwise. Moy, waking at six from deep sleep, would dress, descend, let Anax out into the garden, drink some milk and eat some oats, return to her bedroom, make her bed and lie upon it supine open-eyed for half an hour. This was known as Moy's 'White Time' when she planned her working day or allowed her soul to leave her body; after which, usually, she would set ferociously to work. Sefton rose almost as early, made some tea, ate some toast, and listened to the seven o'clock news; then, except in darkest winter, went into the garden for some brief gardening. Moy fed the birds and stroked the trees, but Sefton tended the plants and mowed the lawn. (There were two small trees, planted after arrival at Clifton, a laburnum and a Japanese maple.) As Sefton was returning to her books Aleph, in dressing-gown, was making her way to her bath. Neither Moy nor Sefton cared much about baths. By this time Louise, who preferred an evening bath, was occupying the kitchen and boiling an egg. Aleph's breakfast came later and lasted until after the eight o'clock news. Louise, when the kitchen was empty again, did the washing up, which Sefton allowed her to do at this time of day only. Sefton did not like the washing-up machine, which was now rarely used. Louise listened anxiously to the movements of the girls, plotting their soft-footed whereabouts. She had come to feel almost in awe of meeting them early in the morning. They had become, year by year, month by month, mysterious to her, her love for them an extended pain, a web or field of force, of which she felt at times the almost breaking tension.

The post, if any, arrived about nine o'clock. On the day in question, which happened to be a Saturday, four days after the birthday party, Louise and Aleph were in the Aviary discussing Aleph's forthcoming holiday with Rosemary Adwarden. Moy, her 'White Time' over, had washed her very long hair and was drying it beside the electric fire in her bedroom, teasing out the damp strands between her fingers. Her blonde hair had red streaks here and there. Sefton's brown hair also admitted many lines of red. Louise spoke of Teddy's 'Viking look'. Anax, let in from the garden by Sefton, raced up the stairs, his claws clicking on the linoleum, and scratched at Moy's door. She rose to let him in and received his leaping and pawing ecstasy as if they had not met for days. Has he forgotten, she wondered. No, it was not possible. Sefton, sitting on the floor in her little room beside the kitchen, was wondering what would have happened if, when Isabella and Mortimer had murdered Edward II, they had also had the nerve to murder his young son Edward III. Perhaps the Hundred Years War would not have occurred?

The front doorbell rang, Sefton jumped up and opened the door, it was the postman. He handed over a letter to Aleph from Rosemary Adwarden (Sefton recognised Rosemary's daft writing) and three packets sealed up in brown paper. She took all these into the kitchen and put them on the table. She noticed with surprise that one of the packets was addressed to herself. Sefton did not often receive packages by post. She then noticed that the other two were addressed to Moy and Aleph respectively, and that the writing upon these packages was the same. She hesitated, was about to call out, when curiosity overcame her and, with the help of a kitchen knife, for it was well sealed, she prised open her package. Inside the brown paper there was tissue paper, and inside the tissue paper was a shiny cardboard box, and inside the box was an amber necklace. She drew it out. Sefton possessed no jewellery except for a string of wooden beads which Moy had made for her. She knew at once that the necklace which she held in her hand was no common thing but something grand, composed of glowing faintly transparent light brown amber, with little silver pearl-like beads here and there between the pieces making a pattern, the necklace joining into a single string weighted at the end by a pendent drop of larger even more glowing amber, lightly carved and warm to the touch. She held it up for a moment, then searched the packaging for a note or message. There was none. She carried the necklace into her bedroom and for a moment put it round her neck. There was no mirror, and she hastily took it off again and thrust it into the pocket of her corduroy jacket. Her swift mind had of course at once penetrated the mystery. She ran out to the foot of the stairs and called the others, 'Post! Presents!'

Aleph and Louise appeared, then Moy, bundling her still damp hair into a thick rope, twisting the rope round and round upon the nape of her neck and securing it with an elastic band. Sefton watched. After interested exclamations about the two packets Louise put the kettle on, Aleph sat down at the table and started reading Rosemary's letter. Moy, deftly using the sharp knife, cut through the thick sealing tape and undid the brown paper. She looked at the writing on it. 'What odd writing, it looks foreign, who can it be from? Look, Aleph has one too.' She undid the tissue paper, and opened the box, Sefton already standing behind her to view the contents. There was a blue necklace inside. Moy, now silent, drew it out. Louise turned, Aleph looked up. Louise said, 'What is it?' Moy said, 'It's lapis lazuli.' 'Oh, heavens – but who's it from?' Moy said, 'It's from Peter.' She sat down at the table beside Aleph. 'Peter – oh you mean – ' 'Yes.' 'How do you know, is there a message?' 'No.' 'Of course, it's a birthday present, how kind! But it must be very expensive.' 'Well, he's rich, isn't he,' said Aleph, putting away her letter.

Moy, sitting motionless, stared at the necklace which she had put down, spilling out of its box.

Louise said, 'Oh – Moy – ' She sat down beside Moy, gazing at her. Moy turned to her and smiled and put her hand affectionately upon her mother's arm, seeking the wrist beyond the cuff.

Sefton said, 'Aleph has got one too, and so have I.' She took the amber necklace out of her pocket and laid it upon the table. Moy fingered it and admired it.

'You can have it,' said Sefton to Moy, 'I never wear jewellery.'

'No, it's yours, *he* wanted you to have it.'

'The blue goes with Moy's eyes,' said Louise, 'and the amber goes with Sefton's eyes, and her hair.'

'Then what about Aleph?' cried Sefton. 'Come on, Aleph, open yours!'

'I can't open the package, it's all glued up. You open it, Moy.'

Moy opened it as far as the box, which she handed back to Aleph.

Aleph, frowning slightly, as if fastidious, opened the box and lifted out a heavy sparkling mass. The others, exclaiming and averting their eyes, could not at first see what it was. Aleph ordered it, holding it up between her hands.

'*Diamonds!*' said Moy.

Sefton said nothing but looked at her mother.

Louise thought, oh – this is *too much* – it's frightening, it's *sinister*. She said in a mute soulless voice, 'I suppose they are real –'

'Louie, of course they are,' said Sefton, 'how can they not be!'

'We can't accept them,' said Louise.

'We've accepted amber and lapis, so why not diamonds!' said Moy, and then laughed one of her rare wailing laughs.

Aleph had now arranged the necklace on the table making the shape of a V-shaped collar. The diamonds sparkled emitting blue and sometimes yellow light. 'They are alive,' said Moy.

'Moy thinks everything is alive,' said Sefton, 'I heard her say sorry to a piece of lemon peel.'

'Whatever are we to do?' said Louise.

'Write him thank you letters,' said Sefton.

'But we don't know his address. And anyway we *can't* – it's not right –'

Aleph gathered up the sparkling mass and dropped it back into its box. She uttered a long deep sigh. Then she rose and left the room taking the box with her. Sefton laughed. The two girls stared at their mother, who was rubbing her hands violently over her face and tugging at her stiff hair which stood up between her fierce fingers.

'Why worry so much, Louie?' said Sefton. 'Don't be so old-fashioned.'

'Don't be a fool, Sefton!' said Louise. Sefton was startled at her tone and looked at Moy, raising her eyebrows.

'Let's ring up Clement,' said Moy.

'You think Clement is the measure of all things!' said Sefton.

'I mean, he probably knows Peter's address.'

'Louie dear, I'm sorry – ' said Sefton.

Moy said, 'I think it would be unkind to refuse the presents.'

'Ungracious,' said Sefton. 'All right, it is a bit embarrassing. But what else can we do?'

'He said he had no family,' said Moy, 'and he wanted us to be his family.'

'Louie,' said Sefton, 'it isn't that we madly want to keep these baubles, it's just a matter of decorum.'

Louise rose and faced her two daughters, Sefton with her short jagged red-brown hair and her green-brown hazel eyes and her sturdy commanding presence, and Moy with her blue Teddy eyes and her hair hastily twisted into a mass upon her neck, making her look older. Louise thought, *what will happen to them* – perhaps just this is the beginning of some awful end. She said, 'Just *think*. Don't you remember that awful scene?'

Sefton said, 'Yes. But let's leave *that* alone.'

'These presents are a bribe. He wants us on his side. He's forcing us to come out for him, to endorse his story, to *decide* for *him*.'

'Well, what do we think?' said Sefton. 'You had a long talk with him, Moy.'

'It wasn't about that.'

'Of course not, silly, but what did you make of him?'

'He's very strange,' said Moy, 'I can see him as an analyst trying to probe people and – help them – then something terrible happens to him – and everything's upside down – But I don't think he's bad. I think really he's kind and good, there's something simple about him, only – '

'So you think he's truthful?' said Louise. 'You say he's strange. Perhaps he's mad – or extremely ill.'

'You see how difficult it is,' said Sefton, 'it's like in history when you simply can't decide. All right, one looks about for evidence – but I for one can't see at all clearly here. I don't think accepting the presents need imply we swallow everything. It is a bit unfair to expect so much of us – '

'Exactly.'

'But if we grandly send the stuff back we can't continue to hover, we're in the fray.'

'But if we keep the stuff we're in the fray too.'

'I don't think so – we can be just passive. It's forced on us, we didn't ask for it. As I said,' said Sefton, 'I am not motivated by any desire to keep this expensive necklace – if it would clarify the situation I'd gladly throw it in the Thames!'

'About mine,' said Moy, 'I feel it as a special personal gift from him, and if I returned it it would hurt his feelings.'

'I wonder if Aleph will want to keep those diamonds!' said Sefton. 'It is a bit pointed, isn't it, as if he were courting her!'

'Has that only just occurred to you?' said Louise.

'As if we, or she, could be bought? I doubt if he's thought of it.'

'Then he is very naive!'

'Perhaps he is naive. Moy thinks he is.'

'I don't know what I think,' said Moy, 'I like him – '

'In spite of his being so nasty to Clement?'

'But perhaps he's dangerous, I think he could be.'

'You mean dangerous to Lucas,' said Louise.

'We've kept Lucas out of it so far,' said Sefton, 'I mean *we* have – '

'I shall go and see him,' said Louise.

'You mean see Lucas?'

'Yes.'

'Don't,' said Sefton, '*don't.*'

'Are you frightened of him,' said Moy, 'or do you think we'd just make things worse?'

'I think we should do *nothing*' said Sefton, 'but if something *must* be done let Louie ring up Clement.'

'All right, all right! I'll ring him later!'

Louise left the kitchen and went upstairs. Sefton was about to go to her own room when Moy showed her a piece of paper which she had taken from her pocket.

'What does it mean?'

'*Virtuti paret robur.* Strength obeys virtue. I wish it were true!'

'Hello Harvey, this is Emil.'

'Oh Emil – good – good morning! How are you?'

'I do not ring too early?'

'No, no, I've been up for ages.'

'Studying of course!'

'Of course!'

'So I interrupt your studies?'

'No, no, not at all, I'm so glad to talk to you! Are you in Germany? Are you having a lovely time?'

'Am I in Germany, yes. Am I having a lovely time, yes and no. And the cleaning lady, she has come?'

'Oh yes, she has come, she's so nice, we have nice chats.'

'Also she cleans?'

'Also she cleans!'

'And how is your beautiful mother?'

'Oh she's all right, she's fine. I've invited her to tea today.'

'You are a good boy. And you get on with your studies. And you have been comfortable in the flat?'

'Your beautiful flat has been heaven to me. I thank you *so much* – '

'Good, good. And your leg is better?'

'No – I mean yes, it is.'

'Is your mother soon going back to Paris?'

'Oh yes, pretty soon – '

'And you can now climb the stairs to your own flat to see her?'

'Oh yes, yes – '

'Good. Forgive my shortness. You know I abominate the telephone.'

'Where are you now, are you in the mountains?'

'No. I am in Berlin. Give my affectionate greetings to your dear mother.'

'Yes, I will. How is Clive? Give him my best wishes.'

'My wishes to Bellamy also. You see him?'

'Well, yes, not just lately.'

'Keep well, Harvey, be a good boy. I shall hope to see you soon, I will ring again soon. May God bless you.'

'So he's kicking you out,' said Joan. It was midday and she was drinking gin. Harvey's 'tea' had been an instinctive fiction.

'Not in so many words. He asked if my leg was better.'

232

'And you instantly said no, I'm afraid it isn't, I'm on crutches, walking is agony, thank heavens for your lift.'

'No, I said it was better.'

'You idiot! You lied! Clive is behind this. He thinks if you were still in the flat Emil might – '

'And he asked if you were soon going back to Paris and I said yes.'

'Only unfortunately I am not going back to Paris.'

'*Maman?* – !'

'So you will have to find somewhere else to live.'

'But I can't – why can't you go away – ?'

'Why can't I go away? Tiresome dull old mother, why can't she go away? Why isn't she dead, the rotten old hag?'

'*Maman*, don't start up, it's so *boring*.'

'Nobody loves her.'

'I love her. Oh do stop whining – '

'I'm not *whining*, you little monster of selfishness. I am selling my flat in Paris, I can't go back there, I must stay here, I *want* to stay here. I have business here.'

'What business? Can't you go and stay with Grandmama?'

'She hates me. I think almost everybody hates me. Aren't you listening? I propose to stay in London. You must find somewhere to live, you must find a *job*.'

'I can't find a job, no one can. Anyway I've got to study, I'm a student – '

'Students are characters in operas. Well, why don't you go to Florence? You can walk now can't you? Why not just go?'

'I can't walk. I've got to stay here for hospital treatment – '

'Aren't there hospitals in Florence?'

'And anyway I've told the people I can't come.'

'You always despaired too soon. But they gave you a grant, didn't they?'

'Yes, but it's cancelled, someone else has it now. *Please* don't talk about Florence.'

'So what are you living on, I'm quite interested to know, who feeds you, who pays the rent of this mouldy little flat?'

'Who do you think, who's always been paying? Lucas and Clement. Oh God, and just when I thought I was becoming independent!'

'Independent! You think you'll just sail into the university next year and it's all found. Not a bit of it. It'll cost thousands to put

233

you through three years of that, your so-called grant is pitiful, in fact now I come to think of it it's a loan, and the government is cutting it too. Lucas and Clement have been supporting you for years, you can't blandly expect them to go on forever. Anyway Clement is out of a job, he hasn't saved anything. He's nearly bankrupt, and Lucas is absolutely unpredictable. I can't help you, I haven't got any money. You'll have to begin helping me.'

'But *maman*, I thought you had this grand job in the fashion house.'

'It was never grand and now it isn't a job. I have nothing to sell except myself. You don't know it, but I've supported you for years by selling myself.'

'Oh don't be *silly*! I suppose you'll get some money for the flat —'

'How selfish you are, how thoughtless! I'll be reduced to Humphrey Hook in the end.'

'By your imaginary friend you mean drugs or *that*! You are just tormenting me, please stop.'

'You call that torment? As for living somewhere, couldn't Louise put you up?'

'Where, in the garden shed? *Maman* dear, come back to reality.'

'Yes, better not. You must marry a rich girl, not one of those penniless princesses. And they are no better than your sisters by now. What about Clement? You could sleep on the sofa. You aren't becoming gay, are you?'

'No!'

'I sometimes thought Emil fancied you, or poor Bellamy of course —'

'*Maman*, look, be serious —'

'Serious? I'm desperate.'

'You say you have business here. What is it?'

'My own business. I mean I want to consider my future. I want to talk to my old friends. Can't you understand that?'

'Yes, that seems sensible. Who are they?'

'Well, Jeremy Adwarden.'

'Oh, him.'

'Yes, him. Also Tessa (oh, her), Louise of course, Clement, Lucas, Cora, Emil —'

'All right, I see, the old gang, yes —'

'Well what did you expect?'

'If them, why Lucas and why not Bellamy?'

'Bellamy has no sense.'

'Neither has Cora. What the hell. I've decided I must go and see Lucas.'

'Really? I advise you not to. He doesn't like you.'

'How do you know? That's what worries me. I don't like not being liked. I want to make peace with him.'

'What about?'

'Oh nothing. And now there's this other business with Peter Mir.'

'Poor Mir is deranged, dotty, mentally ill, a thorough nuisance. I'm surprised Louise let him into her house. I suppose it's because he's rich. She thinks he's got his eye on the girls.'

'*What?*'

'Are you blind? He's quite young, could be round about forty. Anyway, as you say, what the hell. I know, I've been to hell, I've seen it, I've been shown round. I'll kill myself. You'll see, you'll be sorry. You've grown up, you ought to be able to help me, to look after me, even to love me.'

'*Maman*, dear, dearest, you know that I love you!'

Harvey moved his chair nearer to his mother's and took hold of her hand, he tried to kiss her hand but she drew it away, her eyes filling with tears.

Clement, not at home to Louise's telephone call, was with Bellamy. It was raining outside. Bellamy's room was cold.

'Have you got a fifty-pence piece for the meter?'

'The meter?

'The electric meter. The fire has gone out, I haven't got one and it only takes – '

'Yes, yes.'

They were sitting on the bed. Clement, still wearing his overcoat, handed over the coin. Bellamy fed the meter and the little fire came on again.

'He spoke about a solution', Bellamy went on.

'Yes, you said so – he means a final solution!'

'He said he wanted to re-enact the whole scene. There's something very important which he has forgotten and he thinks he might remember it if – '

'Yes, yes. And he told you to tell me to tell you the whole truth!'

'Yes, but, Clement, I don't want – '

'Well, I will tell you the whole truth. I don't know where all this is leading. I imagine he wants to kill Lucas and probably me too, never mind. Oh shut up, just listen and don't look like that. I *was* there, at that scene, Lucas *did* plan to kill me, he even tried to kill me – '

'But this is – '

'With a club, a baseball bat, we used to – '

'But this is all *madness*! He can't have meant to kill you!'

'He took me in his car, to some sort of derelict place where there were trees – I don't know where it is and I don't want to – he said he wanted to show me some glow-worms.'

'*Glow-worms?*'

'Anything would have done, I mean to distract my attention, of course there weren't any, I was looking down, I was drunk, then I realised he had raised the club and was going to hit me, then suddenly Mir intervened, he lifted his arm to stop Lucas, and Lucas struck him on the side of the head.'

'Oh *God* – '

'You know, damn it, I can't help feeling that this story must have been told everywhere again and again, that I must have told it, that Mir must have told it in court, only of course he wasn't in court, he was dying or dead. He fell to the ground and Lucas knelt beside him and then he told me to clear off and keep my mouth shut, and he handed me the club, it would have been evidence, the baseball bat, we used to play with it when we were children – oh *hell*, this is *hell* – '

'Clement, please *stop*, this *can't be true*, he can't have meant it, it must have been a sort of play, he *can't* have intended to kill you, nothing proves it, nothing can prove it – '

'Oh yes. He said, "An angel might have stayed my hand", but that was a joke.'

'A *joke* – ? But this is *impossible* – '

'And something I thought of later, Lucas took my wallet when

I was asleep in the car, he intended the police to think it was a robbery – '

'How – ? Oh, I see. Oh God, how *dreadful*. But still nothing proves – Really, I can't *believe* it – '

'I've been dazing myself with all this, that we can't know, nothing can prove, and reading back from it that he didn't really mean it, it was just to frighten me, and so on, but that's all dream stuff – and we've got to deal with Mir.'

'When he left the hospital why didn't he go to the police – ?'

'That wouldn't be real revenge. He wants to do it his way.'

'Still – Clement – if Lucas was in earnest, Peter did save your life, and if he wasn't in earnest – '

'And so what. I wish Mir *at the devil*. I can't tell you how much I *loathe* it all, it's ruining my work, it's destroying me, everything I do is false, I've lost my *self*.'

'You haven't talked to Louise?'

'About all this? Of course not!'

'Has he?'

'He said quite enough on the first occasion!'

'But they don't know what to believe.'

'He said he'd talk to them in his own fashion.'

'He said this to you at the party? Was he kind to you then?'

'Not very. Louise doesn't want to get involved. What she thinks would be something like "Well, maybe there's something in it, but it's all got exaggerated and the poor man admits he can't remember things". That's the sort of feeble senseless compromise which would satisfy her. Bellamy, don't you *see*, that man has pushed his way in, using the women, he says he's a member of the family, he danced with Aleph – '

'You don't imagine – '

'I imagine anything. He is using you too.'

'He told you to tell me, and you have told me. But you didn't have to.'

'I had to, Bellamy, I would have told you anyway. I can't lie to you, he probably guessed that. He wants another witness. And he wants to make us justify him before *them*, to portray him as innocent, kindly, not dangerous, not crazy.'

'How could we, without accusing you and Lucas?'

'I don't matter, I'm just a liar, Lucas could be left vague for the present. Justifying equals mystifying.'

'I don't understand, did Peter say all that – ?'

'No, I'm just inventing, I'm trying to see into his mind! He has two apparently incompatible objectives.'

'To placate them and to destroy Lucas.'

'He wants to become established as a member of the family. That may take time. Or he may just chuck the family anyway. Then he'll proceed against Lucas.'

'Perhaps if he does join the family he may forgive Lucas?'

'Never. He is crammed full of rage and hate and desire for revenge. Remember that he sees Lucas as a murderer not only of him but of me. This could belong to the second part of his justification, it's a matter of tactics. It occurs to me that this apparently ridiculous re-enactment may be part of some plan.'

'But how – '

'For instance, Lucas might have an unfortunate accident.'

'You mean – but all this is *too awful*! Clement, he isn't a devil! It's madness – '

'Madness is where we live now. Of course he could at any moment get his lawyers busy and set up a court case against Lucas and call me as an accessory and you as a witness, and whatever happened it would be the end of Lucas's career and the end of mine. He is holding all that in reserve.'

'Why me – oh – I suppose – '

'You would truthfully tell what you have just heard.'

'Oh – Clement – '

'But he prefers to do it all himself. Can't you see how cunning he is, and how ruthless? He wants an eye for an eye and a tooth for a tooth.'

'He said that even if it came to pistol shots – but of course he didn't mean – '

'Oh he meant it all right. Perhaps they'll just kill each other. Yes, they are both mad, it's a battle between two mad magicians!'

Harvey's taxi had disappeared into the darkness of the ill-lit street. Harvey was standing outside Tessa's front door. It was the dark damp foggy evening of the day of Emil's phone call and his mother's tears: also the day (though unknown to Harvey) of the Clifton necklaces and Clement's confession to Bellamy. Now a sudden unbearable anguish had driven Harvey to see Tessa.

Harvey's answer to Aleph's question concerning what Harvey and Tessa had talked about at the birthday party had not been entirely truthful. Tessa had in fact not agreed with Harvey's conjectures about Lucas's sex life. When Harvey had stated, what seemed to him obvious, that Lucas had no sex life, Tessa with (as Harvey now recalled it) a mysterious knowing look had said, 'Really? You had better ask your mother!' When Harvey had asked why, Tessa had hurriedly (as of one desiring to cover a slip, as Harvey saw it now) said, oh she meant simply that Joan was a better judge of character and likely to make a better guess. Harvey, preoccupied with his hatred of the party and his desire to leave it with dignity, had not at the time reflected upon this little exchange: now however a sinister conjecture was growing in his soul. When his mother had 'run away to Paris' Harvey had not thought about her possible 'love affairs'. Shy of the whole matter in any case, he felt no impulse to wonder, even less to inquire, about *aventures* whether in Paris or London. Now he had suddenly found himself rehearsing their recent conversation, for instance her (surely slightly accented) reference to 'old friends'. Was this in some way significant, concealing Lucas's name in the list of innocuous others? And how did she know that Lucas disliked Harvey – they must have been discussing him. She certainly didn't want Harvey to visit Lucas. All this suggested concealment. It was Tessa who had unsettled everything, with her imprudent remark and her significant look: Tessa with whom (he could scarcely now believe it) he had lately been in bed! The memory of this dismal episode remained very painful to Harvey, though in a sense it also 'hung in the air' as something unconnected, scarcely real, a non-event. After all, 'nothing had happened'. Harvey did not regard Tessa as being quite, or really, a woman. Perhaps just this had made the experiment possible.

He had put on his soft walking-shoes and was holding his new stick. His crutches were still with him and when he was in the flat he still used them to give his lame foot a rest. For public scenes however he had used the clinical stick which his second physiotherapist had given him. Now he had impulsively bought an expensive-looking, and indeed expensive, stick of some blond glowing wood (walnut?) with an ivory handle representing the head of a long-beaked bird. This was less useful than the clinical one, but gave him confidence. After all, some men still carried sticks just for style, and not because they were lame. Thus armed he had set off and a prompt taxi had carried him to Tessa's door. He was relieved to see two lights on, one in the office and one on the top floor. A little rain had begun to fall, he could feel it on his hair and see it in the light of a distant lamp. He had no umbrella, well that didn't matter. He knocked. There was no reply. He knocked again. Then he tried the handle of the door; the door was not locked, he opened it and entered the shadowy musty little hall and then the little office where the light was on. He called out 'Tessa!' No reply. Dropping his coat and his stick in the hall he went up the stairs to the landing and called again. He turned on the light in Tessa's bedroom where the little narrow white bed was neat and one of Tessa's corduroy jackets hung on the back of a chair. He paused. Did the unlocked door suggest a prompt return? Out of curiosity he climbed the last flight of stairs to where Mr Baxter had once lived out his miserable life, perhaps died, Harvey could not remember. The light was on, the window was partly open, the bed was stripped to the mattress, and a large trunk full of Tessa's clothes stood open. He thought, is she leaving? Perhaps she has gone away in a hurry to stay with her awfully grand friends whom she doesn't introduce to us – or to her other secret sumptuous flat or *house*, where she lives her other life. Leaning over the trunk he fingered, then lifted up, a long blue and mauve silk dress. He thought he heard a sound below then guiltily dropped it. He called 'Tessa!' No answer. He closed the window which the wind was rattling, and after a few moments' reflection closed the lid of the trunk. As he began to descend the stairs he felt suddenly very frightened. His exploration of the house had momentarily driven from his mind his reason for being there. Something flashed brilliantly in his eyes, like a vividly coloured picture shown for an instant upon a screen, a jagged muddled jigsaw of images of Lucas, Tessa, his mother, their faces hideously smiling, or contorted with grief or rage. The phenomenon vanished. He ran down the stairs past Tessa's bedroom and paused panting in the hall. The hall was dark, he felt suffocated, there was an evil smell, he could not find his stick or locate the door to the street. He tried to become calm, standing still and breathing deeply.

Then he became aware of something which had troubled him half-consciously and continuously ever since he had entered the house. It was a rhythmic *sound* like a distant engine. Something out in the road? He listened. It seemed more like something in the house. It was a distressing uncanny sound. He thought, it must be a machine, to do with heating or water or gas, which has *gone wrong*. It can't be meant to go on and on like that. He now located the sound as coming from the back of the house, perhaps even the garden. What should he do, go away and leave it? It was a horrible and dangerous noise, louder from where he now stood in the office. If Tessa had gone away for a long time it might do harm. Should he not tell someone, a neighbour, the gas company, the police, that a machine had gone seriously wrong and must be mended? He was reluctant to go towards it. But supposing the house were to go on fire or be deluged by a broken water-pipe? There was a door at the back of the office which he opened cautiously. The room beyond was dark – he turned on the light, which revealed a table and a typewriter. Everything seemed as usual, no overflowing tap, no gas left on, he quickly checked. The noise was nearer. A door on the far side led presumably into the kitchen. Harvey had never penetrated that far. He opened the door. The sound, more high-pitched, was now almost deafening. The dim light revealed nothing except the darkness of the room beyond. Harvey moved hastily back, then thrusting his hand round the corner of the doorway he fumbled for a light switch which he found at last – a dim, even dimmer light shone upon a little room containing a sink, a gas oven and some cardboard boxes. There was another door, from behind which the terrifying rhythmic noise seemed to be emanating. This door was very slightly ajar. Harvey moved forward. He pulled at the door, it came open revealing another small cramped darkness and a *dark figure*, someone standing there. For a moment Harvey, horrified, thought: it's a person, it's Tessa, and she's *gone mad*!

He moved back hurriedly, stumbling over the boxes, then returning and peering saw indeed in the dark slit, which now seemed like an upturned coffin, the form of a woman, certainly not Tessa, standing there in hysterics, the voice jerking forth like the regular movement of a machine, the high piercing scream, the desolate agonising wail, the raucous drawing of breath, growling then dying to a moan, then the scream again. Harvey retreated into the kitchen. He felt he was going to be sick. He stood beside the sink shuddering and uttering little moaning cries, mimicking the appalling sound. He wanted to run away, to run out of the house, to escape from the hideous nauseating phenomenon. He trembled, putting his hands to his mouth. Then he returned cautiously. He must make that awful noise *stop*. He stood in the middle of the room and called out, 'Do please stop!' The scream and the wail continued. He shouted '*Stop it*! *Stop*!' The sound began to diminish, changing its pattern, the dreadful mechanical regularity beginning to break down. Harvey advanced cautiously toward the dark doorway. His eyes were now accustomed to the dim light in the room and he could see into the dark opening. He could see the woman, standing in profile to him, staring at the wall, clasping her hands to her throat. He saw that the little coffin-like slit was a lavatory. He said '*Please* come out. Come to me.' He spoke now as if speaking to an animal. The woman did not move. Harvey reached in and touched her arm at the elbow, feeling woollen material which he pulled slightly. She began to turn towards him, then almost to fall as if she were going to faint as she took a step into the room. He seized her firmly by the arm, supporting her and making her continue to move. She now, still moaning and sobbing, allowed him to lead her out through the kitchen and on to the office, he guided her to a chair at the table where she sat down covering her face with her hands. He pulled up another chair and sat beside her, stroking her shoulder. He became aware of her sweaty feral smell. The hysterical sound was gone, but she continued to sob, in a rising and falling regular note, almost as if she were singing.

Harvey said, 'Now, please, do stop, I want to talk to you, tell me what's the matter, let me help you.' As she sometimes moved her hands, dragging at her hair and pulling at her throat, he caught glimpses of her face immensely red and swollen. Her face was so disfigured by weeping that he could not guess her age. She was dressed, poorly it seemed, with a shabby cardigan with a hole in one sleeve. Her hair, dyed blonde with a little grey appearing, was a tangled matted mess which she drew down now and then over her face. Harvey, distraught, repeated, 'Please stop crying, do let me help, talk to me, perhaps I could help, oh I am so sorry – ' The woman ignored him as if intent upon her weeping as upon some sort of work or task. Once he tried to take hold of one of her hands but she wrenched it away. After a while he simply sat back and watched her. If only Tessa would come back! He had only just remembered where he was and that Tessa existed. He thought, how can someone go on and on crying like that, how can such crying not kill them or do them permanent damage, why doesn't she become exhausted and faint or go to sleep, how can such grief exist, what can I do, nothing, must I wait with her now, ought I to wait and wait? He felt he ought to wait but suddenly and passionately wanted to get away. He saw on the table a very shabby old handbag which could not possibly be Tessa's, and into it he stuffed a considerable amount of Emil's generous taxi money. After a last plea, 'Please stop, please talk to me!', he got up and went to the door. He looked back at her still heaving and keening, then moved away, picking up his coat and his stick. He closed the front door quietly as he went out. He felt a traitor and a coward.

Once he was outside however, where it was dark and cold and windy, and the rain was soaking his hair and running down his face, a new will and a new energy seemed suddenly at his disposal. It was as if something had, ever so lightly, touched him. It was so surprising that he paused. Must it not be connected with that awful grief? A mean sense of escape? No, this was something else. Perhaps the weeping woman had been a sort of test or trial run. But had he not failed? What hideous violence or what terrible loss had brought about such grief, which he was now leaving behind? He walked on slowly. He felt that he was being moved on as by a revolving door. Suddenly, in another part of the human scene, of the great chessboard of being, his presence was urgently called upon. Where action had hitherto seemed impossible, he was now empowered to act. The ruthlessness of his departure could seem a source of strength. He had just seen part of a tragedy in which he had no role, now he was being sent out to play a role in his own tragedy. What this role was he did not know. But he felt loosened, as if all his sinews had been unbound, uplifted, inspired to run his own risks. He even noticed that, with his new stick, he was walking fast and without pain. It was nevertheless a long way to the tube station. However, fate, in on this act, was mindful of him and within minutes a taxi appeared. He climbed in and gave the driver Lucas's address in Notting Hill.

*

He parted from the taxi at the end of the road and began to walk cautiously along under the trees on the side opposite to Lucas's house. Squeezing the water out of his hair, he noticed that the rain had stopped. He had no cap. His head was cold. He had, he now realised, *kept* so long, like a dangerous treasure, his notion of 'having it out' with Lucas: this was to take the form of some kind of dignified apology, accepted with equal dignity, ushering in an era of some sort of decorous friendliness. Harvey had not dared to write to Lucas, partly for fear of using an inappropriate expression, more because receiving no reply would reduce him to hopeless misery. It had also seemed impossible to arrive unannounced; but given the whole situation, 'unannounced' now appeared as the only possible way. He had for so long wanted so much to heal that wound, which he had never revealed to anyone, the painful memory of that, after all so childish, and so trivial, episode. Did Lucas eternally hold against him that piece of silly clownish rudeness – or was it possible that he had completely forgotten it and would laugh to hear of Harvey's long anxiety? He did not believe that Lucas had forgotten. Now, in any case, it was the time to find out. He had kept in his heart, pure and undamaged, his gratitude to Lucas for, together with Clement, financing his education. How happy he would be if he could at last with an open heart, lay all these things at Lucas's feet.

There was a light downstairs, perhaps in the hall, Harvey could not clearly remember the interior of the house. He stood opposite to it. Other dark thoughts came to him but he banished them. He concentrated, imagining his entry into the house, his standing in the drawing-room among the books, standing before Lucas who would be sitting at his desk, smiling a mild sardonic smile. Oh let it be, he said to himself, holding his hand to his beating heart. He sighed deeply. Last leaves were falling from the plane trees and one of these, as a signal, lightly touched his cheek. Then, as he moved, his foot leaving the kerb, something happened. A person, a *woman,* had *appeared* in front of Lucas's door, and then instantly *disappeared.* It had taken place so quickly that Harvey could even wonder whether he had actually seen anything. Perhaps another leaf had simply floated past his eyes. The door must have opened and closed in a second, so that she seemed to have dissolved into the door. After a minute or two he crossed the road. He stood outside the house on the pavement trembling, then leaning his brow against the wet cold railings and moving it to and fro. He thought, I mustn't go mad, I must be sure, I must *know. She* cannot be in there, it must be an illusion, why should it be *her*, my mother, when it might be anyone or no one. Oh why have I let those awful thoughts come back, why did I go to Tessa's house and find that miserable woman, it was like a curse – is she still crying there, afraid to go home to some violent cruel man? Now, yes, yes, I must search London, I must find out where she is, she *mustn't* be here, she *must* be somewhere else, I must go everywhere, to Clifton, to Cora, to the flat, oh God if only I could fly like Ariel – oh how glad I shall be when I find her *not* here, how happy I shall be then! He was holding the railings and trying to shake them, he seemed to be tied to them, his hands glued to them, should he not be racing away? But the door – the door *couldn't* have opened and shut so fast, so it must have been an illusion. Oh let it be an illusion. Then it came to him, of course the woman had not entered by the door, she had passed along the front of the house beneath the front windows and turned at the side to the gate into the garden. Instantly, picking up his stick which had fallen to the ground, he mounted the steps toward the front door, then stepped down into the paved space behind the railings. He paused, putting his hand against the wall of the house, he leaned his shoulder against the wet wall, listening to his rapid breath, and opening his mouth in silent grief – then levering himself away he walked with long strides along the frontage and round the corner toward the gate. He tried the gate, it was open. He passed on and emerged into the garden and came out on the lawn.

He walked backwards a little, looking at the house. He murmured '*maman*'. If only he could *know*. But what was he doing, standing in this garden, underneath this tree? It was fate indeed, it was all part of the curse, part of his being lame, it was to do with Tessa, he ought not to have gone to Tessa, she had despatched him to hell, through that little door to that doomed woman, and now *here*, to witness this phantom, this *effigy*, of his mother. He felt faint, it was as if a great terror were coming towards him through the darkness. Dropping his stick, he reached out to the trunk of the tree, opening his hand against it, if only he could remember what kind of tree it was. Was it a sycamore? Above him the wind was moving among the branches with a clattering sound. There was something so very odd, so eerie, so awfully *secretive*, about the way that woman, if she existed at all, had vanished. Brushing his wet eyelids with his other hand, he stared at the house. No light, yes, there was a light, curtained, very dim, in an upstairs window, from the room which opened onto the balcony and the steps down to the garden. He walked now, taking long strides over the grass, and gripped the cold wet iron of the staircase. Open-mouthed and panting he hauled himself up, then stood holding his hand over his heart, containing it. A very narrow shaft of light from within, betokening a slit in the curtains, was laid out near to his feet. He moved, thrusting his head forward, trying to thrust his eyes forward. He could see into the room. A chest of drawers, a stretch of bare wall, then a bed. Lucas was sitting on the bed, his head turned sideways. A patch of colour, a piece of material, was draped upon the bed, next to him, touching his knee. It was, it *must* be, part of a woman's skirt. As Harvey leant over a little more, Lucas suddenly turned his head.

Harvey fled, levering himself down the iron stairs in great leaps, then stumbling round the corner of the house. He fumbled with the gate, slithered out along the railings, climbed onto the front door steps, then leapt down them into the street where he continued to *run*. When he had reached the corner of the road he became aware of an acute pain in his foot. He also remembered, as he reached out seeking for it, that he had left his stick behind in Lucas's garden.

'Come,' said Lucas, 'there are disagreements which divide even the gods.'

'They are always disagreeing,' said Peter, 'divine guidance is a matter of compromise. Have we not already come a long way?'

They had indeed, it seemed, come a long way. Bellamy observed the scene, which he had himself in large part engineered, with amazement. They were in Lucas's drawing-room. The room, full of dark shades, the dark Persian carpet, the dark reds and blues of the books from which Lucas always tore the paper covers, the dark brown walls, the big mahogany desk, the leather sofa, was now faintly illumined by the weak morning sunshine, which lighted up the English china dogs, the Italian casket, and the portrait of the Italian grandmother clutching her beads. Lucas was seated at his desk, with Clement sitting a little behind him on one side. Opposite to them sat Peter and Bellamy, Peter on the brown velvet chair with the coat of arms cushion, and Bellamy upon one of the leather-cushioned ladder-backs which he had brought forward from the wall. This set him at a slightly higher level than Peter who was visibly lounging, his long legs stretched out, in the softer chair. Bellamy shifted his own chair a little farther back. He thought, it's like a law court, no, not quite, with Peter sitting like that. Anyway, who could be supposed to be trying whom? It's just what Clement said, it's a *duel*, and, yes, Clement is Lucas's second and I am Peter's second! When Peter and Bellamy had arrived punctually at nine-thirty on the doorstep, Clement had opened the door, turning away at once and going back to sit with Lucas with whom he had no doubt been conferring. Bellamy had hoped to have a word with Clement, at least an exchange of glances, but Clement had quickly, even pointedly, turned his back. Now, sitting behind Lucas like a secretary, his face was cold, and he did not look directly at the visitors.

The impossible situation had been planned with surprising speed. Clement, after his last talk with Bellamy, had mentioned the idea of a 'return to the scene of the crime' to Lucas, who had been amused by it. Bellamy, whose only method of meeting Peter was hanging around The Castle, had asked his 'principal', who was now in a better temper, if he would meet Lucas to discuss it. Peter agreed. Lucas agreed. Clement however, when informing Bellamy of Lucas's 'invitation', said grimly, 'Your man comes at his own risk.' Bellamy too had mixed feelings. He did not really believe in what Clement called the 're-run', nor could he imagine what it could possibly be like. He simply trusted that another face-to-face meeting between the two adversaries might somehow cool the atmosphere and even bring forth some sort of understanding. He had urged Clement to beg Lucas to make some kind of concession, even the smallest conciliatory gesture might do some good.

However, sitting stiffly upon his stiff chair and facing the pair behind the big desk, Clement grim and Lucas sardonic, it seemed to Bellamy that it had all been a great mistake. He thought, they *hate* each other, that's what it comes to, in coming here each of them is hoping to find out how to destroy the other. If they agree to go back *there* it will end in catastrophe, the whole idea is crazy.

Still, Clement had said that Lucas was 'amused', and Peter was apparently collected and relaxed. He looked, Bellamy thought, bigger, sturdier, his abundant curly hair a glowing brown, his rounded cheeks pink from the cold, his ample lips slightly pouted as if with satisfaction and presence, as he gazed about the room. He was neat, as usual, with a suit, complete with waistcoat, of soft dark grey tweed, and a dark green tie. Lucas was wearing, over shirt and trousers, a loose brown smock-like garment which usually appeared at this time in the winter. His dark straight oily hair, tucked back, framed his face, his thin sharp nose, his black slit eyes. His thin lips were parted slightly showing his long white teeth in what was perhaps a smile, while he stroked his eyebrows thoughtfully with one graceful hand. He looked like an official in some foreign place, some eastern place, a consulate maybe, or indeed like a judge or less formal dispenser of laws or fiats, presiding over a court-martial or people's court. Bellamy and Clement, as subordinates, scribes or junior officers, were more simply attired, Bellamy in his usual black jacket and trousers, and white (not altogether clean) shirt, and Clement in jeans and a blue jersey from the top of which his shirt rather carelessly emerged. Bellamy tried in vain to catch his eye.

'A long way?' said Lucas in answer to Peter's question. 'I don't think we have moved at all. What is it you want to talk about?'

After a moment's pause Peter went on, 'You are a historian and will know of cases of men of power who, having hastily slain their enemy, or discreetly arranged his removal, have later blamed themselves for having forfeited the moral pleasure of forgiving him.'

This seemed to amuse Lucas. 'There are such cases but I think that what the men of power, as you call them, were sorry to have forfeited was nothing moral, but simply kudos, fame, renown. Anyway I cannot see this allegory as having any relevance to our arrangements. Perhaps it pleases you to indicate that you are able at any time to arrange my removal, which as far as I am concerned is not news. Please let us not mess around or play about, I am rather busy.'

Peter, unhurried, leaning back in his chair and staring fixedly at Lucas, continued. 'Perhaps it is indeed more gratifying, as well as more blessed, to forgive rather than to punish. It is a pleasure which God indulges in from time to time, we are told. As a Jew you will be familiar with the Psalms, the prayer of David – "Deliver me from blood guiltiness, oh God".'

'You evidently persist in thinking I am Jewish,' said Lucas conversationally, 'but so far as I know there is no evidence for this view.'

'You are Jewish. You look Jewish. You think Jewish. I know you are Jewish. Heine said that being Greek is a young man's game, one ages into becoming a Jew. I believe you are undergoing just this metamorphosis.'

'You wish to establish a bond between us. I reject this bond. Let us not become sentimental. I gather that you expressed a wish to return to the place where, so unfortunately for both of us, we met.'

'You say unfortunately,' said Peter, who had been smiling during these exchanges, 'that seems to me a hasty thoughtless remark. Three people met at that place. Unfortunately indeed for me. But for you and your brother I played the part of a saviour.'

'This ground has been gone over, I think', said Lucas.

There was a silence, Peter staring at Lucas, Lucas leaning his head upon his hand and moving some paper upon his desk, Clement gazing at the picture of his grandmother. Bellamy, looking quickly at the door, thought, if this silence is allowed to go on Lucas will throw us all out. Not knowing what he was going to say he began, 'I think – '

Peter interrupted him. 'May I ask a question which has been troubling me?'

'Yes.'

'Exactly why did you want to kill your brother?'

Lucas, without hesitation and looking mildly at Peter, said, 'Because my mother preferred him to me.'

'I see. I understand completely. I hope you will excuse my asking.'

Bellamy said, 'I think I should say here that – '

'I doubt if you understand *completely*,' said Lucas to Peter. 'You said you were a psychiatrist – or was it a psychoanalyst?'

'The latter – '

Bellamy said, 'I think I should say here that Clement has told me exactly what happened and I believe him.'

There was a moment of almost embarrassed silence. Then Clement, suddenly staring at Peter, said in a cold voice, 'I very much resent the way in which at that recent meeting you forced me to – '

'To tell lies?'

'Who else have you told except for Bellamy?' said Lucas to Clement, interested.

'No one.'

'I didn't force you to do anything,' said Peter. 'I'm sorry I roughed you up a bit after the party. Never mind. Well, what does Lucas think about our idea of a re-enactment? It is several months, I think, a sort of anniversary.'

'What is the point of this celebration?'

'I am afraid that my poor Bellamy, who believes in angels, thinks that somehow a wand may be waved, lies will become truth, war will become peace, all will be seen to be harmless and innocent after all, and we shall embrace each other. I myself cannot hope for a miracle – '

'What then?'

'I'm not sure – a sort of rite of purification – a sort of mystery play – a gamble, a gesture – the intervention of a god – well, why do I not say God – '

'I do not understand you,' said Lucas, 'you begin to sound as mad as your poor Bellamy.'

'But you also said – ' Bellamy began.

'Yes, yes, there is another thing. Ever since that – that first event – I have had difficulties in remembering – well, that is natural, after such a blow to the head. But I feel increasingly sure that there is something, some *great thing*, which that blow has annihilated, as if a huge part of my personality has been blotted out. I feel that if I could only regain it, draw it back to me out of the dark, this could help me – '

'The forgotten thing may be something terrible,' said Lucas, 'that you are better without. However, I understand your wish and your idea, as a psychoanalyst I daresay you have seen such cases. You might be able to resume your work. You might even imagine it into a symbolic revenge without bloodshed, something rather aesthetic and picturesque.'

'I could not be more serious.'

'You mean you are offering me an olive branch?'

'Yes, what else do you think I have been doing since I arrived here?'

'I have little notion of what you are doing, I did not invite you.'

'There is another thing which I would like to ask.'

'What?'

'Could I see it again?'

'See what?'

'The – the – weapon – the murder weapon – '

The pale sunlight had faded and the room was darker, Lucas switched on the lamp. Then he drew the wooden club out of a drawer and put it on the desk where it rolled slightly, then lay, its smooth grainy surface shining, looking *new*. Lucas broke the silence that followed by observing to Clement, 'Do you remember that game of "Dogs" we used to play in the cellar?'

Peter said softly, 'Another witness is now present. So, do you agree with what I am saying?'

Lucas said, touching the club and rolling it to and fro, 'I don't know, you have said so many things. I am afraid you are a romantic and I am not.'

Peter said, even more softly, '*I must be satisfied.*'

Lucas, putting away the club, now looking at him and speaking in a patient tone, said, 'I am afraid you are still suffering from a delusion. You used the word "murder". There was no murder. I didn't murder you. It was an *accident*, you were the victim of an *accident*.'

'Your profound desire to murder *him* inspired you to murder *me*. You were mad with rage because your plan had been frustrated. Because of you I am only half alive. You have ruined my life.'

'So you keep saying. But you are alive, you have recovered, you are better, you are well, I can see you are well, you even have a lively imagination. I have offered you money, you say you have plenty of money, that is good too, innumerable pleasures are at your disposal. I never intended to kill you, I had no motive to kill you, I did not kill you, you were there *accidentally*. I hit you because you accosted me. How often must I say this? Please do not interrupt me, please *concentrate*, you said you had lost your power of concentration, but surely you can *think* enough to see that all your talk about restitution and revenge – and by restitution I think you mean revenge – can have no meaning, there is no *place* here for these concepts. I recognise no obligation to you, I have committed no crime against you, I see no reason why you should speak of forgiving me, the question simply does not arise. Do please look calmly at the matter, you can follow an argument if you try, and see the sheer *rationality* of what I am saying – and for heaven's sake let your curious construction of sin and forgiveness and innocence and revenge and so on fall quietly to pieces. Why do you *distress* yourself so? Try to understand that you simply have *the wrong picture*. Since coming here you have spoken quietly, you have mentioned peace – did you not mention peace? At any rate an olive branch, and I agree with you that this is not a matter for shouting. I want to get on with my work and not be continually disturbed by you, and I am sure that when you have freed your mind of these fruitless obsessions you will find many attractive and valuable things to do with your life. Why torment yourself when you might be happy? You see, I wish you well. So let us part calmly and quietly and terminate this tedious discussion for good.'

During this speech Lucas, sitting upright, his hands stretched out palms downward on the desk, had been looking directly at Peter and speaking slowly in a calm lucid tone.

Peter, who had been leaning back in his chair, sat upright, then leaned forward, drawing in his lips and listening intently. He replied, still speaking quietly. 'You are a devil. This is lying talk and you know it. You are trying to confuse me. Your evil intent against him was turned against me. You are a wicked man and you have performed an evil act. Somebody has to pay.'

Lucas, abandoning his magisterial pose, replied, 'So you are changing your tune. As for forgiveness, about which you rant, my brother has forgiven me, you can see that, he is sitting beside me. If he can do it, surely your forgiveness, if you insist upon it, may be taken for granted without any more embarrassing ceremonies!'

Peter, after a pause, said, 'You think my anger and my threats are just jokes.'

'Not at all, you spoke most realistically about cutting off my hands, like wire cutting cheese.'

'I would like to send you to hell.'

'My dear, I live in hell, and have done so since I was a small child.'

'Since I regained my mind I have thought, and dreamt too, of nothing but of killing you.'

'You can do it any time, if you don't mind going to prison.'

'Only I wanted to see your face again and to know who was your intended victim. You are a vicious animal and you deserve to die. But I don't want to kill you, that is too painless a fate. I assure you I am in deadly earnest. I am used to bloodshed, as I told you I was trained as a surgeon. I want to maim and cripple you, I want to damage your mind –'

'One reward of living in hell is a certain kind of courage. I do not fear anything, certainly not morality, or your foul fantasies either. Should you not be ashamed of them? Let your venom fade, why cherish it so, it must be exceedingly painful.'

'And I have left a note with my lawyer and if anything happens to me, you are to blame!'

Lucas laughed. 'My dear man, I am not threatening you. And let me reassure you that I have not left any such note with my lawyer!'

Peter stood up, kicking his chair violently away behind him. Bellamy leapt up hastily too, knocking over his chair and picking it up again. Clement moved his chair forward. Lucas had put an elbow on the desk and propped his chin on his hand.

Peter picked up his coat and hat from the floor. 'I am your judge.' He spoke thickly, in extreme emotion. 'The heavens – shall be rolled together – as a scroll – '

Lucas was silent. He made a slight gesture, as of sympathy and farewell.

Peter marched out, and, after a desperate look toward the other two, Bellamy ran after him. The front door slammed.

After the sound of the shutting door Lucas remained seated, pensive, gazing at the window. Clement waited for him to say something. As Lucas remained silent, Clement, like a spectator leaving the theatre after the performance is finally over, began to fiddle for his coat which was beside his chair, stood up, put his coat on, and walked round the desk. He walked along the room, picked up the sewing-chair which had been thrown over by Peter's violent exit, replaced the embroidered cushion, and put the chair back near the fireplace. He also moved the ladder-back chair to its place beside the bookshelves. Then he returned and stood in front of Lucas. As Lucas continued to stare at the window, Clement said, 'Well, goodbye then.'

Lucas turned to him and said amiably, 'Don't go away yet. Sit down somewhere.'

Clement retrieved his chair from behind the desk, placed it in front of the desk, and sat down opposite to Lucas. He thought, they are *both mad*, they are both crazy wizards.

Lucas went on, 'It is interesting that he used that image of the heavens rolling up like a scroll. It occurs in Isaiah, and again in Revelation. In Isaiah it is reserved for God's enemies. In Revelation it is described as occurring after the opening of the sixth seal, when there is an earthquake and the sun becomes black and the stars fall and the sky departs. But *that* wouldn't have been Jewish reading. I wonder what sort of religious upbringing he had?'

Clement said, 'It certainly seems to have included the idea of retribution.' He was feeling very tired and anxious to go away.

Lucas continued, speaking pensively in a dreamy tone, 'The painters, you know, the painters, what they did for Christianity! But Christ too is portrayed by Michelangelo as vindictive, presiding over the Last Judgment and raising his fist! I wonder if there is in any sense life after death.'

'Luc, you don't believe that!'

'Not as it is traditionally portrayed, but it is conceivable that the brain may continue to operate in some twilit way, ticking on like a machine, after the body is technically dead, as is sometimes suggested.'

'Yes, but people who recover and describe those scenes were never dead!'

'Yes, yes, but there is a kind of awful plausibility, something like the Buddhist Bardo, or the Christian Limbo – and the Greeks pictured Hades as a twilit world.'

'Luc, how can you talk like that – '

'Of course he's right, he's only half alive, a zombie, a ghastly awful dummy, a puppet. The human mind is a weird place. There, there, Clement, I am just musing. As for the heavens rolling up like a scroll, that is more than plausible, our planet is a freak which we shall destroy by our own wicked senseless activities in the next century. Our history will very soon come to an end. Now that God is dead, we are at last presented with the truth, yes, the truth remains, but it is on a short lead. Anyway, we are nothing and it matters not what we do. Now I must get on with my work.'

'But what did you make of all this? He seemed to be friendly, he talked about an olive branch, then he became awful. You shouldn't have taunted him.'

'My dear boy, *you* taunted him, that was the turning-point. You know, I am now inclined to think that we have played this thing all wrong from the start.'

'You mean we should have insisted it was a joke, a silly game, and you never intended – ? Nothing could be proved – '

'Horribly undignified, unthinkable really. And he took us by surprise, after all we thought the fellow was dead. Oh never mind, what a nuisance he is.'

'He's dangerous, he might do anything. And his idea of return-ing to that place, as if – '

'Oh, I rather liked that, it's interesting, it has a certain charm – something good might happen, he might even manage to get rid of himself, he might go up in a puff of smoke. Symbolic punishment without bloodshed, that would need some concen-tration! Metamorphosis, a final solution! A gamble, he said, yes, yes – tell Bellamy to tell him I like it. You three can fix it up, only don't bother me with the details.'

Harvey had found the front door of Clifton closed but not locked, and had so far been unable to make contact with any of its inhabitants, though he believed that some were in the house. He had not rung the bell. He sat down, first in the kitchen, then on the stairs. It was about eleven o'clock in the morning. Sefton's door was open and her room was empty. After a while he ventured up the stairs as far as the first landing. Aleph's door was open and her room was empty. He peered into the Aviary, saw Sefton lying on the floor, and retired quickly. He could hear, from the next landing, from Louise's bedroom, a conversation including raised voices taking place between Clement and Louise. He returned to his place at the bottom of the stairs.

Had Lucas seen that stick, had he guessed who owned it and why it was there? Of course he has guessed, he *knew*. A compo-nent of Harvey's state of grief and terror was that before he had had that fatal conversation with Tessa about Lucas's sex life, and even after it too, he had so passionately wanted to see Lucas, to *make peace* with him, to *make friends*. He was increasingly haun-ted by that childhood episode, but had come to believe that if he could now as an adult meet Lucas on equal terms, with grace and dignity, he could somehow make a new treaty with him as man to man. He was *fascinated by Lucas*, he wanted to like him, he

255

even wanted to *love* him, he wanted them to be, in some sudden blaze of light, intimate friends. Now everything was crippled, everything was twisted, everything was poisoned, like his foot. And he, Harvey, had done something terrible to his mother, he did not know what, but it was dreadful and forever. He did not want to see his mother, he did not want to think about her. Someone had gone into the house, it might not even have been a woman, it might have been a boy. Perhaps Lucas was a paedophile. And that patch of colour was just part of the counterpane. Perhaps it was all a hallucination. The only real thing was his stick, lying there sending out its terrible truthful signals.

'Well, you're the only person who can really look after her.'

Louise was addressing Clement concerning Joan.

'I don't see why,' said Clement wildly.

'I think she's in danger. She rang me up and talked of being "hooked". Is she on drugs?'

'I don't know. Not yet anyway.'

'But if you don't know – ! When did you last see her?'

'A little while ago. I think she's gone to Paris to arrange the sale of the flat.'

'Yes, she said something about that.'

Thank heavens, thought Clement, who had just invented this idea. Well, perhaps she really is in Paris. 'Louise, I didn't come here to – '

'You know Emil and Clive are coming back, Harvey will need his own flat. Someone will have to take her in, where can she go? We can't have her here, I mean there just isn't room. Supposing Harvey were to move in with you?'

'No! What about Cora?'

'She says she can't stand being bossed about by Cora. Please, Clement – we can't expect Harvey to – '

'Louise, dear, I didn't come here to discuss Joan – '

'Well, what – '

'I came to see you, just to *see* you, to be *with* you, for God's sake!'

'There isn't much for lunch.'

'I don't want lunch, I don't want food!' Clement, who had only lately left Lucas's house after the 'scene', had driven straight to Clifton. It was true, he just wanted to be with Louise, to be calmed by her, to feel her warm loving affection, to be reassured, to get a whiff of ordinary good life. Why was she so hostile, had Joan been talking to her about – ?

Louise had been sewing when Clement arrived, still shortening the long evening-dress which had hung for years unworn in her cupboard, a mere memento. Even now, she thought, as she stroked its soft, still brilliant, striped silk, it could only be a special occasions dress. But did she have special occasions any more? Even the children's birthdays were becoming a little less special. She felt love for the dress as if it were a wounded creature. She thought, perhaps I'll give it to Aleph. She had also thought that what had reminded her of the dress was the white silk scarf which Clement had given her. She had intended to tell Clement this and show him the dress. But when he appeared suddenly, looking so wild and pushing his way into her room so aggressively, she had randomly started to talk about Joan and now they were both upset, standing rigid and staring at each other.

Clement said abruptly, 'Look, I have to see Bellamy, he won't be in yet, if he's not I'll have to leave a message. Could you give me a bit of paper and an envelope?'

Louise, frowning and shrugging her shoulders, found paper and envelope in a drawer and handed them to him. He stuffed them into the pocket of his overcoat which he had thrown on the bed. They resumed their confrontation. Her fear, his fear, their staring eyes.

She said, 'Clement, I'm frightened.'

'Don't be silly,' said Clement, 'what on earth have you got to be frightened of? You're just fussing.' He added, 'Oh – I'm so tired – and I ought to be at the bloody theatre.' He felt a strong desire to lie down on the bed.

'I want to find out the truth, I want to know what really happened.'

'What really happened, what, where? Oh that business, it's all over, there's nothing to find out – '

'You know what I mean, that time – in front of the others – when you and Peter disagreed – it was so confused – and somehow awful – '

He's 'Peter' now, is he, thought Clement. Another sickening idea was occurring to him. 'It was certainly confused. You probably can't remember – and *he* couldn't remember. You must realise he is still a sick man.'

'I want to know whether Peter – I don't want to think he's either mad or lying – it must all have *meant* something.'

'What must have meant something? Don't you see he's a damaged man, he can't think straight, that's all. Oh God, can't you just pity the poor fellow and leave it at that? After all, he's nothing to do with us!'

'Clement – I feel there's something awfully wrong in all this.'

Louise had been on the point of telling Clement about the three necklaces, but decided not to. She had also thought of asking him if he knew Peter's address, but decided not to say this either. She stood with her hands hanging at her side. She looked down at her dress where the sharp needle was trailing its thread. Some light from elsewhere, it must be sunlight, she did not turn to look, kept illuminating the needle and making it flash. She blinked, suddenly reminded of something which had happened before, she felt giddy, a sudden great cleft had opened between her and Clement. He was looking at her almost with hatred.

Clement made an impatient dismissive gesture. He said, 'Is Aleph here? I'd like to talk to her.'

'What about? She isn't here.'

'Is she still going to the Adwardens' place in Yorkshire?'

'Yes. She's gone over to see Rosemary this morning, they're not just staying in Yorkshire, they're planning a whole tour.'

'So they're all back, and the boys too?'

'Yes. Clement, what's the matter with you? Please tell me. I feel you are ill, I feel as if something's eating you, wasting you. I do wish I could help, I wish I could understand. You said such strange things about Peter wanting revenge – I don't believe it – '

'I was drunk when I said all that. You think he's Mr Pickwick. He isn't, that's all. Just leave him alone. You haven't been making any overtures to him, have you?'

'Well – no – not – '

'Good. As far as you are concerned he's *over*.'

'I think I'll go and see Lucas.'

'*What*? Are you *mad*?'

'I want to know what – '

'Louise, don't, *don't do it*, I forbid you – '

'Clement, really – !'

'He would be very cold and very angry and would upset you extremely. I told you not to meddle. You must *not* see Lucas.

You would have nothing but trouble, you would make trouble for yourself and others. Believe me and do as I say.'

'Surely I have a right – '

'You are ignorant and you have no right – '

'Don't shout at me!'

'I'm not shouting. I'm very sorry Louise, I shouldn't have come here. I might have known – I'm so sorry – '

Clement got up and pulled his coat off the bed. He felt ready to weep. He felt *so tired*.

Louise stood back. She said, 'Moy is upstairs. She's decided to leave school. Don't make a noise as you go. I don't want her to know you are in the house, it always disturbs her so.'

Moy, well aware of the disturbing presence in the house, was lying on her bed propped up by pillows. Her legs and feet were bare, her blue shift, crumpled up, scarcely reaching her knees. She was wearing her lapis lazuli necklace which lay, a little slack, warm against her throat. Her long thick plait of blonde hair snaked over her shoulder and down between her breasts. Anax was lying beside her, his long hind legs spread out behind. He had propped his long nose upon her bare leg and upon the hem of her skirt and was staring at her with his uncanny light blue eyes which could sometimes look so cold and remote and undoggy. Moy touched his moist black nose with the back of her hand, then tickled it a little with the tufty end of her plait, inviting him to play. But Anax was not in a playing mood. His soft closed mouth was curled up a little upon one side, the dark line of the lip revealing a white tooth. She stroked him along his nose and over his brow, feeling for his strong shoulders under the stiff black and grey fur. He continued to stare, shifting slightly as if refusing her caress.

Today was a very special day for Moy. It was a Monday and she was not going to school. She was sixteen. It was her right not to go to school. Since her fourteenth birthday she had, at intervals, told her parent and siblings that when she was sixteen she would leave school. Sefton had advised her sternly not to, the other two dismissed the matter, saying vaguely she must wait and see. As the date approached Moy informed her headmistress, who mildly suggested that more schooling might assist her in later life, and her form mistress, who agreed that Moy's talents lay elsewhere.

Miss Fitzherbert, with whom Moy had not discussed her dismal visit to Miss Fox, simply advised her to 'Go on painting, why not'. At home, Aleph congratulated her, Louise argued feebly, and Sefton presented Moy with a list of London art schools with addresses and telephone numbers. This list, which she had not studied, was laid out upon one of the shelves weighed down by a large black stone with a white band upon it. So now she was free. She lay on the bed, oppressed by lassitude, ennui and fear, listening to Clement's angry voice on the floor below.

She had not recovered from her fight with the swan. She still woke at night panting, having to sit upright in bed. The huge heavy white breast reared itself above her like a great shield in nightmare dreams, pressing her down. She was tormented by other images and uncertainties, had the little black duck actually got away or had it already been drowned before she reached it, had she really seen it escaping? Also: had she perhaps *hurt* the swan? She had fought with it so desperately, she remembered, in the fragmented kaleidoscope of their battle, seeing its great black webbed feet like hands, and clutching them frantically to thrust them away. Had the poor swan been hurt, had she damaged one of its feet? She sat up now abruptly, disturbing Anax who jumped off the bed and retired to his basket, stepping into it carefully with slow deliberate paws. She took off her necklace and put it away in a drawer next to the little lapis box which was still occupied by the white stone, and by a piece of paper saying that strength obeyed virtue. Moy knelt down beside the stones which she had now, just lately, as if part of her changing life, removed from the shelves and put into cardboard boxes on the floor. She had become alarmed by her powers of telekinesis and by the occasional naughtiness of some stones which had apparently developed their own mobility and propelled themselves onto the floor. Anax did not like this, he looked baleful, he growled. 'Poor stones, I'm sorry,' Moy said to the stones as she turned them over in their boxes. Who am I, she thought, to interfere with the destiny of a stone? Perhaps they all want to be elsewhere, out in the sun and the rain, out in the sea, where I found them, in their own places, in freedom? She recalled a scene when, as a small child, she had implored Sefton not to drop a stone into a well. Sefton had laughed and tossed it in.

The larger stones had remained upon the floor against the walls. She looked with particular contrition toward the conical stone, still covered with runic scrawls of yellow lichen, which she had removed from the wild hillside near Bellamy's cottage. It had been embedded in a grassy dell, just showing its noble greenish golden head, and seeming to look toward the solitary rock, other denizen of the dell, the grey rock criss-crossed with little cracks, which in some other even older language must have had meaning too: hidden in the dell, the only stone, the only rock, rising up from the long grass. Moy had quickly seized the beautiful stone, pulling it up out of its hole in the earth, and putting it gleefully into her stone bag. Coming down the hill she had met Bellamy who took her heavy burden from her. It was only when he was putting the bag into the car that Moy was stricken by the sense of having committed a crime. She wanted passionately to take the stone back to where it belonged, with its friend, the two of them together upon that remote stoneless hillside. But would she be able to find her way? Now the conical stone with its yellow message was exhibited, dusty as in a museum, in a little rainless room, among other random captives. How unhappy it must be. And she thought of the grey rock far way, lonely in the night and the day, the sun and the storm. Tears came into her eyes.

She rose and went to sit upon the side of her bed. The wound with which she travelled vibrated within her. She thought, I shall never have what I desire. I shall become bitter and defeated and dim, and I shall never really paint, I am a freak, a crippled animal, something to be put down, put to sleep, put out of its misery. I am like the little maimed dragon of Carpaccio – except that the dragon was innocent. From now on my life will become defiled, it cannot be otherwise. How does evil begin in a life, how can it begin? Well, I shall soon know.

Sefton, lying on the floor in the Aviary, was not idly resting, she was reflecting. Where did the Romans come from? If Augustine had not discovered Plato would things have been different? *What* things would have been different? The Renaissance for instance? When she rose and descended the stairs she missed Clement's departure and also failed to see Harvey, who had by now secreted himself in Aleph's bedroom awaiting her return. As Sefton reached the foot of the stairs the second post arrived, depositing upon the floor a scatter of advertisements, a letter in Joan's handwriting addressed to Louise, and another letter lying face downwards.

Sefton piled the advertisements upon the hall stand, setting Louise's letter apart. She turned over the other letter. It was addressed to herself. As she instantly recognised the writing she stood for several moments very still. Then breathing deeply she moved into her bedroom and closed the door. She sat down on the bed, opened the envelope, and read the letter through carefully. The letter ran as follows:

My dear Sefton,
I wonder if you could come and see me on Thursday morning about ten? If you cannot, perhaps you would drop in a note to that effect by hand. Otherwise I shall expect you.
Yours,
Lucas

'What did you dream about last night?'
'A tiger.'
'Burning bright?'
'No. What did you dream about, Harvey?'
'The tower of Siena cathedral.'
'*Tiens*!'
'*Tiens* nothing. It was made of marzipan. Then it turned into a picture by Mondrian.'
'Marzipan, Mondrian. I envy you your aesthetic dreams.'
Aleph had at last arrived, finding Harvey waiting for her. They sat as usual facing each other, Harvey on the bed, Aleph on the chair.
'You're using your old stick, the hospital one. What's happened to your smart one?'
'This one is less smart but more useful. Are the Adwardens back?'
'Yes.'
'And Rosemary and Nick and Rufus?'
'Yes. And, yes, I'm going to Yorkshire with Rosemary. I shall sleep in that four-poster bed. Then we are going to tour the dales and cross the Scottish border. The others are staying in London.'
'I wish they'd invite me. I think Nick and Rufus are against me.'
'No one is against you.'
'My mother is. She wants me to take a job to support us.'

'Why don't you run away to Italy, why don't you just *go*?'

'Would you come with me? All right, that's a joke. Anyway I have to stay here with the doctors.'

'But you're studying, aren't you, you're working? I wouldn't mind living in Emil's flat.'

'That's another thing. Emil and Clive are coming back, I have to move. Sorry, I'm becoming a little misery and I know you hate little miseries. I feel so trapped. *Eternel retour*. I still don't know what it means, but it's what I feel. I saw an awful thing, a woman crying, I mean *terribly* crying.'

'Anyone we know?'

'No. Oh *hell*.'

'This house is full of crying women.'

'Surely Sefton never cries.'

'She was crying last week over the death of Alexander.'

'Aleph, don't you cry. I don't want you ever to cry, I want you to be happy eternally, I want you to be your own perfect self forever. I feel so terrible before you, so wrecked, so broken, so vile, I've never felt like this before, I'm not worthy, I'm under a black cloud, I'm a faithless knight, I ought to be punished, I ought to be sent away for seven years to be some awful person's servant.'

'You think I'd still be there after seven years? Come, now I'm joking!'

'I love you, I want us to be together forever, I can't bear the idea of being separated from you, you won't be away long, will you, I want to talk and talk and talk to you, I want to look at you, you are so beautiful, you are the most beautiful creature in the world, I wish you weren't going away, I want to say so much and to say it *right* – I shall say it later, only don't leave me.'

'You mean it's as if we are in a fairy tale, and there's something we can't say, some word we can't utter, some riddle we can't answer – and if we *did* say it or answer it we would die, or be in paradise together.'

'Yes, Aleph. Only I'm filthy and guilty and worthless, I'm under a spell, I'm under a curse.'

'Harvey, you are asleep. You will awake.'

'You will wake me, you will, won't you – '

'But we have to be noble, both of us, don't you think?'

'You mean wonderful, like people in Henry James?'

'No, noble, heroic, straight-backed, like people in Shakespeare.'

'You mean good brave people in Shakespeare. Yes, we are both under a spell, we are paralysed because we have been so perfectly together all our lives. And so we are – unlucky – anyway I am – '

'Harvey, please don't go on, unless you want to see another woman crying! You know all this is a sort of nonsense.'

'It isn't.'

'All right, I know it isn't. But do buck up, brace up, as Sefton would say, pull your socks up!'

'I think we are really talking to each other, we are really being *with* each other, we are *being* each other. I shall always love you, Aleph, remember that. Let me hold your hand, this is a special moment after all, our special moment in time, as if the gods were near, as if we were really going to be released. Wait, Aleph darling, lovely one, let us just be quiet together, it's like prayer, it's like salvation.'

'Yes, yes. But don't be so tragic, dear Harvey. It's lunch time. Louie is downstairs in the kitchen, and I heard Moy go down. Let's just dry our eyes and go down together. You'll stay to lunch, won't you? Louie will be so pleased.'

'*Lunch?* Aleph, don't be *daft!*'

My dear Father,

I have abstained from writing to you for some time, according to your ordinance, and I hope that you will forgive this communication, which comes without your blessing. I need your advice, I need your prayers. I spoke to you in my last letter about an angelic personage who has entered my life, a man wronged and fighting righteously for justice. I have now become, reluctantly, involved in a fiercer and more dangerous phase of this struggle. I say reluctantly because our (mortal) foe is someone whom I also love. Can one say – I have met with anti-Christ and I love him? The situation is in fact almost infinitely complex, visible in all its aspects only to the eye of God. I have attempted in this, alas one must now call it, *feud*, to act as a mediator and peace-maker, but in vain. I fear extremely for my angel and for his adversary. May I not now visit you? There is little time left. Those here below must be forgiven. For we wrestle not against flesh and blood but against principalities, against powers, against the rulers of the darkness of this world, against spiritual wickedness in high places. Please excuse this thoroughly confused letter. I am in a deadly dilemma and do not know what I should do. At least – I think – nothing here is *my fault*. Yet how can one say that? Blessed is the peace-maker, for he shall be called the child of God. And he who tries and fails to be a peace-maker may ever after reproach himself for not having had the courage to *prevent* what he could not *control*. I cannot explain this in a letter. I beg you to reply to this and let me come at once to talk to you before these two men destroy each other. The sight of your calm holy face would I am sure endow me with the necessary wisdom and *courage*.

Your loving and faithful disciple,
Bellamy

P.S. You said pray at every moment. I have been unable to do that, but I have tried to pray *often*, sometimes using words which I have heard you use. But I have had a curious sensation as if my prayers were becoming *fat*. Can prayers become fat? It sounds idiotic, but I could explain the image. I am not, I hope, going mad. I tell myself that God accepts any prayers, even false ones, if you see what I mean.

My dear Bellamy,
Your letter has been forwarded to me from the monastery. As I was about to let you know, I have left the Order, and the priesthood, and the Church. I have, as the saying goes, lost my faith. I can no longer believe in the God of Abraham, Isaac and Jacob or indeed in any personal God or supernatural (I use this word advisedly) divinity, or in the divinity of Christ or in eternal life. I do not believe in what I once took to be my lifelong mission, the abnegation of the world and the saving of souls. I have no more authority and no more wisdom and I have for some time now felt myself to be a liar as I spoke to humble penitents who possessed a faith which I lacked. I am sorry to have to tell you this, destroying or damaging perhaps some structure in you which I seemed to be erecting and you seemed to desire. However, it would be foolish pride on my part to imagine that you will, after some

brief dismay, feel that you have in truth lost anything of great value. You are a natural (to use that somewhat silly but here soberly apt term) *seeker*, and you will *find out your own way.* As I now have to do for myself. I give no address since I do not want you to (should it occur to you to do so) come and find me. Frankly, you would be unwelcome, and I would be, for your purposes, worthless. Please do not write to me. Any letters sent to the monastery will be, at my behest, destroyed there, so pray do not send any. Bellamy, I am sorry. I hope you will find goodness and happiness – I feel that you are a person to whom both might naturally belong. Be happy yourself and make others happy. You should stay with Christ, that presence need not fade, it can be an icon. But do not be miserable seeking for moral perfection. Remember Eckhart's advice (for which he was deemed a heretic): do not seek for God outside your own soul. My more worldly advice to you is as follows. Leave your hovel in the East End, which by now even you must see to represent a preposterous falsehood. Do not seek solitude. Return to some small flat near to your friends, and get a job (not unlike the one you left) wherein you can be extremely busy every day relieving the needs and sorrows of others. And do, as a sign of sanity, go back to your dog!

Yours most sincerely,
Damien Butler

P.S. I have been, let me say this to you in all honest humility, impressed and moved, even edified, by your ardent, though in some ways illusory, faith, and your, as it happened, impossible, desire to give up the world. You thought that I could teach you – perhaps it is you who have taught me. In taking leave of you I wish that I may, sincerely and without presumption, utter the words of Virgil as he takes his final leave of Dante:

> Non aspettar mio dir più nè mio cenno:
> libero, dritto e sano è tuo arbitrio,
> e fallo fora non fare a suo senno:
> per ch'io te sovra te corono e mitrio.

When he received this letter, which he read sitting in his tiny cold room on the edge of his bed, Bellamy of course began to write a rapid, passionate, incoherent reply. But after a while his pen moved more slowly. Then he sat quiet for some time. Then he tore up his letter. He read Father Damien's letter through again and folded it up carefully and put it in his pocket. Then he sat for a long time upon the bed, leaning forward with his face in his hands.

'So it's fixed for Friday evening, ten p.m.' said Clement to Bellamy on Wednesday evening in Clement's flat.

'Friday evening. It sounds so *normal*, like a lecture or a dinner party.'

'Whatever it is like, it will resemble neither.'

'It may end in a joke or a fiasco.'

'You are optimistic, my dear Bellamy.'

'No, I'm not. What are we doing, are we mad too, can't we stop it? Even now we could sabotage the thing.'

'The result would be fatal, they would go it alone, they're excited, they're *keen*! We have to be there.'

'Just to watch?'

'No, we'll have to *control* it, don't you see, give it some intelligible order, something to keep them going, a beginning, a middle and an end. There must be a termination – '

'Like theatre – '

'Yes, like theatre. It's got to be aesthetic – '

'You think you can charm them, drug them – '

'Well, you think there'll be angels, a reconciliation scene – '

'Peter keeps speaking of a metamorphosis. I don't know what he means. Oh *dear* – '

'What's the matter with you? Look I've drawn a map.'

'Do we need a map?'

'Yes! We can't go blundering about on the way to the spot! Remember, it will be pitch dark – '

'What about the moon?'

'Oh bugger the moon, it'll be behind the clouds as usual, anyway we'll be in under the trees. I just hope it doesn't pour with rain, they're predicting storms. Don't make a noise, and remember to bring a torch. We must synchronise our watches.'

'So you've already been there – ?'

'By daylight. Someone had to! It looks – never mind – '

'I can't imagine what we'll be doing, standing together under the trees.'

'Holding hands! No, we must keep on mentioning what it's supposed to be for.'

'Well, what is it for?'

'Oh Bellamy! So that your man can remember something which he's forgotten! I bet it's about a woman.'

'He said more than that, he said it would be a rite of purification, a sort of mystery play, a gesture, a divine intervention – '

'Yes, yes, anything which will keep Lucas amused – '

'You seem to think it's playing about,' said Bellamy, 'like your juggling and standing on your head.'

'All right. Let's be realistic. Think what we have witnessed, you and I, in the way of pure hatred. Your man is quite capable of bringing a little revolver along and shooting Lucas's kneecaps off. Or he could kill Lucas and involve us as accessories. Or – '

'How awful. Do you think we should search them first?'

'Don't be silly! Your man is as strong as an ape, I told you, he nearly killed me once.'

'Clement, I wish you wouldn't keep calling Peter "your man". Why can't you use his name – '

'All right, Mir, Peter, as you like. I'll tell you something funny. Lucas wants me to bring the bat along, you know the – '

'Yes!'

'He says the scene wouldn't be complete without it! I'm to carry it, I'm his squire!'

'But he's joking, he doesn't mean it.'

'When Lucas makes a joke he means it.'

'He really is anti-Christ.'

'Well, your Peter is demonic too, a demonic psychoanalyst. All right, all right, it's all Lucas's fault. They are a couple of mad magicians. It may come to that in the end, a test of magic. Or call them archangels if you like, that's more your terminology. A battle between two archangels, we must just see to it that they don't destroy us.'

'Clement, I don't even know where the place is.'

'It's a little park in north London, it's changed a bit since the summer, Lucas was quite interested, I drove him up there, some building was going on, but not in *our* area, all the trees were still there. They are Wellingtonias. I didn't notice the first time.'

'What – ?'

'Here's your map, it shows where it is, where to go in, where the building is going on, it's quite open now, and where exactly we are to meet. Of course Mir should know the way, but it's possible that he's forgotten. And also of course the *time*, we don't want to dally, we've got to get it over quickly and in order, like I said. Look at the map, *look* at it, you fool, it's all perfectly clear – '

'Yes, yes, I will look at it, I'll show Peter – oh how terrible it is – '

'All right then. Now you'd better go home. I'll drive you.'

'Couldn't I stay the night with you?'

'No.'

'Oh how I wish it was over and all of us safe and well.'

'Here's your coat.'

'Clement, by the way, could you just look at this?' Bellamy had copied out the lines of Dante from Father Damien's letter.

'It's Dante, the *Purgatorio*, Virgil saying goodbye to Dante.'

'Yes, I know that, but what does it *mean*.'

'Don't you know?'

'No, I don't understand Italian, not everybody does!'

Clement translated. 'Do not expect any word or any sign from me. Your will is free, upright and sound, it would be wrong not to be ruled by its good sense. And so, master of yourself, I crown you and I mitre you.'

When Bellamy had gone Clement sat down again on his leather settee in front of his electric fire, stretching out his slippered feet upon the kazakh rug. He thought about Friday and wondered how four rational beings could have invented anything which was so insane. How had this weird idea been conceived, how had it grown until it seemed inevitable? Peter had suggested it to Bellamy because he thought it might recover a piece of his memory. This was rather daft, but plausible. It could be seen as an act of kindness on the part of the others to assist in this act of shock therapy. Bellamy had adopted it for this reason and also because he had been encouraged by Peter to think of it as some further possible illumination, some change of mind or soul, perhaps, in Bellamy's enlarged view of it, a miracle of peace and reconciliation, even the intervention of angelic powers. Of course they should more often have kept in mind that Peter was, or had been, a psychoanalyst. Was he a follower of Jung, why had they never thought to ask him that? Why had they not been more deeply *interested* in him, asked him more searching questions? Perhaps because he had entered their lives as an accuser before whom they were to be judged guilty – and indeed did they not all of them feel guilty? All that is except Lucas. But did not Lucas, surely, feel guilty? Clement did not like to think about the possible phenomenon of Lucas's guilt-feelings. Then what about Lucas's motives? The baseball bat, which was also to be present, might be treated as just another *aide-mémoire*, the fact that Clement was to carry it a reassurance for the enemy. Could there be a dramatic moment when Clement handed it to Peter? Had Clement not told Bellamy that the encounter would and *must be* theatre? Clement had thought wildly of somehow disposing of the weapon on the way to the meeting, but decided it was too risky thus to toss away so potent an object which might constitute a piece of *evidence*. In any case he could not risk Lucas's anger at the loss of his 'toy' which he was to *entrust* to Clement. How perfectly mad it all was! What was Peter really up to, why had he not so far played his strongest card, his return to the law court, was he not after restitution, justice, was he simply amusing himself by torturing Lucas before handing him over to the law? Another factor in the complex field of force was that of the 'Clifton ladies'. Was Peter perhaps looking precisely in that direction for – what – his ransom, his reward, his consolation prize – his hostage? He had sold them such a touching picture of himself, a man without family, without home, diffident and lonely. And also rich. I suppose he *is* rich, thought Clement. We've all swallowed that too! Here Clement's memory, in which there were no gaps, conjured up the image of Peter dancing with Aleph at the party. Then he thought of Louise and the electric hostility which had existed between them at their last meeting, and the feeling of his hair rising came again, it was as if they were divided by some magic shield, motionless and tongue-tied. What a horrible metaphor, he thought, as if one's tongue were tied up by wire. He could feel his tongue writing in his mouth at the idea. He thought, I'm losing my grip, I'm losing *them*, it's all Luc's fault, he has devastated us and defiled our innocence. He has hypnotised us. Why am I so docile, why am I taking part in this charade, acting as his second, defending his indefensible position, and opposing the righteous stance of a wronged man *who has saved my life?* Is it because I feel guilt for what Lucas called my cruelty to him when we were children? Perhaps I was cruel. Or is it really because I admired him and revered him when I was a child, I looked up to him, I thought him remarkable and amazing, he is remarkable and amazing. I think I loved him, I think I still love him. And now I am leading him into a trap where he will let anything happen, he will let Peter kill him, he doesn't care, he does not value his life at anything. Or perhaps I shall be the victim; after all, as Lucas said, it was all my fault.

It was Thursday morning. Standing in the road near Lucas's house Sefton looked again at her watch, which was taking an incredibly long time to drag its hands on from nine-forty to ten o'clock. Now when at last there was only one more minute she approached the house, and after standing at attention at the door for a suitable number of seconds, rang the bell. There was a brief silence. Then Lucas opened the door, smiled, said 'Ah, good morning Sefton,' then turned, leaving her to close the door and preceding her to the drawing-room. With long strides she followed him. In their other previous meetings Lucas had sat behind his desk and Sefton had sat upon a chair, always put in waiting for her in the middle of the room fairly close to the desk and facing it. Now, reassuringly, the chair was in place, but stationed a little farther away from the desk. Sefton had usually stood until Lucas sat down. Now however, still standing, he motioned her to sit. As usual, she took off her coat and put it on the floor. The room was as usual rather dark since Lucas kept the curtains partly drawn. The green-shaded lamp was alight on his desk. Sefton sat with her hands folded. Her heart was beating painfully.

Sefton, who habitually concealed her emotions, had never

revealed to anyone the extreme nature of her devotion to Lucas. Concerning how far he was aware of it or how he might feel about it she did not reflect, it was not her business. During the time, now more than a year, since Sefton had left school, and up to the day upon which Lucas and Peter Mir had had their fatal encounter, Sefton had regularly, and more frequently than she divulged at Clifton, had tutorials with Lucas. The arrangement, which was his suggestion, could of course at any moment terminate, and after 'that day' and Lucas's subsequent disappearance, Sefton had come to assume that it had ended. She had not expected, or allowed herself to hope for, the present summons. Of course she was afraid of him, and this was generally assumed. In fact the Cliftonians and others predicted that Sefton would simply not be able to stand it! Lucas could certainly be savage and ruthless, not hesitating to wound. But Sefton, with her soldierly courage and her passionate intelligence, had instantly perceived the pearl of great price which was now within her reach. Lucas was not only a good and exacting teacher, he was a great scholar. She had been told, as a child, that Lucas was awfully learned and clever, but this had meant little. Now, coming to him from the agreeable domain of her thoroughly worthy schoolteachers of history and of the classical languages, she felt like an ambling walker confronted by a cliff. The standards which she perceived, though still hazy to her, were terrible ones. She grew pale. But at the same time a new spirit awoke in her, a completely new understanding of what scholarship and learning meant. This spirit was not ambition, it was love. It was a stricter clearer more invigorating sense of *truth* which was love. Her love for Lucas, for of course she loved him dearly, was something close, ancillary, but separate. It was a profound reverential passion. If permitted she would have bowed to touch his feet.

Lucas did not sit down but began to walk to and fro between his desk and the mantelpiece. Sefton's chair had evidently been placed unusually far back in order to keep this pathway clear. Lucas was wearing a white shirt, undone at the neck, and a shabby black-velvet jacket. He walked slowly to and fro in silence, his hands behind his back, his dark Chinese eyes narrowed, his lips indrawn to a line. His dark damp hair hung down neatly over his ears. He did not look at Sefton. She watched him, breathing deeply.

At last he stopped pacing and sat down upon his desk facing

her and said, 'Do not speak please during what I have to say to you.' After a pause he went on, 'A historian, though he may as a teacher specialise, must be a polymath. This cannot be said too often and I have said it to you often enough. He must not only know the whole of history in so far as this is possible in our miserable lifespan, he must be widely acquainted with the structures of human life. To take one instance, if he wishes to discuss slavery he must have a knowledge of economics. Knowledge of languages is of course essential. Fortunately you are a ready learner, you have Greek and Latin and French, you have taught yourself Italian and Spanish, and you have fair German. Your knowledge of German will in due course need to be perfected, it will prove your most important asset after the classical languages. You should also learn Russian, I think you know a little, it is not a difficult language and will reward you with the great pleasure of reading Pushkin. When you were a child you thought of history as stories about heroes. This is a natural starting-point. The cult of the hero is a persistent phenomenon, men will love a monster if he has *bella figura* – and of course there are also good heroes, as we have seen even lately in our own time. We have discussed this. We have even discussed why we both hate Napoleon! Of course you are now aware of the vastly more complex nature of historical studies. Yet meticulous tracings of facts need not exclude the warmth of passions, provided these are controlled by truthful vision. The Lord whose shrine is at Delphi does not say yea or nay but gives a sign. Meditation upon such signs may prove a richer guide than an acceptance of simpler safer conclusions in terms perhaps of general tendencies, the error of Marx. Human behaviour, the property of individuals is often irrational and mysterious. You are still, as you know, only a struggling beginner, an apprentice, a historian *in ovo*, scarcely even that. History is not a science, nor is it an art, though the historian must, as writer, be an artist too, he should write well, lucidly and eloquently, and is not harmed by a lively imagination. What is history? A truthful account of what happened in the past. As this necessarily involves evaluation, the historian is also a moralist. The term 'liberal', mocked at by some, must be retained. Historians are fallible beings who must make up their own minds, constantly aware of the particularised demands of truth. What is seen as odd must be allowed to retain its oddity, upon which later on a clearer light may or may not shine. There are many dangers. History must be saved from dictators, from authoritarian politics, from psychology, from anthropology, from science, above all from the pseudo-philosophy of historicism. The study of history is menaced by fragmentation, a distribution of historical thinking among other disciplines, as we see happening in the case of philosophy. Such fragmentation opens a space for false prophets, old and new. Not only the shades of Hegel and Marx and Heidegger, but also those, you know whom I mean, who would degrade history into what they call *fabulation*. Of course it is a truism, of which much has been made, that we cannot see the past. But we can work hard and faithfully to *portray* it, to understand and explain it. We *need* this if we are to possess wisdom and freedom. What brings down dictators, what has liberated eastern Europe? Most of all a passionate *hunger* for truth, for the truth about their past, and for the justice which truth begets. You stand upon the brink of another century. Upon you and others like you will fall the burden of preserving the purity of scholarship and of the high standards of independent thinking. You must adhere to these old values, continually purifying them and holding them sacred. Above all beware of a relaxed determinism which haunts our increasingly scientific and technological civilisation. You are on your own, thinking your own thoughts, be calm, be patient, endure an infinite slowness, time spent in checking a fact or a reference is not time wasted but an essential part of the sheer blank labour involved in scholarship. Historians too have their dark nights. Love and seek perfection. Remember that this is a lifelong dedication, you are entering upon it as into a religious house, something to which you must give your whole life, you must grow into being a scholar. You must be an ascetic, shun sins, avoid remorse and guilt, these must not consume your time and energy. Do not envy the talents of others or their fame, do not indulge jealous feelings when another is preferred. Travel light, simplify your life. Beware of being involved in the problems of other people, altruism is too often simply a busy exercise of power. Another piece of advice. Do not marry. Marriage ends truthfulness in a life. I think you are in any case inclined toward solitude. Solitude is essential if real thinking is to take place.'

Lucas paused here. He had been looking as he talked, not quite at Sefton, but beyond her, to the dim far end of the room. He now looked at her for a moment – then stood up, walked round his desk, and sat down in his usual chair. Sefton, at a point about half way through Lucas's speech, had begun to weep. Her tears, which she did not attempt to wipe away, flowed quietly down to her chin and dripped onto her corduroy jacket. She had sat motionless, gazing at Lucas, and as if not breathing. Now she drew a deep breath and moved, bowing her head and closing her eyes.

Lucas shuffled some papers on his desk and said, 'Please go now.'

Sefton, who had now found a handkerchief, rose and stood facing him. She did not move towards him. Then she stooped to pick up her coat.

Lucas then said, in a soft gentle voice, 'I shall soon be going away for some time. Goodbye, dear Sefton.'

She could not see his face. She made a gesture, touching her breast with a closed hand, then opening the hand and stretching it towards him. She turned, carrying her coat, and went to the door and out into the hall. As she was opening the door she heard a step behind her.

Lucas, now in a bright humorous tone, said, 'Wait a minute, could you take this to Harvey? He left it behind.'

He put into her hand Harvey's stick with the ivory bird's head. Sefton took the stick. She was outside the door and the door had closed.

Once outside the house Sefton soon ceased her weeping, but not in order to hide her tears. She recalled how, when reduced to tears by Lucas in a tutorial, he had reminded her of how Odysseus in the house of Alcinous had becomingly hidden his tears. Sefton concluded afterwards that the reminder was not really designed to induce her not to cry, or if she must cry to conceal it, but was just a half-jest aimed to restore her to her ordinary cheerful docile state of mind. In fact Lucas had, especially after he had roughly chided her, made many jesting reproaches of this sort, the memory of which she cherished. But now her tears dried because so many terrible emotions and speculations demanded her attention. She gasped, however, tearlessly, and catching her breath sobbed and groaned. (Also like Odysseus on that occasion, she thought as she walked along.) The predominant emotion was fear. She had so many times, when Lucas had disappeared after the court case, listened to the conjecture that he had killed himself. Moreover, and of course, she loved him; but in Sefton's stern code her love had always been chained up, and howled fruitlessly, as indeed it did now. Among her sombre and terrible thoughts a contemptible pang of jealousy kept distracting her. So Harvey had left his stick behind. So Harvey too was admitted to Lucas's counsels, and probably far more intimately. She walked all the way back to Clifton.

As she approached the house she saw a taxi waiting outside. The door of the house opened and Harvey emerged. Sefton hurried forward waving the stick. She came up to him and handed it to him, saying, 'You left this behind. Lucas told me to give it to you.' Harvey took the stick. He said nothing, but shocked Sefton by a look of extreme distress, almost, she thought afterwards, of hatred. He got into the taxi which drove off. Thinking about it afterwards Sefton reproached herself, remembering what Lucas had said about jealousy. And she thought, I am jealous because Harvey sees Lucas – and Harvey is jealous because I do!

'We are too early, are we not?' said Lucas.

'Yes. We'd better wait in the car.'

Clement had parked the car down a side road.

'Yes, indeed. I believe it has stopped raining now. I have brought my umbrella.'

'Are you all right, I mean how are you?'

'What a quaint question. I am looking forward intensely to the performance. It is charmingly unpredictable.'

'You're not intending to – you will keep quiet, won't you – I mean you don't have to *do* anything.'

'I have nothing in mind to do. Would you like to search me to find out if I am armed?'

'No. We want to get this business over quickly.'

'How long do you think it will take?'

'I hope about four minutes.'

'Oh, I hope longer than that. You haven't forgotten the bat?'

'It's in the inside pocket of my overcoat. But what's it for? Is it for me to defend you with?'

'You must make it visible. It may jog Dr Mir's memory. After all, the purpose of this gathering is to make him remember something or other. It has no other purpose so far as I know.'

'I hope it has no other purpose.'

'You think he may be violent?'

'I don't know. Do you?'

'I think there may be some manifestation. I hope there may be one, not too unpleasant of course.'

'According to Bellamy, Peter thinks of it as a mystery play. I certainly think of it as theatre.'

'Well, I have all along taken the view that he is mentally disordered, either deranged by the blow I struck him, or else perhaps generally given to epilepsy or to some similar aberration. He is a very excitable man, an oriental type.'

'Bellamy continues to think that there may be some sort of miracle, a reconciliation scene or an angelic intervention. If he, I mean Mir, wants to play it that way, for heaven's sake will you – '

'Co-operate? Of course I will. But if he requires me to – '

'We'd better go now. We are supposed to be there first.'

Bellamy was sitting in the front seat of the Rolls. Peter had picked him up as arranged at The Castle, where Bellamy had been lurking outside at the mouth of the cul-de-sac. He had climbed in in silence. The silence continued as the car proceeded slowly through the traffic. Bellamy could hear Peter's irregular breathing, deep sighs and indrawn breaths, almost sobs. He turned his head very slightly, glimpsing in the almost dark of the car his companion's profile, his thick lips parted, his gleaming eye seeming to protrude from its socket. Bellamy thought, my God he looks bullish! Is he going to have a fit or something? I wish he would say something. Oh what a mad business, no good can come of it, only chaos, and not just chaos but evil. How did we gradually get entangled in such a terribly dangerous shambles!

At last, in quite an ordinary tone, Peter said, 'It has been raining, I'm afraid it will be awfully muddy. I have brought my umbrella. I hope you have brought yours?'

'Yes,' said Bellamy. He thought, perhaps they will fight with their umbrellas. At that moment he remembered that he had forgotten to bring the torch. 'Is there a torch in the car?'

'No.'

Oh God, thought Bellamy, without the torch I can't read the map!

They had arrived. It was soon clear that Peter knew the way. Perhaps, indeed probably, it was not the first time that he had returned to the place. He turned down a side street and they got out. Bellamy saw that they were parked just behind Clement's car, its number plate illuminated by the headlights, and was about to remark on this but decided otherwise. If the fates were arranging things, it was better to leave it entirely to them. He got out quickly. Peter got out slowly, leaning against the side of the car. Then he fumbled out his keys and locked the car. He was holding up his green umbrella as if in a ritual. Then Bellamy remembered he had left his own umbrella in the car. That too was fate. Peter took hold of Bellamy's arm, leaning upon it, and leading him purposefully along the road. Bellamy was trying to remember the map, searching for it with his free hand, but it was in his other pocket where his body was pressed firmly against Peter's. He thought, it doesn't matter, *he* knows the way. They turned into another, ill-lit, street and leaving the pavement and walking on what seemed to be gravel, passed a pile of bricks and what looked like a cement-mixer, and were then walking upon a gravelled path, then in total darkness upon damp grass. Bellamy thought, thank God he knows the way – I hope he *does* know the way. Then a sudden light flashed ahead, for a second illuminating the low sweeping branches and trunk of an immense tree. They moved on, blundering through longer grass, in the direction of the light. A moment later Clement was gripping Bellamy's arm, pulling him onwards through an even darker darkness. The great trees surrounded them, then, apprehensible by a change of air, they were in some sort of small clearing, where Bellamy, looking upward, imagined he could see the sky. He continued to clutch Peter, whose body felt burning hot against his arm. He now saw the other figure, Lucas, standing a few feet away. There was a terrible silence.

Clement had at first been amazed by Lucas's willingness to set up the weird scene which was supposed to achieve something, reconciliation or remembrance. On reflection however he saw that it was 'just like Lucas' to accept a challenge and join in what might prove a dangerous game. There was also, as he reflected further, so many profound aspects of the relation between these two. Inevitably they were fascinated by each other. And what about him, Clement? It fell to him to *arrange* it all, and this involved, as he had only lately perceived, the return to a place where he himself had very nearly died. It was as if all his inward being, his hopes and fears, his loves and hates, his experience, his *consciousness*, had been so jumbled and shaken up and tossed around that everything had become hopelessly unconnected and out of order. During the time when Lucas was 'lost' he had worried so intensely about Lucas that he had not meditated at all about what had happened, and what might have happened. And when Lucas returned he had been too busy studying Lucas and exploring and adjusting his own relationship with him. Now, forced to arrange the encounter which had come to seem so inevitable, he had had to return alone, to stand by daylight beneath the great trees, and in a sudden violent vision of the past *see*, as upon a screen, the slow motion movements of the three actors. The merest flicker of change, amid the unnumbered millions of possible changes, could have prevented that particular conjunction. Clement had felt faint and sat, almost falling, upon the ground. The trees too had seen what had happened. They were old and had seen much. It was after that, when he had returned home and was working out the details, the 'logistics', of the 'second event', that he saw clearly the enormity of it all, and that when the time came, on that perilous night, *he himself* must be in charge. They wanted theatre and they would get theatre. It was *his* mystery play and *he* would direct it.

He had prepared his speech. Now, speaking in a soft clear sing-song voice, he began. 'Listen, my friends, we are gathered together in this place where an event of great significance to all of us, I include Bellamy, occurred at about this time on that evening some months ago. What exactly happened on that occasion is a question which has been much disputed, but the purpose of this meeting is not to continue this dispute. The three persons involved in that event, which I call "the first event", have all suffered very much indeed in the sequel of what then, by the work of chance, occurred. We may in this sense, and from this point of view, count ourselves as companions in a disaster. I believe that no one here wishes to make of this meeting any useless exacerbation of our mutual differences and our common pain. The idea of a re-enactment or "second event" was I believe first suggested by Dr Mir to my friend Bellamy, who then passed it to me and I mentioned it to my brother. The matter then rose again during a discussion involving all four of us, which began with some suggested reconciliation but did not unfortunately end in an agreement. However, I feel sure that we have all reflected upon what was said at that time, and that this reflection has engendered second thoughts, tending towards peace rather than war. We have all been wounded, and reason as well as forbearance urges us to seek recovery. We need and want to return to our ordinary lives. One purpose of this meeting must be to employ the heightened emotion, which we must all be feeling, to carry us, like a wave, over the barriers which divide us toward at least *détente* and appeasement. I think the word "metamorphosis" was used. Let us believe that change is possible. This meeting must, at least at this stage, bear something of the semblance of a confrontation, and Bellamy and I have observed, not simply in jest, that we have been unwittingly cast as supporters or "seconds", Bellamy to Dr Mir, I to my brother. It is customary on such an occasion for the seconds to suggest to the principals that this is a time to recognise the futility of their ill will and to declare mutually for peace. I now make this suggestion and propose a pause for its consideration. During this pause let us concentrate and consider whether we are not here confronted with a great possibility of choosing good instead of evil.'

Silence followed. Bellamy, hypnotised by Clement's words and his magisterial tone, wondered if he were having a dream. Was Clement reading from a paper? No, after all he was an actor, yet really he must be speaking impromptu and from his heart. How splendidly he has taken charge, yes it is like the theatre, I would not have believed it possible! Listening to Clement, who was standing opposite to him, he had moved a little way from Peter, but could still feel the heat of his adjacent body. Bellamy's eyes were now accustomed to the darkness and he was aware of Lucas, wearing a long black mackintosh, standing beside him. He turned again to Peter, Peter had left his overcoat in the car. How tall and straight he stood, as if at attention, and, as Bellamy could now see, was wearing a black suit, and a black tie. His shoulders were high and square, his head thrown back. Bellamy thought, he looks like a dictator. Bellamy threw his head back too, looking upward to the sky through the opening in the trees. The clouds had parted to reveal a single bright star.

Lucas spoke. He said, 'I confess that I came here out of curiosity, but did not expect to be bored. To celebrate the occasion my brother has made a pompous nonsensical speech. Let us be content with that. We must all be oppressed by this place, and I suggest that we now go home.'

Clement, ignoring Lucas, went on. 'I will now remind you of the other aim of this gathering. Dr Mir has suffered, as we all know, from a considerable loss of memory. He believes that a return to the scene of his mishap may, with an intensification of his mental state, break through the black cloud which obscures that which he desires to remember. I suggest that at this moment he should concentrate extremely hard upon the hidden thing or things which he wishes to recall, and that we should sincerely attempt to assist him by a similar silence and intense concentration.' There was another silence. The silence continued.

Bellamy began to pray. His prayer seemed to be taking the form of a dream. He felt his lips falling apart, his hands hanging limp, his body relaxing, his eyes closing under heavy lids. He thought, there is no God, but what I am feeling now is what God is. I must concentrate, no I must simply stay and wait, because what it is is so powerful, so gentle, and so close. I must breathe and be filled with Peter's anguish, desire what he desires and see what he sees. Oh let this vision be given, let him find it, that which he desires and loves, let it come to him and be with him forever. Let me just with the power which fills me now reach out a little more, joining my will to his, thinking only of *this thing*, oh let me see it, let my eyes be his eyes, to see what he has lost and *must find*, for it is nearer now than it will ever be, it is so near – I can see it, only there is a blackness over it, I can see the blackness, oh let it be withdrawn, it is *there* but covered over, let there be light. Bellamy was aware of lifting up his hands which had become weightless, like two birds lifting him from the ground. He gasped for breath, he felt that he was going to faint, he opened his eyes wide and looked up through the opening in the tree toward the sky. He thought, where is the star? It is still there but it has become so large and is so bright. It is moving, it is *falling* – stars fall through the sky and we see them falling – but this star is coming nearer and nearer – perhaps it is a meteorite – it will fall upon us – oh God, it is *an aeroplane on fire*. Bellamy tried to cry out. Suddenly there was a light shining close to him. He saw Peter Mir as if he were *burning*, only he was not being consumed, he was simply *composed of light*, and grown taller, a pillar of light, burning, shining. In this second there was a devastating crash, a deafening sound of tumbling smashing destruction. Bellamy's mouth opened to scream into the sound. Then he saw that Peter, still rigid, still glowing, was falling, his arms at his sides, and would have struck the ground face downward had not Bellamy moved instantly and received him in his arms, collapsing back with Peter on top of him.

'Are you hurt?'

'No.'

'Is he hurt?'

'I don't know. Oh Clement – how terrible.'

'He must just have fainted. Can't you get out? Just push him up a bit, I'll try and pull him. Damn, where's the torch, I've dropped it somewhere, oh *hell*!' Pitch blackness surrounded them. Bellamy struggled, trying to get some power into his arms and legs, then holding Peter's head up with one hand to prevent it from touching the ground, while Clement was hauling Peter by the shoulders, attempting to turn him over.

'Get out from under, will you, support him, do you want him to suffocate? Where's the bloody torch?'

Bellamy heaved himself partly out, pushing at Peter's inert body feeling Clement's hand near his, grasping at clothing. 'Oh, let him not be dead!'

'Shut up, Bellamy, just *help* me, will you, try to lift him a little, hold onto his head, we must get him onto his back, yes, there that's better.'

The light of the torch played upon the muddied clothes, then upon the face. Peter's face was indeed frightening. It was white, looking like ivory. His mouth was open and his eyes were open, but there was no sign of animation.

Clement said, 'He's been struck by lightning.'

'There was something in the sky like a star falling down – or was it an aeroplane – I saw an aeroplane on fire, and there was a crash – oh Clement, did you see him just before, how he looked – ?' Bellamy staggering to his feet, began to moan and sob. He picked up his glasses from the ground.

'Oh shut up, keep quiet, we don't want anyone to come!'

Clement knelt down. He was aware of Lucas standing beside him. He thought, *it's happening all over again*.

He put his hand under Peter's neck, rolled his head a little, shook his shoulders, and began with his other hand to pull at the neck of his shirt. 'Bellamy, get his tie off, get his *tie* off.'

Bellamy, kneeling on the other side, undid the tie and the shirt. Peter's head and face were wet. The open eyes were dreadful. The rain was falling into the eyes.

Suddenly Peter blinked, he closed his eyes and his mouth, his features moved, his brow wrinkled a little, he turned his head slightly on one side, away from the light of the torch.

'Thank God,' said Clement. He pulled again at Peter's shoulders, trying with Bellamy's assistance to lift his head a little off the ground. 'He seems to be breathing all right.'

Peter uttered a very soft moaning sound. He opened his eyes again, then screwing them up. Clement covered the torch with his hand. Peter, still lying flat, seemed to be animating his limbs in an attempt to sit up. Then he almost inaudibly murmured, 'What happened?'

'You fainted,' said Clement. 'It was all that concentrated emotion.'

'Don't hurry him,' said Bellamy.

Lucas, who had been standing behind them, said, 'I'm going to get a taxi. Goodnight.' He disappeared into the darkness.

Peter attempted to sit up, failed, then managed to rise a little supported by Bellamy. He was panting and breathing deeply. He said 'Lift me – just a little more – I don't think I can get up.'

'Well, you've got to get up!' said Clement. 'We'll take you home.' He said to Bellamy, 'We must get him out of here!' He was thinking, suppose someone finds us here, suppose the *police*, find us here!

'I think I'll – kneel first if I can – if I can turn round – then perhaps you'll both – pull me up – sorry, my legs don't seem – to be there any more. But wait, please – just give me a little time.'

After a minute or so Peter, kneeling, tried several times to rise, supported by the other two. The weight was too much. Bellamy said to Clement, 'We'll have to get help.' Clement said, 'No.' At last they hauled him to his feet.

'Keep him moving.'

'Which way is it, how do we get out?'

'We must get to the path. Come on, Peter, you can walk, just *help us*, will you?'

'Where is my umbrella?'

'Oh hell. Here it is, I'll carry it. Come on. Bellamy, could you take the torch, shine it down, *down* you idiot, cover it with your hand.'

They reached the path, then crept on a little way, and stopped breathless.

Peter said, 'I can't drive.'

'No, of course you can't. I'll drive you home in your car.'

'I don't think I can remember – where I put it.'

'It's just behind Clement's car,' said Bellamy.

'And turn right here, where the trees are, into the drive, then turning left.'

Peter, sitting passenger in the Rolls, had made a considerable recovery. He had directed Clement with prompt skill. The journey had not been a very long one. Bellamy, sitting in the back, had tried to make out where they were going, but soon became confused.

The car, moving slowly along the drive, stopped in front of a large house, which was all in darkness. Bellamy hastened to help Peter out, they both walked him up the steps to the door, where he fumbled for keys, found them and opened the door. This took a little time since the door appeared to have several different locks. Then the door opened and they entered, Bellamy supporting Peter, Peter switched on a number of lights, dropped his umbrella, and sat down on a chair. They looked at each other. Clement said, 'I'd better lock the Rolls.'

'No, no, it must take you and Bellamy home. No need to lock it now, I won't keep you long. I must just sit still for a minute or two.'

'Is all this house yours?' said Bellamy.

Peter said, 'Yes.'

'Sorry. I thought it might be flats.'

'Shall we help you up the stairs?' said Clement. 'Do you think you need a doctor? We could ring for one.'

'No doctor, thank you.'

'How are you feeling?' said Bellamy. 'You've had an awful time, you know.'

'I'm feeling fine.'

'Someone should stay the night with you,' said Bellamy. 'I could stay, if you like.'

'No. I am – all right.'

Clement gave Bellamy a quick look. He said, 'Thanks about the car but we can get a taxi.'

'No, no, it's late, you mightn't find one, I'd like you to take it.'

Bellamy thought, is he offering it to Clement as a present?

Clement said, 'Thanks very much then. I'll bring it back tomorrow.'

'All right – tomorrow – tomorrow.'

'I'll leave it in the drive, I'll drop the keys through the letter-box.'

Peter was sitting on a large curly mahogany chair beside a highly polished walnut table. Above the table there was a distinctly modern expensive-looking green and blue picture. Bellamy could not assemble the picture which seemed to be jumping about, the greens now receding while the blues were protruding, the blues receding and the greens palpably protruding. He felt giddy, he felt *exceedingly tired*. The big bright hall full of yellow light seemed like an immense dream bubble with a tilting slanting floor upon which Bellamy felt unable to balance. There was a vista of a huge staircase rising and turning, and a sort of gallery above. He set his feet wide apart. He noticed that his overcoat, which he had instinctively unbuttoned on entering, was smeared with mud. Peter's shirt and part of his jacket and trousers, also his shoes were muddy. His curly hair seemed dark and wet, his dark grey eyes darker, his large beautiful eyes into which tears were dripping, no not tears, rain. During their odd conversation Bellamy had been staring anxiously at Peter and wondering, is he mad? It then also struck Bellamy as odd that all through the business of getting Peter to the car and then travelling in the car he, Bellamy, had *forgotten* the *manifestation*. Now he recalled it. Peter burning. An aeroplane burning. A star falling, or was it lightning? Peter falling. He stared, concentrating upon Peter's face.

Bellamy said, 'I am seriously worried about you. You are suffering from shock.' Gazing through the golden bubble Bellamy could see a chair, *another* chair. He began to make his way to it, over the parquet floor, then over a priceless oriental rug.

'Shock – yes – but do not be anxious. I am well, I shall sleep well.'

Bellamy sat down on the chair. He thought, we're putting mud everywhere. He heard Clement's voice saying, 'Come on Bellamy, time to go home.'

Then Peter's voice saying, 'Thank you both very much for your help. Now if Bellamy can just assist me up the stairs – '

Bellamy rose from the delightful chair. Peter rose. Clement said, 'I'll wait down here.'

At the bottom of the stairs, Bellamy said, 'I'm terribly sorry, my shoes are still muddy, I think I made marks on that lovely rug. I'll take my shoes off here, if you don't mind.' Leaning down, he managed to undo his shoes and kick them off. Peter took hold of the banisters, Bellamy took hold of Peter's arm. Slowly they mounted the stairs.

Bellamy, never allowed to know where it was, had of course wondered about the house where Peter lived. Why was he so secretive about it? Was he ashamed of it? Was it very small and mean? Perhaps Peter was not as rich as he claimed to be? Or could there be a *woman* there? Peter had said he was solitary, but had it been naive to believe him? Such thoughts, as they drove along in the car, were however far from Bellamy's mind, he had been praying: oh let him live, oh let him be well, let all be well. And: oh why did we put him into such danger!

Now, sitting in an armchair in Peter's large bedroom beside Peter's large bed, he felt suddenly at peace. Somehow coming up the stairs had done it. At the bottom of the stairs Bellamy had felt weak and exhausted, even afraid he would have to call Clement to support both of them. At the top of the stairs he felt some sort of new energy. Peter seemed stronger and was perhaps communicating some of his strength. Now he sat, watching while Peter switched on lights, pulled the big long curtains across the windows, and removed the embroidered quilt counterpane from the bed. He was glad he had taken his shoes off.

Peter, who had evidently now removed his and was moving about, said, 'Would you mind staying with me a little longer?'

'I'll stay all night.'

'No, just for a very little while. My bathroom is here, would you like to go in?'

'No, thank you.'

'I won't be long, I just want to tidy up a bit.'

Peter disappeared into the adjacent bathroom and could be heard splashing the water about. Then he called to Bellamy, 'There's no towel here, could you get me a towel? They're in the cupboard by the window.'

Bellamy pulled a huge towel out of the warm intimate cupboard and put it into Peter's hand which was stretched out through the door, 'Thanks. I won't be a moment.'

Returning toward the bed Bellamy reverently undid the sheet and blankets on one side, folding them neatly back to invite entry. Then yielding to an irrepressible impulse, he climbed onto the bed and lay down and went to sleep.

He awoke, wondering at once how long he had slept. He thought, Clement's waiting downstairs, he'll be furious with me. He next saw Peter standing beside him. His curly hair had resumed its shining brown colour, his eyes glowed, he was smiling. He was wearing some sort of long priestly robe, a black and white kimono, he looked like a king, a god.

Bellamy rolled himself hastily off the bed, and tried to adjust the sheets and blankets. He said at once, 'I must go now.' He added quickly, 'I don't have to go, I'll stay with you – '

'I am perfectly all right, do please go home. Goodbye, and thank you.'

'We'll be in touch,' said Bellamy. A sudden terror had come to him. Something had *happened*. Was Peter, for some reason, now saying goodbye to him *forever*? Was he no longer needed, did this mean *the end* of Peter in his life?

'Don't worry about me. I shall sleep well.' Bellamy followed him to the door, trying to think of something more to say.

Peter opened the door. He looked down at Bellamy with his glowing eyes. Then he said in a low voice, '*I have remembered it.*' Bellamy went through the door which closed behind him.

Clement was not cross with Bellamy. He even indicated a downstairs lavatory for him. Bellamy put on his shoes. They left the house in haste, accidentally banging the front door behind them. For a while Clement drove in silence, frowning. Bellamy kept turning to look at him. He wanted to say many things to Clement but was too tired and confused to decide which ones to say. When he was about to speak Clement spoke.

'Did you notice anything odd about that house?'

'No. It's rather grand, isn't it? I'm sorry I kept you waiting. Peter – '

'That's all right, I spent my time exploring the place. There's something strange about it, indeed distinctly fishy.'

'What on earth can you mean? I didn't notice anything.'

'I did as soon as I came in. It smelt strange.'

'I haven't any sense of smell. I don't know what you're at.'

'That house has not been inhabited for a long time.'

'Are you suggesting Peter just broke in – !'

'I don't know what to suggest. It was just sort of – empty. I madly wanted something to eat, I still do. There was nothing in the larder, nothing in the fridge, no food anywhere. There was nothing lying about in the kitchen, nothing on any surface, nothing to show that anything had been cooked – '

'Well, it's just been put away – '

'And it was the same in all the other rooms, everything extremely neat, but no ordinary signs of human habitation. No book lying anywhere, no hat, no gloves, nothing on the floor, no writing paper, no pen, no towel in the kitchen – '

'No towel – ' Bellamy recalled Peter's request for a towel, which had not struck him at the time as odd. But anyway, why should these things be odd?

'It's just that the servants – there must be servants – are very meticulous, they keep things very tidy and – '

'Tidying away all the food? Not a sign of food, not a crumb anywhere. And a more important piece of evidence – '

'Well perhaps he has several houses, I don't know, why not, it's his business. Or perhaps he'd forgotten where the house was – '

'Bellamy, do come and stay at my place tonight, you will, won't you – there's so much to say – Don't go back to that ghastly hole – '

'Sorry, Clement, I must go home. I want to be by myself. Thank you and please don't drive me there, I'll go by tube, I'm sure the trains are still running – '

'Of course I'll take you there, if you want to go there! Damn, we've been going in the wrong direction!'

'No, no, please just drop me at the next tube station, I can easily – '

'I don't know where the next bloody station is, I'll take you back.'

'No, no, it's miles, Clement, please – oh look there's a taxi, it's just sitting there, I'll get it, do stop, do *please* stop – '

'Oh all right. Have you got any money?'

'Yes. Well, I think so – '

'Here, take this note.'

'Thank you – I'll – ' Bellamy jumped out. Waving he entered the taxi.

Bellamy was sorry to hurt Clement's feelings, but he so *intensely* wanted to be alone where he could confront the awful cacophony of his own feelings. A terrible thought had come to him. Peter had *twice* said, 'I shall sleep well.' Could that mean that he intended this very night to commit suicide? His wonderful saying, 'I have remembered it' – just that could be the very motive for suicide. Should Bellamy tell the taxi to go back? Then he realised that he had no idea where Peter's house was.

Clement drove the Rolls very fast through the now empty streets. He felt savagely miserable. He was extremely angry with Bellamy who had, when Clement *needed* him, refused to be with him. This night, this particular night, he wanted Bellamy to be with him. He feared to be alone with his thoughts.

So, his mystery play, which he had been so certain that he could direct and control had turned into something awful, something *newly* awful, some new *happening* which seemed like a horrible repetition of the first one. Clement could not stop believing that *Lucas had done it all.* Why had he, Clement, allowed himself to become a pawn in that vile contest between those two hateful enchanters? Confound both of them! Why had he imagined that he had to *protect* Lucas? He must have been mad. Why had he *forgiven* Lucas, if that was what he had done? He had been almost magicked into believing that Lucas had never intended to kill him at all. Why had he hung around Lucas, wished to see him when he was back? He was behaving *just as he had done as a child.* Lucas had treated him abominably when they were children, he had pinched him, punched him, put terrifying curses on him, battered his legs in the compulsory game of 'Dogs', lied about him to their mother, knowing all the time that Clement would never accuse him, never complain. When Lucas had disappeared after the court case, Clement had been sick with anxiety! Why had he not rejoiced, thinking 'perhaps the bloody man has killed himself and I shall be free of him at last'? But no, he could *never* have thought that. And now he had set up the 'second event' almost frivolously. If he had not taken it over Lucas and Peter might simply have forgotten the idea. Well, they had both seemed to want it, even Bellamy saw a point in it. But of course Bellamy was waiting for a miracle, for the appearance of an angel or something! Clement should simply have let the whole thing alone. He had stupidly been unable to resist a little drama, 'an evening in the theatre'. He had taken up Peter's words, 'a mystery play', but really he had thought of it as a farce. He had composed those ridiculous speeches, and even uttered them, with some sort of genuine passion (but then when is an actor genuine?), while imagining that people might actually start to giggle. Surely Lucas had treated it ironically, as if he were enjoying what he had called 'a charade'. Had Clement imagined that he could somehow *cure* them all by creating something *absurd*? Salvation by the absurd. A conjuring trick by Clement Graffe. Of course theatre is a kind of hypnosis. Clement had certainly, and instinctively, used that form of its power when, with grandiose rhetoric, almost with sincerity, he had exhorted Mir to 'intensify' his mental state and 'break through the cloud which obscures what he wants to remember'. Evidently Mir had succeeded in intensifying his state to a degree which deprived him of consciousness. For a moment Clement thought he had been struck by lightning. Perhaps he *had* been? What is it like when someone is struck by lightning? Was there not a lightning flash? There had been a great light and some noise. Had he begun to fall before or after the flash? Bellamy had spoken of something falling out of the sky. The whole idea of a 're-enactment' had been *mad*, it had been for all of them a ghastly *ordeal*, which could do no good and could do a great deal of harm. How much harm, eddying outward in fateful circles, Clement was beginning to foresee. He could still feel the grasp of Mir's strong hand upon his neck. And then this evening, taking Mir back to that weird uninhabited house, it was like a bad dream. Suddenly Clement recalled something which he had been about to tell Bellamy, only Bellamy had interrupted him. In that whole tidied-up empty-smelling place he had observed, fallen down beside the refrigerator, one piece of out-of-place disorder. It was a copy of an evening paper. Clement had picked it up. It bore a date in early July.

He parked the Rolls near his flat and went up in the lift. He entered the flat and turned on every light. He took off his overcoat and dropped it by the door. The flat was cold, the heating was out of order again. He noticed with surprise the early picture by Moy which had hung for a long time in the bedroom, but which, for some reason, he had lately moved to the sitting-room. In vivid crayon it represented a child's head, round and pale with large blue eyes, rising above a mass of flowers, perhaps lilies, while in the background a white pillar with a white ball upon it, standing upon a green line, suggested that the child was floating in a pool. He thought, the white ball is the moon, which her head is reflecting, and she is *drowning*. Why didn't I see this before? He picked up two letters which were lying on the floor. One was from his agent, the other from the little theatre in which he was supposed to be taking an interest. Both requested him to telephone. He dropped them in the wastepaper basket and turned on the electric fire. He saw his muddy footprints upon the kazakh rug. He took off his shoes and threw the rug away into a corner of the room. He sat down beside the fire. Suddenly something occurred to him. *The baseball bat*. What had happened to it? He leapt up and discovered his overcoat lying in a heap. He shook it and searched it. It wasn't there. He fruitlessly and stupidly searched the flat. When had he last had it? Lucas had asked him about it when they were waiting in the car. Clement had said that it was in the inside pocket of his coat. He remembered putting his hand in and touching it. What happened to it afterwards? He had not thought of it again till now. It must have fallen out, dropped out somehow in the disorder of the event, and be lying there in *that place*, constituting some final awful *piece of evidence*. Or – had Lucas picked it up, or even removed it somehow from Clement's coat? He now recalled that on the 'first occasion' Lucas had taken away his wallet. And now – was it possible that Lucas, in that darkness, had actually *struck Peter again*? Clement wailed and bit his hands. Should he not now, *must* he not now, go out and *search* for it? He thought, I can kill myself, I can always kill myself. He decided that nothing could be done until the morning. The morning – oh how he dreaded it! He took several sleeping-pills and went to bed, but it was long before his terrible thoughts allowed him to sleep.

The morning came. Bellamy, who had expected to stay awake all night thinking, had in fact, after falling exhausted into his bed, slept soundly. The room was cold, a damp patch had developed over the window, he put all available blankets on top of the bed, together with all his clothes, except for his underclothes which he wore underneath his pyjamas. As he woke up, rising through a dream, his first thought was of Father Damien's letter. He particularly remembered, and repeated to himself, the words: Do not seek for God outside your own soul. He seemed to wake with those words upon his lips. And then for a short time lay, suddenly suspended, in some warm fluid, which was indeed God, the perfect love of God. But then he thought, surely God is not in my soul, I am in God's soul, or rather I am in the womb of God. Why did I never realise this before?

He was thoroughly awakened by shouting in the street. Someone banged on his window. He sat up. He thought at once, but there is no more Father Damien and no more God. He was aware of someone who was trying to reach him through a cloud. Could it be Magnus Blake? Then he remembered what had happened on the previous day. He uttered a sob. He got up and dressed quickly. He must go *at once* to Peter. *Why had he ever left him?* He could so easily have *hidden himself in the house.* Why did that obvious idea not occur to him? He could have stayed there all night, watching over Peter, he could have *saved Peter from suicide.* He must leave *at once.* But then he realised he had no idea where Peter lived, he had no notion even of the part of London, carried in cars he had paid no attention. Perhaps he would *never find Peter again.* He thought, I'll go to The Castle, perhaps the landlord knows. But perhaps if he does, Peter has told him not to tell. Then he thought, Clement must know, he must remember. But suppose he has forgotten? Bellamy pulled on his coat and ran out of the house to the nearest telephone box. It had been vandalised. He ran about looking for another one. When at last he found one he rang Clement's number but there was no answer. He continued to wander about, looking for telephone boxes, agitating his arms and talking to himself.

Clement woke, after what seemed, and perhaps was, a short sleep, to an instant awareness of the situation. He absorbed, as it were in one large gulp, the whole of the last evening's events. Predominant in his mind was the crazy belief, which hung there like a black object, perhaps like the cloud which he had (conceivably) conjured away from Peter Mir's mind, that somehow Lucas had engineered the whole thing. It *had* been like a duel, and *Lucas* had won. Part of all this was the hideous business of the baseball bat, and an image of Lucas raising it up to kill Peter a second time. It was all Clement's fault! Why had he taken it there, yesterday evening, to that place? Because Lucas told him to. Indeed, why had he so idiotically looked after the fatal object during Lucas's absence, and carried it back to him, like an obedient dog, on his return? Why hadn't he destroyed it or, given that it was almost indestructible, thrown it into the Thames? He had laid it down obsequiously upon Lucas's desk. Because after all it was Lucas's property, because it had belonged to their childhood, because it was an accusing reminder of what Lucas had done, because it was a magical object, fatally bound into their long weird relationship? Clement looked at his watch. It was seven-thirty. He thought, I'll go there at once. If it's *not* there it may be anywhere – in Lucas's desk or in a police station. Then he remembered the Rolls. He thought, I'll get rid of the Rolls first, then I'll get a taxi. He ran out, found the beautiful car where he had left it (no parking ticket), and set off across London. But it was the rush hour. The journey, which had taken scarcely more than twenty-five minutes last night, now took him more than an hour. He got lost at the last moment and spent time driving about among similar roads containing large houses. He turned the Rolls into the drive at last, got out and locked it. He dropped the keys through into the hall. There was a dull echo. Silence. He moved away and surveyed the house. In an upstairs room, which he reckoned to be Peter's bedroom, the curtains were still closed. Turning to go he looked at the Rolls and felt a quaint twinge: how much, if things had been different, he would have enjoyed driving that car through London.

There were no taxis. He found the nearest underground station. At the other end (not many stations) he had a little way to walk. Why had he felt compelled to deliver the Rolls first, to 'get it off his hands'? He had wasted time during which *that thing* might be lying there waiting to be found. He hurried. He saw his own little black Fiat sitting there (with a parking ticket). The sun was shining, appearing intermittently between plump greyish clouds which were being bowled along by an east wind. There was a clear light. Some work was being done upon the building-site. The cement-mixer was hurling its contents to and fro, a small bulldozer had appeared. Some way ahead, beyond the gravelled path and the shrubs and smaller trees, the great Wellingtonias were visible. *Everything was visible. The place* was still there, present in the sunshine, instead of being hidden far away in darkness in the confines of some tragic opera. Clement felt sick, anguish squeezed his heart. He must find the thing, take it away and burn it, char it out of recognition, *torture* it. Holding his hand to his painful heart he moved under the dark graceful boughs of the trees. Here was the place, the little clearing, the space above it where the innocent clouds were now obscuring the sun. There was nothing there. He looked, he searched, turning over twigs and leaves and kicking the earth. Had he expected to find it lying there with blood on it? Oh why had he not come earlier! Where was the cursed thing now? He would have to keep waiting for time to show, or not to show. He decided to go and see Lucas, but he dreaded the prospect. He began to walk back to the road, taking a different, he thought quicker, route. As he came to a space of mown grass he saw children playing, laughing and running after a ball. Nearby on a seat two adults were watching them. A boy, aged about twelve, was playing with two slightly younger girls. They were playing with the ball, the girls tossing it to the boy who was skilfully hitting it in various directions with his bat. With his bat. Clement stopped. Yes – *that* was *it*. He thought, I must take that evil accursed thing away from those children. But he stood there watching and did not move. Suddenly the ball, a green tennis ball, came speeding in his direction. He picked it up and threw it back. The children waved to him. The adults waved too. Clement waved back. He watched the game. The two adults rose and called the children. Laughing and talking they all trooped away through the trees, the boy carrying his trophy with him. Clement followed him for a while at some distance. They emerged onto the road through a gate in railings, and climbed into a big car with a Belgian number plate. Clement watched the car out of sight. Then he went to find his own car. He got into it and laid his head down on the steering wheel. Tears came into his eyes.

3

MERCY

Bellamy was standing in the drive looking at Peter's house. After
making two vain telephone calls he had at last reached Clement
who said he had been out returning the Rolls. Clement had also
given him Peter's address. Bellamy had arrived by taxi. It was
now nearly eleven o'clock. Bellamy noticed, as Clement had done,
the curtains drawn in the upstairs bedroom. Bellamy felt exhausted and torn by his fears, and by the misery of not having been
able to reach Clement. Now, seeing the drawn curtains, he felt
horror. He thought, how am I now to go into the future, how
will I be able to endure this dreadful thing which is about to
happen to me, and the *remorse* which will torture me for the rest
of my life. Oh God, why didn't I stay with him! What's the use
of knocking at the door? No one will answer.

The sun was shining. He walked, hearing his feet crunch upon
the rain-wet gravel. He stood at the door. He found a bell and
pressed it. Nothing. He waited. He rang again, a long ring. The
door opened. Peter Mir said, 'Oh Bellamy, good, I was hoping
you would come.'

Not many minutes later Bellamy was sitting in Peter's kitchen,
eating ham and eggs, to be followed by toast and marmalade, and
drinking delicious hot coffee. Bellamy had given up, together with
various other things, breakfast, indeed just lately had eaten little
except bread and tinned beans. He was now faint with relief and
could not stop smiling and saying 'Oh good heavens!' or 'Who
would have thought it!' The knowledge that Peter was pleased to
see him shone about him like a continuous warm clear light.

Peter, dressed in trousers and shirt, his bare feet in slippers,
looked younger, his curly bright brown hair which grew so
smoothly down the back of his neck, glowing in the sunshine, his
dark grey eyes luminous under his copious furry eyebrows. His

high forehead was unlined, his smooth plump cheeks glowed like polished apples, his thick well-formed lips were parted, smiling, sometimes trembling with some concealed emotion. Standing at the end of the table and leaning over it he occasionally, probably unconsciously, lifted his end from the ground, as he looked down upon Bellamy breakfasting. He had, he explained, got up late and already been out shopping, he was so glad he had not missed Bellamy, but of course they would have met very soon anyway. The kitchen window was wide open, there was a glimpse of tall trees in a garden, all the windows visible to Bellamy as he came into the house were open. The sun shone on the garden, it shone into the kitchen – and it seemed to Bellamy that he had never before seen Peter except in dark places.

Of course Bellamy did not reveal his anxiety, now blown so entirely away and almost forgotten, about Peter's 'sleep well' and the curtained window. He explained that he would have come earlier only he did not know the address, and how he had gone about trying to find a telephone box, and anyway Clement was away returning the Rolls. He felt, as he spoke so readily and easily to his smiling host, the words tumbling over each other with merry eagerness, I am *chattering*, I am like a child telling its day to a loving parent! As he watched Bellamy, Peter kept laughing, and then Bellamy laughed too.

Bellamy said, 'You know, this is not very far away from where I used to live, only you live in the *rich* part! Why, that's how you found Anax – he was making his way back to my old flat!'

'Yes, that was a great thing, it opened the door. I shall say more about this later. So you all got back safely last night?'

'Oh yes – '

'And Lucas, how did he get back, did he drive Clement's car?'

'Oh no, he doesn't drive. He got a taxi.'

'It was rather a – confused scene. I must have startled you, falling over like that. You and Clement were very kind to bring me back here.'

'Not at all, we were glad to help, of course we were terribly worried, but – '

'Bellamy, do you mind telling me what exactly happened last night?'

Bellamy had not expected this. He was silent, dropping his eyes and bowing his big head. He took off his glasses and put them on the table, and took firm hold of a lock of his straw-coloured hair. He had been so continuously anxious about Peter's welfare, about whether Peter was alive or dead, last night, he had not reflected upon 'what had happened' or attempted to determine what *had* happened. He realised however in this moment as he laid down his glasses that he had *intuitively known* what had taken place. They had spoken beforehand about a 'metamorphosis', a visitation, something like a miracle. He had for a moment seen Peter as an angel. It was as if his holy, other-worldly, body had been for a second revealed. He had burned and glowed. That was the change which had been, for a moment, too much for his worldly body, so that thereby he might indeed have died. This was what had happened: this and what this *meant* and would *bring to pass*. But if Peter himself did not know it, how could Bellamy tell him? He raised his eyes, dreading to see Peter now anxious, uncertain, relying suddenly upon Bellamy. But Peter looked calm and untroubled, gazing a little quizzically at Bellamy, someone who has asked a question to which he knows the answer. Bellamy thought, he is testing me.

He said, 'Peter, I think you know what happened. Something extraordinary, something miraculous happened.'

Peter, still looking quizzical, raised his eyebrows. 'Oh? Like what?'

'Like the road to Damascus.' This comparison had only just occurred to Bellamy.

Peter laughed. He said, 'Oh, that – '

'You died and rose again. You became an angel.'

'Well, we may return to these matters later. There is something important, not unrelated.'

'What is that?'

'You have not asked me what I have remembered.'

Bellamy had indeed forgotten Peter's words which he had whispered to him when they parted last night. He had forgotten simply because minutes later he was overwhelmed by the idea that Peter was going to kill himself. He now thought, what he remembered may be some terrible thing, something which may destroy him – he felt himself blushing and he put his hand to his throat. He said humbly, 'I am very sorry.'

'You see, whatever we may think about last night, it did bring about one of the things which it was supposed to bring about. And it may prove to have brought about the *other thing* as well.'

'Please tell me what it is that you have remembered?'

297

'God.'

'*What?*'

'God – I have remembered God.'

This vast statement should have shaken Bellamy and, as he realised later, made him bow his head in reverence. But alas at that moment his instant thought was, *after all, he is mad.* He stared at Peter owlishly, his mouth open, as if something very banal had been said to which one might answer, 'Oh, really.' Bellamy struggled for words.

Peter watched him with amusement. He gave the table a final shake and then sat down. 'Don't worry, dear Bellamy, all will be explained. No, not all, much will be explained if we have time, and why should we not have time? I will tell you soon what is of immediate importance – for there are, after this – miraculous, if you like, return of my memory, things which must be done soon – and you must help me do them.'

'I will do anything for you. But what do you mean by God, how does one forget God and then remember him?'

'You told me that you wanted to enter a religious house.'

'Yes. But now I have decided not to.'

'I also have sought enlightenment, not in Christianity, but in Buddhism. When I was young I was wild and wanton, I was very selfish, full of greed, full of envy and jealousy, hurtful to others. Then I felt suddenly that I *must change*, I must change myself or die, change by dying to my awful self. I was fortunate at that time to meet a holy man, a Buddhist, now alas dead, and I spent a time living far away from the world – I will tell you more of this later – then, still following the Buddhist discipline, I returned to the world – '

'But Buddhists don't believe in God.'

'In a personal God, no. I used the word as a brief way of indicating a spiritual path.'

'Do not seek for God outside your own soul.'

'Yes. So speaks Eckhart. As Buddhists speak of the Buddha in the soul. As Christians might speak of the Christ in the soul.'

'But you are Jewish.'

'What is that "but" doing? I am a Jewish Buddhist. Judaism too seeks God in the soul. Not in a man-made man-like idol. Remember the Second Commandment. It is too often ignored.'

'But, Peter – '

'I am now simply trying to explain what it was that I had

forgotten. I simply did not remember the years I had spent as a Buddhist, it was as if all had been compressed together and I was the same as the "angry young man" of my youth. I could feel the continual *pressure* of what had been lost, I felt it as a strange dreadful presence.'

'But could you not get help, you are a psychoanalyst, you must have known such cases of amnesia, you could have asked some colleagues, some friend – '

'Yes, yes, seek help, that sounds easy. But I did not know what I was seeking, and sometimes I feared it might be some horror, as if *I too* had committed a crime and deliberately forgotten it. And during this time I was also obsessed by grief at what I knew I had lost, my ability to do my work, and by my passionate desire for revenge. I was consumed by *hatred.*'

'Yes – I see – how strange – Buddhists say that enlightenment is found by a blow – '

'My dear, I have never been near enlightenment, I am just a beginner! And certainly *that* blow took away the little light which I had. That is what I meant by forgetting God.'

'But, you see, the first blow took it away – the second blow brought it back. Last night you were *struck down*, an angel struck you, and you became that angel – I saw you become very tall, I saw your spiritual being – '

Peter laughed, 'You speak wildly. If an angel was present it was Lucas.'

'*Lucas?*'

'An angel is a messenger of the divine, a messenger is an instrument, sometimes an unconscious one.'

'So it was right to act it all again – Peter, Peter, do you remember how in that pub, The Castle, when I first talked with you, I said I wanted you to enter my life, enter my heart, with a great beating of wings like an angel. Oh now let me be with you! I asked you for a sign, and a sign has been given. Let me be your patient, let me be your servant, heal me – '

'Stop, please, *stop*! I need to heal myself. Yes, we shall talk later and be together. I said there were things to be done, and here I need your help.'

'I will do anything for you.'

'Listen. First I must make peace with Lucas. I said earlier that that strange encounter, our second event, had brought about one

299

good thing, the recovery of my memory. Now, soon, I hope it may bring about another good thing, our reconciliation.'

'You mean you don't hate Lucas any more or want revenge–?'

'Those things have gone away. The light has shone upon them and they are shadows, they are gone. I do not want anything except peace. Listen. Today I shall send a letter to Lucas informing him of the change – the metamorphosis – and suggesting that we meet.'

'What can I do today – may I stay here?'

'You can do nothing today. Just go away and keep your mouth shut. Tomorrow – '

'Tomorrow – '

'Tell Clement what has happened. And – also – '

'Also?'

'Those ladies – '

'The Clifton ladies.'

'I want you to tell them too. Tell Louise, tell Alethea. I mean – tell them I have recovered my memory. But – I think – *not* about last night. That might upset them.'

Bellamy had, at Clifton, on the evening of the following day, a spellbound audience. The meeting took place in Sefton's room so that Anax, shut up in Moy's room, should not hear Bellamy's voice. The kitchen might have been more convenient, only the kitchen door did not shut properly, was indeed scarcely a door at all. The little room was crammed. The folding table, together with a lot of books, had been put out in the hall. Bellamy sat on a chair placed against the bookshelves which were beside the window. Louise sat upon another chair, Clement and Aleph and Sefton sat on the bed, Moy and Harvey on the floor. Many books were under the bed. In the morning Bellamy had gone straight to Clement's flat where they had talked for a long time, and it was agreed that Clement should be present when 'the ladies' were told.

Bellamy had taken off his round glasses and was holding them in his hand like some tool of instruction. He was in black and white as usual. His old black jacket had with age acquired a greenish patina. He had searched in vain for a clean shirt. He had been moving his big round head to and fro as he talked, turning his amiable pale brown eyes upon each of his hearers in turn. What he said had (as Sefton put it later) sounded more like teaching than like revelation – it was as if he had known it all since long ago. Now it was question time.

'You mean he had been practising this religion, or whatever it is, for years and *forgot* it all?' said Louise.

'Yes.'

'How many years?'

'Well – I don't know. Some time. You see, lapses of memory like his often work like that. You can remember all kinds of ordinary things but not important things. Like shell-shocked people in wars who forget who they are or who they're married to and so on.'

'Yes,' said Harvey, 'that does happen. I saw a film about it.'

'So he forgot he'd been good?' said Moy.

'Did he also forget how to be good?' said Sefton.

Harvey and Aleph laughed.

'I don't know,' said Bellamy. 'I think he's always been good. But don't let us argue about that.'

'I think it's an important point,' said Sefton. 'I suppose now he'll go back to psychoanalysis.'

'And he told you and Clement all this at his house?'

'What's his house like?' said Harvey.

'Posh,' said Bellamy. 'A big house with a garden all round and lots of big rooms. I didn't see much of it.'

'So you've only just seen it?' said Louise. 'You said you didn't know where he lived.'

'He wasn't living there,' said Clement.

'That's what you think,' said Bellamy.

'The house hadn't been inhabited for ages,' said Clement, 'it was obvious he had only just arrived. I thought it a bit odd. Perhaps he wanted to avoid someone or something.'

'Perhaps he wanted to avoid Lucas,' said Sefton, 'perhaps he thought – '

'Or the police,' said Harvey.

'Perhaps he had forgotten where it was,' said Moy.

'It can't be that,' said Bellamy, 'the house is near where I used to live – '

'So that's how he found Anax!' said Sefton.

'He doesn't live there, but visits it secretly at night!' said Harvey.

'I was going to say,' said Sefton, 'if he accosted Lucas and Lucas acted in self-defence, then he might believe that Lucas wanted to attack him, but – '

'Surely it was the other way round,' said Louise, 'he *thought* Lucas was attacking *him* – '

'Well, Lucas *did* attack him,' said Moy.

'I was just going to say that,' said Sefton.

'Please please,' said Bellamy, 'all this is entirely irrelevant, I am telling you that he has regained his memory and wants to make peace – '

'I don't think it's irrelevant, but let us leave it for another time,' said Louise.

'You say he was a Buddhist,' said Sefton.

'He *is* a Buddhist.'

'What kind of Buddhist? Is he Zen?'

'I'm afraid I don't know.'

'Has he lived in India or Japan?'

'I don't know.'

'I expect he forgot that too,' said Harvey.

'There seems to be a lot about him that we don't know,' said Louise. 'Are you sure he's genuine, that he isn't deceiving you, or just imagining things? As you say, he has been suffering from shock.'

'I am sure, I am getting to know him better – '

'That seems to imply that you feel you don't know him well enough.'

'I know him very well. He is a good man. He is going to make peace with Lucas.'

Clement said, 'I think you've said enough now. Let's leave it at that, shall we.' He motioned to Bellamy and rose, expecting the others to do so too. As they did not, he sat down again.

'But this is very interesting,' said Louise. 'What you've said is very interesting, and splendid if it's true.'

'Perhaps he's going to confess that he was a thief?' said Sefton.

'No, *no*, he's *not* a thief! He's just giving up hatred and revenge! He regards all those things as shadows, they are gone.'

'Shadows?' said Louise.

302

'You mean it was all a dream?' said Harvey. 'Whose dream was it?'

'Don't Buddhists think that everything is unreal?' said Moy to Sefton.

'Not quite like that,' said Sefton. 'It's more like Plato.'

'Oh. I see.'

'Let's leave Lucas out,' said Clement. 'What Dr Mir has decided to say to Lucas is his business. I think we shouldn't speak about it.'

'But it has been spoken about,' said Louise, 'and this seems an opportunity to get things clear. We are told a lot of strange things and then told not to discuss them. All this new stuff is thrust at us and we're being expected to swallow it and say no more, even if it doesn't make sense!'

'Oh do be calm, Louise,' said Clement. 'Don't get excited.'

'I am calm, I am not excited!'

Aleph, who had been sitting with her feet tucked under her, stretched out her legs and put her feet on the ground. She said, 'I think the main thing that Bellamy wants to tell us is that Peter has regained a part of his mind, and as a result he has become quiet and peaceful, I think this is wonderful, Bellamy has told us something wonderful.'

'I agree,' said Sefton. 'I wish him well with his Buddhism. I think it's quite the best of the world religions.'

Clement rose, Aleph rose, Sefton got up from the floor. Various voices were raised. Clement marched Bellamy to the door.

'Well, what do you make of all that?' said Harvey to Aleph.

Clement and Bellamy had gone. Louise was in the kitchen. Sefton, having rearranged her room, had returned to her studies. Moy had taken Anax for a run on the Green. Harvey and Aleph were sitting in the bar of The Raven. Harvey had insisted on walking there.

'What do I think? I think it's splendid. Don't you? Peter is a complete person again. He has regained his whole nature, he's able to love and to forgive. When he said it was all shadows he meant that so much of evil is unreal. I mean, he saw the futility of blaming Lucas or wanting revenge. One must rise above that. I think I shall become a Buddhist!'

'If Buddhists think evil is unreal they must be mad! Thinking evil is unreal is holding hands with evil under the table.'

'I put it badly. Of course evil itself isn't unreal, but certain kinds of thoughts we feel about it, like revenge and hatred and so on, are useless, made up of fantasies. Wouldn't you agree that we should not spend time wanting to revenge and punish?'

'Punishment isn't the same as revenge. There are crimes and there must be punishments – '

'Vengeance is mine, sayeth the Lord. Hate the sin but love the sinner. Of course I'm not suggesting that we should abolish Law Courts and imprisoning people! I mean something quite simple really, we should try to overcome our egoism and see the unreality and futility of so much of our instinctive thinking. We occupy too much time blaming and hating and envying other people and wishing them ill. We shouldn't do it!'

'Where does all this sermonising come from? Have you been having tutorials with Peter, like Sefton used to have with Lucas?'

'No, I'm just thinking, I'm growing up!'

'Are you in love with Peter?'

'No.'

'Are you going to marry him?'

'Harvey, *dear*!'

'I suspect the study of English literature is doing you no good, it's full of all sorts of romantic high-flown nonsense. You've been reading Shelley.'

'I plead guilty to that crime.'

'I think Bellamy is daft, even dafter than you. Peter Mir has told him a lot of lies to put him off the scent.'

'Off what scent?'

'Didn't you hear what he said about how Peter stayed away from his house in order to avoid people? These people might be the police.'

'So you hinted! One might have all sorts of reasons for avoiding people. It's none of our business.'

'So you side with him against Lucas. Not that I side with Lucas. I think they're both liars.'

'Surely you don't think that Lucas – '

'No, I just don't like him. But at least Lucas is wantonly rude and unkind and doesn't pretend to be saintly. Whereas according to Bellamy, Peter Mir has become perfectly virtuous and wants to be admired, especially by you and the others! Why can't he be good in private? He *asked* Bellamy to tell us all about it!'

'It's *relevant*, don't you see? We are involved too. Why are you being so mean?'

'I don't see why we're involved. If we think we are, we're just meddling.'

'I'm sorry, my dear. I just think that love is what is important, that is forgiveness and tolerance and mercy – and we shouldn't enjoy ourselves censuring people and thinking we're better.'

'I also think that love is what is most important, though I don't think it necessarily contains all those other fine things you were extracting from it – and I don't know what love can do for the *terrible* things of life. I love you, Aleph, I've always loved you. I need you all the time. And I'm very sorry you are going to be away so long with Rosemary Adwarden.'

'Not long, dear Harvey, I'll be back!'

'Yes, yes, you will, won't you, I shall look forward to your return as to a release from prison, I shall feel like a criminal who has served his term, or a hostage who is suddenly unchained and set free. You speak as if you have discovered some new wisdom. Perhaps at last I am finding some new kind of wisdom too.'

'Look at this,' said Lucas. He handed over the letter. Clement read it. The letter ran as follows.

Dear Lucas,
You were kind enough to attend that curious gathering where our original encounter was commemorated, and where I distinguished myself by fainting. As your brother explained, one purpose of the meeting was to generate some will for a reconciliation. The other purpose was to jog my defective memory concerning some aspect of my life which I was conscious of having forgotten. The former objective is still unclarified, the latter has been achieved. As I have explained

305

to Bellamy, who will explain to your brother and to the ladies at Clifton, I have, to put it briefly, remembered my religion. I am, as I told you, Jewish (and, as I told you, I believe that you are too). But I am also a Buddhist, and have undergone a considerable period of disciplined meditation. The shock of that second encounter or 'event' has brought me back again to my 'right mind'. This is to admit that the view of me as 'deranged', held I think by you and others, was in a sense a correct one. I had lost my moral consciousness – and have now regained it. I was filled with hatred and desire for revenge. Now I have no hatred and no desire for revenge. The threats and insults which I directed against you I hereby cancel and revoke. I have no ill will toward you, I am very sorry for my aggressive behaviour, and I ask you to forgive me. I now see that vindictive rages and vengeful intentions are but fantasies, the superficial frothing of the ego. I am now able to overcome these selfish and purely phenomenal manifestations. There are moments for war and there are moments for peace. You are no doubt familiar, on this topic, with the discussion between Krishna and Arjuna. Why did Krishna tell Arjuna to fight? Many well-intentioned thinkers have puzzled over this question. The ready answer is that Arjuna, sunk in egoism, could not have made the decision not to fight with a pure mind, his motives would have been self-righteous, his action valueless. Thus far any novice might stumble. But *why* did Krishna tell Arjuna to initiate a battle in which thousands of men would die – simply in order to perform what he 'really' or 'naturally' felt to be his duty? (We might discuss this case some time, I would like to hear your opinion.) Philosophy, in which I have dabbled, has long bemused itself with the contest between the right and the good – to which the saint's cry of *ama et fac quod vis* is a potent contribution. At any rate, in our affray, a decision for peace can I think be made easily and with a quiet mind. I have in the past (it seems now a very long time since our first meeting) moralised in an intemperate manner concerning your motivation, what you were about to do and why, what made you do what you did do. The clarification of this whole situation in the cause of justice was formerly my main objective. I wished to remove the shadow cast upon my own motives, and to extract from you some sort of retribution. I also wished to see you in the role of one suing for pardon. I have never, and I trust you understand this, had any craving for publicity or wish to drag you back into a law court. This was to be a matter between you and me — as indeed it continues to be. I want now to erase and wash away the whole of that situation, as I have washed away that state of my mind which promoted it. My desire for revenge, an eye for an eye, the humiliation and destruction of my enemy, is now understood by me as an impulse of unenlightened egoism, a submission to determinism, an evil fantasy, which I now hereby repudiate and make to vanish. May I hope that, as I offer you not a mere olive branch, but the total renewal of my soul, you will co-operate with me in ending a 'feud' which was itself unreal, and a painful wastage of time and spirit by both of us. May I come to see you? I am now back in my own house (a healthful image!) and my telephone number is above. I venture to add that when we meet (which I hope will be, at your convenience, very soon) that I shall ask you to grant me one small favour, which I shall then explain to you. Also, please may your brother, and he only, be present at our meeting.

Yours in peace and reconciliation,

Peter Mir

Clement read the letter through carefully and handed it back to Lucas. Lucas was seated at his desk, Clement standing facing him. Clement wanted Lucas to speak first, but as he did not speak Clement said, 'You will see him, of course?'

'I'm not sure about "of course", but I shall certainly see him.'

'Out of curiosity.'

'Out of what he might call an "enlightened" curiosity.'

'When did you get the letter?'

'I found it yesterday evening, delivered by hand. I assume that Bellamy informed you, and has informed the ladies.'

'Yes. You imply that you will receive him in an affable manner. I expect he will give you every opportunity to "come off" just as you wish.'

'You use an elaborate vocabulary. I think he is an ingenious man, and I respect ingenuity.'

'Won't you be relieved to get rid of him?'

'Get rid of him? It doesn't seem, whatever happens, that I or

307

we will be able to get rid of him! He makes himself out in the letter to be as light as a feather and as innocent as a little bird, his sins washed away by the wand of Zen. But what I fear is that he will prove to be an old man of the sea who will continue to hang about our necks.'

'You mean the Clifton ladies?'

'Oh, he will want to get hold of *them*. He may even fancy one of them – Aleph say – or even Louise. He is, I am prepared to believe, very rich, and is also, in spite of his protestations of simplicity, very strong-willed and very clever, or let us say smart. His ostentatious reference to the *Gita* shows that he has completely misunderstood that affair.'

'But if all he wants is to make *them*, somehow or other, into his family, does not that in the end leave you free? Or do you think he wants to have you too?'

'And you, Clement, and you.'

'He has certainly captured Bellamy.'

'When he does come here, and I join him in hoping it will be soon, he will act the part of a holy simpleton. But he will want his reward all the same. He may even want my friendship.'

'He does not as yet know you very well.'

'Indeed, he may be in for more than one disappointment. But all *that*, which may be indefinitely prolonged, will constitute an emotional situation. I suspect he enjoys such things. He hopes for a baring of bosoms.'

'Well, he will never see yours. I wonder what the "small favour" will turn out to be. That may be the great snag. He will want you, after all, to confess to him, to say you're sorry, to give him free and for nothing all the things he was so aggressively demanding! At least you must be relieved to know that he has apparently no plans to murder you.'

'We shall see.'

'Or else he may want you to sign some incriminating statement, which he will then treasure as a weapon against you.'

'Nothing of that sort. Anyway we shall soon know. Could you fix it, my dear, there is his telephone number. Any day this week at 10 a.m. will suit me.'

Harvey was sitting curled up in an armchair reading *I Promessi Sposi* when he heard the strange sound of a key in the front door. For a second he thought, it's a burglar! Or is it the cleaning lady? No, she always rings. He leapt up, decanting his book onto the floor. The door of the drawing-room was open. It was Emil.

'Emil! How wonderful, you've come home!'

'Harvey! I interrupt your studies! What have you been reading? Ah, very apt and suitable to your age. Have you been happy here?'

'Oh, ever so happy! I'm awfully sorry – I should have moved out after you rang up. I – I just delayed – my mother was still there and – I'm so sorry, I'll pack up and get out at once – '

'It needn't be at once, please do not blame yourself. Oh, how nice it is to be home!'

'You have such a wonderful home to come to, I wish I – Well, I'll just go and get my things together.'

'No, no, don't hurry please, I am so glad to see you, let us talk. What is the time? It is nearly twelve o'clock. Why not stay for lunch? Please stay. I have brought back some goodies in my luggage. Yes, if you could help me to bring it in from the landing. We can have a celebration lunch, and you can tell me all the news.'

The next hour and a half was spent in the kitchen, where Harvey had hastily cleared away the remains of his breakfast. On the large kitchen table (Emil said 'It's nicer in here.') they had placed a white damask cloth with lace frills (never of course utilised by Harvey) and had laid out Emil's beautiful best plates and glasses for lunch. Emil had of course a big handsome dining-room where these lovely things, also untouched by Harvey, lived in a large long mahogany sideboard. For lunch they had, from Emil's goodies, bread, caviar, rollmops, salami, pumpernickel, schnapps, and two bottles of Rhine wine, and, from the house stores, oatmeal biscuits, butter, cheese and Cumberland jelly. Emil commented on the fact that Harvey had not touched any of the fancy tinned foods which were stored in the larder. Whatever had he lived on?

Harvey did not like rollmops and hoped he could get away with only pretending to eat them, but he liked everything else and as he sat down opposite to Emil and lifted the little round glass of schnapps which had been placed beside the tall thin glass of white wine, he felt a sudden lift of his spirits. Perhaps after all, somehow or other, with Emil's return, a new era was starting and his luck was going to change! Harvey liked Emil very much, though he had not (partly because of Clive's jealousy) come to know him well. He was cheered and heartened by Emil's kindness, by his affectionate smile, by his evident *appreciation* of Harvey. Emil was tall and soldierly, rather stern and dignified in appearance, with a long sharp straight nose and a well-shaven bronzed complexion and a very high brow with short straight blond hair sleeked well back and closely adhering to his head. Clive used to tease him by saying that he wore a wig, which was patently untrue. His narrow eyes were pale blue, his firm lips suggested determination, perhaps because the full lower lip projected beyond the thin upper lip. Cora Brock, who was very fond of him, said he had 'truthful lips'. He had been, and to some extent still was, a picture dealer. He was said to have come to England to escape a tyrannical father who disapproved of his sexual preferences, but left him all his money.

As they attacked the good food and drink Emil started to ask questions.

'Now I must hear all the news. I have been travelling and out of touch. How is your foot? You said on the telephone it was better. But I see you limping.'

'I think it probably won't get any better. I'll have to "live with it", as they say. I'm constantly told that a limp is romantic, like Byron you know.'

'Dear me, that is not good enough. We must hope for a complete cure – you are young and youth cures well. You are having some treatment I hope?'

'Yes, but it doesn't help.'

'I know a man in Harley Street – '

'Please let's not talk about my foot, it's such a bore.'

'All right, but we shall return to the matter and I shall want details! And how is Lucas?'

'Lucas? You know he is back?'

'Yes, but no more. I received such a letter from Bellamy. Then I unexpectedly left the address I gave, but letters will have been forwarded to here.'

'Oh, there are lots of letters, I put them in a box.'

'Good, good. And how is it with Lucas?'

'Well, you know the man he killed, well, he didn't kill him, the man turned up and wanted some damages.'

'So he returned from the dead and wanted money from Lucas, after having tried to steal his wallet?'

'I don't know. You'd better ask Lucas.'

'And dear Bellamy? I hope he has not gone into his monastery.'

'Not yet.'

'And the lovely Andersons?'

'Lovely as ever.'

'Especially Aleph?'

'Especially Aleph.'

'And your beautiful mother, gone back to Paris?'

'She's, well, actually – '

'You will be able now to get up the stairs to your attic?'

'Yes, it – I've got used to it. I'll go after lunch – well, now we've really *had* lunch, and such a wonderful lunch, thank you so much! I'll just pack up my stuff, I can go by taxi – Emil, you were so very kind to give me that taxi money, I'd have died without it. I expect Clive is arriving later – '

'I will tell you something, Harvey. Clive will not be arriving later. We have parted company. Or I should say, he has left me. He has found someone else whom he better loves. He is gone from me.'

'Oh Emil – how awful – you have been together so long – I am very sorry indeed – I do hope – you may find someone else – sorry, I am putting it badly, I am just so sorry – '

'You put it very well, my child. To find someone – oh yes – that is the problem. To have mutual love, that is so difficult indeed. I hope you may achieve it, Harvey, I hope the gods will guide you to where happiness is. As for me – there is another partner waiting for me, a teacher whom I knew long ago – his name is solitude. I am glad to be back here among my English friends, I will, oh yes, ring up everybody, I shall make out some *übersichtliche Darstellung*, as Wittgenstein used to say. But I shall come back here to an empty flat and close the door, and I shall lean back against the door, as I recall I used to when I was young, and breathe deeply and feel the *deep* relief and liberation of coming home to solitude, coming home to *myself*.'

It was fifteen minutes to ten. Lucas and Clement were waiting for Peter Mir to arrive. The long curtains had been carefully adjusted, pulled first this way and then that. The sun was shining but the wind was carelessly shifting some little clouds around. Clement was sitting on Lucas's desk. Lucas was walking to and fro, the length of the room and back. Clement had had some trouble in setting the stage. At first he had arranged the chairs so that, Lucas of course sitting at his desk, Clement should be seated beside him, only a little behind him. While Peter should sit on a chair isolated in the middle of the room. Lucas however had vetoed this arrangement. Now it was to be that Lucas would of course take his usual place behind the desk, Peter's chair would be approached, placed very near to the desk, almost up against it, while Clement was to sit a long way off, well down the room towards the door.

Lucas said, 'I want to see his face at close quarters. What colour are his eyes?'

'Dark grey – I think.'

'Not perhaps a very dark green? The colour of some coniferous trees? No, black I believe.'

'Oh damn his eyes. For heaven's sake don't let him get too close. Or anyway let me sit just behind him.'

'No, I want you at a distance, up near the bookshelves.'

'As I told you, it's very possible that all this remembering and becoming good and so on is a pretence, he may want to get near to you simply to attack you. He'll start with some soothing account of how he's given up revenge and so on, and then when we're both off our guard – '

'I don't think that will happen.'

'Don't say it so casually, as if it were about will it rain tomorrow. He says he's changed, but this may mean anything. Your life may be in danger. Perhaps you don't care.'

'Think, Clement, he can easily kill me at any time, or get some villain to kill me. Or do you imagine that like you he's a man of the theatre?'

'Theatre. Yes. I'm afraid of it here.'

At last the bell rang. Clement hurried to the door. Against a bright background of sun and racing cloud Peter Mir stood smiling, his smooth rosy cheeks glowing in the bright light, his large eyes shining, dark grey, or were they really very dark green? He was wearing a green and brown tweed jacket, a blue striped shirt open at the neck, very narrow brown tweed trousers, and, not seen before, a black cap which made him look very Russian. He also wore, which particularly impressed Clement, a broad leather belt with a silver buckle about his waist. He carried his mackintosh and his green umbrella. It occurred to Clement that, exiled from his house for mysterious reasons, he had just regained access to his full wardrobe. He looked extraordinarily youthful and full of energy, like a young man setting out upon a delightful mountain walk. He looked happy and excited. He doffed his cap with a flourish. Clement gave, gravely, a slight bow. Peter, with a humorous conspiratorial smile, bowed too. He followed Clement into the drawing-room.

The room seemed dark, after the blaze of colour through the front door, and Clement instinctively and against Lucas's wishes, pulled the curtains back a little more. Meanwhile Peter made for the nearest chair. Clement hastened back, touching his sleeve, and conducting him to the chair in front of the desk behind which Lucas was sitting in his usual place. Clement returned to the more distant chair, quickly moving it a little further forward.

Lucas said to Clement, 'Pull back that curtain again, please.' Clement did so, and returned to his seat.

There was a moment's silence during which Clement gazed at the floor. Peter put his mackintosh and cap and umbrella down beside his chair, then sat quiet, staring at Lucas. Lucas spoke.

'You wished to see me. Please get on with what you want to say.' His tone was weary, and he leant his head down on one hand.

Peter began at once. 'My letter will have informed you of my recovery of my being. The person who confronted you earlier is no more. You see now a new person.' He paused, expecting or allowing Lucas to speak. Lucas, gazing intently at him, said nothing. Peter went on, 'Memory is a strange thing. A loss of memory can, evidently, induce or be a change of character. A wisdom which I had learnt over years was lost to me. My sense of value, my moral sense, was darkened and depraved, reverting to that of my previous unenlightened self. I hasten to add that I am not, in any proper sense, and will never be, a truly enlightened man, but let us say that now I see light, the light which I had lost, and have found again.' There was another pause. Lucas maintained his serious studious gazing. Peter said, 'During the strange time, the dead time as it were, between our first meeting and your reappearance, I busied myself, as soon as any consciousness returned to me, in studying, with what material was available, your career and personality, and I kept watch, as you know, upon your family. You are a learned man, what is called a polymath, and must know something, however superficially, about Buddhism, and about the use of a shock or blow to induce wisdom. Let me say here, in case you wonder how I came to be a Buddhist, that I learnt this discipline during visits to Japan, made in the course of my professional work. In fact Buddhist teaching is not at all remote from the asceticism of mystical Judaism or Christianity, and indeed not alien to psychoanalysis. Travel a little further and you will see it as pure common sense. What I am now rehearsing will not be strange to you. How was it that you and I met on that dark summer night? You of course were there with intent, I as the most accidental of strollers. A minute either way and we would never have met. In any case, whatever we may think of here as fate, the outcome, which caused so much terrible grief and about which I was so ferociously angry, has proved to be, not a catastrophe, but a blessing, the release of a great spirit. I have found my true self, I have been returned to the Way, and what is even more remarkable is that I find myself, upon the Way, at least a little *farther on*. My understanding has been deepened, my vision clarified, I can see my path ahead, my task and my mission. I am aware of my frailties, the weakness of my will, the vast distance between good and evil. But a violent shock, and a glimpse of death such as I have had, may produce incurable depression, or else a liberation into a more pure, more free mode of living. When I die, what goes away? Nothing. As we grow older the body devours the soul. But it may also be that the soul, shocked into awareness, is able to chasten the body.'

Peter here paused, putting his hand to his breast and breathing deeply. Lucas said at once. 'Wait a minute. Are we to understand that your new being, upon which we congratulate you, has now opened to you the possibility of some extreme asceticism? Do you intend to leave the world, to join some monastic order, perhaps in Japan, where you can continue in peace your journey toward enlightenment?'

Peter, raising his finger, with the air of a teacher who is glad to be interrupted by an intelligent pupil, said, 'Ah! For so much I can scarcely hope. Do not be misled by my boasting, which is in part a product of a new happiness and, at my modest level, a sense of freedom. Now I am grateful for life itself –'

'But you spoke of a mission and a task. Perhaps you will return to your practice of psychoanalysis.'

'No, I think not. I see only a little way ahead – what I can achieve later I shall discover later. I possess, as I think I told you, a great deal of money. I have to decide how most wisely and satisfactorily to give it away. I need advice, I need *friends* – '

'Such as Mrs Anderson and the Misses Anderson.'

'Yes, indeed, I already regard those excellent and beautiful people as my family. As I think I said earlier, I have no family. Now, after my liberation, I find it is not too late to create one.'

During Peter's long speech Clement had been gradually moving his chair forward, at first out of anxiety, later out of a desire not to lose a single word of the interesting tirade. Lucas, now noticing his position close behind Peter, frowned and with an angry gesture motioned him back. Clement unobtrusively receded toward his previous post.

Peter's speech had been accompanied by various gestures (Clement, leaning sideways to watch, thought of them as Jewish or oriental gestures): a lifting of the left hand together with a modest or humble extension of the right hand as if to receive, a lifting of the shoulders with an opening, on each side, of both hands as if in some sort of surrender, a movement of the right hand, drooping from the wrist, then moving gracefully upward palm open and fingers apart as indicating some trick or gift, then as in humility, or perhaps blessing, lowering the forefinger to the thumb, then a slow passage to the breast, and placing of the closed left hand inside the grasp of the right hand. At Lucas's last question, or statement, Peter had stretched out both arms at shoulder height, then moving them upward in a gesture of joyful liberation.

Lucas, who had watched this final gesture with raised eyebrows, then said, 'Well, thank you very much, Dr Mir. You have rehearsed for us in vivid terms what you explained perhaps more simply and clearly in your letter. I am glad that you have so entirely recovered, and returned to a happy and fruitful life. I, and also my brother, wish you very well indeed. Thank you for coming here to tell us of your good fortune.'

Lucas now made as if to rise, but was arrested by Peter who instantly reached out his long arm and pointing finger across the desk. 'No. Wait. Please wait. The most important part of my discourse is yet to come. *Please* oblige me with your continued attention.'

Lucas said, 'We have listened to you patiently for some time, and our meeting seems to have reached a satisfactory conclusion, would it not be wise to leave it here? Surely there is nothing more that can profitably be said.'

'There is indeed more, but I will try to be brief. What I have been saying has left out one thing.'

'What is that?'

'The original act.'

'What original act?'

'The original event when you struck me violently with a club and nearly deprived me of my life.'

'Oh that. But did you not explain in your letter that this whole affair, increasingly wrapped up in obscurity and uncertainty, could now be consigned to the past? Your own emotions, you even generously suggested, were to be regarded as fantasies and illusions of egoism. And you asked for my forgiveness. This is going far, very far, it is enough. Enough for you, and enough for me. Let us now, having reached this remarkable degree of understanding, leave it all alone for good.'

Lucas, leaning forward, spoke in a gentle persuasive tone. He spoke indeed, Clement was sure then and later, with profound sincerity.

Peter, who until this moment had seemed full of confidence and energy, the master of the scene, now began to show anxiety. He raised his left hand, putting the back of his hand against his mouth. He looked at Lucas soberly, even sternly. He lowered his hand and said in a new soft voice, 'No. It cannot be so consigned. It must, I am afraid, be clarified, I mean looked at in a clear light, shall I say *worked over* – somehow – before it can be – overcome.'

'Oh dear,' said Lucas in a brisk sprightly voice, audibly shuffling the papers on his desk, 'do we have to start all over again? Surely *just that* is what you seemed so pleased to be free of. Surely one replay is enough?'

Peter, breathing deeply and looking down at his now quiet hands, said, 'Please let me go on talking, thinking and talking. We have reached, may I say, a great high peak, or plateau, an open space, in our – contest – I mean our relationship. Yes, I have been set free, I can sit quietly and breathe, I am *at peace*. Instead of the image of blind Justice with her sword and scales I have that great clear space, rather perhaps like a green field, a pure light, quietness, the sudden absence of the terrible pains of anger and hatred. But then – ' he paused – 'but then, still, *what about you?*'

'I am not sure that I understand you. If you are thinking of my welfare, moral or otherwise, I assure you that I can look after that myself. Is it not now your *duty*, your surely not unpleasurable duty, to *leave me alone?*'

Lucas, sitting up straight, was staring at Peter who, rigid, was staring back. Clement, banished to the back of the room, saw, or more deeply felt, as never before, his sense of them as two great rival magicians.

Peter turning his head away and relaxing his body, said in a worried tone, 'Well, not quite like that. I want peace of course. But I also want reconciliation. And reconciliation involves two people. Do you see? I used to want retribution, now I want reconciliation – I want something clear – like an equivalence – only not like it was before – '

'It is,' said Lucas gently, as if speaking to a child, 'at this stage in our proceedings, useless, and even dangerous, to seek for clarity or speak of equivalences. Do you want me to confess to a crime, or make some gesture of submission, so as to be with you in that green field? It won't do, you know, it won't do.'

Peter did not reply to this at once. He looked at Lucas, then looked away again. He said, 'I daresay I am thinking about myself, about my peace of mind. I know what you mean, about the *danger* of this, as it suddenly is now, argument or – contest. But – yes – I want something which is not just an empty form of words. There is a lack of completeness. Something deep is making its demand. I want to move all this, all that we have talked of, all our words, on a little farther, on toward something needful, a kind of action. Keeping in existence the understanding which now, now this very moment, exists between us. I think, I hope, that now you will see what I mean.'

They continued to stare at each other. Lucas nodded slightly, waiting for Peter to continue.

Peter continued. 'I said in my letter that there was one small favour which I was going to ask.'

Lucas nodded again.

'Well, now, this favour, may I – ?'

Lucas said, 'Go on.'

Peter suddenly stood up.

Startled out of the hypnotic state which the 'contest' had

induced in him Clement rose too. Lucas said to Clement sharply, 'Sit down.' Clement sat down.

Peter then picked up his chair and, holding it in one hand, walked round the desk. He put the chair down beside Lucas's chair, but sideways to it and close against it. He sat down. Lucas turned his head towards him.

Peter then said to Lucas, 'Please take off your jacket and your shirt and – '

Clement rose again and took several paces forward. He thought, Peter Mir has *gone mad*.

Lucas, and Clement could see a strange smile upon his face, took off his glasses, took off his jacket, then his shirt and his vest, tossing them away behind him, still facing his interlocutor.

What happened then seemed to Clement to occur in a dream, in a hypnotic vision, or another dimension. He stood paralysed and spellbound. He saw that Peter was holding in his left hand his familiar green umbrella. Peter's right hand had seized the slightly curving handle of the umbrella. He drew it away. Out of the inside of the shaft, materialising quietly, not suddenly, but as if by magic, there appeared a long gleaming steel knife. Clement did not move, he could not. Lucas, looking down at the knife, did not move either. He looked back at Peter. The other part of the umbrella fell to the floor with a soft sound. Peter now looked down toward the point of the knife. With his left hand he gently touched Lucas's side. Then he advanced the knife and thrust it in between the ribs.

Clement tried to move, he tried to cry out, he uttered an incoherent sound. He fell to his knees, then stretching out his hands lay prone on the floor in a dead faint.

'Pull him up onto the chair, get his head down between his knees, that's right, leave it to me.'

Clement felt sick, he felt he was suffocating, a black canopy was hovering above his head, his eyes were blinded by something, perhaps tears, he uttered sounds, protesting incoherently as Peter's large strong hand, gripping his neck, thrust his head down. The pressure was removed. He sat up, his head drooping. Peter caught hold of him again as he was about to fall from the chair. He lifted his head and sat open-mouthed, gasping, breathing deeply, seeing in a haze the faces of Peter and Lucas bent solicitously towards him. He heard Peter's voice saying, 'He's all right now, he hasn't hurt himself. You haven't hurt yourself, have you, Clement?'

Clement, not sure whether this was true or not, murmured, 'No, no – ' He saw, as if reflected in a round mirror, Lucas standing near, smiling, holding his shirt in his hand. There was a small red smear upon Lucas's side.

Sitting steady on the chair Clement was able to see, now clearly, the two of them, smiling at him and actually *laughing*. 'You are all right, aren't you?' said Lucas. 'You came quite a cropper.'

'I am perfectly well, thank you,' said Clement, looking with amazement as Lucas dabbed his side with his shirt and then put the shirt on. Clement said to Lucas, 'Are *you* all right?'

Lucas replied, 'Yes, very much so.' He and Peter began laughing again.

Clement looked about him. There was no sign of the long knife. He saw Peter's green umbrella lying innocently on the floor, now in front of the desk. What had happened, what had he *seen*?

Ignoring Clement now, and moving away from him, the two were talking to each other. Lucas was saying, 'I always knew that you were something of an artist.'

Peter said, 'I was afraid, you know.'

'I can imagine that. You are a brave man. It was well done.'

'I needed you – to make this – it was necessary – '

'I entirely understand.'

'I thought you would.'

'The sword and the scales have had their day.'

'That is well put. Of course it was a flaw in my – '

'In your new being.'

'Yes. I suppose I ought to have quenched that tiny spark of – '

'Quite!'

'Like in a fairy tale, everything is right except for one little thing – '

'Now it is gone.'

'With your co-operation.'

'I said it would be dangerous to get things clear – '

'But now things are clear. You agree?'

'Yes.'

Clement listening to this conversation thought again: they are mad, they are behaving like drunks, what on earth are they talking about, what do they mean, it doesn't make sense! It was true that Lucas and Peter, now standing face to face near the desk, were punctuating their elliptical conversation with expressive gestures and frequent bursts of laughter. They seemed indeed to be intoxicated with their subject and enchanted with each other, it was as if at any moment they might start to waltz. At last however they stepped back and gazed at each other. Peter picked up his umbrella and mackintosh and cap.

He said, now visibly exhausted, in a quiet solemn tone, 'So, I take my leave. We shall meet again. All is well.' He bowed. Lucas bowed. Turning towards the door he seemed suddenly to notice Clement. 'My dear Clement, how are you, are you feeling better?'

Clement rose to his feet. 'Oh yes, much better.'

'Good, good.' He moved towards the door, then turned. 'I quite forgot something important. I am going to give a party.'

'A party?' said Clement.

'Yes, a *party* to celebrate – my recovery, my return to my own house – that shall be quite soon, next week perhaps, I shall send out invitations to you, to you all.'

Lucas stood smiling, then leaning back against his desk, Clement opened the drawing-room door for Peter, then ran before him to open the front door. It was raining. Peter descended the steps, donned his mackintosh and pocketed his cap, and began to put up his umbrella as he waved goodbye.

When Clement returned to the drawing-room Lucas was sitting behind his desk, where he had turned on the green-shaded lamp. He had put on his narrow spectacles and was examining his pen. He looked up at Clement as if mildly annoyed at being interrupted. 'Thank you for coming. Now please go. I must get on with my work.'

Clement picked up his chair and carried it forward and placed it opposite to Lucas. The chair which Peter had lately occupied had been moved back against the wall. The final phase of the argument, or duel between the two mages had taken place standing. Clement now seemed to *remember* this as if it had all taken place long ago.

Leaning his arms on the desk he said to Lucas, 'What happened?'

'You saw what happened.' Lucas frowned slightly but did not immediately repeat his dismissal. He removed his glasses and began to clean them on a piece of yellow duster.

'No, I didn't, I fainted.'

320

'Oh yes, of course. Well, nothing happened when you were unconscious except that we rushed forward anxiously to revive you.'

'Yes, but before – I don't understand. There was a knife, wasn't there, I saw a knife.'

'There was a knife.'

'And – I think – I saw blood.'

'Yes, there was blood. I'll show you. Dear me, this is like doubting Thomas. Do you want to touch me too?' Lucas set down his glasses, turning pulled up his shirt and showed Clement a small red slit between two of his ribs. 'Is that enough?'

'But – is it a deep wound? Oughtn't you to go to the doctor? Oh *dear* – '

'Of course not. Please don't faint again. It was the merest pinprick. A little blood was drawn, that was all.'

'I thought he was going to kill you.'

'Did you? It was kind of you to be so upset.'

'But did you expect – I mean – was it all a show – I mean was it fixed beforehand, did you know – ?'

'No, of course not! Anything like that would have been senseless.'

'So he might have killed you. With that long knife, he could – '

'Well, he was a surgeon once. I'm sure it would have been painless.'

'Luc, don't *jest*.'

'I am not jesting. I am just trying to find for you a mode of explanation. In fact there is, now I come to think of it, no reason why I should offer you any explanation. I assume you followed his argument. If you did not you are a fool and better off left in ignorance.'

'Please, Luc – suppose I hadn't fainted, would he have gone on, would he have killed you?'

'So you think you saved my life?'

'*Please* – '

'I doubt if he ever intended to kill me. But of course I wasn't sure. That was the essence of the matter.'

'So you would have sat there and let him do it?'

'At that point resistance would have been useless. He is far stronger than I am.'

'So you *offered* yourself?'

'As I told you before, Clement, he could kill me, or have me killed, at any time. He still can. Only I think now he probably won't.

321

He is an artist and a gentleman. He chose to despatch me with a symbolic retribution. That's all. He is a very remarkable person.'

'So you'll meet him again, you'll go to his party?'

'You know I never go to parties. Now please go away, will you, dear boy. You have been the privileged spectator of what I hope is the conclusion of a rather strange drama, about which I know that you will *never* speak. Now let us at last say farewell to this matter. Please be off.'

Clement continued to lean his elbows on the desk. He said, 'But what about me?'

'Well, what about you?'

'I'm left out. Oh dear, I'm so confused – you said I must have followed his argument, but I can't follow it. Was it all about forgiveness?'

'Roughly.'

'So he let you off?'

'A crude expression.'

'But *what* about me?'

'What indeed?'

'I thought he was against you not only on his account but on my account.'

'I daresay he thought that you could look after yourself and deal with your own case in any way you thought fit.'

'You are deliberately confusing me.'

'I am trying to offer you a bit of clarity, but if you don't want it, never mind – just go away.'

'Luc, please tell me – now – did you intend to kill me?'

'No, of course not. Now go. And let that matter too go to rest.'

Clement got up. He felt giddy, and wondered if he were going to faint again. Where was his overcoat? Oh, out in the hall. He began to walk slowly toward the door. When he reached the door Lucas suddenly called after him. 'Wait a moment. I have something more to say to you.'

Clement turned. 'What?'

'I forgive you.'

'*What* ?'

'For all the suffering which you caused me when we were children, I forgive you.'

'Oh – thank you – '

'Now clear off.'

*

322

'*Maman*, please, I must go, I said I'd see Aleph before she goes away with Rosemary.'

'She'll miss the party.'

'Oh hang the party!'

'So we've all been invited!'

'When are you going to Paris?'

'I'm not going to Paris. I'm staying here.'

'You can't stay here, we'll go mad!'

For two nights now Harvey had slept on the floor in the narrow space between the extended bed and the bathroom door. The bed, on his mother's insistence, remained extended all day, instead of being folded into its cupboard. Progress from the front door to the bathroom was over the bed. Harvey had been unable to sleep. He lay on his back listening to his mother's quiet snoring and thinking how increasingly awful his life was becoming. It was as if he were being squeezed out of the world. For two mornings he had gone to the local library to work, but could only continue to read *I Promessi Sposi* which was beginning to bore him. He 'went shopping' for food. He bought cheap white wine. He refused to buy champagne, even with his mother's money. In any case she kept on announcing that she was penniless. He went to his bank and cashed a cheque. He did not dare to ask how much money there was in his account. He could not ask Emil for any more taxi money. He assumed that Clement and Lucas were continuing to finance him. But suppose they had forgotten, or suppose Lucas had decided to stop paying. Bellamy of course could not now be expected to contribute. He did not believe his mother's penniless story. How was he going to get her out? No one seemed to be inspired to assist him. Supposing she became ill? She seemed to be living on white wine and oranges. Lying in bed, now wearing an old pyjama jacket which Harvey imagined he could remember from his childhood, she consumed oranges, dropping the peel around on the bed and on the floor. He hated to see her eat the oranges, she was like an animal. Harvey spent his time tidying and cleaning the flat. This activity provided his only form of satisfaction. He cleaned the bath, he even cleaned the windows. On the two previous days when Harvey had returned from the library, carrying wine and oranges and tins of beans and ravioli and macaroni cheese, he had found her gone. The bed was chaotically undone, her nightdress and pyjama jacket half buried in it, her one suitcase overflowing with garments. There was nowhere in the flat to hang anything up except a hook on the door. She returned, on each occasion, about nine o'clock in the evening. To annoy her, he did not ask where she had been. Also, on each occasion, they had both promptly become thoroughly drunk together on the white wine. Was this strange mode of life to go on and on? It seemed already to be establishing a regime. Since Harvey had perforce moved in with his mother he had not shaved. Why? Was this the beginning of some long penitential incarceration during which he would be destined to grow a beard? Aleph had once said how beautiful he would look with a golden beard, like some heroic Scandinavian. Harvey hated beards. Perhaps the omnipresence in the bathroom of Joan's strong-smelling cosmetics made him realise that *he* was the intruder. He could not look at himself. He tidied up her clothes, including her night clothes and her underclothes. Sitting on the side of the bed he ate half of a small tin of macaroni cheese with a spoon. He had no appetite. His leg was hurting. He lay down on the bed and gazed at the ceiling. On the first day he had telephoned Clifton but had found only Moy, who was incoherent and unhelpful. 'Going into one of her trances' as Bellamy used to say. On the second day he rang again and got Louise, who warned him of Aleph's imminent departure. She said, 'Do come tomorrow, Aleph wants to see you before she goes in the morning, she's leaving about eleven, she's just rushing about today.' Harvey then thought in order to pass the time, of going to see Bellamy in his awful cell, but shuddered away from it. That place was unclean, his flat, despite his efforts, was unclean, his mother's clothes were unclean, there was orange peel in the bed, he could not shave, he could scarcely even eat. Now it was the morning of the third day and he had engaged himself in a horrible time-consuming row with his mother.

'You are a coward. Why didn't you just go to Italy, never mind your foot. You just wanted an excuse. Why don't you take a job?'

'Oh shut up, *maman*, I haven't any skills. Look I must go – '

'You could be a waiter, anyone can be a waiter.'

'Besides, I've got to *read*, I've got to *study* – '

'I don't believe it. Who is supporting you, I presume someone is.'

'I don't know. Who is supporting you, if it comes to that?'

'I have been selling myself to pay for you.'

'Don't play that dreary old card. I don't understand why you don't go back to Paris, if you don't want to you can sell your Paris flat, didn't you tell me you were selling it?'

'I can't, I don't own it, I only pretended to, someone else owns it! Oh *God*, I need a man!'

Harvey had by now set aside his notion that he had seen a woman at Lucas's house and that that woman was his mother. He had been so overwhelmed by the shock of the loss of his stick and its even more terrible return that this anguish had somehow swept away his earlier speculations. He had even begun to conjecture that the 'woman' whom he had 'seen' might have been a boy, or else an illusion created by the dim light and the rain. He passionately *did not want to think* about Lucas.

'Oh please, *chère maman*, let us not have this *senseless* argument again! I must go to see Aleph!'

'Couldn't you occupy her room while she's away?'

'Perhaps you could!'

'Well, we both know we can't. Who'd want us in that house? It would just embarrass them. There remains Clement, he loves me, I shall ring him up.'

'Oh, it's all so *contemptible!*'

'I know. Why are we both so stupid? We are both cowards. I shall have to resort to Humphrey Hook after all.'

'The final solution. *Maman*, do not frighten me.'

'At least I'd have peace then and no more worries!'

'Oh stop it!' He had searched his mother's luggage for drugs or sleeping-pills but found none. However, he knew that she had left several cases with Louise at Clifton, and probably others with Cora.

Harvey was sitting on the end of the bed. His mother, barefoot, clothed now in smart narrow black trousers and a loose dark green shirt, was leaning back against the pillows, raising her head awkwardly. Her mass of hair was tangled, her face devoid of make-up looked pale and hungry.

He thought, how beautiful she is, she is *profoundly* beautiful, she is a gipsy. Staring at Harvey she touched her hair as if timidly with her frail hand. She said, 'It's cold.'

Harvey leaned forward and kissed her cold feet, enclosing them in his warm hands. Her eyes closed, then sparkled, then slowly filled with tears.

'Oh darling *maman*, I love you so much! I *must* go now.'

*

Harvey relied on finding a taxi. He usually had luck with taxis. When he appeared, a taxi appeared. This time, however, he was not lucky. He walked, turning his head this way and that, increasingly upset as he looked at his watch and saw how late it was. He walked slowly, leaning on his stick, the clinical one, not the smart one tainted by Lucas. Thoughts about his mother soon vanished, he was possessed by anguish about Aleph. How had he idiotically spent so much time arguing with his mother? Distant live taxis were constantly seized by others. He stood at crossroads impotently waving his stick. Nearly half an hour had passed. Harvey was almost in tears. At last the longed-for cab obeyed his signal. He climbed in and leaned back closing his eyes. He thought, Aleph wanted to see me alone. Still, surely I won't be too late. Oh why is she going away just when I want so much to be with her! She is the answer to the riddle of my life.

He reached Clifton and paid the taxi. There was a long sleek black car outside. Rosemary Adwarden's car. As he hurried toward the door of the house it burst open and, with a medley of voices, the Cliftonians poured out onto the pavement. Rosemary was opening the boot of the car and putting in Aleph's suitcase. Rosemary was as tall as Aleph, a lithe blonde destined by her barrister father for the legal profession. She already had a place at Edinburgh University. Harvey, who liked her, had not seen her for some time. She was the first to notice him. 'Why, Harvey, you poor lame duck, I'm so sorry! Get better soon, won't you!' Sefton, standing by, said censoriously, 'You're late!' Aleph, handsome in her tweed travelling clothes, was being kissed by the others. She threw her overcoat and mackintosh into the back of the car. She turned to Harvey. He wanted a message but there could be none. She kissed his cheek, clasping one of his hands and squeezing it. 'Goodbye, Harvey, thank you for coming, goodbye!' She stepped into the car. The car sped off, Aleph's hand fluttering at the open window. Harvey did not wave. He felt a stone on his heart, the terrible weight of remorse. She had wanted to talk to him alone, and he had not been there. Would he ever be able to win back what he had in this minute lost? He thought, she will never forgive me, she will lose her love for me forever.

Sefton had moved back into the house. Moy had run in after her and released Anax who had been shut in the kitchen. Louise, still on the pavement, said to Harvey, 'Come in, my dear, and have a cup of tea.'

Harvey followed her in. Moy, followed by Anax, was disappearing up the stairs. Sefton had entered her own room and shut the door. Louise went into the kitchen. Harvey said, 'I want to talk to Anax. I'll be back in a minute.' He followed the bounding dog up the stairs and on up to the top landing. Moy, turning and seeing him, looked startled. She pushed open the door of her room. He sat down on the top step and tried to attract Anax's attention while Moy watched. The dog calmed down and, called by his name, came to Harvey who patted him, uttering endearments, and then stroking his long back from which the thick soft fur fell down so neatly, stroking him over his sleek head and over his long grey muzzle and his black whiskers, gently touching his black curling lips and his white teeth and his moist black nose. Anax gazed at him with his blue eyes which were so distant and so strange and so sad. Harvey, looking up at Moy, thought suddenly, Anax loves Bellamy, Moy loves Clement, I love Aleph. And here we all are shipwrecked. Oh what a fool I am! 'When will she be back?' he said to Moy. Moy made a vague helpless gesture. Evidently she didn't know.

Harvey rose and made his way cautiously down the stairs. The kitchen door was open and Louise was sitting at the table. Harvey thought, this house which I know so well and have known so long ought to be my home. Only it is not. My mother is right. Less and less will I be welcome here.

'Harvey, sit down, have some tea. Why don't I see you more often? I wish you would regard this place as your home like you used to do. Have some of this lemon sponge cake, I made it for Aleph only she wouldn't have any. How is your mother? She is neglecting us too.'

'Oh she's all right. You know Emil is back? Clive has left him.'

'Yes, Emil rang me up, he wanted all the news. He told me about Clive. So sad, isn't it, after so many years.'

'Yes. He wants to be alone now.'

'I quite understand. So you are sharing your flat with Joan? Isn't it much too small?'

'Yes, but I think she's going to move in with Clement.'

'To move in with Clement?'

Harvey had no sooner said this at random than he felt another pang of sharp and painful remorse. If he had been a grain more sensitive he should have realised that Louise was on the point of offering him Aleph's room. If only he could have lived in Aleph's house, slept in Aleph's bed, the magic power which he so desperately longed for would have been granted to him.

Yes, 'everyone' had been invited to Peter's party: the Cliftonians of course, Lucas, Clement, Bellamy, Harvey, Joan, Tessa, Emil, the Adwardens (but only Jeremy and Connie could come, Rosemary was away touring with Aleph and the boys had returned to their boarding school), the landlord of The Castle, and Cora Brock who had, as Joan put it, 'Got into the act somehow as usual.' Anax had also been invited, but of course with Bellamy there his presence was impossible.

The invitation said simply *Peter Mir at home 6 p.m. onward*, but Peter had assured Bellamy who told Clement who told Louise that besides, of course drinks, there would be 'things to eat'. 'I suppose we shall have to eat standing up, which I *abominate*,' said Clement. There were also reflections about who else, strangers, other friends of Peter's, might be present. This remained unclear, though Bellamy reported that Peter had said 'family only', meaning what he called his 'new family'. 'He wants to thank us for being kind to him,' said Louise. Clement found this very funny. Joan suggested that he was gathering us together to blow us up. Altogether there was a good deal of not unpleasant mystification, including problems about what it would be correct to wear. How long a skirt? What sort of tie?

Clement, putting on a dark blue bow tie, was in a very unhappy state. Joan had telephoned him asking if she could come and stay in his flat, 'Only for a few days,' she said, while Harvey was finding somewhere else to live. Clement had felt instantly that he *passionately* did not want Joan in his flat, if she were there he would *go mad*. Why? Because he was in love with her? Certainly not. He *hated* her, he *hated* himself. The horror of that scene with the knife had not left him. How could *that*, which he had witnessed, have really happened? Clement's *dread* now concerned not only the sight of the knife and the blood, but perhaps even more the *dance*, as it now seemed to him, performed by the two of them after the event. The word 'event', now recurring to him again, made it all seem increasingly like the slow enactment of an awful pantomime. What he had lately seen might be called the 'third event', or Act Three. They had laughed, they had capered round each other, they had positively delighted in each other, they had surely *touched* each other. It was like watching mad goats dancing. Thank heavens, he thought, as he fumbled with his tie, Lucas, who never came to parties, would not be present at this one! Or, in the new nightmarish scenario into which they were now entering, *would* Lucas come, would he decide to *manifest* himself? Perhaps this would turn out to be Act Four. I'm sure, thought Clement, that something terrible and *absolutely unexpected* will happen at this party. Time had unravelled itself with a baneful slowness since that unspeakable *first moment*. Then there had been the law case, Lucas's disappearance, the miserable interim, then the *tête-à-tête* with Lucas which had had some meaning which now escaped Clement, then the horror of Peter rising from the dead, then the 'trial' and Peter's conquest of 'the ladies', then the metamorphosis, then the climax, the knife, the blood, the dance. Then Joan proposing to move into his flat. 'No!' he had cried on the telephone. 'No, it's too much, no, you can't, no, no!' Afterwards he had felt sickening remorse, but could not ring her back since Harvey had no telephone and anyway what 'apology' could be offered short of telling her yes, of course, she must come and stay at once! The idea, which also occurred to him, that he might take in Harvey instead, was of course equally out of the question. It would be an affront to Joan; and in any case Clement had developed curious feelings about Harvey, perhaps guilt, perhaps even jealousy. But all this was mad. Thank heaven Aleph would not be at this party. Oh poor Joan, had he now made her his enemy forever? And this morning, when his agent had telephoned him, mentioning an interesting part in a new play to be put on in Glasgow, but likely to reach the West End, and he had refused, his agent had said that unless he did *something* very soon he would be *totally forgotten*.

Peter's house was indeed 'lit up'. By now nearly all the guests had arrived, complaining of the cold (snow was forecast) and basking in the huge warm shell of space and light. Drinks were swiftly placed in every hand. Peter, in the drawing-room, had greeted

329

those he knew and been introduced to those he did not. Bellamy had already explained to him that Lucas *never* answered invitations and *never* went to parties. Peter also introduced everyone to Mrs Callow the cook (old retainer), Patsie (Mrs Callow's niece) and Kenneth Rathbone, landlord of The Castle (evidently old friend and already known to Bellamy). The guests were encouraged to 'stroll about everywhere', and some, not all, eagerly did so, penetrating, on all three floors, drawing-room, library, study, dining-room, kitchen, scullery, empty rooms, garden rooms, cloakrooms, bedrooms, bathrooms, dressing-rooms, laundry rooms, boxrooms, and what Joan called 'ambiguous boudoirs'. All the doors stood open. Clement's anxiety about 'eating standing up' was soon dissipated by a glance into the dining-room set for a sit-down dinner, and his other anxiety about not getting enough to drink was removed by the sight of a large table at the far end of the hall where a crowd of drinks, including a recommended 'special', were continually replenished for the strollers. Sausages and cheese biscuits and other dainties were also available in large bowls placed here and there. Clement kept on amazing himself by noticing how totally the house had changed since his last visit: another metamorphosis. Peter too, dressed in a very dark suit and a luxuriant green silk cravat, was smiling, moving about with happy ease among his guests, even wandering after them up the grand staircase. Clement also noticed, and mentioned to Bellamy, that their host, gracefully opening his hand and then raising it, was *touching* all the people with whom he conversed. 'I suppose he is blessing us all,' Clement said. 'He patted me. Now he can hardly take his hands off Emil.' Bellamy, beaming with pleasure, replied, 'Accept his blessing. He will do us all good. Can you not feel a kind of warm enlivening force?' 'Yes,' said Clement, 'but I am afraid it is that "special". I wonder what's in it.'

Moy and Sefton had decided after a brief conference, to wear their necklaces. They did not consult their mother. As Sefton pointed out, this was their first opportunity to thank the donor, to whom they could then explain that they would have written 'thank you' letters only they did not know his address. On the other hand, would the donor be embarrassed if, wearing the necklaces, they thanked him publicly? Perhaps he would not want anyone to know he had given them such expensive presents, perhaps indeed, as Sefton surmised, he had simply wanted to give something to Aleph, and had included them only out of politeness?

As it happened, the Clifton contingent arriving first, and being let in by Patsie who told them where to put their coats, had been welcomed profusely by Peter, who exclaimed at the necklaces, touched them, and said how well they suited their owners, and that he had chosen them with care. He seemed to be about to kiss Louise, but instead held her hand in both of his and squeezed it for some time. He said, 'How sad about Aleph, I mean about her not being able to come, it is sad for *me*.' 'Well, indeed,' said Louise, and withdrew her hand. Emil then arrived and was introduced. Later in the evening Louise glimpsed Peter and Emil sitting together, deep in conversation in the library. Moy and Sefton had wandered away by themselves. Moy was wearing one of her long shifts, an auburn one, round-necked, upon which to show off her lapis lazuli. She had considered putting her hair up, but decided not to. It did not always stay up. Her thick blonde plait hung down to her waist. She seemed to have become a little taller and a little slimmer. Sefton was wearing a long dark green skirt, pulled firmly in at the waist, with a white blouse and a very old black velvet jacket. She nervously fingered the amber necklace, which tended to hang down invisibly inside the jacket. Her uneven reddish-brown hair was, quite by accident as she had just washed it, more orderly, fluffy, less jagged, more like a halo. She looked about her sternly, even aggressively, her mouth compressed, as if she were searching for someone, which she was not.

Clement, abandoning Bellamy who was following Peter around, set out to look for Joan, whom he had seen in the distance talking to Cora Brock. He found them still together. Cora, the only one wearing an ankle-length skirt, was a rich handsome woman of fifty, certainly eccentric and brusque, but secretly generous and yearning for friendship. She put on a bluff chatterbox manner to conceal her shyness. She was still mourning for her husband, Isaac Brock, who had died ten years ago. She was childless.

'Hello Clement, I hear you have given up the theatre.'

'No, Cora, the theatre has given me up.'

'Well, it is a miserable profession. You know, this Peter Mir is attractive, you misled me, Joanie. I am looking forward to my turn to talk to him. Yet he is a bit like a schoolmaster too, don't you think? And his eyes, his eyes, those dark murky eyes, and they are quite bulging, surely he is something of a fanatic. Joan says he is religious and I am not surprised. Isn't he Jewish? He looks Jewish. I believe he is. That's good. Look how kind and attentive he is to everyone, though a little fussy too, don't you think? I'm sure you wonder how he knew that I existed, I thought Joan might have mentioned me, but, no, it seems that he asked Bellamy to gather in a few other members of *our circle*. I didn't know I belonged to a circle, but evidently I do. As Joan puts it, he just wants to enlarge his acquaintance in our milieu. Well, I won't argue with that. I gather he is a psychoanalyst, one can always do with one of those. Someone said he was just coming back to this house and that's what the party's for, perhaps he's been letting it at some phenomenal rent. You know, I let my house last year, only it wasn't worth it because the people were so awful, one has to be careful. I take it dinner is to be late, I didn't realise there was dinner. I asked little Patsie, such a charming girl, and how pretty those two younger Andersons have become, of course Aleph is dazzling, and when she is present nothing else can be seen, but those two are not at all bad-looking, Moy's plait is quite a work of art, but why doesn't she set her lovely hair free, like other girls do nowadays, whatever will happen to Moy I wonder, is she as daft as ever? And talk of daft, isn't Tessa Millen coming I'm told, I haven't seen *her* for ages.' As Cora continued Clement was trying to catch Joan's eye, but Joan kept on looking at Cora with an amused indulgent smile. Clement gave up and went to collect some more 'special', where he saw Emil talking to Bellamy. They waved to Clement and almost at once moved away still talking. Clement realised he was drunk and sat down on a chair in the hall.

Emil said to Bellamy as they ascended the stairs, 'The noise down there is dreadful. But fortunately this house is crammed with rooms. Let us sit in here, I imagine it is a servant's bedroom, no, Bellamy, not on the bed. Here are two chairs, draw yours over. I want to give you a lecture. But first of all let me say how impressed I am by your Peter Mir. He can have a serious conversation instantly and then proceed at once to chat. He is good-looking too, a spiritual man I should say. Of course such a man could not be a criminal or a thief, he has taken it all very well, and he looks the picture of health, God be thanked. Such a pity Lucas is not here, but there, we know what Lucas is like! But is not this an odd sort of evening, why are we, who all know one another, the guests, has he no other friends? Perhaps he has quarrelled with his friends and decided to collect some new ones, why not! And his library, have you seen it? I had a quick look, there seem to be no medical books, or scientific books unless you count books on agriculture, perhaps as he is so rich he has somewhere a toy farm? There are also some Russian books, my Russian is poor, but I see Tolstoy and Dostoevsky, Turgenev, Pushkin, in fine old editions, he is of course a cultured man – but otherwise in English, detective stories, Conan Doyle, Thomas Hardy, Kipling. Well, I had only a glance, and no doubt he keeps his medical textbooks at his consulting rooms. Or perhaps this is his consulting rooms. Or perhaps this is only one of his many houses! But now I must lecture you. I have been hearing about you, living in the cold room in the East End and visiting that monastery.'

'I haven't been to the monastery lately.'

'But you plan to go, you hope to go, I tell you not to. It is *not* for you. *Experto crede.* I had such thoughts when I was young. That path is for very few. Most tragic of all are those who are silent prisoners of an asceticism which for them is pure hell. Thus whole lives can rot away. Indeed, Bellamy, it is a way to hell, believe me, for such as you it is. You have a warm heart, you must work in the open with people, aid them as you used to do, be with ordinary men. I think that deeply you see this and believe it, you need only someone to shake you, to beat you a little, to pull you out of that miserable dark dead end. You are a romantic, you must follow your heart. Come back to your flat – '

'I have sold my flat.'

'Then come and stay with me. Be brave and make the break. Come to me, and *recover*.'

Clement had at last cornered Joan, running after her up the stairs and pursuing her along the landing. They paused.

'Joan, I'm so sorry, forgive me – '

'What for? You're drunk.'

'About on the telephone – I was awful – it's just that I can't bear it – I just couldn't – I must be alone – '

'You are afraid of being alone with me.'

'Yes, I suppose so. No, it's not just that. I can't stand anyone. Please forgive me, you do, don't you, I'm just Clement, your old friend.'

Joan said, 'Let's go in here. Why are all the doors open?'

'Our host wants to prove he has nothing to hide.'

'Well, let's close this door.'

They went into a small room filled with cupboards, evidently a dressing-room. Joan closed the door. Clement hugged her.

'Harlequin, will you marry me?'

Clement, not expecting this question, released her. He answered instantly, 'No, I can't, I *won't*, I mean it won't do, I'm very sorry – '

'But why – is it because you think I belong to someone else? I don't, I swear I don't!'

'No, I don't think, I don't think anything about you, I – '

'Don't say that. You do think about me, you do love me, I know it. I'm still Circe, you are Harlequin. It's still like that – oh let that be – let it be forever – remember Vercingetorix – '

'Dear Joan, please don't ramble on about the past. Of course I care for you – '

'You are unhappy. I can make you happy. We were so happy once together, have you forgotten? You can transform me. I can transform you. Only I know you, only I understand you – '

'Joan, please don't *bother* me, I have troubles, I don't want to marry you or anybody, *please* shut up and leave me alone – '

'I know you have troubles, I want to share them, I want to help you, I can help you, I love you. Don't you think this night is somehow enchanted? It's a sign. We are all changed into our real selves, we are all beautiful, we are saved, you are beautiful, I am beautiful – '

'Darling, you are drunk!'

'You see, you call me "darling". Tonight it's like being in a fairy palace where everything is lit up and beautiful and everything is understood and forgiven and truth is told and love declared – and as you said, there is nothing to hide! Oh don't you feel this, this liberation, something is offered to us, given to us, something we must take and hold in this magic time which brings us together – '

'Dearest Circe, it's no good – '

'You love me, Clement, I know you do – '

'It's no good, we are old friends, we must just go on being old friends – '

'Yes, make each other happy, be together – that's called marriage – oh be brave! Rescue me, I am desperate.'

'No, no. Forgive me.' He opened the door and drew her out onto the landing.

Harvey had brought his mother to Peter's house by taxi. He was not looking forward to the evening. Peter, who had greeted him rather briskly, had spent a little more time with Joan, during which Harvey had retired and hidden himself in the library. When he emerged he saw Joan talking to Cora. Pretending he was going somewhere, he limped about holding a drink, then made for the kitchen where Patsie and Mrs Callow kindly enquired about his 'disability'. After he left them a few people, Emil, Sefton, Mrs Adwarden, waved to him but did not approach him. He thought, I hate this party, I hate everybody here, I want to leave, but I can't without *her*. I suppose we'll get a lift from someone. But they'll all stay for *hours*. I have to go to the hospital tomorrow. Why do I have to go there? Just because it's something to do. We're broke, we have no money. I'll have to support *her*. I'll have to give up the university. She keeps on hinting about suicide. She's sure to get drunk, I'll have to keep an eye on her. I'm getting rather drunk myself. Where is she now? She's not with Cora, Cora's talking to that man from the pub. I'll have a look in the drawing-room. The drawing-room was a huge magnificent white and golden room with a high ceiling, much grander even than Emil's drawing-room. One long wall at the far end was covered by a tapestry depicting the return of Odysseus, which Sefton was explaining to Moy. Jeremy Adwarden, always said to have been sweet on Louise, was sitting next to her on a sofa. Louise was wearing the pink blue and white silk evening-dress, she looked flushed, animated and young. She and Jeremy waved to Harvey. Sefton said, no she had not seen Joan lately. Moy said she really must go and find a lavatory. Emil, looking in from the hall, beckoned to Sefton, he had always liked her, they sometimes had serious discussions about the future of Europe. Harvey turned away toward the stairs and began to mount them slowly. Now he must search the bedrooms, expecting to find his mother lying drunk upon a bed. He looked into one bedroom, where Connie Adwarden was admiring herself in a long mirror. Harvey was feeling very tired. With self-punishing slowness he mounted the next flight of stairs to the top floor. He just needed, for a short time, to be absolutely alone. He opened two doors. One of the rooms was like a little study, with a table and two chairs. Perhaps a place where some servant or bursar had added up accounts. Harvey came in, closing the door and dropping his stick on the floor. He sat down. He put his hands on the table, he laid his head on his hands and fell asleep.

Louise, before being led into the drawing-room by Jeremy, had not failed to notice Clement pursuing Joan up the stairs. She had been unexpectedly shocked by Harvey's casual remark that his mother 'was going to move in with Clement'. She thought that Harvey must instantly have noticed her reaction. She herself had been surprised by it. Yet why was she surprised, had she not always known the irrational jealousy of her disposition, her quiet possessiveness which she hid, she imagined, so well? How easily one is hurt. Or is it only I who am so stupidly vulnerable. Oh if only Teddy were still here, his great wise being solved all problems – oh Teddy, my love, my darling. Now I am all wounds. Yet even in this perhaps I deceive myself – I am all selfishness, all ingratitude. The girls are wonderful. They will go, but that all mothers suffer. I love Harvey with a secret locked-up passion which I conceal with a coolness which must gradually lose him. I hugged and kissed him when he was a child. Now I am distant, matronly, old. Once I wanted him to marry Aleph so that he could be my son. But he will not marry Aleph. He is already slipping away. He would not even come in time to talk to her before she left. They are fated to be brother and sister, but at an increasing distance. The bond will snap. My God, what these next few years will bring me – and I am one of the luckier ones. And I have carelessly, wantonly, stupidly lost Clement. Have I only just, now, realised how much I love him and how much I need him? I *need* him, and that need has made me take him for granted. When Teddy died I was grateful for Clement's love which he could not conceal from me – but for so long I was paralysed as if asleep, and when I woke up Clement had become used to me as a sisterly friend. I put up with his actresses, he told me about them, I was sympathetic, and so I have become not just a sister but a mother. I have made it my task to be passionless. My path is a quiet one now, on into the decent solitude of old age.

When Harvey woke up Peter was in the room. Harvey attempted to rise but found it difficult. Peter motioned him to keep still, closing the door behind him, and stood looking down at Harvey. Harvey felt frightened. He had never been alone with Peter, or even, apart from perfunctory exchanges at the birthday party and this evening, had anything like a conversation with him: nor had he at all made up his mind what he thought about this perhaps untrustworthy even dangerous person. He sat up rigidly in the chair, ready to rise.

Peter, interpreting his attitude and clearly aware of his

emotions, smiled slightly, then drew up the other chair and sat down. He said conversationally, 'How's the foot, Harvey?'

'Awful. I mean all right. People say you have to learn to live with something. Well, I'm learning.'

'You think it will be a long time before it gets better?'

'I don't think it will ever get better. The doctors have given up. I just have therapy to make it less painful, not to cure it, it can't be cured. Never mind that. What a super party, thank you so much for asking me! That "special" drink is wonderful. Oh dear, I think I was asleep.'

'I'm sorry you missed going to Italy, but you *will* go. And you will be at the university next year.'

'I suppose so.'

'Why just suppose?'

'Well, we're short of money. But one mustn't say that! Of course we'll manage, and someone will help. It's just that I don't *hope* any more, I've lost my nerve. Sorry, I'm talking nonsense, it must be that "special".'

'Would you mind if I looked at your foot?'

'Looked at – ? Well, it's *horrid*, and there's really no point.'

'Please oblige me.' This sounded like an order.

'Oh, all right, but it's *nasty*, I'm ashamed of it, and I should have had the bandage stuff renewed only I didn't go – '

Leaning down Harvey struggled with his shoe-laces. Since the accident he had worn broader larger ugly shoes. He looked with displeasure, with anger, upon the tangled mess of lacing on the ugly shoe. Peter made no move to help him. Why the hell does he want to look at my poor miserable foot, thought Harvey, oh why can't people just *leave me alone*! With the lace now half undone he began to shake his foot ferociously, then had to pause and renew his struggle. He shook his foot again and the shoe flew off leaving a dart of pain. Angrily he tore off his sock, and with difficulty undid the elastic bandage.

Looking up he saw that during this operation Peter had risen, taken off his jacket revealing a white shirt, loosened his green cravat, and undone the top buttons of the shirt. He had also put on his glasses. He put his chair out of the way, then knelt down and inspected the foot. Harvey stared at it too. He lifted it a little. It was swollen, red, also tinged with blue, it was hot, it hung there miserably at an odd angle, it smelt. Harvey thought, poor maimed object, I hurt it, I damaged it forever. He felt ready to

337

weep. He was upset and annoyed that Peter had asked to see it and he had agreed to show it. He said, 'Lots of people have looked at it and pulled it about and tied it up and injected it and put rays through it, they even tried acupuncture. You're a psychiatrist, sorry psychoanalyst, you probably believe in psychosomatic ailments, perhaps there are some, sorry, I hope you don't think I'm being rude, but honestly it's no good. I'm lame for life.'

Peter said nothing. He took Harvey's hot swollen foot in both his hands and held it firmly. Harvey, who was about to continue his tirade, fell silent. Of course, cool hands holding a hot foot bring relief. Harvey felt the relief. He stayed still. He closed his eyes. He could feel Peter's hands moving slowly around, under his foot, over his foot, round his ankle. He felt an electrical thrill in the sole of his foot. Then it seemed as if an electric shock, then another, had passed on up his leg. The shocks were warm, slightly painful, but exhilarating. His leg jerked. Peter's hands retained his foot. Harvey opened his eyes. He felt dazed as if he had actually slept for a moment. Perhaps it had all been going on for a long time. He still felt rather drunk. He saw Peter's face rapt in concentration, his thick lips slightly apart, his murky grey eyes enlarged by the spectacles, his thick eyebrows lowered and the lines of a frown above them, his curly hair, now longer, falling forward onto his cheek. Harvey's foot now seemed to be filled with electrical movement, like the ripples of a swift stream. Then Peter removed his hands, removed his glasses, and stood up. He fixed his shirt and his cravat and put on his jacket. Harvey hastened to say, 'It feels odd, it feels better.'

Peter said thoughtfully, frowning again, 'It may help. Perhaps I shall try it again later on, if you don't mind.'

'Oh yes, please.'

'But you must work too. You must have courage. Healing is a mysterious business. Rest just a little, while they come down. Dinner is to be served. There now, Harvey, goodbye for the moment.'

Harvey found that 'There now' infinitely comforting. He sat still for a while, then awkwardly did up his bandage and put on his sock and shoe.

Bellamy had for some time been searching for Peter, narrowing his 'beech brown' eyes and peering about through his glasses. Peter had said practically nothing to him since his arrival, though he had talked at length to other people. Bellamy had begun to feel frightened, as if he could actually see before him a grey void full of bubbling atoms. He thought, I am going to have a migraine, I haven't had one for years. Perhaps everything he had hoped and imagined about Peter had been simply *a mistake*. The metamorphosis was just a charade after all, a great mysterious blunder, the final breakdown of *everything*. He had so carefully put on his 'uniform', and was unusually clean and tidy. He had combed his straw-coloured hair carefully, even carrying a comb in his pocket for regular attentions. He wore a shabby black suit, a clean white shirt, and a thin very dark blue tie. His jacket was neatly buttoned up. He had enjoyed the party at first, watching with Clement how Peter was going round patting everyone and giving them his blessing. He had also passed a pleasant time making friends with Kenneth Rathbone, who turned out to be Australian, and whom he had hitherto known only as the rather aloof landlord of The Castle. He had even come to the conclusion that Rathbone knew quite a lot about Peter, and Bellamy determined to find out what Rathbone knew. So far however he had not managed to do this. Rathbone had subsequently disappeared into the kitchen to 'slant a beaker' and 'give the girls a hand' since they were 'running late'. Bellamy, following him, had offered his services too, but had been told by Kenneth in a friendly way to 'fuck off'. After that he had perfunctory conversations with Cora and Connie and Louise, while keeping his ever-roving eye on Peter and hoping to be summoned. Then he realised that Peter was no longer visible. He searched downstairs then upstairs. In the search he had of course entered Peter's big fine bedroom of which he had such delightful memories. He returned there. Of course all the wandering guests had by now visited the 'master bedroom' and gone away. The 'crush' was over. Bellamy lingered a while, breathing deeply. To calm himself he looked at the watercolours above the bed.

Peter entered hurriedly. He stared at Bellamy with surprise. Then he smiled. Then he said, 'I'm just going in here.' He disappeared into the bathroom. After all, he is human, Bellamy reverently thought. When Peter emerged he looked at his watch, he closed the door, he sat on the bed. Bellamy stood before him.

'Listen, Bellamy, I've got something to say to you, perhaps I should be saying it at more length later, but since we are together I may as well put something into your head to think about. I'll be very brief, then we must go down to dinner.'

'Oh, what is it, I hope – '

'First I must ask you one or two questions. Are you going into a monastery?'

'No. I have decided definitely not to.'

'Is that true? Are you sure? You are not entering into any engagement, going away to serve some novitiate or – ?'

'No, no. I'm just here. I'll have to find some ordinary job.'

'You're not saying this only in order to please me?'

'No, I mean of course I want to please you, but, you see I've lost my faith, the priest I used to – '

'Yes, all right, we can talk about that later. Listen, I have a proposition to put to you, which I want you to think over carefully. Now that I have remembered myself I have to make some plans. I am a rich man, I have been a reasonably benevolent man. But now I want, while I still have time, to put all my money to work, I want to set up a benevolent institution. In doing this I shall need to employ people. But first I shall need a secretary. Would you be interested in being my secretary?'

Bellamy threw his head back, he tugged at his pale hair, his mouth opened, he took off his glasses. He gasped, 'Yes – I can think of nothing more – I couldn't have dreamed – I can't tell you how much – '

'I would like you to go away and consider this.'

'I won't go away, I won't consider, I want to be – '

'All right, all right, don't *you* faint, please think it over. It may involve your coming to live in this house.'

'Peter – you know – '

'Now come along, we must go downstairs.'

When Peter and Bellamy came down the stairs they found a number of guests already standing at the door of the dining-room, waiting for what Peter had described as 'a simple repast'. News had soon gone round that they were not to be subjected to the agony of a stand-up buffet supper, but there was a real dressed-up dinner-table with candles in silver candlesticks, and even a *placement* with everyone's name written on a card in beautiful italic script. There had in fact been some trouble about the *placement*. Peter's first arrangement had placed himself at the head of the table with, in sequence, on his right Louise, Lucas, Cora, Bellamy, Tessa, Jeremy, on his left Joan, Clement, Connie, Emil, Sefton, Harvey, Moy, with Kenneth Rathbone at the end of the table. However, Bellamy, Clement, Louise, Jeremy and Emil had all separately informed Peter that Lucas *never* went to parties.

The second arrangement then ran Peter at the head, on his right Louise, Bellamy, Cora, Jeremy, Tessa, Sefton, and his left Joan, Clement, Connie, Emil, Moy, Harvey, and Kenneth at the end. Later still, Peter, after calling some of his more mature friends together, decided that Tessa was not coming. This left Sefton next to Jeremy. This picture was further disturbed by Moy whispering that she wanted to sit next to Sefton. Emil meanwhile, diplomatically or in innocence, expressed the wish to talk to Harvey. So finally, Moy, now thoroughly upset at causing so much trouble, was placed between Jeremy and Sefton.

When the guests had filed in and found their places and stood waiting in the candlelight, there was a moment of silence. Was Peter going to say grace or something? He was not. He sat down, ushering the others to do so, which they did, and after another short shy silence everyone started talking. The first dish was smoked salmon with scrambled eggs and caviar, and stilton and spinach pie for the vegetarians. Mrs Callow and Patsie, now in smart dresses, darted deftly round the table. Peter was saying to Louise what a pity Aleph was not with them, but no doubt she was having a happy time with Rosemary, where did Louise think those girls were by now? He hoped in time to meet Rosemary, also Rufus and Nick. Cora said to Bellamy, 'Why did we have to drink so much before we could eat?' Bellamy replied at random, 'Peter couldn't get his full staff, he's only just got back here.' Cora said, 'Well, where was he before, and what's the matter with you, you're floating on a cloud?' Joan, finding herself next to Clement, at once thrust her leg against his. Clement attempted to move his, hers followed. He turned a stern look upon her, then they laughed, then they sighed. After that Clement resolutely turned to Connie Adwarden whom he had earlier, vaguely, felt to be a bit out of things, and asked her if she had written any more children's stories lately. She said she have given up. 'My children talked me out of it. Children aren't what they used to be. They have lost all that great tract of innocence which we used to have.' Clement agreed. He thought, I just hope Joan won't start saying things to Louise. Emil, after praising the German wine which had been served with the smoked salmon, was lecturing Harvey on improving his German. A great language and a great literature, now a great united country. 'Our poets do much for us – Goethe of course, Hölderlin, Rilke, Celan. I suppose you have read Celan?' Harvey who had not heard of Celan, said no. 'You must read him, read poetry, Harvey, read the great poets of Europe, Europe will be saved by its poets.' Sefton, who could talk to anyone on a serious subject, was questioning Kenneth Rathbone about the mythology of the Aborigines. Meanwhile Jeremy and Moy, after a slightly sticky start, were getting on like a house on fire. It turned out they had both noticed that Peter was a collector of watercolours, of the Norwich School, some by famous artists. He also possessed a Samuel Palmer, they discussed Samuel Palmer and Moy said how much she liked his self-portrait which reminded her somehow of the Polish Rider. Cora was now congratulating Bellamy on his return to sanity, news of which had reached her, and describing the rigours of her childhood in a convent school, and what a relief it was to marry a Jew, and how sensible Judaism was without any bother about the divinity of Christ and life after death. Meanwhile Peter was talking to Louise and Joan, asking them to describe their schooldays together, a topic taken over by Joan whose stories of her own exploits reduced all three to helpless laughter. The first course had been taken away and the second course (said to include a very special *coq au vin*) was eagerly awaited. Other glasses had now been filled with Beaujolais Nouveau. It was nearly the moment when, in an orderly and decorous dinner-party, each guest, inventing some plausible creative topic, stops talking to the person on their right (or left) and turns toward the person on their left (or right).

At that moment the front doorbell rang, making itself clearly heard above the din. Several people exclaimed 'It's Tessa!' Peter stood up. Then he sat down again, and said to Bellamy, 'Could you answer the door?' Bellamy threw his chair back and hurried out, saying to himself as he crossed the hall, 'I am Sir Peter Mir's private secretary!' He opened the door. It was Tessa. 'Tessa, how splendid, you've arrived at last, come in!'

But there was something wrong. Tessa was dressed in trousers and boots, not for a party. Hearing the chatter, which had broken out again, she seemed surprised. She looked round. Visible in the bright light above the door was a tall man who was just behind her. Further back two other men were standing beside some sort of small van which was parked on the drive. A little snow was falling.

The tall man came forward, passing Tessa. He said in a soft polite voice to Bellamy, 'Good evening. My name is Fonsett. I have come to see Mr Peter Mir. Is he available?'

Bellamy thought, it's the police! He said to Tessa, 'What on earth is this?'

Tessa said, 'What's all the noise?'

'It's Peter's party. You were invited, weren't you?'

'I haven't been down at my place lately. I'm sorry, if we'd known there was a party – '

'May I come in, please?' said the tall man. He stepped forward into the hall, brushing past Tessa. Tessa followed.

Peter was standing at the door of the dining-room. When he saw his visitor he closed the door behind him.

Fonsett said, 'Hello, Peter.'

Peter said, 'Hello, Ned.'

Bellamy shut the front door upon the two men outside, who in fact showed no sign of wanting to thrust their way in.

Fonsett said, 'I hope you agree that it's a fair cop. We're sorry about the party, we've only just – '

Peter said, 'Let's go into the drawing-room. Good evening, Tessa. Bellamy, please go back to the others.'

Bellamy said, 'I'd rather stay with you.'

They marched into the drawing-room. Tessa closed the door. Peter sat down on a sofa near the tapestry of Odysseus. Fonsett drew a chair out from the wall. Bellamy and Tessa stood.

Fonsett said, 'Well, well! We nearly caught you on the evening of the dog! Then you and the dog got into a car and disappeared.'

Peter, though evidently disturbed, preserved a calm demeanour. He fingered his cravat. He said, 'I think I had better explain your identity to my friend here.'

'Go ahead.'

'This gentleman is Sir Edward Fonsett, a very distinguished doctor, a psychiatrist, who has been in charge of my health. I owe him a great deal.'

'You are not very grateful though, are you,' said Fonsett, 'to disappear like that, just when our treatment was doing you so much good! Honestly, we didn't know whether you were alive or dead! Thank heavens we've caught up with you, we've had a man watching this house at intervals ever since you vanished.' He turned to Bellamy and said, 'Mr Mir discharged himself from our clinic without permission and disappeared, thereby seriously endangering his health. That's a serious offence!'

'It's not a legal offence!' said Bellamy. 'Why shouldn't he leave, he isn't certified, your clinic isn't a prison!'

'Of course it is not a legal offence and of course he is not certified, far from it, but it is an offence against his own health, and such conduct is, to say the least, unfair to *us*! Miss Millen here, whom we have lately had the pleasure of meeting, has been investigating the background of Mr Mir's recent activities, and eventually found her way to us with a lot of useful material.'

Bellamy cried, 'Tessa! You led them here!'

'Not at all,' said Fonsett, 'as I told you the house was being watched. Our patient has now been good enough to return to it and must have entertained the notion that we might turn up. In fact his coming back here is a signal of his desire to return to our care. Isn't that right, Peter?'

The drawing-room door opened and Emil came in. He said, standing in the doorway, 'Sir,' (for he had not yet presumed to advance to first names), 'I have been asked by Mrs Callow to ask you whether she should serve the next course.'

'Oh, serve it by all means,' said Peter.

Emil, showing some sign of being invited to stay, left after a short pause.

Bellamy looked at Peter. He was sitting with his hands folded, his face calm and thoughtful, his eyes dreamy, like someone who, after a long walk, has found out suddenly how tired he is. He now looked at Fonsett and smiled a gentle friendly smile.

'Well, Ned – '

'Surely you expected us, didn't you?'

'No, not exactly, perhaps not so soon. I simply couldn't go on hiding. The fact is that I have had a profound change of mind, a large part of my memory has returned – '

'Just as I predicted! Later we shall discuss all this. You know you are my most interesting patient. Now, I expect you have a bag packed, a Jewish custom I think you once told me, one never knew when one would be routed out and moved on! I think a quick break would be easiest for all, especially for you. I trust you not to vanish through the back door. Your old room awaits you. You should not upset yourself by emotional apologies to your guests. I am sorry we chose party-time, we didn't know. You agree to come, do you not?'

'No, he does *not* agree!' said Bellamy. 'Really, what nonsense is this, who are you? Peter, who is this person, breaking in like this, it's like the Gestapo. Do tell him to go away!'

344

'You are making this worse,' said Tessa, 'please don't raise your voice. Everything will be explained.'

'And what were you up to, Tessa, playing the detective for these awful people? Peter, surely, please – '

'I'm sorry,' said Tessa, 'this is all very upsetting, and I hope that Mr Mir will excuse me, I meant well. It was just that I felt suspicious of him, the way he presented himself, and when I found out that something he had said was untrue I felt that I ought – '

'Keep calm, Miss Millen,' said Fonsett, 'let us not say "untrue". We are most grateful to you for your researches, but there is no need to go into those matters now. So let us go, shall we, Peter? Someone can collect all your things and bring them round in the morning, we are not going to the moon!'

'No, no, no!' cried Bellamy distractedly. 'He is not to go, we shall not let you take him, I shall call the others – '

'Please do not,' said Fonsett in a soft voice, 'and do not wave your arms about in an aggressive way.' He rose. 'Let us go in peace, quietly without fuss. Peter himself will reassure you. Please do not shout, sir. I do not know your name.'

'My name is Bellamy James, I am Dr Mir's secretary. If you try to remove him we shall all prevent you. Peter, we won't let them take you away! He left you of his own free will, he has, by his own wisdom and courage, *cured himself*. He is not ill, he is well, he is *better* than any of you cranks, he is a *spiritual* person – '

'We shall certainly want to know and study,' said Fonsett sitting down again, 'everything that has happened to him in this interim. Yes, Peter, you shall tell us about your adventures, and this telling will make you better. You have evidently been living a stressed and tiring life, just what you ought *not* to have been doing. You must rest, you must *recover*. Your help, Mr James, may prove valuable to us later on. But now – '

'Bellamy,' said Peter, 'I go of my own accord. I am sorry for this – '

'But where to, they'll hide you, it's a kidnap, I must come too – '

'Dr Fonsett will give you the name and address of his clinic, you can visit me – '

'But not at once!' said Fonsett.

'I have to speak with my friends. I fear that I have in one way misled them and I must take this chance to explain. First of all, please Bellamy, would you fetch Clement?'

345

There was an extremely uneasy atmosphere in the dining-room. Mrs Callow was serving the *coq au vin*, and the vegetarian lentil curry. When Bellamy appeared at the door there was silence. Bellamy said, 'An old friend of Peter's has arrived. Clement, could you come for a minute?' Clement followed Bellamy out. Before they reached the drawing-room they were followed by Emil who said, 'And I shall come too.' The trio entered the drawing-room.

Tessa had selected a chair and Fonsett had turned his so that now, with Peter in the middle, those who were seated faced those who had entered. Bellamy closed the door.

Fonsett said at once, 'Introductions please.'

Clement, ignoring him, said to Peter, 'Please tell us what is happening, we are rather worried.'

Peter said to Fonsett, 'This young man is an actor, his name is Clement Graffe, and this gentleman is Emil Wertheimer, a picture dealer I believe, he is one of my newest friends.'

'You are a quick collector of friends,' Fonsett observed. 'Graffe. Are you related to Professor Lucas Graffe?'

'He is my brother.'

'Ah *yes*. Well, well. Now Peter, is this your audience? Now go ahead. We must all look at our watches.'

Clement said, 'Peter, whatever has happened, why is Tessa here, who is this man, is he from the police?'

Peter said, 'This is my doctor, Sir Edward Fonsett, who wants to take me back to his clinic for more treatment, and I have agreed. I am very sorry that this happy evening has been disturbed – '

'You don't mean you're going now, you're being taken away, immediately, now this evening, that's impossible – '

'I agree it's impossible,' said Bellamy.

'It is not just possible, it is essential,' said Fonsett. 'And Peter knows why. I don't want him to vanish again!'

The door opened and Jeremy Adwarden came in. Bellamy closed the door after him.

Clement said, 'This is Mr Adwarden, a lawyer.'

Fonsett said, 'Now Peter, say your say, or would you rather not? After all, later on will do, in fact later on will be better, when you have had time to clear your head and think things out. So let us be off, shall we?' He stood up.

Emil said in his most grinding voice, 'Wait a moment, Sir Edward, you seem to have intruded rather brusquely upon our host, and I for one do not like your tone. It is scarcely good manners to remove someone in the middle of his dinner party. I imagine you do not propose to carry him away by force?'

'He has two thugs on the doorstep,' said Bellamy.

'Really!' said Fonsett. 'My very experienced sympathetic minions can scarcely be called thugs. One of them is I think already known to Mr Mir. That is Jonathan, you remember Jonathan, Peter?'

Peter smiled and nodded.

Bellamy felt such anguish at that moment that he had to clasp his face violently between his hands to stop himself from screaming.

Clement said, 'Look, we don't understand all this, I think it would be best if we talked to Peter alone, without Dr Fonsett.'

'That is I think an excellent idea,' said Emil. 'You go away, we will talk to Peter alone.'

'Be very brief then,' said Fonsett, 'you may go to another room.'

'*You* will go to another room,' said Bellamy, 'I shall show you one.' He opened the door. Kenneth Rathbone and Louise were standing in the hall.

Dr Fonsett reached out his hand and touched Peter's knee. Peter smiled and nodded. Fonsett rose. 'All right. But make it snappy. I know you'll play straight.' He followed Bellamy who led him into the library. All the lamps were on. Bellamy noticed there was a key in the keyhole on the outside of the door. As soon as Fonsett had entered he closed the door and turned the key.

Clement said to him, coming out into the hall, 'Shall we summon the others? Or let them carry on with their dinner if they want to?'

'All must come,' said Emil.

Kenneth Rathbone said to Bellamy, 'Listen, sport, I want to know what's happening to my mate? Who was that bastard you were conveying?'

Clement answered, 'A doctor. Peter is all right, he wants to talk to us. Go into the drawing-room but do be quiet.' Kenneth and Louise went in.

Clement and Bellamy went to the door of the dining-room. After the brightness of the hall the candle-lit room seemed like a long dark cavern. Clement turned on all the lights.

Remaining in the dining-room were Joan, Connie, Cora, Sefton, Moy and Harvey. By this time the general view in the dining-room was that the police had arrived and Peter was being arrested.

347

Connie was in the process of telling them that they need not worry, Jeremy would sort it all out.

Clement addressed them. 'I'm sorry, but I must ask you to come over to the drawing-room. There's nothing to be alarmed about. A doctor has come, a friend of Peter's. Peter wants to talk to us about something.'

They all got up and came out into the hall exchanging anxious glances. Cora said, 'I must go to the loo first.' Mrs Callow and Patsie were standing at the door of the kitchen. Patsie immediately offered to lead the way and Cora disappeared with her. Mrs Callow, who was obviously very upset, said, 'What about the bread-and-butter pudding?'

Clement said, 'It had better wait.' He added, 'Don't worry.' He and Bellamy led the remaining guests to the drawing-room.

There was an eerie silence. Peter was still sitting on the sofa in front of the tapestry at the far end of the room. He had taken off his green cravat and was holding it in one hand. He had a mild startled look which Bellamy had not seen before. His lips were parted, his brow slightly frowning, his eyes narrowed. He was looking about – like someone lost in a crowd in a railway station, Bellamy thought, indeed like a *young man* lost – lost, but brave, noble, resolute, pure in heart – and, oh, he had never looked *so young*. All this Bellamy thought in a moment, and he shivered with horror and with fear. He felt cold, he thought, the house is becoming cold, perhaps the radiators have already been turned off. Peter rose, dropping his cravat on the floor, and said in a calm voice, 'My dear friends, I am very sorry about this, but there is nothing to be alarmed about, please sit down.' There was some shuffling about. Joan, Louise and Connie sat on a sofa which Jeremy had turned round to face Peter, Jeremy sat on the arm of the sofa. Clement and Bellamy pulled out chairs from the wall. Cora, arriving, sat in an armchair, Emil in another armchair. Kenneth Rathbone, refusing to sit, stood at the back. Sefton sat on a chair in the front which Tessa had vacated. Tessa said to Peter, 'Do you think we should let Jonathan and Michael in? It must be cold in the van. I don't mean ask them in here, just into the house.' Peter said, 'Yes, of course, I should have thought of that, do let them in.' Tessa, opening the front door, let more cold air into the house. It was snowing outside. Tessa could be heard admitting Jonathan and Michael and handing them over to Mrs Callow and Patsie. Tessa returned and sat on the floor near Sefton, refusing Sefton's offer of her chair. The drawing-room door closed, the kitchen door closed. But two people remained in the hall. Harvey, who had drunk deep of the 'special' before dinner, and had continually emptied his promptly filled glasses at dinner, was feeling rather sleepy once again. He had felt, after Peter had held his foot, a general not unpleasant lassitude. At dinner, after their first intelligent conversation, he had found his eyes closing and had to be nudged by Emil. Now, rising sleepily, he had got as far as the hall. At the far end, tucked in a little under the stairs, Harvey had earlier noticed a tall chair with high sides like a box, perhaps an old sedan-chair, amply upholstered within. As the others went into the drawing-room he made his way to this chair, snuggled himself inside it, and went to sleep. The other non-entrant was Moy. Ever since that loud ring of the doorbell she had felt a cold sickening premonition. She could now neither eat nor drink and sat there shivering, flushed with terror and with a sort of dark shame. She knew that something dreadful was going to happen, was indeed happening, some evil deed was being done. When the others left the dining-room and hurried into the draw-ing-room, she lingered behind, she could not go in. She stood aside, watching the emergence of Tessa and the admission of Jonathan and Michael. The drawing-room door closed. When Mrs Callow asked her if she would like to come and sit in the kitchen, she refused. The kitchen door closed and there was a sound of animated voices as Mrs Callow and Patsie questioned Jonathan and Michael, plying them with food and wine. Moy had noticed Harvey's defection and even went to look at him curled up inside his sedan-chair like a hibernating bear. She returned to the drawing-room door and listened. Then she sat down on a chair in the hall. She put her hand upon her warm lapis lazuli necklace.

When everyone, after some shoving and stumbling about, had settled down, Peter, standing, began. 'Let me say again how sorry I am that our happy, for me at any rate very happy, gathering has been disturbed in this entirely unexpected manner. I thought it possible that such a visit might occur, but I did not expect it or bring myself to arrange it. Let me explain. I assume that all of you present know something of my recent history, how I received an almost fatal blow on the head delivered by Professor Lucas Graffe. I was then in various hospitals and latterly in the clinic run by Dr Fonsett, who has visited me this evening and desired

me to resume, for a while, his course of treatment. I have agreed
to this. I should say, and I must *emphasise* this, that Dr Fonsett
and his colleague Dr Richardson saved my life and my sanity and
I owe them an incalculable debt of gratitude. When I felt that I
had recovered sufficiently I discharged myself clandestinely from
the clinic. I was moved to this ungrateful act by a pressing desire
to visit Professor Graffe, that is Lucas, and discuss what had
happened, concerning which I had a certain sense of grievance.
Lucas meanwhile had disappeared and I had to wait some time
before seeing him. During this time, and after, I have lived, not
in this house, but with my friend Kenneth Rathbone at his pub,
The Castle. I did this because I was afraid that Dr Fonsett would
find me and urgently require me to return to the clinic. In due
course Lucas arrived back and we were able to have some conversations. I should say that, as some of you know, I was concerned
to demand of Lucas not only clarification, but retribution. In fact
my state of mind at that period was that of a very angry man. I
was at the same time unhappy with this condition because I was
constantly aware of something which I was unable to remember
– this sensation was much more painful and compelling than any
ordinary case of forgetfulness – it was as if a large part of my
being had fallen into oblivion. However, with the help of kind
friends, most especially Bellamy, I have been able to recover that
lost, more worthy, part of my soul and so empowered to overcome
my vindictive passions, and to make peace with Lucas. This is an
achievement, or godsend, which I value very much. In this better
frame of mind I also decided to come out of hiding, and living in
this sense a false life, and to return to this house.'

As Peter paused here a curious thumping sound, like that of a
machine, could be heard. Connie said, 'What's that?' Bellamy
said, 'It's Dr Fonsett. I locked him into the library.' Peter said,
'Oh dear! Release him please!'

Bellamy left the room and returned with Dr Fonsett, who was
looking distinctly annoyed. However, he instantly removed the
annoyance from his face. 'Well, Peter, have you now explained it
all? We must not dally, it appears to be snowing, and Michael
and Jonathan are still outside. I had not reckoned that the operation would take so long!'

Peter said, 'They are inside now. And I'm afraid I haven't
finished yet. Would you mind sitting down?' Bellamy offered his
chair and Fonsett sat on it. Bellamy remained standing with his

arms crossed. Cora whispered to Joan, 'This is absolutely *fascinating*!'

Peter stood silent for a moment, perhaps to regain the thread of his thought. He was standing very erect, his feet slightly apart, his shirt undone, his head thrown back, his curly hair, which seemed to have grown longer, framing his face. His attitude, as it now seemed to Bellamy, was that of some youthful liberator of the people.

Peter went on, 'You will have noticed that Dr Fonsett arrived here accompanied by Tessa Millen.'

Bellamy, who had been longing to say this, interrupted, turning to Tessa. 'Yes, why did you bring these people here, why did you interfere, why did you betray him, he has done no harm, he has done nothing but good.'

Fonsett, smiling, said, 'Oh we would have arrived fairly soon anyway, Miss Millen just supplied us with some interesting details.'

'What details?' said Bellamy aggressively to Tessa. 'You said something he said was untrue. What was it?'

'Not untrue, just a fantasy,' said Fonsett.

Tessa, who had been sitting on the floor, stood up. With a glance at the doctor, she said, 'Well, he claimed to be a psychoanalyst. But I saw at once that he could not possibly be a psychoanalyst.'

'But he *is* a psychoanalyst,' cried Bellamy, 'he said so, I mean he said he *was* one, and he told us that he was now not able to be one.'

'I'm afraid he was never a psychoanalyst,' said Tessa.

'Well, a doctor then, it's just some other name.' Bellamy turned to Peter.

Peter looked grave. Then he said in a quiet confidential tone, 'I am sorry, Bellamy, I was never a psychoanalyst or a doctor of any kind. Dr Fonsett kindly said I have had a fantasy. In fact I had simply told a lie.'

There was a moment of shocked silence.

Then Jeremy Adwarden said, 'Well, if one may ask, what was your occupation?'

'I was a butcher.'

There were several exclamations. Then a silence during which people looked at one another. Cora covered her face.

Then Louise said, 'Then why didn't you tell us? We wouldn't have minded, we don't mind, why should we?'

Peter said in an apologetic tone, 'Yes, I wondered myself why I said it, it was quite impromptu, almost a joke – well, that's not right – I said it and then let people believe it. It was false pretences. I'm sorry. I said it first to Lucas and Clement. Perhaps I felt it was more dignified, that it gave me more status. I was confronting what I took to be a powerful enemy. I wondered later whether they hadn't heard about it in court, where unfortunately I was not present, but evidently not. I am very sorry. I ought not to have done it, I apologise to you all. I don't think I've told you any other lies.'

Fonsett, who had been smiling during these exchanges, said, 'I like that, "dignified", that's good! I must say when Miss Millen told me I couldn't help laughing! However, you must not mislead them further. As far as "status" goes, you are at least a very *rich* butcher.'

'Well, yes,' said Peter, 'I mean I have not been standing behind the counter handing out the meat. My grandfather did this when he was young in Odessa. My father, who was born in England, built up the business, and I have built it up further.'

'In short, you are a tycoon,' said Fonsett. 'You earn infinitely more than I do! So you needn't worry about not being a psycho-analyst! At least you thought you were some sort of healer in your Buddhist phase, remember? Now show them your toy, just to prove you really are a tycoon. Look, there it is, it's over there on that table.' He pointed.

Clement looked. He stood up and took some paces back, carrying the chair with him. He put his hands on the back of the chair. The 'toy' was the green umbrella. Sefton had already risen. She picked up the umbrella and handed it to Peter. 'Thank you, Sefton.' Looking at her he took the handle and slowly drew the long knife out. There were exclamations.

Fonsett said, 'Now read to them what it says.'

Peter said to Sefton, 'You read it, see, it is engraved here.'

Sefton, holding the knife up and tilting the blade, read the inscription. '*To Peter Mir, with the respectful esteem of his fellow directors and the employees of Mirco, on the occasion of his fortieth birthday.*'

There was a murmur.

'It's a real butcher's knife, isn't it,' said Fonsett, 'or rather a ceremonial version, like a ceremonial sword.'

Peter took the knife from Sefton and slid it back into its sheath. He gave it back to her. Only then did he look at Clement. Clement, remembering that look afterwards, wondered what sort of a look it was. It was only visible for a second. He stumbled forward, then sat down on his chair and put his hand to his brow, covering his face. Joan hissed to him, 'Don't laugh!'

Sefton put the umbrella back on the table. Then she said in her calm clear voice, 'How can you be a butcher if you are a vegetarian?'

Peter replied, 'I cannot be and now I am not. I will talk to you about this – '

'But not now,' said Fonsett, standing up. 'Come on, let's go, it's past your bedtime. Please fetch that suitcase which I'm sure you keep packed. Never mind if you leave things behind – '

There was more murmuring. Jeremy Adwarden said, 'Wait a minute. It is not at all clear to me that our host wants to go! By what authority are you taking him away?'

'That's right,' said Bellamy. 'Who are you, anyway – how do we know – ?'

Fonsett replied, 'The authority is his. Is it not, Peter? As for who I am – '

Peter said, 'It's all right, Jeremy. This man saved my life. I go of my own accord – '

Bellamy cried out, 'You must not go, we will not let you go, you must stay with us – !'

Fonsett said, 'Please do not be hysterical, Mr James. You will see him again and in much better health. Now, Peter, if you would like to collect some of your stuff – '

Peter suddenly moved, making for the door. There was a loud rustling and bumping as everyone sprang up, pulling their chairs out of the way or pressing forward to see what was happening. Peter emerged into the hall, followed by Bellamy who pushed his way through after him.

Moy was sitting on the stairs. She rose hastily and stood aside. Peter, mounting the stairs, paused for a moment as if about to speak to her, then hurried on. When Bellamy had passed her Moy ran down the stairs.

Bellamy followed Peter into his bedroom. Peter, who had evidently expected Bellamy to follow him, closed the bedroom door and said, 'Ned was right about that suitcase. I have always kept it packed. Now, Bellamy, sit down while I pull it out.' He went over to a large cupboard at the far end of the room.

Bellamy did not sit down, but followed him. 'Don't go to that place, it's *impossible*, it's a *nightmare*, stay here, tell the doctor you'll come and see him sometimes, that's all that's necessary, stay here and all will be well, I don't trust those people, bringing that van and two thugs, you were right to escape from them, don't go back now, you are well, you are happy, you are *free*, don't you see that you are *cured*, oh why did you come back here to be captured again – !'

Peter was pulling a large suitcase out of the back of the cupboard. He said, 'Well, I got tired of being on the run, it was living a lie, it was living with fear. Now I can go straight on *through* it all.'

'What do you mean? You mustn't go, these people are scientists, they'll drug you, they'll damage you, they simply won't *understand* you, they will destroy your peace.'

'I owe them my life. But it isn't just that. Bellamy, do stop wringing your hands. This sudden intrusion is probably all for the good, I am forced to realise that I am very very tired – I have been taking everything too fast. My enlightenment, I mean just my rediscovery of myself, is not something I can seize upon and run on with. It must be lived into at a slow pace. I don't want to be in danger of a sudden collapse.'

'Yes, yes, you are tired, you want peace, but you can rest here, you can have peace here, you can recover here, in your own home. Peter, I can't bear it, my heart is breaking, I'm so *frightened* for you. And what about your great foundation, your doing good, my being your secretary – I could protect you, I could see that you rested, and that everything happened slowly – I was so happy, for you and for me – and now I'm terrified.'

'Bellamy my dear, we shall come back to all that. This is just a necessary interim. Think that I am simply going into retreat. I shall return. Now we should go downstairs. Please don't excite the others. Don't be afraid, Bellamy, we shall meet again soon. But wait, I shall need an overcoat, and a scarf and some other shoes –'

Meanwhile everyone had hastened out of the drawing-room into the hall, where they gathered round Dr Fonsett with something of the quality of a menacing crowd. He was surrounded by angry voices and at one moment Jonathan and Michael felt it necessary to move forward to make sure that he was not likely positively to suffer violence.

Louise was saying, 'He has always seemed to me perfectly well. At first he seemed to us a bit eccentric, but we have got to know him, his oddity is simply that of being a good man! After all, when you think of what he has been through – what are you going to do with him, why are you in such a hurry – it's like a kidnap!'

'You ask what I am doing,' said Fonsett. 'I am simply doing my duty as a doctor and a man of science. I am not a magician. Peter and I know each other very well, we have done much work together and will do more. He is still my patient.'

Jeremy Adwarden said, 'I am a newcomer to this scene, but I agree with Mrs Anderson in thinking that your methods are too hasty and insensitive. You say in this possessive way that he is your patient. Your attitude is suspiciously authoritarian. I for one do not feel satisfied that our host is going away with you of his own free will. I should warn you that your possessiveness could land you in difficulties with the law. There is a faint smell of abduction, the abduction, as it seems and will appear, of a rich man.'

'That's right,' said Cora, 'he is doing it for money. He keeps telling his patients they are ill, and pocketing their large cheques!'

'I suggest,' Jeremy continued, 'that you go away and let our host reflect upon his situation. He has only just returned to his house, and should now, in my view, be left here in peace.'

There were murmurs of 'Yes indeed,' 'Leave him alone.'

Fonsett said, 'I am sorry, the circumstances of my arrival are entirely accidental, and unfortunately contain an element of drama. I would have preferred a quiet arrival and a friendly talk. But you have, I believe all of you, had only a brief acquaintance with Peter Mir, whom this lady has admitted to be an unusual and eccentric person. There is a case history here of which you know nothing. He came into your lives, a short while ago, as the victim of a terrible accident from which, it seemed, he had made an amazing recovery. He kindly says that he owes his life to me and to Dr Richardson. In fact he overlooks, or more likely has forgotten, other gifted doctors who fought hard initially to save him. We have all been watching him for a long time! In running away from our clinic, and having what I may call an adventurous episode, he has followed a well-known manic-depressive pattern. He has passed through a period of hyperactive exaltation, and now, as he himself recognises, and as his return to his house demonstrates, is moving into a period of melancholy exhaustion leading perhaps to despair, even to suicide. He is in need of expert help – '

Emil said, 'What methods do you use?'

Fonsett replied, 'I am not sure what your question means, and in any case an explanation could take a long time. Briefly, we are not psychoanalysts, we are psychiatrists. We do not make conjectures based upon our patients' dreams, or their early childhood – '

'So you give them drugs.'

'That is one part of our method. I imagine you are sophisticated enough not to be made uneasy by the word "drug".'

'I am made uneasy,' said Emil. 'I have only lately made the acquaintance of this intelligent and clear-headed man, and I cannot believe that he is in need of your "treatment", whatever that may be.'

'Hear, hear,' said Kenneth Rathbone. 'I guess I've known him more than most here have, and I say he's the best chap I've ever met and also the wisest – '

'Yes, you see he is a Buddhist,' said Joan, who had for some time been wanting to speak, 'he's a spiritual person, like a holy man. He doesn't need doctors! It's you who need him, not him who needs you!'

Emil said, 'There are indeed spiritual things which you scientists do not understand and these are the deepest things upon which man's being rests.'

Fonsett spoke patiently, in no way put out by the aggressive tone of his critics. 'So he has told you he is a Buddhist! Well, he may indeed have picked up a smattering of Buddhism on one of his trade missions to Japan. Incidentally, he is a fishmonger as well as a butcher, as he failed to tell you! I agree with you' (he indicated Emil) 'that there are deep spiritual matters on this planet. Buddhism is a deep matter and one which cannot be quickly mastered. A rapid impression of it must be superficial, and in the case of a mind given to fantasy, must remain at a completely unreal level. You accuse me of haste, but you have all, it seems to me, come to rather hasty conclusions! Peter seems to have collected a lot of new friends remarkably quickly! He was

356

certainly getting tired of the big-business community. And you all seem to have taken him rather promptly to your bosoms! What do you think about him?' Fonsett said suddenly to Clement.

Clement had been expecting this question, though he could think of no reason why he should be chosen. He said coolly, 'I am very sorry for him.'

'Yes, but what do you *think*?'

'I don't know him well enough to have any clear impression. Like everyone else, I think he is some sort of remarkable person.'

'Some sort – what sort? Can't you say any more? Your opinion interests me.'

'No, I can't say any more!' said Clement. Then he abruptly added, to his own surprise, 'Oh go to hell!'

'Well said, cobber,' said Rathbone.

Moy, on the outside of the circle round Fonsett, said suddenly, 'I think he is a good man.'

There was a murmur of approval. Cora Brock said, 'Moy is right. He is a saint!'

'I am sorry to hurt anyone's feelings,' said Fonsett, 'but claims of this kind, which people are often moved to make, are almost invariably romantic. How much do we know of any other human creature, how much do we know of ourselves? We scientists know, in our own field, many things. But any so-called moral or religious knowledge, is of its nature imprecise. This distinction is a fundamental and indelible aspect of human being. Religion is connected with the fantasising aspect of the mind, it is connected with sex. These are large generalisations. I suggest simply that you have all, with various deep motives, elected Peter, about whom you know very little, to be your guru!'

'Well, what's wrong with sex?' said Joan. 'It's liberation, it's life, it's like Easter Day, we have all been drinking nectar, we were in hell, we are raised up, we are saved, we are beautiful, that's why we love him, that's why we need him, a great spirit has been released!'

'That's it!' said Rathbone. 'We need him, you take him from us, we'll come and get him!'

At that moment Peter, accompanied by Bellamy, was seen coming down the stairs. There was a confused cry of mingled grief and exaltation. Peter was carrying his overcoat, Bellamy was carrying Peter's bag. Jonathan and Michael moved to the bottom of the stairs. The group surged forward then parted. Fonsett took hold of Peter's arm as they moved onward. Emil and Kenneth were already barring the door. Jeremy joined them. Bellamy was following close after Peter, still in possession of the suitcase.

Jeremy said, 'Wait please, don't hurry so. Put down that suitcase, Bellamy. Why not at least wait till tomorrow? We want to be certain that Peter wants to go with you.'

'Whether he wants to go with you ever at all!' said Kenneth.

Fonsett said nothing, but turned toward Peter, releasing his arm.

Peter said to the guardians of the door, 'Thank you, thank you with all my heart, but as I have explained to Bellamy, I do go willingly. And I agree with Ned that it is better to make this move quickly.' He turned then so as to include the others who were standing round the doctor. 'I apologise for this hasty departure. I wanted to talk to you all, but there has not been – enough time. We shall meet again. Thank you, dear Louise – dear good Louise – ' He hesitated here, as if trying to compose briefly what could only be said at length. He said, 'You understand.' Then, 'My thanks to you all who have so kindly wished to rescue me – and – the children – do not cry, Moy, you and I know each other, and noble Sefton will do great things, and Harvey will get well, and Aleph – Aleph – yes – please forgive my stumbling words – and I see my old friends, Mrs Callow and Patsie, please do not grieve, my dears, I shall be back – and then there will be another party which will not end in tears. Now may I say, please stay and finish your dinner, please, for me, do that, please stay!' Patsie was mopping her eyes with her apron and Mrs Callow was crying audibly. Peter paused, seeming to have finished. Then he turned suddenly toward Clement, who was standing a little apart from the group, near the drawing-room door. For an instant Clement and Peter gazed intently at each other. Peter said in a loud clear voice, 'Look after your brother!' Clement gave a soft exclamation like a sob.

Fonsett said, 'Here is my card with the address of the clinic. Who shall I give it to?' Jeremy Adwarden reached out for it. 'Come on now, Peter, give them your blessing and let us be gone.'

Peter turning to Louise said, 'Tell Aleph – ' Then, as Fonsett was plucking his sleeve, he raised his hand with open palm and turned toward the door near which Jonathan and Michael had already placed themselves. Emil and Jeremy and Kenneth moved aside, the door opened, and Fonsett and Peter went out, followed by Bellamy. The bright outside light revealed the falling snow, the plain van, and Jonathan opening the doors at the back, while Michael climbed into the driver's seat.

'Here's your suitcase,' said Fonsett, taking the bag from Bellamy and thrusting it inside. He took charge of Peter's overcoat and tossed it in.

Bellamy clutched at Peter, grasping his hand and his jacket. 'Take me with you!'

'No, my dear Bellamy, later, you will be with me later, not now.'

Bellamy said to Fonsett, 'Let me come, he needs me, I am his secretary, he wants me to come with him.'

Fonsett said, 'I don't think he wants you, he has just said he doesn't, anyway you can't come, sorry.'

Bellamy continued to hold on to Peter. Peter said, 'Bellamy, thank you.' He kissed Bellamy on the cheek, then climbed into the back of the van followed by Fonsett. An iron bar in the shape of Jonathan's arm thrust Bellamy back. Jonathan got into the van and closed the door. The van backed a little, its wheels hissing softly in the fallen snow, turned, and glided down the drive and out of the gates.

'Come on in, Bellamy,' said Clement, 'unless you want to be a snowman.'

Clement stood in the doorway from which the others had moved away. Bellamy came in slowly. Clement dusted the snow off his friend's jacket and out of his hair. He then piloted him down the hall and into the library, the scene of Fonsett's incarceration. He shut the door, pushed Bellamy down onto a dark red club-style leather sofa, and sat down beside him. Moy was sitting on the stairs crying. Sefton, sitting with her, was holding and stroking Moy's long plait. Louise, now joined by Connie, was crying on one of the sofas in the drawing-room. Moy, who had no handkerchief, had been wiping her eyes upon her arm until Sefton had produced a large male handkerchief from the pocket of her velvet jacket. Louise was sobbing into a daintier handkerchief which, now soaked, was taken in charge by Connie, who gave her an equally small hankie of her own: then, watching Louise's sorrow, was unable to restrain her tears. Patsie and Mrs Callow, who had taken their grief back to the kitchen, were burying their faces in tea-towels.

Louise was thinking, it's such a little time since we saw him from the window, out in the rain with his umbrella, and didn't know who he was, and we were afraid of him, and in a way we've always been afraid of him, and then we were glad to know he was alive and Lucas had not killed him, and then he wanted to get to know us, and that was so odd, and he wanted to call us his family, and he said all these strange things about how Lucas was going to kill Clement and how he saved Clement's life, and we didn't believe him and we thought he might be a thief and then we thought he was ill and confused and I still don't know what to think, and then he brought Anax back and that seemed like a miracle and a sign and we loved him for it and I asked him to make peace with Lucas and he said women always want to make peace, and he came to Moy's birthday party and called Aleph princess Alethea and seemed like being in love with her and Clement was so much against him and said he wanted revenge and then he sent the girls those necklaces as if he wanted to buy them, and then Bellamy told us he'd had some sort of conversion and given up wanting revenge and become a good man, and now it seems he *is* a good man, and I wish I'd trusted him and believed him from the start, and good heavens what about Aleph, does he want to marry her, what does she think, and he is so rich, but really I couldn't be with him when he was so against Lucas and I *didn't go to see Lucas*, and I *ought* to have done and I *will* do, and I haven't *been with* Lucas and he has been alone and I have been stupid and *afraid* to go to him, and I haven't even looked after Harvey properly, though I do love him so much, and now he's gone too, and now Clement and Joan are together and I'm sure Joan was his mistress once and I have not done what I ought to do and I have muddled everything and lost everything *because I am a coward*! The bitter tears poured from her eyes as she sobbed into the limp handkerchief with her wet mouth.

Meanwhile outside in the hall Jeremy, Emil, Kenneth, Cora and Joan were giving consideration to Peter's suggestion that they should stay and finish their dinner. They drifted into the dining-room, which turned out to be occupied by Tessa who was wearing her overcoat and sitting alone at the head of the table drinking wine. When they appeared she got up. Jeremy said, 'Don't go.' Joan said, 'What's your new career, private detective agency?' Tessa replied, 'As it happens I have a new career, I have decided to help mankind in a more practical and reliably successful way,

I have become a medical student.' 'Well done you,' said generous Cora. 'But what about the Refuge?' 'It will be taken over by a woman called Pamela Horton who will be considerably more efficient than I was.' 'Stay and tell us more,' said Jeremy, who had always liked Tessa. 'No, I must go, goodnight.' She left the dining-room and quickly sidled out of the front door, closing it quietly behind her. 'She has guilt feelings,' said Emil. 'If so they are unnecessary,' said Jeremy. 'Peter's capers would have been found out anyway. I like his pretending to be a psychoanalyst! And of course that knife – that was why the police said he was carrying an offensive weapon!' 'How will Tessa get away?' said Cora. 'Didn't she come in the van?' 'How thoughtless of us,' said Jeremy. He ran and opened the door. The snow was falling thickly, silently, like a curtain close before his face. Tessa had vanished. He returned. 'She will survive,' said Emil. Mrs Callow appeared at the door and said, 'Would you like bread-and-butter pudding or cheese?' Cora and Joan said bread-and-butter pudding and cheese, the others said cheese only and Jeremy asked her to bring in two more bottles of Beaujolais Nouveau. They settled down together. A few minutes later Connie came in and joined them, saying that Louise was feeling better and had gone into the kitchen to help with the washing up. Jeremy said 'Typical!', adding, 'Bless her!'

Moy too had recovered a little and gone off in search of a lavatory and somewhere to wash her face. Sefton, left alone, went into the empty drawing-room where the chairs, facing all directions, were occupying the middle of the room. Following her instinctive desire to create order out of disorder she put the chairs back in their places, including the ones which had come in out of the hall. Returning to the drawing-room she saw the green umbrella upon the table where she herself had put it. She stared at it, then she picked it up, she examined the handle, then she undid the catch and drew out the long knife. Tilting it toward the light she read the inscription again, cautiously she tried the sharpness of the blade, then she shuddered and slid it back into its place, and put the innocent-looking umbrella back upon the table. As she moved away to leave the brightly lit room she saw something lying on the floor. It was Peter's green cravat which he had taken off and held dangling in his hand. She picked it up and then automatically put it into the pocket of her jacket. She felt suddenly very tired and overwhelmed by grief. She thought *some-*

thing awful has happened today, it has happened to Lucas, no it has happened to Peter. It is a nightmare, no it is a *catastrophe*. Oh what suffering there is. I feel so tired, I want so much to go home and to *sleep*. As she reached the door she met Louise.

'Where's Harvey?'

'I don't know,' said Sefton, 'he isn't in here, didn't he stay out in the hall?'

'But where is he now? He can't have gone home by himself.'

'Perhaps he's upstairs, he may have gone to lie down.'

'No, I've looked everywhere, so has Patsie, we can't find him, he must have gone out into the snow!'

'Keep calm, Louie,' said Sefton, 'we'll find him!'

They emerged. Moy appeared, now on her way to offer her services in the kitchen. Sefton called, 'Moy, have you seen Harvey?'

Moy came across to them. 'Yes, he's asleep, I'll show him to you.'

They followed her down the long hall. The little door of the sedan-chair had been pulled to. Moy gently opened it, revealing Harvey as near to being curled into a ball as it is possible for a human to be. His eyes were closed, he was breathing quietly, his fair glossy curly hair had spread itself out upon the cushions like a halo, one hand, extended towards his chin, held a strand of hair, straightening it out. His face was benign and calm. 'Well, thank heavens he's all right!' said Louise. 'We won't wake him just yet. You children must be taken home. I'm going to stay with Mrs Callow, she is very upset and there's still a lot to do.'

In the dimly lit (for Clement had turned out most of the lamps) library, sitting upon the dark red leather sofa, Clement and Bellamy had been having a long serious conversation.

'Bellamy, you keep calling him an angel and saying he has rescued your life, but you also say you are broken, finished, plunged in eternal darkness and so on – what would he say if he were here, wouldn't he chide you?'

'But he is not here, and I shall never see him again.'

'Of course you will, he's in a hospital in London, Jeremy has the address, I'll get it from him! You just seem to have folded up the future.'

'It is folded up.'

'Well, he did talk about the heavens being rolled up like a scroll, but that was for the end of the world!'

'It is the end of the world. My world. I'm sorry to be so stupid and *awful*. You are being very kind to me. Why don't you go away, go back to your flat.'

'And what will you do, stay here!'

'No. I can't stay here. I shall never come here again. I just don't want to bother you, I don't want to bother anyone.'

'My dear, going on like this you will succeed in bothering everyone! Look, come home and stay with me, and don't just stay tonight, stay as long as you like, and – '

'He is an angel, I saw him on that night, you know, when he was changed – '

'Yes – '

'He is an avatar – '

'Yes, yes – '

'I wanted him to teach me, to enlighten me, I wanted to be with him forever, for all of my life, and now the powers of darkness have carried him off – '

'My dear creature, you are *drunk*, that is what you are, *drunk*! Now please let me carry you off!'

'Dear Clement, you are making jokes and trying to cheer me up. Yes, I am drunk, but I am also perfectly rational. I am in mourning for what I have *lost*. Peter told me this evening that he was going to use his money to set up a great good foundation and he said I was to be his secretary and live with him in this house.'

'Oh really, did he say that? But in the future, why not? It may be quite soon – '

'It's not just being his secretary and living here and helping him – I saw a path with a light shining on it, I saw everything I've been *looking for* – wanting to be in that monastery was a false way – then suddenly at last I found *my* way – wanting to have goodness is not enough, it's work, finding the way is part of the work, I felt I had *come home*.'

'Good, then you *are* home! All this despair is just false, it's a show, you refuse to admit you'll see him again and you're banking everything on that, but even if you didn't see him again, wouldn't you still be on the way?'

'No – it was all too brief, I couldn't sustain it without him. Without him I shall sink back into being the useless whining self-deceiving empty person that I know I really am – all those letters I wrote to that monk, they were all daydreams and romance – '

'Oh all right, let's try the other tack, there's every possible reason why you will see him again, he's not ill, he's just going to rest, he'll be back here in a few weeks, anyhow he can discharge himself whenever he likes, Jeremy can help him if necessary, he hasn't been abducted!'

'I had a glimpse, then the door was closed again. Those men will destroy him. I have lost the one I love.'

The door opened and Louise looked in. 'Sorry to disturb you, Clement, I wonder if you would mind driving the children home? I'm staying here a bit longer to help clear up.'

Clement rose. 'Yes, of course, I'm just going to take Bellamy home with me, I'll take the children too, there's room for all of us in my car.'

Bellamy got up. 'I can't stay with you, I must go back to my room, I must be alone there, I shall take a taxi. Where is the telephone?'

'Oh *all right*, I'll drive you back to that hell-hole.'

They came out into the hall. The inhabitants of the dining-room were emerging too. Moy and Sefton were waking Harvey up. Sefton was shaking him gently, plucking at his shirt, even pulling his hair, while Moy repeated his name at intervals, a little louder each time. Harvey awoke. He showed no surprise but smiled sleepily at the girls. Unfolding himself he said, 'Oh is it time to go? I've had such a happy dream!' Emil marched over to Bellamy, 'Come along, Bellamy, you are coming home with me in my car.' Clement said, 'He insists on going back to his own place and I'm driving him.' Bellamy murmured 'Sorry,' as Clement, gripping his arm, propelled him along. Louise assembled the children, Cora said she was taking Joan. Jeremy Adwarden, after liberally tipping Mrs Callow and Patsie, collected Connie, who was carrying glasses into the kitchen, and also Kenneth who had no car having arrived by taxi. They all found their coats. Clement opened the front door.

The snow had ceased falling. The light above the door, and the distant street lamps shining through the trees, showed the sparkling cold pathway of the drive where the marks made by the van had already been sifted over, the sugary laden branches of conifers, the windless silence. No one, it now appeared, had been bold enough to park in the drive, which was now being patterned by reverential footprints. Clement left first with Bellamy and the children, then Cora with Joan, then Jeremy with Connie and

Kenneth. Louise, who with Patsie was still dealing with the chaos of the dining table, said she would get a taxi home later on. Meanwhile, however, Emil had persuaded Mrs Callow that they should 'Leave the rest until tomorrow.' Mrs Callow agreed, saying tearfully, 'Well, *he* won't be there, will he!' No, they didn't want a lift, she had her car in the garage and they would lock up and turn on the burglar alarm. Louise left with Emil, walking in silence over the trampled snow and along the road to Emil's car. When, turning round, they drove past the house, it was already dark.

As the big Mercedes sizzled quietly through the empty well-lighted streets over the frosty snow Louise began to cry again. Emil, glancing at her, said after a while, 'What is it, my dear? You are so sad about that man?'

'Yes. It's partly shock. Forgive me.'

'Oh Louise, Louise – weep on, it is to be envied in you women, I wish I could weep.'

'Emil, I am so sorry about – '

'Yes, yes. But now you. Is he then a good man?'

'Yes, I think so. But it's all so complicated – '

'And Lucas? Have they met, are they friends? What is it with that? And why did he say to Clement to look after his brother?'

Louise thought, of course Emil *doesn't know* about it. But what *is* it? Would it soon begin to seem like a dream – it had somehow the qualities of a dream, where incompatible things seem true. She said, 'Emil, I don't know. You had better ask Bellamy.'

Before they reached Clifton Louise had mopped away her tears. Emil got out and held her arm to walk through the snow to the door. He hugged her and kissed her in silence. She entered the house and Emil's beautiful car hissed away alone. Yes, it was like a dream.

The lights were on, there was no sound in the house. But there was a sound. As she stood on the stairs she could hear the soft voices of Moy and Sefton talking in the Aviary. She thought, how good they are, how innocent they are – and her heart ached with fear for them. She reached her bedroom door, then called 'Goodnight.' They came to the door of the Aviary and called up to her. She went to bed and to sleep.

4

EROS

Bellamy was standing in a garden upon a smooth grassy lawn. Behind him was a lake. Before him was a path between little box hedges, and beyond the box hedges on either side were big rose bushes covered with flowers. He thought, this is a wild garden, yet this part isn't wild, 'it is the *rose* garden'. At the end of the path steps led up to a terrace, and at the top of the steps there was a statue. Screwing up his eyes, for there was a lot of light, Bellamy made out that it was a statue of an angel with towering wings. Beyond the steps, across the terrace, was the front door of the house. The door, which was closed, was surrounded by stone carvings. Bellamy thought, I would like to look at those carvings. He thought, it's a big house, very big yet not too big, it is just the right size. The house was long, with a low sloping roof, it was built of stone, the neat rectangular stones being of different sizes and different colours, some pale grey, some light brown, some faintly pink. Bellamy thought, it's like an eighteenth-century house. Then he thought, why do I say it is 'like an eighteenth-century house' – surely it *is* an eighteenth-century house. And yet – it isn't. With this he felt a shock in his breast, like a blow, and he thought, how could I *forget* – He suddenly felt fear. Then, as if set in motion by an alien force, he began to walk slowly forward toward the steps. As he came nearer he became aware that what he had taken to be a statue of an angel was a real angel dressed in red and golden silk robes, and now he could even see the long glossy feathers of its wings. As he approached nearer still it moved, gliding off its pedestal onto the smooth paving stones of the terrace, and moving like a domestic bird, not fleeing but simply moving away along the terrace, along the face of the house, away from the door. Bellamy followed, not daring to come too close in case it took flight. When it neared the corner of the house Bellamy called after it, 'Tell me, is there a God?' It called back at him, turning its head slightly, 'Yes!', then in a swirl of coloured robes disappeared round the corner of the house. Bellamy followed, now hurrying, but when he turned the corner the angel had vanished. He walked slowly on, walking, he noticed, not upon smooth stone but upon stony gravel scattered with little green leafy plants. Then as he walked he heard a sound, the sound of someone walking behind him upon the gravel of the terrace. At once Bellamy knew who it was who walked behind. He thought – *it is He*. He did not look round. He fell forward upon his face in a dead faint.

Emerging from his dream Bellamy felt breathless, excited. He thought at once, but I didn't go into the house, as I ought to have done. He thought, I'll go another time. Then he thought, but there will never be another time! Then he was aware once more of those footsteps upon the stony gravel behind him, and he allowed himself to be possessed by an ecstasy of prostration. He woke up gasping. Then he remembered. He sat up. Then he sat on the edge of his bed, pressing a hand against his fast-beating heart. He was wearing his vest and pants underneath his pyjamas, as he usually did. He had imagined that he would not sleep, but he had slept. Sorrow can sometimes induce sleep. The room was cold. He turned the light on. He took off his pyjamas. He relieved himself into the wash-basin and dabbed his face with cold water, which was all the taps provided. He put on trousers, a shirt, a jersey, and some slippers over the socks he had worn all night. He thought, this is what every man does, this is how men live, if they are lucky enough. He filled the kettle at the basin, turned on the gas-ring, found the matches, put the kettle on, and put a coin in the meter for the electric fire. He did not want to shave, he had shaved yesterday, now he would never shave again. He could hear above his head the usual racket of the Pakistani family getting up, he could hear the children chattering. He felt a terrible contempt for himself, it came to him like a grey suffocating storm. The kettle boiled. He found a mug and put a tea-bag into it, he held the mug over the basin and poured the boiling water from the kettle into it, scalding one hand as usual. He sat down again on the bed, putting the mug on the floor. He got up and went to the window, pulling back the flimsy cotton curtains and looking through the dirty net ones. It was raining, the snow was gone. He turned out the light, he returned to sit on the bed. If only he could blot out of his mind that golden period of time, an hour perhaps, during which he had pictured himself, and in such *elaborate detail*, Peter's secretary, Peter's friend, helping Peter to build up a great organisation for the relief of human suffering. He had, in that brief time, imagined so much, as if in a cosmic vision of the salvation of the world. Now wiped out. The wiping away of the horizon, the drinking up of the ocean. That was what it was like, what it was *all* like. All the misery surrounding him now at this very moment in these streets, in these rooms. How had he imagined that he had the *energy* required to alleviate one atom of it? Father Damien gone, Peter Mir gone. They had been reality, or rather they had seemed to be his reality. Suppose he were to go along to that clinic, that doctor had left the address with someone. Or had he? Could that place be found, did it exist? Anyway they would not let him in to see Peter – and even if they did, *it would be a different Peter.*

Time passed. The tea in the mug was cold. He must do something, he must put on his shoes, he must go for a walk, he must make the bed, he must clean the room. At least he could read the Bible, which was there before him on his bedside table. He picked it up and opened it at random, and read how God had told Ezra to tell the children of Israel to put away their alien wives and the children of such wives. Oh the weeping and the sorrow, the tears of women, the cries of children. He thought, I have no wife and no children, I have put away my dog and he has forgotten me. Magnus Blake has forgotten me and I have forgotten him. He closed the Bible. During this time the memory of his dream had been departing from him, and remained only like a coloured blur. He recalled however with great clarity the words of Virgil to Dante, which Father Damien had written to him and which Clement had translated. 'Your will is free, upright and sound, it would be wrong not to be ruled by its good sense'. Only I haven't *got* such a will! thought Bellamy – rather he pictured Virgil turning away into the twilight knowing that he and his beloved pupil will never meet again. Tears came into Bellamy's eyes. He chided the tears. Someone was tapping on the window, but he paid no attention. He thought I am weak, I am useless, and I *feed* upon my own weakness. The tapping grew louder. Bellamy looked up, he stood up. He pulled back the net curtain. Someone was outside looking in. It was Emil. And beyond Emil in the roadway was Emil's big Mercedes.

*

368

Clement mounted the steps to the door of Lucas's house and rang the bell. Silence. He rang again, a more lengthy ring. After waiting for a while he moved back onto the pavement and examined the windows, for the day was dark enough to warrant a light inside. Nothing.

Two days had passed since the events at Peter Mir's house. On the previous day Clement had visited his agent and had one of his usual inconclusive talks. He had also visited the incompetent little theatre whose affairs he was supposed to be concerned with and discussed the usual lack of money. Then he had lunch at a little Italian restaurant in the Cromwell Road. Then he had gone to see a much acclaimed film about a wife killing her husband's mistress. Then he had some drinks and a cheese sandwich at a pub in the Fulham Road, returning then to his flat where he switched off the telephone. He had no wish to converse with any of the persons in yesterday's drama. He felt as if something had been completed and he would never see any of those people again. He watched some football on television. He took a sleeping-pill and went early to bed.

The next day, waking to a sense of variegated misery, and still unwilling to hear Louise or Bellamy moaning or speculating about Peter, he began to feel at first a desire, and then an anguished passionate need, to go and see Lucas. He was now haunted by Peter's words 'Look after your brother'. Why had he not gone yesterday to see Lucas, why had he not *run* to Lucas at once? He felt a devouring wish to see Lucas, to hear his scathing ironical voice, to *tell* him everything that had happened, even perhaps to *discuss* it with him. It had occurred to him that he, and everyone involved in Peter's ghastly 'party', must be feeling guilt – helpless guilt perhaps. (Or is helpless guilt *not* guilt?) They had muffed it, there had been a betrayal. Something should have been done which was not done. Now he wanted to hear Lucas laugh, he needed Lucas's protection, he had always needed it. He went back to the steps and along the paved path inside the railings, found the gate open and went down the passage into the garden. He stood back on the lawn where the rain, which had ceased now, had muddied the remains of snow. He surveyed the house, it was dark. He went up to the drawing-room windows and peered in. Supposing Peter's knife had contained a deadly poison which would take effect later and not be detected? Would he see Lucas lying dead upon the floor? All was as usual. The portrait of

369

Clement's grandmother gazed at him from above the fireplace. He climbed up the cast-iron steps to the balcony, he peered into the bedroom. No inert figure lying on the bed. He even called out 'Luc! Luc!' No one. He laid his head against the cold damp glass and groaned. He climbed down the wet steps and went back along the passage to the front of the house. He crossed the road and stood there again staring at the house. 'Look after your brother.' Had he looked after him? Clement recalled their last meeting. He forgave me, I forgave him, he knows I did. Did that mean unbelieving what had happened? Oh Christ, does it matter now what happened? Anyway, if Lucas has done away with himself, it certainly won't be because of guilt feelings about *me*! It had started to rain again. He blinked. Just at the door some shadowy apparition seemed to have, at that very instant, composed itself. The figure of a woman, raising up her hands. The woman vanished. Clement moved. Then he saw her again standing on the pavement. It was Louise. He crossed the road.

'Why, Clement, you startled me.'

'You startled me. There's no one there.'

'Are you sure?'

'Yes. Why did you come here?'

'I suddenly felt terribly anxious about him – and I wanted to see him, to talk to him and – and ask him things – '

'Don't ask him things, Louise, anyway he wouldn't tell you, he'd just upset you. Now I'll take you home in my car.'

'Why did you come here?'

'Because he's my brother.'

'Because Peter told you to.'

'No.'

'You don't think he – '

'No. Come on, we're getting wet. Why should we *bother* about that tiresome quarrelsome blighter? He can look after himself. Louise, stop being so *sentimental*.'

'Well, you came – but of course you are – I do wish I had come to see him earlier, I blame myself very much – '

'There's my car. Are you coming with me or not?'

'You're sure they won't mind our being in the Aviary?'

'Of course not. Are you afraid of them? Moy's gone to see Miss Fitzherbert, you know, her painting teacher. I'm glad someone is taking her in hand. Aleph's in Scotland, we had a card from her today. Sefton's in the British Library. It's just as well Moy is out, you know she's so bothered when you're in the house.'

'Poor child. I hope she is recovering.'

'Yes, it's just a childish crush. Would you like a cup of coffee?'

'No thanks, you have one. Oh *God*!'

'Clement, don't be upset. You look as if you're going to cry! We shall see him again soon.'

'Lucas is such a – '

'Sorry, I didn't mean Lucas, I meant Peter. I thought of going to the clinic, Jeremy rang up and gave me the address. But Jeremy thinks we should leave it for a while – I mean, I believe, that Peter really needs to rest, and if we all turn up, if any of us turn up, it will over-excite him.'

'Yes, I agree, better leave it.'

'Emil thinks so too. He rang up, he says Bellamy is staying with him.'

'Really? I wanted Bellamy to come home with me. Oh – never mind – '

'Emil is generous. How's Joan, is she still with you?'

'As far as I know she's with Cora. She'll look after her.'

'But wasn't she staying with you?'

'No.'

'Aren't you *worried* about her?'

'Well – no – yes.'

'Harvey said he thought she was considering suicide. She uses some phrase like going somewhere – going to Humphrey Hook, like going to the devil – meaning suicide, or drugs – '

'Who's Hook?'

'He's the devil.'

'I'm going to him too.'

'Perhaps we should ring up Cora and warn her – no, that would be too interfering.'

'I agree.'

'Somebody should be keeping an eye on her all the same.'

'Are you implying that I should? You seemed to think, or professed to think, that she was staying with me. She was not.'

'You know her best.'

'Nothing follows from that. *You* are the one who looks after people, *you* are the great mother figure, you are *mother* to us all! Let's change the subject. When is Aleph coming back?'

After Clement had gone Louise went upstairs to her bedroom and looked into her mirror at her staring eyes, her eyes wide with terror and remorse, about to fill with tears. She thought, why am I deliberately *destroying* myself? Am I *mad*?

'So you agree we should not try to see him at once?'

'I suppose so.'

'*You* especially.'

'I'd upset him. Christ, how I think how I'd upset myself!'

'He has been on the crest of the wave. He has exhausted himself. Now comes the nemesis, which he must be helped to endure.'

'You mean he is a manic depressive and needs medical help.'

'I would not quite put it so, I do not *know*. I just think it wise to have an interval. And he himself accepted the doctor's authority. Indeed, in coming back to his house, he asked for it.'

'Yes – but I see it – with another meaning.'

'You know, Bellamy, I am not saying these things with any selfish motive. I am selfish, I have selfish motives, but here I am trying to see clearly.'

'Emil, I understand that you are not saying this just because, etc. You say it out of your wisdom, in which I profoundly believe. It's just that there is such a strong – force – which draws me to him – and I must believe in that force too.'

'Love, yes. But sometimes love must sacrifice itself in order to remain love. And indeed I too must give up – but enough of that. You will see him again, your abstention is just for this time. You will stay with me for this time? So we need not argue about that any more?'

'I will stay – for now – thank you.'

'Good. Many of your things came in the car, and we will fetch the rest tomorrow. You have paid the rent, have you not?'

'Yes, I've paid this quarter and the next quarter. I suppose someone will want that poor little room. What an awful thing poverty is. Oh Emil, what anguish it all is, it *all* is. When I wanted to go into the monastery it was just because of *that*. But I wasn't worthy, I was pretending. Please understand, Peter *remembered* his goodness, he discovered himself again, and that he had a mission – '

'Yes, yes, there was a revelation – '

'He will need me, he will need you – you know what that sort of faith is – '

'So in a way I am still just a simple-minded Lutheran, it was in my childhood, these things go deep. With what charming simplicity he told us about the lie, that he was not a great doctor, but just a rich butcher!'

'Emil, you still don't understand – '

'I do, I do, I respect your saint, these things are mysteries. Have some more whisky.'

'No, no, I've already drunk too much, I must go to bed. Oh, Emil – thank you – you know – '

'Yes, yes, I know. But one further thing before you have that bath you've been dreaming of.'

'Yes?'

'You must get your dog back. He shall live with us. I love dogs.'

Two more days later (it was Saturday) Moy, always up first, had, in this order, run downstairs in her nightdress, let Anax out into the garden, dressed, given Anax his breakfast, drunk some tea, eaten a piece of toast, washed up, and set the breakfast table for the others. She saw with disapproval the careless way in which Louise had piled up the dinner plates, putting the plates with the flowers on in the same pile as the plates with the birds on. She divided the piles, so that each plate was with its family. Today Moy had planned to pay a visit (involving a train and a bus) to her painting teacher Miss Fitzherbert, who lived south of the river in Camberwell. South of the river was a strange romantic land, like another city. Moy had briefly, tactfully, omitting the swan, conveyed to Miss Fitzherbert her failure with Miss Fox. Miss Fitzherbert, who had by now overcome her annoyance at Moy's sudden absence from school, had suggested that Moy should come and see her to discuss other art schools, and, equally important, other modes of approach to them. Sefton came down, then Louise.

Moy who did not like 'hanging about', finding it was not yet time for her to leave for Camberwell, considered taking Anax for a run on the Green, decided not to, and sat in the kitchen drawing Sefton. Louise, who had become (the children noticed this but did not comment) unusually preoccupied and aloof, went out early to do some shopping, refusing Sefton's usual Saturday help. Sefton, abandoning Moy and her sketch, disappeared into her room. Moy came out of the kitchen and sat on the stairs. She tried to think of Peter and how he had said to her 'You and I know each other'. But now all his words seemed senseless, utterances of incoherent despair. Louise never spoke of him, and Sefton refused to. It was as if they were ashamed. Moy decided that, after all, there was time to run Anax upon the Green. She rose and put on her coat and picked up Anax's lead. Hearing the familiar jingle he came tearing down the stairs nearly knocking her over. She managed to fix the lead to his collar while he kept jumping up at her and licking her cheek. The postman arrived, thrusting some letters through onto the floor. Moy, who hardly ever received any letters, usually put the few that arrived on the kitchen table without looking at them. This time, picking them up, she looked through them (there were only four and two were bills) in case there was another card from Aleph. What she saw at once however was an envelope which was *addressed to her*, Miss Moira Anderson. She put the others in the kitchen, and quieting Anax sat down again on the stairs and opened the strange letter, wondering what it could be. She could not place the writing which looked faintly familiar. The letter ran as follows:

My dear Moy,
Please forgive me for writing to you, I think it's better than by telephone. As I expect you know, I am staying with Emil for the present. I expect we are all suffering from shock after that terrible evening at Peter's house. But we must wait in *hope*. I am sure we shall see him again before long. My own life has changed lately and in drastic ways. I will tell you more about this later on, perhaps when you are older. I write to say this: I think, as matters stand now, that it was a mistake, a fruitless grief for both of us, to separate myself from Anax. I have missed him terribly and I have no doubt that he has missed me terribly. I am *very grateful* to you all, and you especially, for looking after him during this period,

when I have been, as it were, in retreat – or in eclipse, or in never-never land – somewhere else anyway! I think now I am able to take Anax back, and I do hope you will not mind parting with him. I can imagine, when you are still at school, and most of you out all day in any case, he must have been a mixed blessing! I would like to come, if possible, tomorrow, that is Saturday (when you will have received this letter), to pick him up. I'd like to come at about eleven. If that's not convenient, then would you telephone me *chez* Emil, the number is above. I am *so grateful* to you, dear Moy, and to all of you! I would not have entrusted him (or, as I thought then, given him away) to anyone else. So if I don't hear by telephone I'll come at eleven. I look forward to seeing you, and on some other occasion we must have a good talk! With much love, yours

Bellamy

P.S. Please have his collar and lead ready. And, it occurs to me, as he will be so extremely glad to see me, I mean he'll bark and jump about, could the reunion take place in the Aviary? I hope he won't knock things over! I think it would be best if you were to shut him into the Aviary, and then let me in quietly, I shall say nothing till I see him. Then you could leave us together! *Thank you*, dear Moy –

Moy put the letter in her pocket. She knelt down again and took the lead off Anax, leaving his collar on. He started once more to lick her face. She put him aside gently, then went to the telephone and rang Miss Fitzherbert to ask if she could come tomorrow morning instead. Sefton emerged from her room and seeing Moy's face said, 'What is it?' Moy said, 'Bellamy wants Anax back, he's coming to fetch him this morning.' Sefton, who understood, said 'Oh – Moy – ' She put her hand on Moy's arm. Without looking at her Moy touched her fingers. Watched by grieving Sefton she climbed the stairs to her attic. Anax ran after her, frisking about her feet. It was just after nine o'clock. There were two terrible hours ahead.

Moy spent the two hours with Anax, at first trying to draw him. (Of course she had drawn him many times.) Then sitting on the floor hugging and caressing him and looking into his blue eyes

which could express such ecstasies of joy and love. Then lying
flat on her bed with the dog warm and quiet beside her, his heart
beating near her heart. As it neared eleven o'clock she went down
with him to the Aviary and shut him in, leaving his lead on the
floor near him. Sefton had gone to the library, Louise was out
shopping. Moy sat on the stairs near the door. Punctually the bell
rang and she opened the door. Bellamy stood on the doorstep in
the cold sunshine, his round face beaming, his pale hair lifting in
the breeze. Behind him she could see, drawn up at the kerb, Emil's
big car and Emil at the wheel. Emil waved, Moy waved. Bellamy
stepped in and Moy closed the door. He whispered, 'Oh thank
you, thank you,' clumsily grasping for Moy's hand. She put her
finger to her lips and led him up the stairs. She opened the door
of the Aviary, Bellamy went in, she watched from the doorway.
Anax was curled up on the sofa, his copious tail covering his nose
and eyes. Hearing the door he looked up. He did not bark but
screamed. He sprang down, he ran to Bellamy, he leapt up at
him, nearly knocking him over, Bellamy sat down on the floor,
then lay down, embracing the moaning scrabbling body of the
dog. Moy left them together. From her room upstairs she heard
the long piercing howling cries of ecstasy. Then the door opening
and the descent to the street. Bellamy called out something. Then
the door closed and the sounds died away. Moy wept.

'You've just missed her,' said Sefton, opening the door to Harvey.
'She's gone to the clinic.'
　'Oh, so he's better?'
　'No, I mean there's been no news. She just felt she had to go.'
　'I bet they won't let her in.'
　'That's what I said.'
　'So she'll be home soon.'
　'She said she was going on somewhere else afterwards, visiting
or something, she has compulsions.'

'My mother has them too,' said Harvey. 'I've just been having lunch with her at Cora's place.'

'Look, do you mind if I close the door? It's letting in the cold air. Can you decide whether you want to stay out or come in?'

'Oh, all right, I'll come in.'

'I didn't mean to influence you one way or the other.'

'You haven't influenced me.'

Harvey stepped inside and Sefton closed the door.

'Moy is out too, she's gone to see her painting teacher. Did you hear, Bellamy has taken Anax back, he came and apprehended him yesterday in Emil's car. Moy was in tears. How's your mother?'

'All right. Thank heavens she's with Cora.' Harvey did indeed feel relieved that his crazy mother was staying with dotty exotic yet somehow sensible Cora. But his satisfaction had been checked when, just as he was leaving, Joan had whispered to him, 'I don't like it here. I'm not going to stay. It's the end.' What did 'It's the end' mean? Did it just mean 'it's awful'? Probably, knowing his mother, it meant nothing, not even an intention to leave.

'I'm just going to have some lunch,' said Sefton.

'*Lunch*? But it's after three o'clock.'

'Is it? I thought it was earlier. Would you like some?'

'I've told you, I've had lunch with Cora!'

'Well, would you like some tea? Come into the kitchen anyway, it's warmer. It looks awfully cold out there, perhaps it's going to snow again.'

Harvey hung up his coat in the hall. He said, 'I'd like some coffee, if you have any. I feel a bit drunk, actually.' He realised with dismay that what he really wanted now was another alcoholic drink. Sitting at the kitchen table he watched gloomily while Sefton produced coffee for him, tea, bread, butter and cheese for herself.

'What do you think about all that, Sefton, I mean the Peter Mir business?'

'I don't know. I feel very sorry for him. There can scarcely be anything worse than surviving something which shatters your mind and leaves you obsessed with revenge.'

'But he recovered, he repaired his memory.'

'But did he really get his mind back? I think he was probably just a decent good man before, and then suddenly got it all back but in a lurid light.'

'How do you mean?'

'I don't know. Meditation is good. I sort of meditate myself.'

'What do you do?'

'I just sit.'

'How spiritual. So you don't think he's some sort of fraud? He lied about his job.'

'That was superficial, almost a joke, as he said. I think there has been terrible suffering for both of them.'

'Both of them? You mean Lucas too? Can *he* suffer?'

'Yes, but we can't see inside. It's like Moy's spider.'

'Moy's spider?'

'Yes, Moy had a spider she was very fond of in her room, a big chap, I saw him, living in a crack in the boarding which he'd covered over with a furry thick silky web like a curtain, with a hole in which he sat, and if he was disturbed he ran back through the hole into the crack, it was like a little house, Moy called it his house. Then one night she saw another spider, rather like him but a bit larger, walking along the wall. When Moy's spider saw the other spider he ran back into the crack and the big spider came and followed him in. Moy says she watched it all with a kind of fascination, the new spider was so large and a slightly different colour, she didn't realise at once, though she says she *ought* to have done, that this was the female of the species who had travelled perhaps from far away, walking wearily and long, surmounting all kinds of obstacles, to find her mate. Moy then got terribly upset when she told me about it the next morning, she cried. She ought to have understood and instantly captured the female in a glass and taken it away and let it go in some very distant place from which it would never be able to find its way back. As it was, she could just sit and look at the little house and could not stop herself from picturing what was happening inside. She said it was like something in a play, or perhaps it must have been an opera, like in *Rigoletto*, when the music plays loudly and the stage is darkened when a murder is going on behind a closed door. She went to bed but she couldn't sleep, and she got up early in the morning, and she thought perhaps after all her spider would be there again, sitting so pleased with himself in his hole in his web, only of course there was no one there, and very quickly the web fell into disrepair and began to fall away. A little bit later on, I forget how much, perhaps almost at once, Moy saw the female spider walking away along the wall and she said she knelt

378

down and as she put it, "startled the spider", menaced it somehow, and it ran away quickly. And afterwards Moy said she felt
ashamed of herself for senselessly and wrongly threatening the
poor spider who had only done its natural duty and enabled the
continuation of the race. And of course *her* spider would probably
have died of old age quite soon anyway, if he hadn't been eaten.
But she kept looking for him, just in case he was still alive, and
remembering the moment when she could so easily have saved
him by capturing the other spider.'

While she was telling this story Sefton had eaten her bread and
cheese and drunk her tea. Harvey did not like his coffee and had
set it aside. He offered feebly to wash up. She refused his offer,
washed up rapidly, and then began to move back towards her
room. Harvey followed her into her room and sat on the bed.
The room was rather dark. The red and blue Turkey carpet was
covered with books. Sefton knelt down and began to sort the
books, then stood up and put them back swiftly into their places
on the shelves. The bookshelves entirely covered one wall of the
small room and crept round beside the narrow window, making
with their coloured bindings, a kind of tapestry.

Harvey watched her. The sleeves of her shirt were rolled up.
The red and blue of the carpet were leaping to and fro before his
eyes. He said, 'I don't see how Moy can go on existing, she
identifies herself with all sorts of beings down to the tiniest ones,
and they are all suffering.'

'She is strange and wonderful. So is Aleph, only in a different
way.'

'But you were saying that those spiders in the little house are
somehow like Peter and Lucas. But which of them is devouring
the other?'

'Oh I didn't mean it was like in that way exactly, just that – I
don't know – just that they are bound together, they are tied
together, somehow struggling with each other, and their suffering
is in the dark, it's a mystery.'

'But about Peter being a Buddhist or whatever it was, do you
think that was something real?'

'Yes – I suppose one could try to find out – but I certainly
don't want to. Perhaps Lucas exalted him somehow – first a
demon, then a saint. Maybe when he comes out of *that* place he'll
be ordinary again. Poor man – he said he had no family or friends

379

– so he took up with *us* – and we can't protect him, we can't help him.'

'So inside that dark house you think both of them are suffering, even Lucas is?'

'Yes.'

'You don't think he's a cruel sadistic cynic?'

'No. He suffers terribly all the time. He lives in fire.'

'How do you know?'

'I just know. Sometimes I think he will become quite desperate – with the pain of simply being himself – he might do anything.'

'But Sefton, he has already *done something*!'

'I don't know what he has done. I am thinking of what he might do.'

Sefton, who had now put away all the books, was sitting on the floor leaning against the end of the bed, her legs, clad in brown corduroy trousers, outstretched. She was not wearing her jacket. She unravelled the sleeves of her shirt, then frowned and turned them up again. Her shirt and trousers were old, impeccably clean, pleasantly faded by innumerable washings. She drew her fingers through her roughly cut brown hair in which, it occurred to him, the strands of red were increasingly visible. She raised her golden-brown eyebrows pensively as if staring into a far distance. He looked at the pale reddish hairs shining upon her strong forearms. She had always alarmed him a little. He thought, she is full of power, she is a *phenomenon*. This classification pleased him a little. He thought, she is already thinking about something else, not about me, about some crisis in the reign of Hadrian! I had better go. He moved as if to get up.

However, Sefton was thinking about him. She said, 'I think you didn't bring your stick with you. Did you bring a stick? I didn't see one.'

'No, I didn't bring one – '

'So your leg, your foot, is better!'

'Not really. Well, yes a bit. I use taxis!'

'Why were you so cross with me on that day that I brought you back your stick which you'd left with Lucas?'

Now she was looking at him with her green eyes.

'Oh Sefton – I'm sorry – '

'What did you talk about with Lucas?'

'Oh – nothing – I mean I didn't talk – ' He thought, she's jealous, she'll hold it against me.

380

'Well – never mind – ' She smiled, observing his embarrassment.

He thought, *are* her eyes green, or are they brown? A sort of greenish brown. She's being kind to me. She has lucid truthful eyes. He felt uncomfortable sitting on the bed, and looking down at her, so he slipped into sitting on the floor with his back against the bed and his knees up. He felt awkward here too. Now she laughed at him and wondered if he were blushing. He thought, she doesn't believe me about Lucas. At that moment the room suddenly became brighter. The sun was shining. He said, 'The sun is shining!' He looked down. The Turkey carpet had become even brighter and more lively.

Sefton said, 'Harvey, on that evening when you fell asleep in the sedan chair – '

'Yes, wasn't I silly!'

'You said you'd had a happy dream. Can you remember the dream?'

Harvey was about to say no, when he suddenly remembered the dream. 'I dreamt you were pulling my hair.'

'But I *was* pulling your hair, I was trying to wake you up!'

'How strange – when I was waking I made it into a dream.'

'A happy dream.'

'Yes.'

They were silent for a moment, side by side, looking at each other.

Harvey said awkwardly, 'How odd, I forgot the dream, and now I've remembered it, only it wasn't a dream.' He felt a curious electrical force which was somehow moving into his body and taking charge of it. He thought, of course I'm drunk, I even feel a bit faint. Sefton looked away at her books, then at the window where the sun still shone, then back again at Harvey. Her hand, supporting her, was beside him on the floor. He put his hand on top of her hand. Her hand moved like a little captive animal, gripped his hand for a moment, then retreated. They were looking at each other again. Harvey now stretched out his arm along the resistant surface of the counterpane and let his hand touch Sefton's shoulders, feeling through her cotton shirt her warm back, her bones. They continued to look at each other, their intent questing gaze dissolving in a kind of blinded stare. Harvey let his knees slip sideways and levered himself a little forward with his other arm. He leaned forwards and his lips very lightly touched her cheek. He saw her close her eyes. He closed his eyes. Their lips,

381

moving hastily, but with a quiet precision, like birds flying in the night, met for a second.

They drew apart and gazed at each other with a questioning astonishment, with fear, almost with terror. They were trembling, shuddering. It was as if some great blow had paralysed them. They sat thus for a short while, awkwardly shifting their positions, panting, their hearts racing. Then Harvey again pursued Sefton's hand and held it, stroking it, while they sat open-mouthed. Sefton then withdrew her hand and looked away.

Harvey said at last, almost in a whisper, 'Can it really happen like this? Evidently it can.'

Sefton, not looking at him, said in an anguished voice, almost peevishly, 'Well, what *has* happened? I'm not at all sure.'

Harvey said, 'Do you mind if we lie on the bed?'

He slipped out of his jacket then arched himself up, edging back over the counterpane. He kicked off his shoes. Sefton somehow followed, lying inertly face downward. Harvey lay on his back, he stared up at the ceiling, noticing a crack, then that his teeth were chattering. He closed his mouth and breathed slowly and deeply through his nose. He felt and seemed to hear the noisy tumbling of his heart, he could also feel Sefton's heart beating against his side. Turning he put one arm across Sefton's back, then led his hand to touch the silky tangle of her hair, then to touch her neck which was burning hot. He opened his mouth again and bit his lower lip. He found himself moaning very softly. Withdrawing his outstretched arm he moved back against the wall, making a space for Sefton to turn towards him. Obeying or seeming to obey his movement she rolled over onto her back in the middle of the bed. Harvey undid his belt. Leaning on an elbow he touched her hot cheek, then began to undo her shirt. Her hand arrested him.

'Sefton, don't be angry with me. I love you.'

After a moment Sefton said, 'Yes. Something has happened. But I think it is a form of madness.'

'Yes, yes, it is!' said Harvey, now undoing his trousers and attempting to pull off his shirt and vest with one hand, since Sefton was still holding the other hand. 'Oh Sefton, Sefton, I want you so much, I love you so.'

'Harvey, *don't*. We don't know who we are, I've never felt so utterly strange to myself – we have become monsters, we are suddenly – *monsters*.'

'Don't be frightened, my darling Sefton.'

'I'm not – frightened – I think – just – amazed, appalled – '

'We're nice monsters, good monsters, oh my dear, please let me undress you a little, just a little – '

'No, *no* – '

'Look, I'm undressing too, just let me pull all this stuff – off.'

'Stop, I don't want to struggle with you, stop, *please*, Harvey, be guided by me – it's all so terribly strange – and I do want it to be *all right*.'

'Yes, it will be all right, Sefton I want you, I've never felt like this before – '

'Nor have I, but – '

'I'm overcome, I'm like – crushed, run over – I must have all of you forever – '

'Think how very strange your words are. Listen, Harvey, *listen*, this, whatever it is, has only just happened to us, it happened in seconds – '

'Thank God it happened to both of us – '

'When we were sitting on the floor, remember, it seems ages ago – '

'I have known you for ages, we were made for each other, millions of years ago, I have known you forever – '

'Harvey, it's all beautiful – it's something the gods dropped on us, it's a weird awful beauty, like nothing we've known before, but wait, we have gone far enough now – '

'You mustn't speak like that, you deny your own words, we've found each other, we must *go on*, don't *torment* me.'

'You don't understand, I'm not denying or tormenting, we must prove this thing, we must respect it, we must try it – '

'Yes, let's try it now, Sefton, I'm in agony – '

'Someone may come in at any moment – '

'Oh hang them! Just let me *be* with you – '

'Harvey, be gentle, be quiet – there's tomorrow and tomorrow. Let us put on our shirts and look at each other like sane people. Let me go, I'm getting up.' She slipped from him.

Harvey lay groaning, then slowly adjusted his shirt and vest, his trousers, his belt. He sat up on the edge of the bed. Sefton stood before him. He thought, who is this strange beautiful woman, her face is transfigured, it's radiant, it's so gentle, but was this all a dream perhaps, just this and nothing more? 'Sefton, sit beside me, that's right, let me just touch, do what I ask.'

383

She sat beside him and let him undo the buttons of her shirt. Sefton, as Spartan, wore, in the coldest weather, no brassière, no vest. Harvey touched her breasts, closing his eyes, then leaning down his heavy head against her. He did not resist her when she pulled his head up, tugging his hair like in the happy dream. They then began to kiss each other hungrily, fast. At last Sefton said, 'You must go.' 'I can't leave you.' 'I'll come to you.' 'You'll come to my flat?' 'Yes.' 'Tonight, tomorrow?' 'No.' 'Sefton, don't kill me, I have *got* to see you.' 'Listen, Harvey, I am older than you are, I am thousands and thousands of years older than you.' 'Sefton, I know that, but it is not relevant now!' '*Listen* – let us *not* meet tomorrow –' 'Don't say that –' 'Let us meet the day after. Harvey, this is holy, we must be worthy of it, tomorrow let us be quiet, and rest, let us be like – in penitence, in prayer – I want this, I want it like this –' 'You want time to recover and tell me to go to hell.' 'No. I believe all this is real. Just do as I ask. And please go away now.' 'Well – I have to obey you – I'll obey you to the end of the world.' 'I'll come at ten, the day after tomorrow.' 'All right, my dear love, my dear.'

Sefton adjusted her shirt, buttoning the buttons and tucking in the tail. She rolled up the sleeves as they had been before. She opened the door.

Harvey stared at his overcoat hanging up in the hall. It was as if the overcoat *didn't know*. He went out and put it on. Sefton opened the front door. It was misty outside. Cold mist moved into the house. Harvey raised his hand and went out. The door closed. He walked down the road smiling like a madman.

Sefton lay supine on the red and blue Turkey carpet, breathing in long deep breaths so slow that it seemed that between one and the next she might quietly die. She felt pinned to the floor by a gentle but insistent force. Her eyes were open, her face serene, her lips slightly parted in a faint quizzical smile. Her limbs were relaxed, strengthless, flattened as if by the passage of a vast silent wind. At intervals she framed words, holding them concealed in her mouth like sacred charms. She thought, I am now in a vacuum, I am nowhere and nothing, transparent, uncreated, substanceless, drifting in limbo, between being and non-being, where one may choose not to be. I am dissolved by fear and violence into a timeless peace. How little I have expected this overthrow, this sudden awful presence of the god. Perhaps after all not to have been born is best. How near the human soul must be to nothingness if it can be so tossed.

Moy came in. She closed the door quietly as she usually did, and went into the kitchen and put the kettle on. Then she went and knocked softly on Sefton's door, saying, 'Would you like a cup of tea, Sef?' She often did this. There was a silence. Then Sefton replied, 'Thanks, dear, I'll come.' A few minutes later, just as Moy was making the tea, she came in.

'What's the matter, Sef?'

'What do you mean, what's the matter?'

'You look funny.'

'How funny?'

'As if you were getting the 'flu. Do you feel all right?'

'Yes, of course! I'd love some tea. How did things go with Miss Fitzherbert?'

'Oh very well, she's so kind. I wonder if we could invite her round.'

'You know we never invite anyone round.'

'She said I'd been cowardly and must be brave and wild.'

The telephone rang. Sefton upset her tea. Moy went out into the hall.

'Hello.'

It was Clement. 'Hello, Moy.'

'How did you know it was me.'

'You have a special lovely voice.'

'Oh. I'm afraid Louie is out, she's gone to the clinic.'

'Has she? Well, well.'

'I'll tell her you rang.'

'Moy, don't ring off.'

'Sorry.'

'I might want to talk to you. What's the art school news?'

'Miss Fitzherbert said I should paint more in oils. Only it means buying canvases.'

'I'll buy you some canvases.'

'No, *no*, I don't mean that, I wouldn't accept them – '

'Don't be silly! Just say I rang. I'll ring again.'

Moy returned to the kitchen. Sefton was mopping the table where she had spilt the tea. Moy said, 'It was Clement, he'll ring again.'

Moy drank some tea. Then she went slowly upstairs. Anax used to run up the stairs in front of her, push open her door, and jump on her bed, turning to her with his wild lively always expectant foxy face. She went in and closed the door behind her. The silent room seemed full, full of something, as if all the atoms had grown and were crowding upon one another, atoms of silence. She breathed them in through her nose and mouth. Looking toward the Polish Rider she met his calm tender gentle thoughtful gaze. She thought, what he sees is the face of death. He sees the silence of the valley, its emptiness, its innocence – and beyond it the hideous field of war on which he will die. And his poor horse will die too. He is courage, he is love, he loves what is good, and will die for it, and his body will be trampled by horses' hooves, and no one will know his grave. She thought, he is so beautiful, he has the beauty of goodness. I am a freak, a crippled animal, something which will be put down and out of its misery, I am a hump-backed dwarf. She turned away toward her stones, which had so much worried Anax, upon their shelf, and reached out her hand, nearer and nearer. A stone moved to her hand. She thought, my stones, oh, my stones. She warmed the cold stone in her hand, and she thought too, as this thought came suddenly at such times, of the rock upon the hillside, and its stone which she had taken away. She thought, I shall die of misery and pain. Then she thought, when I am eighteen I shall go to India where all things, even the tiniest things, are holy and sacred. And she thought, I don't yet know what pain is. The world is full of *terrible pain*. *He* could see that too.

Soon after Moy had gone upstairs Louise returned. Sefton was still sitting in the kitchen. She sprang up. 'Oh Louie, have some tea, I think the pot is still warm.'

'I'll put the kettle on just in case. Have you had tea?'

'Yes.' Sefton watched her mother, still with her coat on and her woollen cap pulled down over her ears, filling the kettle at the sink, and it brought back to her some memory of early child-hood, and its special security, and for a moment Sefton thought about her father.

'Where's Moy?'

'Upstairs.'

'Oh dear, she must be missing Anax. Do you think we should buy her a dog?'

'No. It would just get run over. What happened at the clinic?'

'Nothing – it was no good.'

'I thought so. It's too early to start visiting. What's the place like?'

'Terribly grand and expensive – and terribly quiet and as it were barricaded! I didn't get past the girl at the desk. She asked me to wait in a room full of flowering plants. Then she came and told me Peter was recovering and they would let us know when he was ready for visitors. She already had our address. She said Bellamy had called earlier and been told the same.'

'So they know all about us.'

'Yes, I'm rather glad of that. I asked for Dr Fonsett but they said he wasn't available.'

'Of course!'

'Did anyone ring up?'

'Clement called. Moy took the call.'

'Oh dear, she gets so upset talking with him by telephone.'

'And Harvey dropped in.'

'I'm sorry I missed him. I'll ring Clement now.'

Louise went into the hall and rang Clement's number. No answer. She returned to the kitchen. Sefton had gone back to her own room. Louise emptied the lukewarm tea-pot, put in some more tea and poured the boiling water into the pot. She sat down at the table. She had not mentioned to Sefton a visit, equally fruitless, which she had made after leaving the clinic. She had gone again to Lucas's house and rung the bell. No answer. She went through the gate into the garden, but did not climb the iron staircase. She returned to the front door and rang again, and called his name. Silence. She thought, he is dead. Now tears came to her once more, familiar tears. Something which Louise had never divulged to anyone was that, soon after Teddy's death, Lucas had made her an offer of marriage.

'What did you do yesterday?'

'I worked as usual. I thought about you. What did you do?'

'I couldn't do anything, I just was – I couldn't eat or drink or speak – I walked about London. I was in heaven and hell.'

The sun was shining into Harvey's little room, it shone upon the bed which was extended across the room. The bed was neatly made up with a neat Indian counterpane upon it. Sefton, who had just arrived, stood by the door, Harvey was near the window beside his little writing-desk. They looked at each other across the bed.

Harvey's left hand was holding his right hand firmly by the wrist. The sun shone upon his yellow hair, he had combed it carefully, its strands fell in very slightly curling straight lines. He was taller than Sefton. He released his right hand and stretched it out towards her across the bed. They shook hands. Then they both sat down on the bed on opposite sides, turning to see each other. Harvey thought, this is one of the most weird and *dangerous* moments of my life. As Sefton did not reply to him he said, 'I suppose you wanted us to cool off.'

Sefton said, 'I wanted us to know that it was *possible* that what happened the day before yesterday was an odd event which just happened once and had no sequel.'

'Well, I want a sequel. Perhaps you don't?' He added, 'Perhaps you think we don't suit each other?' Sefton shuddered. 'So you do think so?'

'No. I think your terminology is ludicrous. Whatever is between us now is far above – all that – '

'All what?'

'Discussions of compatibility.'

'Well, I don't think much of your terminology, either. Get up, would you?'

Sefton stood up and watched Harvey tear off the counterpane and haul back the sheets and blankets. Then he began to undress, pulling off his shirt and kicking off his shoes and his trousers.

Sefton had never seen a man entirely naked. She had instinctively found the male organs, unless excused and made innocent by great art, rather pathetic and ugly. She took off her coat and dropped it on the floor. Then she sat down again on the bed and watched him. Harvey, now undressed, knelt down on the floor against his side of the bed, as if modestly hiding himself from her.

Sefton said, 'Of course you know I've never done this before.'

Harvey, crossing his arms on his chest and lowering his eyes, said, 'Neither have I really – I had an experience – which I'll tell you about later.'

'Well, for heaven's sake don't tell me now.'

'I have taken precautions, so you needn't fear – '

'I have taken precautions too.'

'So you believed in the sequel.'

'Yes but – you see – *this* might be a single occasion too – and I want it, if it happens, not to be – that's what yesterday was about – '

'You haven't said that you love me. If you don't there's still time to say so.'

'I love you, Harvey.'

'You are not to go away. I see you are wearing a skirt.'

Sefton took off her shoes and her long socks and her knickers and dropped her skirt on the floor. As she did so she saw Harvey delving into the foot of the bed and bringing out an object which turned out to be a hot water bottle. She looked at it with revulsion and horror. She began to unbutton her long shirt.

Harvey had stretched himself out on the bed. 'Take it off, Sefton, and come to me.'

Sefton took it off and lay down beside him trembling and closing her eyes.

'I do hope it didn't hurt?'

'Only for a moment.'

'And – oh dear dear Sefton – you did like it, I did please you?'

'Yes, yes – '

'You have given me such joy, like I didn't know existed, it's like being made into an angel, you have made me into an angel, you have made me into a god, it's like being blinded by blazing happiness, like the sun coming down and down and one is exploding into the sun, oh Sefton you have made me so happy, so joyful, I love you forever, I worship you, I am in heaven, you are so beautiful, you are happy too, you do love me, it is wonderful for you?'

'I love you.'

'I feel so strange, as if I were living in a myth – '

'Myths are dangerous places.'

'But *we* are safe, aren't we, aren't we, my dear dear one?'

'Yes – be quiet, my darling – '

'We are good monsters, we are happy monsters, we have been changed into divine beings, we are glorified – '

'Yes, rest now – I am going to put some clothes on.'

Sefton rapidly put on her shirt and her knickers, then put her skirt on and buttoned it at her narrow waist. She sat on the bed, tucking her bare feet away under her skirt. 'Harvey, put your shirt on.' Sitting up, he put it on. They looked at each other.

'Sef, don't say now that you don't like me, that you don't want me. I shall die if you say that.'

'I love you. That is everything. Please let us rest together now.'

They reposed, leaning upon piles of pillows, looking at each other and gently touching. Harvey unbuttoned Sefton's shirt and put his hands upon her breasts.

'Sef, you're not afraid of sex? Some girls are to begin with.'

'I'm not afraid.'

'Fancy, I've just discovered sex! It's everything they say, only far far more! Bellamy said to me once, "Be patient, it will all come to you, some god will explain it to you, it will all be clarified, it will all be *easy*!" And so it is!'

'Bellamy said that to you? I'm glad.'

'You're thinking perhaps that Bellamy was the person – I had that experience with – it wasn't him, it was Tessa – and it was nothing, *nothing* happened – I just wanted to try it on someone, I wasn't in love with her, she was just being kind to me – I'm terribly sorry, I wish I'd waited, please don't mind, you do forgive me, don't you?'

'Of course I don't mind! And I wasn't thinking of that about Bellamy at all – I'm just glad the god has explained it. We must do our work – '

'This is our work! All right, I know what you mean, we will work, I shall work far far better, my foot will heal – '

'Let me look at your foot.'

Harvey displayed it. Sefton took it gently in her hands and massaged it, then stroked it as if it were an animal. 'Sef, it's better already. You know, Peter did that for it on that night, when he was taken away.'

'Perhaps he'll do it again.'

'And *you'll* do it again. Suddenly anything is possible. We'll leap over all the obstacles.'

'And we'll tell each other the truth.'

'Oh Sefton, we're here, we've arrived, this is it – trip no further, pretty sweeting – I'm so happy, I'm crazy with happiness, the world is brilliant, it's shining – '

'Do get dressed, my darling, I want you dressed.'

'We are transformed, we are blazing with light, I tremble before you.'

'I tremble too.'

'Yes, I'll get dressed. We are made for each other, no one else will do.'

'About obstacles, we shall have to think, we shall have to be careful.'

'Sefton, we shall be married, we shall be together.'

'We must tell the others.'

'What others?'

'Your mother, my mother, my sisters, Clement, Bellamy – '

'But why "careful"? I don't like that "careful".'

'Harvey, we've got to think what to say, how to say it, in what order, in what words, they'll be amazed, they'll be shocked, they may be upset, they may be angry – '

'Oh to hell with them. We'll just announce it!'

'For instance, what about Aleph?'

'How do you mean, what about Aleph?'

'People have expected you to marry her, perhaps they still do. Perhaps *she* expects it. You love her.'

'Oh Sefton! I love her as a sister! We understand each other, we've known each other forever. We know that *that* is impossible between us!'

'Yes, but your understanding with her may envisage your marrying someone else, but not your marrying me.'

'So you will reject me to please Aleph!'

'Don't tease me.'

'I'm not *teasing* you.'

'I'm sorry, forgive me – '

'I forgive you. I love you.'

'I love you. Oh Harvey, I feel so strange, so wonderful, so devastated – now I'm going to cry, and after that I shall go home, I must be alone for a while.'

Sefton, at home in her little room, did not lie down on the red and blue carpet, but knelt beside her bed burying her face as if in prayer, then slipping sideways huddled with her arms about her knees. She had taken off her skirt and put on her old corduroy trousers. She was listening to a voice, a much loved voice, a voice of authority, which said: simplify your life, travel light, do not become involved with family problems, possessions, or the troubles of others, do not marry, marriage ends truthfulness, live with solitude, solitude is essential if real thinking is to take place. She thought, he will never forgive me, he will despise me and cast me out, he warned me against the ambiguous Eros, the deceiver, the magician, the sophist, the maker of drugs and poisons. Of course I am in love, yes, this *is* love, and I am *sick* with it – but what follows? Do I really believe that I shall give over my life, the whole of my life, which is only just now *really beginning* to another person? Shall I cease forever to be the cat that walks by herself by her wild lone? What has happened to my soldierly completeness with which I was so content, my satisfaction and my pride? At the first trial I am broken. Something *terrible* has happened to me, something which I never thought of as ever concerning me, I am a different person, I feel that difference in every atom of my captured and invaded body. I am distracted from myself. I am *losing* myself, I am in a state of *warfare*, of confusions and compromises and base dissension and deceit. I must not become this other person, this cowardly overthrown defeated person. By what act have I betrayed myself? There was an invasion and a pain. What I felt then was *his* exaltation, *his* joy, and my love for him leaping over all obstacles. Can this be right and true, the truth of a life, of my life? Oh I am so confused, I want my solitude. And what of Aleph, how does she stand, my dear sister whom I have loved forever with such an innocent and guileless love? How can I gauge Aleph's mind? Is it possible that she sees Harvey as her property, something *kept* all this long time *in store*, waiting for the grown-up moment which may be now so nearly ripe? Could she not indeed at any time reach out her hand and take Harvey from me? Or else, this changeless step which we two have taken, which must destroy the happy childish harmony in which we have all lived so long, could it not also ruin Aleph's life – and in ruining hers, ruin ours! I have never had such terrible deep thoughts – and must I now forever live with such thoughts? Perhaps poor Harvey simply wanted sex, and lacking Aleph took me up instead, a substitute, a sort of puppet, instead of Aleph, even perhaps to spite her, not really loving me at all. What do I know of Aleph's thoughts, of that long long conversation between

her and Harvey, from which I have been excluded? I must *stop*
this thing, I must not go back to Harvey, I must tell him that I
cannot come to him, that I must draw back, that we must be
apart forever. What an agony, what a tearing pain, what horrible
and evil thoughts darken my mind – oh why did this awful thing
have to happen, my peace and my innocence are gone from me
forever.

She thought, I'll write a letter to him now, and deliver it at
once. I won't see him, I'll just drop it in. Then I shall feel free.
She wrote.

Dearest Harvey,
Please forgive me, I cannot proceed, I cannot go on with
what has happened to us. It is wrong for me, I cannot commit
myself to anything so absolute – and anything less than
absolute is not what is in question. I must return to my
freedom which I now realise is something so essential that it
makes my love for you seem like death. I am *so very sorry*.
Also I am extremely disturbed about Aleph. You must think
deeply about her, about her feelings, about your very long
and deep friendship with her. For this, *you too* must be free.
We acted hastily, carried away we have assumed too much.
We must step back from each other, we are too young. We
must regard what happened as a beautiful episode – it need
not be a secret from Aleph – I leave that to you. Of course
we shall see each other, and so on, almost as before. Please
understand, dear dear Harvey. I love you. But what I say
now is wise and right, and I hope you will respect it. Oh my
dear – forgive me, in all this I want your happiness – I am
so very sorry –

She quickly sealed the letter and ran out of the house. Already it
was getting dark. How had the day gone so quickly?

Louise, coming down the stairs, saw Sefton returning.
  'Oh Sefton, there you are, where have you been?'
  'Just delivering something.'
  'Are you all right, you look a bit flushed.'
  'I'm all right, Louie.'
  'How do you feel? I hope it's not that 'flu that's going round.
Have you got a temperature?'

'Of course not. I feel fine.'

'I was going to ask you, have you had a card from Aleph, lately I mean?'

'Not lately, no.'

'I haven't heard for several days. Did she tell you when they were coming back?'

'I can't remember her saying anything definite.'

'I keep thinking they may have had a car crash. Rosemary drives so fast.'

'Of course they haven't had a car crash.'

'I tried to ring Connie yesterday but there was no reply.'

'I expect they're in Yorkshire.'

'I can't find our telephone number book, and they're ex-directory. Where is that book, can Aleph have taken it away with her? Can you remember the Yorkshire number?'

'No.'

'It's yards long. Oh dear. Would you like some tea?'

'No thanks.'

'I suppose you've had some lunch?'

'No, I mean yes.'

'Sefton, come into the kitchen, you are over-tired, you are working too much. You *must* have some tea.'

Sefton followed her mother into the kitchen and sat down.

'I hope those girls are all right. I think Connie is cross with us.'

'Why?'

'For involving her and Jeremy in that extraordinary evening with Peter Mir.'

'I thought she was enjoying every moment of it.'

'I do hope he'll get out soon. I think he does us good.'

'By being religious – or giving us jewels?'

'Fancy his giving Aleph that diamond necklace.'

'He's a millionaire, he gives them to all the girls.'

'Here is your tea. Would you like some cake or a biscuit?'

'No, thanks.'

'I'll try the clinic again tomorrow. Sorry, I feel terribly restless.'

'Give Clement a ring.'

'I don't think he's there. He – oh never mind.'

'Well, Bellamy then, I suppose he's still with Emil.'

'He talks so on the telephone.'

The telephone rang and Louise ran out. She returned. 'It's Harvey, he wants you.'

Sefton went out, closing the door behind her. She could be heard making laconic answers. She returned.

'I suppose he wants to know if Aleph is back.'

'Yes. Louie, thanks for the tea, I think I'll go and get on with my work.'

'Do stay with me a little longer, can't your work wait, stay here and relax. I think I'll call the Adwardens' London number again, or I suppose I could try Jeremy's office, I know that number is in the telephone directory.'

'You could ring Cora for the Yorkshire number.'

'I don't want to bother Cora.'

'Oh don't *fret* so, Louie! Aleph will turn up soon, and she'll be cross if you've been fussing everyone else!'

'I think I'll just try Connie again.'

Louise went into the hall and dialled the number. She heard Connie's voice.

'Oh Connie, I'm so glad you're there, I've been trying to ring you.'

'I just dashed to Paris for the exhibition, just got back, I'm *exhausted*! How are you?'

'All right, I'm just thinking about Aleph and Rosemary.'

'Yes, such a wonderful tour!'

'Quite a long one.'

'Rosemary always wants to see everything. She'll drive a hundred miles to see some crumbling castle, especially if Mary Queen of Scots or someone was imprisoned there!'

'You relieve my mind – '

'How's our recent host, Peter Mir, are they keeping him inside?'

'For the present I think, he'll be out soon. So do you know when they'll be back?'

'When who'll be back?'

'Aleph and Rosemary.'

'Well, Rosemary's back, or rather she isn't, she's in Paris, or she was, and Aleph's with you.'

'No she isn't, she hasn't come, we haven't heard from her – '

'Rosemary took her to your place before coming on to us.'

'*What*? No, she didn't, I've said, she hasn't come back, she isn't here – you say Rosemary's back from their tour – ?'

'*Yes*, she came back a couple of days ago, she told us all their adventures!'

'But Aleph isn't with you – '

'No, I keep saying, Rosemary took her to your place, I've no idea where she is!'

'Did you see her with Rosemary?'

'No, of course I didn't, Rosemary had already delivered her to you!'

'But she hasn't, she didn't, Aleph isn't here, she hasn't come back, we don't know where she is! Look, could I talk to Rosemary, have you got her number in Paris?'

'Well, I'm afraid she's left by now, she said she was going on to Chartres, I don't know where she's staying – or whether she actually went to Chartres, she's so vague! She said she'd be back in England on Thursday or Friday – '

'Connie, *please* could you tell Rosemary to ring me – and do please could you ring me if you hear anything?'

'Are you worrying about Aleph?'

'Yes!'

'Well, you're more likely to hear something than I am – but what are you worrying about? She's probably gone on somewhere else with some friend. She is grown up, you know.'

'Yes – of course – anyway – thanks, goodbye.'

Louise returned to the kitchen. Sefton said, 'Well – ?'

'Connie says Rosemary came back two days ago, and said she'd brought Aleph back here. Rosemary's somewhere in France now. Connie says Aleph has probably just gone on somewhere else with a friend.'

'How could she – ? Louie, *please* – '

'Aleph wouldn't do that. So it means something must have happened to her. Oh Sefton, what can have happened – she has had an accident, she has been attacked – '

'We'd have heard. Look, do ring Clement again.'

Louise rang Clement's number, again no reply. She said, 'Where's Moy?'

'Upstairs, I'll get her.'

Moy could not offer any clues. No, she had heard nothing from Aleph, and Aleph hadn't said anything.

The doorbell rang. Moy ran to the door and admitted Harvey. Sitting in the kitchen, Harvey too was questioned, but could provide nothing but exclamations of distress. Moy went back upstairs. Louise was telephoning Emil's flat and speaking first to Emil and then to Bellamy.

Harvey and Sefton sitting side by side spoke in low voices.

'How can you have written me such a letter! We have only just found each other!' 'Where's Aleph, do you know?' 'Of course I don't know! Are you mad?' 'Harvey, I do mean it about leaving me alone, I've got to be alone. And now this awful thing about Aleph.' 'You care about Aleph more than you care about me.' 'Harvey, I want you to *think* about Aleph, to think about what she means to you – and to me. We can't just – ' 'You want to sell me to Aleph, you want to make her a pretext for dropping me, you think it was all an illusion, you are causing me terrible pain.' 'I'm in pain too, I want you to have some ordinary time with Aleph – ' 'What can be ordinary now?' 'I want you to *be* with her, she may simply be waiting for you, just wait and *think*, anyway we are far too young, we have been too hasty, I don't want us to do any more, God, don't you *understand*?' 'No, I don't. Do you want me to propose to Aleph and if she turns me down, try you?' 'This is a horrible conversation, I'm sorry, it's all my fault, I oughtn't to – do please just stay away, only *forgive me* and don't be angry with me, I *can't bear it*.' 'Sefton, you are sending me to hell.' 'Don't you care about Aleph?' 'Look, I'm in love with you! Perhaps she's gone to Peter Mir. People can do mad things.'

Louise returned. 'Bellamy and Emil can't help.'

Sefton said, 'Harvey thinks she may have gone to Peter Mir, he seemed to be in love with her.'

'He may have told her to go to some place,' said Harvey, 'and he'd join her there. Of course he's a bit mad.'

'He gave her a diamond necklace,' said Sefton.

'*Did* he?' said Harvey.

'Do you think I should telephone the clinic?' said Louise.

'No,' said Sefton, 'Harvey is talking nonsense.'

'I don't think it's nonsense, I'm going to telephone them.' She went back into the hall. Moy had returned and was sitting on the stairs.

Sefton moved away from Harvey where they had been sitting shoulder to shoulder and where she had resisted his hand. She stood up. 'How mad all this is. We are all mad now. It had to happen. Aleph has gone away to other friends, like Connie said, she's just fed up with living here and being watched all the time.'

Louise stood in the doorway. 'They wouldn't tell me anything. They said they never discussed patients by telephone. Oh dear, what can we do, we must do something!'

Harvey said, 'Perhaps she's with Clement. That seems likely, after all – '

'After all what?' said Sefton.

'Clement isn't there,' said Louise. 'I'm going to call the police.'

'Oh *no*, Louie!'

Sefton followed Louise into the hall and sat down beside Moy on the stairs. Moy was trembling. Sefton put an arm round her.

Louise rang the police who listened politely, said they had had no report of any relevant accident or assault, yes, they were noting the telephone number.

Harvey came out of the kitchen. Moy was now retreating up the stairs. Harvey said to Sefton in a low voice, 'I'm going. Walk along the road with me. Please.' And to Louise, 'I must be off now.'

'Oh Harvey, won't you stay to supper? It is nearly supper-time, isn't it, I'm so confused – '

'I'm so sorry, I must go.'

'How will you get home? Shall I ring for a taxi?'

'No thanks. I'll walk. I'll find a taxi.'

'I'll walk with you,' said Louise, 'just a little way. Sefton will look after the telephone. Come on, where's your coat, where's mine? It's terribly cold out and now it's foggy too.'

The door opened and the cold brown atoms of the fog rushed into the house. Sefton gave a soft plaintive cry like a bird's cry. Harvey went out through the door followed by Louise. Huddled in their overcoats they gasped, inhaling the thick bitter air and stepping cautiously upon the frosty pavements. Louise put her arm through Harvey's. 'Harvey, you know you are one of the family. We all love you very much. I wish you would make your home with us. Don't worry, dear dear, Harvey. I'm sure Aleph will turn up tomorrow and explain everything.'

'I hope *you* won't worry too much,' said Harvey. 'She'll be all right, she can look after herself.'

'Yes, of course, you are wise, you understand her so well, probably much better than I do, you have both been so close. What made you think she might be with Clement?'

'Oh, not for any special reason. He's one of the family after all.'

'Why, yes, of course. Look, there's a taxi, I remember you said you could conjure them up! Goodnight, my dear dear child, we'll be in touch, don't be upset. Have you got enough money for the fare?' She hugged him and kissed him twice upon his cold cheek.

Louise walked back to the house, tracking their footprints which were still clear in the thick powdery frost. She had come out without her key, but Sefton had put the door upon the latch and it opened silently at her pressure. She closed it, unlatching the lock and shooting the bolt. The kitchen was empty. Louise dialled Clement's number again but there was no answer. Sefton appeared. 'Sefton, come and have some supper.'

'No thanks, I've made myself a sandwich. I made one for Moy too. I think she's gone to bed. The kettle has boiled, by the way.'

'You can't go to bed! Come and sit with me in the kitchen.'

'Sorry, Louie, I'm awfully tired, I'm ready to collapse with tiredness.'

Louise poured the boiling water upon the fresh tea-leaves and inhaled the calm familiar aroma. A loaf was upon the table, with some butter and cheese from Sefton's sandwich-making, also some biscuits left over from tea-time. Sefton's door was closed. Louise left the kitchen and began to mount the stairs. Upon the second flight she found Moy sitting and crying, still clutching her uneaten sandwich in one hand.

'Moy, don't grieve little one. Come down and sit with me. I'll make supper for you. Nothing bad has happened, all will be well.'

'Yes – I hope – oh I'm so unhappy. And I miss Anax so much.'

'Come on down and we'll have supper.'

'I couldn't eat anything. I'm just going to bed. Oh I'm – so sorry – ' Moy rose and went on up the stairs, disappearing into the darkness at the top of the house.

Louise went back to the kitchen and poured some tea into a mug. She thought: something awful has happened and the children know it. She put away the butter. Carrying the mug she went up the stairs. The door of Aleph's room was open. She thought, I ought to search that room. But she went into her own bedroom, and to the window where the curtains had not yet been pulled, and looked down at the place where so long ago she had seen Peter Mir standing, half expecting to see him again. She left her bedroom door open, hoping and dreading to hear the telephone. She sat down on her bed in the darkened room and sipped the tea, but it was still too hot. She thought, this is the end of happiness, darkness begins here.

'Where's Cora?' said Clement.

'Gone to bed, I think.'

'Gone to bed? Oh I see. Leaving us alone together.'

'So it appears, dear Harlequin. What an innocent you are!'

'She said "a dinner-party". Then there's only three!'

'And now there's only two.'

'And soon there will be only one, because I'm going home.'

'No you aren't, darling Harlequin. You are going to have some more whisky.'

Joan was right. Clement poured a small quantity of whisky into his tumbler and added a lot of mineral water. He sipped the mixture. He had reached a stage where he felt an overwhelming necessity to go on drinking. He had unsuspiciously accepted Cora's invitation, assuming that Joan might be present among others, but not anticipating the device evidently set up by Joan and her generous match-making hostess. Not that it mattered, he would soon walk out. He drank the whisky.

Clement liked going out to dinner, really anywhere with anyone. He liked dressing-up for dinner, not just in the traditional black and white which suited him so well, but in carefully selected brightly coloured shirts and ties. He enjoyed the *problem* of what to wear. Tonight he had on a brilliant pink shirt with a silver bow tie and a dark blue and now very old velvet jacket. He had, as dinner proceeded, loosened the tie and undone a button of his shirt. His very dark glossy hair, disarranged during dinner by his nervous hand, now framed his face with wild locks. His lips were red, his cheeks, stirred by alcohol, were also red. His eyes seemed darker, blacker. Gazing at Joan, he drew his hand over his brow, then down the Grecian profile of his long nose. Joan was wearing a *décolleté* evening-dress which, as she and Cora had explained during dinner, was one of Cora's cast-offs which Joan had altered to fit her slimmer figure. The dress was silvery grey, somewhat the colour of Clement's tie as they had observed, made of a silky material which emulated fish scales, three-quarter length and dubbed by Cora as hopelessly art deco.

'I like your dress.'

'It's one of Cora's, well we told you that, didn't we. I'm getting drunk too. Cora is getting fat, poor girl.'

'You are as slim as a dolphin.'

'Aren't dolphins rather plump, the dear things? You are drunk, my sweet, my beautiful.'

'Yes. I must be. Your eyes are flashing like neon signs.'

'Read the signs, my angel. At least in this dress I can show my legs. Legs are forever.' Turning sideways she pulled up her skirt. She had grown her dyed dark-red brown hair longer than usual, and allowed it to fall in curling gipsy tangles. Her eyes, prominent in the dark circle of her make-up, sparkled at him, her long eyelashes flickered.

'I must go,' said Clement. But he stared at her and did not move.

'Clement, may I show you something? You won't have to go far. You can walk can't you?'

'Of course I can walk.'

'It's just out here.' Joan sprang up. Clement detached himself from his chair and followed her, holding onto his glass of whisky. Following her, he crossed the hall and mounted the stairs. Joan threw open a door and Clement found himself in a bedroom.

'Well, what was it you wanted to show me? Then I must go.'

'Oh you poor slow beast! To start with, look at this, it's Spanish.' She pointed to the huge magnificent bed, its dusky headboard painted with swirling roses. The sheets had been pulled back.

'All right. Joke over. I'm going home.'

'No, you're not. I've locked the door and hidden the key.'

'Oh Joan, don't be so *boring*. I don't want to be nasty to you. I'm tired and I've got a lot of troubles. Just don't play these silly fruitless games, you ought to know by now – '

'Indeed, dear Harlequin, you must not be nasty to me, you must *not*, because then I would cry. Just let us talk for a little bit.'

'Well, first of all put the key back in the door.'

'I didn't lock it, I just said that, the door has no key, look – ' She swung it open, then closed it again. 'Now do let's sit and talk, where shall we sit, say you there and I here.' She pulled two big chairs, evidently also Spanish, away from the wall and set them closely opposite to each other. Clement sat down. Joan sat down, her knees just touching his.

'Was this little dinner joke your idea or Cora's?'

'Oh, both – you know Cora has such a big heart, I think it's something to do with not having children, and she mopes for Isaac all the time, and she loves looking after people.'

'Yes, she's kind, but you are naughty.'

'Oh Clement, how delightful!'

'What – ?'

'You calling me naughty! It's such a sweet endearment! Yes, that's just what I am, naughty! Oh how sweet you are!'

'I didn't mean it as any sort of compliment. Joan, please learn to leave me alone.'

'I can't. You say that, and you come to dinner. Why not face the facts? *You* can't leave *me* alone! Oh, Harlequin, don't look at me like that!'

'I'm sorry if I have misled you. I cannot love you in the way that you require.'

'How pompous you sound, it's the drink. But then you *do* love me in some other way. You imply that, don't you? So can we not teach each other how to love each other, since we are so close? We are close, really we are closest – you do love me, old friend, you do – don't you?'

'Well, yes, I suppose so.'

'What an old miser you are. And I am so humble I can be pleased by your grudging words! But seriously, we are very old friends, aren't we?'

'Yes.'

'Then call me "Circe" like you used to.'

'Oh wicked Circe, you turn men into pigs. You have turned me into a pig, and now you complain about my piggishness!'

'So, maybe I do turn men into pigs, yes, perhaps I do, considering most of the men I've got to know. Perhaps automatically turning men into pigs was a curse laid upon poor Circe by the gods. Whenever she ran into some nice man he instantly turned into a horrid pig! Oh Harlequin, my heart is so heavy.'

'So is mine. But there's nothing to be done about it. We must each carry our heavy hearts along our separate roads.'

'You want to marry Aleph. But you are afraid to ask her. Maybe you think she'll run away and join you one day! So why not ask her, I dare you to!'

'I'm not in love with Aleph.'

'Clement, I know that you desire her, any man must. Peter Mir desired her. How that man has stirred us up, I think he's liberated us somehow! I feel liberated.'

'I don't.'

'I feel good. I mean goody good. I suddenly have confidence in my goodness, I have faith in it. I can't think why all these years

I've thought I was bad, everyone has told me I was bad, you have, even Harvey has.'

Clement laughed. Joan's knee pressed his, then retreated. 'Dear Joan, I'm glad that you have discovered your goodness! I wish I could discover mine. I just feel hopelessly morose at present.'

' "Morose" is a fine word. I think your trouble is that you're in love with Louise, you know that Louise is dowdy and spiritless and dull, but for some reason you feel you have a duty to love her. Perhaps you think the shade of Teddy has commanded you to love her. But, Harlequin, can't you just *get out* of it? Peter has moved everyone but you! Look how Bellamy and Emil have shacked up! No sooner is Clive gone than Emil grabs Bellamy.'

'I don't believe in your conversion to goodness. What you say about Louise is mean and spiteful and untrue.'

'All right, I know it is, I was just trying to provoke you and make you reveal your feelings! And think how close you and I are to each other so that we can talk in this way, we are free beings together, we *get on* together, we tell each other the truth, isn't that so?'

'In a way, yes.'

'And how rare that is. Dear Clement, I love you, I've always loved you, you know that. Listen, listen. I want to marry you, I want to be your wife and to be with you always and forever. And I'll be a good good wife, I'll learn to cook, I'll look after the house and your clothes and everything and be your secretary and I'll learn to use a computer and I'll *serve* you and do all the little jobs that you feel waste your time and every night in bed we'll hug each other and make love and then if we wake in the night we'll each know the other is there and we'll reach out and hold hands and in every way we shall keep each other safe, and live happily and simply and truthfully with each other, oh Clement, that's what I have always wanted and dreamt of, please please marry me, I love you so much – '

Tears were streaming down Joan's face. Clement, reaching out to her, said, 'Joan, do stop crying, or else I shall start to cry too.' For a moment she clutched his hand. Then Clement pushed his chair back, releasing her hand. '*Please* don't be so upset, *please* try to understand, I just don't want to marry you, I don't love you enough, we don't suit each other, we could not live together, it wouldn't do, it's out of the question, please don't imagine it as possible – '

'You think I'm bad, you think I'm promiscuous, and wouldn't be faithful to you, but I *would* be, I'd want to be with you all the time, if I had you I wouldn't *dream* of anybody else – '

'It's not that, I'm sure you'd be faithful, I just don't want you! Now do stop crying *please*!'

There was a silence. Joan dried her eyes on the silvery sleeve of her dress, Clement pushed his chair further back, then got up and stood behind it.

Joan said huskily, not looking at him but at her soaked sleeve. 'You said that at the end of the world you would take me in – '

'Maybe I did, but – '

'Well, now it's the end of the world.'

'No it isn't, and don't threaten me with "Humphrey Hook", Harvey told me all about "him"!'

'But, Clement – '

'You won't hang yourself or take to drugs, you're far too sensible, you love yourself too much, you love life, you'll always find a way – Look, if you need money I can give you some, don't say no, money always helps – don't be angry with me, Joan, I am still your old friend if you will let me be – '

Joan stood up and began trying to pull her tight-fitting dress off. She managed to pull the top part down as far as the waist. She sat down awkwardly upon the bed. 'Come to me, Clement, stay here tonight, just for this night, I know you want to, be with me, like we once were, remember, in the rue Vercingetorix, oh please do stay, my Harlequin, my darling, just give me this night – '

Clement turned and ran from the room. He hurried down the stairs, found his coat, and let himself quietly out of the front door. Oblivious of the freezing air he walked all the way back to his flat, moaning quietly to himself. When he got back he took a sleeping-pill and fell into a deep slumber. He was wakened the next morning by his telephone and Louise telling him that Aleph was lost.

On the next day, Clifton was like a besieged encampment. There was intense chaotic activity but no good news. Well-intentioned people kept turning up and departing. The telephone was in constant use. Something seemed to be happening in every room. Clement arrived first, coming round immediately after Louise's early phone call. By then the meagre post had been scrutinised. Bellamy then arrived, followed soon by Emil. Sefton left early, saying she must go to a library. Harvey then arrived and sat in the kitchen. Kenneth Rathbone, informed by telephone, arrived with a case of lager, which he thought might help, and stayed a little, also sitting in the kitchen and drinking the lager and talking to Louise, who, assisted by Moy, was continually making tea and coffee. It occurred to Clement that he ought to ring Cora and tell her to tell Joan. Cora was a bit stiff with Clement, said she would certainly come round (though Clement had not suggested it since she had no helpful information) but that she would not bring Joan. Bellamy, in the kitchen, tried to console Harvey, who was taciturn, while Emil, with a cup of coffee, went up and sat by himself in the Aviary. Louise rang up the police and received the same friendly courteous reply, and yes the hospitals had been checked too. She rang the clinic and was told that the doctors were busy and she should arrange an appointment. When Bellamy later went up to find Emil Louise suggested to Harvey that he might like to sit in Sefton's room, but he declined. Kenneth Rathbone left. Tessa Millen, whom they had failed to reach by telephone, arrived accidentally, wishing to introduce Louise to her friend Pamela Horton, who was to be the new director of the Refuge. Tessa also, it was evident, wished, after her dubious role in the matter of Peter's arrest, to reinstate herself in the affections and respect of the Cliftonians. Told of the situation, she suggested that Aleph's room should be searched for clues, perhaps an address or telephone number. Tessa and Pamela set about searching the room, opening drawers, shaking out garments, undoing the bed, even lifting the carpet. Harvey left the kitchen and went up to the Aviary, but finding Emil and Bellamy in conference, went to sit on the stairs. Then Connie Adwarden arrived, accompanied by Nick and Rufus who (released at half-term) could scarcely conceal their enjoyment of the whole scene. Connie announced that she had discovered in Rosemary's room the addresses and telephone numbers of two hotels in France. She had not attempted to ring them herself as she wanted Louise to be with her. They hurried to the telephone and in fact, at the second attempt, actually located Rosemary. Connie handed the phone to Louise. But all that she could establish, on a bad line, was that Rosemary had taken Aleph to somewhere in central London (near Harrods, Rosemary said) and dropped her there at Aleph's request, since Aleph said she wanted to buy something, and that was the last she saw of her. Cora arrived by taxi and joined Louise and Connie in Sefton's room.

By now it was nearly lunchtime. It was raining. Tessa and Pamela reported that they had found nothing, and after many expressions of goodwill and hopes for further meeting, departed. Emil told Bellamy he was hungry and took Bellamy away. Jeremy Adwarden arrived with his car to pick up Connie and the boys, and offered a lift to Cora who accepted it. Miss Fitzherbert arrived, also by accident, bringing a small canvas she wanted to give to Moy. Clement asked where one could buy canvases, she told him and departed with a rather confused impression of the scene. Clement and Louise, thinking they and Moy now had the house to themselves, discovered Harvey sitting in the Aviary. Louise asked him to stay to lunch but he said he was going away but would come back later. Lunch was a miserable affair, indeed it scarcely existed. Louise had laid the table, Clement, leading Moy by the arm, took her to see the little canvas which Miss Fitzherbert had brought and which had been put into Sefton's room. Moy shuddered. Clement picked up the canvas and put it on the stairs. He tried to lead her gently into the kitchen but she resisted, glaring up at him like a wild animal. Louise had made sandwiches. Moy accepted one and ran away up the stairs picking up the canvas on the way. In the kitchen the sandwiches had established some kind of momentary reality and rational calm. Louise ate one. Clement ate several. They sat in silence. Louise made some tea. The telephone rang but it was only Emil who, guilty at having taken Bellamy away, was asking for news. Louise rose saying she was going to rest in her bedroom and disappeared up the stairs. Clement opened a tin of Kenneth Rathbone's Australian lager but decided not to drink any in case his breath should smell of alcohol. He opened the front door and breathed in the bitter foggy air and watched the cars passing. He closed the door and found that he was muttering aloud. He returned to the kitchen and washed up two plates. The tea, which he had refused, was now lukewarm. He stood beside the sink, murmuring softly, 'Oh, oh, oh – ' An awful solitude swept over him like the cold air. Whatever had happened, some great finale was taking place. He went softly up the stairs and knocked on the door of Louise's bedroom.

'Come in.'

The curtains were drawn. She was lying fully dressed upon the counterpane, outstretched stiffly on her back, her arms rigid by her sides.

'Have you heard anything?'

'No.'

'Pull back the curtains will you?'

'I hope you slept a little.'

'Perhaps. It wasn't like sleep.'

'Would you like to get up? I'll make some more tea.'

'Not yet, in a little while. Is Sefton back?'

'No.'

'Where's Moy?'

'Up in her room, I suppose. Shall I go and look?'

'Not yet. Stay here with me, Clement. I feel everything's gone mad. All those people coming in this morning, it was like a crowd scene in a theatre – or else like – they were all coming to look at us, they were *voyeurs*, they were pleased, their eyes were bright. Tessa and that other girl loved tearing Aleph's room to pieces, I heard them laughing.'

'Most of them were our old friends, they really cared, we're lucky to have friends.'

The front doorbell rang. Louise began to struggle up. Clement was on the landing. He leapt down the stairs and opened the door. It was Harvey.

'Has Aleph come back?'

'No, and there's no news. I suppose you haven't found out anything?'

'No. Is Sefton here?'

'No. Come in. Louise is resting. Moy's in her room.'

'I'll sit in the kitchen. Don't worry about me.'

Clement ran back up the stairs. Louise on the landing had heard the conversation.

'Yes, it's Harvey, poor dear boy, I'm glad he's come.'

'Louise, come and sit in the Aviary. Harvey and I will make you some tea and bring it up.'

'No, I'll come down.'

'Well, sit in the Aviary just for a while, just to please me.'

'All right. Where's Moy?'

'Up in her room.'

'I'll go and see her. No, you go and talk to her now. I must change my dress. Then I'll go to the Aviary. Please put the lamps on, it's getting so dark. Oh how strange and terrible it has all become. It's like living in a slow motion mental home. It's really like the beginning of going mad. Everything is different, *everything*.'

Louise was wearing her usual light-brown day dress. As she began to pull it off, Clement left the room. He went softly up and tapped on Moy's door. There was no answer. He opened the door slowly. It was dark in the room. He could see Moy sitting on the bed. She looked up at him, bowing her head sideways, and her eyes seemed to gleam like the eyes of an animal. Clement spoke slowly, as if to someone infantile or very old. 'Would you like some tea? Would you like to come downstairs? Are you all right?' Moy turned her head slowly away, then murmured, 'I'm all right.' Clement tried to think of something encouraging to say. He murmured lamely, 'Oh well – I'm so sorry.' He closed the door and put the light on on the landing. He thought, of course she's upset about Aleph – but oh when will she stop being in love with me? I should have sent Harvey up instead, it would have given him something to do! Oh if only Aleph would return and give us back our wits! I can't believe anything's happened to her, I think it's something *wanton*, and *quite simple*, she'll be back tomorrow. He ran down the stairs and turned on all the lamps in the Aviary. Then he went on down, putting on the lights in the hall, in the kitchen, and in Sefton's room, where Harvey had been sitting in the dark. Clement said, 'It's very cold,' and Harvey agreed.

When Clement came up to the Aviary with a tea-tray Louise had changed into a light woollen dress with red and black stripes. Clement thought, even in a catastrophe a woman may want to change her dress. But why did he now think of a catastrophe? He had been busy all day protecting Louise, yes *protecting* her. Why had he so determinedly not imagined that Aleph might be in terrible trouble, lying nameless in a hospital, raped, kidnapped, drowned, violently attacked in a dark place like Lucas had been? No, like Peter had been. He had laid out Louise's tray with bread and butter and cake and cups and saucers and plates and knives and spoons and a sugar-bowl and a milk-jug and a tea-pot. She was sitting on the sofa. He put the tray on the sofa beside her and drew up a chair opposite. Louise said, 'Is Harvey still here? Tell him to come up.' Clement went down and called Harvey up. He thought, I've never seen such a miserable boy. Of course he loves Aleph. I love Aleph. *Oh God.* Louise drank some tea. Harvey accepted a piece of cake and went to the other end of the room, took a book out of the bookcase and sat down and pretended to read it. Clement could see him pretending. Clement felt cold. He thought, this house is terribly cold. He felt a clammy crawling sensation all over his body as if his skin were turning into scales with little insects underneath the scales. Fish have lice and fleas, he thought. All animals have them, all animals are in torment. It's a kind of evil boredom, an ache of fruitless empty despair, accidie, Aleph knows all about that. Louise said that she was going up to see Moy and would Clement ring the police again? Louise went upstairs, Clement went downstairs, Harvey followed him downstairs. The police gave their usual negative reply. Harvey said vaguely that he would wait a while. Clement went back upstairs. Louise had returned, saying Moy was all right, she just wanted to be quiet. Louise sat on the sofa, and putting the tray on the floor, Clement sat beside her.

'Do eat something, eat some cake.'

'No, thank you, the tea was fine.'

'But you've eaten nothing all day – you look so pale – '

'Oh Clement, don't *bother* me so. Sorry. If there's no news tomorrow will you come with me to the clinic?'

'I'll come with you anywhere.'

'You know I can't help connecting this with Peter. *It's something to do with him.* With the way he's disturbed us all.'

'You don't think she's with him in the clinic?'

'I don't know.'

'It's a perfectly mad conjecture.'

'Perhaps he knows where she is. Even if she's not with him or connected with him, I mean if he doesn't immediately know, he might know by *concentrating his mind*, he could somehow – find her, you know, the way people find things – by intuition or telepathy – or something.'

'All right, let's try anything. Like Moy used to find things.'

'If she could have done it, she would have done it.'

'Would you like me to drive you round now?'

'No, I can't bear it, I'm too tired, Peter would be tired, I wouldn't be able to help him. I'll go tomorrow when I'm stronger. I'm sorry to feel so feeble, what a nightmare of a day, I've never known such a day, it's been so long, and all those people. Do you think I'm stupid? Aleph will turn up tomorrow and explain it all. She sent a letter which went astray. I shall feel a fool for making so much fuss. Girls everywhere are running off and their parents don't get into such a state. Only these girls could *never never* just go away and not tell me, it just *cannot be*. I feel I'm making a miasma all round myself, like a grey web. Look, please go down and if Harvey's still here tell him to go home, somehow the thought of him sitting down there makes everything even more awful. Has Sefton come back, she can't have or she'd have come straight to me.'

'She's not back. Perhaps she's out looking for Aleph.'

'Yes – I thought that too.'

Clement went down. Harvey was sitting in the kitchen. He seemed to be asleep. He woke up, then jumped up. Yes, he would go home, yes, he would find a taxi. Yes, thank you, he would come back tomorrow. He put on his overcoat and slid noiselessly out of the door. Clement looked into Sefton's room and automatically drew the curtains. The house was very cold. He went back to Louise. The Aviary was very cold. He told Louise that the house was cold and could one turn up the heating?

'Yes, there's a switch in the kitchen, a thing you turn, only I can't remember how it's done, one of the girls usually does it.'

'Never mind.' He sat down again beside her and took her hand. Her hand was cold. He laid it against his cheek to warm it.

'Oh Clement, what has happened to time? Perhaps there'll be a letter tomorrow and everything will be explained and will be quite simple and ordinary and all this anguish will seem like a bad dream. But oh – time has become such a torture, a *slow* torture. One tries to capture a piece of time that lies ahead and is full of light, like thinking that a letter will come, or Aleph will suddenly come in through the door and wonder what we were all worrying about – but thinking about that just makes this awful black time even blacker.'

There was the sound of the door opening. They both ran out onto the landing. It was Sefton.

Sefton looked tired. She said, 'Any news?' They said no. Had she any news? No. She hung up her overcoat which was wet. Evidently it was raining outside. Clement carried Louise's tea-tray down to the kitchen and put the cups and saucers in the sink, and asked if Sefton could turn up the heating, which she did.

'Sefton, go up to your mother, I'll make us all some sort of supper down here.'

Clement found bread and butter and cheese and put them on the table. He put out clean plates with knives. He put the kettle on. He found powdered soup in packets. He could hear the two women talking softly upstairs. He began to feel absolutely exhausted. There was a silence. He thought, Sefton has gone up to see Moy. He hurried up the stairs.

Louise had been crying. She made a helpless gesture to Clement.

'My dear, won't you come downstairs and have supper? Isn't it supper-time? You *must* be hungry. We'll *all* have supper. Please, you *must* come down!'

'No, dear Clement, you go and eat. I'm going to bed.'

Sefton had come down the stairs from Moy. 'What's happened to Aleph's room? Has the devil been in it?'

'We were just looking for clues. Sefton, you'll have supper, won't you, and Moy – and Louise will come down, *please* come.'

Louise got up and said again, 'I'm going to bed.'

'You *must* eat something, some hot soup, I'll bring it up.'

Louise left the Aviary and mounted the stairs to her bedroom.

Sefton said, 'Don't press her. I'm just going to take some grub up to Moy. I'll give Louie something. Thanks for holding the fort.' She disappeared downstairs.

Clement, who had not considered the matter, now thought, perhaps I ought to stay the night here. He followed Sefton down.

'Do eat something, Clement. Or have you already had supper?' Sefton disappeared with a laden tray. Clement sat down. He was ferociously hungry. He tore the loaf apart and covered the large fragments of it deeply in butter and lumps of cheddar cheese. He tilted some powdered soup into a mug and poured hot water upon it. He suddenly felt like crying. He said aloud, half-choking, 'Oh I'm so tired, I'm so *tired*.'

Sefton returned. In silence she put some remaining bread and cheese and an apple onto a large plate. She said, 'Would you like an apple?'

'No, thanks. Sorry, Sefton.'

Sefton, standing with the plate in her hand, said, 'Don't be sorry. You've been here all day.'

'Yes.'

Sefton put the plate down. Clement stood up. They hugged each other. Clement found himself moaning quietly as he had done earlier in the day, how much earlier, in what a day.

Releasing Clement, Sefton, picking up her plate, said in her usual casual manner. 'Well, I'm off to bed. You'll find all sorts of things in the larder. Goodnight.' She departed, closing the kitchen door behind her.

After a short time Clement ascended the stairs and knocked softly on Louise's door.

Louise was in bed, her bedside lamp was on. She said, 'Sefton brought me something to eat, but I can't eat it, at least I tried to, could you put the tray out of the way? It's there on the floor.'

'I'll take it down. But, Louise – '

'I think I'll go to sleep now. What time is it? No, don't tell me.'

'Have you any sleeping-pills?'

'Yes, yes, I have them. Clement, can I ask a favour of you?'

'Anything you like, my darling.'

'Could you stay here tonight?'

Clement felt a strange momentary shock. 'Yes, of course.'

'Don't go away, it must be so late – I'm feeling so afraid, it's an awful fear like I've never had before.'

'Of course I shall stay with you, I'll – protect you, I'll – '

'I'm sorry to trouble you, with you in the house I shall feel safe – you don't mind, do you?'

'Louise, you *know* that I don't mind, I – '

'You can sleep on the sofa in the Aviary. There are blankets and pillows in the landing cupboard. Please forgive me for being mad all day.'

'Louise, we are all mad. Do sleep, take the pills. You've got them, have you? I'll be here, I'll be nearby, I'll guard you.'

He leaned down and kissed her and she put her arms around his neck. He left the room and stood on the landing, standing rigidly at attention for some while, listening to the silence of the house. There were no sounds. He tiptoed to the cupboard and pulled out blankets and pillows. As sheets had not been mentioned he did not look for them. As he was about to go to the Aviary he heard an odd sound, like a little bird. He thought, it's Moy, she is having a dream. He turned off the light on the landing. The house below was dark. Carrying his bedclothes he found his way down to the Aviary and turned on one of the lamps. He thought, I am so dead tired but I know I shall lie awake all night – in *torment*. But as soon as he had turned off the lamp and settled himself on the sofa he fell instantly into a black abyss of sleep.

Clement had achieved his great ambition at last. He was playing Hamlet. He was dressed in black and white and so were all the other members of the cast, since the director had decided that this was to be a black and white production. It was also, as it happened, a ballet, but Clement had no difficulty in learning the steps. He was only a little surprised to find how easy ballet dancing was after all. He could already float across the stage without touching the ground. A continual beating, almost thumping, of heart-rending music accompanied him. He was flying, flying was easy too. He thought, this is like Peter Pan. Good heavens, perhaps it *is* Peter Pan? No, it can't be. Now he was down on the ground confronting a woman, only this woman was two women, and the two women were his mother and Ophelia. They were dancing too, standing one behind the other and swaying to and fro as if they were the *same person*, they were teasing him, they were *tormenting him*, the music was faster and louder. He thought, I *can't dance* any more, in a moment I shall fall, I shall *faint*. I need help. He tried to scream.

He woke up. Sefton, having tapped on the door, had entered. He sat up quickly, remembering where he was. He clasped the neck of his shirt, he felt his heart.

'I thought I'd better wake you. There's some breakfast downstairs.'

'Oh – is everyone up?'

'Yes, but we all get up very early.'

'Is there any news?'

'No, but the post hasn't come yet.'

'Did I scream?'

'What?'

'Did I scream?'

'I didn't hear you scream.'

Sefton lingered for a moment, then went out closing the door. Clement dressed with great speed, folded up the bedclothes and put them back in the cupboard. He could not recall his dream but the horror of it stayed with him. He dreaded coming downstairs. He thought, I can't stay in this house, it is *doomed*.

He came into the kitchen and found Louise, Moy, and Sefton all sitting sedately at the table. A place had been laid for him. Louise and Moy said 'Good morning.' He said, 'Good morning.'

The next question must be: Did you sleep well? Louise said, 'Did you sleep well?' 'Yes, very well.' Sefton offered him eggs and bacon, which he refused, and toast, which he accepted with no intention of eating it. He also accepted some coffee. No one else was eating.

Clement, pulling himself together, said to Louise, 'Do you still want to go to the clinic?'

Louise said, 'Do I still want to? Of course I do.'

'Why go there?' said Sefton. 'Surely they'll tell us if there's anything to tell.'

'I think Peter could help us,' said Louise. 'I mean help us to find Aleph. I feel their fates are bound together.'

The girls exchanged anxious glances.

'It's worth trying. I'll drive you there. At least it's something to do.'

Louise said, 'Sefton, you'll stay here, won't you?'

'I'll stay here,' said Sefton.

There was a gloomy silence. Clement tore up his piece of toast and pretended to eat some of it. He felt a bit light-headed as if he might faint. He thought, it's simply hunger. Except that I can't eat. I want to go home. Only I've got to drive Louise to the bloody clinic. I had some awful dream. Then he recalled with terrible vividness the sight of Peter's knife approaching Lucas's naked side, he saw the line of the ribs and the point of the knife entering the skin and the blood flowing. He got up hastily, then sat down again. He felt he was going to be sick. He said to Louise, 'I'm just going up to the Aviary. Please come up when you're ready and we can make a plan.' He thought, I want to lie down somewhere. But I can't and mustn't lie down.

He got up again and went out into the hall. At that moment the post arrived, with several envelopes fluttering to the mat. Clement at once noticed an envelope with the name of the clinic conspicuous on the outside. He picked it up and went back into the kitchen. 'Louise, it's from the clinic.' Louise, also already risen, seized the envelope, and after scratching it vainly with her hasty fingernails, managed to tear it open. She drew out the white typewritten sheet and read it. She handed the letter to Clement across the table. She sat down. Clement read it quickly.

My dear Mrs Anderson,

It is with the greatest distress and sorrow that I report to you
the death of our patient Mr Peter Mir, who died quietly and
peacefully yesterday evening. I hasten to bring you the sad
news, since I know how much you and your children and
friends cared about Mr Mir; and he for you, as he spoke of
you all as his 'family'. You will be consoled to know how very
much your support and affection gladdened and enlivened the
later days of his life. Hoping to recover, he spoke of you
often and looked forward to a meeting which can now alas
not take place. I am, I may say, well aware of the anxiety
with which you parted from him on that evening. Let me
assure you that his interests were, by our intervention, best
served. He would not, in any case, have survived. It is indeed
a miracle that, after the violent blow which he received, he
has lived as long as he did. He was kept alive by his courageous will to accomplish certain ends (you will I think know
what I refer to) and, these accomplished, he relaxed into a
calm submission to an inevitable death. I write this letter to
you, taking you as being the 'mother' of the 'family', and trust
that you will, at your discretion, inform his other friends. He
was, in his way, a great man, certainly a remarkable man,
and within his last year found the affection and warm friendship for which he had so long craved. He was, in the end,
after the amazing burst of energy of which you were all at
times witnesses, exceedingly tired and ready to sleep. My
colleague, Dr Richardson, joins me in sending our sincere
sympathy.

> With kind regards,
> Yours sincerely,
> Edward Fonsett

Clement said to the girls, 'Peter Mir is dead.' He put the letter
down on the table. Sefton picked it up and read it, and passed it
to Moy. Louise was sitting still, one arm stretched out on the
table where she had reached to give Clement the letter. She was
very pale, her eyelids drooping, her lips trembling and parted in
a woeful grimace, as she gazed down at her other hand which lay
upon her lap. She murmured, 'Their fates are bound together.'

Clement said sharply, 'Louise, don't talk nonsense! As the

doctor says, Peter was certain to collapse after all that manic activity. I expected this. We all did.'

'I didn't,' said Louise.

Moy was crying. Louise began to cry. Sefton went out into the hall. Clement sat down beside Louise and drew her towards him, putting his arms around her.

Out in the hall, Sefton picked up the letters which were still lying there. There were two bills. Underneath, there was another letter, with a London postmark, addressed to Louise. Sefton recognised Aleph's writing. She held it and stared at it. She moved on into her bedroom and closed the door. She sat upon her bed. She opened the letter.

Dearest dearest Louie,

I write this with grief, though also, as I shall explain, also with joy. I have never never wanted to hurt you, even the tiniest bit, and I know that what I have to say will hurt you – but I hope and believe that later on you will understand and be able to be glad in my gladness. I am sorry I am not writing a good letter – I delayed writing for reasons which will be plain, and now write in haste, as I know how worried you must be. I am going to America with Lucas. When you receive this letter I shall be there. He will take up a university post. (He has had lots of invitations.) I shall continue my studies. We shall be married. I have, all my life, been deeply in love with Lucas. He is the only person I could dream of marrying. I love him absolutely, he loves me absolutely. I know that we shall make each other happy. He has not known too much happiness in his life. I am daily and hourly glad to see how much happiness I can bring him now. Please please believe that our union is inevitable and will be happy. I am very sorry that I concealed all these things from you, and from Sefton and Moy. At first it was almost 'too good to be true' for both of us, and then, during the period in which Lucas was away, after the episode with Peter Mir, he just had to be alone. During this time we corresponded – he disguised his writing, I was so afraid one of them might be opened by accident! We have both of us gone through an ordeal in perfecting our relationship, which makes us now all the more certain of our felicity. This letter comes simply to bring the news, which, when the shock is over, you may not find after all so dreadful! We will meet again before long, dear dear Louie, you will come to America, you and Sefton and Moy will come, and we shall visit you in England. I know that you will forgive us, you will *have* to forgive us, and when you see us together you will know everything is right and good. Oh my dear mother, you desired my happiness, and Sefton's and Moy's. I hope and pray that they will, when the time comes, be as happy as I am, and I hope that you will always be happy because you are so good and so true, and that you will also and always be happy in my happiness.

We shall be moving about a bit, but when we have a settled address I will send it. Then please, my dear dear mother, write to me and say that you forgive me and that you wish us well! I am very sorry that my sudden departure may have caused you anxiety. I shall write later to Sefton and Moy. Give them my eternal love. And to you, with my eternal love,

Yours,
Aleph

Sefton closed her eyes. A violent flush burnt in her neck and blazed in her face. Holding the letter in her hand she bowed her head down to her knees. She groaned, she *wailed*. She gasped for breath. She stood up and looked out of the window. Outside it was frosty and still. The leaves had fallen from the trees. A few snowflakes were wandering in the quiet air. A great sword pierced Sefton's heart. She too had loved Lucas with her own kind of deep secret love, and it seemed to her in this moment that, if he had asked her, she would have gone with him anywhere. She had treasured that secret love, never revealing to anyone her profound feelings about her great teacher, enlivened by the belief that, though he was utterly inaccessible, *she*, in her own humble way, was *nearest* to him.

Sefton, the soldier, threw back her head and checked tears. She thought, I have lost Aleph too, whom I love, yes, with an eternal love. We shall meet, but as strangers. It is the end of an era. A whole part of my life is torn away. And oh poor Louie, poor poor Louie. She went back into the kitchen.

Moy, still crying, was washing up. Clement was sitting beside Louise with his arm round her shoulder. Louise saw Sefton's face and thrust Clement away. She took the letter which Sefton handed to her. Clement moved away and stood up. Moy moved from the sink, putting her hands up to her face. Louise read the first part of the letter and then put it down. 'She has gone away with Lucas, they have gone to America, she is going to marry him.'

Clement said, 'Oh *no!*' and turned away and leaned his head against the wall. Moy sat down close beside her mother, caressing her arm and nestling against it.

Sefton, trembling and shuddering, sat down at the table and buried her face in her hands. Louise finished the letter and gave it to Moy, who read it. Moy passed the letter to Clement. Clement read it and then, afraid of the terrible silence, said to Louise, 'Anyway, she's safe and well and even happy!' He went on wildly, 'So I suppose now ordinary life can continue. We don't have to worry about her any more. We've been mad for two days. Now we can be sane and get on with our own lives!'

Louise said, 'Don't blame her.'

'I'm not blaming her,' said Clement, 'I'm sure no one here is blaming her – I'm just suffering from shock! I think she could have spared us these two days. Perhaps it didn't occur to her that we'd worry!' He added, 'Isn't it strange! Peter brought them together after all. Lucas couldn't have endured Peter getting Aleph! As for all those letters, can they have been love letters? When did he decide to grab her, I wonder?'

Moy got up and went back to the sink and continued to wash the cups and plates and put them in the rack.

'There now, look at Moy, she's gone back to ordinary life already! And in a few minutes Sefton will return to her history books, and I shall go to my agent and get myself a job, any job. And Louise will go out shopping.'

The doorbell rang. Everyone jumped. Sefton ran to the front door. She called back, 'It's Harvey. I'll tell him.' She closed the kitchen door.

Louise gave a little moan and then began to sob. Clement moved in beside her. 'Louise, stop crying, I command you. I love you. Here's my handkerchief. Don't cry so, *I can't bear it.* I'm suffering from shock too!'

Louise, checking her sobs, said, 'He will destroy her.'

'Oh nonsense, how can we judge, they may just as well be very happy. Or else she may come back, she could come back tomorrow!'

Louise said, 'She will never come back.' Then, 'I'm going up to my room. We must send the news around. Would you mind ringing the others and telling them about Aleph and about Peter? Tell them not to ring up and not to come round. I'm terrified somebody will come.' She got up and ran up the stairs. From the upper landing she called down to the hall, 'And then leave the telephone off the hook.'

'Louise, wait, *wait*. What shall I tell them – I mean about Aleph – shall I just say that she's written and she's all right, or that she's gone to America, or that she's run off with Lucas, or what?'

Without hesitation Louise replied, 'Say it all.' Her bedroom door closed. It opened again. 'And, Clement, please after that *go home*, will you. *Don't stay here.* Go and see your agent, like you said. I'm very grateful to you. But please *go home*.' The door closed again.

Sefton and Harvey emerged from Sefton's room. Clement had forgotten about Harvey. He mechanically said, 'Hello, Harvey.' Sefton said, 'Harvey and I are going for a walk. Please don't go away, dear Clement, stay here with Louie.' She stretched out her arms to him, clasping his shoulders, then hurried out of the front door, followed by Harvey.

Clement thought, I *won't* go away, I'll stay here. He turned to the telephone and rang Emil's number. Clement said, 'Emil, it's Clement, I'm at Clifton, listen to two bits of news. Peter Mir has just died, we have a letter from the clinic. And we have a letter from Aleph, she is alive and well, she is in America with Lucas. Please could you tell Bellamy? He'll be very upset about Peter I'm afraid. Also, I would be awfully grateful if you would telephone all this news round to the others, you know, the Adwardens, Cora, I think Joan is with her, Kenneth Rathbone, the people who were at the party, the people who called in yesterday. And please tell them all *not to come round*. Louise asked me to say this. I'm sorry to bother you, but I have a lot to deal with here.'

Emil replied, 'How very terrible and surprising. I will do the telephoning. Bellamy is with me here. He will be very distressed, I am very distressed. And Tessa, we shall tell her too, yes? I have a telephone number for her. But what exactly is it with Aleph, is she with Lucas on some tour or scholarship, or in some other way?'

'Time will show I expect. She says they're going to be married. If you can just tell the others what I said.'

'Oh, I will do so. How strange and frightful. Clement, I would like to see you soon, Bellamy will also want to see you soon. How is Louise?'

'As you can imagine. I must ring off now. I am very grateful to you.' Clement put down the receiver, then picked it up again and laid it down on the hall table. He stood still, holding his head in his hands. He felt hot tears rising in his eyes.

He went into the kitchen and finished the washing up and dried the china and the cutlery and put it all away once again. He came out into the hall and looked at the telephone which was lying like an amputated arm upon the table and fizzing slightly. He went up the stairs and looked in on the chaos in Aleph's room, resulting from Pam and Tessa's well-intentioned search for clues. He began to straighten out the bed and pick up the clothes from the floor. He was touching Aleph's clothes which she had run away forever without. He went into the Aviary and lay down on the sofa. The house was silent.

Harvey and Sefton had reached the Green and sat down on a seat.

'Why were you away the whole of yesterday?'

'I'm sorry. I was so terribly upset.'

'So was I. I nearly went mad.'

'There was just too much, and I had to think. I felt I had to concentrate on Aleph. I thought I might find out something. Of course I didn't.'

In fact Sefton had spent the day more or less randomly walking about London, as if she might actually *meet* Aleph. One strange thing was that in her wandering she had passed and looked at Lucas's house. About this, of course, she said nothing.

'You were avoiding me. I could have come with you.'

'I wanted you to concentrate on Aleph too.'

'You wanted me to be as it were alone with Aleph.'

'Yes.'

'I thought about you all day.'

'But you must have thought about her too, about all the long years when you talked to her, you had a continuous conversation with her, you must have felt it would go on forever, you must have *relied* upon her more than on anyone, you must have loved her more than anyone, how can you not have loved her – '

'Those were children's conversations. What they were really about was that *it* was impossible between us since we were brother and sister.'

'You say that now. But she is so beautiful and so witty, I used to hear you both laughing so much, she must have *pleased* you so, she must have *delighted* and *amused* you so – '

'There was nothing deep.'

'There *must* have been *deep* conversation, consoling and full of spirit, like you could have with no one else – '

'Don't go on with this, Sefton. *It* just wasn't there. We were children teasing each other.'

'Yes, all right, but then you grew up. What was suddenly possible with me came as a complete surprise to both of us. That surprise could just as well have happened with her. I feel as if you have come to me by mistake, thinking I'm Aleph, as if I were wearing the head of Aleph over my head, like in myths or fairy stories when a god or a magician makes one person look like another person. And now people will think you turned to me just because you had lost her – '

'Stop, stop, *wake up*, don't be so foolish and unkind! Give me your hand.'

She gave him her hand. She began to cry.

'Sefton, darling, don't be angry with me, don't be cruel to me, I love you so much – '

'Yesterday, we didn't know that Aleph had run away and that Peter was dead. And Peter dying *just now* – oh why did he die, why did we let him die, why didn't we keep him with us – It's so strange, and so weird and sad, Louie thought he would help us to find Aleph, she said their destinies were bound together.'

'I wonder if she thought that Aleph might marry Peter. Perhaps Lucas thought that too – and now, well, who would have guessed – '

'Now it's happened it may soon seem possible, likely, even necessary. Aleph was such a prize and he was such a pirate.'

'My mother said that Aleph would be carried off by an older man, by a tycoon – well, I suppose Lucas qualifies – but how can they be happy? That seems impossible.'

'I can see them as happy.'

'Beauty and the Beast. Women love Beasts.'

'Lucas can be – not like he seems.'

'I was afraid of him. He was rather horrid to me when I was

421

a child. I wanted to make peace with him, but I couldn't. He haunted me like a sort of demon. Aleph used to quote a piece of *Beowulf*, I forget, about a shadow-goer who came in the night – that was Lucas – perhaps she already knew.'

'Yes. So suppose she comes back with broken wings and a broken heart? Then you would feel guilty, then you would run to her.'

'Sefton, *please* – oh my darling, don't cry so – '

'Anyway, she wouldn't come, she's too proud, if she lost him she'd find someone else who was worthy of her. Oh Aleph, Aleph, my dear dear sister – everything has changed. I feel – just now – we're in a sort of no man's land, a desert, a place of dust and ashes and awful mourning – it's like being in retreat, or being punished or in prison or something.'

'You mean we feel guilty. That must pass. We must carry our love on through the darkness. Will you come back to my flat?'

'No, I must go home. I've got to be with them. We'll cry together.'

'Will you tell them about us?'

'Not yet, let's wait – they've had enough shocks.'

'You're not having second thoughts, my love, my angel?'

'I love you, I love you. We'll say goodbye here, then I'll run back to Clifton.'

'Moy, I've brought you some coffee and biscuits.'

Clement, plucking up his courage, had knocked on Moy's door. As there was no answer he had cautiously opened the door.

Moy was sitting on the bed, just as she had been on the previous day. Her long thick yellow plait was hanging forward over her shoulder and down onto her lap. The room smelt of paint. Clement put the cup and plate down on an empty shelf. Why empty? He saw, turning, that the floor round Moy's feet was covered with stones. He thought, she has been crying, she has put her stones about her to comfort her.

Moy said, 'Thank you, I don't want coffee but never mind, thank you for the biscuits. Where is my mother?'

'She is lying down.'

'Is Sefton here?'

'No, but she's coming back soon. I'll get you a cup of tea.'

'No, thank you.' She took hold of the end of her plait and

began tugging it fiercely, looking at Clement with her royal-blue eyes which so reminded him of Teddy Anderson.

After a moment's silence he thought he had better go, but then decided that he ought to stay. He had tended to avoid Moy because of her 'crush' and out of kindness to her, but now, seeing her so lonely and so desolate, he felt that he must think of something more to say.

He pulled a chair away from the wall and sat down, being careful not to put his feet on the stones. Moy, still playing with her plait, observed him with a grave sad look.

'There's a nice smell of paint. What have you been painting?'

'I've been painting over the canvas Miss Fitzherbert gave me, just putting on a first coat.'

'A first coat?'

'With oils one must paint into paint.'

'Oh. I see. I'll buy you some canvases. I know where to buy them. You must let me bring you – well anything you need for painting – '

'Thank you, but please don't trouble.'

Seeking another subject Clement said, 'Remember when I found you when you had gone to look for Anax, and you came home in my car. That was an adventure, wasn't it!'

Moy frowned, cleared the frown, and for a second smiled a strange crooked smile. 'Yes.'

Clement was taken aback. He recalled how, returning in the car, he had chided Moy for her ridiculous attachment to him. How could she forgive him for doing so, and for recalling it, and offering it to her now like a sweetie to a child! And how terribly tactless of him to mention Anax! She was no longer a child. Without his noticing she was becoming a grown-up. He saw her now for the first time as a young woman, slimmer, taller, wearing a dark blue dress with a belt, certainly not to be called a shift or an overall! He was about to say to her 'You've grown up.' Instead he bowed his head, hoping that she would understand.

He got up and said humbly, 'I must see your mother.'

Moy, now grave and sad once more, nodded. Clement raised one hand with an open palm. She raised a hand very slightly, scarcely visibly, in recognition. He left the room. He thought that perhaps some important communication had passed between them, but he was not sure what it was.

He knocked softly at Louise's door. He had done so a little earlier, had no reply, and concluded she was asleep. Now there

423

was a murmur. He entered cautiously. The curtains were pulled and the room was dark. Louise, raising herself up, put on a lamp beside the bed. 'Oh, it's you.'

'Yes. How are you?'

She sat up on the edge of the bed. Her thick brown hair which usually so easily adjusted itself was tangled, almost fuzzy. Her pale face was shining as if with sweat, or perhaps, he thought, face cream to conceal her tears. She looked at him hostile, wrinkled and frowning. 'I said you should go, you must not waste your time here. We can look after ourselves.'

'Sefton went out for a while and asked me to stay.'

'Is she back?'

'Not yet.'

'Where's Moy?'

'Upstairs. I have just been talking with her.'

'Is she crying?'

'Not now, no.'

There was a sound downstairs of the front door opening and closing. Louise looked up, Clement hurried to the landing. 'It's Sefton.'

'Now please go, Clement, please.'

'All right. But I'll come back.'

'No, *don't* come back. I mean, we must mourn, not you. I mean – I'm sorry – I'm in such a desolation – '

'Louise, darling – '

'*Please go.*'

Clement passed Sefton on the stairs. She raised a hand to him, then went on into Louise's bedroom.

Clement picked up his overcoat and came out into the street, closing the front door quietly. He pulled his coat on and pulled his scarf out of the pocket. He had left his gloves in the car. He creased his face against the cold. He wanted to cry, at least to cry out. He walked to his car and pocketed the parking ticket. He sat in the car. Desolation, yes, *desolation*. Where can I go now? I'll go to Bellamy. No, Bellamy is living with Emil. And *they* don't want me, now Aleph is gone. I have been leading an empty life. I must work again, I must get *work*, I'll go and see my agent, I'll accept *anything*. He went on sitting in the car with his mouth open, screwing up his eyes and trying to weep. Deep, deepest inside his wounded heart, he felt the new pain, the pain which would now travel with him always. *Lucas*, oh *Lucas*.

*

'So that is how it is?'

'That is how it is,' said Bellamy.

Bellamy was sitting in an armchair with his legs stretched straight out. He was wearing his bedroom slippers. There was a hole in the toe of one of them through which his sock was now protruding. He looked at it, then cautiously withdrew his leg.

'But why not stay here all the same? It seems to me there are two questions and you have answered only one. I want to see into your soul.'

'Emil, you may see into my soul at any time, and I will attempt to assist you –'

'Well, why do you not want to stay here? Are you afraid?'

'Of course not! I just want to be *by myself*. I came to that conclusion some time ago. Then I thought it meant becoming a hermit. Then I gave that up.'

'And gave up God.'

'What does that mean. Yes, all right.'

'But have you always lived alone? You see, I have known you a long time, but I do not know these things about you.'

'I have never lived with anyone, though I once –'

'And you at once thought it was immoral?'

'No, I don't think it's immoral!'

'That was your monkish idea, you felt inclined to chastity –'

'Not just that, I just like *being alone!*'

'I too have liked it. Well, so later, as we all know, you did want to be a monk.'

'That was romanticism.'

'But you lived in a little room in a poor place so as to be a monk in the world to help people.'

'Yes, but I helped no one and just made myself miserable!'

'Then there was Peter Mir, and you thought him to be an incarnation, an avatar, some sort of high being.'

'Well, not at first –'

'Ah yes, he wanted revenge on Lucas.'

'But then he was not himself. Then he recovered his good real self and made peace.'

'Would you have lived with him?'

'Emil, I don't know! And now –'

'Yes, now it does not concern us. It was – like his mission. What does one know of Jesus before his time came? And what sort was Peter's mission? They seemed to think he was a magician

– well, they thought that of Jesus too. And do you think that he has saved you.'

'I'm not saved! Haven't we now answered the question and dealt with the problem?'

'Let us say that is one thing. But there is the other thing.'

'What's the other thing? I can't see any other thing.'

'The other thing is me.'

'How do you come in?'

'Bellamy, you are naive, sometimes you are positively obtuse. No, listen. A man may want to live for years alone. Then for some reason he may change his mind. I am the reason.'

'Dear dear Emil, if I could be persuaded by a reason, you more than anyone else might persuade me, but – '

'Really, it seems that there are two questions. Do you want to be chaste? Do you want to live alone? It seems that you want to be chaste, all right. But that need not prevent you from living with another person. All right, you have not wanted to before, perhaps because you could not find a worthy person. Here I present myself. As we know, you have already, if I may use the traditional phrase, rejected my advances. All right, all right. That matter will not be pursued. The point is that you have been living here successfully for a while, we are old friends, we know each other well, we are on the way to knowing each other very well. Why not simply stay here? I need you, I think you have discovered that you need me. Think about it dear Bellamy. Here you can be happy.'

'I don't care about being happy.'

'You deceive yourself. All beings strive for happiness, but it has many names and what is sought is often something else. I grieve so for that poor girl. He will cut her throat and then his own. However cruel he becomes she cannot leave him. This is what she will endlessly attempt to call her joy. Be glad that you are free, Bellamy. You have done no harm. You can still attain your open busy life, helping other people. Why not have innocent happiness as well? You know we love each other.'

Louise longed for sleep and dreaded waking. With waking consciousness came for a second her old bright happy being from the past, then the recall, the black awareness of a world destroyed, and the deep sharp pains of remorse and wild regret. The house was mortally wounded. Louise took her quick scanty meals alone in the kitchen. The girls came in and out. Nobody cooked. Everything was slow, as if in consonance with the slow sad puzzled movements of the grieving soul. She spent long periods in the Aviary, no longer feeling that it belonged to 'them', indeed not able to feel that there was any 'them' any more. The girls shunned the Aviary, their continuous bird-like chatter was no longer heard there in the long evenings. There was no laughter, indeed no voices. The piano remained untouched. Everyone tiptoed. Louise wandered about in the long room, looking at the bookshelves, which contained a mixture of Sefton and Aleph's books. History, classical literature, poetry in several languages, novels. She went across into Aleph's room. It had been perfectly tidied and even dusted by Sefton. There was more poetry and more novels on Aleph's shelves. Louise picked out a copy of *Pride and Prejudice* and took it back to the Aviary. She had abandoned *A Glastonbury Romance* since she suspected that some of the people she liked might come to grief. Nobody rang up, nobody rang the doorbell. Of course she had asked Clement to tell everyone not to come because she and the children wanted to be quiet for a while. She said or thought, 'I want to be with the children', but even in saying or thinking it she realised that now 'the children' meant something utterly different. What were 'the children' without Aleph, could there be children? Of course they loved her, the two remaining ones, they hugged her, they had mingled their tears. But they could not converse with her. Sometimes she felt herself as being a strange quiet animal, perhaps a rare animal, who was to be stroked and petted but not communicated with. She could utter no sound. The children loved her but shunned her, or perhaps she herself was instinctively setting them at a distance. Three days had passed now since the day of Aleph's letter. No other letter had come yet. As time passed Louise dreaded this next letter; and dreaded that there might be no letter. Well, letters did come, from Oxford, admitting Aleph to Magdalen and Sefton to Balliol. Time was different, long, heavy, lazy, grey. Sefton was out of the house much of the time. Moy sometimes went out briefly, 'for walks', she said. Louise saw her once, sitting immobile upon a seat on the Green. Mostly Moy was upstairs in her room where she spent long periods, working she said. Louise called in on her at intervals and always found Moy at work, though she could not be sure whether this were a semblance of work set in motion by the sound of Louise's feet on the stairs. There was evidence of work. Already the small canvas donated by Miss Fitzherbert had been painted over in wild unusual brilliant colours, representing, Moy said, the old cat Tibellina. ('Do not fear the colours,' Miss Fitzherbert had said to Moy, and Moy had mentioned this once to Louise.) The fresh rich oil-paint smell pervaded the room. Upon the sloping sky-lights the rain battered down from the thick dismal clouds. How little light there was for Moy to work in. Louise in her new way, in her utterly changed scenery and way of life, was suddenly worried about Moy. Moy had always been the clever little mouse who could do everything, make bags out of raffia, paint Easter eggs, make masks, make necklaces, sew lovely garments. Thus she had lived as, it occurred to Louise, they had all lived, under Aleph's great brilliant canopy, in her light. 'Moy is such a happy little thing, always busy!' Now this picture seemed to be changing into something much darker, even more macabre. Louise recalled the episode of the fight with the swan. 'Of course Moy *would* fight a swan to rescue some beastie or other!' They had made too little of it, they had not questioned her enough, they had assumed that, whatever it was, Moy must have exaggerated it a little, made it picturesque. Perhaps she had really *fought* with the swan. Perhaps, on the other hand, she had invented some of it. They had not gone on talking about it, they had forgotten it. They had not helped Moy to find an art school, they had left that to Miss Fitzherbert. They had casually let her leave school. Was that right, would not another two years have been a precious advantage, something she would later grieve for having lost? They had not made her pause, not argued with her or made her reflect, perhaps about how, later on, she would earn her living. Well, Sefton had raised some objection but did not persevere. They had joked about Moy, calling her fey, paranormal, a little witch. Now suddenly she was a mystery, a stranger, perhaps a *case*, falling into solitude, into the dark, into depression, into a nervous breakdown. Oh, if only Teddy were here, all that is ill would be well. She recalled Joan's words, 'They are like a drawn bow, they compose a field of force, it is time for them to fly apart.' Now with Aleph gone the harmony, the union of souls, the balance of power, is broken. Such good children, such ideal children. Oh how can she do it to us, how can she! But really it is my fault.

She waited for the letter, for the transatlantic telephone call. Or for the sound of the key in the door, and Aleph weeping in her arms. But she thought too, whatever happens she won't come back, not like that. Only perhaps later on to *show us her children*. This idea was hideous. And now in her deep heart an even sharper pain was stirring, a pain which would stay with her always. Lucas had wanted to marry her, her, Louise. She thought, after Teddy died and Lucas came to me and wanted to marry me and I said no, it seemed as if our relations simply had to cease altogether. His pride would have prevented any more real communication. I must have wounded him deeply, I could not conceal my surprise, which he must have interpreted as repulsion. No wonder he withdrew, not only from me but from the others. I ought not to have accepted that withdrawal. I ought to have approached him and held onto him, after all I had learnt to admire him, and to love him, Teddy's friend, Clement's brother – I ought at least to have tried to show him how fond I was of him, how much I cared, how much we all cared, how much he belonged to us, I should have tended him, visited him, made him come to Clifton – but I was selfishly concerned with my own grief and then later on it was somehow too late, I neglected him and mislaid him, through a puny lack of nerve, and I became *afraid* of him. Now, after the catastrophe with Peter, after Lucas had run away and hidden, I ought to have welcomed him back, run to him *at once*, and helped him to recover – I ought to have shown him affection, love. I thought of going to him, but I kept putting it off, and Clement discouraged me. I might have saved him if only I had been near him from the start – perhaps then he would not have built up that terrible hatred of Clement – oh God, if only – then I would have saved Peter – and saved Aleph. Everything would have been different – and it is all my fault. Now he has taken her away and made it impossible for him and me ever to meet again.

Clement had visited his agent. (Telephone calls were no good.) The agent had now suggested some quite interesting things to him which would normally have cheered him and brightened his eyes. He had said in each case that he would pursue the matter, but he lacked energy. He kept saying to himself, it is a time of mourning, a time of dust and ashes, a time of penitence. He had twice telephoned Clifton but Sefton had answered, saying Louise was resting. He went to bed early and lay sleepless. He kept thinking about Peter. Ought they to have stopped that doctor from carrying him off? But he wanted to go and what could they do, really they knew nothing about Peter, he was a visitor from another realm. He recalled Peter pinning him against the wall and gripping his throat. How was he to think about it all now that Lucas too was gone? Did Lucas's crime, the awful abduction of Aleph, suddenly make everything different? Had Lucas decided to take Aleph as an act of revenge, taking her away from Peter? But that was the wrong way round. It was Peter who wanted revenge, and had then forgiven Lucas and as it were set him free. And Peter forgave me, thought Clement, as he tossed restlessly in the dark seeking vainly for sleep, and good heavens, Lucas forgave me too! But what about Aleph, had I ever wanted to marry her, could I have married her, did I love her? That did not seem like reality, more like a fairy tale and now more like something dark and awful, Clement's guilt for not having protected Aleph, his guilt for having been cruel to Lucas when he was a child. Yes, was not that how it all began? Am I to go on believing all my life that Lucas hated me so much that he wanted to kill me? That is more real than his 'forgiveness'. And now what matters, Aleph's happiness? Will Lucas betray her, humiliate her, strangle her? Or will they be a happy academic couple living out their lives on some American campus, giving drinks parties round the swimming-pool? All that will go away and perhaps we shall never know. So what is fundamental? For me it remains that Peter saved my life and gave his life for me. Then sleepily Clement found himself thinking about the baseball bat, which was shining suddenly like a holy relic. That toy, with all its childhood memories, must have put into Lucas's head the idea of taking revenge. And how very strange to think of that awful weapon now far away in Belgium, the innocent plaything of Belgian children!

As Clement turned his head upon the pillow, closing his eyes at last to the advent of sleep, he suddenly recalled the evening at

Clifton when they had lost Anax and Peter had brought him back, and when Peter had gone they had all said who he reminded them of, and Aleph had said 'the Green Knight'. At the time Clement had vaguely assumed that she was referring to the green umbrella with which he had first appeared to them. But was there not perhaps a deeper meaning, was there not some Middle English poem about a Green Knight? He now thought he recalled reading a translation of it when he was at Cambridge. What was the story? Arthur's knights are at the Round Table when a huge entirely green knight appears and challenges one of them to cut off his head, after promising to visit the knight for a return match in his own realm on the same day next year. Gawain takes up the challenge and cuts off the knight's head. The knight picks up his head and holds it up in his hand and reminds Gawain of his promise. Next year Gawain sets out gloomily to meet his adversary, but loses his way and is entertained at a castle by a Lady whose husband is out hunting. The Lady tempts Gawain but he resists her charms. At last he gives in as far as to accept the significant gift of her green girdle. He leaves the castle and finds the meeting-place, the Green Knight appears with his axe. Gawain, expecting instant death, kneels down, the axe descends – but makes only a small superficial wound upon his extended neck. The knight, who is of course the Lady's husband, congratulates Gawain on his courage, but chides him for his moral failure in accepting the girdle, for which he has mercifully received only a mild punishment. Gawain declares he will wear the girdle forever after as a token of his sin, in giving way to temptation and staining his perfect chastity.

Why does all this suddenly come upon me, thought Clement, why is it suddenly so significant? Had Aleph had some sort of intuition, a kind of mystical insight, when she gave Peter that name? Pieces of the story are there, but aren't they somehow jumbled up and all the wrong way round? Lucas cut off Peter's head, and Peter might have cut off his, but because he was noble and forgiving he only drew a little of Lucas's blood. It isn't really like the poem, yet it is too, and it is something much more terrible. Lucas was brave and Peter was merciful. Or would Peter have killed Lucas if I hadn't been there? So am *I* also in the story? And Aleph, wasn't she the temptress, wasn't she what they both wanted? But that isn't quite right, the Lady was the wife of the Green Knight, and the Green Knight was good, though he was also a magician. Now Lucas is a magician too, and Lucas is not good, but Aleph is Lucas's wife. Yes, it's all mixed up. Lucas cut off Peter's head twice, he killed him first instead of me and second because he wanted the Lady. But how could Aleph have mysteriously conjured up this tale and this ending? What had Aleph meant when she called him the Green Knight? She may have intuitively seen farther, seen him as a sort of instrument of justice, a kind of errant ambiguous moral force, like some unofficial wandering angel. He could have claimed a just retribution by killing Lucas, or better still perhaps maiming him. That was his first apparition. But then later he forgave him and punished him only by that small symbolic shedding of blood. Will Lucas cherish that scar, Clement wondered, will he ever *tell* anyone, will he tell Aleph? Of course the Green Knight in the story was testing his opponent from the start, provoking a violence to which in honour the chivalrous fellow had later to submit himself. Not only that, there was the ordeal of sexual temptation, in which the performance of the chevalier was certainly not perfect. Only now, things are all confused, Clement said to himself inside his wild thoughts, and *I'm* getting confused. *There* the first blow was struck as a provocation to a mysterious adventure, *here* the first blow was struck by an evil magician whose victim reappeared as another, ultimately good, magician. And what about the temptress who in the story was the good magician's wife? I wonder if Aleph when she spoke up so promptly already saw herself as playing a part, perhaps as a temptation laid before both the evil one and the good one. Now the good one has gone, receding into his mystery, and the beautiful maiden has been awarded to the evil one. Is this the end of the story? Perhaps for *us* it is the end. But, Clement said to himself, as he had said once to Lucas, *what about me?* Am I some *alter ego* of my brother, enacting some minor ordeal of my own? But why minor? Ever since that first moment I have been in hell. Only I am not a hero, not a chevalier, not a demon, not even a small demon, just a wretched sinner and a *failure*. A dispensable object. I have no courage. I have failed two women, no, three, and must wear the badge of failure for the rest of my life.

Now Sefton was often absent, Moy, always at work, was silent, there was no news from Aleph. Louise longed for darkness and sleep. By day she wandered about the house, tidying things and cleaning things and moving things about. People had begun to ring up, Cora, Connie, Bellamy. Louise said yes she was perfectly well, no, there was no news, no she did not want visits. Bellamy asked her if she had seen Clement. No, she had not seen Clement. Bellamy said Clement did not answer the phone and when Bellamy had twice gone round to his house there was no answer to the bell – perhaps he had left London. Louise said perhaps. Perhaps he had gone to Paris. Yes, perhaps. She was beginning to be short of breath, she was frightened. She rang Clement but there was no one there. She wondered where Clement was, perhaps he had actually gone to America. Why? Perhaps he knew where Aleph was, and where Lucas was. Louise had, over the years, seen, what many others had not seen, Clement's *love* for his brother. Perhaps they would live *ménage à trois*! I am going mad, she thought, I am in some sort of silent raging grief of which I shall die, everything has gone. Another thought, a rather sad and bitter thought, came to her. Perhaps he was with Joan. Well, why not? Joan was lonely, she was beautiful, she loved him. Louise thought of ringing Cora but decided not to. She had been rather short with Cora when Cora had rung to sympathise. She rang Clement again but no answer. These mounting anxieties about Clement had begun to torment her. He had always been beside her, always at hand. Why had she sent him away? If only Moy were not in love with him. But would not Moy get over it, she was only a child after all. Or was she now a woman? Louise kept saying to herself, I am only worried about Clement like Bellamy is, that's all. Only such strange and awful pictures kept coming into her mind and haunting her sleep. The idea began to take hold of her that he had really *gone*, Clement, *gone*. His world too had been shaken to pieces. Perhaps he had gone to America to stay there forever, where Lucas and Aleph were living now, forever. Or else – he had committed suicide and was lying on his bed in his flat holding the bottle of pills in his drooping hand. After all, *he had loved Aleph*. She tried to keep calm, it was only an interim, Aleph would write, Clement would appear. Though coaxed by the children she did not leave the house. She sat in the evening in the Aviary, so quiet, unable to read or to sew. Moy, who did not read books, was sometimes silently with her. And Sefton, who was reading the

433

poems of Propertius and trying to render them into English. They listened to music on the radio as they used to do. Yes, Moy was a young woman, sitting there motionless holding the end of her thick golden plait upon her lap with one hand, her blue eyes vacant with thought, or turned with sadness upon her mother or her sister. Now that she ate so little she was almost slim. Of course no one played the piano.

On the next morning Louise rang Clement again, no good. She rang Emil and talked to Bellamy, who told her he would soon be moving out, no he had no knowledge of Clement. She then rang Cora, no news, except that Joan had left and Cora did not know where she was. Louise announced to the girls that she was going out 'to get some fresh air', and 'might be away for some time'. She put on her thick overcoat and a woollen cap and gloves and boots. The coldness surprised her, she had forgotten the outside world. There was no wind but an absolute coldness, so cold as to seem to silence the sound of the cars. The sky was white. Her breath made quick puffs of cloud around her. She walked a bit at random and saw with surprise in a newsagent's shop, Christmas decorations, Christmas cards. Of course, before long it would be *Christmas*. The coldness had already brought tears to her eyes. How could so much time have passed, had they all been in a trance? She thought, and am I going to commit suicide too? The idea formed itself like a pendent notice hanging in front of her eyes. But this was non-sense, *she* was not going to commit suicide, how could she if it was nearly Christmas and she must buy presents for the children – for both of them. Or should she not send a present to Aleph – if she knew where she was? The idea was horrible. She paused and looked at a dog. It was a black and white collie with brown eyes, but it reminded her of Anax. She patted it and it smiled up at her and wagged its tail. Its owner also smiled at Louise. A taxi appeared and Louise got into it and gave the address of Clement's flat. Here she paid the taxi man and rang the bell, but there was no answer, she had not expected an answer. As she walked away an idea, a most obvious idea, came into her mind. Where was he? Perhaps with Joan? Perhaps with the ladies of the theatre? After all, what did she know of his life, who he went to bed with, who he really loved? His time with her and with the children had been only a little interlude, only a little whiff of domestic life, not the real world. Louise stopped and stood for some time motionless, with her gloved hands deep in her pockets. Someone, staring at her, even spoke to her, asking if he could direct her or help her in any way. No thank you, I am beyond help. She walked on slowly. So now I must go home, where else can I go, I cannot find out anything, even about where he is. Anyway, what business is it of mine? What am I doing, walking about like this and grieving for him? Was there anyone now whom she could decently *ask*? No. She had never been curious about his other life, she could remember nobody in it! Nobody, that is, except his agent, a man called Antony Sloe, about whom Clement used to make jokes. Having remembered this Louise also remembered the road where this man lived. She thought now as she walked more purposefully along, I'll go home and ring him up. Then she thought, no I'll go to see him *now*. I must find out –

Antony Sloe, after Louise had arrived by taxi to see him, was not very helpful. He was cautious and uncommunicative. Yes, Clement was, he believed, still in London, but really he might be anywhere. Why was she looking for him? Was she herself in the theatre? Louise said, which was reasonably truthful, that somebody was ill. After a bit of frowning and staring Sloe wrote down the name of what he said was a small '*bijou*' theatre, now derelict, in which Clement was interested, adding however that as likely as not Clement wouldn't be there. Louise ran out and hailed another taxi.

The theatre, south of the river, and indeed small, had a pretty Georgian façade of grey stone. Louise cautiously pushed one of the doors. It yielded. The foyer was empty. There was a smell of old upholstery and dust. She stood there for some minutes, holding a hand over her heart and listening to a dark silence which seemed to emanate from within. She also wondered why she had come here, come this far. She stuffed her gloves into her pockets and moved forward and mounted some stairs, breathing the silence and the dusty smell. Treading softly and cautiously she pressed a door ahead of her which swung suddenly open and, as she stepped through it, closed behind her, leaving her in thick pitch darkness. She tried to retreat but she had lost the door and stretched out her hands, beating the dense dark, seeking for a surface. She found a wall and leaned against it. She dropped her handbag but, scrabbling on the floor, found it. At last she felt a yielding surface, a door, which she pushed, seeking for daylight. The door gave way, she edged through, but not into the light of day. She was standing in a huge silent dimly lit space, with some sort of gaping hole before her. The door behind closed quietly. She was on the balcony of the little theatre, looking down the very steep rows of seats toward the empty stage. From where she stood the stalls were invisible. She felt giddy, as if she were being impelled to fall or fly downward. She reached out for something to hold onto, gripped the back of one of the seats, and sat down. A soft dim light came from invisible sources. In the intense opaque apprehensive silence she could hear her heartbeat and her fast breathing. The air was cold and damp and smelt of rot. She feared the emptiness of the theatre, its coldness, the brooding dead exhausted air, the little puny empty stage, with its mean space and its wordless futility. Supposing all the lights were to go out. All she desired now was to get away safely. She rose hastily and went back to the door, holding it open to shed a dim light onto the corridor. She paused and turned back to look again. The stage was no longer empty. A man was standing on it, the man was Clement. He was standing with his hands in his pockets and his head bowed. He had not seen her.

Louise slipped quickly through the door letting it close behind her, hurried through the darkness, fumbled for the other door and found it, hurried down the stairs into the foyer, and ran out into the street. She walked along slowly, panting, ready to cry. She came to some iron railings where big dark sacks of rubbish had been put out onto the pavement. She paused, she looked at the sacks and at the railing, the spear-shaped tops of which had in places been broken off. She reached across to the railing, touching it with her ungloved hands. Then she turned back and walked slowly back toward the theatre. She crossed the foyer, not this time mounting the stairs, but following an arrow which pointed behind them. She passed quickly now through a door, across a dark corridor, and back into the big dimly lit space. The stage, now on a level with her, seemed surprisingly near. Only it was, once again, empty. Louise stood for a few minutes looking at it. She felt intense disappointment, even a kind of guilt, as if she had missed something, perhaps forever. He had been there, she could have spoken to him. Could she call out now, cry his name? It was impossible. She felt again the terror, the sense of being a criminal in fear of discovery. However, she walked a little forward, looking to right and left. There was no one there. She went on, walking slowly and silently upon the shabby threadbare carpet. She felt

436

now a curious obsessive impulse to reach the stage and *touch* it. She reached it and laid her hand upon the torn velvet which covered the wood. The wood was warm. She saw some steps and mounted them, turning round now to look at the whole silent auditorium. She moved a little. The boards creaked.

'Louise! What on earth are you doing here!'

As soon as she saw Clement standing at the back of the theatre and heard his voice her terror vanished. She slipped off her coat and dropped it on the dusty floor and shook out the skirt of her dress. It was almost as if she were *acting*. It was a moment before she could command her voice, but when it came it was calm and clear. She was even able to experience a kind of reassuring irritation.

'What do you think I'm doing? I heard you were here and I thought I'd drop in and look at the place.'

'How clever of you to find me. But who told you?' Clement was coming down the centre aisle.

'Oh, someone told me. I think it was your agent, yes of course it was. But what are you doing? This place seems to be a wreck.'

Clement mounted the steps. He approached her and picked up her coat. 'Yes, but I hope it can be rescued. There was talk of pulling it down. It's terrible when a theatre dies.'

'The boards creak.'

'Yes, and that will never do! And there's dry rot in the boxes.'

'Are there boxes? Oh yes, I see them now, they're tiny.'

'Got to have boxes, it's a matter of prestige! But Louise, why – ?'

'Where will you get the money from?'

'We'll stir up the usual sources and mount an appeal – maybe we'll find a millionaire – you see, it's so pretty – '

'Will it be *your* theatre?'

'Well, if it survives, sort of, I hope – '

'Look, do you mind if we go out into the daylight? It's so awfully damp and cold in here.'

'I'm so sorry, come this way, follow me.' He led her off the stage, not through the auditorium, through various mysterious spaces, collecting his overcoat and turning out lights behind him, down some stairs, and then, suddenly pressing a bar, out by a side exit into the brilliant daylight of a street where there was even a hint of sun. They walked along the side street to the front of the theatre where Clement locked the front doors.

'Could I have my coat?'

'Oh, I'm so sorry.'

Louise put her coat on. She said, 'Well, I must be getting back home. Would that bus take me?'

'No, it goes to Clapham Junction. Any Aleph news?'

'No –'

'I assumed you'd let me know.'

'Yes.' Louise noticed they were standing beside the railings where the iron spears had been decapitated, and she reached out again and touched the bitterly cold iron. 'Well, thank you for showing me your theatre. Now I really must go.'

'Why go, why not stay with me and have lunch? There's a little Italian restaurant which I've discovered, quite close. I'll have to go back to the theatre this afternoon, but –'

'No, thanks. I'd better get back, I don't eat lunch now anyway, and Moy is holding the fort. I'll just get a taxi –'

'There aren't any round here.'

'Well, where's the nearest tube station?'

'Look here, I'll drive you home, if you don't mind walking to my car?'

'Oh no, certainly not, I mustn't waste your time, I'm sure you –'

'Louise, do as I say, it's not far to the car, and I can get you back quite quickly, come on.'

They walked to the car in silence.

'I wonder when you'll hear from Aleph?'

'How do I know? I expect a letter soon, telling us about their arrangements, where they'll be. I don't know whether Lucas had any particular university post in mind. Did he tell you?'

'Tell *me*? No! How's poor Moy?'

'She's very quiet. I sometimes wonder if she's going mad.'

'Oh dear.'

They were silent. The car crossed the river and began to run along beside the Thames. Clement suddenly turned to the right, drove a little way, then stopped under huge leafless plane trees in a little square.

'What is this, where are we?'

'Where indeed, Louise? I don't know.'

'Oh – really – !'

'Please don't.'

'Don't what?'

'Be so cold and – *bloody tiresome.*'

'I'm sorry, but – '

'Can't we *talk* to each other any more, have we *lost* each other?'

'I hope we haven't lost each other, Clement.'

'Such awful things have happened – Lucas and Aleph, and Peter – maybe we have to be in mourning for a while – but – '

'But?'

'You came to the theatre.'

'Yes, perhaps I shouldn't have. It means nothing.'

'I think it means everything. It means you need me, it means you love me. Isn't that true? All right, cry, do cry – perhaps I shall cry myself – '

'So you've got used to it at last.'

'What an odd way of putting it.'

'Well, it is startling, I am startled.'

'Because it is so sudden.'

'Because of what it is.'

'Yes, it is like nothing on earth.'

'*We* are like nothing on earth.'

'We are made divine. Let us be worthy.'

'We shall be.'

'To say we are sure may seem rash.'

'And naive.'

'But we *are* sure.'

'We are lucky. You feel it had to be?'

'Yes.'

'All those years it was making itself, like a creature in a chrysalis, buried in the moist earth.'

'Yet there is accident – like you falling on the bridge.'

'I would have been in Florence now.'

'The gods tripped you up and you had to be here. But we could not be as we are without that long knowledge of each other, we are not people who have just met.'

'Yet we are people who have just met.'

'You were so close to Aleph – so many evenings, we, Louie and Moy and me, heard your soft inaudible conversations and your laughter – '

'All that was simply a weaving of our impossibility.'

'You loved each other.'

'Only in a childish way.'

'You were ceasing to be children.'

'Sefton, don't torment me with this. I love you, I love only you, I worship you, I am you. This is the truth and we are in it.'

'Yes, yes – we must be always in the truth. Oh my angel, I feel transfigured, I feel dazed with light.'

'Come closer, let me hold you again, your heart against my heart – '

'Oh my sweet boy – oh my love – '

Later, dressed, they sat on Harvey's bed, enlaced, feet and legs tangled, facing each other, hands round each other's necks, like Indian gods, Sefton said.

'We must tell them soon.'

'How will they take it? They may not like it!'

'They will be very surprised and then very pleased. My mother has always loved you, she wanted to keep you with us, she once said to me that she wished you were her son.'

'I felt she was putting me at a distance.'

'She was afraid of showing too much affection and seeming to appropriate you. She was sensitive about your mother's rights. And she may have thought too much affection might put you off! She'll be so glad.'

'I hope so. And Moy?'

'She'll be delighted too. Of course she's fixated on Clement, but she's always liked you.'

'If we're going to tell Clement and Louie, we must somehow tell my mother at the same time, she mustn't hear it from them.'

'I wonder how *she* will take it?'

'Amazement, horror, relief, delight.'

'She wants you to marry a rich woman. She also wants you to marry someone she can dominate. I am neither of these. She is still with Cora, isn't she?'

'Sefton, you must love her, you must, she will long to love you, and she will love you – she has that sort of brittle mask, but it's just acting – she is so gentle and so vulnerable and so kind, and she has had such a rough time, she longs for love, she longs for security – '

'How can we give her security, we are penniless students?'

'I mean the security of loving kindness. Sefton, don't be afraid. You have more fears than I have. I fear your fears.'

'Then I shall send them all away! We have so much love, let it overflow, you are right.'

'She may even learn to be happy at last.'

'I hope that we may all make Louie happy too one day. I fear – that word again – that she may mourn for Aleph all her life.'

'Perhaps Aleph will come back, or – '

'No, never. And Aleph will never speak to us truthfully again, and we will never speak truthfully to her. Now you stay here please, I shall go home.'

Walking back to Clifton in the cold still afternoon among wandering snowflakes, Sefton thought, how was the path so suddenly cleared for us, so that we could speed along it? Did we somehow unconsciously know that Aleph was leaving, did we feel her going, her absence, and how everything would now be different? He has taken me instead of Aleph. Aleph he could not take, something which perhaps I shall never know stood between them and made it impossible. It may be that they had so thoroughly, working it out over the years in those long long conversations, made themselves brother and sister. Perhaps he thought I was Aleph, and for an instant, *that* instant, I was Aleph, the possible Aleph, as if her head and shoulders were laid upon me like one of Moy's masks. I was the Aleph yet not Aleph that could be desired. But my Aleph mask will fade and become transparent and dissolve away. Is this a myth, is it all a myth? It is just a dream of mine, a fear-dream, and that will dissolve and fade away. I am in love, truly in love, and I am happy, blazingly happy, with a happiness I never knew existed, which gives me back the world and all the things in it brilliantly coloured and divinely blessed. 'Travel light, simplify your life.' I have set aside *his* advice, and *he* has set aside his own advice, and both our lives are to be very different from now on. I am no longer the cat that walks by herself on by her wild lone. Well, I shall simplify my life by love and work and truth. But what has really happened to *them* I shall never know.

*

441

Dearest Louie,

I am so sorry I didn't write sooner again, we have been travelling a lot and visiting various universities. I think our final home will be at Berkeley, but at present we are in New York where Lucas is giving some lectures and we are staying with a friend, a former colleague of his, at the address above – we will be here for at least a month, and I will of course send other addresses. Please excuse a short letter now just to let you know where we are. I *love* America, and have seen some wonderful things in our travels. Lucas is showing me America! California is wonderful, so is New York. I hope you will come and see us at Berkeley, where we are going to rent a house with a view of the Bay! (Berkeley is just by San Francisco.) When we are settled there I shall join the university and go on with getting my degree and then my doctorate. My dear dear Mother, I am so sorry about the trouble and distress which I may have caused you all – *words cannot express this* – and I hope that you have now 'got used' to my absence, and that your love for me has not been damaged. I rely upon this love and crave for it and ask for it. This I say to you and to Sef and to Moy. I look forward to the time when you will visit us in California and we can show you America! *Please* understand, *please* forgive, and do please write to me as soon as you receive this letter at the address above to tell me you are not angry and that I am still your daughter whom you love. Lucas sends greetings! With much much love, my dear, my dear, ever your

Aleph

Dearest Aleph,

We have all received your letters with great relief, as of course we were worrying terribly about you when we didn't know where you were. Of course we were surprised! But surprise fades and love as you say is eternal. Please send news, write often, let us have addresses, and be sure that we think about you all the time, and of course wish you and Lucas every possible happiness and joy. Please do not be distressed or imagine for a second that we could be angry with you! We miss you very much – we shall look forward to seeing you again before very long. Please, please be happy, be well, and do visit us when you can. This is just to say that I have your precious second letter. My dearest Aleph, my dearest daughter, from me and from all of us, much much love,

Louie

'Well,' said Louise to Clement. They were sitting side by side on the sofa in the Aviary. Clement had just read Aleph's letter, then Louise's reply. It was the day after Louise's adventure in the theatre. They both felt by now that all that had been decided yesterday had been decided long ago, perhaps many years ago.

Clement said, 'I don't know what to say – '

'I don't, didn't know what to say – and I don't know what to think either.'

'One cannot say what one feels.'

'No. What does one feel?'

'We have lost them both.'

'There is a great emptiness. It comes home now doesn't it, I can't quite believe it, I have to go through it every morning when I wake up, remembering it, and then trying to *think* it.'

'Both of them gone – it's a terrible blow. One feels that now seeing them must always be a lie.'

'As my letter is a lie – and hers too. Yet the love is there, the love *is* there – only it's as if it's so wounded it has curled up and gone into a black hole.'

'I hope the love will recover though it can never be as it once was, it can never again be really expressed. Or is all this nonsense? We are suffering from shock. Perhaps in a year or two we'll be spending our holidays with them in California!'

'I hope so. No, I don't hope so, I mean I can't see it, it's impossible. Being with them affectionately, openly, with mutual love?'

'With Aleph conceivably. Lucas will be polite, but will be away at the university, giving seminars, attending meetings, *she* will show us around, drive us about in her big car – '

'At least I hope she *will* go on at the university. But suppose he ditches her, will she come back here, will she be with us? Or will she stay in America and find an American husband?'

'She won't come back here. She'll stay in America and find an American husband. But he won't ditch her. And do you know, I can imagine them happy together – and Lucas, really happy, for the first time in his life.'

'Clement, you haven't changed your mind since last night?'

'No my love, I feel we arranged all this ages ago, it's so simple, it's so right, it's just that we have idiotically delayed it. For this we must forgive each other.'

'But now we must tell the others. Sefton will be delighted, I know she will. Only Moy – you know how Moy feels about you – '

'We must be firm and sensible about that. These were feelings she had as a child, in a childish game. But she is grown up now and probably already embarrassed that we were ever able to notice them.'

'We must just assume she's got over it. She'll be all right, she's shedding her childishness very fast. She's taller and she's becoming quite beautiful, have you noticed?'

'Yes, she'll survive. Where's Sefton, out slogging away as usual?'

'She works too hard. Wait, listen, Sefton is just coming in now, someone's with her. Why, I think it's Harvey! Sefton, Harvey, hello, come up, Clement and I are up here!'

Two radiant beautifully dressed young people entered the Aviary. Sefton was wearing a dark green dress of very fine corduroy pulled in at her waist by a red belt. Her abundant reddish brown hair, grown a little longer, was combed back from her brow, her green hazel eyes shone, her firm lips were parted, her pale face, blushing, glowed. Harvey, tall, slim and noble, the raffish prince, had put on his best second-hand suit of dark brown tweed, with a blue striped shirt and a red and green tie, his glossy flowing blond hair falling neatly to his shoulders, his fringe carefully trimmed, his large gentle brown eyes narrowed with joy. Clement and Louise, rising to meet them, were wearing respectively, Louise a pale blue velvet dress with a lace collar and a dark blue cardigan, and Clement a light golden brown suit, with a dark red shirt and a light red bow tie. Louise, smiling though also near to tears, looked flushed, her stiff hair combed upward and backward making a crown. Clement alone looked solemn, lifting his long nose, pouting his red lips, running his hand with a graceful movement through his copious dark hair. They were a handsome foursome. There was an instant's silence. Louise looked at Clement. Harvey looked at Sefton.

Louise said, 'My dears, I'm so glad you've come. How smart and pretty you both look! We have something to tell you.'

'We have something to tell you too!' said Sefton.

'Who shall tell first?' said Louise.

'We shall,' said Clement. 'Listen, dear children. I am going to marry Louise.' He put an arm round her waist.

Sefton and Harvey gasped, then laughed, then wailed with joy.

Sefton said, 'Oh how perfectly wonderful, and listen, listen, I am going to marry Harvey, and Harvey is going to marry me!'

After an instant they all began to talk at once, till talk was taken over by helpless laughter, and they were waving their arms and kissing each other. Clement sat down at the piano and began to play Mendelssohn's wedding-march. Then Sefton cried out, 'Where's Moy?'

'Yes, indeed, quiet Clement, we must tell Moy, I'll fetch her, no you fetch her, Sefton, she's working as usual, she must think we've all gone mad!'

'All right, Louie,' Clement and Louise looked at each other as Sefton rushed away up the stairs. She returned with Moy. 'I haven't told her,' Sefton said.

Moy stood in the doorway, then came in and closed the door behind her. She smiled at her mother, then became grave. The others became suddenly grave too. Moy was in her new being. She had become taller and slimmer. She was wearing a blue dress with a round neck and a belt, not like her old shapeless shifts, very nearly a smart dress, as Clement said later. Her thick golden plait was hanging down over her left breast. She was carrying her painting overall, which she had hastily taken off after Sefton's summons and absently tossed over one arm. Her blue eyes, which matched her dress, gazed anxiously only at her mother.

Louise said, turning to the others as if for permission and support, 'Moy, my darling, we have to tell you two – new things – I am going to marry Clement, and Sefton is going to marry Harvey, so there, you see – what a happy family – we all shall be – ' After this Louise burst into tears, and Clement led her to the sofa and sat down beside her. Sefton, also in tears, ran to Moy and hugged her and kissed her. Harvey, breathing deeply, went to the window and looked out, adjusting his tie. Some real snow was falling. Of course Moy shed some tears too and said how glad she was. Clement said there should now be champagne, and then they could all sing together. Harvey said he thought he and Sefton should now go on to tell his mother, who was still with Cora. It was then voted that they should all go to Cora's house, and Louise ran downstairs to telephone Cora (without giving anything away) that she and Clement and the children would so much like to come over. Sefton said she would run out for a bottle of champagne, and Clement revealed that he had brought a case, it was in his car. They began to troop down the stairs and put on their warm clothes. Moy said she was sorry, she was in the middle of a picture, and disappeared back upstairs.

'What's all this?' said Cora, opening the door.

Clement carried the case of champagne and put it down in the hall. He had been thinking on the way over that after all it was unseemly and unkind, and perhaps unwise, to arrive in just this way to inform Joan of his intentions. How would she react? Was she really still with Cora, perhaps she was not, he now hoped she was not. But of course she had to know soon, indeed at once, and he must tell her. The presence of others might indeed be helpful to them both, precluding drama – so he hoped. Also, his heart at this moment strangely went out to Joan and he thought of her more lovingly perhaps than he had ever done before. He thought, she's tough, she's *brave*. She will take it calmly, proudly, without a shudder, probably without even an exchange of significant glances. And he thought, she will think: poor fool!

'May we go into the drawing-room?' said Clement.

'Yes, who's stopping you. Joan is in there.'

They trooped in, leaving their slightly snowy coats in a pile in the hall. Joan, who had been sitting on the window-seat, stood up. They could not avoid the significant glance. Clement thought, perhaps she understands already. As agreed beforehand, Harvey, stepping forward, addressed his mother. '*Maman*, please don't faint, listen, I am going to get married. I am going to marry Sefton.'

Joan replied instantly but calmly, 'Don't be silly, Harvey.' Her crackling eyes flashed at Clement.

Ignoring her, Harvey turned to Cora and said, 'And Clement is going to marry Louise – so, you see, this is how it is – ' His strong voice trailed away.

Cora, sturdy, said, 'How absolutely marvellous! Was that champagne I saw out there? Let's celebrate! We have something to celebrate too. So bring in the bubbly, and I'll get glasses directly.'

There was a bustle with everyone moving about, bringing in bottles, handing glasses.

When they were more or less gathered again, Joan, who had briefly disappeared, said in her loud commanding voice, 'May I say, on behalf of myself and Cora, how glad we are to hear your news. I'm sorry, Sefton, for that slip of the tongue, not a good start for a mother-in-law. I didn't mean anything personal, I just thought Harvey was too young to marry, but now I see he isn't and I think you are ideal, you will keep him in order.'

'So may we raise our glasses?' said Clement.

'No, wait a moment. There is something to be added to this happy scene. Shall – I – Cora – ?'

'Yes, yes.'

Joan went out, crossed the hall, and returned after a minute followed by a tall handsome middle-aged man with a large head and a lot of almost colourless straight fair hair. He was smiling shyly, showing long white teeth. His light blue eyes were narrowed among wrinkles.

Joan took his hand. She said to him, pointing. 'This is Clement, who is going to marry Louise, this is my son Harvey who is going to marry Sefton, this is Sefton, she is Louise's daughter.' She then said, addressing Clement, 'And this is my *fiancé*, Humphrey H. Hook from Texas.'

Fortunately for her hearers, Hook took charge at once, approaching Harvey with his long stride and his broad glinting smile and taking his hand. 'So, I'm going to be your step-father, Harvey, is that OK?' Harvey, dazed, said, 'Oh, yes, sir, that's OK, certainly that's OK.' He rescued his hand from the iron grip. Clement reached out his hand to Joan. Joan kissed him. He said, 'My dear, I wish you every happiness, *well done* – I mean – ' Cora was pouring out the champagne, as Hook shook hands with the others.

Joan was explaining, 'You see, Humphrey wanted us to live in America where his business is, and I wanted us to stay in England, so we couldn't get anywhere, but do you know what suddenly arranged things for us? The Fax machine! With the Fax machine any businessman can live anywhere, so we're going to buy a house in London and one in the country.'

Clement murmured, 'The Fax machine, oh the Fax machine!' Hook was explaining that his extra H stood for Harold, and that his ancestors were Scandinavian, and that he and Joan were going to have their honeymoon in Norway. They drank the champagne and toasted one another and tears came into the eyes of all the women and also into Harvey's eyes. They stood in Cora's big drawing-room, moving among themselves as in a dance, no one sat down. Joan said, 'All we need now is Bellamy marrying Emil!' The word 'happiness' was often used, although, since they were all in their own ways sober and reflective people, each one wondered for a moment or two *what* it was and *how* they were destined to achieve it. (At least one thought for a second, 'Am I mad?') Cora alone felt detached, *her* fate was not in the balance. She thought, I am always helping other people to be happy (for these were not the only matches which she had facilitated). But I can never be happy without my Isaac. Better not to think about happiness at all. Cheerfulness will do. And I do like looking after people. It was Cora also who, with the dead in mind, suggested they should all drink a toast to Peter Mir. As they, more solemnly did this, Clement said suddenly, 'How strange, do you remember that drink which we had at Peter's place before dinner, that "special"? Now we see what it was – it was a love potion!' And Joan said, 'It's as if all spells are broken and we are all set free!' Everyone laughed, then became solemn, thinking of Lucas and Aleph. There was no toast to them, and no one mentioned their names. Before they all parted, Humphrey Hook took Harvey aside and spoke to him gravely, saying he much looked forward to their being good friends, and that he would do everything in his power to make Harvey's mother very happy. He also captivated Sefton, calling her his stepson's lovely bride. Harvey, cautiously ready to like Hook, thought: *Maman* said Sef would keep me in order. I think this man will keep *maman* in order!

Meanwhile at Clifton, not long after they had left, Moy was busy struggling with a pair of scissors. She was trying to cut her long golden plait off at the nape of her neck. It was not easy. The scissors were rather blunt. She did not unplait the hair, as it would be harder to deal with spread all about. The closely interwoven mass of hair, so thick at the top, resisted her, it did not want to be cut. Moy went downstairs to the kitchen and found the big kitchen scissors. She was ready to try the secateurs next, only at last she could feel the dense stuff giving way, coming away, parting, yielding bit by bit to the steady tugging of her left hand. The

scissors made a strange sound, partly a little shrill, partly a deep
hissing shearing sound. She kept on steadily sawing, keeping the
blades at work, until suddenly the whole long thick thing came
away in her hand and she could look at it, hanging heavy and
drooping and dead before her. She climbed back up to her bedroom carrying the severed plait. She did not know what to do with
it. She threw it into the basket in the corner with the cushion in it,
which she had left untouched since Anax left.

'But how did you get in?' said Bellamy to Kenneth Rathbone at
The Castle. It was early and the pub was empty.

'I climbed in by a window at the back. I planned it before, did
myself up shabby in overalls and carried some tools. A cobber in a
white coat saw me, but he thought I was a maintenance man!
Then it was dead easy. There was a big board with the names and
the numbers of the rooms. I just slipped in. It was more than half
an hour before the nurse found me!'

'He was glad to see you?'

'He was! He held my hand. He asked after all of you. He
wondered why you didn't visit him.'

'Oh *God*!'

'I told him the docs said we mustn't come.'

'But you came. How I wish – '

'We had such a talking, I've never had such a talk, we could
have gone on for hours.'

'Of course you must have got to know him well when he was
living here.'

'Fairly, but he was still a bit of a mystery man, I couldn't make
him out. You know, at the start I thought he was a criminal hiding
from the police!'

'What did you talk about, I mean when you saw him at the
clinic?'

'Oh he fairly poured it out, all sorts of things, about himself.'

'About himself? What things?'

'Well, he said it was between him and me.'

'Surely he wouldn't mind your telling me. Did he know he was dying?'

'I don't know. He said, "I'm going home!" but what he meant by that I don't know, might have meant anything, mightn't it?'

'You said you couldn't figure him out at the start. But what did you make of him later on?'

'I don't know. I think he's some sort of holy being. Or was, I should say, I can't think of him as not existing.'

'Nor can I. I think of him as an avatar, I mean an incarnation, a pure sinless creature, a very special visitor to this awful scene, like an angel – I can't express it.'

'You've expressed it very well, mate. But who's going to believe us? Perhaps he'll come back – but not in our time. Same again?'

'No, thanks, I've got to start to pack up – '

'So you're off to the seaside.'

'Yes, to my cottage. I tried to sell it, but fortunately no one bought it. I'd like you to come down and stay, and we could go on talking about Peter – '

'Yes, you wanted to be a monk, didn't you. My mother wanted me to be a monk.'

'Really? So you are a Catholic?'

'Yes, or was. Now I'm a publican and sinner.'

'I'll call in again when I'm back, I do want you to tell me – '

'Well, you'll have to make it snappy, I'm leaving here next week.'

'Oh, I'm sorry – '

'Yes, it's shift, boys, shift. I'm going home too. I'm going back to dear old Oz where I belong, where the sky is where it ought to be, way up far above in heaven, not sitting on top of your head the way it is here.'

5

THEY REACH THE SEA

Bellamy had intended to be alone with Anax in his cottage beside the sea, but after a quick preliminary visit he had found the house intact and unburgled, yet cold and solitary and sad. So, impulsively, he had asked Clement and Louise and of course Moy, and Emil, to come and stay. Emil, detained by picture business, was yet to arrive. He wrote letters to Bellamy every other day. The others had already come. Harvey and Sefton were in Italy, endowed with holiday money by Harvey's new father. A somewhat confused and perfunctory Christmas was over. Now it was January.

The square squat stone-built house stood near to the estuary of a little foaming stream as dark as Guinness. The thick grass, cropped by black-faced sheep, sloped down to orange and grey and black speckled rocks with little foothold steps and innumerable pools containing tiny fish and anemones, undisturbed it seemed by frequent high tides. Beyond, the beach was heaped with dark grey stones streaked with white geometrical patterns, each one unique, and huge old greenish oyster-shells, ossified, fossilised, adorned by the pale stony droppings of prehistoric worms. Brown ever-wet seaweed banded the lower levels of the tide, continually raked by the grim powerful grey waves with their bitter grinding undertow. Inland, at all seasons, the misty rain descended upon the huge forest trees, pines and firs and great yews and ancient tangled graceful oaks.

Bellamy was tormented by his conversation with Kenneth Rathbone. If only it had never happened, if only it had not occurred to him, consumed by a desire to talk with someone about Peter, to go that morning to The Castle. A little later, and Kenneth would have gone, and he would never have known, never have received that torturing picture of Kenneth by Peter's bedside, holding his hand. Why had not *he* had the wit and the sensibility and the consuming *love* to climb through a window and find Peter and hold his hand and *kiss* his hand, and then be told those wonderful precious things which now he would never know? Just two days later Bellamy had come running back to The Castle, but Kenneth had already gone, back to the land where the sky is where it ought to be, leaving no address and taking all those precious secrets with him. I would have *understood*, thought Bellamy, as he prepared to go to bed. I would have known what to ask him, he would have been able to say much more to me, and been sure that I would be able to *think* about it, to treasure it, to use it, to teach it. He may have thought of me as his messenger to the world. After all, he said I was his secretary. Perhaps, oh God, he was *waiting* for me! Oh if only all *that* had happened, all that he promised me, how I was to be with him and help him, I can't stop picturing it as it might have been! He said to me, 'All these things are shadows.' He could have shown me the reality. Now I am devoured by the demons of remorse, I think hideous thoughts, I shall be ill again, the old depression will come back. It is all my fault, I could have saved him, I could have rescued him, I just lacked courage, I lacked imagination. He was an angel, I saw him bathed in light, I saw him *transfigured*. All this I have lost by accident, and it is as if I killed him by accident. He will be belittled and forgotten, I can see this happening already, *they* are diminishing him, calling him mad, letting his image fade into something pitiful and banal. He was too great and strange for their little world. He said to me, 'Later, you will be with me.' Perhaps he simply meant that he would survive. Oh if only I had *proof* – but what of?

Bellamy took a sleeping-pill and crawled into bed. Anax, already in the bed, snuggled up against him. Stroking the dog's warm body Bellamy thought: Anax too will die.

It was the morning of the next day. Bellamy had gone for a walk with Anax. Moy was out climbing among the rocks and inspecting the stones. Clement and Louise, now man and wife, were still at the breakfast table. They were, as they kept on saying to each other, very tired. They had been through too much. Clement had hurried the matter through as fast as possible. They were married in a registry office, also present being Sefton, Moy, Harvey, and Bellamy. After the ceremony they all drank champagne with Connie and Jeremy, also present being Rosemary, Nick, Rufus, Emil, Cora and Tessa. Joan and Humphrey had also got married in Florida, *chez* Humphrey's mom. Tessa, invited as an old friend in spite of her dubious role in the abduction of Peter, was now a medical student. She advised Bellamy to consider this profession, it was not too late. Clement and Louise sent a cable to Aleph and Lucas announcing their marriage and received a cable by return bearing suitable congratulations. Louise had attempted, but failed, to write a letter. No answer had yet come from Aleph, though perhaps there was one waiting at Clifton. Louise dreaded that letter. She felt she knew what serene palliatives it would contain.

'Moy is being sensible, isn't she.'

'You mean not moping about your having stolen me away?'

'She is quite natural with you, more than before. And cutting off her hair makes her look older.'

'You thought it signified the end of the cult of me.'

'Have you noticed how much she looks like Teddy with her hair cut? I wonder what she did with that long thick snake of golden hair.'

'One cannot ask.'

'Sefton has become more beautiful too. Perhaps she always was, only she had that remote austere look. Now she is gentle and loving and everything shines.'

'Yes, they are transfigured. And you, my darling, have also secured Harvey.'

'It was clever of you to guess how much I always wanted Harvey.'

'And he has acquired a lovely mother-in-law and a rich step-father.'

'Suppose Mom vetoes Joan.'

'She won't. Joan will charm her. Joan will love America, she will become an American, she is naturally American.'

'Oh Clement – there is so much to make us happy, but so much that is terrible and awful and black. I sometimes think I shouldn't have burdened you with so much – absolute grief. It's the feeling of death, there have been three deaths – '

'You mean Peter and Lucas and Aleph.'

'When we were at Cora's you said that Peter had given us a love potion which set us all free to love and be happy – but how can we be happy, how can we ever be happy now? Peter didn't die *for* anything, he died accidentally, senselessly – he appeared out of a mystery which I have never understood, and now he has vanished leaving all *this* behind – if he had not appeared Lucas would not have coveted Aleph – '

'If he had not appeared I should probably be dead – but never mind that!'

'And your marrying me makes any reconciliation with *them* impossible forever. I can't bear having lost Aleph, I can't bear it, I dream she is with me, I wake up and think she is here, but she isn't and never will be – and I am burdening you with all this and it will poison you. Oh why can't we be happy – '

Clement moved his chair up close to his wife and put his arms around her and hugged her fiercely. Her head was against his shoulder and the torrent of her tears was soaking his jacket. This was not the first time since his marriage that he had received this speech and these tears. He had been suddenly so purely blindly happy when Louise had come to him in the theatre. Why had not this happened earlier, he wondered, long ago. Well, it was wonderful that it was happening now. All that had seemed impossible, too late, a dream, had suddenly become possible, even natural and inevitable. But now all *this* had to be lived through, seeing her weeping, overcome by misery and terror, biting her hands to choke back her sobs, giving way to frenzies of grief which, however, she indulged only when alone with Clement. After several of these fits Clement was seriously frightened, though also relieved by the control which enabled her to smile at Bellamy and Moy, and take an interest in Bellamy's chaotic kitchen, of which she was now mistress, and train the others to separate the knives, forks and spoons and the big plates from the little plates and to put the pretty crockery away for special occasions. Also going shopping in the distant village, where Clement always accompanied her, seemed a consolation and a return to reality. He thought, I had not realised how much Aleph was her favourite, like her flagship, her *front* to the world. She was so proud of Aleph, of Aleph's *magnificence*, though she must have felt perpetual deep anxiety about what the future held. And he thought, she has something about Luc, which probably she will never tell me, and anyway I don't want to know, there's some terrible twist of the screw there. She's going through it, facing all the *worst* things, the things that *can't* be explained, all the shattered hopes

454

and the remorse and the *demons*, and she's working it all out on me, and I hope and pray and believe she'll recover, she'll *tire*, she'll fall down exhausted, and then I shall pick her up and carry her home. In bed with her was good. He had feared, when he realised how strong the demon of grief was in her, that it might be otherwise, that she might have built up some defensive dislike, even horror, of the idea of sex. This possibility had disturbed him deeply even earlier on when his love for her, which had always been alive though quiescent, had suddenly and prophetically wakened and increased. But on the first night she had said, 'We are in heaven, and it is all *silent*.' They discussed calmly and sensibly Aleph's second letter and Louise's reply. It was when they had come to the sea, even, Clement felt, at the *sight* of the sea, Louise had begun more violently to enact, in her soul and body, the deep horror of all that had happened. Clement, but briefly, had thought that this sickness might bring upon her that very revulsion of which he was so afraid. But it was not so, she gave herself to him now not quietly but wildly, desperately, as one rushing out into a tempest. Sometimes, however, in the night, when she rested with him and he held her and protected her, he could feel as if they were floating upon vast calm waters.

Louise, moving away from him, mopped her face with Clement's large white handkerchief which she had taken from his pocket, then blew her nose. She went on, 'I think Moy is going mad.'

'You said she is sensible!'

'It's probably my madness. She cried so terribly when she broke that plate. She cries a lot. Well, so do I. I keep thinking about Teddy. How terribly quickly things go away into the past and people become ghosts, first vivid ghosts, then pale ghosts, then just names, then – nothing.'

'We shall always think about Teddy.'

'Yes, that is an eternal wound. I was thinking about Peter. He is vanishing already. Of course we never really knew him. It's as if he were made of some sort of soluble material, he crumbles away.'

'I think we never felt that he was real at all, he was an intruder, he ought to have been somewhere else, it was all a mistake, he didn't belong to our scheme of things at all, like some bizarre instrument of justice, coming from some other court upon some other planet.'

And so, thought Clement, we betray him, we explain him away, we do not want to think about him or puzzle about him or try to make out what he was in himself. Bellamy thinks he is an angel, and I am glad he thinks so, that may preserve him for a while in some form of being. But for the rest of us he is an embarrassment, as if something huge and strange has shot up in our midst and we simply cannot conceptualise it and so we imagine that it isn't there, like the New Zealand natives who could not conceptualise Captain Cook's ship and simply ignored it. Perhaps we are surrounded with such beings, heavenly or demonic, for whom we have no concepts and who are therefore invisible. We may indeed diminish Peter and make him into a mere nightmare or a retired butcher – but really he is something alien and terrifying. After all, the Green Knight came out from some other form of being, weird and un-Christian, not like Arthur's knights. But he was noble and he knew what justice was – and perhaps justice is greater than the Grail. Lucas came to understand him, and indeed they understood each other, it was as if they were bound together. Peter saved my life, he gave his own life for mine. And Clement recalled vividly, as he was des-tined to continue to do, their first tragic meeting – and with it the image of Lucas and Peter, after Lucas's ordeal and after Clement had fainted, the two sorcerers, delighted with each other, dancing together like goats in a love-scene. Now he remembered suddenly, as something indissolubly connected, Peter saying, his last words spoken to him: 'Look after your brother.' These words had impressed Clement deeply, inscribed upon his heart. Well, he thought, I tried to look after him, but it wasn't possible. Did I ever really try? Then for the first, but not for the last time, it occurred to him: perhaps these words can *refer to the future*. And he thought, I shall go on blindly and secretly jumbling all these things together and making no sense of them as long as I live. Maybe every human creature carries some such inescapable burden. That is being human. A very weird affair.

Clement pulled Louise to her feet and led her to the window. Low down above the sea, the sky was filled with large majestic clouds, rounded like piles of bubbles, moving in slow procession, pure white above, golden below. The sea, a pallid glitter at the horizon, nearer where the forms of the waves were discernible a darkening grey, crested with flutters of foam as it neared the shore and hurled itself choking among the rocks.

'Look, Louise, the sea, and all your birds, the cormorants flying in formation, and the black-headed gulls, and the oystercatchers and the terns, and there is a heron flying back inland. And there is Moy among the rocks, you can see her blue dress, she is looking into a pool, and there, just coming over the hill, is Bellamy, and Anax running in front of him toward the house – '

Louise, holding Clement's hand, surveyed the scene. 'Yes, yes – all the same I'm worried about Moy.'

'Perhaps we should get her a cat?'

'No, she loved Tibellina so much, I don't think any other cat would do. And I'm worried about Sefton and Harvey.'

'They promised they'd wait a year before getting married. They will wait a year, and they will get married. *They're* all right.'

'Yes. But I made them promise. That may not have been wise.'

'I told them it was an ordeal! That amused them, they are so romantic – and they are so much in love, they know *that* doesn't matter, they are for eternity.'

'I hope nothing awful will happen to them in Italy. I wonder where they are now, at this very moment.'

At this very moment Sefton and Harvey were on the bridge, the long high famous bridge which so many persons, including some distinguished ones, had committed suicide by leaping from. The sun was shining from a cloudless sky upon the deep valley, the slopes densely covered with cypresses and umbrella pines, the dark awful chasm, the glimpse far on of the river and the ruined Roman bridge. The immobility, the silence, the solitude. The two observers were alone on the bridge. Harvey had informed Sefton (who knew all this already) about its date, its suicides, the town, its duomo, its handsome square, its war damage and its connection with Crivelli. They had reached the town by a linkage of buses that morning, established themselves at a hotel, and then come straight to the bridge. As for the promise to delay their own marriage for a year, they gave it readily. (A ruling about chastity

457

would have been another matter.) They were so intensely happy with each other, what after all was a year in the eternity of their love. They were also very satisfied with the acquisition of Clement. Sefton had worried very much about Louise's particular grief about Aleph, into which Sefton saw more deeply than others. Sefton had her own grief about Aleph and her own anxiety about Moy. She had had discussions with Harvey about Moy, and they had decided henceforth, tactfully, to *look after* Moy. It almost began to seem then that Moy was their child. Other children they talked of too.

They had walked across the bridge to the far side and were looking down at the trees below, the rounded green balls of the pines, and the elegant darker green spears of the cypresses which seemed almost black in the fading afternoon light. They had been discussing suicide, why on earth people did it and how they did it. This was a subject which always made Sefton think about Lucas. She had made the connection, instinctively, when first occasionally, then more often, she came to him for tutorials. Studying her teacher she discerned something extreme to which she could not easily give a name, something ruthless or reckless, something desperate. Of course she heard him much spoken of, but when her opinion was asked she had little to say. Very early in her dealing with him she grasped what was required of her. She was to sit quietly, to listen attentively, when asked a question to answer carefully, not to say anything hasty, vague or muddled, but to give a clear and definite reply, daring, if need be, to be in the wrong. When, in speaking to her, Lucas paused, Sefton was to intuit whether this pause was an interval in his thinking or an invitation to her to speak. When castigated (for a 'howler' or evident stupidity or failure to do her 'prep') she was not to exclaim 'So sorry!' or 'Oh dear!', but simply to lower her head slightly. No laughing was to occur, and of course no chat or general or personal remarks before, after, or during the session. An ironical remark by Lucas, if not a reproof, might elicit a faint smile. An equally brief smile might appear at departure, not arrival. When coming and when going Sefton bowed and Lucas nodded. During this period between them, that is on her side, a vast absolutely secret structure of unspoken emotion and repressed joy and fear had come into being. Herein Sefton had built up a picture of Lucas's character, or part of his character, a profound part. About his sex life, if any, she did not reflect. Not that she assumed there

458

was none, but it was not her business. She felt a deep sorrow, a deep wound within him. When he had said to her, at the end of their last meeting, 'I shall be going away for a time,' she instantly conjectured that he might mean that he was going to kill himself. But she spoke of this to no one. She treasured, and would always treasure, the only endearment she had ever received from him. 'Goodbye, dear Sefton.'

The swift paths of thought had, in a few seconds, led Sefton far away from the bridge, away from Harvey, into the now so utterly intensified and unfathomable mystery of Lucas. She was looking away back across the bridge where still no one had appeared to join them. She became aware of a movement beside her, a shadow fell. She turned sharply. Harvey was above her with one knee upon the parapet. For a black moment she thought that he was going over the edge. He drew up the other knee, and pressing upon the parapet with his right hand, stood up. Sefton remained perfectly still, not uttering a sound. He began to walk. She watched paralysed, icy. Then she began to walk, at his slow pace, about ten paces behind him, so as not to be visible from the corner of his eye. About the middle of the bridge he stopped for a moment, put a foot forward, then hesitated. Sefton stood still, aware of her open mouth, her trembling, the violence of her heart. He continued to walk, slowly. She followed. Time passed. The pines and cypresses on the far side, which had been invisible, came slowly into view. She thought, or remembered later thinking, he will fall at the last moment, *he will not be able to get down, he will fall.* The woodland came closer, the terrible presence of the chasm receded, the end of the bridge was in view. At last, though still before him, the trees were nearer. When he reached the end of the parapet he stopped. Sefton moved forward, taking long quiet strides, then began to run. As she reached him he bent his knees and put one hand on the parapet. She thought he was going to spring; but he sat, and then slithered down the wall into her arms. They walked in silence off the bridge, onto the path which led back into the town. There was a seat. They sat down. Sefton leaned forward, holding her head in her hands.

'Sefton, I'm sorry, don't be cross with me – '

Sefton lifted her head, now pressing her hands to her tearful eyes. 'Never, never, never do anything like that again!'

'Of course I won't, there isn't anything like that to do anyway. You're not going to faint, are you?'

459

'You are – I don't know what you are – '

'A wicked monster. I'm sorry!'

'Did you plan it beforehand?'

'No. I imagined it beforehand. But I didn't intend to do it till I did it, and then I *had* to.'

'You didn't have to because Bellamy dared you. And now to impress me – '

'It was rather to impress myself. It was a kind of homeopathy.'

'You jumped down. You must have hurt your foot again.'

'You held me, it didn't knock the ground, it's been getting better and better. I felt if I did this it would complete the cure.'

'You are *mad*. You nearly destroyed yourself and me.'

'You know – I've only just thought – if I hadn't taken Bellamy's dare I would have been in Florence all that time, and I might never have discovered you – '

'Oh shut up. Let's get away from here.'

They walked back slowly arm-in-arm. 'There won't be a *passeggiata*, I'm afraid, not in this weather, but we can sit in the café and admire the square. You do forgive me?'

'I'll think it over!'

But Harvey was wrong, there was a *passeggiata*. The people of the little town were walking together, round and round the square. Quickly, his arm round Sefton's waist, he pulled her into the slow crowd. They moved slowly, as in a march, as if in a great demonstration or a religious procession, carried along by the flow of people, by their physical pressure, pushed, brushed, gently jostled. There was a soft murmur of voices, like distant birds, like the sound of silence. Some resolute stalwarts walking in the opposed direction stared, smiled, sleeves brushed sleeves, hands brushed hands. Beautiful faces appeared, joyful faces, inquisitive faces, friendly faces, dejected bitter faces, faces like masks with round empty mouths and eyes. Harvey held Sefton closely to him, his thigh against her thigh, as if their adjacent legs had grown together. Harvey had cut his curling yellowish hair a little shorter, Sefton had grown her wild reddish hair a little longer. She was almost as tall as Harvey. They felt that they resembled each other, they were twins, as, crushed together, they turned and gazed into each other's faces, their lips parted in a dazed smile of joy. Some Germans, sitting in the café, voted them the handsomest couple.

*

Moy had secretly carried with her, in a large bag in Clement's car, the big conical stone with the golden lichen runes upon it. As soon as she had heard that Bellamy had not sold his cottage and that she was to go and stay there with Clement and Louise, she had planned to have another try, perhaps a last try, to bring the lichen stone back to its place on the hillside beside its friend the rock from which she had so unkindly separated it. She had lately, just before the news about their visit to the cottage, had a dream about the stone, that it had escaped from the room and was walking down the stairs, that she had followed it and found it scratching at the front door. She had opened the front door and watched it walk away down the street. After that, in her dream, she had terribly regretted letting it go out alone into the streets of London, and had run out trying to find it, running to and fro through all the nearby streets in vain.

Clement and Louise had gone on saying to Moy and to each other how very much she was going to enjoy being beside the sea. She was given the pretty attic room with the loveliest view. She had rocks to climb on, pools to investigate, stones to pick up. There might even, she was told, be seals. All this, thought Clement and Louise, and Bellamy, would divert her mind from recent shocks and sorrows. However, it was not so. Of course she did climb over the rocks and look at the tiny creatures racing about and hiding in the pools. She also looked at the stones, but so far (Bellamy noticed this) had not picked up any to bring into the house. The presence of so many things which ought to have delighted her and been her friends brought home to Moy how little delight she could now feel and how alienated she now was from all the beings to which she had once felt so close. She had already noticed before leaving home that the curious powers which had once alarmed her had now been withdrawn. The stones in her bedroom no longer moved, there were no more rebellions, or things coming obediently to her hand. They lay now inert, her things, no longer related to her by mysterious ties. Moy connected the fading of her fey powers with something natural in her growing up. She was not surprised. But she was also distressed, even frightened, by the loss of contact with innumerable entities whose relationship with her she had taken for granted. Perhaps this 'dead' feeling was also brought on by an intensification of her old secret sorrow. Perhaps one day this sorrow might end. But she did not think it would end or see how it could end.

Sleeping up in the attic she had bad dreams. She dreamt about the swan. She had hurt the swan, broken its foot, the webbed foot hung, half-severed from the leg, red with blood. The swan was hopping on its one leg. Only now the river had turned into a shop, a poulterer's shop, where the swan, still alive, was hanging from a hook. She dreamt about the black-footed ferret, that it was stuffed in a glass case in the Natural History Museum, and when Moy came to look at it she saw it opening its little mouth to say something to her, only as she watched a keeper came and hand-cuffed her and led her away, and all the lights went out. She dreamt about the little house where the spider lived and that she had become very little and was in the house with the spider, and the spider was frightened and kept saying to Moy 'Save me, save me!' and Moy was crying and saying, 'I can't save you, I'm too small, I'm too little.' She dreamt about Colin her hamster and how an evil cat was carrying him away into a wood to kill him, and how she tried to run after the cat, but could only move very slowly, and the trees and the bushes were reaching out their arms to hinder her. She dreamt about Tibellina the Good Cat, and how she had lain on her death-bed and Moy had stroked her and she had looked up at Moy so piteously and could not even mew. She dreamt she was the little dragon whom Saint George was about to behead. She dreamt she saw the Polish Rider passing slowly by and he was weeping and she called out to him, but he turned his head away. She dreamt that she was drowning in the pool of tears.

Those were the tortures of the night. The tortures of the day consisted in pretending to eat, pretending to play, pretending to be happy, passing the hours, enduring the sympathetic looks and the loving remarks. Louise's conjecture that Moy was going mad was now sometimes being entertained by Moy too. She had tried, walking about behind the house and along the shore, to remember where, in what fold of the grassy hills, was the rock to which the lichened stone belonged. She several times walked up into the hills, feeling for some sense of direction or god-given orientation, but none came. She recalled that the grass had been fairly long, there had been no trees, a bush perhaps – and it was in a little dip or dell. Had there been a stream? Near a path? She could not remember. Today (it was the day after Clement had shown Louise the sea and the beauty of the world), not in any hope but in order to do something, perhaps simply to 'give up', Moy had carried the stone down surreptitiously to the sea. At low tide it was possible to walk around the little headland into the next, also small, bay where there was a different vista of the hills. Moy had already tried this view in vain. What she wanted now was simply to be out of sight of the house. She walked down the beach to a line of low rocks and took the heavy conical stone out of its bag. Then climbing up a little, she placed it on top of a flat rock. Perhaps the stones could signal to each other? But could she interpret the signal? She climbed down and walked back and wandered about near the shore upon the grass between the stones and the hills but felt nothing and saw nothing. She wondered whether she should leave the stone here upon the rock, where it was rather conspicuous. Perhaps someone else would find it and take it home. Could that be a good thing or a bad thing? Or should she put it into the sea? Would it like the sea? It was not a sea stone. Yet, in hundreds and thousands of years it would become a sea stone, the runes would be washed away, its sharp cone would be softened into a hump and sea creatures would live upon it. She started to climb up the rock again to retrieve the stone, then decided not to. What did it matter? It was just a stone. It was nothing. She was nothing.

Bellamy was sitting in his bedroom. Spread out beside him on the bed were all the letters which Father Damien had written to him. Anax was lying on the bed, partly on the letters, looking at Bellamy, blinking with his sly blue eyes, slightly stirring his bushy tail when his master looked at him. He had extended himself in an attitude which Bellamy loved, stretching out his long hind legs behind him. 'Move over, Anax.' Bellamy pulled the letters out and arranged them.

He had decided at the last moment to bring the letters with him. Earlier, he had thought of destroying them, they upset him so profoundly. He thought: and *he* never knew Peter! Everything had happened so topsy-turvy. It was as if it would take years for him to *understand* what had happened. But what would he be doing during those years, how would he live, would he not simply *forget*? But then how would he exist, having forgotten? He would become some sort of inert sleepy animal like a toad. He had had a terrible dream in which he was lying on the ground soaking wet, having become long and grey and without arms, and people were treading on him. This dream suddenly reminded him of some other old dream in which he had been 'Spingle-spangle'. But *who* was 'Spingle-spangle', and how did *he* connect with the Archangel Michael, leaning on his sword, and looking down with satisfaction upon the suffering of the damned? Bellamy had brought a note-book with him, intending to copy out parts of the letters. But when he began reading them he was overcome by emotion, and found himself reading and re-reading certain sentences as if they composed part of a continuous litany, as if a distant clear voice were speaking them and he were murmuring the responses.

You are deeply stained by the world, the stain is taken deeply, as the years go by, you cannot become holy by renouncing worldly pleasures, you must not look for revelations or for signs, these are mere selfish thrills which you mistake for adoration, what you take for humility is the charm of masochism, what you call the dark night is the obscurity of the restless soul, by picturing the end of the road you imagine you have reached it, you cherish magic which is the enemy of truth, you think of the dedicated life as a form of death, but you will be alive and crying, the way of Christ is hard and plain, it is a way of brokenness, we seek the invisible through the visible, but we make idols of the visible, icons which are made for breaking, the agonies of that pilgrimage may consume a lifetime and end in despair, your wish to suffer is a soothing day-dream, the false God punishes, the true God slays, the evils in you must be killed, not kept as pets to be tormented, do not punish your sins, you must destroy them, go out and help your neighbour, be happy yourself and make others happy, that is your path, not that of the cloister, be quiet, humble, know that what you can achieve is little, desire the good which purifies the love that seeks it, pray always, stay at home and do not look for God outside your own soul.

As Bellamy put down the last letter (they were only roughly in chronological order) he found tears in his eyes, and lifted his hands to dry them. He sighed a long deep sigh. He thought, surely some day I will go to him and I shall bow down to the ground before him in the Russian manner. Only, alas, I would not find him, and I must not find him, he told me to expect, or indeed seek, no signal, and I must think of him as vanished utterly and gone forever. Now he is just Mr Damien Butler and I shall never see him again. I wonder if he has some other name and has already become Mr John Butler or Mr Stanley Butler. How agonising it must be for a priest to give up all that magic power – magic, yes, he feared it, power over souls. If he despaired, what must I do? Does he not tell me? Not to seek solitude, to go out and help my neighbour. I suppose I shall do that. The drama is over – why do I call it a drama – he would understand, he has been through it all, and he has learnt therein things which I shall never know. And he thought, finding it suddenly the most terrible of those sayings: the way of brokenness. And he thought sorrowfully of his parting from his dear mentor, and the last words with which he had left him, the parting words of Virgil, your will is free, upright and sound, it would be wrong not to be ruled by its good sense. Have I got a sound upright will, Bellamy wondered. I'm not sure that I have. Indeed I am sure that I have not. Anyway, Dante was not setting off alone into the wilderness, he was going on into the magnetic region of the Divine. And what was that stuff about crowns and mitres? I'll ask Emil about it, he knows everything, and I'll ask him about my will too. And as he thought this Bellamy felt a sudden surge, as of a warm wind, a breath of warm air. He thought, yes it is true, I love Emil, and Emil loves me, I shall get that job helping people, and we shall live together and stay together.

Bellamy had been vaguely aware for some time that Anax was restless. He had lifted his long muzzle and now was whining slightly, then as Bellamy gave him his attention he jumped off the bed and ran to the door. It's past his walk time, thought Bellamy, besides I want to be outside breathing the fresh air, I have found new thoughts. He put on his overcoat and scarf and his woollen cap which Clement derided, and went downstairs following Anax's rush. As he opened the front door admitting the cold wind the dog began to run, running up toward the little headland – they called it a headland but it was really a hillock – which divided the house from the next bay. Bellamy called 'Anax, wait!', but the wind blew his voice away. He hurried on after the dog, who by now had disappeared. A few minutes later, as he hurried on, he could hear Anax barking; it was Anax's hysterical bark. What could be the matter?

Moy picked up the bag. It was not empty, it contained something else which she had forgotten. She drew it out, a long yellowish snake, her plait of hair. It had already lost its sheen, its light, its life, it was a dead thing. Moy advanced toward the sea, as she did so pulling the elastic band off the end of the plait. She put the elastic band in the pocket of her coat. The mild weather had departed, an east wind was blowing, at the horizon a continuous wall of cloud was moving steadily along, joining the sky and the sea. Nearer, overhead, the sky was a pale pregnant spongy grey. Moy was wearing her winter overcoat with a woollen scarf, stout boots, warm trousers, and a mackintosh hood over her, as she felt it, shaven head. She stepped carefully over the band of seaweed onto a stretch of pebbly sand. She noticed stones, wet and shining. She came down to the edge of the sea, stepping into the strong running foam. The sea now seemed to be above her, a ragged wall of grey sliding curves and boiling white crests. A cold light as of its own making hung over the sea, a mist of instantly dissolving spray caught by some dull gleam from the rain-filled sky above. Not far out now, the tall waves were breaking with a ferocious booming sound, smashing themselves into the curling racing waters which rushed forward and as wildly receded. Moy took a firm hold of the thinner end of the rope of hair, and whirling it, hurled it with all her strength out toward the great heads of the breakers where it vanished instantly. She thought, I can't throw it very far, the tide will bring it in again, it will look like seaweed, and anyway I – anyway – I –

Moy's terrible secret sorrow which she had told to no one was this. She was not, she never had been, the least bit in love with Clement. She was very fond of Clement. But she was, and had always been, desperately in love with Harvey. An early joke about her being 'keen on Clement' enabled her to hide her dreadful love and her dreadful hope. She had counted the days and the weeks and the years until she should be old enough to tell her love. She had watched him, she had studied him, she had imagined, she had pictured it a thousand times, how she would reveal it to him. She had looked into the mirror, trying to see herself through his eyes. She had felt desperation, then increasing hope, then new fears, then new hopes. She had not imagined that he would marry Aleph. Indeed, she was glad of his friendship with Aleph since it removed him from other temptations, reserved him, she now so often felt, *for her*. Beyond her declaration of love she could not

466

see. But as she rehearsed the intensity of her passion she thought that he *must*, when the time came, *respond*. The desire to, at the right time, *tell* him became, as the years moved forward toward that time, increasingly painful, like a poisoned wound that must heal itself by breaking open. She *now* thought in anguish of the times, the recent times, when she could have told him, and had been afraid to, and had clumsily withdrawn, when she could have attracted him and drawn his attention to her. When she had watched over him when he was sleeping in the sedan-chair and could have wakened him with a kiss. If only she had *let him know*, then she could more easily have borne his not preferring her. He was ready to fall in love – and if he had *known* – he must have loved her – if he had known how much she loved him. The pain of this loss burnt her in every waking moment, that awful 'if only'. She had lost him, and lost him through her own fault. There were no more pleasures now in life, her stones knew it, they were dead. She moved forward into the swirling water.

Then she saw them. She thought, but *people are swimming* in the wild sea, many people, many faces turned towards her, big eyes gazing at her. Then she realised – it's the silkies, they have come for me – *my* people have come for me at last. She took off her overcoat and threw it behind her. She plunged forward, stumbling in the high violent breaking waves. As she fell she heard the distant sound of Anax barking.

When Bellamy reached the top of the slope and looked down into the next bay he saw Anax on the beach, right up against the breaking waves, rushing in toward the waves, then running back again, continuing to bark hysterically. *Whatever is it?* Then Bellamy saw the seals. The little bay was full of seals, their wet grey doggy heads bobbing in the wild-crested waters, just a little beyond where the huge waves were breaking. He thought, how wonderful, the seals are here, they are back, I thought they had gone forever, and so many I can't even count them! No wonder Anax is excited! He slackened his pace, striding down the hill through the thick wet grass. He thought, I must stop Anax from barking, he'll frighten them, he never barked at them before. He called out, 'Anax!' fruitlessly into the wind. Then he saw something else. Something like a human person was in the sea too, in the chaos of the breakers, no, now beyond them, overwhelmed by the huge waves, disappearing from view. At that moment Anax rushed forward and leapt his high leap over the top of the next breaking wave – and he too vanished. Bellamy ran, crying out, stumbling down the steep way, through old dead bracken and gorse bushes, hearing himself gasp and moan as he ran, then over the cropped grass onto the stones, the big wet stones shifting under his boots, clambering over the rocks, then over the slippery seaweed onto the sand which was strewn with smaller stones. He stopped, panting, hearing now the deafening *cracking* sound of the breaking waves, seeing nothing except the chaos of waters ahead. He threw off his encumbering overcoat and crossed the sand and entered the sea, stepping awkwardly, clumsily, concentrating on continuing to stand up. Water came pouring into his boots, he was walking upon sand, stopping at every step as he advanced, meeting the repeated violent blows of the breaking waves, hearing himself calling, crying out into the tearing wind, his mouth filling with sea water. There was no question of swimming, if he lost his balance he would drown. He concentrated on standing, then beginning to retreat as he felt then the strong fierce receding water clawing away the sand from under his feet. He knew of nothing now but survival, not losing his balance, not being able to *walk* – then his legs gave way and his arms were without force and the sea took him and he saw above him the inner hollow of the tall wave breaking over him and he saw its dome of translucent green light as he fell backwards under it, choking with water, experiencing death. The next moment he found he was still alive, scrabbling in the ferocious undertow. He saw something near him, something round, something dark, tumbling for a moment in the boiling foam which awaited the next wave. He reached out towards it, taking hold of something, a sleeve then an arm, he tried to find his legs again, then found, as the water struck his back, that he was kneeling in the sand. He crawled frenziedly, still holding on to the human arm, then managed to rise to his feet. As he recalled it later, that rising was like to a resurrection, perhaps what the risen dead would feel at the end of the world. He advanced, pulling the child, for that was what he had realised it was, behind him like a heavy sack, dragging it up the slope out of the violent beating waves, out of the power of the sea. And he thought, as he remembered, even then, *Anax has drowned* trying to save a child, and tears came into his eyes, and he felt their warmth upon his cold cheeks. He sat down upon the wet sand with the thing beside him, and thought, for he imagined the child must be a boy, and *he*'s dead too. He tried to command his breath and to remember what one is supposed to do when someone is drowned, get the water out of their lungs, then breathe into their mouth, or something. He was still crying and sobbing as he sat up, then knelt to see what could be done. At that moment Moy moved and uttered a faint groan, then opened her eyes, and Bellamy recognised her. She was breathing. He stood up and looked back at the sea. There was no sign of Anax. Bellamy uttered a terrible cry of anguish which the wind tore away, blowing it away with the wind-swept seagulls and their stormy shrieks. Then he saw a long grey form crawling out of the chaotic foam and the wildly running shallows and onto the beach, then standing up and shaking itself. He knelt down again beside Moy. She was panting and trying to sit up, he lifted her a little and supported her against his knee.

'Moy, Moy – '

She kept shuddering and murmuring and uttering little soft sounds and breathing deeply and choking and gasping, then, she whispered, 'I'm sorry.' Bellamy felt something warm. It was Anax's warm tongue licking his hand.

'You must get up and walk!' He pulled Moy to her feet. Then he saw, further on toward the land, his overcoat and Moy's overcoat lying near to each other on the sand, and he thought, thank heavens the tide is going out, and the weather has changed too. The wind had dropped and there was more brightness in the sky, and he thought, that was the light which I saw when I was under the dome of the wave. Leaning upon him, Moy began to walk.

'Come on, Moy, we must get you home quickly. Whatever possessed you to go swimming!'

He did not expect her to answer, but she said. 'It was the seals, I had to – ' then she said, 'It's so strange, the water was warm.'

'Not for me! Look, here are our coats, and they are dry!' It was difficult to get the coats on over their wet sticky garments. He helped her on with hers, then donned his. 'We must hurry now, thank heavens I arrived in time, it was Anax barking, he really rescued you. Where is he – oh look at him!'

Anax, running ahead of them, had climbed up onto the flat-topped rock where Moy had left the conical lichen stone. He was sitting in profile, his front paws extended, beside the stone, looking at it. 'Look, Moy, he's just like something out of ancient Egypt!'

Moy looked. She stared at Anax and at the conical stone. She looked between them, looking at the hillside beyond, and she *saw the place*. It was not far away, it was quite near after all, not distant as she had imagined. 'Bellamy, sorry, there's something I've got to do.'

Leaving hold of him she ran away with amazing swiftness, reached the rocks and clambered up. She seized the stone.

'What – ? Moy!'

But already she was running away toward the grassy slope and the meadow beyond.

'Moy, wait! Anax!'

She ran on upward through the longer grass, stumbling but never falling, and Anax ran after her, then passing her ran before her. Bellamy, exhausted, blundered on behind.

As soon as Moy had touched the stone she felt her body become warm and agile, she could run and keep running, the stone seemed weightless, she followed Anax. Breathless at last she slowed down. Yes, she recognised the particular formation of the land, the shape of the hill, the thicker grass, the dip beyond into the little dell. Anax had already run over the grassy edge and into the dell. Moy followed him, hugging the stone. Yes, there was the rock, rising high, high out of the grass, a smooth grey pyramid, criss-crossed with hieroglyphics, quite unlike the rocks of the sea, unique, solitary, sacred. Holding the stone, leaning against the rock, Moy sat down in the damp grass. But where had the stone been in relation to the rock, where had its place been? She said, bending over the stone, hugging it against her breast, 'Seek, Anax, seek!' Anax was already sniffing about. Then he began to dig in the grass at the side of the dell. Moy rose and went to him. Beneath the grass there was a hole. She looked back at the rock. Yes, that was where it had been, where they could see each other. Anax moved aside. Moy lowered the stone into the hole. It fitted exactly. Moy felt something snap inside her as if her heart had snapped. The heart-string, she thought – what is the heart-string? Tears came into her eyes. She touched the stone, pressing it firmly into its hole. Kneeling, she kissed it. Then she hurried to the rock and kissed it. Then, after caressing the mysterious messages of its criss-cross cracks, not looking back, she ran quickly out of the dell and onto the open hillside. Anax was frisking wildly beside her. Bellamy was half way up the hill.

'Moy, whatever are you up to? Do you want us to die of exposure? You must come back to the house at once, you must be freezing cold, we must have hot baths, Anax must be cold too, we must hurry back – !'

They began to walk briskly down to the path, at the horizon the sun was shining on the sea, they were talking, chattering and smiling at each other, the words tumbling out of their mouths.

'They'll be cross with us!'

'They'll be cross with *me!*'

'No, with *me!*'

Think of those hot baths, thank heavens there are two bathrooms!'

'And Anax can lie by the fire.'

'We'll light fires in all the rooms, it's time to do it now.'

'That will help us dry our clothes.'

'It's good that we left our coats behind!'

'We didn't have much time to reflect, anyway I didn't! But why did you go in at all?'

'It was just – the seals – '

'You are absolutely daft, but never mind, we can talk about this later – well, it's such an adventure we shall talk about it forever!'

'I feel warm now, do you?'

'Well, warmish. I'm glad that wind has given up. But get a move on, after your bath you must go to bed, you must be suffering from shock.'

'I'm not, not a bit.'

'Well, I am. It's wonderful that the seals are back. I expect they came to say hello to you.'

'Well – yes – I think – they did – '

Bellamy thought, what's happened, something's happened – I'm afraid she will collapse when she gets back, such an extraordinary girl, and I shall probably collapse too, but not for long, perhaps it's reading all those letters, no, of course not, Moy and the seals, and how on earth did Anax *know*, and what were they doing up there on that hill, well, I won't tell about that, how brave she is, I've got so much to do, I'll find that job he spoke of, and yes he was right about happiness, don't be miserable thinking you can't be perfect, isn't the *Bhagavad Gita* about that, living above one's

471

moral station, I must ask Emil, and there was something about the presence of Christ not fading, I'll look after Moy, and Emil will help her to get into an art school, perhaps we could adopt her, or sort of –

'Bellamy, thank you so much – '

'Don't worry. You made the seals come. I wonder if they saw the seals. Emil is coming in a day or two, you like Emil, don't you?'

'Oh yes, I love Emil.'

'We'll get you into an art school, I mean you'll get yourself into an art school – '

'Yes, I shall get started here, and then – '

'And then what?'

'I think I'll go to India when I'm eighteen, I'd like to live there.'

'Oh -- I wonder if – '

Would Emil and I be happy in India, he wondered. I suppose I might become a Buddhist there. Well, we'll deal with that problem when the time comes.

'Look Moy, see the chimneys, they've lit all the fires, they must have known we were going to try to drown ourselves. And Anax is running on ahead to bring the news.'